DATE DUE

GAYLORD			PRINTED IN U.S.A.

SOUNDPIECES 2
Interviews With American Composers

by
COLE GAGNE

photographs by
Gene Bagnato
and
Lona Foote

The Scarecrow Press, Inc.
Metuchen, N.J., & London
1993

Also published by Scarecrow Press:

Soundpieces: Interviews With American Composers, by Cole Gagne and
Tracy Caras, 1982.

British Library Cataloguing-in-Publication data available

Library of Congress Cataloging-in-Publication Data

Soundpieces 2 : interviews with American composers / by Cole Gagne.
    p.   c m.
   Includes bibliographical references and index.
   ISBN 0-8108-2710-7 (acid-free paper)
    1. Composers — United States — Interviews. I. Gagne, Cole,
1954- .
ML 390.S6682   1993
780' .92'273—dc20   93-34663

MR
780.92
SOU
3/95

Dedicated to my sister Dawn
and her husband Greg,
in memory of John Cage and
in memory of Lona Foote.

CONTENTS

PREFACE

With the eighteen composers in *Soundpieces 2*, I have tried to represent a wide spectrum of musical attitudes and techniques. Taken together, these interviews should illuminate for readers the areas of crucial concern to our music in the second half of this century.

John Cage (1912-1992) began composing with indeterminate procedures in the early 1950s, and music hasn't really been the same since. His epochal decision to create non-dramatic scores that were free of his own tastes and memory has inspired generations of composers worldwide in their use of indeterminate, aleatoric, minimalist, theatrical, meditative, improvisational, and experimental techniques. Christian Wolff, Pauline Oliveros, "Blue" Gene Tyranny, and James Tenney have all been associated with Cage to varying extents over the years, and their different approaches to chance, no-mindedness, and spontaneity reflect that contact. La Monte Young and Anthony Braxton, who might more reasonably be considered admirers from a distance, have also been deeply affected by Cage's ideas, and say as much in their interviews. That distance of admiration can even span light-years of musical differences, judging from the visible delight of Sun Ra and John Cage when they performed together at Coney Island in 1986. Lou Harrison wrote in his *Music Primer* (C.F. Peters, 1971), "I would generally rather chance a choice than choose a chance," but his friendship with Cage dates back to the 1930s, and the two were fellow percussionists as well as compositional collaborators in the early '40s. Even young composers such as Glenn Branca and John Zorn, who have felt the need to rebel in their own ways against Cage's example, have created indeterminate scores that owe their existence to the doors opened by Cage's music.

vii

The prophetic work of Harry Partch (1901-1974), who built his own instruments and tuned them in just intonation, continues to be vindicated by the range of composers who have struck out on the paths he blazed. The new scores for Partch's instruments written by Anne LeBaron and John Zorn are only the most recent instance of his legacy. The design and construction of new instruments has vitalized the musics of Lucia Dlugoszewski, Glenn Branca, Moondog, Lou Harrison, and Pauline Oliveros. The number of composers who work outside equal temperament also continues to grow, and is represented here by the harmonic-series-based tunings in compositions by James Tenney, Glenn Branca, La Monte Young, and Lou Harrison, and by the improvisations of Terry Riley and Pauline Oliveros on justly tuned keyboards and accordion, respectively. (Even Moondog and Alan Hovhaness, who have worked almost exclusively in equal temperament, confess their dissatisfaction with it in their interviews.)

Some readers may be surprised to find improvisation even being mentioned in a volume of interviews with composers. More than half the people to whom I spoke, however, regarded improvisation as fundamental to their composition. Its role is obvious for composers in the tradition of great African-American music, namely Sun Ra and Anthony Braxton. But improvisation has also been of formative and enduring value for Terry Riley, Pauline Oliveros, and La Monte Young. Christian Wolff has devised specialized strategies for improvising musicians; "Blue" Gene Tyranny and Anne LeBaron know how to get out there and play; John Zorn is dedicated to doing both. In the hands of Laurie Spiegel, even the computer has become an instrument for realtime improvisation.

That quantum leap in capability is only one of the recent breakthroughs in electronic music. Morton Subotnick has expanded the boundaries of electronic composition, with completely synthesized works as well as pieces for live performers and interactive electronics. Both areas of composition are also prominent in the musics of Pauline Oliveros, James Tenney, Terry Riley, and "Blue" Gene Tyranny. Additional fallout from the electronics explosion ranges from the static sound environments of La Monte Young to the virtuoso synthesizer playing of Sun Ra. Laurie Spiegel's groundbreaking work in computer music looks ahead to an even wider dissemination of electronic composition: The *Music Mouse* software she devised for her sophisticated improvisations is commercially available for use by professional and amateur musicians.

Of course, none of the above is meant to suggest that tonality has had its day. For melodists as gifted as Lou Harrison, Ned Rorem, Alan Hovhaness, and Moondog, tonality is as much a constant as it has ever been in Western music. Sun Ra's approach in his sets with the Arkestra is usually to juxtapose tonal pieces (both standards and his own) alongside his radical compositions and arrangements. Other composers in this book, particularly Terry Riley, Laurie Spiegel, Anthony Braxton, James Tenney, "Blue" Gene Tyranny, Anne LeBaron, Christian Wolff, Glenn Branca, and John Zorn, use tonal structures and techniques in compositions that also employ atonal, indeterminate, improvisational, and/or minimalist methodologies.

If there is a common denominator to the composers I've interviewed, it relates not to any single medium or technique or sound; rather, it exists in their use of music as an opportunity to overcome their conditioning and change the way they think. My hope is that readers will find this book not just informative, but inspirational.

To conclude, I'd like to mention a few details regarding the contents of this book. My purpose in doing these interviews was to provide a forum for the composers, and so they were all given the opportunity to edit and revise the text of their interview and its supplementary material prior to publication. Thus, some subjects that we discussed were considerably truncated or dropped altogether. But the final results stand as a faithful documentation of these composers' ideas.

The bibliographies, discographies, and catalogs of compositions which follow each interview are as complete as I could make them, again thanks to the help of the composers. (I welcome any corrections or updates that readers would care to share with me.) Only the composition list for Moondog breaks the format of strict chronology: With the help of Ilona Goebel, he has just begun cataloging his vast output, and many of his works have not yet been dated. All the other composition lists, however, should give readers a working idea of the composer's development over the years. In the case of Anthony Braxton, I was able to include only the composition number for his scores; I regret the omission of their graphic and coded titles, and am grateful to him for his indulgence regarding this limited representation of his work. With the music of Sun Ra, the most sensible approach was to substitute his discography for a composition list — a selected discography at that, in light of the enormity of his recorded output. For this reason, his is the only discography arranged chronologically by the date of the recording session (cited parenthetically after the record title, when known); all the other discographies list the recordings in the order of their release date.

Regrets? I have a few.... No project ever turns out exactly as planned, although this book certainly came close to my goals. The only real disappointment was the unavailability of Ornette Coleman, Cecil Taylor, and The Residents to be interviewed. They of course have my highest regard, and I urge readers to hear and learn more about their musics.

Acknowledgments

My thanks go first and foremost to the composers, who took time from their busy schedules to be interviewed, to read and revise the texts, and to pose for photographs. Extra special thanks go to "Blue" Gene Tyranny, for helping me in my research on several of his colleagues, and for his advice and encouragement.

My work was greatly facilitated by the scholarship of several eminent musicologists. I am especially indebted to Richard Howard, both for his book *The Works Of Alan Hovhaness* (Pro/Am Music Resources, 1983), and for his generosity in sharing with me his subsequent research in cataloging Hovhaness's scores by Opus number. Other sources of valuable information were Graham Lock's *Forces In Motion: The Music And Thoughts Of Anthony Braxton* (DaCapo, 1988), Arlys L. McDonald's *Ned Rorem, A Bio-Bibliography* (Greenwood, 1989), and Heidi Von Gunden's *The Music Of Pauline Oliveros* (Scarecrow, 1983).

Last but not least, my thanks go to the friends and colleagues who helped me: David and Melanie Carp, Elaine C. Carroll, William Colvig, Frank de Falco, Ralph Dorazio, Judy Dunaway, David Fuqua, Bruce Gallanter and the Downtown Music Gallery, David Garrick, Don Gillespie, Ilona Goebel, Rudolph Grey, Shelley Hirsch, Hinako Hovhaness, Mimi Johnson, Joan LaBarbara, Kevin Lally, Sue Latham, Alan Licht, Tom Maresca, Manny Maris, Iris Papagian, Barbara Petersen, Lauren Pratt, Kathryn Riser, Henry Schuman, Steven Swartz, Spencer Weston, and William Winant.

Cole Gagne
New York City, January 1993

photo: Gene Bagnato

GLENN BRANCA / Introduction

GLENN BRANCA was born in Harrisburg, Pennsylvania, on October 6, 1948. He attended Emerson College, studying theater, but dropped out and came to New York City in 1976. While working there on theatrical projects, he became friends with composer/musician Jeffrey Lohn, and the two formed the band Theoretical Girls. In its own way, the band was as experimental as Branca's theater, as was the case with his next band, the Static. His experience with the densities and loudness of electric guitars sparked ideas too complex and austere for Branca to pursue in a rock-band format, and he began working with other musicians on the performance of his own compositions. Starting with *(Instrumental) For Six Guitars* (1979), he created a series of landmark works for ensembles of electric guitars playing with the high-voltage drummer Stefan Wischerth. With *Lesson No. 1, The Spectacular Commodity* (both 1979), and *The Ascension* (1980), Branca unleashed a visceral, high-volume music unique to rock or new music, culminating in his Symphony No. 1 (1981), which combined his guitarists and drummer with keyboards, brass, and percussion.

Through the interaction of their amplified harmonics, Branca's guitars were creating a hallucinatory range of acoustic phenomena. He began composing works to bring them more to the fore, such as *Indeterminate Activity Of Resultant Masses* (1981) for ten soprano guitars and drums. For his Symphony No. 2 (1982), he devised mallet guitars for his musicians, giving them more open strings with which to work. The breakthrough for Branca was his Symphony No. 3 (1983), in which his interest in alternate tunings and instrument building were vitalized by his research into the harmonic series.

Branca dedicated that score to composer Dane Rudhyar, acknowledging the insights he'd gleaned from Rudhyar's book *The Magic Of Tone And The Art Of Music* (Shambhala, 1982), regarding what it termed pleromas: "differentiated vibratory entities are made to interact and interpenetrate in order to release a particular aspect of the resonance inherent in the whole of the musical space.... These pleromas of sound have musical meaning in the total resonance they induce ... not only in the ears of a listener but in his or her psyche — far more than in the component notes and their precise frequencies." Such a concept has haunted American composers in this century, from Ives' multiorchestralisms, Cowell's tone clusters, and the electronic densities of Varèse to the aggregates of sound let loose by Cage, Feldman, and Nancarrow. Its major exponents included in this book are Alan Hovhaness, massing like voices in free rhythm; La Monte Young, constructing an aurora borealis of interacting partials; Anthony Braxton, redefining harmonic relationships through ensembles of soloists and ensembles of orchestras; Laurie Spiegel, creating electronic densities with her mighty *Music Mouse*; and Sun Ra, unleashing volcanic eruptions both Arkestral and synthesized. In Glenn Branca's music, guitar or orchestral, pleroma composition achieves its most radical expression to date.

After several years of studying and composing with the harmonic series, Branca received his first commission for an orchestral score. Although since cannibalized into several other works, his Symphony No. 7 (1989) released that genie from its bottle, and the orchestra has become his primary focus as a composer. He still can be lured, however, by commissions to write music for ensembles of electric guitars, such as his Symphony No. 8 (1992).

Branca has written scores for choreographers Eiko and Koma, Twyla Tharp, and Elisa Monte; playwrights David Mamet and Matthew Maguire; and filmmakers Dan Graham and Peter Greenaway. He has received awards from the National Endowment for the Arts and the Creative Artists Public Service Program. Readers interested in learning more about Glenn Branca's guitar music are directed to the essays and interview in my book *Sonic Transports* (de Falco Books, 1990).

Glenn Branca currently lives in New York City. When I spoke with him at his Manhattan studio on July 16, 1992, I was particularly interested to learn more about his recent scores for concert instruments, and to discuss how these innovations in his composition have affected his involvement with the harmonic series.

GLENN BRANCA / Interview

Q: *In Passions Tongue*, your operatic scene based on Georg Buchner's *Woyzeck*, was the first time you composed for traditional concert instruments. How did that opportunity come about?

BRANCA: It just came out of the blue from Greta Holby, a New York choreographer who had used my music with some of her dances. She had also been getting gigs as an opera director and she knew people in the scene. Through her contacts she was able to get a commission from the Opera Tomorrow Festival sponsored by the Minnesota Opera. It was intended to encourage composers who hadn't been writing opera. We started working together as librettist and composer — she had never written a libretto but she wanted to try.

Q: The commission was to develop an opera that would then be staged in Minnesota?

BRANCA: Yeah, potentially. They were commissioning very few new operas at that point, but they did have hopes that maybe something might work. It was really a pie-in-the-sky kind of thing to believe that they would go ahead and commission the full work. As it happened the collaboration between Greta and I didn't work out, but I still did end up going ahead and writing a scene from *In Passions Tongue* for the festival. I could have done it for my ensemble, but I really didn't have any ideas about writing an opera using amplified instruments. I actually was interested in the conventional idea of an opera. Since there was also the access to the orchestra, I thought, well, this gives me a chance to finally work with an orchestra. It seemed that it was going to be years down the road before I ever got the chance. But they were looking for composers who weren't part of the academic scene — a window of opportunity for someone like me.

Q: Your subsequent orchestral works give me some idea of how you'd write for those instruments. I'm curious about the music you wrote for the voices in that operatic scene.

BRANCA: It was actually incredibly easy, because I'd simply sing it. I didn't have a libretto but I had the text of the play in front of me and just sang the lines out loud. I did have an idea about how the music was going to sound: entirely in half-steps — which also made it easier for an untrained singer such as myself. I was also using glissando, happening through the half-step changes, sometimes moving over as many as two-and-a-half or three steps, but very slowly. I wanted nothing approximating a dissonant interval. So that determined how the harmony was going to work. Once I had written one of the parts, the other part had to fall into place. I felt very comfortable with it. The easiest things are very often the best things. It's a very slow, very heavy scene, but I'd chosen one of the heaviest scenes in the play. The whole opera was not going to be written just like this part. It does describe a state of extreme intensity, to say the least! It's not the murder scene but one of the scenes leading up to it, in which he confronts her with her infidelity.

The couple of reviews were pretty good, and they did seem to get it. One particular review that I remember, the writer states that they were singing their subconscious, which was what I was going for 100 percent. That's what I think opera's about. At least for me. It doesn't have to be absolutely literal — nobody sings to each other in real life. So this gives us an opportunity to use music to resonate with what's really going on in someone's mind, not necessarily what's happening on the surface. The words are there for that; the music tells you what's happening in the abstract. A perfect marriage. I think the scene was quite successful to that extent.

My original conception of that opera was somewhat complex, and this has been a problem with my work. I had conceived a very theatrical idea. I wanted to have three scenes performed at the same time, with three sets of actors all playing the same characters. The first scene in the play would be performed in the very front of the stage; on a platform behind that, or on a second stage, the second scene would be performed; and on a platform behind that, the third scene. All at the same time. And of course the first scene would be the loudest and the one you could see the best; the second scene wouldn't be quite as loud, etc., which made a very interesting musical challenge, I thought. And then, of course, when it's time for the second scene, the second scene takes the front of the stage, and the third scene is second and then the fourth. What interested me theatrically and musically about the idea is that I wanted to create a connection between all three scenes which of course would then somehow have to work with the next set of three scenes which would include two of the previous scenes and on and on till the last scene which would of course include the first two scenes. A definite mindfuck.

Q: Is this opera something you're hoping to develop further?

BRANCA: No, I've completely shelved it at this point.

The piece I have to write right now is actually another opera: *The Tower Opera*, which has been in the works for quite a while now. The funding organization had given us two years to produce the piece, and now I finally have some time to do it, so that's the next thing I'm going to write. The only reason it's going to happen is because at the moment I'm in a position to produce a pretty good orchestral sound from the computer. Which means we can actually use the computer tape in the production if it's not possible to hire a full orchestra.

Q: Is your approach to the vocal writing for *The Tower Opera* more ambitious than what you've described doing for the scene from *In Passions Tongue?*

BRANCA: No, not at all. I'm going to treat the voice as an instrument. It will be what I consider to be an orchestral piece which will contain voice as one of the instruments. I usually like to double the voice with the instruments because I don't like the ambiguous intonation of the voice.

The way the piece is conceived, it's going to be entirely consonant at least to the extent that I'll be avoiding the use of clusters and concentrating more on relatively differentiated melodic themes. I want to compose something that's very upbeat, in contrast to the feel of the libretto. I think the music can put a whole other twist on the work. I don't think the music has to literally reflect the surface, as I said before. I think the music can carry on a completely different line which can deepen the intensity of the work.

Q: In the recording of your orchestral piece *The World Upside Down*, I was struck by the unusual monochromatic quality created in the timbres and balances of the instruments.

BRANCA: In many of those movements I was still trying to get a field of sound. A non-differentiated kind of sound. In the past I've liked thinking of the orchestra as a single instrument. I didn't want anything to stand out. For instance, in the first performances of *The World Upside Down*, the trumpets just didn't blend. There was just no way unless you muted them, and when you did, the sound changed. And at that point, once they were muted, why bother to use the trumpets? I actually had the trumpet parts played by B-flat clarinets in the second version of the piece.

There's no doubt that, in the future, I am going to work more with orchestration and orchestral colors. But for a long time I was completely immersed in the idea of the composition, and I completely ignored orchestration itself as a compositional tool; actually, I avoided it. It partially started out from working just with the string orchestra, first in the scene from *In Passions Tongue*, and then in the music for the Peter Greenaway film.

Q: Did the mixing facilities in the recording studio give you a chance to get an even more precise monochromatic effect from the orchestra than you could get in a live performance?

BRANCA: All of that music is almost completely unmixed. Although *The World Upside Down* was recorded in a 24-track studio, the sound in the room was so incredibly dry that we had to go with the stereo room mics almost exclusively. We couldn't bring up the close mics because they were unbelievably dry — about three or four times drier than the sound of the room mics. We had to run incredibly high levels of reverb. I just couldn't abide such a very, very dry sound. At that point I wished we had just recorded it on DAT in a concert hall, which would have been a lot cheaper as well. We did use the close mics when we had to bring up the sound of an instrument on a couple rare occasions, but we don't have a close mic'd sound. Again, I wanted this blend. Plus the fact that we just didn't have time; it was the difference between paying for two mixing sessions or ten. And I don't think the results would have ended up being that much different. So we put the reverb in to increase the blend. Borden Auditorium at the Manhattan School of Music has a fantastic sound, and that's where I've heard most of my music played. It just sounded exactly the way I wanted it to sound: like an orchestra from heaven — the sound of an orchestra in a dream. I think that if you know that's what I'm going for on that record it becomes more interesting to listen to.

Q: Orchestras tend to be perturbed at the idea of playing unusual tunings. Has that been a problem for you?

BRANCA: I've had no problems with that whatsoever. I've had at least three different orchestras play microtonal notation, and they've played it perfectly, first shot out of the box. I've been surprised by the kinds of things that give them trouble and the kinds of things that don't. The trouble, the difficulty is balance, pure and simple. I've written some pretty difficult parts by this point — microtonal parts, difficult rhythmic things, and the problem is hooking in with the group that you're sitting beside, if that group isn't playing exactly the same part — especially if you're used to having that group playing exactly the same part! In orchestral music they're used to having one dominant line, and everything else is either a kind of obvious counterpoint to that line, or is peripheral and coloristic. But when you're scoring four or five different rhythms that are all meant to intermesh and create this single line, that is very, very difficult. This is a well known fact. This is why composers like Bartók write that type of thing only for string quartet. But I want to hear it for the orchestra! And they do try — we have gotten some pretty difficult things to work. It's a matter of rehearsal, and if there's only two rehearsals, there's only so much that can be done.

Q: Your music for the film *The Belly Of An Architect* used the same instrumentation as *In Passions Tongue?*

BRANCA: Exactly the same size orchestra, 48 strings. Originally, *The Belly Of An Architect* was going to be for string orchestra, chorus, and amplified ensemble (not all playing at the same time). But as the budget got smaller and smaller and smaller, I had to decide, "OK, I'm going to go only with the orchestra." I knew that was dangerous because I still didn't feel confident enough about my orchestral writing; we're talking about several months after I had finished my first orchestral piece, and all of a sudden I'm writing this film score for orchestra. Peter Greenaway had said, "Do whatever you want," and the producer pretty much agreed with him — although I had a feeling that the producer really didn't want me to do the score, but Greenaway was behind it. So I took it upon myself. I had never intended the entire score to be orchestral; it was going to be half harmonic-series instruments (played by my ensemble), half orchestral, and a chorus. As it turned out, with all of the union problems, it wasn't even physically possible for me to record with my ensemble; I would have had to go to England and record with an English ensemble. I had to decide on one or the other, and I went with the string orchestra because I was still wanting to take advantage of orchestral opportunities that were presenting themselves to me. Again, both this and *In Passions Tongue* I could have done with my own ensemble. And with my ensemble, the things that don't work get thrown out or revised in rehearsal. Well, when I went to London to lay out the hour of music in front of the orchestra with two recording sessions, the ones that didn't work just didn't work; there was no way to replace them. That was an education. But we did come out with a few good things.

Q: Was there much music that was recorded but never used for the film?

BRANCA: About 20 minutes of the music was recorded, and they used about nine minutes of that in the film. They gave me no idea of how much music they wanted, so I wrote an hour when they only needed about 25 or 30 minutes, really — one theme, "Augustus," was used five times. I could have spent my time a lot more economically if I'd had any idea of what they really wanted. I did try. I went to England while they were editing the film. I stopped in the studio hoping that Greenaway would give me some idea of what he wanted. I did not receive any kind of detailed idea until two weeks before I was supposed to leave for London for the recording sessions, and I told them, "The only thing I'm doing now is finishing up the score copying and organizing parts. The piece is finished." There were 16 short pieces. The preparation of parts is so much more time consuming than anyone ever realizes.

Q: Is there music that was never used in the soundtrack which you've since used in another context?

BRANCA: I have used bits. The third movement of the Symphony No. 6 is from *The Belly Of An Architect*. It's rewritten, but it uses many of the same chords and it's similar in structure. Part of the Symphony No. 8 also contains part of the scene that I wrote for *In Passions Tongue*. It was the only thing of this sort that I'd ever written, and I knew that the opera was never going to happen.

Yeah, stuff that doesn't get used, I always find a way to use it somewhere, like from this *Woyzeck* thing — I hate to see it just sitting on the shelf. I developed my approach to clusters and dissonance about as far as it could possibly go, in the *Belly* soundtrack. So when I wanted to work with it in another piece, like the Symphony No. 7 or in *The World Upside Down*, I would draw on some of those ideas.

Q: Symphony No. 7 was your first score for full orchestra?

BRANCA: No, the first thing was the incidental music for Matthew Maguire's *The Tower*. *The World Upside Down* and Symphony No. 7 were written in a true continuum. They were interpolated into each other. The Symphony No. 7 was supposed to be written first, and immediately after that I had just enough time to get back in the chair and write *The World Upside Down* for Elisa Monte's deadline — she needed to have the music to write her ballet. But she wanted some music from me before I started writing the Symphony No. 7; she desperately wanted at least ten minutes. So before I started writing the Symphony No. 7 I had to start working on the piece that I was going to write after the Symphony No. 7. So I did the first movement of the ballet for her, and then started working on the Symphony No. 7. I had spent a lot of time on that first movement, and limited the amount of time I had for the symphony, so I had to draw on some music that I had already written for *The Tower* and use that as movements of Symphony No. 7 — actually, this gave me the opportunity to do some more work on those, some expansions and changes. Then I started working on the new music for the symphony. When it was performed, I wasn't happy with it — as usually is the case. Virtually every major piece I've written since Symphony No. 4 has been completely and totally rewritten whenever I get a chance to do it again. When we go back out on tour, I rewrite the piece; I usually throw out at least one or two of the movements. The Symphony No. 6 even had two different names, the pieces were so entirely different.

I wasn't happy with the Symphony No. 7, but I wanted to continue working with the ideas. So when I got home from Austria, I tore apart the piece and rewrote some of the movements for the Elisa Monte ballet, I also wrote some new movements, and, of course, I had already finished the first movement. So at this point, the Symphony No. 7 has been completely cannibalized.

For a while, I had a reputation for being prolific, constantly turning it out. I'm not prolific, I'm very slow. So the pieces originally written for *The Tower*, as far as I'm concerned, are not Symphony No. 7, they exist as unique pieces: *Freeform*, *Shivering Air*, *Harmonic Series Chords*. They were actually never performed live or even in their entirety as part of *The Tower*.

Q: When the Symphony No. 7 was premiered, what we've come to know as *Freeform*, *Shivering Air*, and *Harmonic Series Chords* were part of that work?

BRANCA: Most of those were part of that symphony. It was about an hour and 15 minutes of music, and they comprised about 25 minutes of that.

Q: And the other 50 minutes of music?

BRANCA: Much of that was rewritten for the Elisa Monte ballet. Although when I listen to it now I realize that it's clearly different music and might sound interesting if it was performed by a full 90-piece orchestra. At the time I thought that in the ballet I could make some of the same ideas work a lot better.

Q: In conducting your earlier Symphonies, you had the option of reshaping the piece in performance — especially to extend the duration of material to release unusual acoustic phenomena. If you're writing everything down for someone else to conduct, you have to decide in advance exactly how long and to what effect everything must be.

BRANCA: It would be nice to get a gig as a resident composer with an orchestra. I could spend a year with the orchestra and write one orchestral piece during that time. I could hear ten minutes of the piece during a rehearsal, go back home, rework it, take it back next month, hear five more minutes of it, and keep working it. When you're going for something which is not a standard convention of orchestral writing, how do you know how to get it? The fact is, I did achieve it to some extent in *The World Upside Down*. In the sixth movement, I did get some of the acoustic phenomena. Most of it is in the low and midrange instruments. Again, with a full orchestra I think it would be heard to a far greater degree.

But there are other things which interest me besides acoustic phenomena. I'm going to start putting more emphasis on those ideas.

Q: Can you tell me more about those?

BRANCA: It's mainly about the manipulation of thematic material. I'm interested in great complexity and this has been something that has interested me for a long time.

Q: Your guitar Symphonies employed what you've called an emotional structure that kept finding its way into your music. Has that gone by the wayside somewhat since you've begun composing for orchestra? Is it something that you want to try to develop in that medium?

BRANCA: I don't think about that idea much anymore. I really took my music to such visceral extremes so many times that I just can't see continuing in that direction. Right now I think more in terms of free composition which is probably related to that idea but more of a head trip. In the past I've just allowed myself to go with the emotional part of it. Now I want to get more into the technical, heady kind of ideas that I've thought about, whether it was theater or music. That to me is what the orchestra is for: transparency — you can have a lot of things going on and hear them all separately at the same time. You just can't do that with electric instruments — the ceiling is very low! Even a triad, when played on a keyboard, has so much harmonic density, that you can't really expand on it too much further or it just becomes mud.

Q: Yet your orchestral music so far has sought to create a single sound-producing instrument out of the musicians, rather than a weave of differentiated voices and lines.

BRANCA: I have been treating the orchestra brutally. My rough worker's hands have not been sensitive enough. Now I have a better idea how that delicate instrument needs to be handled.

Q: On the other hand, listening to your orchestral music has made me appreciate a lot more just how contrapuntal your previous music has been; it tends not to sound that way because of the instruments.

BRANCA: It doesn't come through; it gets muddied and you don't hear it. I had always wanted to redo *Lesson No. 1* for orchestra because there's always been so much more going on in that piece than could be heard.

Q: Despite your *Harmonic Series Chords* piece, would you say that your work with the harmonic series has gotten pushed onto the back burner in your music for orchestra?

BRANCA: I did create an approximation of the harmonic series specifically for use with the orchestra. There are two pieces that involve the harmonic series in *The World Upside Down* — the third movement and the sixth are based on harmonic-series chords. The difference with those pieces was that I used the chords freely; they were in no way determined by any structural process in the series. But the chords themselves are fairly exact duplications, which really worked. And if you listen to *Harmonic Series Chords*, you can hear that those chords really sound very much like the same chords in the first part of the Symphony No. 3. To me it's really obvious — anyone who's familiar with Symphony No. 3 would say, "Oh well, this is just the first part of Symphony No. 3 for orchestra." And it is very similar. The difference was, the chords were from a different part of the series. They are very different chords, and if you compare them, you would see that it's actually quite different.

Q: Is that sort of music difficult to notate accurately for concert instruments?

BRANCA: It's very easy. Microtonal notation has been around for 60 years —
that was the easiest part. That's what I meant by "approximation," I only had to
create an analog for "conventional" microtonal notation in the equal-temperament
system. I chose three values: a little higher, a lot higher, and a little lower. For my
purposes a small arrow above the notehead pointing up would be an eighthtone
higher, and one going down would be an eighthtone lower. A notehead with a little wedge above it means a quartertone higher — I didn't expect anyone to play it
literally a quartertone higher. Musicians understood that because they've been
playing Penderecki for years. I made a chart which gives me a very exact, graphic
representation of the series of equal-temperament notes directly overlaid by the
harmonic series (if you've chosen a specific fundamental frequency). So I was able
to physically see just how far off each note was from its equal-temperament part-
ner. The approximation is really good, and I would say that if anyone was ever
interested in working with the harmonic series in the equal-temperament system,
this is the chart to use; it's fairly exact. The problem is, of course, that you can't
write anything that's to difficult to play. The musicians will try to play anything
you give them; they will try. And they like something new, they like a challenge.
But if it's too hard, if it's obvious that they can't get anywhere near the intonation,
if it's too fast, they'll do it, but it won't be in tune. So I have kept it slow and easy
and the intonation has been surprisingly good.

Q: Are you still interested in composing for instruments designed to work with
the harmonic series, or do you think you'd rather give that a rest for a while?

BRANCA: Yeah, I'm giving it a rest. There's absolutely no doubt that I want to
get involved in it again eventually. But it was really very necessary for me to consciously stop working with the harmonic series. I would have ended up writing no
music whatsoever — it was becoming far, far too theoretical. And too far away
from anything that could realistically be performed, even on my instruments. I
mean, the incredible amount of time involved, with musicians having to learn to
play the instruments as well as learning parts. For what I need to do now, it was
just out of the question — building more instruments, for instance, and getting
involved with everything except writing music. The truth is, my work has really
been about structure, right from the beginning. And that is the single motivation
that's been beneath it all. It's been about structure and the manipulation of structure and the creation of structure. What I learned from the harmonic series
taught me a lot about structure and mathematics. But for me to stay with it
would lead to becoming a purely theoretical composer. For instance, Hans Kaiser,
who was the greatest scholar of the harmonic series, wrote no music whatsoever
for the harmonic series — and he did compose. He wrote quite a bit of orchestral
music: None of it was for the harmonic series. It was all very conventional. It can
become such an academic thing, a mind trip that's separate from music, because

we're so far from being able to really work with these ideas. It will be years from now, when music is being played entirely by computers, that working with the harmonic series will make a lot more sense. A composer could score an oboe part for the most complex possible piece in harmonic-series tuning, and there would be absolutely perfect intonation in every single note. Actually, such a program is possible even now. It just would take years for me to develop it. But microtonal programs already exist, and all of the samplers are totally capable of playing the finest microtonal intonation. It's just a matter of developing a program which can read and process microtonal notation. Ideally the kind of program I would like to have would simply be an interface between a mathematical algorithm and a microtonal score program. When such a thing exists for the home computer, we will then truly see a change in the face of music. If composers who actually write music still exist! The computer becomes more and more interesting to me in direct proportion to increasingly restrictive union rules for the commercial release of live orchestral recordings.

Q: Was going back to composing for guitars with the Symphony No. 8 a compromise for you, or was it a welcome opportunity?

BRANCA: I didn't want to do it; I definitely did not want to do it. Once I did, yeah, I got totally involved in it. I still think there are plenty of interesting things that can be done with guitars. Those ideas are just nowhere near as interesting to me as what I want to do with the orchestra.

Q: The people who commissioned you specifically wanted guitar music?

BRANCA: They said, "No orchestra." People haven't known that I've written orchestral music, so obviously they aren't commissioning me to write orchestral music. But in every single case, when I've been commissioned for the ensemble, I've said, "Is it possible we can do something with an orchestra?" If it's a big-enough festival, they've actually been able to say yes. This was a big festival (Expo '92 in Seville) but my agent in Europe, Maria Rankov, doesn't like my orchestral music; she likes my guitar music. She negotiated the commission, and she said, "This has to be for the guitars or you don't get it"! So that's simply where that was at.

Q: Did the three or four years you spent away from the guitars change your approach to composing for them?

BRANCA: Absolutely. This was very different: We were using fuzzboxes and digital delays — just to make the sound a little fuller; I wanted it to be a little more intense. And I used conventional guitars and conventional tunings. Since the days of Theoretical Girls, I'd never used a conventional guitar tuning, E A D G B E. But I wanted to try having the musicians playing stuff that was a little bit more difficult. There's only one way to do that, and that's to give them the guitar that they know how to play. That was fairly successful. There were three movements: One of them has been completely thrown out, one will be rewritten, and then I'm going to write two more for the next time we do it, which will probably be next year for an ensemble tour which seems to be in the works and which I suppose I can't afford to turn down. Although I'd really rather just be sitting at home writing music than jumping around onstage. There was the possibility of a downtown-music festival here in New York, which I wanted to support, but that's not going to happen. There's no plan to do the show here. It seems crazy not to do it in New York, but if nobody wants to book it, I'm not going to pursue it. I should do these things. People liked it, we got good reviews and all that. I actually had a lot of fun because I wrote it as though I was writing for orchestra. It was all in staff notation. I was reworking some of the ideas that I had already written for conventional instruments, as well as using the same kind of techniques: I was writing it on the computer, everybody had beautifully printed-out parts. All of the musicians had to be able to read, but as it turned out, every single person who'd been in Symphony No. 6 (except for one) could have done it, as far as the reading was concerned. So as it turned out, everybody in my group could read, no problem. And by the end, when I was making large changes in the last few rehearsals, I was able to bring stuff in, put it down in front of them, and they were pretty much able to play it the way an orchestra would play it, cold, right off the bat. So that was definitely a kind of revelation, that I was able to work with my ensemble, and treat it almost exactly the same as I would treat an orchestra.

Q: Did ideas regarding the harmonic series play a role in Symphony No. 8?

BRANCA: No, because we didn't use any of the harmonic-series guitars. The instrumentation is almost exactly the same as for Symphony No. 6: guitars, keyboards, and drums. Only the tunings are different — but there are no harmonic-series tunings in that one either.

Q: In writing for orchestra, have you found yourself going back to other orchestral composers who in the past hadn't interested you but now seem more attractive or instructive?

BRANCA: There's really not as much of that as you might want to think. It seems like that should be true; it seems like all of a sudden I should become interested in serialism — because as far as sophistication of orchestration, and subtlety, and complexity, Elliott Carter is the king (not that he writes strict serialist music). And his idea of what the complex is does relate to my idea of the complex. Basically, I'm interested in something that's complex, but in which the manipulation of the material is recognizable. And that's one of the problems with tone-row music: The tone row is being manipulated in really interesting and sometimes mathematical ways, but isn't it meaningless if it can't be read by the listener? One reason why the largest audience for that kind of music is musicians is because they can sort of follow a little bit of that. But even most musicians can't really follow it. I love the idea of using formulas and of manipulating ideas, but if it's not read, it's worthless. The complexity that I want to make is with a clear theme. When I say "theme," I don't necessarily mean a melody; it could be a percussive thing, a certain kind of rhythm that's recognizable. Then you manipulate that rhythm, not necessarily as a theme and variation. I did experiment with these ideas in the *Vacation Overture* and the String Quartet, I wanted to see how some of these things would work. I really want to put together very disparate-sounding ideas, but make them blend into one single fabric. I know what the music has to be. I can't necessarily hear it — I wish I could really hear it, but I can't. I know what it has to be, and I know it's possible to create a sound with the orchestra which is something we have never heard. I know it's possible to do it, but I think it does require manipulation of themes through various kinds of repetition in the context of an involved, interpenetrating structure. I think the computer makes it much easier to do this kind of thing, because of the editing function: It becomes possible to interpolate and collage material in ways that previously only existed in the realm of Cageian-type random process, but which now can be far more consciously determined while still retaining a spontaneous quality. Very abrupt changes of every sort, not just tonal or rhythmic, but every kind of change. Again, that in itself is not necessarily so difficult to do. To create a work that seems to have form, seems to make sense as a piece of music, and still contains disparate elements, is the idea that I'm working towards. But a piece like this requires an incredible amount of time to organize. It can't just be written from the heart; as I was saying, this is a mind-trip kind of piece. If it's a piece that does have to make sense, then it becomes necessary for me to be able to retain a lot of diverse information in my head at the same time. I've got to be able to recall the entire gestalt at each moment. The computer is still only a tool, it doesn't write the music.

I see it like writing a very complex novel — I see the different themes as being characters. The most well written and interesting novels, as seamless as they may seem, actually contain a lot of very detailed technical ideas. There's a constant series of climaxes and resolutions going on throughout any good novel, on all different levels. You've got the large shape, and within that large shape there are usually two or three smaller shapes, and within each one of those there are another five or six, going all the way down to the single page — I'm talking about good novels, the ones where it really works, constantly throughout the book, while maintaining tension and suspense right to the end. This is what a really good piece of music has to be, as far as the long form is concerned. And the long form is what interests me. I like the idea of writing two-hour pieces of music which don't stop. Now, things like that are virtually impossible for an orchestra to play. But if I ever write a piece that's good enough, I would demand that an orchestra play it. It's not fair to demand that they play bad pieces of music which are very difficult, but when it's good enough....

So I'm talking about not only complexity, but also complexity over an extended period of time. And that is like architecture, I need to be able to map the piece; I need to be able to start to see the piece. The whole piece needs to take on a character — it's not simply a matter of small sections sewn together, or of a minimalist idea of a continuous, overt, and obvious development. In *The Belly Of An Architect* music, for example, I had gotten to what I think of as the first level; I now saw the whole piece, the entire one hour. It wasn't detailed in any way, but I knew the sweep of the piece; I knew the ebb and flow of the piece. And the piece had a character. I now wasn't thinking about everything else in the world. I was thinking about the character of this piece. So now my character started to tell me what it was. It's as simple as that. Then the thing starts writing itself. This is the way a piece of music has to be written, and again it's a function of time. It's like a photograph coming into higher and higher resolution as it sits in the chemical solution. This is the way, for me, a long-form piece of music has to develop. And at this point, it's the only way it can develop. I have actually, mentally, somehow subconsciously refused to write a piece of music unless I can begin to develop this idea. Or let me put it this way, it's become very difficult for me to write any other way. But this is where, eventually, it has to go, for me. It may mean having to find some kind of working situation outside of New York.

So what happens is, the more highly defined the piece becomes, the easier it is to maintain a mental picture of it. The key is, you have to see the whole thing. How can you write one single part unless you know everything that went before and everything that's going to go after? You have to know how that part fits into the whole structure. So you have to be able to retain a picture of the whole piece at all times. I'm not interested in writing novelistic or narrative music. I think that might be fine; I even like the idea, at this point, of programmatic music — it may be one way of approaching this idea at the beginning. It can be a non-musical thematic idea. Many people have done something like that, started with a poetic idea that had nothing to do with music. But the point is, and the reason why it's a function of time, is that mentally you have to be able to hold the piece in your mind, and no matter how brilliant anyone's mind is, there's still going to be a limit to the amount of information we can retain at any one time — I'm talking about at least an hour of music, and that's a lot. So I think that, for the people who have succeeded in doing it, in most cases it's been when it's been possible to continually be approaching this same character many, many times over a long period. As you become more and more familiar with it, it's no longer so difficult to retrieve, and it is then possible to continue to create it in greater and greater detail. Plus the fact that, as I said, since the kind of music I'm talking about writing is far more complex than anything that I know of, that increases the difficulty to a great extent. It's not that I have to be able to envision every measure, you know, but I have to know not only the large shape but also the little ebb and flow.

Q: It's a question of getting together the gig that would enable that kind of creative process to take place.

BRANCA: Yeah, I can't imagine that an hour of music like this could be written in less than a year. And realistically, if I say a year, we're talking at least a year and a half of very concentrated effort, where I'm not doing business and the distractions become reduced to a minimum. My goal a few years ago was to write good music. My goal now is to create a situation in which it's possible to write good music! All I have to do is decide that that's going to be my main priority. So right off the bat, the notion of taking commissions is completely out of the question. I have to be able to determine the piece I'm going to write, I have to determine when I'm going to write it, I have to determine how long I'm going to spend writing it. And there can be no deadline; there's no way that someone can say to me, "Now it's finished." It has to be finished when it's finished. That's the only way. If you can create that situation, then when the commission comes along, you say, "Well, here's the piece. I finished it last year." I have not been able to do that. I've had to work on this ridiculous deadline thing, and that's just no good.

Q: For the kind of large-scale piece you're describing, is it a foregone conclusion that it would be for orchestra rather than for amplified instruments?

BRANCA: Oh no. I want to write for more interesting timbres than are available to me in the orchestra. The name of one of these pieces is simply *Music For Strange Orchestra*. And I want to put together an orchestral sound — you see, I love the orchestral sound — but I want to introduce all kinds of other instruments that I love. It's not unusual to do that; many composers have become very successful doing it. But I'm not talking about introducing just a hurdy-gurdy or just bagpipes. I'm talking about hurdy-gurdy, bagpipes, sarangi, sitar, tamboura, musette, steel drums — a whole spectrum, a massive orchestra that would include all of the orchestral instruments as well and would be treated as a Western orchestra. That's the difference, there would be no attempt at an Oriental or Middle Eastern sound of any sort. I'd still be writing super-Western, super-uptight music! There's no way around it, that's the kind of music I want to hear. And I want to use instruments that I've built as well: my harmonic-series instruments, which actually can be used at low volumes and could blend with an orchestra. And then invented instruments; there's a whole instrument-building scene in the United States now that pretty much revolves around a magazine called *Experimental Musical Instruments*. People are doing some really cool things and I want to incorporate some of that into this Western idea of an orchestra. And talk about time and money! Now we're really talking about serious time. You're not just handing out the parts, you know; you're teaching how to play the instrument. So my idea is to set up what I'm going to call the Institute for Harmonic Research. The original Institute for Harmonic Research is in Vienna, and it was started for the purpose of archiving the writings of Hans Kaiser, the person who's done the most work on the harmonic series of anyone who ever lived. So I would start mine, which actually would have nothing to do with the harmonic series other than as another tonal system. My idea is to set up a library/music archive/workshop situation outside of New York City, in the country somewhere — which is for me the only place where I can really work — and try to create a situation that would have to revolve around my own work at first, because it would be too large to go beyond that. Eventually I would open it up. It's simply a matter of opening up the access to facilities — rehearsal space, workshops, equipment — to young musicians, and have them work with experienced composers in a kind of intern situation. I see a piece like *Music For Strange Orchestra*, once it's been written, as something that would have to evolve over a period of two or three months, as far as the unusual instruments are concerned. And I really mean evolve; I'm not talking about a two- or three-week rehearsal schedule, I'm mean months of really working — the musicians not only learning about the instruments, but in some cases building them. For people who are interested in serious music — whether they're instrument builders or composers or musicians — there's no place for us to congregate in any way. There are a few festivals and there are a few institutions, but they're mainly centered in universities, and it's a very academic thing. And if you don't want to become part of that university system, or you want to do some kind of music which clearly doesn't fit into that system, then you can't be part of this support network. And there are more and more people everyday who are working independently outside of that system. There's nowhere for us to go, and I think it would be important to have such a place where people could visit or work, hear music, perform. Just hang out, talk about music, think about music, work in a non-hostile environment. There'd be a listening theater, an extensive library, all manner of computer research and networking. I like the whole idea of it being a kind of global resource. Hooking up different groups so that there's a feeling of some kind of community. There's too much competition, even in the downtown scene, as small as it is; it's just a pity to see people competing for this tiny, tiny, tiny slice of the pie. It's ridiculous, ridiculous, when we should be thinking about creativity, we should be thinking about making beautiful music, not about who's going to get their name in the paper and who's going to get the grant. There's got to be some other way, there's just got to be. I think there can be much better music than what we're hearing if we create a sane and supportive environment for new music. It could certainly help people make the music that they feel they really want to make, not what they think people want to hear or what's going to make them the most money. It's just such a pity, I've seen so many people lose the sense of why they did it in the first place. But I can certainly understand why. I've had great opportunities and it's still difficult for me to do it properly, the way it should be done.

COMPOSITIONS

1973	*Scratching The Surface* play
1975	*Anthropophagoi* music/theater piece written in collaboration with John Rehberger
1975	*Percussion, Electronics, And Mouth* five short pieces for the Dubious Music Ensemble
1976	*What Actually Happened* music/theater piece written in collaboration with John Rehberger
1976	*Ballet Continuo* movement piece
1977	*Shivering Tongue Fingers Air* solo music/theater piece
1977	14 songs for Theoretical Girls
1978	*Cognitive Dissonance* theater piece

1978	20 songs for the Static
1978	*Inspirez/Expirez* instrumental composition for the Static
1979	*Ernest Kitzler, 1964-1977* gallery exhibition
1979	*The Whole Field* performance piece written in collaboration with Barbara Ess
1979	*(Instrumental) For Six Guitars* composition
1979	*The Spectacular Commodity* dance score
1979	*Dissonance* composition
1979	*Lesson No. 1 (for electric guitar)* composition
1980	*(Instrumental) For Six Guitars* expanded version in three parts
1980	*The Ascension* composition
1980	Music for a film by Dan Graham
1980	*Light Field* composition
1981	*Lesson No. 2* composition
1981	*Mambo Diabolique* one section of this composition is also the piece *Structure*
1981	Symphony No. 1 (*Tonal Plexus*) in four movements
1981	*Indeterminate Activity Of Resultant Masses* for ten soprano guitars
1982	Music for the dance *Bad Smells*
1982	Symphony No. 2 (*The Peak Of The Sacred*) in five movements
1983	Symphony No. 3 (*Gloria*) music for the first 127 intervals of the harmonic series
1983	*Acoustic Phenomena* music written as a performance collaboration with Dan Graham
1983	Symphony No. 4 (*Physics*) in four movements
1984	Symphony No. 5 (*Describing Planes Of An Expanding Hypersphere*) in seven movements
1985	*Classical Space (Forms Of Infinite Regress Within A Finite Field)* gallery exhibition of 20 drawings derived from the harmonic series
1986	*Chords* for refretted guitars and drums
1986	*Music for the Murobushi Company* for fretless, harmonics, mallet, and bass guitars and drums
1986	Scene from *In Passions Tongue* opera
1986	*Hollywood Pentagon* for untempered steel-wire guitars and drums
1986	Music for *Edmond* theater score for four guitars, keyboards, bass, and drums, on tape
1986	Music for *The Belly Of An Architect* film score for 48-piece string orchestra
1987	Symphony No. 6 (*Angel Choirs At The Gates Of Hell*) in four movements for guitars, keyboards, and drums
1988	Symphony No. 6 (*Devil Choirs At The Gates Of Heaven*) revised version in five movements
1989	*Gates Of Heaven* for chorus

1989	Symphony No. 7 in three movements for orchestra
1989	*Shivering Air* for orchestra
1989	*Freeform* for orchestra
1989	*Harmonic Series Chords* for orchestra
1990	*The World Upside Down* dance score in seven movements for orchestra
1991	*Vacation Overture* for orchestra
1991	String Quartet No. 1
1991	*Les Honneurs Du Pied* dance score in two movements for orchestra
1992	Symphony No. 8 for guitars and drums

All compositions published by Brancamusic, c/o P.O. Box 96, Prince Street Station, New York, NY 10012.

DISCOGRAPHY

1978
"You Got Me" (Theoretical Girls)
Theoretical Records single

1979
"My Relationship," "Don't Let Me Stop You" (the Static)
Theoretical Records 02 single

Live At Riverside Studios (the Static)
Audio Arts of London cs

1980
Lesson No. 1, Dissonance
99 Records 01 ep

1981
The Ascension, Lesson No. 2, The Spectacular Commodity, Structure, Light Field
99 Records 001 lp

"Fastspeedelaybop"
Just Another Asshole #5 lp

1982
Music for *Bad Smells*
Giorno Poetry Systems 025 lp; ESD 80722 cd (1993)

1983
Indeterminate Activity Of Resultant Masses (excerpt)
Crespuscule 116 cs

Symphony No. 1 (*Tonal Plexus*)
ROIR A125 cs
Danceteria 081 cd (1992)

Symphony No. 3 (*Gloria*)
Neutral Records 4 lp

Acoustic Phenomena
Kunsthalle Berlin (limited-edition single)

1985
Acoustic Phenomena (excerpt)
Tellus 10 cs

1986
Music for *Edmond*
Gema 02 (limited-edition ep)

1987
Music for *The Belly Of An Architect*
Crespuscule 813 lp, -2 cd

1989
Symphony No. 6 (*Devil Choirs At The Gates Of Heaven*)
Blast First 71426-1 lp, -2 cd, -4 cs

1992
Symphony No. 2 (*The Peak Of The Sacred*)
Atavistic 05 cd, cs

The World Upside Down
Crespuscule 960-2 cd

BIBLIOGRAPHY

"Running Through The World Like An Open Razor." *Just Another Asshole #6.* Eds. Barbara Ess and Glenn Branca. New York: JAA, 1983.

ANTHONY BRAXTON

photo: Gene Bagnato

ANTHONY BRAXTON / Introduction

ANTHONY BRAXTON was born in Chicago, Illinois, on June 4, 1945. At age 11, he began studying at the Chicago School of Music. In 1963, after a semester at Wilson Junior College, he joined the Army. Stationed with the Fifth Army Band in Highland Park, Illinois, and then with the Eighth Army Band in Korea, Braxton played clarinet and alto saxophone. After his discharge, he returned to Chicago, studied philosophy at Roosevelt University, and attended the Chicago Music College. He also played alto and tenor in the houseband for the Regal Theater, where he performed with Sam & Dave, the Impressions, and the Del-Vikings.

In 1966, with the encouragement of Roscoe Mitchell, Braxton joined the newly formed Association for the Advancement of Creative Musicians (AACM), and began performing with many of its members, particularly Leo Smith and Leroy Jenkins. Two years later Braxton recorded his first lps: *Three Compositions Of New Jazz* and *For Alto*. Both were landmarks in the development of his music: the former a statement of his belief in multi-instrumentalism, and the latter an investigation into the vocabularies available to a soloist. These records also established the musical priorities in which he would eventually become an acknowledged leader: closed- and open-form composition, systematic improvisation, and extended performance techniques.

In 1969 Braxton formed the short-lived Creative Construction Company with Smith and Jenkins, which gave performances in France with Steve McCall. Returning to the States the following year, he formed Circle with Chick Corea, Dave Holland, and Barry Altschul. The quartet split up a year later, and Braxton continued performing with musicians throughout Europe and America. In the mid '70s he began releasing a series of lps on Arista Records, documenting his music for a variety of performers, from his own solo and ensemble works to his *Composition No. 82* (1978) for four orchestras. Braxton's involvement with Arista ended with the '70s, but he has if anything increased his output of recordings in the '80s, principally on the European labels Black Saint and Hat Hut. He also continued to perform internationally in an array of musical combinations, with perhaps the most recognition being achieved by his quartet performances with Marilyn Crispell, Mark Dresser, and Gerry Hemingway. The '80s also saw the start of his series of *Trillium* operas, and the writing of a group of prose works, *Tri-axium Writings 1-3* and *Composition Notes A-E*.

Over the years Braxton has worked with numerous musicians and composers, including European artists Derek Bailey, Evan Parker, Gunter Hampel, Giorgio Gaslini, and Gino Robair; Americans Max Roach, Roscoe Mitchell, Dave Brubeck, Alvin Lucier, Joseph Jarman, Richard Teitelbaum, Muhal Richard Abrams, Frederic Rzewski, George Lewis, Anne LeBaron, Alvin Curran, and

David Rosenboom; and traditional masters from the East, such as Japan's Meisho Tosha and India's Nageswara Rao, Anuradha Mohan, and Vidyadhar Vyas.

Braxton has received a Guggenheim Fellowship and a National Endowment for the Arts grant. He is the subject of Graham Lock's book, *Forces In Motion* (Da Capo, 1988), which features extensive interviews with Braxton and documents a 13-day tour of England with his quartet. In 1985, he joined the faculty of Mills College as Darius Milhaud Associate Professor of Music. He left Mills in 1990, and currently teaches as a Professor of Music at Wesleyan University in Middletown, Connecticut.

I interviewed Anthony Braxton in his office at Wesleyan's Music Department on November 13, 1992. As both teacher and performer, demands on his time are relentless, yet he graciously gave the opportunity to speak with him about some of his most celebrated recordings, as well as his special sense of tradition in music, and his resistance to the label of jazz composer.

ANTHONY BRAXTON / Interview

Q: On your first recording, *Three Compositions Of New Jazz*, the musicians begin by singing, and over the course of the lp they perform on a range of instruments. Was there a desire on your part to redefine the musicians' sense of themselves, so that rather than identifying with their instruments and regarding themselves as a sax player, a violinist, and a trumpeter, they could be three people at work in an expanded field of music-making?

BRAXTON: In the middle '60s, part of the challenge of redefinition would involve redefinition in the context of instrumental dynamics, redefinition in the challenge of composition, and redefinition in the dynamics and hope of synthesis. On the plane of multi-instrumentalism, the AACM in the time period of the middle '60s would reinvestigate what multi-instrumentalism could mean in a dynamic sense. I'm thinking of the work of Eric Dolphy and the early work of Coleman Hawkins. In the middle '60s, I myself would start to investigate and research syntax as a context to reexamine language and vocabulary. And that decision was not separate from the challenge of second-plane initiations — that being concerns about a collective improvisation, and that which is "greater than the individual," the collective. In that context, we sought as instrumentalists 1) to always play one instrument that was not mastered — or at least this was my decision, even though in fact I saw this same attitude in the other musicians as well, to always have one instrument that was not polished; 2) to always be involved in percussion, that is, to have some percussive instrument. Sun Ra in the early period would help us to understand the significance of percussion; 3) I was particularly interested in finding a position for the creative artist, which would transcend just the role of the instrument, and so singing would be a way to expand our options. It would also be a way of having an involvement with normal, non-trained voices. We were not trying then or now to present some kind of professional vocal stance; rather, we sang in our normal voices and tried to create a context of possibilities for the individual, as opposed to "I want to play alto saxophone like Paul Desmond for the rest of my life," or "I want to follow John Coltrane, imitate his style, and use that for the basis of making a living for my whole life." We were interested in the discipline of creativity, as it has been defined through the last two or three or four thousand years from the African mystic tradition, the European mystic tradition, and the world mystic tradition; having to do with creativity as not separate from spiritual dynamics, creativity as not separate from the phenomenon of evolution, and creativity as not separate from self-realization.

Q: So the newness described in the lp title isn't about being, say, more dissonant or less tonally centered than other musics, but rather a new attitude in making the music and in what it could signify for the people who hear it.

BRAXTON: This was in conjunction with what had opened up in the middle cycle. By that I'm only saying the work of Ornette Coleman, the work of Cecil

Taylor, Bill Dixon, Albert Ayler, as part of the trans-African restructural tradition — as well as the trans-European restructural tradition: I'm thinking of, for me, Arnold Schoenberg, the great man; Karlheinz Stockhausen; John Cage; Harry Partch; Ruth Crawford Seeger; Hildegard von Bingen. That work and that continuum would be very important for me as well. And finally, from the world tradition, the work of the great Robert Marley; the work of Frankie Lymon and the Teenagers, of course; John Philip Sousa and Scott Joplin would help clarify a synthesis model, along with Ali Akbar Khan and Ravi Shankar.

Q: Would you say that the new jazz brings to the surface the sense of spirit which had characterized the musics of Morton and Armstrong and Ellington and Smith and Waller and so many others, but which wasn't expressed overtly because their work functioned on pop and entertainment levels for audiences?

BRAXTON: For myself, I know nothing about jazz, but I think I understand what you're saying and I can relate to it. The problem of jazz for me has been its relationship to the jazz-business and -defining complex. I feel that the great American musics of the last hundred years have been profoundly distorted. There have been distortions about lineage, when in fact every component of the music has a universal axis. There have been distortions about individual input and evolution, as if the music could be based solely on Armstrong's shoulders, when in fact in every region of our country there was a response to the spark of creativity and change, and that all of our people at every point in time have helped contribute and advance us as a species to this point in time, vis-à-vis all of the information channels. I think current concepts of New Orleans being the genesis of every component of the music is profoundly in error, and is a political tool that is not separate from how the jazz-business complex works, having to do with defining the model of correct for what is black, what is white, new images related to black exotica, present-day attempts in the post-Reagan/Bush time space of creating a neo-classic jazz continuum that uses Eurocentric values to put down Europe and also to distort the polarities between African-Americans on the plane of African-Americans. I see all of these matters as connected to political considerations, having to do with the need of the marketplace to reinvent spectacle-diversion focuses as a way to keep the market components active.

Q: To define and package the work so it can be sold more profitably.

BRAXTON: Thank you, that's what I'm saying!

Q: Of course, you want as much as anybody for your music to get out there too, but it has to be made available as what you've actually done, not as someone else's redefinition in an attempt to make it more marketable.

BRAXTON: Totally correct. I was never against at any point receiving four billion dollars for my music. I was against only having to change my music to receive the four billion dollars. Although as I get closer to fifty, I find myself thinking maybe I'll even change —

Q: Take it down to two billion?

BRAXTON: Two billion, right, but no taxes! A man has to draw the line someplace!

Q: You were discussing multi-instrumentalism as part of a new attitude in making music with your first lp. But after that, you released *For Alto*, a double lp of music for solo saxophone. Was there the feeling that you'd offered a challenge or thrown down a gauntlet in making music?

BRAXTON: The decision to become involved in solo alto saxophone music was a direct result of having exposure to the solo musics of Fats Waller, the solo musics of Arnold Schoenberg, especially Opus 11. I was also very taken by Scott Joplin's piano music and Karlheinz Stockhausen's piano music. I found that part of the beauty of solo music for me was its ability to give a better understanding of architecture and syntax; what would constitute genesis devices for better understanding what a concept space was. My decision to get involved with solo alto saxophone music was consistent with the decision I made in the time period, that decision being I wasn't interested in freedom, I wasn't interested in not-freedom, I wasn't interested in jazz, I wasn't interested in classical music. But I was profoundly affected by all of these continuums. I wanted to create a context of recognition on the tri-plane (tri-plane being, in this context, individual consciousness, group consciousness, and synthesis consciousness), and on the third tri-plane, that as an individual, I would not get lost in some existential concept of freedom, where nothing mattered and no value systems could be applied to it, when in fact I found that intellectual condition to be alien to my life experience — since in the act of discovering music I discovered areas (focuses) I was not attracted to, as well as musical situations I was more attracted to. Value systems and the phenomenon of attraction are always taking place in the experience of hearing music and sonic activity.

Nevertheless, the decision to create the alto saxophone music would involve finding those devices that could help me not repeat myself. Because on the most basic level, the first solo concert I gave, after three minutes of what I thought was brilliant playing (but which I now think was mediocre playing), I discovered myself repeating myself, and I'd go someplace else and repeat it again. By the time the concert was over, I understood that the concept of existential freedom, where you just go out and play, might be interesting in a poetic sense, but in a practical sense, in terms of having a viewpoint that got results, in fact something more would be needed. Because I wasn't interested in putting myself in a position where I had to be totally inspired from beginning to end. No, that isn't how it works. There have to be some internal components that can help for the 90 percent of the performance which is not super-inspired. It's at that point where the consideration of theory and discipline becomes relevant, and it was at that point, just because of the need to not repeat, that I would begin to look for those devices that could clarify recognition. It would be at that point where I would begin to focus on syntax as a way to discover the primary components of my work which in that time period was "a work in progress," as far as discovering those things that I liked and looking for what would unify that activity on the tri-plane. In the 25 years after that experience, I would come to view my work as a tri-partial sonic entity that seeks to demonstrate a context of architecture, a context of philosophy, and a context of ritual and ceremonial synthesis. As such then, to go back to your question, the original solo music was the first attempt to clarify fundamental points of definition: architectonic definition in the sense of looking for the 12 sound-types in my system — the DNA of my material. And from that point, I would look for the geometric scheme that would extend the model. I would look for the identity state that would synthesize what those processes could mean in the sense of real music material, and it would be at that point that I would begin to generate processes of vocabularies, processes of languages. Later, I would use the "classical balances" related to world-culture pedagogy. That is, Johann Sebastian Bach was an improviser who wrote down his music and who was also a theorist; Duke Ellington was an improviser who wrote down his improvisations and began to produce his compositions and created his own theory; Ornette Coleman; Pauline Oliveros; John Cage; Harry Partch, the great man that no one ever talks about anymore, who would in fact function as an instrumentalist, as an instrument-maker, as a theorist, as a synthesist, he would seek to find the "new balances" for his system. And so I would arrive at the same point in terms of seeking to define 1) a context to better understand myself; 2) a context that could help me better understand relationships; and 3) a context that could help me better have hope for the next cycle.

Q: In dedicating pieces on *For Alto* to Cecil Taylor and John Cage, there's the idea that both men have done work which is useful and available to anyone attempting to make creative music, and that they're not mutually exclusive or somehow restricted to separate ethnic and/or aesthetic areas.

BRAXTON: That's why it's important to keep the table of definitions open. That's why I'm happy to see President Bush retire. He had a great life and was able to work for those forces that he is aligned with. I'm hopeful that the next time cycle will give us a fresh set of balances that might give us more possibilities for all of our people and for all of our vibrational persuasions. My model, the system I seek to build, is a model that respects the polarities and the balances, which says, "Wherever you are at in the circle, there is a way for you in my system."

Q: Your use of graphic images in place of verbal titles for your compositions strikes me as, on one level, an effort to encourage people to rethink how they're going to listen, in that they aren't being directed toward familiar formal models or standard emotional/poetical allusions.

BRAXTON: The generating number of my system is the number three. I have tried to use the number three to express every primary component in terms of the major points of the system. In terms of the titles of the compositions, every structure has three titles: There is the image title, or graphic title; there is the formula or coded title; and finally the Opus number in terms of the order of the composition, as far it being composed first, second, third, fourth, or fifth. In the beginning, the graphic titles would seek to express processes in the music from a dialectical standpoint: rhythmic logics, pitch logics — not totally serialistic processes, since I would find very early that serialism, even though I found it attractive, was not my way. I needed to have a system that would give me the possibility to parachute out for a moment, based on whatever correspondent dynamic I needed to get me through that moment. I needed a model that would demonstrate a context of mutable logics, stable logics, and synthesis logics, and that could be readjusted, just as in improvisation, to skid on a moment.

Q: The graphic titles also offer a structural overview of the pieces, don't they?

BRAXTON: Yes. From the early musics, I would move from the formula titles to the alternative-coding titles, factoring in my hero Bobby Fischer, his chess moves. From the coding titles, I would move to the dimensional-drawing titles, which would begin more and more to look at the schematic musics from beginning to end. From the schematic musics, I would move into the composite structures which would seek to integrate color and intention in the scheme of the processes. From that point I would begin to investigate hieroglyphic structures as a way to begin to move into the tri-metric spaces, to move into correspondence variables, and finally, moving into the image musics, the ritual and ceremonial musics, which would seek to portray the 12 attitudes that underlie my system. And from that point into the storytelling musics.

Q: The use of graphic titles also takes the compositions out of the world in a certain sense: the music whose name cannot be spoken. Yet it's still a very deliberate engagement of the listener's sensibilities, and includes this more overt acknowledgment of spirit which we were talking about earlier.

BRAXTON: Part of what excites me about the next time cycle is the challenge of poetic logics as a way to override two-dimensional definitions concerning process. As such, I would move into the image space, the space of storytelling, the ritual musics, as a way to expand outside of the structural decisions, just on the plane of structural decisions. I'm not interested in structure; I'm not interested in not-structure. I'm interested in the cracks, or at least the veil of the music. Sound is only one component of those forces which have attracted me to this area. It is the veil behind the sound which I find myself more and more concerned with. Architecture in that context then is to look for the 12 doors as they relate to the identity scheme of the composite-summation model. But let me back up on that. In my system, which is three of three of three, that being a tri-metric system, every piece is an orchestra piece; every piece is a solo piece; every piece is a synthesis piece. But it goes even further than that. The bass part in *Composition 83* can itself be extracted and played by orchestra; can be extracted and played by solo bass; can be extracted and played by trumpet. In the consideration of tempo in my system, there is no tempo: Every composition is a fast piece, is a medium piece, is a ballad. In terms of harmony, I have designed a context of tri-metric pitch sets. By pitch sets in this context, I'm saying that the harmonic logic of my system is a tri-metric logic that says a given harmonic logic is only an imprint whose components establish an identity state of relationships in terms of 1) the traditional act of composing a piece for orchestra with particular instruments, as in the classical European musics which I love, 2) that same information expanded through dynamic transposition since it can be played by any instrument in its second stage, and 3) that same material taken and mixed with another set of materials. It becomes a genetic soup that demonstrates mutable logics, stable logics, and synthesis logics. And in every case, its micro/macro correspondence establishes a clear relationship, from the DNA of the solo music to the primary summation identity of the composite system.

Q: So a string quartet, say, could take any four parts from any of your compositions, play them together, and be presenting a perfectly valid interpretation of your music.

BRAXTON: That's it exactly.

Q: Would playing two of your records simultaneously have less validity because the musicians aren't actually working together?

BRAXTON: No, I'm open to different interpretations. The body of work that I hope to work with, that I have the great honor to kick about, is not about a Eurocentric (or even African-American-, middle-class-centric, for that matter), two-dimensional concept of the golden performance or the golden composition. Rather, this material will be offered as a giant Erector set or giant bowl of clay or giant city-state conglomerate (like in the United States of America), which will contain and respect the 12 different consciousness focuses/peoples and their internal relationships. I seek to, with this model in the city-state version, establish the lanes of correspondence between those perspectives/paths, and what that could mean in terms of stable-logic connections — laws, codes, states of environment — and mutable synthesis, in terms of responsibilities for the individual, and individual rights, because each individual has his or her rights. I seek finally to develop a context of navigation through the forms, through the sonic space, through the stable space, and through the synthesis space.

Q: Your musicians are being asked then not just to play a score or to improvise, but to adopt a unique, expansive vision of reality.

BRAXTON: I encourage the musicians who work with me to have fun, do their best, make a mistake, let us all work together. But meanwhile, don't work only with me. Also, I encourage each of my musicians to develop their own music, and work and learn to fight for your music, and figure out what it is that motivates you. So that the next context will be about more than the individual. We need to use this next eight-year time cycle to realign the dynamics, and to prepare our children for the next state of planet particulars, because the geo-political particulars of this time period seem to be in a state of profound realignment. At this point in time, our children are not in a position where they are able to keep up with these changes. If you really want to learn about American culture, you have to move to Europe or you have to move to Japan, because the information is not made available to our children in an intelligent way in America in this time period.

Q: I take it you see the coming turn of the century as epochal in more than just calendar time.

BRAXTON: Yes, I feel that the challenge and beauty of the next thousand years will be awesome, and I only can bow to the Creator for the fact of physicality and consciousness, the fact that we can even be in a body and wake up and be in the same body and have memory. All of this is incredible. At the same time, when I look at America, I find myself thinking that unless serious decisions are made in the next time cycle, we will find ourselves in a position similar to Great Britain. Not only that, this time period in many ways seems to hint at variables a hundred years ago, as we found ourselves entering into the 1900s. I'm thinking of 1) the nationalism taking place in Europe; 2) the complexities here in America, in terms of the economic cycle we're dealing with, and the unemployment that's taking place; 3) the banks scandal, the BCCI scandal, and what that has meant to social programs, and what that will mean if changes are not made; 4) the debt we are leaving to our children. This has become serious now, we're talking about three trillion dollars, that's serious. And unless something is done, our children will have to feel the effects of what that will mean in real terms. So I find myself thinking that the next eight years will be extremely important to reaccelerate a curiosity. Understanding too that in the 1960s, we landed a person on the moon. And we've forgotten about that. That can't be right for something as monumental as that achievement to suddenly be lost on Americans, and we suddenly find ourselves not able to face the future. My hope is that now that the Cold War is over, now that by 1992 the collapse of Communism has taken place, we've gone through a war already, we've experienced riots in Los Angeles, maybe we might find a way to retune our children to the future as opposed to the trauma of the Cold War era. Something has to be done to redirect us to the next time cycle, and my hope is that that realigment will contain a profound nod towards universal dynamics, respect for differences. It's not a question of having everyone agree on everything — that is a monodimensional way of looking at life. We need a respect for differences as well as for things similar. I think the strength of America is its universal component. If we can create the right model, a model that can accept differences and roll with our energies, I believe our diversity contains the seeds for the next thousand years.

Q: Being little more than 200 years old, America has always lacked a sense of its own past and traditions. And any nation that piles up a massive deficit and doesn't fund education plainly has no sense of the future. We've been conditioned to focus on making a killing right now. Your music describes how an awareness of history can work with a new sense of what can be manifested, personally and socially.

BRAXTON: This is because I never rejected the tradition. I love the tradition. But part of the tradition is the tradition of creativity and innovation, and the tradition of seeking to establish a postulation related to the time cycle and time-cycle variables one is born in. This is why I find it so disturbing that, as we find ourselves in the '90s, looking at the next thousand years, the marketplace would have us believe that the genesis devices in the music have been reached, and that the only possibility now for our children is to recreate those devices which propelled us to this point in time. I can't agree with that viewpoint. That viewpoint is a marketplace viewpoint that has completed the transformation of bebop in the same way that the New Orleans musics became Dixieland music. They've taken the shell of bebop, aligned with academia (who have taken the music and misdefined it from a Eurocentric perspective). Bebop has suddenly become big business, but there's no respect or understanding of John Cage. Bebop's not even being taught correctly: They talk about Louis Armstrong — what about Lil Hardin Armstrong? What about our great women? When are we going to build a model that gives a truer picture of progressionalism?

Q: The two pianists of *Composition No. 95* are instructed to perform in costumes "for the purpose of 'preparation' for coming change (either vibrational or actual)." Could you elaborate on the kind of change the piece seeks to prepare?

BRAXTON: In the ritual and ceremonial musics, I would seek to better understand intention, and I would find myself seeking to intuit some understanding of the next time cycle, in terms of what the music itself seems to be suggesting. *Composition No. 95* was composed as a signal composition to indicate preparation for change states. I feel for instance that our country has already entered into another change state. We are in a transition and the present change state has not been completed — still, symbolically, the fact that we have a new President-elect hints at the nature of the change cycle we're going through. *Number 95* then would be one of the preparation-structures call — this is a call for being alert. I find myself hoping in the next time cycle to better understand functional musics and the role of functional, ritual musics in the next time cycle. The *Trillium* opera complex is an attempt to build a context of definitions related to the *Tri-axium Writings*. All of this is part of the model that I've been attempting to build — or at least, this is what I've been able to learn about my own work.

Q: I wanted to ask you about the *Trillium* project. I understand that it will ultimately consist of 36 operas.

BRAXTON: Yes. At this point five components have been completed.

Q: You're also the librettist and have written all the texts yourself?

BRAXTON: Yes. The libretto for the *Trillium* operas is the second partial of the philosophical system, that being the *Tri-axium Writings*. In the *Trillium* operas, I make a story from one of the philosophical arguments. From that point, the opera becomes a context of dialogues debating a particular argument. In this way, like the music system — that being the system starting from long sounds, trios, and from that point moving that into an orchestra, stable-logic context as a second component (and later into a ritual-synthesis component) — the same is true for the philosophical system, from philosophy to discussion of philosophy in the operas to symbolic belief.

Q: Only one of the operas has been performed so far?

BRAXTON: Just one.

Q: Has there been any interest from opera companies here in the States regarding this series?

BRAXTON: No. I have been looking for people; I'm constantly seeking and looking for possibilities, but at this point in America I have nothing to report in terms of something that has potential.

Q: Is it possible that recording some of this music could help provoke interest, or do you not want it performed unless it's staged as a full opera?

BRAXTON: I would like to have it staged. It doesn't have to be the golden performance, but I would like to hope that the next cycle for me will involve an opportunity to experience the operas.

Q: Over the years, you've led many large ensembles in performances of your music. But I was struck to see that you weren't listed as having conducted any of the six pieces on the *Creative Orchestra Music 1976* lp.

BRAXTON: I think on the two ballad compositions, the second composition on side one and the second composition on side two, I did conduct. But for the most part, because we had a creative orchestra in the tradition of the so-called jazz orchestra, there was a need to have as many saxophones as we could have, and I wanted to, because of the nature of the music, throw myself into the sectional work as well — so that we could all suffer the music together and fight to play it together. In making that decision, it required me to participate as an instrumentalist, especially for the more active rhythmic numbers, and that was why I didn't conduct.

Q: What about conducting one of the four orchestras that played in the recording of *Composition No. 82?*

BRAXTON: The original plan was for me to conduct one of the orchestras, but I was not able to arrive in Oberlin early enough. In fact, there were only two rehearsals — I think it totalled about three or four hours.

Q: It's incredible to think of a two-hour-long piece for 160 musicians being recorded under those conditions.

BRAXTON: I could not think then or now of the golden performance. I knew if I was not able to slip it in under the table in that time period, there would probably not be another opportunity. As such, we did record *Composition No. 82* for four orchestras — but the tempos were slower, and we were not able to get a totally accurate performance. For instance, if the piece had been performed as conceived, each performer would have been in a chair that could turn 360 degrees, spreading the sound as such. That aspect of *No. 82* was not realized at all. And we were also not able to position the orchestra in terms of layout correctly. We did a quick-session version of *82*. It was all that was possible. And yet I feel especially grateful to the people at Oberlin who made this possible, because they did not have to give me any opportunity. Even the small amount of rehearsal time we had, in the end, there is only profound gratitude to these people. I thank them for the experience.

Q: I understand about a third of the score had to be deleted.

BRAXTON: That's right.

Q: Can you give me an idea of what was left out?

BRAXTON: I had genetic pointillistic materials and trajectorial materials, materials which would lead the individual listener in a live performance down a given path. I made the decision to take some of that material out, since in terms of the recording, the directional components would not be heard as such anyway. And so I was really dealing with time: Do this project and get what we can get out of it before they discovered it was not going to be a jazz orchestra, and before they discovered that there was a string section and a heavy notated component. All of this of course is totally unacceptable for the "jazz" musician, even though I have been saying I'm not a jazz musician for the last 25 years; in the final analysis, an African-American with a saxophone? Ahh, he's jazz!

Q: Have you been able to continue writing the other works in the series of progressively larger multiorchestral scores, which you'd projected at that time?

BRAXTON: I'm very far behind schedule. Since coming into academia, falling behind has become a way of life. But yes, I'm still working on that series.

Q: You've worked closely with people who are deeply involved with electronics, such as Richard Teitelbaum and David Rosenboom. Is it your preference to leave that medium more to your collaborators, or are there areas in it with which you'd like to work more directly, either as composer or performer?

BRAXTON: I will have by next week a Macintosh in my office. I have just got a Kurzweil 2000 keyboard, and my plan for the next time cycle is to accelerate my efforts to learn about electronic and computer musics. I have my own agenda in terms of what I want to do with this medium, but it will not be inconsistent with the nature of the model that I have been building. Computer technology will give me the possibility to send a given logic through an extended time parameter. I'm very excited about electronics, but as part of a family of three children, my wife, and myself, my problem for the last 25 years has been to have enough money to have food on the table. It's only been recently that I've been able to get a computer for my family — we have a computer at home and the children use it — but I didn't have enough money to get another computer so that I could have one to work with. Well, now I have one coming, and my hope is to learn more and more and to become totally involved in electronics and computer music.

Q: I know you attended Wilson Junior College, studied philosophy at Roosevelt College, and went to the Chicago School of Music. Did you stay with any of these places long enough to receive degrees from them?

BRAXTON: No.

Q: That's true of most of the composers I've spoken to, who were born after the Second World War.

BRAXTON: It's incredible, but how many Ph.D.s can we cite who have been able to evolve a dynamic music? Not many, because in America in this time period the platform for Ph.D.s seems to drain the individual of those balances that could help that individual understand something fresh. Instead, our Ph.D.s are molded into a cast in the same way as our neo-classic beboppers. And so I went to the second year in college and I said to myself, "Well, it was great. Goodbye, and let me go and work on music." Because I noticed that none of my heroes were connected to academia in terms of their music, and I also noticed that most of the academic contemporary music was the least interesting music for me. Later, as I got older, I would of course try to develop more respect for academia, and of course later I would find myself connected to academia. But I find it ironic that a person who was as far away from academia as I was should find himself in the middle of academia. Fortunately, I have my sense of humor!

Q: In teaching at Mills and at Wesleyan, have you found yourself swimming against the tide, or has there been a greater openness to transforming that experience, both for your students and for yourself?

BRAXTON: I've had very positive experiences teaching. It's frustrating in the sense that I wish I could have more time to do my own work. This is one of the primary complexities of academia, that it takes so much time and energy. But I have had many positive experiences. Teaching can be very beautiful. And the process of arranging material and research, I was always involved in that anyway, and so that aspect of academia is consistent with how my life had been going anyway. I find that the 30 years I spent fighting for my music and running all around the planet, I'm very glad I did that. The problem of academia is, because 99 percent of the professors have never actually gone out and done it, the theory, the concept of theory assumes an importance that might not be healthy. If you've never tried it yourself, theory becomes a way of validation which can be dangerous. I mean no disrespect to the beauty of probabilities, or to the particulars of a given system. I'm only saying that individual experience and the challenge of an artist dictate that whatever position one arrives at, that theory should not be separate from the whole process of postulation. I can relate to individuals like George Russell or Ornette Coleman or Harry Partch; I think that part of the challenge of the next time cycle is going to be to understand the difference between Eurocentric and trans-African model building and world-cultural model building; to arrive at a new summation understanding of theory and architecture and transformation.

Q: In your recent performances in New York, I've heard you play with traditional musicians from Japan and India. Can you talk about the importance of non-Western musics for the development of your composition?

BRAXTON: I feel it's important for the individual to find his or her self, but also to get out of the self and understand the polarity. Plus, the beauty of being on the planet with all kinds of different people and possibilities, I would imagine, would be to learn as much as possible about the dynamics related to that. If one really loves music, it's kind of hard to erect a barrier in front of what music is, and say, "Well, reality for me exists from Charlie Parker to John Coltrane, or from Louis Armstrong to Duke Ellington to Herbie Hancock, that is what the music is." I feel that those individuals who are seeking to define the state of possibilities in this time cycle in that manner are giving our children a limited sense of what's happening. I'm proud that I was born in Chicago, and I tell my students here at Wesleyan and in my travels, whoever you are, wherever you're born, that is good enough. The music doesn't come from New Orleans, it doesn't come from Chicago. It comes from everybody. Every life is relevant, and there are many different ways to experience and participate in creativity. As such, having a chance to play with the Japanese master Sato and having a chance to work with Indian masters, is part of my education. There are many great traditions of music. That is why I made the decision many years ago to become a professional student of music. That way, I could continue to learn — not to mention I never wanted to give up making a mistake. If I would take away my mistakes, I wouldn't have any music!

Q: What you've described about Western and non-Western musics strikes me as analogous to questions concerning composition and improvisation: Erecting barriers between methodologies only hinders the development of creativity.

BRAXTON: I agree completely. I found myself in the '70s listening to the all-improvisational schools, moving more and more to talk of improvisation as superior to composition. That's just as dangerous as the composers who seek to emphasize composition and choke off individual dynamics and input. When the problems of African-Americans become more important than the problems of human beings, there's a problem. When the problems of the Democrats become more important than the Republicans, there's a problem. When the feminist movement extends to a point where human values are less important than the agenda for women, there's a problem. When everybody hates white men, you better believe something must be wrong. When the "ism" becomes more important than the "is," it's time to clean the mirror. Because in real life, the components are more complex than left or right or up or down, and we need a platform that can negotiate the differences in a way that can be evolutionary.

Q: Have you written scores with no improvisatory aspects for the players?

BRAXTON: The piece for four orchestras is totally written. One third of my system is in the stable logic space, one third of my system is in the mutable logic space, and one third of my system is in the synthesis logic space. I have a category of totally notated musics; I'm not against totally notated music. Sometimes it's the only thing I want to hear. Sometimes I only want to hear a march. Many of the jazz journalists will find themselves putting my music up or down for the wrong reasons. In fact, I'm not interested in having the same kind of music for every record. Part of the challenge of recognition in my opinion is the possibilities to create different kinds of musics: musics which are not exciting; musics which are very active; musics which are totally notated; musics which have no notation; musics which seek to explore possibilities for the high-sonic spectrum; musics which seek to explore the low register. I've tried and I will continue to try, just so that I can stay interested in my own work, to look for diversity.

Q: This sense of complete availabilty is a very American phenomenon, isn't it?

BRAXTON: Yes. It's part of the secret of our country, and yet it's not always understood.

Q: Would you say that, in your music for groups of like instruments — 100 tubas, say, in *Composition No. 19*, seven trumpets in *Composition No. 103* — you're moving beyond the realm of vertical harmony and into a situation in which aggregates of sound are released that have their own unique character and dynamics?

BRAXTON: You have hit it right on the mark. In my opinion, the challenge of the next time cycle will see extended possibilities, just because of where we're at in terms of technology. In that context, present-day concepts of harmony will be replaced by relationships, and relationships as a point of definition for sonic activities, but the nature of those activities will be fresh, because of the possibilities for setting forth a logic that will create its own moment that's separate from a two-dimensional, defined action that will be repeated in the same way every time. Computer technologies, virtual-reality systems are all leading towards this. So we're really talking about navigation in the three-dimensional space. In that context, what is harmony in the three-dimensional space? For my system, harmony is tri-metric pitch states. Inside of that, I'm really talking about tri-metric pitch relationships, which become a point of definition for energies which are sent out, in a fundamental state or in an expanded sense in terms of a stable solo composition, or intervallic formings as it relates to multiple logics in a combinational structure that can relate to the individual.

   There's another component to this also. I've talked of tri-metric pitch sets as a point of definition for expanded logics. There would also be the stable-logic manifestation of what that means. At present, part of the experimentation I'm doing is trying to create a music that would be analogous to a giant choo-choo-train set, where you have three tracks: stable, mutable, and synthesis tracks. We need to switch tracks to bring two musicians together, three musicians together; to cross tracks; you're driving on a highway and you see 84 going this way and 94 going this way, three vans are moving in this direction — directional logics, navigational logics; the concept of playing, for instance, *147*, but while *147* is playing, half of the people in the orchestra, who are moving through that space, will leave to be replaced by other energies. In other words, a total state of movement, stability, primary identities, secondary identities, correspondence, transitional corridors — in this way, the summation system seeks to demonstrate physicality, the physical-universe experience. The summation aesthetic is for all of these processes to be happening at once. What that means for my system would be for all of the compositions to be played at once, and for all of the improvisational logics to happen at once, with all of the meanings.

Q: So the music becomes a way of perceiving the world and functioning in it, in a manner that creates new possibilities for the individual.

BRAXTON: It will create new problems too. The work of Plato and Aristotle did not have to be used in the way that it has. But our species is dynamic, and we always find a way to use the information "to the hilt"!

COMPOSITIONS

1968   *Composition No. 1* for piano
1968   *Composition No. 2* for any four single-line instruments
1968   *Composition No. 3* for any eight single-line instruments, piano,
        and two percussionists (one playing inside the piano)
1968   *Composition No. 4* for five tubas
1968   *Composition No. 5* for piano
1966-72 *Composition No. 6a-p* sixteen compositions for the creative
        improvisational ensemble
1969   *Composition No. 7* for orchestra
1966-69 *Composition No. 8a-k* eleven compositions for solo instrumentalist
1969   *Composition No. 9* for four amplified shovels
1969   *Composition No. 10* for piano
1969   *Composition No. 11* for creative orchestra
1969   *Composition No. 12* for woodwind quintet
1970   *Composition No. 13* for any four single-line instruments
1970   *Composition No. 14* for solo instrumentalist
1970   *Composition No. 15* for any four instruments
1971   *Composition No. 16* for four pianos
1971   *Composition No. 17* for string quartet
1971   *Composition No. 18* for string quartet
1971   *Composition No. 19* for 100 tubas
1971   *Composition No. 20* for two instruments
1971   *Composition No. 21* for recorded tape with or without instruments
1971   *Composition No. 22* for four soprano saxophones
1971-74 *Composition No. 23a-p* sixteen compositions for the creative ensemble

1971	*Composition No. 24* for orchestra
1972	*Composition No. 25* for creative orchestra
1970-74	*Composition No. 26a-j* ten compositions for the creative solo instrumentalist
1972	*Composition No. 27* for orchestra
1973	*Composition No. 28* for six musicians and dancers
1973-75	*Composition No. 29a-e* five compositions for piano and two wind instruments
1973	*Composition No. 30* for piano
1974	*Composition No. 31* for piano
1974	*Composition No. 32* for piano
1974	*Composition No. 33* for piano
1974	*Compositions Nos. 34, 35, 36* three compositions for synthesizer and two instruments
1974	*Composition No. 37* for saxophone quartet
1974	*Composition No. 38a-b* two compositions for one single-line instrument and synthesizer
1974	*Composition No. 39* for creative orchestra
1974-76	*Composition No. 40a-q* seventeen compositions for the creative ensemble
1974	*Composition No. 41* for chamber orchestra
1974	*Composition No. 42* for creative orchestra
1974	*Compositions Nos. 43, 44* two compositions for the creative quintet
1975	*Composition No. 45* for creative orchestra
1975	*Composition No. 46* for ten instruments
1975	*Compositions Nos. 47, 48* two compositions for the creative quintet
1975	*Composition No. 49* for one to twenty musicians with or without dancers
1975	*Composition No. 50* for two instrumentalists and two synthesizer players
1976	*Composition No. 51* for creative orchestra
1976	*Compositions Nos. 52, 53, 54* three compositions for the creative quartet
1976	*Composition No. 55* for creative orchestra
1976	*Composition No. 56* for creative orchestra
1976	*Composition No. 57* for creative orchestra
1976	*Composition No. 58* for creative marching orchestra
1976	*Composition No. 59* for two soloists and thirteen instrumentalists
1976	*Compositions Nos. 60, 61, 62* three compositions for piano and one wind instrument
1976	*Composition No. 63* for two soloists and chamber orchestra
1976-78	*Compositions Nos. 64, 65, 66, 67, 68* five compositions for creative instrumentalists
1976-79	*Composition No. 69a-q* seventeen compositions for the creative ensemble
1976	*Composition No. 70* for quintet
1977	*Composition No. 71* for creative orchestra

1977   *Composition No. 72a-h* eight compositions for one single-line
        instrument and string bass
1977   *Composition No. 73* for three instrumentalists
1977   *Composition No. 74a-e* five compositions for the creative duo
1977   *Composition No. 75* for three instrumentalists
1977   *Composition No. 76* for three instrumentalists
1977-80 *Composition No. 77a-j* ten compositions for solo instrumentalist
1977   *Composition No. 78* for creative orchestra
1977-78 *Compositions Nos. 79, 80, 81* three compositions for piano, two
        woodwinds, and brass
1978   *Composition No. 82* for four orchestras
1978   *Composition No. 83* for orchestra
1978   *Composition No. 84* for any number of instruments
1978   *Compositions Nos. 85, 86, 87, 88* four compositions for one
        woodwind instrument and string bass
1979   *Composition No. 89* for creative orchestra
1979   *Composition No. 90* for any number of instruments
1979   *Composition No. 91* for creative orchestra
1979   *Composition No. 92* for creative orchestra
1979   *Composition No. 93* for creative orchestra
1980   *Composition No. 94* for three instrumentalists
1980   *Composition No. 95* for two pianists
1980   *Composition No. 96* for orchestra and four slide projectors
1966-84 *Composition No. 97a-j* ten compositions for any instrumentation
1981   *Composition No. 98* for four winds, two brass, and piano
1978-83 *Composition No. 99a-k* eleven compositions for solo instrumentalist
1981   *Composition No. 100* for fifteen instruments
1981   *Composition No. 101* for one multi-instrumentalist (wind or
        brass) and piano
1982   *Composition No. 102* for orchestra and puppet theater
1983   *Composition No. 103* for seven trumpets
1966-84 *Composition No. 104a-l* twelve compositions for any instrumentation
1984   *Composition No. 105* for quartet
1982-85 *Composition No. 106a-m* thirteen compositions for solo instrumentalist
1983   *Composition No. 107* for two multi-instrumentalists (wind or
        brass) and piano
1984   *Composition No. 108a-d* four compositions for any instrumentation
1966-84 *Composition No. 109a-l* twelve compositions for any instrumentation
1984   *Composition No. 110a-d* four compositions for quartet
1970-84 *Composition No. 111* for any instrumentation
1983   *Composition No. 112* for creative orchestra
1983   *Composition No. 113* for one soloist, a large photograph, and
        prepared stage

1984	*Composition No. 114* for any instrumentation
1984	*Composition No. 115* for any instrumentation
1984	*Composition No. 116* for four instruments
1984	*Composition No. 117* for any instrumentation
1984-86	*Composition No. 118a-l* twelve compositions for solo instrumentalist
1985-86	*Composition No. 119a-i* nine compositions for solo instrumentalist
1984	*Composition No. 120a Trillium — Dialogues A* opera
	Composition No. 120b Zackko Ring for any instrumentation
	Composition No. 120c for solo baritone saxophone
	Composition No. 120d for solo instrumentalist and dancer
	Composition No. 120e for solo sousaphone or tuba
1984	*Composition No. 121* for piano, any two single-line instruments, and percussion
1985	*Composition No. 122* for piano, any two single-line instruments, and percussion
1985	*Composition No. 123* for solo flute, slides, and constructed environment
1985	*Composition No. 124* for any instrumentation
1986	*Composition No. 125* for solo tuba, light show, and constructed environment
1986	*Composition No. 126a Trillium — Dialogues M* opera
	Composition No. 126b Joreo Ring for any instrumentation
1986	*Composition No. 127* for four instrumentalists and dance ensemble
1986	*Composition No. 128* for solo wind instrument and two dancers
1986	*Composition No. 129* for five woodwind instruments
1986	*Composition No. 130* for four instruments
1986	*Composition No. 131* for four instruments
1986	*Composition No. 132* for two dancers, six mobile soloists, organ, and two chamber orchestras
1986	*Composition No. 133* for any instrumentation
1986	*Composition No. 134* for creative orchestra
1987	*Composition No. 135* for twelve instruments
1987	*Composition No. 136* for any instrumentation
1987	*Composition No. 137* for creative orchestra
1987	*Composition No. 138a-e* five compositions for the creative solo instrumentalist
1988	*Composition No. 139* for piano
1988	*Composition No. 140* for four instruments
1988	*Composition No. 141* for six instruments
1988	*Composition No. 142* for six instruments
1988	*Composition No. 143* for two instruments
1988	*Composition No. 144* for five instruments
1988	*Composition No. 145* for seven instruments
1988	*Composition No. 146* for fifteen instruments

1989	*Composition No. 147* for three clarinets and ensemble
1989	*Composition No. 148* for four instruments
1990	*Composition No. 149* for any instrumentation
1990	*Composition No. 150* for any instrumentation
1991	*Composition No. 151* for twenty-five instruments
1991	*Compositions Nos. 152, 153, 154, 155, 156, 157* six compositions for one wind instrument and string bass
1991	*Composition No. 158* for four instruments
1991	*Composition No. 159* for four instruments
1991	*Composition No. 160* for four instruments
1991	*Composition No. 161* for four instruments
1991	*Composition No. 162a Trillium R* opera
	Composition No. 162b Shala Ring for any instrumentalist
	Composition No. 162c Shala "Crowd" Movements for ten or more instrumentalists/dancers and/or singers
	Composition No. 162d Shala "Sitting" Movements for any amount of performers — in solo or group
	Composition No. 162e Shala "Chinese Dragon" Path Connections for ten or more voices
	Composition No. 162f for solo oboe
1991	*Composition No. 163* for twenty-four instruments
1992	*Composition No. 164* for twenty-two instruments
1992	*Composition No. 165* for eighteen instruments

All compositions published by Synthesis Music. Inquiries about scores should be sent to Frog Peak Music, Box A36, Hanover, NH 03755.

DISCOGRAPHY

1968
Compositions Nos. 6e, 6d
Delmark 415 lp; cd (1991)

Compositions Nos. 8a, 8f, 8h, 8(a/b), 8d, 8c, 8g, 8b
Delmark 420/1 lp

1970
Composition No. 6g
Byg 529 315 lp
Affinity 15 lp

Compositions Nos. 6h, 8k, 6f
Byg 529 347 lp
Affinity 25 lp

1971

Composition No. 16
Musica 2004 lp

Compositions Nos. 6k, 6j, 6a, 22, 6i, 4, 6l, 6m
Freedom 400112/3 lp
Arista 1902 lp

Composition No. 6f
Blue Note LA472-H2 lp

Composition No. 6f
ECM 1018/19 lp

1972

Compositions Nos. 20, 21
Delmark 428 lp

Compositions Nos. 23l, 23k
America 6122 lp

Compositions Nos. 8i, 26a, 26j, 26b, 26d, 8j, 26c, 26i, 26f
America 011/2 lp
Inner City 1008 lp (1976)

Composition No. 25
Ring 01024/5/6 lp

Compositions Nos. 6n, 6(o), 6p
Trio 3008/9 lp

1973

Compositions Nos. 23n, 23p, 23m, 23(o)
Nippon Columbia 8504-N lp
Denon YX-7506-ND lp

1974

Compositions Nos. 26b, 26h, 77b, 26e, 26f, 26g
Ring/Moers 01002 lp

Compositions Nos. 23b, 23e, 40(o), 40m, 23f, 23d
Ring 010010/11 lp

1975

Composition No. 36
Sackville 3007 lp

Compositions Nos. 23b, 23c, 23d, 38a, 37, 23a
Arista 4032 lp

Compositions Nos. 23h, 23g, 23e, 40m
Arista 4064 lp

1976

Compositions Nos. 30+31
Finnadar 9011 lp

Compositions Nos. 51, 56, 58, 57, 55, 59
Arista 4080 lp; Bluebird 6579-2 cd (1988)

Composition No. 6f (excerpt)
Douglas 7046 lp

1977

Compositions Nos. 40n, 23j, 40(o), 6c, 6f, 40k, 63
Arista 5002 lp

Compositions Nos. 60, 40p, 62
Arista 4101 lp

Composition Nos. 64, 65
Moers 01036 lp

Compositions Nos. 40q, 74b, 74a
Sackville 3016 lp

Composition No. 69q
ECM 1-1109 lp

1978

Composition No. 76
Arista 4181 lp

Composition No. 82
Arista A3L 8900 lp

1979

Compositions Nos. 77a, 77c, 77d, 77e, 26f, 77f, 26b, 77g, 26e, 77h
Arista 8602 lp

1980

Compositions Nos. 69c, 69e, 69g, 40f, 69f, 23g, 40i
Hat Hut 19 lp

Compositions Nos. 17, 26e, 26i, 77d, 77e, 77b, 26b
Sound Aspects 009 lp, cd

Compositions Nos. 69g, 40f, 69m, 40d, 40i, 69h, 69k
Moers 01066 lp

1981

Composition No. 98
Hat Hut 1984 lp

Composition No. 42
Nessa 20 lp

Compositions Nos. 40b, 69n, 34, 40a, 40g, 52
Antilles 1005 lp; 422-848 585-2 cd (1990)

1982
Composition No. 95
Arista 9559 lp

Compositions Nos. 69b, 69a, 23j, 6a, 69p, 6n
Cecma 1005 lp

Composition No. 101
Dischi Della Quercia 28015 lp

Composition No. 107
Hat Hut 2030 lp, cd

1983
Compositions Nos. 105a, 69m, 69(o), 69q
Black Saint 0066 lp

Composition No. 6k
Hat Hut 1999/2000 lp

1984
Composition No. 113
Sound Aspects 003 lp

1985
Compositions Nos. 114(+108a), 110c, 115, 110a(+108b), 110d, 116
Black Saint 0086 lp, cd

1986
Composition No. 62 (+30+96)
Mills College 001 lp

Compositions Nos. 131, 88(+108c), 124(+96), 122(+108a+96),
101(+31+96+30)
Black Saint 0106 lp, cd

1988
Compositions Nos. 40d(+108a+108b), 136(+96), 86
Rastascan 002 lp

1989

Composition No. 129+
Sound Aspects 023 cd

Compositions Nos. 141(+20+96+120d), 142
Victo 02 lp

Composition No. 96
Leo 169 lp

Compositions Nos. 138a, 106d, 118f, 138b, 77g, 118a, 138c, 106j, 77c, 26f, 119i(+99e), 119g, 99b, 106a, 138d, 106c
New Albion 023 cd

1990

Compositions Nos. 99, 101, 139, 99b(+97c, 117e, 117h+118h), 107
Hat Hut 6019 cd

Compositions Nos. 40d, 40g(+63), 40j, 110a(+1b+69j), 6j
Hat Hut 6025 cd

Composition No. 98
Hat Hut 6062 cd

Compositions Nos. 69c, 69e, 69g, 40f, 69f, 23g, 40i
Hat Hut 6044 cd

Compositions Nos. 85, 87
Sound Aspects 031 cd

Compositions Nos. 105a, 110a, 114, 69h
Sound Aspects 038 cd

Compositions Nos. 136, 140(+112+30), 62, 116
Music & Arts 611 cd

1991

Composition No. 107 (excerpt)
Centaur 2110 cd

Compositions Nos. 112, 91, 134, 100, 93, 45, 71, 59
Black Saint 120137-2 cd

Compositions Nos. 40f, 23j, 40(o), 6c, 40b
Hat Hut 6075 cd

Compositions Nos. 110a(+96+108b), 110a(+96), 60(+96+108c), 85(+30+108d), 105b(+7+32+96), 87(+108e), 23j, 69h(+31+96), 40(o)
Leo 200/201, 202/203 cd

1992
Compositions Nos. 147, 151
Hat Hut 6086 cd

Compositions Nos. 160(+5)+40j, 23m(+10), 158(+96)+40l, 40a, 40b, 161, 159, 23c+32+105b(+30), 23m(+10), 40m, 67(+147+96), 140(+47+139+135), 34a, 20+86, 23g(+147+30), 69(o)(+135), 69b, 107(+96), 101, 23n(+112+108a+33)
Hat Hut 61001/4 cd

Compositions Nos. 6n, 6o, 6p
Hat Hut 6119 cd

Compositions Nos. 156, 152, 40a, 157, 155, 154, 153
Music & Arts 710 cd

Composition No. 165
New Albion 050 cd

Compositions Nos. 92+(30,32,139) + (108c,108d)
New World 80418-2 cd

arrangements

1974
In The Tradition, Volume 1
Steeplechase 1015 lp

In The Tradition, Volume 2
Steeplechase 1045 lp

1985
Seven Standards 1985, Vol. 1
Magenta 0203 lp, cs

Seven Standards 1985, Vol. 2
Magenta 0205 lp, cs

1988
Six Monk's Compositions 1988
Black Saint 120116-1 lp, -2 cd, -4 cs

1990
Eight (+3) Tristano Compositions (1989) for Warne Marsh
Hat Hut 6052 cd

collaborations

with Muhal Richard Abrams:
Duets 1976 Arista 4101 lp (1976)

with Derek Bailey:
Duo 1 Emanem 3313 lp (1975)
Duo 2 Emanem 3314 lp (1975)
Royal, Volume 1 Incus 43 lp (1986)
Moments Précieux Victo 02 lp (1987)
Royal, Volume 2 Incus 44 lp (1987)

with Derek Bailey's Company:
Company 2 Incus 23 lp (1976)
Company 5 Incus 28 lp (1977)
Company 6 Incus 29 lp (1977)
Company 7 Incus 30 lp (1977)

with Circle:
Live In German Concert CBS Sony 19XJ lp (1971)
Gathering CBS Sony 20XJ lp (1971)
Paris-Concert ECM 1018/19 lp (1972); 843 163-2 cd (1990)
Circling In Blue Note LA472-H2 lp (1975)
Circulus Blue Note LA882-J2 lp (1978)

with the Creative Construction Company:
Volume One Muse 5071 lp (1970)
Volume Two Muse 5097 lp (1970)

with Giorgio Gaslini:
Four Pieces Dischi Della Quercia 28015 lp (1982)

with Joseph Jarman:
Together Alone Delmark 428 lp (1972)

with Roscoe Mitchell:
Duets With Anthony Braxton Sackville 3016 lp (1977)

with Neighbours:
With Anthony Braxton GNM vol. 3 120 754 lp (1980)

with Max Roach:
Birth And Rebirth Black Saint 0024 lp (1978)
One In Two — Two In One Hat Hut 2R06 lp (1979)

with Gino Robair:
Duets 1987 Rastascan 002 lp (1988)
"She Left Him For A Her" Elemental / T.E.C. Tones 90902 cd (1990)

with Gyorgy Szabados:
Szabraxtondos Krem 17909 lp (1984)

with Richard Teitelbaum:
Open Aspects '82 Hat Hut 1995/6 lp (1982)

guest artist

with Muhal Richard Abrams:
Levels And Degrees Of Light Delmark 413 lp (1968); cd (1991)
1-OQA+19 Black Saint 120017-1 lp (1978); -2 cd, -4 cs (1990)

with Ran Blake:
Rapport Arista-Novus 3006 lp (1978)

with Marion Brown:
Afternoon Of A Georgia Faun ECM 1004 lp (1971)

with Dave Brubeck:
All The Things We Are Atlantic 1684 lp (1976); cd (1988)

with Jack Coursil:
Black Suite BYG 529 349 lp (1970); America 6111 lp (1971)

with the Globe Unity Orchestra:
Jahrmarkt / Local Fair Po Torch JWD2 pl (1976)
Pearl FMP 0380 lp (1978)

with Gunter Hampel:
The 8th Of July 1969 Birth 001 lp (1969)
Familie Birth 008 lp (1972)
Enfant Terrible Birth 0025 lp (1975)

with the David Holland Quartet:
Conference Of The Birds ECM 1027 lp (1973); 829373-2 cd (1988)

with the Instant Composers Pool:
[untitled] ICP 007/8 lp (1970)

with Leroy Jenkins:
Silence Freedom 40123 lp (1970)
B-X°—NO/47A Byg 529 315 lp (1970); Affinity 15 lp (1970)
For Players Only JCOA/Virgin 2005 lp (1975)

with George Lewis:
Elements Of Surprise Moers 01036 lp (1977)

with John Lindberg:
Trilogy Of Works For Eleven Instrumentalists Black Saint 0082 lp (1985)

with Roscoe Mitchell:
Noonah Nessa 9/10 lp (1977)
LRG/The Maze/S 11 Examples Nessa 14/15 lp (1978)
Sketches From Bamboo Moers 02024 lp (1979)

with the New York Section of Composers of the '70s:
New American Music, Volume 3 Folkways 33903 lp (1976)

with David Rosenboom:
A Precipice In Time Centaur 2110 cd (1991)

with Woody Shaw:
The Iron Men Muse 5160 lp (1977)

with Archie Shepp & Philly Joe Jones:
[untitled] America 6102 lp (1970)

with Alan Silva:
Lunar Surface BYG 529 312 lp (1970)

with Leo Smith:
Three Compositions Of New Jazz Delmark 415 lp (1968); cd (1991)
Silence Freedom 40123 lp (1970)
B-X°—NO/47A Byg 529 315 lp (1970); Affinity 15 lp (1970)
Budding Of A Rose Moers 02026 lp (1979)

with Paul Smoker:
QB Alvas 101 lp (1984)

with Richard Teitelbaum:
Time Zones Arista 1037 lp (1977)
Concerto Grosso Hat Hut cd (1989)

with Walter Thompson:
Four Compositions Dane 001 lp (1980)

with Three Motions:
Impressions RAU 1010 lp (1979)

with Andrew Voigt:
Kol Nidre
Sound Aspects 031 cd (1990)

BIBLIOGRAPHY

The eight volumes of Anthony Braxton's writings — *Tri-axium Writings 1-3*
(1985) and *Composition Notes A-E* (1988) — are published by Synthesis Music
and available through Frog Peak Music, Box A36, Hanover, NH 03755.

LUCIA DLUGOSZEWSKI

photo: Gene Bagnato

LUCIA DLUGOSZEWSKI / Introduction

LUCIA DLUGOSZEWSKI was born in Detroit, Michigan, on June 16, 1934. She attended the Detroit Conservatory of Music, where she studied piano and composition, and was a pre-med student at Wayne State University from 1949 to '52, where she received her B.S. in chemistry. In 1949 she also gave her first concert of "everyday sounds" in Detroit, which consisted of the sounds of daily activities. Frustrated by the sexism and ageism that blocked her attempts to enter medical school, she abandoned her idea of becoming a doctor and instead accepted an opportunity to move to New York and study piano with Grete Sultan in 1952. While there she gave another concert of "everyday sounds" and studied composition with Felix Salzer at Mannes College. Around this time, she wrote scores for productions by The Living Theater. Soon thereafter she began studying composition with Edgard Varèse.

In 1951 she devised her innovative "timbre piano," a unique preparation of the instrument which she has since employed in a variety of pieces. The following year, she encountered choreographer Erick Hawkins, who was looking for a pianist for his dancers, and by the mid '50s she was writing scores for his company. She has been an indispensable fixture in his company ever since, producing scores for many of his most enduring works, including *Here And Now With Watchers* (1957), *Geography Of Noon* (1964), *Lords Of Persia* (1965), *Black Lake* (1969), *Of Love* (1971), *Angels Of The Inmost Heaven* (1972), and *Cantilever Two* (1988). For Hawkins's dance *Eight Clear Places* (1960), she devised over a hundred percussion instruments which were constructed for her by sculptor Ralph Dorazio and which she has since used in many of her compositions.

Dlugoszewski's radical innovations in rhythm, timbre, and instrumental technique attracted increasing attention in the '60s. During this time, she also composed scores for films by Jonas Mekas, Ben Moore, and Marie Menken. By the '70s, her music began to be recorded and received performances by such noted conductors as Pierre Boulez, Lukas Foss, Joel Thome, Gunther Schuller, and Dennis Russell Davies. Her work underwent a tragic eclipse in the '80s with the protracted illness of her mother. After her mother's passing in 1988, Dlugoszewski began putting the pieces of her career back together, and in the '90s has premiered new compositions and resumed performing, both with Erick Hawkins and in concerts of her music.

Dlugoszewski has taught at New York University, the New School for Social Research, and the Foundation for Modern Dance. She has been awarded the National Institute of Arts and Letters Award and the Koussevitzky International Record Award. An accomplished author, she has also received the Tompkins

Literary Award for Poetry. She is the recipient of Guggenheim and Thorne Fellowships, and grants from the National Endowment for the Arts, the Martha Baird Rockefeller Foundation, and the Creative Artists Public Service Program. Her music has been commissioned by numerous sources, including the Ingram-Merrill Foundation, the New York Philharmonic, the Louisville Orchestra, the Lincoln Center Chamber Society, the American Brass Quintet, and the American Composers Orchestra.

I spoke with Lucia Dlugoszewski at the Erick Hawkins Dance Studio in New York City on July 15, 1991, and again at my home on January 10, 1993. The freedom of composing scores for Hawkins has long been a double-edged sword for Dlugoszewski: She could pursue her inspiration without hindrance, but her music would be heard mostly by people who weren't primarily listening to it. As a result, her long and distinguished career has received scant documentation from the press and the recording industry, which has made her a difficult subject to research. So I was eager for this chance to learn more about her development as a composer, performer, instrument-designer, teacher, choreographer, and aesthetic theorist.

LUCIA DLUGOSZEWSKI / Interview

Q: When you attended the Detroit Conservatory of Music, were you also composing or were you only a piano student?

DLUGOSZEWSKI: I was a composer right off the bat. I went there when I was nine years old, and they had me do a little concert. In fact, I was the first one to do an all-Bach concert at the Detroit Conservatory — because I wanted to do it. I also had my own pieces right away. I mean, I don't know.... But I had my own pieces, what can I say?

Q: What were they like? Do you recall at all?

DLUGOSZEWSKI: They all thought I was kind of unusual! I was the first one to demand to play the Ravel *Sonatatine*. And the rest of them in the Detroit Conservatory said, "How do you know that you're not playing wrong notes?" I just knew I wanted it, but why, I wouldn't know. My mother gave me my first lessons — they were just little piano lessons — and she had not had too much training. Both my parents were very bright, but they didn't have too much formal education. So it was all on my own. I was just a strange one, right from the start!

When I went to high school, I had been playing the piano for a long time and composing. Then I majored in science, and so from college I have a Bachelor of Science in chemistry — because I did not want to earn my living through music. I just wanted the music to be very pure, so that I could have the maximum adventure possible, without somebody doing a mind trip on me because of the marketplace.

Q: Were you pre-med while at Wayne State University?

DLUGOSZEWSKI: I was pre-med, yes. My father obviously was a very free spirit and very bright. Like all fathers, he wanted a son, but one of the great things about him was that he had me and he educated me to be a free spirit too, as if I had been a son. So I was very lucky, I didn't have that stigma that girls of my age had: "You can't do this." So the first blow came when I applied for medical school. I was only 15, and I think I looked 10. My grades were great, but at that time, the male-chauvinist business was so great in pre-med. And a girl — and with a Polish name on top of that? Forget it.

But the joke is that I had this crazy idea that I would earn my living as a doctor, the way Chekhov did or the way William Carlos Williams did, and then do the music! I mean, can you imagine that? It would have been a battle just to become a doctor then. And then the music too! But the blow of being rejected that first time around at medical school was a very big trauma. I just couldn't understand it, and my parents couldn't understand it. Then I got the offer to work in New York City with a concert pianist named Grete Sultan — and I took it right after graduation.

Q: How did that offer come about?

DLUGOSZEWSKI: She was a friend of another concert pianist, Katje Andi, who was a very good friend of Edward Bredshall, the pianist I was studying with. I guess I always got a lot of attention, but people always thought I was very strange, and I think Edward Bredshall just felt that Grete Sultan was such a far-out concert pianist, that this would be something I should be doing. When I came to New York, I also began to study analysis with Felix Salzer. He wrote a book called *Structural Hearing* and it was very good but it never acknowledged Schoenberg. Actually, we got along very well in terms of the analysis — he's a very nice man — but when I was asked to write a piece of my own, I knew I was going to write a piece. When he began to look at my music, he didn't say anything to me for two weeks, and then he looked very unhappy and said, "I don't think I'm the teacher for you." But he did send me to Ben Weber and to John Cage and to Edgard Varèse, and he said, "You could study privately with these people."

So I took my little piece to them, and they all were very complimentary. But I always say that that's when I really had my first great lesson in composition, because they wanted to know who were the others that I was going to see. And the minute they found out who the others were, they would put them down, totally. Of course, we know about that, but I thought then, "These are Masters, and if one Master fights another Master, what does it mean?" And in a funny way it reinforced this wonderful thing I got from my father, of never putting anybody's head over my own. Which I think is a great thing to have when you're going to do creative work, because in the end, that's what you've gotta do anyhow. It takes so long for some people, but I had it. This so-called strangeness comes from the fact that my Dad was this free spirit. I was born in the heart of the Depression, so my father was always around because he wasn't working. There was nowhere to work — and he was very idealistic. What a combination! I remember coming home from school, and saying, as a child will, "Daddy, the teacher said this or this," and he'd say, "That's nonsense." And I'd look at him and I'd say, "But the teacher said that." And he'd say, "He's just a man" — or "she's just a woman" — "so just remember that. You have a brain just like theirs."

I remember going to John Cage, and I think he would have liked me to be his follower that way, but I just thought that whole chance direction wasn't for me; I felt I saw flaws in it philosophically. And he wasn't too happy about that. But I remember when he wanted to know who else I was going to see, and he said, "Oh, you're not going to see Edgard Varèse! All he does is write wrong notes." And when I went to Varèse, he said, "You're not going to go to John Cage! He has no form."

Actually, I ended up with Edgard Varèse. I had never heard his music before — not in Detroit, Michigan. And then I heard it and I just flipped. My instinct took me there, and I think that was the best solution for me. He didn't teach — not really. You teach yourself, he'd said. Another man like my father. And we were very, very good friends in constant dialogue until he died.

Q: At the time you went to him — around 1953, '54 — wasn't he gathering the sounds for the taped sections of *Déserts*?

DLUGOSZEWSKI: That's right, that's when I was so excited. I went to the

Town Hall concert where he had his retrospective, where *Déserts* was, and that was just a fantastic concert.

Q: Did it ever seem to you that Varèse was trying to draw you into electronic composition?

DLUGOSZEWSKI: Naturally, he had the feeling that it was going to be the hope of the future, and I guess I backed away from that the way I did from John Cage's chance. At the time that Varèse was working on it, it was a very exciting possibility for new sound. But I think it's beginning to show itself up since then. First of all, in everything that I've done, I don't think I have ever been limited by just using live music. I think I have certainly created areas of sound which equal anything electronic. I've never heard anything that I coveted which I haven't done some other way, with the added, most important dimension of aliveness. And the big thing for me is that you bring in the live musician and that sense of spirit. Now they have those keyboards were you press a key and you open up a whole universe — some universe! And so you don't feel the passion and the evolution of how you got those sounds. The machine has just gone into play, but what have you yourself done? Nothing. Whereas a violinist works so hard to get those tones, and his ear has to be so aware, and all that. I think that the element of the live musician, and the spontaneity of the live musician, has always been the thing that I felt I missed in electronic music. It's not that some people haven't written very interesting stuff, but I always feel that deadness — that's just what I feel.

Q: After you arrived in New York, you gave a concert which involved listening to the sounds of ordinary actions. How did someone at that time get from studying at the Detroit Conservatory of Music to playing such a concert?

DLUGOSZEWSKI: I guess I was like that already, right from the start. That's how my verbal poetry was, and that's why I think Chester Kuhn was so interested in me. Actually, *The Structure For The Poetry Of Everyday Sounds* was an extreme experiment in what Zen Buddhism calls "suchness." The New York piece was performed in the loft of a wonderful sculptor, Ralph Dorazio, and the whole New York school of painters and poets and composers were there, including John Cage and Morton Feldman. John loved it and said I created a whole new kind of theater. That "everyday" stuff really made John flip. In fact, he and Morty had a fight over it that night, because they both came and Morty obviously was very possessive about John and was determined to put me down, and John just argued with him all night long about that, and kept telling him he was wrong about me.

Q: I've read different accounts — was the everyday-sounds concert in '49 or '52?

DLUGOSZEWSKI: There were two different concerts: One was done in Detroit in '49, and the other in New York in '52.

Q: I'm fascinated that you already had an ear for that.

DLUGOSZEWSKI: I don't mean that this is the whole story, but I think that intervallic music always expresses direct emotion, and there's no getting around it. I mean, it just does, I don't care if you're Stockhausen or Hovhaness or whatever. And there are aspects of human emotion which limit our deepest imagination because they're involved with our egos. The music that depresses me the most is the kind that uses that intervallic, melodic thing to manipulate us, and it's always moaning around. This "neo-Romanticism" is not Romanticism, it just sounds like self-pity constantly going on and on. So in the end, with music at its worst, people are manipulated emotionally because of the melodies, but they haven't really heard, sound by sound. A passionate melodic ear, on the other hand, is the one of Hovhaness; and then the long pure journey of luminous melodic invention of Lou Harrison; and then Ned Rorem, the poet's joy, who truly embraced their words with his rich melodies. These three devoted their lives in different ways to the purity of melodic vision. And then this clunky neo-Romanticism in its totally calculated way really pollutes this freshness and authenticity.

The Western tradition — I don't know what else to call it now — has acted as if timbre is a superficial thing, because of their philosophic point of view. They think that there's the thing in itself and then there are the properties, like timbre, around it. But in Eastern mysticism, especially in Zen Buddhism, they feel that the actual immediacy of the sound is extremely valid, extremely significant. With the everyday sounds, I was just fascinated with the idea that you could get sounds that wouldn't stimulate your emotions but would stimulate your sense of wonder. I think that was something in me, and it's still in me — I mean, it's a very deep core that makes me love the Zen Buddhist artists of classical China and classical Japan so much. With my everyday sound, I didn't know it at the time, but I was creating a historic experiment in extreme Zen suchness.

I also feel that, in the current stream of things, the idea of knowing what beauty is became almost suspect. So I think it takes a special courage to try to know what beauty is. But even more than that, I wanted to make those leaps, like rituals of immediacy, into that sense of aliveness. Meister Eckhardt said that God created the world now. I heard that and I liked it. It's the enlightenment idea: You created it now and you created it now and you created it now. And that's immortality; once you're in the now, that's immortality. It's the only one I can think of which we've got.

Q: At the New York concert of everyday sounds, you screened off the performers so the audience couldn't see them?

DLUGOSZEWSKI: Right. And then Cage insisted that we take away the screens and play it again.

Q: Had the players also been screened off in Detroit?

DLUGOSZEWSKI: No, they were visible. I was just trying it out, with the group where I was writing poetry, because they were the most far out on the campus. I just felt a wonderful flowering in that, so they gave me a lot of courage

— especially the teacher of the group, Chester Kuhn, who teased me that I was his Rimbaud.

Q: I take it part of the point in screening off the New York players was to make the sounds less categorized and more themselves for the listeners?

DLUGOSZEWSKI: Right. Now I think we shouldn't have; I think it was just nerves. I was going way out on a limb at that time: Nobody else was doing this; there was no *musique concrète* (that I knew of — maybe there was). Some of my friends at the time said, you'd better, because it's going to distract everyone. Now I think I would leave it open. I actually wrote a third *Structure For The Poetry Of Everyday Sounds* for the Living Theater's production of Jarry's *Ubu Roi*, for two performers, Ralph Dorazio and Mary Norton Dorazio. She's the one with the very strangely poetic dangerous ears.

Q: With the unusual percussion battery of *Radical Quidditas For An Unborn Baby*, there seems to be a real concern that people should see how the sound is being made.

DLUGOSZEWSKI: Absolutely. I thought that visually it was terrific to see all those percussion instruments, and one player playing them. And ultimately, music is the making and hearing of a sound.

Western philosophic ideas about reality I think are linguistic distortions; as a matter of fact, I think what the Zen koans are all about is just to crack linguistic distortion. In the West, the idea of theater is that it always has to be an illusion. But in classical Eastern theater, everything is real. With Western Puritanism, dancers were kicked out of the whole official culture, because the body was dirty. But music was left in. Why? Because it is considered so "spiritual." It's mysterious, invisible, it doesn't paint tables and chairs, and therefore it's called "spiritual." It was always in the pit, where no one could see them do anything, and it came up invisibly, like a "spirit." I just saw for the first time in Japan a Noh play that lasted four hours. And all the musicians were on the stage, right with the actors — they were not ignoring the reality of what was happening; everything was real. I think you get a tremendous vitality that way; you get tremedous excitement. That idea of immediacy that only the live performer can bring, I think, is spiritually just a thrilling, thrilling thing.

Q: The sense of mystery in the sound is greater when it's played out front than when it's hidden.

DLUGOSZEWSKI: Absolutely, because then everyone in the audience can empathize. The musician is an actor or a ritual figure, re-enacting the drama of making it happen, and everyone is there with him or her, making it happen.

Q: How do you feel about your music when it's recorded?

DLUGOSZEWSKI: I think it just is never as wonderful as a live performance. To tell you the truth, I believe in the live performance, but I get very vulnerable in modern society, whether you're getting grants or whatever, and in an effort to have some kind of currency, I would like more people to know that I exist — but that's just a human, egocentric need.

Q: It's also easier to make the work if it has more of an audience.

DLUGOSZEWSKI: Absolutely. I haven't had a recording since *Fire Fragile Flight*. I think it's harder to do now, you have to work at it politically — and I have a hard enough time just surviving and writing my music and keeping pure to my vision; that career hang-up is really more than I can handle.

Q: You play the percussion part in the CRI recording of *Tender Theatre Flight Nageire*.

DLUGOSZEWSKI: That's right. I'm playing the kind of invented instruments that you saw in *Radical Quidditas For An Unborn Baby*.

Q: I understand that you've designed a hundred of these instruments.

DLUGOSZEWSKI: Erick Hawkins commissioned me to do an hour-length, uninterrupted piece of music for a dance that he choreographed, which was just pure meditation on nature. I think that's what gave me the impetus to do it. I started to write it for traditional instruments that had the melodic possibilities, and then I realized that, particularly in that work, they would interfere with the purity of his nature meditation. Then I began to look at the percussion instruments, but our traditional percussion instruments are so ... what? So masculine in the wrong sense. Remember the contemporary orchestral pieces with all that "aggressive" percussion? It makes me think, the way they treat those drums, that they're really beating up women with their mallets.

I began to think of things that could be done, just the way Varèse was thinking in terms of the electronic — all new territory. I guess my hobby is to think; I like to just sit and think. To build things is not necessarily my area, but I do have, I don't know what you would call it, on one level a systemic mind: When I get an idea, I see the gestalt, I get the whole thing. So once I had one ladder harp, then I had a choir of ladder harps; once I had a tangent rattle, I had a choir of tangent rattles. So that's how they got invented. It's not that I was out to invent instruments, but that I wanted to create an ego-less sound possibility, a suchness possibility, so that you would help the ear just to hear the sound for its own sake. I invented those different percussion instruments because I wanted something non-intervallic, so emotions wouldn't interfere. I'm redoing that piece for ordinary instruments because of the logistics of the fragility of these invented instruments, but with these same unusual ideas. This new evening-length work is called *Suchness Concert And Otherness Concert*.

Q: What's the biggest hassle with having designed so many percussion instruments — storage?

DLUGOSZEWSKI: Storage, yes. Now that I have Bill Trigg so excited about my work, he's going to be the one to help "love" these delicate, "unrealistic" instruments — he has a loft. He's a thrilling musician. He said, "I'll be for you what Danlee Mitchell is for Harry Partch."

Q: Is it literally over a hundred?

DLUGOSZEWSKI: Yes. A lot of them are not big. There are closed rattles and what I call unsheltered rattles, which are things that hang. They're made out of wood, skin, glass, paper, and metal. After I invented them and made them so that I loved their suchness sound, then my sculptor friend Dorazio re-made them so that each one is also one of his mysterious, lovely pieces of sculpture.

Q: Are you still designing instruments?

DLUGOSZEWSKI: No. As I say, I like to think, I like to go into imagination. I think one of the great things about music is that you can become such a fantastic imaginary architect: There are these very reckless things that you can build, which no one would dare build in the real world. I enjoy making structures like that. One could be inventing all kinds of things, but if you're doing that, you're not just sensing the wondrous possibilities of creating music; you're busy in the inventing.

Q: All of those percussion instruments were the result of that single piece from 1958, *Suchness Concert*, which was the score of Hawkins' dance *Eight Clear Places*?

DLUGOSZEWSKI: I stopped it after I did *Eight Clear Places*. That single piece was a big culmination — I mean, it's an hour long — a big new architectural structure, like my hour-long *Archaic Timbre Piano Music*, which also has that kind of reckless new architecture. And Varèse said of both pieces that maybe they were more exciting than his electronic sounds. That was the period, about three or four years, when I did just everything that I thought would be fun to try. Now I use them in the percussion section of anything I do, because they're lovely sounds. But I think I then began to find more new playing techniques for traditional instruments. After all, I did that whole thing on the timbre piano — John Cage did his prepared piano, but I think I did something different. I think it was Robert Sabin, who was editor of *Musical America*, who found the term "timbre piano." He said, "Lou Harrison did something, Henry Cowell did something, John Cage did a lot, but you did something more, and so we'll call it a timbre piano." And that was a whole new set of techniques for bowing the inside of the piano. And then there's the percussion, string instruments, brass — I mean, look at *Space Is A Diamond*.

Q: Have you ever played brass yourself?

DLUGOSZEWSKI: No.

Q: How did you know you could get all that sound out of a trumpet for *Space Is A Diamond?*

DLUGOSZEWSKI: What I do always is find an adventuresome musician who's willing to take a chance, who's poetically inclined and will follow me on my creative adventure. Then I'll say, "Hey, you know, what I'd like is this-and-this kind of sound. What if you did thus-and-thus with your horn." And they try it. If it's great, we both say, "Hey! That's great!" And if it isn't, we try some more. Gerry Schwarz, the trumpet player; Linda Quan, the violinist; David Taylor, the trombonist; David Stanton, the clarinetist; Bill Trigg, the percussionist; Claire Heldrich, the conductor — those are all musicians that are excited by such an adventure, and suddenly we are all adventuring together.

Q: So you would closet yourself with the performer and develop a vocabulary.

DLUGOSZEWSKI: That's right, stretch the instruments.

Q: Then you'd have to come up with a notation to describe the sound and its performance technique.

DLUGOSZEWSKI: That's right. Some people have gotten very much into calligraphy, like Stravinsky and Lou Harrison and John Cage and George Crumb, and that's all very lovely. But in the end, those are only fingers pointing for what you're going to have. I know that my notation could still be refined, but I just felt that I would not hold myself back from the wonderfulness of the sound to take time to agonize over the notation.

All notation has to be is a correct kind of communication between composer and performer. If I could manage that, so be it. You can invent symbols, and I did a lot. And where it has to be verbal, it's verbal. But look how much in traditional music you have to read between the lines, between the notes. Some of my favorite music is the late Beethoven, like the "Hammerklavier," and the Bach Goldberg Variations and the late Schubert sonatas. And everybody acted as though the late Schubert sonatas were ridiculous, too long and so on — I remember when I was kid and read music criticism, they said, "Oh, the Schubert sonatas, you can go to sleep during them." It was only years after he was dead, that Artur Schnabel (who was kind of connected with Grete Sultan; there was that tradition) found a way of phrasing them. After all, Schubert was doing a lot of leaping, the way that architecturally and kinesthetically thrills me in my own adventures. He'd had these long lines with these strange things happening, but it was all one phrase, this wonderful, long, totally non-linear phrase. It's only when we found these wonderful phrases that the late Schubert began to make sense.

So I suppose I should take heart. One critic reviewed *Abyss And Caress* and said, "That's nothing but sound effects." And that means he's caught in the Western tradition of linguistics, where the properties of the thing are not important. The thing becomes a common-sense postulation. There are so many factors in the human mind which interfere with our sense of aliveness and our sense of reality. They're all there to protect us, to solve our problems, to make us emote in relation to the rest of the world, to do a hundred other things. But not that wonderful, gemlike moment of just experiencing directly, which certainly the Eastern spiritual doctrines, especially Zen Buddhism, feel is enlightenment. And what is enlightenment? I realized that it is that sense of utter aliveness. That's what my music is trying for, the pursuit of aliveness. One time someone asked me, "What is your music all about?" That wonderful question! I didn't know what to say, so I thought about it and said, "Well, I guess it's involved with realness and with spiritual refinement." This realness, this sensing what is real in that most alive moment, just doesn't happen very often for anyone, but what a goal for artist or saint.

I got to reading the haiku poets a lot. The usual feeling about them is that they write these charming little nature poems. But they are very fierce and very deep poets. Through a sense of observing nature and then writing it down, they're concerned with giving you a ritual that will trigger that aliveness. They offer a sensitivity about the natural world, and then they offer a totally diverse sensitivity about the natural world, and the mental off-balance in between so exacerbates the protective, deadening areas of the mind, that you suddenly see for the first time the sensibility that they most wanted to share with you. What an impressive ritual, what subtlety of perception, of living one's life. I thought, "This is what I've been looking for. This is what I want." That's when I began to realize that form really is how the ear listens. It's how you put these things together in such a way that you do get this wonderful experience of aliveness, that sense of immediacy. I feel every piece I write has a new form. I'm constantly putting form to a test. I worry about form, probably more than any composer I know — it isn't like I slap this sound and that sound together.

The problem of form in composing has concerned me since I was 12 years old. I could never really appreciate why certain musical forms were what they were. You'd get these inadequate answers from teachers: "It gives shape." And then you'd say, "But why that shape? There could be other shapes." (That's what was so great about Erik Satie — I think his mind was a little like mine in a way: *Three Pieces In The Shape Of A Pear.* It's just entrancing.) Or they'd say, "It gives unity." And then you'd say, "Why do you need unity?" I was always the one who'd ask all those questions — they wanted to throw me out! But I think to ask why is so refreshing. When I teach, I let everybody ask me every "why" possible. I never shut anybody up — it's a moral decision. I remember reading a fascinating book by Lewis Thomas, named *The Lives Of A Cell.* He said that, in the inorganic world, there's probability. But in the organic world, everything is held taut against probability. And that thought fascinated me — that special vigor to recognize something that's improbable, maybe impossible, and yet true. Then I suddenly realized that form is a cliche. And that's when I began to newly experiment very deeply with all art in general, but especially music. Music is so special an artform for me because I think you can be the most dangerously creative, the wildest, the most subtle — it permits the courage of the delicacy of daring constructions. You can build the most incredible architectures because they are part of the refinement of our spirits. I'm constantly thinking about the form of these architectures, and as far as I can tell, the symmetrical, Western forms were actually mental cliches, just "safe" ways to keep things from falling apart.

Q: In a real way, they're cues to stop listening, because the more familiar you are with the form, the less you need to hang on to every moment of the sound.

DLUGOSZEWSKI: Absolutely, that's exactly it. That's exactly what the mind does. My music is constantly trying to put the mind into a ritual so it never stops listening. You know how people talk about hearing for the first time? That's a religion to me. When you're a baby, you hear for the first time, and babies have that sense of wonder about them. Great musical artists should make us hear for the first time. Over a period of years, I've evolved several strategies of how to do that. One involves what Artaud called "thusness"; the Zen Buddhist poets called it "suchness"; James Joyce called it "quidditas"; and that wonderful friend of mine, the terrific American philosopher F.S.C. Northrop, called it "art in its first function" and "poetry as pure fact." This is that unique, delicious so-called "thing in itself" — actually not a "thing" at all, but experiencing directly. And this, of course, I've loved all my life. Simone de Beauvoir wrote a very beautiful introduction to Violette LeDuc's *The Bastard*. She said, "What made LeDuc great is that she was able to show us those encrusted, slightly tarnished flecks that were glittering in the steps of the metro station. She was able to show us those because she loved them." I feel that, if I can just love that sound so much and show it to you — that's how I see the idea of suchness. I say, "Look, this trumpet tone, oh, ah." Suddenly courage, artistic courage loves and wills the world. I sometimes kid my students and say, "I think I'm going to start a whole new sect of Zen Buddhism, the Dlugoszewski sect, in which I'll point out that when Buddha sat under the Bo tree and got enlightenment, what happened is that he had an intense aesthetic experience, and it just sharpened him into immediacy." That's what the haiku poets are all about. They write verbal poetry, but I feel that there's no reason why sound shouldn't be just as wonderful — actually more wonderful because the verbal poets are still always just finger-pointing at things, but sound is nakedly just that soft, lovely being something in process.

This thusness suchness quidditas nakedness of sound enveloped my imagination through 1969 and the big *Nine Concerts* piece for Erick Hawkins' second breathtaking meditation on nature, *Black Lake*. Then in '71 and '72 came the transition, two brass pieces: *Tender Theatre Flight Nageire* for Hawkins' *Of Love*, with the invented percussion and the musicians moving in space, and *Densities* for Hawkins' *Angels Of The Inmost Heaven*. And even before that, '65-'66, *Balance Naked Flung* for Hawkins' *Lords Of Persia*. In these I was beginning to "leap for the flexibility of the soul," and this was different. Then came 1974 and the prize-winning *Fire Fragile Flight*, where every moment was a leap to a new place — all development shattered, all immediacy hopefully gained. And in 1980-81 *Cicada Terrible Freedom*. I was somewhere beyond suchness, only I did not quite know consciously that ferocious possibility of otherness. I think that our intellectual life and our emotional life have their own power, but they do limit our aliveness — that exquisite, exacerbated, luminous aesthetic sense. And our naive realistic intellectual life, our common-sense life, that does it too, but even more so because it is so deceptively dishonest as well. Joyce talks about being, and he says, "For the millionth time, to wrest being from non-being." What does he mean by that? If it's being, don't we have it? But these things like naive realism do get in the way — Whitehead called it "the fallacy of misplaced concreteness." That's a mouthful, but it means a lot. It means that we think we're living but we're not living. When Simone de Beauvoir went to Japan with Sartre, she saw the Noh drama for the first time. She said of what they were doing that they had a language that makes the presence of "Other" in each person a fact. That was Sartre's philosophic idea, and he applied it brilliantly psychologically and philosophically. But she suddenly was applying it aesthetically — and I think that's the best way it's ever been applied! She said, "They want to enter the world that is 'Other' absolutely. They are an absolute refusal of imitating ordinary reality." Ordinary reality is this common-sense thing that we have in language: tables, chairs, and so on. And we think that we're experiencing those things, but we're not; they're still concepts. When the Zen people did those koans — look at how crazy that is, you know, the sound of one hand clapping — they were trying to put you off balance from that naive-realistic thing. She says, "It's through the shattering of this reality" — which is what the koans were doing — "that meaning is isolated in brilliant purity." I was suddenly enchanted with her, as nothing else about her so enchanted me.

Otherness became my new obsession. But you don't have to call it otherness — that can be kind of chic French intellectual, right? You can call it strangeness. And why the strange, why the surprise? Gertrude Stein — a good apple-pie American — said you've got to put a little strangeness in a sentence to make the noun come alive. By that she means just what we're talking about. I began to think that so much of what we think is form is fixed, finite, and cliched, ultimately naive realistic "ordinary reality" which the Noh artists were constantly shattering. I wanted to shatter, too, and look at form from the point of view of otherness. The haiku poets use two terms: They talk about "suddenly" and "carefully." For me, "suddenly" is otherness — you're using a ritual to shatter things in order to bring the mind to nakedness. And "carefully," which is this suchness, already is naked, and you're deeply living it. You're deeply living those Violette LeDuc encrusted, tarnished little flecks glittering in the metro station, which she loved so much.

Q: Your approach to form has been to find ways of accommodating both suchness and otherness.

DLUGOSZEWSKI: There's a wonderful thing that the Chinese Zen (they call themselves Chan) artists used to say: "The 'i' painters grasp the self-evident that cannot be imitated, and give the unexpected." The best of all worlds! Suchness is like grasping the self-evident that cannot be imitated. "To give the unexpected," that is something else. That's the strange theater, the surprise. There have been an awful lot of things with chance and accident and all that going on, but finally they became systems. I realized that we don't even need that, because we have an inner creative core that's pure unexpectedness, if we can only tap it. My strategies are to find a way to tap it. It used to be said, "If you don't use chance, you're just relying on personal taste." God forbid — no, no, no. That's not what I'm talking about. It's something inward I'm playing around with, something totally naked. In the *Radical Otherness Concert*, I would say to myself, "I want hugeness strangely understood." Or I'd use a lot of outrageous junctures, which probably blew some people away — in the wrong way. But I think if you could ride on that, and go into those deep little pockets of sudden otherness — "suddenly" becomes a spiritual refinement. In the *Radical Otherness Concert*, premiered in 1991, I wanted "absolute shattering of ordinary reality," constantly — just all kinds of reckless ambiguity spatters of this otherness, wild, absolute, free.

In 1992 I began to think of something totally different. I found myself saying, "I want to love and will and otherize and also subtilize the world." This concept of subtlety! I think music is capable of more subtlety than any other art: It just blows past your ear, it's elusive, it's ungraspable. I think the height of elegance is what is ungraspable; I call it the elegance of the ungraspable. There's a wonderful saying by Daruma, the man who brought Zen Buddhism to Japan: "Awaken the mind without fixing it." That has constantly challenged and thrilled me for 25 years. With this new piece, for the first time I really wanted to utterly challenge myself with subtlety. That's why I called it *Radical Narrowness Concert*. At the end of his life, the great haiku poet Basho said lightness was the most important thing for haiku. He called it *karumi*. Lightness, something almost not happening, the delicacy of the new, something fierce waiting to be born, what Hue Neng called "show me the face before you were born," that constant subtilizing movement from gross to subtle. In the first rehearsal, my young friend Bethany Morgan heard the suchness unbelievably in it, but she's a very subtle young lady. In a way I thought, "Challenge yourself to be more subtle than Mozart, more subtle than Webern, more subtle than even the haiku poets, and see what happens." I don't know — you can come hear that piece this February and see what happens! All I can talk about to anyone is my goals; whether I succeed or not, listen and see. I'm going on my adventure. In a way, I'm not that interested in talking about individual pieces — each one has some of these things in it. And subtlety takes special courage these days because it is considered "effeminate," God forbid!

Q: Can you describe how the haiku poets gave you insight into working with both suchness and otherness?

DLUGOSZEWSKI: The haiku poets practice otherness — they literally do. As I said before, they take a sense of suchness about the outside world, and then they take another sense of suchness about the outside world, totally different, a disparate element. The tension between those two rattles the mind. I always say I want form that will shatter the chaos of my mind. It shatters the mind in such a way that suddenly, for a little moment, you are alive, and you are hearing or see-ing for the first time. And when the haiku poets know they've shattered you beautifully, then they tell you something particularly exquisite or mysterious or fiercely nakedly hearing for the first time. There's a poem by Basho: "The belfry without a bell" — well, that already is strange, isn't it? Your mind is a little bit off-balance, and then they come in: "The young leaves." And then you see those young leaves for the very first time, exquisite delicate green. I find this such incredible art, such incredible sensibility. I think that, when he was at his best, James Joyce was sensing this sort of thing in the *Portrait Of The Artist* and the *Dubliners* stories and in *Ulysses*. Then he got to be a linguistic virtuoso, and that's OK, but that was different. When he was operating on the quidditas idea, that was definitely the suchness sensibility. Apropos of one of the haiku poets, some-one said, "The inanity of things was suddenly destroyed by the human spirit." So what do they mean by that? Most of the time we think of our consciousness, the world, everything, as absurd. That is the human disease. The other human dis-ease is boredom. And if we like to camp or fool around that way, then we infan-tilely keep on outraging the bourgeoisie. But a lot of us get depressed by that, because we feel unalive; there's no realness, our ears stop being terrible with hear-ing. So somehow you perform a strategy to cut through that. Otherness, the strangeness, the shattering, a tremendous possibility. I sometimes say to myself I'm looking for a grave intense alien other — as if no one was listening. That grave intense alien otherness-poet Basho wrote, "A bowel-freezing night of tears. The sound of an oar as it strikes a wave." Thoreau heard that same oar in Walden Pond, but the haiku poets knew you had to get bowel-freezing tear naked before your ear would be naked and terrible enough to hear that oar.

What fascinated me the most about the haiku poets is that they really practiced otherness, and why they did. I said I was concerned with realness and the spiritual refinement. Strangeness is a ritual to stretch the mind, opening secret doors, a new vista. And then, in another way, that strangeness actually creates something new. And the only reason for the new is to refresh the mind. Because the mind grasps things so quickly, they become cliches. There's nothing wrong with a cliche, except that it becomes deadening, and anything that's deadening, I don't like. It's something that the mind has chewed up and spit out — we want to keep the mind chewing! The other thing that this strangeness does is that it purifies our ears to the percepetion of what is, suchness! The new also gives the mind immediacy, and when you have immediacy, you're again deeply in aliveness, you've shed the non-alive past as well as the nonalive future for the very alive immediate. I remember seeing a Japanese architecture where, for no reason, there was off to one side a stairway. Talk about surrealism! It's like surrealism, only it has a hundred light-years' more depth than surrealism. It was just there. And I always call it the dis-parate stairway. And I realized that the one strategy to practice otherness is to bring in that disparate element: "The belfry without a bell," or "the huge trees, their names unknown." It's like Hue Neng trying to pass from a novice to a master. He was the dumb one in the monastery; he could never get his words straight. The abbot lined up everyone and put a pitcher out in front of them and said, "Now tell me what this is if it's not a pitcher." And all of them were very learned, and said it was cosmic forces and so on. When he came to Hue Neng who was standing there like an idiot, they all started to laugh because he stuttered and couldn't get any words out. In desperation, Hue Neng went over and put the pitcher on its side. Have you ever repeated a word until it sounds silly? That's when it begins to become alive; it's not a finger pointing that you're reading, it is itself.

Q: That's also when it becomes music.

DLUGOSZEWSKI: Absolutely. And so that pitcher on its side was not the pitcher anymore. Hue Neng made his point, and so the dumb one became abbot of the monastery. I love that man. Maybe I'm one of those dumb ones in that sense.

I feel that the haiku poets take junctures between apparently unrelated things, which create these wonderful sparks that absolutely shatter the mind where it is interfering with direct, immediate aesthetic experience. Suddenly there you are, naked to the world, and you're given this thing and your ears hear for the first time. So I've sometimes said, "The best thing you can do is become disparate stairway mad." Plato talks about divine madness. That madness is not negative, Romantic drug-taking; it's a madness the way you would think someone is mad when they stop being practical. That's un-American! That's mad, right? But it is so thrilling because suddenly you're very, very deeply and dangerously alive. In that sense, I think it is an uneasy mind; in that sense, I think it is a terrible ear; and in that sense, I think it is a sudden universe, because the whole thing just pours into you. Was it Kierkegaard who said, "the fear and trembling of encountering the world"? And then there's an Eskimo saying, "Be not afraid of the universe." And they're both right, in the sense that everything — ourselves, the universe, everything — is fragile and violent and strange and dangerous. All those things, because it isn't easy to get on that tightrope of hearing for the first time, or to get on the tightrope of being a live human being. I am trying constantly to refine musical strategies to make something like this happen.

The other thing that happens is an absolute appeal to our freedom. Absolutely the most beautiful spiritual refinement! Our capacity to choose makes us different from other animals, and that's pretty scary. But then we have that endless, dangerous, creative capacity for freedom inside. But things get encrusted and we get so frightened. This otherness strategy is forever shaking things up. It takes a special kind of courage to match otherness with form — something that is probably improbable and usually impossible and yet true. The other consequence of otherness is the constant anxiety of nothingness — you're always plunging into the unknown. But what better way to live, in terms of spiritual refinement? What better way to live, than this resumption of the world as freedom. I think the haiku poets are just constantly in the anxiety of nothingness. I probably am too. But the stakes are terrific!

Q: I was very struck by the strong feeling for nature in your music, even though there's no attempt to represent the sounds of birds or animals.

DLUGOSZEWSKI: When I was on the brink of writing *Radical Narrowness Concert*, the exciting painter John Phillips invited me to come and work in his barn in Columbia County. He became a sudden convert of suchness and otherness, and the result was a series of 12 paintings of my process. He had seen the old Japanese gardens in Kyoto, and he suddenly said, "I understand your music now because I see it is really like the Japanese stone gardens." When Daruma brought East Indian spirituality and confronted Taoist nature meditation, it became the greatest synthesis of inner and outer of any spiritual doctrine — it became Zen. The Zen gardens are nature and spirituality at the same time, and this thrills me.

I keep an aesthetic diary of things that happen every day, just to sharpen my suchness "soul." New York City has wonderful skies — when the wind blows and cleans up all that pollution, and the evening star is there, like a little tear. Or at dawn in August, the constellation Orion just starts up, and Sirius, the biggest star, is suddenly in this light blue sky — well, it's so beautiful, and my east window just pierces with delight. Something like that happens every day. I remember when I was ten years old and going for my piano lesson at the Detroit Conservatory of Music. I had to walk over a railway bridge, and as I walked over that bridge, I felt the air and emptiness underneath and I just got so excited. Then I read a haiku poem: "Walking over the hanging bridge, and beneath it the voice of the *hototogisu*." That's another one of those weird gorgeous disparate stairway juxtapositions. Danger also is an otherness element — the dangerous bridge — it exacerbates your sensibility, and suddenly you hear this bird. And I thought, "My God, I felt that when I was ten years old." Someone said, "Why do you bother to watch that evening star?" And I said, "Well, you know, I search for myself in the beauty of the star." One time in August I remember I saw the evening star and then I heard a cicada, that little dry rattle, totally different. And that rattled my mind so much — I was walking along and there was just a piece of crabgrass in the sidewalk, and this came through: It was real as nothing before had been so real, and I knew I wanted to write such a kind of aloof, austere, dangerous music. These experiences do happen. Someone once asked me, "If you had your choice, how would you want to be?" I said, "I'd like to be tear-star high-strung, bridge intense, and I'd like to burn with a tear growl scarecrow light" — the haiku poets are always talking about wonderful scarecrows. Did that answer the question?

I think I do try to behave a little like a haiku poet where nature is concerned and why I think nature is so important. I had a friend, a Jesuit priest who was a painter. He went to see Mu Chi's "Six Persimmons," a very beautiful Chan Chinese painting, now in a Japanese monastery. So he went to Kyoto and the abbot there took him aside and said, "Oh you Americans, you make me sick. You're all coming to see that 'Six Persimmons.' Actually, that stone is just as good." So he came back and said to me, "Wait till I tell you what happened!" — because of course I loved that painting too. And I worried about that for a long, long time. What is the virtue of Mu Chi? I had just heard some contemporary music, and they were trying to go into some of these ideas, because it was fashionable at that point in time to fool around this way. There were a lot of synthesizers, and the idea presumably was what Mu Chi was doing so exquisitely. But it was wretched because all this high-tech stuff was so unimmediate. The machines had stolen immediacy from us. The high-tech, problem-solving human mind had everything neatly grasped and had nothing. Nature is the alternate of the grasping, solving human mind. Nature can be cruel and whatever, but it is always inexplicably, elusively, mysteriously beautiful. Nature is always beautiful as the human being is not. When Mu Chi paints something like the "Six Persimmons," he helps us become beautiful as nature is already beautiful. Am I making any sense?

Q: If you know how to look at a painting like that, it can sharpen your ability to see the stone in a meaningful way.

DLUGOSZEWSKI: Absolutely, absolutely. All it is trying to do is bring us back to life again. In fact, that "created now, created now" idea, that flung-into idea in the music, is now another level on which I've been working. When you create something now, that's the one time you're cheating death; that sense of newness which the otherness creates is an anti-death surprise. It's really death-shedding, death-throwing. I guess what made me not compose very much in the '80s was that I had people very close to me who were dying. And I had a nervous breakdown, because I love probably too well. What saved my sanity was that I began to realize that this idea of the "created now, created now," that ritual of immediacy, is our immortality — it throws death aside. It's like something just waiting to be born, that anticipation, that wonder. That's again what I'm after. Nobody could have sudden artistic conversion 24 hours a day — you'd go mad. Maybe there are some people who do, and then they do go mad. But I do think that in a work of art, you can try for it — especially in a time art, because that's the subtlest of the arts, I think. You can try to get a sudden artistic conversion, you can wait like a cat in front of a mouse, until you get one, and then another one and another one. And the other thing which I spoke about already, the ungraspable exquisiteness, that subtlety. Someone asked me about my *Radical Narrowness Concert*, and I said, "I want it to be aloof, vast, strange, dangerous music, as if no one was leaving." I wanted it to be disparate stairway mad.

Marie Von France, the sweetheart or pal of Carl Jung, wrote books too. Jung wanted everything and so he wanted an aesthetic theory, but he was basically not an aesthetic person. She was. She wrote that, in archetypal images, everything doesn't equal everything; there are qualitative differences, but it's the intuition that decides. She also told of this one fairy tale of a princess who was trying to save her prince. She has this ring he gave her, and she's told she has to jump into the very center of the ring, where there's nothingness, in order to save him. But of course, by jumping into the center of the ring, she does what they call the spontaneous act. The spontaneous act — the hardest thing in the world to do — the core of creativity. I always say to myself, "Come on, let's be that person who jumps; a person who's not afraid of the anxiety of nothingness." I'll say to myself, "hugeness, strangely understood." In this new piece, *Radical Narrowness*

Concert, I suddenly wanted lightness, that first snow of the year we had two days ago in New York City. To love and will and otherize and subtilize the universe. From the gross to the subtle. Music is fabulous that way.

Q: When you played the percussion part for the recording of *Tender Theatre Flight Nageire*, was it completely notated?

DLUGOSZEWSKI: Yes. People often said that it seems like it's improvised, and I work for that, the spontaneous act. My objection to things like improvisation or jazz is that the whole reason for improvisation is the sense of spontaneity. But how often are we spontaneous? Only once in a while. Otherwise, we're just regurgitating things that are already in our heads, so we can keep going. It's just those wonderful flashes where the spontaneity is. That's a special way to compose — to sense those few flashes and leaps.

Q: How important is it for a composer to be a performer?

DLUGOSZEWSKI: I think a composer who is a performer will always be more into the immediacy, because performance by nature is the exquisite danger of time, which is one of the most beautiful things about music. I think a composer who is only doing things on paper tends to remove himself from that reality. And I think it is important, but on the other hand, if you're so caught into performance, in the sense of doing, then you will never just sit back and take those wonderful risks of imagination. So there are both — the wide silent imagination of the mind and the absolutely amazing ritual of being alive, which is the danger of performance.

Q: Having been a performer also makes it easier to instruct other performers.

DLUGOSZEWSKI: Oh yes. There's no point writing something that someone can't do. Now, sometimes people can't do it this year, and then five years from now they can do it. I've certainly had people mad at me because I've done such hard things — things they call hard — and now they're getting easier. Constantly stretching that is really exciting.

Q: Your own years of percussion playing must have been poured into the writing of *Radical Quidditas For An Unborn Baby*.

DLUGOSZEWSKI: Oh yes, of course.

Q: Did you also find yourself asking the player to do things that you'd never quite been able to do?

DLUGOSZEWSKI: Well look, I'm not a professional percussionist, I'm a pianist. Bill Trigg has this terrific stick technique, so I was enjoying that, with him using traditional instruments like the marimba, mixing them with the other instruments of mine. So in a sense that piece was mixing those two things together. And sometimes my instruments sounded more reckless than his sounded. But then you had to make those others sound reckless, and I hope I succeeded that way. I don't know. In that piece, I was trying to make the marimba sound as reckless as those tangent rattles. And do you think a marimba could have suchness?

Q: In *Radical Quidditas For An Unborn Baby* or *Space Is A Diamond*, there's only one person onstage.

DLUGOSZEWSKI: And I certainly give them a forum, don't I? It's hard for the composer, because you have such limited parameters.

Q: Are you interested in the theater of the virtuoso soloist?

DLUGOSZEWSKI: No, of course not. That could be a real trap. Obviously you want a very, very fine musician, but I don't think I think "virtuoso" at all. And theater — it all depends on what you mean by "theater." Western theater is still kind of a little bit of a dirty word. For me, theater is seeing something living happening before your eyes. And that ritual is certainly of the highest purity. I think what I'm interested in is that bedrock of poetry which is true in any art. I happen to be involved in sound, and I would like to achieve it on any level. So I don't even know where I'm going — I'm trying to go the pathless way to find the most intense poetry that you can do with sound. There are other ways you can do it, with words or with paint or with movement. I have also choreo-graphed — because they're related — but I guess of all the things, whether it's using bodies or sounds or words (which are three areas that I have done), I think sound has the capacity for the most elusive, subtle recklessness that there is, and that attracts me specially. The subtlety, the elusiveness, the recklessness — all those things about sound attract me. And that capacity for the deepest poetic expression. That's really what I want. And I think that word "quidditas" really means that bedrock of poetry which Buddha felt when he suddenly just heard things and saw things — the wondrousness of consciousness, of being alive, the immediate terrible ear. I feel that Buddha's insight was an aesthetic one, I really do. I think when you have a deep aesthetic insight, it becomes ego-less, and you just hear; you just hear the sound. And I think that's a very thrilling thing.

It's really very hard to compose that way, and so you find endless rituals to make that wonderful spark happen. I think that, formally, I'm the one that went farthest into the leaping of strangeness of the material, strange juxtapositions, and the leaping in dynamics (rather than the gradual dynamic which is the standard). That again is because you get this now, then this now, then this now, and it really does something wonderful to the mind. (I sort of think in those terms I could play the late Schubert sonatas in a dazzling new way.) I decided I was going to use the *nageire* idea, "flung into," in *Fire Fragile Flight*, from beginning to end, so there's a new sound leaping into the consciousness from beginning to end; the very last are sounds that you never heard until the very end. Those were just things I wanted to see how it would happen.

Q: I was fascinated to read your comments that *Tender Theatre Flight Nageire* and *Abyss And Caress* were involved with "the poetic roots of erotic experience."

DLUGOSZEWSKI: Well, that's also possible. I was trying to bring a feminine point of view of tenderness into music, the element of tenderness. The funny thing with me is that I can get very excited, and I can become very reckless and very explosive, and I don't know why, but people hear only that and they don't hear the tender parts. I thought, for instance, the beginning of *Radical Quidditas For An Unborn Baby* was very delicate and very tender. One of my best friends was having a baby — not that I was thinking of the baby; it was the piece — but that sense of tenderness I think is just another very beautiful thing that music can do.

Q: It isn't something ordinarily explored in music.

DLUGOSZEWSKI: No, but I wanted to. That's another dimension of me. I guess I'm so quidditas-oriented, but I'm also a lover; I love eros and I love that sense of warmth and that sense of tenderness. Especially tenderness — my mother was very much that way. When I was little I would make my parents laugh by saying that my mother smelled with tenderness. I think you can be quite exact in music in terms of tenderness; I think music lends itself to that, in almost every way. I think in all my pieces that it enters in; I think it's there. The two trumpet solos at the end of *Abyss And Caress*, I thought they were just full of tenderness. The funny thing is, that's when Gerry Schwarz's first baby was being born, and I was thinking of that too.

Q: You were mentioning choreographing before. I understand that you actually perform as a musician onstage with the dancers in the Erick Hawkins works *Eight Clear Places* and *Geography Of Noon*.

DLUGOSZEWSKI: That's right.

Q: Is that what got you interested in doing your own choreography?

DLUGOSZEWSKI: No. I enjoy the time art of choreography. But you know, there's only so much time. It's like I write poetry just for myself, and I put it on the wall to excite me to be a composer. I'm obsessively a composer. I might be able to write books of poetry, but I think that music is my greatest love and I think it takes all of one's energy just to do that.

Q: Do you see yourself as a composer being in the situation of also physically choreographing the musicians? I'm thinking especially of *Radical Quidditas*, where the percussionist has to leave the stage at certain moments and play from other points in the hall.

DLUGOSZEWSKI: I do, I think I have that feeling. I don't think most musicians are too choreographically inclined, but Bill Trigg certainly was. I love to have sounds move from space to space. I did it in Detroit in 1949.

Q: *Radical Quidditas* is an extremely balletic piece, just in terms of working through that field of equipment.

DLUGOSZEWSKI: Oh yes. But he loved it. I couldn't have done it without him.

But I was doing things where people were moving around at the time that the everyday sounds were done. After all, Charles Ives did say, you know, "You hear the marching bands and you hear these different things," and I believed it. And then I began to think how wonderful it is to see a sound moving. And then you hear it from in back, and then from this ear and then you hear it from that one. I've been doing that for a long time. I don't know whether I was the first. I think we're so competitively avant-garde-oriented — you know, who's doing this new and who's doing that new — but I did it very, very early. I know I did it before John Cage was doing the walk-around music. I think it's just, again, a very lovely thing to do, so when I feel like it I do it still. In *Tender Theatre Flight Nageire*, one trumpet player walks with that long, long note to the back of the auditorium and plays from there and then comes back. You see, that's where you have to have a live performance — you can't have just the records!

Q: I understand that you've taught composing music specifically for dance, as distinct from just teaching composition.

DLUGOSZEWSKI: No, I've taught music composition, of which music for dance is a very specialized and difficult kind of music. I've also taught choreography. I think I've probably done more in creating a new musical form that's serious for writing for dance than anybody else has. I think I've made dance, formally, as important as, say, the libretto in opera; here, you have the movement instead of the words for performance.

When I was just getting started, the official uptown school thought I was just wild, silly and wild. Some of the more avant-garde composers wanted followers, and I don't think, if you're going to be a decent composer, it's useful to be a follower. Anyway, it didn't work for me. And they controlled a lot of concerts, so in a funny way the serious-concert world was shut for me. Then suddenly Erick Hawkins came along and he got very excited about my music, and so it was an outlet. And he is a fantastic artist. Until Virgil Thomson began to champion me, it was a way to earn a living. But what excited me was that it was virgin territory; no one had really done very much in music for dance, nothing serious. And of course, if I was going to do it, I have to go all the way in everything. I started to work with Erick in '53, I guess, so from '53 maybe to '64, my performances were only with him. Because I just wasn't given a chance anywhere else. And he was thrilled with whatever adventure I took.

So I made a whole philosophy of it. I realized that it's two things going on at the same time and that they have a lot in common but there are important differences. I analyzed dance so thoroughly because I think if you're going to collaborate with any art form, you should know about it. That's how I was then able to choreograph too, because the poetic principles are the same. From the point of view of time and energy levels, they're almost simultaneously related. From the point of view of color, like timbre or melody, or that music doesn't use space except imaginary structural space, they're different. My attitude was there were two ways of doing music for dance: You do the music first, and then the choreographer has the full responsibility of making the final work, or you do the choreography first — and Erick at that time wanted to do it that way, which was thrilling for me because I had the last word. Now people had written music for dance after the choreography was done, but it was mainly accompaniment. I analyzed his dance thoroughly from the point of view of time, from the point of view of dynamics; in fact, I really analyzed what he was doing intuitively. He's very unusual in what he does dynamically, he leaps in dynamics. He was just doing it, but I made a whole dynamic structure.

There's an equivalent in the Noh drama, where the way you structure any time art is that all you need to do is, at the right moment, give the audience a flower. So what I would do is discover all the wonderful flowers in the choreography. Then I brought in — and I think this is quite unique with me — that there is also a very special flower of that sound with that movement, and the excitement of that juxtaposition. The dance was done first for *Black Lake*, and then I did the music. That one is quite extraordinary for the way the music and the dance go together, for showing that sound with that movement. The parameters of the dance were from there to there, and these were the flowers, and this was the dynamic structure and this was the rhythmic structure. Then what I felt was that you could either go with it or go against it, and you had that wonderful counterpoint — on every level: time-wise, dynamically, and the flowers could be in different places in the music. After you said, "Well, you can't make it 30 minutes long if the dance is only 20," after you had all your parameters — and I had them so intricately, so many of them — then you took that and then you just forgot it and made the most independent piece of music you could. So that each one could be done separately and be beautiful, and then could also come together.

Q: You've written about the kinesthetic base in Virgil Thomson's music, and obviously there's a similar base in yours.

DLUGOSZEWSKI: Well, the kinesthetic sense is in music, it's in all music. It's just that we're such an unkinesthetic people in some ways. It's Puritanism. It's really fun because now we're more kinesthetic with the disco scene and all. But the greatest excitement is still considered to be when evil takes place, and all this Satanism — I don't get it. I think the kinesthetic sense is mainly the playfulness. You know, when the body moves, there's a sense of real danger; when you do things in music, it's only imaginary danger. But the body is always on a tightrope, in a funny way, in relation to gravity, and that sense of immediacy is probably the most extreme.

So much of music gets brainy. I guess I'm brainy too, and that's wonderful. When I wrote that "the revolution is in perception, rather than conception," I didn't mean I'm not interested in concepts; it depends what concepts. That's why I like D.H. Lawrence so much, because for all his troubles, he tried so hard to be in tune with his own body. He used to talk about the body as not doing something but a soft subtle being something. And I think sound can do that and I like that a lot. I mean, you just hear a paper rustling, and your sense is quickened in a very delicate, wonderful way.

Q: Regarding that revolution in perception: How far along have we come in the 40 years you've been composing?

DLUGOSZEWSKI: I don't know. I would have liked to have been more aggressive career-wise, so I'd have a wider group to understand where I'm coming from. Maybe I'll catch up now. I think there was a wonderful period, just like in a lot of modern art, like the New York school of painting and all, where the sense of immediacy and poetry was very strong, and there's been a kind of backlash, just as there's been in politics. I think we've gone backwards a little bit. That neo-Romanticism — I mean, people that you think would know better, writing those pieces. I have a little bit of contempt for people who were doing 12-tone, and now they're doing not very good Romanticism — certainly their melodies aren't very beautiful, and that's the great thing about the Romantics, their melody. But I guess some people are just trend-oriented; it's not only the critics.

I wrote that quote in 1960, and I think I've broadened my point of view now to say that what is deeply poetic encompasses more than just the perceptual. I think not to hear, not to listen, is not to live, and of course I think the electronic situation has foisted upon us, especially in terms of sound, so much that's not good, that people have stopped listening; I think their ears have gotten blunted. People who act as if there's no difference between the pop field and the serious field have done a lot of harm. That doesn't mean that the pop field doesn't have some interesting things happening, but however you look at it, a great deal of the motivation is commercial. I love money for what it can do for me, but if you are creating music only to make money, the end result always is going to be the lowest common denominator. There's also some kind of morbid fascination with dark things and all this Satanism. It's so paltry, it's so tawdry in comparison to the thrilling thing that music can do.

Q: *Angels Of The Inmost Heaven* is the only dance score of yours which has been recorded; all the others are concert pieces. Do you think that emphasis on disc creates a lopsided perception of what your music is like?

DLUGOSZEWSKI: Well, I think it would be great to have some of those dance scores recorded, because I put everything into them. But I don't think that my dance scores are that different from my concert scores. I don't see dance in the Western sense as frivolous or trivial. I think it's a very serious art and it has many dimensions. I don't think I probably would write for any other choreographer except Erick, because I find him so unique and so musical and so poetic. So there's no friction. Sometimes it's harder to write for dance, it takes more work, because you do have those parameters. Also, your audiences most of the time don't hear. But that was nice for me for those ten years, because I didn't have *The New York Times* on my neck; I was creating and having my adventures. I only had dance audiences who basically didn't listen, and I just created. By the time the music world was ready for me, I had a whole new world.

In '58, when I first did *Here And Now With Watchers* (the big timbre-piano piece, an hour and ten minutes long, which I did with Erick Hawkins), I met the very first critic that started to champion me. It was Virgil Thomson. We were on a panel and he teased me mercilessly — I thought he didn't like me, but he was just testing me. And then he wrote about me in *American Music Since 1910* and was so terrific. That was my first breakthrough. And after Virgil Thomson began to champion me, Leighton Kerner also began to. Jamake Highwater heard my music first years ago, when I did *Here And Now With Watchers* in a little theater that he was running in San Francisco in 1958. Then we lost track of each other until he became music critic of the *Soho News*, and he came when Boulez did *Abyss And Caress*. I got the commission for *Fire Fragile Flight* from Dennis Davies' ensemble in 1974 — I guess that was with Virgil's help — and then in 1975 the commission from the New York Philharmonic for *Abyss And Caress*. Both Leighton Kerner and Jamake Highwater chose *Abyss And Caress* as the piece of the year, and that sort of made me official a little bit. I have a feeling that if both my parents hadn't fallen apart then with mortal illness, it would have been a wonderful period for me, I would have just gone on and on and on. But it was a very hard, tragic hiatus. I wasn't going to lock them away somewhere. I was the only child, and my father died in '75 and my mother in '88. That whole interval was very hard, especially from '81 to '88. I was just taking care of her because I loved her, I loved the poetry she gave me. When I was a baby, she went out in a snowstorm with a dish to show me the fun of snow. She was my haiku poet friend. I think a man might have just walked away from a responsibility like that, probably, because his career would be first, but I couldn't turn my back on my haiku friend of years. So my composing suffered then — *Radical Quidditas For An Unborn Baby* was the first big premiere I've had since I think '83. Wouldn't it be nice if I'd have a renaissance now. I hope so. I do hope so.

Q: Your use of duende in your recent works is a reflection of the personal tragedies you've suffered, isn't it?

DLUGOSZEWSKI: I've always been attracted to the idea of duende, but it was sort of outside my aesthetic stream until the '80s. I realized that no matter how exquisitely I thought, or how poetically I thought, or how much suchness or otherness I tried to encounter, how much immediacy, when I was confronted with people that I was very close to dying, somehow it all fell apart. And that's when I began to think about duende. Then it suddenly hit me, that there's the lightness of Zen and the heaviness of duende. And you put those two together. Duende is an old Spanish word, the deep song of the flamenco singers; it's dear to the heart of Lorca, and he tells about a great flamenco singer named El Libryano, who says, "When I sing with duende, nothing can touch me." It's as if you're looking into the abyss. So you're not doing the immediacy of death-throwing. You look into the abyss and you survive. How that's going to come through, I'm not sure yet. But it thickens the plot. You know, I don't create systems, and I'll tell you why. I have the kind of brain that can create systems at the drop of a hat, but I'm also disparate stairway mad at the same time. And with systems, the minute the mind grasps them, everybody is cloning those systems — even something as beautiful as a fugue. But everybody has their own unusual creative adventure. If you don't put yourself at that great, glorious risk of listening, you haven't lived.

I am now in the process of finishing a commission for the American Composers Orchestra, and it is touching duende for the first time. I usually put my structures and my philosophies right into my title, and this title is *Radical, Strange, Quidditas, Dew Tear, Duende.* Radical meaning extreme; Strange for otherness; Quidditas just for the innocence of each sound; Dew Tear, some evening-star nature meditation to clean up my act; and Duende, to give me courage. *Radical, Strange, Quidditas, Dew Tear, Duende.*

Getting back to the duende. The duende is the material bonds to which our life is tied; that's the thing that can get sick and die. And then there is the unmutilated, beautiful, created-now experience that I court. And the funny thing is that they are both in the troubled mind of the poet; they're both there for me now. How I'm going to synthesize those two, I don't know — maybe I won't. They're sitting there. The universe itself has all kinds of dimensions of duende in it. After all, it almost didn't happen, just as we almost didn't happen, just as a piece of music almost doesn't happen. That is its great treasure of essence, that exacerbated elusively dangerous exquisite precariousness.

COMPOSITIONS

1949	Piano Sonata No. 1
1949	*Moving Space Theater Piece For Everyday Sounds*
1950	*Melodic Sonata* for piano
1950	Piano Sonata No. 2
1950	Piano Sonata No. 3
1950	Flute Sonata
1952	*Transparencies* for string quartet
1952	*Everyday Sounds For e.e. cummings With Transparencies*
1952	*Desire Trapped By The Tail* theater score for upright timbre piano and voice
1952	*Ubu Roi* theater score (*Structure For The Poetry Of Everyday Sounds*)
1952-53	*Openings Of The (Eye)* for flute, timbre piano, and percussion dance by Erick Hawkins
1953-80	*Silent Paper Spring And Summer Friends Songs*
1953	*Tiny Opera* for four poets, moving voice, dancers, and piano
1954	*Arithmetic Progressions* for orchestra
1954-57	*Archaic Timbre Piano Music*
	Here And Now With Watchers dance by Erick Hawkins
1955	*Orchestral Radiant Ground* for orchestra
1956	*Naked Wabin* for flute, clarinet, timbre piano, violin, bass, and percussion

1956	*Flower Music For Left Ear In A Small Room* for eight players
1956	*Visual Variations Of Noguchi* film score of everyday sound
1958	*Music For Small Centers* for piano
1958	*Music For Left Ear* for piano
1958-60	*Suchness Concert* for 100 invented percussion instruments
	Eight Clear Places dance by Erick Hawkins
1959	*Rates Of Speed In Space* for ladder harp and chamber quintet
1959	*Flower Music* for string quartet
1959	*Delicate Accidents In Space* for five unsheltered rattles
1960	*Concert Of Many Rooms And Moving Space* for flute, clarinet, timbre piano and four unsheltered rattles (theater score for *Women Of Trachis*)
1961	*Five Radiant Grounds* for timbre piano
	Early Floating dance by Erick Hawkins
1961	*Archaic Aggregates* for timbre piano and percussion
1961	*White Interval Music* for timbre piano
1961	*Guns Of The Trees* film score
1964	*Four Attention Spans* for piano
	Cantilever dance by Erick Hawkins
1964	*Skylark Cicada* for violin and timbre piano
1964	*To Everyone Out There* for chamber orchestra dance by Erick Hawkins
1964	*Geography Of Noon* for 100 invented percussion instruments dance by Erick Hawkins
1965	*Beauty Music* for clarinet, percussion, and timbre piano
1965	*Beauty Music 2* for percussion and chamber orchestra
1965	*Beauty Music 3* for timbre piano and chamber orchestra
1965	*Violin Music For Left Ear In A Small Room* for violin
1965	*Percussion Airplane Hetero* for 100 invented percussion instruments
1965	*Percussion Flowers* for 100 invented percussion instruments
1965	*Percussion Kitetails* for 100 invented percussion instruments
1965	*Suchness With Radiant Ground* for clarinet and percussion
1965	*Swift Music* for two timbre pianos
1966	*Balance Naked Flung* for clarinet, trumpet, bass trombone, violin, and percussion
	Lords of Persia dance by Erick Hawkins
1966	*Dazzle On A Knife's Edge* for timbre piano and orchestra
1967	*Naked Quintet* for brass quintet
1968	*Hanging Bridges* for string quartet
1968	*Kitetail Beauty Music* for violin, timbre piano, and percussion
1968	*Naked Swift Music* for violin, timbre piano, and percussion
1969	*Cicada Skylark Ten* for ten instruments
1969	*Tight Rope* for chamber orchestra dance by Erick Hawkins

1969-70 *The Suchness Of Nine Concerts* for clarinet, violin, two
         percussion, and timbre piano
         1. pure p'o nageires
         2. sabi music
         3. karumi-beauty-muga music
         4. pool theaters
         5. total karumi
         6. swift p'o
         7. wabin — karumi falls
         7-1/2. pool p'o
         8. wabin — karumi pure flight
         Black Lake dance by Erick Hawkins
1970   *Space Is A Diamond* for trumpet
1970   *Swift Diamond* for timbre piano, trumpet, and percussion
1970   *Velocity Shells* for timbre piano, trumpet, and percussion
1970   *Pure Flight* for string quartet
1970   *Sabi Music* for violin
1971;78 *Tender Theatre Flight Nageire* for brass sextet and percussion
         Of Love dance by Erick Hawkins
1971   *A Zen In Ryoko-In* film score of everyday sound
1972   *In Memory Of My Feeling* for tenor and chamber orchestra
1972   *Densities: Nova, Corona, Clear Core* for brass quintet
         Angels Of The Inmost Heaven dance by Erick Hawkins
1972   *Kireji: Spring And Tender Speed* for chamber orchestra
1972   *The Heidi Songs* opera (work-in-progress)
1972   *Naked Point Abyss* for timbre piano (work-in-progress)
1974   *Fire Fragile Flight* for 17 instruments
1975   *Abyss And Caress* for trumpet and chamber orchestra
1977   *Strange Tenderness Of Naked Leaping* for string orchestra, two
         trumpets, and two flutes/piccolos (work-in-progress)
1978   *Amor Now Tilting Night* for chamber orchestra (work-in-progress)
1979   *Amor Elusive Empty August* for woodwind quintet
1980   *Amor Elusive April Pierce* for chamber orchestra (work-in-progress)
1980-81 *Cicada Terrible Freedom* for flute, string quintet, and bass trombone
1981   *Startle Transparent Terrible Freedom* for orchestra (work-in-progress)
1981   *Wilderness Elegant Tilt* for eleven players (work-in-progress)
1982-83 *Duende Newfallen* for bass trombone and timbre piano
1983   *Avanti* for seven instruments
         dance by Erick Hawkins
1983   *Quidditas Sorrow Terrible Freedom* for orchestra (work-in-progress)
1983   *Song Sparrow Lifted Snow* for orchestra (work-in-progress)
1984   *Quidditas String Quartet*
1987   *Radical, Strange, Quidditas, Dew Tear, Duende* for orchestra
         (work-in-progress)

1988	*Four Attention Spans* for piano and full orchestra; for solo piano and flute, clarinet, trumpet, French horn, bassoon, trombone, violin, bass, and percussion
	Cantilever Two dance by Erick Hawkins
1991	*Radical Quidditas For An Unborn Baby* for 100 invented percussion instruments
1991	*Radical Otherness Concert* for flute, clarinet, trumpet, trombone, violin, and bass
1991	*Radical Suchness Concert* for flute, clarinet, trumpet, trombone, violin, and bass

1. tear pure focus
2. precipice accelerations speed elegance
3. ineffable naked
3. speed radiant naked
4. empty ambiguity spatters
4. huge falling for miles
5. uncompromising extreme ineffables
6. speed fierce leaps
7. grace naked, vulnerable, on a swing
7. grace-reckless
7. speed grace-reckless fierce radiant keystone
8. fierce focus
8. austere suchness rims of silence
8. second focus
8. outrageous quod libet rims of many silences

1992	*Radical Narrowness Concert* for flute, clarinet, trumpet, trombone, violin, and bass

All compositions published by Margun Music Inc., 167 Dudley Road, Newton Centre, MA 02159.

DISCOGRAPHY

1972
Space Is A Diamond
Nonesuch 71275 lp

1975
Angels Of The Inmost Heaven
Folkways 33902 lp

1978
Tender Theatre Flight Nageire
CRI 388 lp

1979
Fire Fragile Flight
Candide-Vox 31113 lp

BIBLIOGRAPHY

"Notes On New Music For The Dance." *Dance Observer*, 24 (November 1957).

"Is Music Sound?" *Jubilee*, 10 (1962).

"Composer/Choreographer, Choreographer/Composer." *Dance Perspectives*, 16 (1963).

"What Is Sound To Music?" *Main Currents In Modern Thought*, 30 (September-October 1973).

"Erick Hawkins: Heir To A New Tradition." *On The Dance Of Erick Hawkins*. Ed. M.L. Gordon Norton. New York: Foundation For Modern Dance [undated; 1974?].

"The Aristocracy Of Play." *Parnassus*, 5 (Spring/Summer 1977).

LOU HARRISON

photo: Gene Bagnato

LOU HARRISON / Introduction

LOU HARRISON was born in Portland, Oregon, on May 14, 1917. His family moved to California not long after, and he grew up in San Francisco. He attended San Francisco State College and studied composition privately with Henry Cowell. He also wrote music for plays and ballets, and produced a group of scores for percussion ensemble, including his collaboration with John Cage, *Double Music* (1941). In the early '40s, he studied composition with Arnold Schoenberg in Los Angeles. A few years later Harrison relocated to New York City, where he studied composition with Virgil Thomson. He also renewed contact there with Henry Cowell and John Cage, and wrote music criticism for the *Herald Tribune*. In 1946 he prepared the score of Charles Ives's Symphony No. 3 for performance, and conducted its premiere. (When the 36-year-old score was awarded the Pulitzer Prize, Ives shared the money with Harrison.)

In 1954 Harrison returned to the West Coast and settled in Aptos, at the foothills of the Santa Cruz mountains, where he continues to reside. He became friends during the '50s with Harry Partch, whose book *Genesis Of A Music* (University of Wisconsin, 1948) had launched Harrison's interest in just intonation. In the early '60s he was invited to an international music conference in Tokyo. During his stay in Asia he studied Korean and Chinese musics, and was soon producing scores which demonstrated a deep understanding of Asian musical structures and techniques. He has since traveled extensively throughout the East, studying, teaching, and performing music. By the early '70s, Harrison and William Colvig had built an American gamelan, for which he composed such major scores as his choral piece *La Koro Sutro* (1971). A series of works for gamelan, alone and in combination with Western instruments, followed over the years, including his celebrated Double Concerto for violin, cello, and Javanese gamelan (1981-82).

Harrison has taught music at numerous schools, including New York City's Greenwich House Music School, Black Mountain College, San Jose University (where he is Professor Emeritus), and Mills College (where he holds an Honorary Doctorate of Fine Arts). He has been composer-in-residence at the Atlantic Center for the Arts, the Universities of New Mexico, Louisiana, and South Florida, the Sarasota Springs Performing Arts Center, the Cheltenham Festival, and the Cornish Institute.

He has written scores for many choreographers, including Jean Erdman, Robert Joffrey, Remy Charlip, and Erick Hawkins, and for filmmakers Paula Heller, Molly Davies, and James Broughton. Harrison has been awarded the Rome prize and the Phoebe Ketchum Foreign Award, and has received Guggenheim, Fulbright, and Thorne Fellowships, as well as a grant from the Rockefeller

Foundation. He is also a member of the American Academy and Institute of Arts and Letters. He is the subject of *A Lou Harrison Reader* (Soundings Press, 1987), to which readers are directed for more information about Harrison, as well as a chance to read some of his essays and scores (and to appreciate his handsome calligraphy). Harrison is also an adept at Esperanto, and has used the language for the texts of several of his pieces.

I spoke with Lou Harrison on November 1, 1990, in his Manhattan hotel room in between rehearsals for the world premiere of his *Last Symphony* (which the composer has since revised and retitled *Fourth Symphony*). Beyond learning more about his new composition — and the irresistible questions about his friendships with Cowell, Ruggles, Schoenberg, and Partch (Harrison has already been interviewed extensively about his association with Ives) — I was particularly interested to discuss with the composer his music for gamelan and his experiences writing scores in just intonation for traditional Western instruments.

LOU HARRISON / Interview

Q: Your *Symphony On G, Elegiac Symphony*, and Third Symphony all had fairly long gestation periods: The first two have material dating from the 1940s, and the third from the '30s.

HARRISON: The reason I'm so quasi-accurate in all that dating is because some of the sketches go way back and they're among my things. One can see the difference, the changes and so on. In fact, they sort of grow over the years, and every so often I'll think, "Where's that page that I did way back then?" Now I know what to do with it, you see, and it suddenly comes up. Often times I can't find it, so I make an approximation. Once I lost the development section of a piece! And so, nothing daunted, I did it over. And it was better; I finally found the original, and the new one was better.

Q: Does this hold true for your new symphony?

HARRISON: Yeah, but not quite as far. It goes back to 1983, some parts of it. The commission for this symphony was just last year. Dennis Russell Davies asked me for a new symphony. He said, "Why don't you start thinking about a new one?" And I thought, "Your wiles again...!" Of course, as I've said publicly, with Dennis, who's so wonderful and such a good friend, all he has to do is say something like that and it's already triggered. I can't help it, the subconscious is already at work the minute that happens.

So it accumulated. He secured this very large commission for me. It's very big — quite staggering, in fact. I think I made myself sick twice, overworking, simply because to a man of my age, having my background and history, the amount was so much that I overworked!

Q: I understand your new piece is called *Last Symphony*, not Symphony No. 4.

HARRISON: That's in parenthesis: "(Fourth Symphony)." But it's *Last Symphony*. As you know, my symphonies all have special names: *Symphony On G, Elegiac Symphony*, and Third Symphony. You would be surprised how hard I work to make critics and program annotators say Third Symphony instead of "Symphony No. 3." What they want is that we should all be serial persons! But I like them to have some special characteristic, even verbally. I thought, at my age, it's unlikely that I'll write another one, so I called it *Last Symphony*. But suppose I do? Then of course it's amusing: I can do a *Very Last Symphony*, or an *Ultimate* one, or a *Very Very Last*, and so on — there are all sorts of maneuvers.

Q: Is this use of material ranging over many years something peculiar to writing large pieces?

HARRISON: Well, it is for me. Things collect around a basic idea or stimulus, and that's why I say, "Where's that? — now I need it." When I use things from the remote past, they get really transmogrified. You would have a hard time recognizing, for example, the third movement from my Third Symphony from the original sketch. When they're in locale with the other parts, they get changed again in relation to those other portions of the work.

Q: Many of your pieces involve the retuning of Western instruments out of equal temperament. Does the challenge of redirecting the skills of traditional musicians excite you, or is it more a necessary evil in your effort to get them to play the music you want to hear?

HARRISON: No, I enjoy that. For example, when Keith Jarrett called me, we were actually the next day leaving the house for New Zealand, and were in the middle of packing. He and I had a long conversation, and he explained why he didn't write a concerto for himself, why he didn't ask a member of his peer group, and why he was selecting me. Of course, he'd played a lot of my music, and I always liked the way he did it — we have a kinetic sense that's very similar, so it worked. At any rate, I told him yes, I'd be happy to write a concerto for him, and then I jumped right in. I said I'd always wanted to write a "pianos" concerto, in which there'd be, say, three pianos on stage, each tuned in a different tuning, for the three movements. And he said, "Oh, that would be very interesting." So we left it at that. Then he said he wouldn't bother me; he wasn't going to call up every month and say, "Where's my piece?" And he didn't; he never said boo till it was ready.

When I got to New Zealand, I thought, to tune three pianos.... He'd play it everywhere, and it takes about two weeks for a piano to settle into a new tuning. That's going pretty far. So I decided not to saddle him with the whole bit, and just chose my favorite keyboard tuning, which is the Kirenberger number two. So far there's been no problem, but there were at the beginning. When the Piano Concerto was first done, A.C.O. called me and said, "What kind of piano do you want?" I said, "Well, Keith's the soloist, ask him." So they did and they chose a seven-foot for rehearsals and then a big eight- or nine-foot for the stage. And both were tuned in the temperament I asked for. But I got panic calls from the tuner, all the way across the continent. I don't think he thought that I knew what I was doing! But I talked tuner talk with him for a while, and he began to suspect that maybe I did know what I was talking about. Then I directed him to Johnny Reinhard here in New York, who knew what was up and soothed him. And so they tuned it very well. Then another problem: It seems that all of the Steinways in Carnegie Hall are either loans from Steinway or else it has some lien on the pianos, so there was the question of permission. They gave permission, but a director from Steinway came to the concert. They did admit that it was beautiful, and so we have permission to tune Steinways in Kirenberger number two!

Then for a while, everyplace it was done, either there would be panic calls from the tuner, or, if they managed well (as they did in Saratoga Springs), some new thing happened: There would be articles in the newspaper about the tuner, showing him tuning it. It gave a whole other thing to the tuners, and now, in California, they fight for it! So it's fascinating to go just slightly off. That's not very far out of the tradition, but it's enough, because you're tampering with the tuning system, to cause a little commotion. Yet everyone agrees that it's beautiful, so the point is being made.

Also, about Keith: The minute he got the work and knew the tuning, he had his own pianos at home tuned that way. By the time he recorded it in Japan — there was fifteen minutes of waves of applause at that concert, and they wanted him to improvise, of course — he knew the tuning so well that, there being only the Kirenberger number two on stage, he improvised in it. By that time, he knew it backwards and forwards. It's one of the most beautiful improvisations you've ever heard. I begged him to put it on the record with my concerto, but he's already completely signed up — I think it's with ECM — for all of his improvisations, so he apologized and said he couldn't do that. But I have it, and I must say, it's just ravishing. When I played it once in class in Seattle, there was silence afterwards, and then a young lady said, "How could he ever return to equal temperament after that?"

A month ago, I called Keith about another matter. We hadn't talked in a long time, and he was very excited and said, "Just as you called, I dismissed my tuner because he was mistuning Werkmeisters number three," and I thought, "We're winning!" Keith is on our side; he's an amazing man.

Q: The orchestra is not in equal temperament in the Piano Concerto. Have the different ensembles been difficult about giving up the way they've been trained to play?

HARRISON: Sometimes. Everybody was so nervous in the orchestra at the first rehearsal, Dennis asked me to explain what it was. But number one, I had thrown out any instrument that couldn't play it; two, there were instructions for tuning. So they did tune to the G and D instead of the A — the A is the only tempered tone in the whole tuning — because all strings have them. They started out tentatively, and in no time at all they loved it, because it's in perfect pitch with what they do; there's no temperament problem to upset them. So that worked very well.

Years before that, in Louisville, I wrote a piece called *Strict Songs*, which also requires the retuning of the orchestra. It's much more complicated than this Kirenberger tuning because the orchestra is involved along with the piano and harps. Again, I threw out all the equal-temperament ones, woodwinds and so on.

Q: The instruments that couldn't be retuned.

HARRISON: Right — or who couldn't do it except in adagio, where they can bend to get a temperament. But in the allegro there's nothing you can do, they're going to play equal temperament. So I did retune the full orchestra for *Strict Songs*. And as a matter of fact, I had fun with Harry Partch at one point, because I suddenly became aware about the harp and those little twister things that pull the strings into three positions: Those can be adjusted for any degree you want.

Which meant that, with two harps, Harry could have had, what, 42 tones. And I said, "Harry, why don't you do this?" And he said, "Well, I don't like the harp!"

But I would say that quite a number of professional musicians are interested and in fact enjoy doing something that's not standard. They get bored, you know, sitting there and hacking out the old repertoire. And if you bring up some fundamental fact like retuning or some new technique that interests them, they really like it. So I've had not much problem there at all.

Q: If exposure to the range of tunings was in their education prior to their becoming professional musicians, you could imagine what we'd be hearing. But it's one area that's still not generally taught.

HARRISON: Oh I know, yeah. It would be wonderful. I've long thought that I would love a time when musicians were numerate as well as literate. I'd love to be a conductor and say, "Now, cellos, you gave me 10/9 there, please give me a 9/8 instead," I'd love to get that! Someday, maybe; or at least some groups, maybe.

Q: You mentioned Harry Partch. I understand that it was after reading his book *Genesis Of A Music* in 1948 that you got interested in just intonation.

HARRISON: Oh yes.

Q: But I've also heard that not too many years earlier, as a critic in New York, you'd written a negative review of a concert he gave. Had you been interested in the tuning but just not liked what he'd done with it?

HARRISON: No, I'd never heard of it at all when I reviewed that concert. Remember, I was a pupil of Schoenberg, and I couldn't imagine not doing a 43-tone serial music. It just didn't make its point. But the minute Virgil Thomson gave me that book — when it was first issued (I still have it) — and said, "See what you can make of this," I got started. And within a week I had bought a tuning hammer for the piano, and away I went. And I haven't really looked back. It's utterly fascinating. And then I got very well acquainted with Harry; Bill and I were very good friends with Harry.

Q: Did he ever hold that review against you?

HARRISON: No, he realized what had happened. He was a very brilliant man. You keep forgetting, because of all the razzamatazz about it, but you open that book almost anywhere, and you're just startled by the acuity and the literary style and the general verve of the whole thing. It's amazing. It's one of the better books of the century — as well as telling the truth.

Q: Can you tell me about when you rebuilt the family phonograph?

HARRISON: I was in Stockton — I don't know how old I was then — and I realized, I guess through a magazine or something, that if you made a larger horn, you'd get a better sound. So I took apart the little portable and built a bigger horn.

Q: Did your folks get mad at you for that?

HARRISON: Oh no. Dad and Mother were always very helpful. They didn't mind what I did as long as I didn't get into too much trouble. And I was always mechanically minded, making things and so on, ever since childhood. Right after that I started making a little tiny violin. I got the top of it done, as well as the fingerboard and the scroll, but then I didn't get any further. Later, in New York, because I couldn't work late in the apartment, I made what I call a cigar-box clavichord. And that led to the invention of two new forms of clavichord, because it curled up — they all do, you know, because of the broken-box syndrome. So I reinvented the clavichord. One of the inventions has never been really made, and it would be beautiful, because it makes a kind of celeste sound. Someday, maybe. I have a very good instrument-builder friend — maybe we can do it in my old age or something, for the fun.

But I continue to do this; Bill and I are still building instruments. We're going to do a whole new set of bonang now because I invented a new form of the bonang: sort of a mixture from the Philippines and Java and our own techniques. But it sounds exactly like traditional bonang. So we're going to run up a set.

Q: Doesn't *Last Symphony* have instruments made specifically for it?

HARRISON: Yes, Bill made two big boxes for it to my prescriptions. They work too. During the next rehearsal I have to make them a little more raucous — it should be quite rackety but they're being timid about it!

Q: Is there any concern about performances of the pieces being more difficult because of the need for specialized instruments?

HARRISON: There is that problem. But I don't see any substitute for what I've done; I can't think of any. In fact, I use two Javanese instruments in this symphony too, one of which there's really no substitute for. What I usually do is give them to the publishers, or put them on alert that they're easy to send out right away wherever it goes.

I've done a number of pieces in which practically the whole orchestra has to be gotten from us. One of them is having terrible trouble: *The Heart Sutra*. It's beautifully recorded, but even before it was recorded, we had to ship this whole orchestra around. (It's called the Old Granddad Gamelan because it was the first American-built gamelan of that kind.) This last year, it really got to be too much. There were two performances in Texas, and Cal Arts wanted to do it but they couldn't get the instruments in time to do it, even by air. Not only that, but there's a back-up string version with the publishers, and they didn't have enough strings to do it! So we had to lose out on that one. New performances of *The Heart Sutra* are coming up, and we're going to have to ship this thing all over. We should probably make a duplicate set. In fact, someone wanted to make three sets for different regions of the country — it's a choir piece, and lots of choirs want to do it. There should be other sets around for that.

Q: By building the instruments, then, you weren't trying to guarantee your own involvement in the performances.

HARRISON: No, I just wanted those sounds and that tuning. That particular tuning is an absolutely pure just intonation in D-major. And everything in it is in some part of that, except for the next-to-the-last movement. That's why the harp's there, because I didn't have the heart to ask Bill to make a whole new set-up, so I just added the harp — which turns out to be a nice relief.

Q: Your *Music Primer* describes building an instrument as "one of music's greatest joys."

HARRISON: It is, actually; it really is — to test the new instrument, see what it can do, and hear it. Yes, it's wonderful, I love it — still do.

Q: But it can also be one of performance's biggest hassles, simply in terms of getting the piece out and played.

HARRISON: Yes, that's true, but you see I have very seldom thought of that. I'm still really a little incredulous that there are people who are fascinated by pieces that I did when I was a kid. When I was doing them, it never occurred to me that anybody would be interested beyond that performance. So some of the manuscripts don't exist. But it's astonishing the number of people who are interested in those things. It took me a long time to get routined in the matter of making a score and having things available and all that. I've just gone on with my musical interests and not really paid any attention to being professional in that sense. I've always envied John Cage: He used to write one major piece a year; it was all neat, the score was right, all the parts were available and so on, it was properly filed, and he got a publisher so that it all stacks up very neatly. I'm too messy!

I really don't have any urge to get things out — never really have had. I write more on a personal and for-the-occasion basis. This symphony is really an occasional piece, if you think about it, because it was for Dennis. He asked for it, so I wrote it for him. He got the commission, and that sort of settled the piece. For months now, while getting it ready, I wondered what the Brooklyn opera house looked like — I'd never seen it. I think always of occasions and people and so on. It just happened that the publisher, Peer International, asked for it, as C.F. Peters asked for the Piano Concerto and the Third Symphony. But even at that, I have a lot of pieces that they won't take, or at least that have not been asked for. So I just publish them under my own Hermes Beard Press, and we've got quite a list now. And that's good because BMI helps support its publishers, and I'm affiliated with BMI. And Margaret Fisher is marvelous. She's done all my copy work, from the Piano Concerto on, and she's practically without fault. In the Piano Concerto, there was just one mistake: She left a flat off an E in the cello part. Dennis had left a half-hour in rehearsal to get the bugs out, and there weren't any! So naturally I glommed onto her right away. Now she's learned *Finale* and she can do the computer work like a whizz. She's holding off for my final changes on *Last Symphony*.

Q: Are you still rethinking features of this piece?

HARRISON: We found some bugs in my manuscript — not in her work. I'm revising two movements.

You know, on the Third Symphony, I did something like five versions of the finale, and only this last year did I finally pull it together — just before the recording.

Q: *Symphony On G* had a wholesale revision of its finale.

HARRISON: Yes, right. And two years ago, I revised the *Elegiac*: two movements practically completely. More and more I realize that my attitude in the matter is like a painter repainting, painting out, painting in, etc. And that I am one of the lucky few who have a conductor/friend who makes it possible for me to hear various versions until the final one has satisfied me. I realize that this attitude is regarded in the speedy professional world as the attitude of an amateur, and so be it. A painter gets to make changes within half an hour to an hour. Months, sometimes years typically intervene before a composer gets to hear his changes — if he ever does.

Q: I was fascinated by your idea of the Mode Room, enabling a person to study the full range of musical modes devised throughout history. What shape is that project in now?

HARRISON: It's not; it got transmogrified into Bill making monochords and strips.

Q: Paper strips that show where the modes actually fall?

HARRISON: That's what it is, so you have your own personal Mode Room. Bill made 25 or 30 of those, and they're all over the world. We would like to standardize the model and put out strips that are on material that doesn't shrink or expand — you have to worry about that.

I'll be doing a lecture at Notre Dame in the Architecture Department, because I'm involved with the Director of Architecture there in a retranslation of Vitruvius, the Roman architect. He has two chapters on Greek music theory and the tuning of an auditorium, Greek- and Roman-style. They did it with bronze bowls. So I'm to give a lecture on Vitruvius and Greek musical theory. And the monochord has been shipped out with that, and also a modified guitar that Bill made me, which has eight strings and you play like a ch'in, so I can tune modes on it. He's also getting me a harpsichord and maybe a harp too. So I can have fun with that; I enjoy all that.

Q: Did working on the Mode Room provide useful material for you as a composer?

HARRISON: Oh yes, and still I'm involved with that. When I started that idea, I was working in part with John Chalmers, who has now finished his book *The Divisions Of The Tetrachord*, and we planned that together. The object was to find out how many useful tetrachords there were within the limit of the 81/80. He ran the computer program and has all the material from all of history. I think he found there's something like 238 usable tetrachords, and that's quite a lot, particularly if you change them; you don't have to have them the same top and bottom. So if you mix them, it's gigantic. Each one is a world, it's marvelous.

Q: You'd been working with gamelan intensively since the early 1970s. Did this symphonic commission seem like an interruption, or were you attracted to writing for orchestra?

HARRISON: Again, it was a request from Dennis, and I'd do most anything for him. Also, Dennis himself is interested in gamelan, and when we went to Chicago last year, he asked the management there to bring the whole gamelan, so we did; we brought Si Betty that Bill made and played there. And he and Romuald Tecco played the *Grand Duo* on our program. So it was really quite something. Dennis is very pro-gamelan. (We did a program at the Cabrillo festival, and it drew the highest-paying crowd of the entire history of the festival — as far as I know, that's still true.) He loves gamelan and as a matter of fact we wrote a piece for him, the *Gending Dennis.* I wrote the Second Piano Concerto with gamelan, and the piano is tuned to it. That's been played around a little, and we have a recording which may come out.

Q: Do you feel that it's somehow anachronistic for you to work with the orchestra at this point?

HARRISON: No, as I say, I have a lot of interests and a lot of things I like to do. Also, my next commission is a gamelan commission — as the one just before was, too. A young scientist in Canada commissioned a work for the family gamelan of a very distinguished scientific family in Jakarta, Indonesia. Every big, good family has a gamelan in Java, if they have status — you have to have a gamelan, it's seen as part of your routine. But I never could find out what the constituents of this gamelan were, what tuning it was, where it was from, and so on. So I just wrote a three-movement work for him. (I think his original reason was because he was in love with one of the daughters, but then the family decided they had too many American husbands, so that didn't work!) We premiered it last year at Lewis & Clark, in Portland, Oregon, with a gamelan that Bill had tuned. But it was an enormous old Javanese gamelan. You should have seen him tuning: Bronze is poison and you have to wear a mask. And stinks, it just stinks, it's terrible. But it's a beautiful tuning. I've had two Indonesians remark on how beautiful the slendro is. One of them called me up twice and said, "Oh, this tuning touches my heart"! So we won. It's a just-intonation tuning too.

The next work is for the Pacifica Foundation. They're building new headquarters in Berkeley, and I was composer of choice for the opening ceremonies. It's already been paid for, so Bill and I put it in a certificate for deposit in the bank until I finished the piece. Charles Amirkhanian, who's director, asked me to base it on gamelan. So I'm going to do gamelan and maybe a couple of other instruments. One of our best gamelan players, who is trained in two styles, is also a professional harpist, so I'm going to write for harp and gamelan. I've used that before and it works beautifully, but never with a great big professional harp, so we'll see.

Q: It's amazing to see how interest in gamelan has grown in the States over the years.

HARRISON: Oh yes, and it continues to grow.

Q: What do you suppose that interest implies about Americans and what they want to hear?

HARRISON: Well it implies two things: that we like to hear new sounds, and also that we're groupies. You know, we're forming committees all the time, and a gamelan is after all a group activity. It tends to form little communities; a gamelan will produce a community almost overnight. So it fits very well. And besides it's so much fun and so beautiful.

Q: Out of all the recordings of your gamelan music which I've heard, your Double Concerto has the most unusual sound. The density and richness of the gamelan textures is amazing.

HARRISON: I chose the place to record it in.

Q: It's the hall that really made the difference?

HARRISON: Yes, it's the art gallery of Mills College, with the glass coffers in the roof. It was very rich — there were no electronic tricks there.

Q: What about the actual gamelan for that performance, Si Darius and Si Madeleine?

HARRISON: It's very rich, yeah — it's the second biggest one that Bill has built. You know, that record is in the courses in Indonesia, and it is very much admired indeed; Indonesian criticism ranks that very high. And students have to study it! That's very pleasing to know.

Q: You wanted to record it in that space deliberately to hear it with that particular resonance?

HARRISON: Yes, I wanted that rich resonance.

Q: To an extent, that density tends to obfuscate pitch. Was that a specific compromise on your part?

HARRISON: No, in fact I don't notice what you're talking about; I still hear all those pitches, you see. I don't have any problem there. It was the ambience of reverbs which I liked. Because if you don't do that, they feed them in anyway!

Q: Was this effect something peculiar to the nature of the Double Concerto, or would you want to hear more of your gamelan pieces done in such a space?

HARRISON: No, I'd have lesser interest in that. That was the best available at Mills, and we had to do it fast before the concert. It was my 65th birthday or something like that, a big concert — for which, incidentally, Pak Chokro (Wasitodipuro; Wasitodiningrat now) wrote us a magnificent piece under NEA sponsorship. It's a real masterpiece. It's called *Purnomo Siddi*, which means "the joy of the full moon" in Javanese. I'm going to push for an American recording of it, and I think we'll get it.

At any rate, there's sufficient interest in gamelan so that the owner and recordist of the label Music Masters have both come to me twice about gamelan. So I have a little packet and I'm going to work with them. They want to record a lot of gamelan. This is another sign of the growing interest in it.

Q: I've read that you've described Javanese gamelan music as beginning from a melodic impulse.

HARRISON: Oh, it's all melody, and stripped melody too. What you start with is in Javanese is called a balungun. It's simply a melody and it's very plain, actually, for the most part; they can get fancy, but the classic repertory is really quite plain. It's a cantus firmus or something like that. Because everything else that happens is due to the processing you put it through, or garapan — the taste of working the melody. Everything, the entire orchestra from top to bottom is that. The basis is just this cantus firmus. It's stated in four octaves throughout the piece, and then all the rest happens as a result of that. So that writing a gamelan work, if it's traditional, is both enticing and very disciplining. Because in slendro you have only seven tones, and your melody has to make sense and be beautiful for as long as it goes on, within those seven tones. It's quite a discipline, and I find that enormously interesting and fascinating. And in pelog, you have seven tones with no repeats; there are no octaves, just seven tones. That's the minor mode. Both are utterly fascinating, and to me, as a melodist, one of my joys is to work with that. I'm very proud when I've produced a good piece. And I was very proud indeed at Lewis & Clark. There were about six or seven major Javanese musicians there, and they played in it too. And Bill and I were accepted as seasoned Javanese musicians, and they spoke to me as they would never have done before: "I thought first that it was too long, but then I heard it again and I decided not, it's OK." They would never have said that previously. So we're obviously part of the family now. In fact, this last work, one of the dancers wants to choreograph it, and another dancer said he wants to choreograph the entire work, and these are Javanese dancers. So this is a very great compliment, because that's almost never done. I'm very happy to feel a part of that family; I feel as though I've got another tradition of which I'm a real part now. So it's a joy.

Q: Your music also springs from a melodic impulse, doesn't it? Even the percussion pieces — the line has to sing.

HARRISON: Yes, that's right. I'm a melodist, I just can't get around that.

Q: That's one factor that made writing for gamelan so natural for you.

HARRISON: Yes. And I've even tied it in with Schoenberg's advice to me. I'd written myself into a corner and took the piece to him — was bold enough to bring it, because his assistant said he wouldn't look at a serial work. But he didn't bat an eye. He went through the work and we came to my block. It was a big movement, and what had happened was I'd really written myself into a corner by too much complexity. And he said, "No, only the essentials. Thin it out, only write the essential, the basic thing." And boy, I've never forgotten that — only what is important, that's all I was to write. And I wonder sometimes if writing gamelan isn't exactly what Schoenberg was saying!

Q: The cliche about your music is how Eastern it is, and of course that's there. But when I think of how all-encompassing your interests are, and the range of your pieces, what strikes me is how American the music is.

HARRISON: Well, I'm glad you think so too. Because I agree, I think we have a very rich culture, and I think it's silly not to see that point and enjoy it.

Q: But is that a chauvinistic response on my part? Or do you think that maybe there is something peculiarly American about feeling the freedom to move back and forth within what's available to us culturally?

HARRISON: Yes, I think so. Because of course we have a wall of separation, we don't have to believe any one thing! I went to an ethnomusicology conference about five years ago, something like that, and did a little paper myself. And I was astounded at what we've got here in this country. I began to think about that, and yes, this whole open thing, this rich culture, is part of being American. I had to argue with a man in Cheltenham, England, who was sort of racist. "In the United States," I said, "we treasure these differences and this richness." He was very funny about that. But of course then there's the opposite side: I just learned the other night on video that there are autonomous Indian nations in this country, and they're not on the maps. For example, the Navajo nation is as big as Virginia, and it's not on the map. Here in New York state, the Onondagas are autonomous and sovereign, as the Navajos are sovereign; the Lummis in Washington, and there are others in this country. I spoke on NPR yesterday, and I said, "I want to see a map in which the truth is shown." I'd like to know what this country really looks like with its sovereignities.

Q: In light of the the range of your work, and its optimism and strength, I was struck to have read your comment that, prior to meeting William Colvig, you were in what you called "another period of hating music."

HARRISON: Yes, but that happened because of my breakdown in New York. There was only one person I could talk music with: It was Robert Hughes. There's something about his personality and something about his sweetness and everything. I could talk to him. Otherwise, I would just get into a kind of rage. After a year or so of teaching ethnomusicology at San Jose State University, I was asked if I would talk to the young composers at the university. I said, "Well, I'll only growl at them," and the man said, "Well, why don't you come growl at them?" So I went and growled, and then very gradually I kind of relaxed and finally I was part of the composition faculty as well. But they let me do anything I wanted. I founded a gamelan there, I taught Chinese music, and I gave two or three sessions of my world-music course, which got better and better every year for 16 years. Considering that it was a state institution, they gave me an enormous amount of leeway and encouraged it too. As a composer I could do anything I wanted. It was wonderful. I look back on it and realize that they were very helpful indeed. And then finally they made me Professor Emeritus, a year or so ago.

Same thing with Mills. I went there when I was 19, and I would say, "This next summer we must bring John Cage," so we'd bring John Cage for that summer; "Next summer we must bring Lester Horton up from Los Angeles," and we'd bring Lester Horton. I was a 19-year-old kid, and when I think of what Mills invested in both confidence and actual work and money in me, I can hardly believe it. So I've always felt this deep debt of gratitude to Mills, and joy — and still do: I'm going back in March for a series of lectures.

Q: This notion of your hating music: Was it anger against music itself or against people who couldn't hear that music had value?

HARRISON: It was a combination. I had had a nervous breakdown in New York: Everything was just too much. And music, since it was the basis of my activities, got to be hateful. And during that period, I had to earn a living, so first I was a forest firefighter for the state Ranger system. They wanted me to stay on because I could speak well; they wanted me to be a dispatcher. But I didn't. Next was about five years of working as an animal nurse in a veterinary hospital. I always have a gag about that: "It's the only other profession in which you can caress the customers all day."

Q: You were also composing at that time, weren't you?

HARRISON: Yeah, I was. I was working eight hours a day at the animal hospital and I was exhausted, and finally I began to take marsalid under my doctor's orders. That's a monoamine-oxidase inhibitor. When you wake up, you start immediately producing monoamine oxidase, which is a chemical that, if you get enough of it, will put you to sleep, period. So if you stay up long enough and keep producing this stuff, you'll eventually fall asleep no matter what. Well, there is a chemical series that will inhibit the production of it, so you don't need sleep. There's a man here in New York who only gets an hour and a half or two hours every night, and lives double lives. It's hard on the family, but you can live a double life. And so I started doing that. I would work an eight-hour day at the hospital; I'd come home, have dinner, maybe read a little bit; and then do another eight-hour music day; then take maybe an hour and a half or a couple of hours, and go back to work.

Q: Was that debilitating for you?

HARRISON: No. You don't really need to sleep except for detaching the synapses at least once during the 24 hours — otherwise you go nuts because your neurons won't take it. But you don't really need that amount of sleep. Except now they're discovering this recent thing, that your brain fires every hour and a half while you're asleep and produces dreams. So there is that. But I did produce an enormous amount of music in that period — I think it was about a year that I took it, and I produced a lot. In fact, my Second and Third Symphonies have a lot culled from that period. But I finally thought, "What the hell am I doing this for? It doesn't make sense." So I stopped it and got a more orderly life. And about that time I was asked to teach, and that was fun. I enjoyed it because I'm really very much of a student at heart; I can't stop studying and learning. And that I did up to the point where I had to retire from teaching due to health. Now I could go back, I think. I miss those checks, but now the commissions are making up for it, and the royalties.

Q: What's the state of your book on Korean music?

HARRISON: It's still pending. I know what I need to do, but I have to find time to do it. That's another thing that I might do when I just take off in the camper; take things like that with me and finish them up. There's a lot dangling and I don't want too much to go dangling over my death, you know. I'd like to finish a few things. My opera *Young Caesar* is one of the things I want to finish: It needs arias. Because it goes on chattering like *Pelléas And Mélisande*. Two years ago, the Portland Gay Men's Chorus mounted *Young Caesar* in the big theater; it wasn't a puppet opera anymore. Also, it wasn't for my friends who could play everything from all over the world; it's now just for European instruments. So now it has to be even further revised, because on the big stage it turns out to be a sort of chatterbox thing, and it needs big arias as signposts along the way. It's still a good piece, and it's the only overt gay opera, so I want to leave a good one. Once I get this next commission over, I'm going to declare a period when I write operas.

And I have other ideas, things I want to do, but I don't want deadlines anymore. I'm too old for them. There are a lot of things I'd like to do: I want to write and paint and do things like that; I always did them all my life, why shouldn't I continue? I have two invitations to put out my collected writings and I'd like to do that.

Q: I understand that in composing *Double Music,* you and John Cage worked independently on your parts, and after you heard everything performed together, no one had to change a note.

HARRISON: We didn't need to. We were so close then that each knew what the other fellow was going to do: I'd come to certain points and say, "I know what John's going to do there," things like this. And he knew what I was going to do. So it fit almost perfectly right away.

Q: Was this kind of collaboration, either with Cage or other composers, something you were interested in pursuing further?

HARRISON: Well, it was John's suggestion. We were doing a concert of our musics which we alternated, and then John said, "Let's do something together at the end," and I said, "Fine." So we contributed the design and instrumentation and rhythmicals. And we didn't cheat, which is a problem if you're going to do a co-op piece; You have to have everybody really do the setup, otherwise some joker comes in and says he didn't like that, and then it's gone. But we didn't cheat and it worked.

And I've done that with other people. Later of course I finished pieces by Ives and Henry Cowell — I finished Cowell's Seventeenth Symphony, something like that. I've always had a way of getting into other people's music. I can't do it anymore; I've been asked to do something like that, but I'm just too old for it. There are other, younger people who have that same ability, and they can do it now.

Q: There's also the collaboration with Cage, Cowell, and Virgil Thomson for the *Party Pieces* which were recently published, but I take it that was really more an entertainment for yourselves.

HARRISON: Oh, that was fun, yes. That was like meeting now, and we'd pass around the paper! But I was the guy who saved it, you see. I'm like a pack rat or a magpie: If it's pretty, I save it!

Q: Today, reading of your associations in New York with Cowell, Cage, and Thomson, the image one gets is that a kind of gay networking was going on. Was that the idea at the time?

HARRISON: No, we didn't have what is now known as gay life. We were all individuals. No, that just happened that we were gay. There were a lot of people that weren't: There was Wallingford Riegger, Otto Luening. But there wasn't a sense of gay unity or social adhesion; we just happened to be, and that was interesting and enjoyable. But it certainly wasn't a social phenomenon.

Remember too, I grew up in San Francisco — I've never really grown up, but the gesture was made in San Francisco! — and there's never been a problem that I could tell in San Francisco.

Q: You've commented elsewhere that New York was far more uptight when you first came here.

HARRISON: Yes, I was astonished when I got to New York to find out how different it was. And that was during the '40s, even when it was wide open because of the war. Then later I found New York really closed down, in a way.

Q: Was there the sense here that one could be whatever one was as long as you kept quiet about it?

HARRISON: Yes. Well, that's something Virgil said: "You could do anything you want, but don't tell anybody." Don't talk about it, that was the main thing. But in San Francisco you talked about it all the time!

Q: You're justly celebrated for all of your work on certain of Charles Ives' scores. But I understand you also played an important role in preparing Carl Ruggles' *Evocations* for publication.

HARRISON: Yes I did. I got them in shape by constant ... begging! I managed to extract them from him. We gave him a party while I was editor of *New Music Edition*; we showed his paintings and gave a very noisy and happy party. In New York, you can tell if it's a successful party by the amount of decibels, and this was a very successful one. We played some music too. Later of course I conducted some Ruggles. Then I finally sort of parted company with him — the character was too much for me.

Q: How do you mean?

HARRISON: Anti-black, anti-Semitic. And loudly, in public. It was just too much, and I finally decided I didn't have to put up with it. I think he was innocent in his heart; his biases were just part of... I don't know what it was. Anyway, it was too much for me. I found out after I'd conducted *Angels* that I'd been invited to do that by the young Richard Franco Goldman — he wouldn't conduct a work of Ruggles, because of the anti-Semitism, you see. But he was nice enough to have programmed it. And I didn't know that was why he was having me do it at the time.

That's also when I learned the use of the word bis. Varèse was backstage when I came off from conducting, and people were shouting "Bis!" in the audience, and I said, "Varèse, what do they mean?" He said, "They want you to repeat it!" Varèse was always wonderfully nice to me and got me performances. So I learned what bis meant, and I did repeat it.

Q: As a teenager, you had spent a long time with Ives' music.

HARRISON: Yes, he had sent me this crate of his scores early on.

Q: Did you feel like you had to set that part of your musical character aside once you began studying with Schoenberg?

HARRISON: Oh no. It was just another thing. Well, the first thing I took to Schoenberg was a neo-classic piece — typical American boy being naughty right off the bat. And my estimation of Schoenberg just went up miles, because he couldn't have cared less about the idiom; he was only interested in the musicality, how it was done, and so on. Later I took him serial pieces, anything — he was not interested in those things, in technicalities and styles. It was something else, some essence, some essential thing — like he told me, "only the essentials."

We got along very well, and I've never understood people who said he was a tyrant. There were a lot of people who thought he was dreadful, but I got along with him very well, I had no problems. In fact, I enjoyed it, it meant a lot to me. And as I've written, when he found that I was going to go to New York, he wanted to know why I was going. And I said I didn't really know, and he said that he did know: I was going for fame and fortune. And he said, "Good luck." And then he added, "Don't study with anybody, you don't need to. Study only Mozart." So I got Mozart piano sonatas and so on and studied only Mozart! But I thought later that that was kind of interesting: I must have passed my polyphony and counterpoint well, because on his own desk he had Bach and Mozart. I was to study only Mozart, so I clearly passed the counterpoint test!

Q: Was it through Cage that you came to study with Schoenberg?

HARRISON: No, it wasn't through him at all. It was Henry Cowell, actually. Henry at one point gave a concert in San Francisco, and some instrumentalist was late — he had to play at the opera and then run over, something like that — so Henry improvised a speech. He was good at this, what he used to call "jollying people along." And he spoke of his admiration of Schoenberg, that Schoenberg was the greatest composer since Beethoven and so on. It was very impressive, and I was already studying Schoenberg's music in the San Francisco Public Library which had almost everything up to that date. (I got an enormous education from that library: French opera and ballet, Spanish folk art, Spanish organ history, everything you can think of is there — and Schoenberg.) And there was a time when I could really enjoy only the music of Schoenberg. I had scores out all the time, and that was all I listened to and thought of.

Q: But you hadn't met him or worked with him yet.

HARRISON: No, no. Then I did meet him in San Francisco at Olive Cowell's house. He came up to conduct his own *Pelléas And Mélisande* with the WPA Orchestra in Oakland, and that's when I first met him, in the car then. Later I went down and studied with him, but by this time Henry had already taught me how to write a serial piece. And I enjoyed working with Schoenberg very much. It was a small symposium. (Otto Klemperer, who would occasionally have illnesses, came to class once and sat there, trying to recover.) When we didn't have anything to show him or one another, then he would analyze things, Beethoven and so on. Once we asked him to analyze one of his quartets, and he said, "Why, it's very easy, I'll show you how I wrote it." And of course anybody could see that you could write his First Quartet, just like that! — or the Second, I don't remember which it was. But he made it so simple, you clearly could have done it!

Q: Regarding Henry Cowell: Is it true that you were with him the day after he was released from prison?

HARRISON: Yes, I was. Olive Cowell invited me up to breakfast that morning. And we sat across from one another as Olive prepared breakfast, and he didn't say a word until all of a sudden he looked up and he said, "Oh, I'm sorry, we weren't allowed to talk in prison." And then he started in, just as always — the change was just like that. So away we went, and chattered ever since!

I was also with him the day before his arrest, as a matter of fact. He took me to Stanford, in the Women's Gym there. He was writing music for underwater swimming, to be broadcast into the pool. And then he played for me in the gym, and we had a grand time. Then the next day I was startled to read that he'd been arrested.

Q: Peter Garland has argued that there was a political slant to Cowell's arrest, that some people were out to get him.

HARRISON: Lots of people have felt that. And he was very liberal.

Q: He'd been to the Soviet Union too.

HARRISON: Right. I think I still have the copy from the Russian state edition of one of the pieces, *Tiger*, I think.

Q: Obviously, with the so-called "morals charge," this was also a homophobic attack against him.

HARRISON: Oh, yes. They tried to make a Wilde case of it in San Francisco.

Q: Did that case have a chilling effect, pushing people back into the closet? Because you've been out all your life.

HARRISON: Well, that's what I was about to say: I wouldn't know, because it never affected me! It only affected me insofar as I had to travel over to see him in prison, as often as I could, which was fairly frequent. And I'd have a lesson through the bars, in effect; and we'd talk of what we'd done, and so on. Then of course later I heard more about it when we were living in New York.

Q: You were still a teenager when he was arrested. I was wondering if it had been traumatic for you to see someone you admired struck down like that by society.

HARRISON: Yeah, I know. But by that time, I had decided that society was no damn good anyway!

COMPOSITIONS

1934	*Peter Pan* incidental music	MS
1934-43	Six Sonatas for cembalo or piano	PSO
1936	*Changing World* ballet score	MS
1936-60	Suite For Symphonic Strings	CFP
1936-83	*Counterdance In Spring* for percussion	HBP
1937	*Choephore* incidental music	MS
1937	Prelude And Sarabande for piano	TP
1937	*France, 1917 — Spain, 1937* for string quartet and percussion	HBP
1937-82	Third Symphony for orchestra	CFP
1938	*Electra* incidental music	MS
1938	*The Trojan Women* incidental music	MS
1938	*The Winter's Tale* incidental music	ML
1938;70	Third Sonata For Piano	HBP
1939	Concerto No. 1 for flute and percussion	CFP
1939	*Green Mansions* ballet score	MS
1939	*Something To Please Everybody* ballet score	MS
1939-54	*Mass (to St. Anthony)* for SATB, trumpet, harp, and strings	PSO
1940	*Johnny Appleseed* ballet score	HBP
1940	*Omnipotent Chair* ballet score	MS
1940	*Sanctus* for contralto and orchestra or piano	HBP
1940	*Canticle No. 1* for five percussionists	MFP
1940	*Song Of Quetzecoatl* for four percussionists	MFP
1940-63	*Jeptha's Daughter* theater kit for two flutes, percussion, one or two auxiliary musicians, narrator, and dancers	HBP
1941	*The Beautiful People* incidental music	MS
1941	*Canticle No. 3* for ocarina or flute, guitar, and percussion	MFP
1941	*Double Music* for four percussionists (composed with John Cage)	CFP
1941	*Fugue For Percussion* for four percussionists	MFP
1941	*Labyrinth* for eleven percussionists	MFP
1941	*May Rain* for low voice, prepared piano, and tam-tam	HBP
1941	*Pied Beauty* for low voice, trombone, cello, flute, and percussion	HBP
1941-69	*Orpheus* for solo voice, chorus, and percussion orchestra	HBP
1941-75	*Elegiac Symphony* for orchestra	PSO
1943	Suite For Piano	CFP
1943-46	*Easter Cantata* for solo voices, chorus, and orchestra	HBP
1944	*Alleluia* for orchestra	TP
1945	*Party Pieces* for chamber orchestra (arranged by Robert Hughes) (composed with John Cage, Henry Cowell, and Virgil Thomson)	CFP

1945	*Schoenbergiana* for wind quintet	HBP
	(arranged by Robert Hughes)	
1945	*Siciliana* for wind quintet	HBP
	(arranged by Robert Hughes)	
1946	*Motet For The Day Of The Ascension* for seven string instruments	TP
1946	String Trio	CFP
1946	*Air* for flute	HBP
1946	*Praises For Michael The Archangel* for organ	MS
1946	*Fragment From Calamus* for alto, baritone, and piano	HBP
1947-48	Suite No. 1 for string orchestra	PSO
1947-48	Suite No. 2 for string orchestra or string quartet	MM
1948	*The Perilous Chapel* ballet score	PSO
1948	*Western Dance* ballet score	HBP
1948-61	*Symphony On G* for orchestra	PSO
1949	Suite for cello and harp	PSO
1949	*The Only Jealousy Of Emer* ballet/drama	HBP
1949	*The Marriage At The Eiffel Tower* ballet score; orchestral suite	CFP
1949	*Solstice* for flute, oboe, trumpet, celeste, tack piano, two cellos,	
	and bass	PSO
1949	*Little Suite For Piano*	EBM
1949	*Alma Redemptoris Mater* for baritone, violin, trombone, and	
	tack piano	PSO
1950	*Almanac Of The Seasons* ballet score	MS
1951;87	*Io And Prometheus* for men's and women's voices and piano	HBP
1951	*Praise For Hummingbirds And Hawks* ballet score	MS
1951	*Praise For The Beauty Of Hummingbirds* for chamber ensemble	PSO
1951	Suite for violin, piano, and small orchestra	CFP
1951	*Holly And Ivy* for low voice, harp, and strings	HBP
1951	*A Political Primer* for soloists, chorus, and orchestra (incomplete)	HBP
1951-52	*Chorales For Spring* ballet score	MS
1952	*Seven Pastorales* for four woodwinds, harp, and strings	PSO
1952	*Serenade* for guitar	MS
	arrangement for harp	MS
1953	*Peace Piece Three* for low voice, violin, harp, and strings	HBP
1954	*Rapunzel* opera	PSO
1954	Serenade in C for woodwinds	HBP
1955	*Simfony In Free Style* for seventeen flutes (three to four players),	
	trombone, bells, drums, five harps, and eight violas	CFP
1993	(arranged for computer synthesis by David Doty)	
1955;92	*Four Strict Songs* for eight baritones and orchestra;	
	for full chorus and orchestra	GS
1957	*Cinna* incidental music	MS
1959	*Koncherto por la violino kon perkuta orkestro* for violin and	
	five percussionists	CFP

1961	*Moogunkhwa Se Tang* for Korean court orchestra	MS
1961	*Quintal Taryung* for two flutes and changgo	MS
1961	*Concerto In Slendro* for violin, cello, two tack pianos, and percussion	CFP
1961-69	*Psaltery Pieces*	HBP
1962	Prelude for piri and harmonium	HBP
1962	*A Joyous Procession And A Solemn Procession* for chorus, trombones, and percussion	CFP
1962	*Nova Odo* for chorus and orchestra	HBP
1963	*Pacifika Rondo* for chamber orchestra of Oriental and Western instruments	PSO
1963	*Majestic Fanfare* for trumpets and percussion	HBP
1964	*At The Tomb Of Charles Ives* for chamber ensemble	PSO
1965	*Avalokiteshvara* for harp and jahlataranga	MS
1967	*Music For Violin And Various Instruments, European, Asian, And African*	PSO
1968	*Harp Solo*	MS
1968	*Beverly's Troubadour Piece* for harp and two percussionists	MS
1968	*In Memory Of Victor Jowers* for clarinet and piano	HBP
1968	*Peace Piece Two* for tenor, two harps, organ, three percussionists, and string quintet	HBP
1968	*Haiku* for unison chorus, shiao, harp, and percussion	HBP
1971	*La Koro Sutro* for mixed chorus and American gamelan with added percussion instruments	PSO
1971	*Young Caesar* puppet opera for five players of various instruments and five singers; for Western orchestra, men's chorus, and soloists	PSO
1972	*Peace Piece One: From The Metta Sutta* for unison chorus, trombone, three percussionists, and orchestra	HBP
1972-73	Concerto For Organ With Percussion Orchestra	PSO
1972-73	Suite for solo violin and American gamelan; for solo violin and string orchestra (composed with Richard Dee)	PSO
1973	*Nuptiae* film score	MS
1974	*Arion's Leap* for justly tuned instruments and percussion	HBP
1976	*Gending Pak Chokro* for Javanese gamelan	HBP
1976	*Lancaran Daniel* for Javanese gamelan	HBP
1976	*Lagu Sociseknum* for Javanese gamelan	HBP
1977	*A Waltz For Evelyn Hinrichsen* for piano	CFP
1978	*Main Bersama Sama* for Sudanese gamelan Degung with French horn	HBP
1978	*Serenade For Betty Freeman And Franco Assetto* for Sudanese gamelan Degung with suling solo	HBP
1978-79	*String Quartet Set*	PSO

1978	Serenade For Guitar With Optional Percussion	PSO
1979	*Threnody For Carlos Chavez* for Sudanese gamelan Degung with viola	HBP
1979	*Discovering Korean Art* film score	MS
1979-80	*Scenes From Cavafy* for baritone, small male chorus, and large Javanese gamelan	HBP
1981	*Gending Alexander* for Javanese gamelan	HBP
1981	*Gending Hermes* for Javanese gamelan	HBP
1981	*Ladrang Epikuros* for Javanese gamelan	HBP
1981	*Gending Hephaestus* for Javanese gamelan	HBP
1981	*Buburan Robert* for Javanese gamelan (revised)	HBP
1981-82	Double Concerto for violin, cello, and Javanese gamelan	CFP
1981-82	*Beyond The Far Blue Mountains* film score	MS
1981-83	*Gending Demeter* for Javanese gamelan	HBP
1982	*Gending Dennis* for Javanese gamelan	HBP
1982	*Lancaran Molly* for Javanese gamelan	HBP
1982	*Gending Pindar* for Javanese gamelan	HBP
1982	*Gending Claude* for Javanese gamelan	HBP
1982-83	*Gending Palladio* for Javanese gamelan	HBP
1983	*Gending Sinan* for Javanese gamelan	HBP
1983	*Gending James And Joel* for Javanese gamelan	HBP
1983	*Ketawang Wellington* for Javanese gamelan	HBP
1983	*For The Pleasure Of Ovid's Changes* for Javanese gamelan	HBP
1983	*The Foreman's Song Tune* for chorus and Javanese gamelan	HBP
1983	*Lagu Victoria* for Cirebon gamelan	HBP
1983	*Lagu Elane Yusef* for Cirebon gamelan	HBP
1983	*Lagu Lagu Thomason* for Cirebon gamelan	HBP
1983	*Devotions* film score	MS
1984	*Ladrang Pak Daliyo* for Javanese gamelan	HBP
1984	*Gending William Colvig* for Javanese gamelan	HBP
1984	*Philemon And Baukis* for violin and Javanese gamelan	HBP
1985	Piano Concerto	CFP
1985	Three Songs for male chorus, piano, and strings	PSO
1986	*Gregorian Mass* for male chorus	HBP
1986	*Gending Vincent* for Javanese gamelan	HBP
1986	*Gending In Honor Of Aphrodite* for Javanese gamelan	HBP
1986	*New Moon* for chamber ensemble	HBP
1987	*Four Coyote Stories* for baritone and Javanese gamelan	HBP
1987	Concerto for piano and Javanese gamelan	HBP
1987	*The Clay's Quintet* for trumpet, French horn, mandolin, harp, and percussion	HBP
1987	*Ariadne* for flute and percussion	HBP
1987	*Varied Trio* for violin, piano, and percussion	HBP
1987	*A Summerfield Set* for piano or harpsichord	HBP

1987	*The Scattered Remains Of James Broughton* film score	MS
1987	*Lagu Pa Udang* for Sudanese gamelan Sunda Slendro	HBP
1987	*Faust* for soloists, chorus, orchestra, solo harps, and gamelan	HBP
1988	*Grand Duo* for violin and piano	HBP
1988	*Air For The Poet* for orchestra	HBP
1989	*Soedjetmoko Set* for female vocalist, mixed chorus, and Javanese gamelan	HBP
1989	Pedal Sonata For Organ	HBP
1990;92	*Fourth Symphony* for baritone and orchestra	HBP
1990	Piano Trio	HBP
1991	*Homage To Pacifica* for Javanese gamelan, mixed chorus, solo harp, solo bassoon, solo Ptolemy Duple, narrator, and verse choir	HBP
1991	*Threnody For Oliver Daniel* for harp	HBP
1992	*Tandy's Tango* for piano	FLP
1992	Suite for four haisho and two percussionists	HBP

DISCOGRAPHY

1952
Suite for cello and harp; String Quartet
Columbia 4491 lp
New World 281 lp (1976)

1954
Suite For Violin, Piano, And Small Orchestra
RCA 1785
CRI 114 lp (1958)

1957
Mass (to St. Anthony)
Epic 3307 lp

Canticle No. 3
Urania 106, 5106 lp

1958
Song Of Quetzecoatl
Period 743 lp
Orion 7276 lp (1972); 642 cs (1984)

1959
Four Strict Songs
Louisville 58-2 lp

1961
Canticle No. 1, Double Music
Time 8000, 58000 lp

1962
Suite For Symphonic Strings
Louisville 621 lp

1969
Symphony On G
CRI 236 lp

Pacifika Rondo, Four Pieces For Harp, Two Pieces For Psaltery, *Music For Violin With Various Instruments, European, Asian, African*
Desto 6478 lp
Phoenix 118 cd (1991)

1970
Suite For Percussion
CRI 252 lp; 6006 cs (1985); 613 cd (1991)

Canticle No. 1
Mainstream 5011, 85011 lp

1972
Concerto For Violin And Percussion Orchestra
Crystal 853 lp; 850 cd (1992)

Concerto In Slendro
Desto 7144 lp
CRI 613 cd (1991)

1975
Fugue For Percussion
Opus One 22 lp

1977
Concerto For Organ And Percussion Orchestra
Crystal 858 lp; 850 cd (1992)

Concerto For Violin And Percussion Orchestra
Turnabout 34653 lp

1978
Gending Pak Chokro
Cambridge 2560 lp

Elegiac Symphony
1750 Arch lp

1981
Main Bersama-Sama, Threnody For Carlos Chavez, Serenade, String Quartet Set
CRI 455 lp; 6006 cs (1985); 613 cd (1991)

A Waltz For Evelyn Hinrichsen
Nonesuch 79011 lp

1983
At The Tomb Of Charles Ives, Party Pieces
Gramavision 7006 lp

String Trio
New World 319 lp

Double Concerto
TR 109 lp
Music & Arts 635 cd (1990)

1985
Concerto No. 1 for flute and percussion
Bis 272 lp; cd (1987)

1986
Sonata No. 2 for cembalo
Mills College 001 lp

A Phrase For Arion's Leap
Tellus 14 cs

1987
Scenes From Cavafy, Favorite Tunes From *Young Caesar*
Hermes Beard Press cs

1988
La Koro Sutro, Varied Trio, Suite For Violin And American Gamelan
New Albion 015 lp, cd

Piano Concerto, Suite For Violin, Piano, And Small Orchestra
New World 366-1 lp, -2 cd, -4 cs

1989
Ariadne, Concerto No. 1 for flute and percussion
CRI 568 cd

Elegiac Symphony
Music Masters 60204 cd, 40204 cs

Concerto for violin and percussion orchestra
New World 382-2 cd

The Perilous Chapel, Air In G
Opus One 129 lp

1990
Suite from the ballet *Solstice, Ariadne, A Summerfield Set, Canticle No. 3*
Music Masters 60241X cd

Canticle No. 3, Plaint And Variations On "Song Of Palestine," A Waltz For Evelyn Hinrichsen, Serenado For Gitaro, Serenade For Guitar And Percussion, Suite No. 1 For Guitar And Percussion
Etcetera 1071 cd

Double Music
New World 80405-2 cd

1991
Third Symphony, *Grand Duo*
Music Masters 67073-2 cd

Varied Trio
New Albion 036 cd

1992
Piano Trio
Music & Arts 687 cd

Seven Pastorales
Music Masters 67089-2 cd

Philemon And Baukis, Cornish Lancaran, Gending Alexander, Homage To Pacifica, Buburan Robert
Music Masters 67091-2 cd

Serenade For Guitar, (Little) Serenade For Guitar
Newport Classic 85509 cd

BIBLIOGRAPHY

"Ruggles, Ives, Varèse." *View* (November 1945); reprinted in *A Lou Harrison Reader.* Ed. Peter Garland. Santa Fe: Soundings Press, 1987.

About Carl Ruggles. Yonkers, New York: Alicat Bookshop, 1946; reprinted in *A Lou Harrison Reader.*

Lou Harrison's Music Primer. New York: C.F. Peters, 1971.

"Lines Of 11 & 3 On Harry Partch" (1973). *A Lou Harrison Reader.*

"Four Items" (1974). *A Lou Harrison Reader.*

"'Such Melodies And Clutter': Thoughts Around Ives, 1974." *Parnassus,* 3 (Spring/Summer 1975).

"Happy Birthday Virgil." *Parnassus,* 5 (Spring/Summer 1977).

"Nines To John Cage On His Sixtieth Birthday, 1977." *A Lou Harrison Reader.*

"Of A Matter I've Not Seen Written Of In Javanese Music Theory, or Slippery Slendro." *Selected Reports In Ethnomusicology,* 6 (1985).

"Tens On Remembering Henry Cowell" (1986). *A Lou Harrison Reader.*

Joys And Perplexities. Asheville, North Carolina: Jargon Press, 1992.

photo: Gene Bagnato

ALAN HOVHANESS / Introduction

ALAN HOVHANESS was born in Somerville, Massachusetts, on March 8, 1911. He began composing music even before starting school, and received his early training in piano from Adelaide Proctor and Heinrich Gebhard. At the New England Conservatory of Music he studied composition with Frederick Converse. In 1942 he won a scholarship to study at Tanglewood. Although he valued his composition studies there with Bohuslav Martinu, Hovhaness left the school and began a serious pursuit of his own musical language.

With the encouragement of his friends, the painters Hermon diGiovanno and Hyman Bloom, Hovhaness followed his interest in learning more about the culture of his ancestral Armenia, and began playing organ in the local Armenian church. His discovery of the music of Yenovk Der Hagopian and Komitas Vartabed proved to be a breakthrough for the composer, and Armenian qualities soon became a cornerstone of his music, from such enduring works as *Armenian Rhapsody No. 1* , Op. 45, and *Lousadzak*, Op. 48 (both 1944), to his Symphony No. 65, *Artsakh*, Op. 427 (1991).

As the above Opus number would suggest, Hovhaness is one of America's most prolific composers (despite his decision to destroy most of the music he composed in the 1920s and '30s). Yet his interest in different kinds of music sometimes seems to rival the scope of his composition list. Along with his studies of 7th-century Armenian music, Hovhaness became increasingly devoted to Eastern music, and traveled extensively throughout the 1950s. He studied the classical music of South India, Japanese Gagaku, the orchestral music of T'ang Dynasty China, and Ah-ak of Korea. Masatoro Togi, a Japanese Gagaku musician, was Hovhaness's instructor in ancient Japanese music and instruments. In the 1960s, his years of study bore fruit with numerous Asian-inspired scores, including *Nagooran*, Op. 237, No. 1, for South Indian orchestra (1960) and *Fantasy On Japanese Wood Prints*, Op. 211 (1964).

Hovhaness has received innumerable commissions over the years, with sources ranging from the Martha Graham Dance Company to the International Center for Arid and Semi-Arid Land Studies in Lubbock, Texas. When Leopold Stokowski, seeking a work for his first program with the Houston Symphony in 1955, commissioned Hovhaness for a score, the result was what has become the composer's most popular piece, his Symphony No. 2, "Mysterious Mountain," Op. 132. Equally beloved orchestral works include the *Prayer of St. Gregory*, Op. 62b (1946), and *And God Created Great Whales*, Op. 229, No. 1 (1970), a commission from André Kostelanetz and the New York Philharmonic.

As a pianist and conductor, Hovhaness has performed his music internationally. He has also recorded many of his strongest scores, including the Symphony No. 19, *Vishnu*, Op. 217 (1966), and *Fra Angelico*, Op. 220 (1967), on the Poseidon label, which he launched in the 1970s.

Hovhaness has taught at the Boston Conservatory of Music and at the Eastman School of Music. He has received the Samuel Endicott Prize, two Guggenheim Fellowships, grants from the Fulbright and Rockefeller Foundations, and an award from the National Institute of Arts and Letters. He is also the recipient of honorary doctorates from the University of Rochester and Bates College. He currently lives in Seattle, Washington.

I spoke with Alan Hovhaness in his Manhattan hotel room on October 3, 1991, in between rehearsals for his 80th-birthday gala celebration at Carnegie Hall. I was especially interested to speak with him about his development as a composer — including his legendary immolation of his early scores — as well as his devotion to non-Western music and his attitudes regarding composition in equal temperament.

ALAN HOVHANESS / Interview

Q: In the Crystal cd reissues of your music, the bios give your name as Alan Hovhaness Chakmakjian. Are you concerned now with reintroducing your full name?

HOVHANESS: I never tried to. I don't mind it, because that was my name. But Hovhaness was easier for people. My high-school librettist — we did operas together in school — he liked Hovhaness very much and said, "Why don't you use that?" My mother had made Hovhaness into Vaness, so everybody thought I was from some Northern European country, which I'm not. I guess my father and mother had some difficulties. My father tried to teach me Armenian secretly. He was a great walker — we climbed mountains many times too — and he tried to teach me Armenian when we were walking, but it didn't stick very well. And I think my mother felt afraid that we'd be persecuted in the suburb of Boston where we were. We were on the wrong side of the railroad tracks! So she wasn't anxious to have me known as an Armenian. But of course I don't have that feeling.

Either way would be all right, but I got out of the habit of Chakmakjian. And it's a difficult name for many people to pronounce correctly.

Q: So those bios are just Crystal's attempt to be complete. If you're listed under "H" in this book, that's all right.

HOVHANESS: It's all right. I didn't know it was in there like that — I guess I haven't seen it. I never listen to anything because I've got so many things going on in my head and I have to get those on paper. What's already done is done. Even if I don't like it, I can't do anything about it.

For my friends and the people in Seattle, certainly Hovhaness is much easier! Although there are beginning to be quite a few Armenians there too. I don't know what they're escaping this time, but they're in a tough position. I'm worried about them — especially if they become free. But it didn't do any good when they weren't independent, because Gorbachev was afraid to do anything to protect them against Azerbaijan. Azerbaijan has Turkish people, and on the other side is Turkey. So the Armenians are surrounded by Turks, which is unfortunate because these have been their enemies all the time and they suddenly start fighting for no apparent reason. So they're in a difficult position and even Gorbachev was afraid he would have revolutions all over Russia, that all the Mohammedan groups would rebel, if he helped the Armenians. So he was suddenly very mean to the Armenians.

Q: You mentioned your high-school librettist. You'd actually been composing for many years prior to then, hadn't you?

HOVHANESS: In junior high school we'd done an opera on the biblical story of Daniel. My mother liked that idea and one of the fellows in school made it into the form of a libretto. So after that he became sort of a poet and he was always writing texts. Some of them I'd set for school — it was the sort of thing the school enjoyed.

Q: I've read that you were writing music by the age of five.

HOVHANESS: Well, I made some attempts at four! But that was because my mother was very religious and had this little harmonium where she was always playing Baptist hymns. And I thought that that instrument could do something besides that. I was just a little kid and so I wrote something, putting together the treble and bass clefs as one clef — which would be a 10-line clef, but it had to include middle C, so there were 11 lines. I wrote that for the organ, and she said, "I can't read that, it's not correct." So I thought, "Oh well, I was planning to be an astronomer, so I guess I'll be an astronomer." But I did find after all that there was a period in early European music when they used an 11-line staff. So it may have been that I'd used it in a past incarnation!

That went on until I was about seven years old. I was out sick one time and came back to school, and they were playing classical music. I heard a song of Schubert's, and I thought, "This song has a very beautiful melody and it's written by Mr. Schubert. So perhaps I should put down on paper the melodies I hear in my head." Because I was always hearing melodies but I thought everybody had this affliction.

We kept that harmonium all through my childhood. Later my mother would use the vacuum on it, and we'd lose various pieces of it — cloth would come out of it and then it wouldn't play!

Q: When you started writing your own melodies, had you had some training to prepare you for working with musical notation?

HOVHANESS: Not in the beginning. I had a soprano voice when I was a little kid and was apparently the best singer in the school at that time. When my voice changed, I was moved from where the larks sit to where the crows sit! I was thinking of Shakespeare: "What a fall is this"! But I felt good because I thought I'm a little more manly now, so I didn't mind!

But I knew how to read music because I read as a kid, singing. And so I started writing my melodies after I heard that Schubert song.

Q: Your Opus 1 is a 1926 revision of a 1922 score — meaning you'd first written it when you were ten or eleven years old?

HOVHANESS: That's right. That was written for violin and piano. I wrote several things then. There was a sonata which was one of my best pieces, I think, from that same period or a little after, and that unfortunately is lost. The boy whom I wrote it for was in school with me. He was a good violinist and became a conductor later. But then he died, so I never did get the manuscript back from him. That would have been interesting because it was a good piece in an early style.

Q: So much of your music from the '20s and '30s is gone now. I've read commentaries that describe you burning up an enormous quantity of scores. Did you actually destroy a lot of your music?

HOVHANESS: I did. I happened to be staying in a place where there was a tremendous fireplace, and so I thought, "I can't have all this stuff — it's in the way." So I burned it all. But that sonata wasn't among those things; I wouldn't have burned that.

Q: How much material went up in that conflagration?

HOVHANESS: It must have been about 500 things, including an opera and sketches — possibly up to a thousand pages. It was too much stuff to worry about, and I wanted to make a new start anyway. That was when I was about 19 or 20; I destroyed an awful lot of stuff then.

There was another time too — I had two destructive periods. The second one was after Tanglewood because I'd decided I didn't want a connection anymore with European music as it was going. I was given a scholarship to go to Tanglewood and study with Martinu who was a very good man; I liked him very much. But I had a bad experience in Tanglewood when we were supposed to play our music for each other in the composers' group. I had an acetate record of a very good performance of my First Symphony, the "Exile" Symphony, with the BBC orchestra; Leslie Heward was the conductor. The record wasn't really loud, but if you listened to it carefully it would be fine. But when they played it, it was interrupted all the way through by Aaron Copland. He was talking loudly in Spanish, to intentionally drown out my music. Then he said, "This is a lullaby, not a symphony." When it was over, Leonard Bernstein went to the piano and said, "I hate this dirty ghetto music." So I thought, "I think I'll go back to the ghetto. I don't like this snobbish attitude here, I don't like the music they're writing, and I don't want to write anything in the style that they like."

Q: But the symphony that was played at that session was something you didn't destroy.

HOVHANESS: That one I kept. There were some other symphonies before, one that I won the Endicott Prize with in about 1932 or so, which was played by the New England Conservatory. I'd also won a scholarship with Frederick Converse — he was a very good man. I used the first movement of that particular symphony again; it's the opening movement of "All Men Are Brothers," which is a little more Romantic than the other music I was writing later. I felt that was a good piece, and Converse liked it very much. Later I studied counterpoint with Converse and went very deeply into that. But I destroyed a lot of work after this Tanglewood thing; I thought I'd start all over again.

Q: Which also meant leaving Martinu.

HOVHANESS: Martinu I was sorry to leave because we'd had a good session together, privately. One session only — the rest of the time he was just teaching people to develop their ears: What note is this, and then from there what note is that, and so on. That was very boring to me because I didn't have a bad ear and didn't need to concentrate on that; I always knew what note it was. But we did have one private session when I went over a symphony with him, and he seemed to be rather moved by that symphony and he approved of it. But I couldn't stay there after that trouble I'd had with Copland and Bernstein, so I just left the next day and went back to Boston.

But I'm grateful to them that I did leave, because I found my direction in music through my painter friend Hyman Bloom. He was an expert in Oriental music and Indian music and all kinds of cantorial music from the unreformed Jewish church. (He didn't like the reform music.) He would play some of the cantors for me, and these were very beautiful. He also brought Six Dances of Komitas Vartabed with him. And he introduced me to Yenovk Der Hagopian, the greatest Armenian troubadour. He was not appreciated at all by the Armenians: They thought he was a barbarian because he sang in the true ancient style. He was the son of a priest, and his father was a great singer. He'd lived with the Kurds too and knew how to sing Kurdish style — his Kurdish songs were magnificent. We made a recording of it – Hyman and I and a few friends put what little money we had into recording him. I think I still have a copy of it at home. He was a great inspiration.

Q: You transcribed some of his music into Western notation, didn't you?

HOVHANESS: I did. My *Armenian Rhapsody* is entirely based on his material. He wanted me to do it; he wanted me to copyright these things so the wrong person wouldn't get hold of it! He trusted me and so did his oud player, and so I made a rhapsody on that. And I made the *12 Armenian Folksongs*. That and this rhapsody are both based on the tunes he sang.

Q: Did Hyman Bloom introduce you to Komitas Vartabed's music, or had you already known it?

HOVHANESS: I knew vocal music of Komitas Vartabed. My father brought home one record when I was a kid, which was made in 1911 with Komitas Vartabed and Shamaradian who was a tenor. Shamaradian visited our house a few times because my father was fairly well known among the Armenians — he'd made a great Armenian-English dictionary. He was working on that when I was born.

Q: Would it be fair to say that, despite the studies you've had, you're essentially a self-taught composer?

HOVHANESS: Pretty much so, yes. I went back to Converse at a certain time and said, "I want to study counterpoint." He thought I was very advanced and said, "What do you mean? You know counterpoint. You do it very well." I said, "No, that's all fake. I'm a good fake, but I don't know it. I want to seriously have a real study of it as a system — and it has to be absolutely accurate." And so he put me in his most advanced class. At the end of the year, instead of writing a fugue on the theme he gave us, I wrote a whole book of fugues and a quadruple fugue at the end, on that theme. So he said, "Next year I want you to come back and teach me."

He was a very friendly fellow. We had a very good relationship. I saw him just shortly before his death: I had a tape or disc of a violin sonata which I played for him, and he loved it. "Your music is absolutely natural now," he said. He was very happy about it. There's something else he said which I've always appreciated. I'd brought in a piece with a melody he liked very much, and he said, "If I heard a bird singing in this melody in the forest, I would know who had taught him." I think that was a very beautiful, poetic way of putting it.

Q: Your scores from the 1920s and '30s, which are now your early Opus numbers — are they works you thought were good enough to keep or are some of them pieces that had gotten out too far for you to reclaim and destroy?

HOVHANESS: Some of them were good enough to keep: The Cello Concerto I like very much. We tried it out in Bellingham, Washington, where the conductor is a good cellist, so I conducted it. I love that work — that's more or less like I am now.

The Opus numbers are a bit deceptive. They were put together years later, and I couldn't remember the order in which things were written. But this friend from England, Richard Howard, came to visit us and he liked my music very much and wanted to make a list.

Q: He's done a spectacular job of cataloging your works by Opus number. The catch is, seeing them arranged that way doesn't give a clear sense of your development as a composer, because the Opus numbers are really a jumble in terms of the sequence of compositions.

HOVHANESS: It is a jumble.

Q: Until about the later '70s; from then on the works are pretty much sequential in Opus number.

HOVHANESS: Well, that's when his list was made. I guess I could be more accurate by then!

Q: Is it true that your Opus numbering began with your Second Symphony at the suggestion of Leopold Stokowski?

HOVHANESS: That's right. He said, "You know, people are funny — they like Opus numbers and they like titles." He was joking, but I gave it a title, "Mysterious Mountain." Then I said, "I don't know what to do because I've got a lot of compositions — I don't know how many I have." So he gave me that number, 132: "Would that be about right?" So I accepted it, and numbered things backwards from there. But there wasn't enough room, so some things are Opused after that but were actually written before.

Q: And others have to share the same Opus number.

HOVHANESS: That's true, that's what happened. So it was sort of artificial. Stokowski had a good sense of humor. He did a lot of my music and was very helpful.

Q: Besides composing for Western instruments, you've also written for the instruments of India, Korea, Japan, and Java. Back in 1965, you were quoted saying, "The study of Eastern music is my life work." Did you really feel that way then?

HOVHANESS: I felt that way, yes; I felt very serious about it. Because some lost concepts of ancient times are actually very modern concepts, really better than what we have. For instance, Gagaku music which I studied with wonderful teachers in Japan. This music originally came from India, way way back, two thousand years ago — and China in the T'ang dynasty. It still goes on but it's just played for the emperor on his special occasions. So I learned the instruments and played with the students' orchestra. I had a wonderful time with that music — it's very complex and very beautiful, very modern. They had orchestras of thousands in ancient times in China, and they'd play out of doors. So when Berlioz wanted to create an orchestra of a thousand during his career, and imagined it imitating nature and everything, I thought he must be the reincarnation of a Chinese composer of two thousand years ago — he sounded just the way they sound. He never quite succeeded: He didn't have the money, poor man!

My friend Hyman Bloom was very musical: He would listen to Indian music and invent instruments that were like Indian instruments, and he would improvise on them. I got a lot of encouragement from him. We would invite people from India who'd come to Boston to study at MIT. (Science, I guess — they wanted to get into something that would make more money.) But they were homesick, so they'd bring their instruments. We learned a lot about North Indian music from them: They would play for us and we'd listen and I'd take notes and so on. So I'd listen to the style and later I would improvise on these instruments myself.

Later, I had a Guggenheim fellowship to study South Indian music. I went to India and studied the style and made a book of South Indian ragas.

Q: I've read that around 1960 you performed in Madras, improvising on South Indian scales. You were playing Indian instruments?

HOVHANESS: I improvised on Indian instruments — I did that before I went to South India. But in South India I didn't do much playing. I wrote music there in my own style, but which was in Indian forms. "Arjuna," my Eighth Symphony, was a piano concerto; I'd actually written it before I went to South India but we performed it in Madras. And in this concerto I played entirely in an Indian manner. I called it by the Indian name "Arjuna"; the Indian title suggested this kind of heroic style. It's quite brilliant and all one melodic line from beginning to end, no repetition — the melody is always changing. This was never recorded and it should be. If it's played by a pianist who understands Indian music and ancient Armenian music, it will be very effective. I played that myself with a string orchestra in Madras. But that was long after it was written. We also did it in Japan, and somebody said it was the most Oriental piece their symphony orchestra had ever played!

Q: You worked as an improvising organist in the Armenian church back in the '30s. Was there ever a point where you thought your own music-making might go more in the direction of improvisation rather than composition?

HOVHANESS: No, I didn't separate the two because composition is sometimes so instantaneous that it's like an improvisation, except you have to write it down, which takes time. I should look into this computer they have now which writes it for you when you play it — I had somebody who wanted to study with me, and he brought me music that was done by computer. But that'd make me too lazy, I think!

Q: Playing various non-Western instruments also exposed you to a range of tuning systems.

HOVHANESS: Yes. The ancient Gagaku orchestra, especially its preludes for the Bugaku dances, are very complex. They have these simple, short preludes that are very poetic and very beautiful, which introduce the instruments almost separately. The big preludes are contrapuntal, but not in our style of counterpoint; it's a totally different style, very complicated, of chords against chords. This wonderful high instrument, the sho (I have one at home), has an absolutely celestial sound. You see it in all the old paintings of various angelic figures coming from heaven and playing these instruments as they come down to earth. I guess these instruments are supposed to have come from heaven, and they sound that way, they really do.

Q: In the C.F. Peters monograph on your music, you said it flat out: "Equal temperament kills melody." Does that still say it all for you, or does that sound a bit too harsh now?

HOVHANESS: Well, it may be a bit too harsh. But still, the instruments that are most fitted for melody are instruments where you instinctively don't stick to the system, where you have more freedom, like the violin or wind instruments or the voice — the voice can do these very subtle things and doesn't have to stay within such a narrow system. I think Lou Harrison probably felt this way very strongly, because he's become very interested in Oriental music of various kinds. I may have been agreeing with him when I said that.

Q: Most of your music has been written for Western instruments in equal temperament. Has that felt like something of a compromise for you — a translation of what you're actually hearing?

HOVHANESS: It is a slight compromise because if you put it in our system with our notation, you don't really get it. With our instruments it can sound very ugly because they can't do it. You have to have players who've been trained in the Oriental systems. That piece named after a Korean painting, *Mountains And Rivers Without End*, had a performance in Detroit where I couldn't be at the rehearsal; if I could have, I could have gotten it closer to what I wanted. But they made it sound very ugly and it shouldn't sound ugly — this little difference in intonation makes all the difference in the world. This was a piece for chamber orchestra, and they were trying so hard to do things that these instruments don't do. Unless you're very skillful, you get an ugly sound trying to do those things. I guess they thought I was being very snobbish, writing music nobody could understand except myself. But that wasn't what I was trying for.

Q: *O Lord, Bless Thy Mountains* is written for two pianos tuned a quartertone apart.

HOVHANESS: That was dedicated to one of my pupils, John Dierks, and his wife Thelma. He's a very sensitive fellow and I appreciate what he does, so I wrote it for him and his wife. He's very much interested in quartertones — that was his particular style and what he wanted to do. They're a little too mechanical for me, but I wrote a piece to try to make it beautiful. He wrote me a very nice letter about it: He liked it very much and was very happy with it, so I'm glad. He was one of the very talented pupils I had when I was teaching at Eastman — he and Dominick Argento I enjoyed very much. It's nice to teach somebody who has already done very well!

Q: Have you ever been interested in using tape or other electronic means to produce these unusual intonations?

HOVHANESS: I think of this in terms of instruments, but I know there are all kinds of possibilities. I've thought about it, but I've never had any experience with the machines that could do those things. I guess I'd have to be here in New York to get it, and I like the mountains where I am, so I'm in the wrong location!

Q: When you work with massings of like voices — sometimes in chamber pieces for, say, four harps or three flutes, sometimes in orchestral pieces where you may focus in on a cluster of instruments — you're not just thinking vertically anymore, are you? Beyond the actual chords, there's also a larger sonic situation, a new resonance, made by the activity of resultant tones and harmonics.

HOVHANESS: Yes, the spacing of sounds.

Q: You have more on your mind and in your ear than simply three pitches when the trio of flutes are playing *Spirit Of Ink*.

HOVHANESS: That's true, that's true. Sometimes it is three notes, but yes, it can be anything; it can be free rhythm.

Q: And along with your free-rhythm scoring, there's also your use of multiple glissandi, or of long, sustained drones that release unique resonances. I hear this sensibility in your piano playing too. I know you're concerned with documenting your playing — is part of the thinking that you want pianists to hear these sounds so you don't have to try to explain them verbally in a score?

HOVHANESS: It is, that's true. Yes, I do think that I try to do that in my playing — my playing has deteriorated greatly in the last few years.

Billy Masselos was wonderful about doing that. He was one of the finest pianists and a very fine person, one of my very best friends. He was wonderful with Ives, he really brought Ives to life tremendously. We'd sometimes appear in the same program in one way or another — I'd be conducting and he'd be playing, or we'd be playing a two-piano piece. He'd play *Achtamar* or some of my other piano pieces, and he'd say, "When I have to play on a bad piano, your music is just right for it!" He said it full of enthusiasm, and it can be true. He was on tour all the time, playing in all kinds of places, and when he would have to play on an out-of-tune piano, then he would immediately use my music, because it would still sound good. Sometimes a bad piano is better than a perfect Steinway for the slurring and the sounds between pitches and all that.

Q: As a conductor of your own music, has it been hard to get musicians to play parts without bar divisions, or do they adapt to it quickly?

HOVHANESS: I think now they adapt to it quickly. Things have changed — it was difficult at the beginning. If they understand the linear style and the freedom of it, then they should be comfortable with it. Because they have a choice too, to a certain extent: They can hold a little longer or not, as they feel. I like to write passages like that for solo instruments in an orchestra piece, and let the rest of the orchestra just murmur or do something in free rhythm or with no rhythm at all, just on their own. I have a couple of passages like that in this new Symphony, "Artstakh." I do it many times — I haven't done it so much just now. In conducting, I start right away with it: At the beginning I feel a little nervous because I know that some of them may not understand what I want. But we had a successful rehearsal; it was very good. I really appreciate the other composer, Karel Husa, who'll be conducting my work: He's doing the work which everybody does, but he's doing it better, he's doing it wonderfully. He's a wonderful musician, first rate in every way. He loves that work and he does it with love. I've listened to him rehearse, and he's much more thorough than I am as a conductor.

Q: He'll conduct your Second Symphony at this upcoming concert. Has that piece become something of an albatross for you? Are you tired of its following you around? For some reason, it's really stuck in the public's mind.

HOVHANESS: Well, it may have a message that gets across to people more readily than some of the others. It has the basis of what I'm after: It has a kind of visionary experience in it. I'm not ashamed of it; it's a work which I believe in.

Q: I read that even though the New York Philharmonic commissioned your 19th Symphony, "Vishnu," they played a drastically cut version for the premiere, which was conducted by André Kostelanetz.

HOVHANESS: Oh yes. That's why I finally did it myself. It was too long for a Pops concert. Kostelanetz became a very good friend and I appreciated what he did for me: He popularized my music very much. And most of it he did very well. That piece, though, I'd put my best in it. I did that when I was composer-in-residence with the Seattle Symphony, and I really wanted to do my best with that. It was commissioned by the New York Philharmonic, so I thought that since they commissioned really first-rate pieces, I should have a chance to do what I want to do. But being on the Pops program, of course it had to be cut pretty badly.

Q: The idea of taking an ax to that one-movement score just seems impossible — it would have to turn out ruined.

HOVHANESS: That's it: Every once and a while, when something really exciting was going to happen, it was cut. He said, "You know, my audience, they won't understand this thing." The cuts bothered me and I felt it really wasn't done right at all until it was done by Richard Bales — I liked him very much; he always did my music right and beautifully.

Q: Is it true that some of the Poseidon recordings of your orchestral music, which you conducted, were done without rehearsing the orchestra, because of financial limitations?

HOVHANESS: Oh yes, we had to go right into it. I had a hell of a time with *Celestial Gate* — by that time the players were tired or something like that. But we got through pretty well, finally. I've generally not had trouble with that, though. If I have an orchestra that's capable, it's a joy to record it.

I conducted *Ani* about two years ago at the Metropolitan Museum. I was about to give up conducting, but they got me such good players that I felt I really could do it very well. So now I have the courage to do it this time.

Q: You'll be leading the premiere of your 65th Symphony at this concert. Do you want to continue conducting?

HOVHANESS: I don't know. I always say I'm never going to conduct again, because I want to give my energies to something else, rather than to something that makes me nervous.

I gave a concert in Paris of my 13th Symphony, conducting a small orchestra. (I had a wonderful review from that; somebody really understood what I was trying to do.) Dane Rudhyar was there helping me with the rehearsals, and the concert itself went very well. But just before the concert, I went back to my hotel room and I got into the wrong pants! The pants were too small and I had great trouble pinning them up for the performance. I was afraid the pants would burst, so I conducted with the smallest motions. We ended with *Prayer Of St. Gregory* and I heard a sound in the audience, which was like hissing. I thought to myself, "My opponents are in the audience," so I made a stiff bow and walked away. Later I went back to the hotel room, and in the closet I found my pants — the pants I was wearing weren't mine (and had many holes)! Dane Rudhyar asked me, "Why didn't you play the encore?" What I thought was hissing in the audience was "Bis," "again" in French, which means encore.

Q: Has your work as a conductor and pianist made the difference for you financially, or is it really as a composer that you've supported yourself?

HOVHANESS: Now, it's as a composer; but of course, for many years I supported myself as a pianist. When I was a kid, I studied with Heinrich Gebhard's assistant, Miss Adelaide Proctor, and that woman did so much for me, sent me all over to concerts — she did many things besides teaching. If I had a good lesson, we'd do symphonies for four hands. I loved that, so I always had a good lesson! She gave me a scholarship and sent me to Heinrich Gebhard when I was older. People used to hire me whenever they had trouble — if any pianist got sick or something like that, they'd need somebody who could sight-read a whole program, and they'd always call on me. So I earned a living that way — plus other performing things, performances of Handel oratorios or Mozart operas with just piano accompanying the voices.

Q: You've written a good deal of your texts for song cycles, cantatas, even operas. Was supplying the words harder or easier than writing the music?

HOVHANESS: I took it just as seriously, but I don't pretend it can stand up especially. I tried to do things that expressed my philosophy or that were based on dreams — I used to dream operas a great deal, strange ones, and I'd try to make something out of them.

Q: Is it true that "Mysterious Mountain" also has material in it which you had dreamed?

HOVHANESS: Yes, in the third movement. When I was composing the music, I became exhausted and had to lie down and sleep for a while. In my sleep I heard the music and saw a Master leaving the Earth, and all nature, trees and flowers, were weeping. Then I was no longer tired and I wrote it down. Later I was copying the orchestra parts of "Mysterious Mountain." When I got to the third-movement flute part, I experienced the same scene and music — but I realized that, in my copying, I had missed one measure in each phrase.

COMPOSITIONS

	OPUS		
1922;26	1#1	*Oror (Lullaby)* for violin and piano	CFP
1922;26	1#2	Suite for violin and piano	MS
1922-35	53#1	*Jesus, Lover Of My Soul* for voice, SATB, and organ (or piano)	CFP
1926;62	9	*Quintet No. 1* for string quartet and piano	CFP
1927;62	34	*Watchman, Tell Us Of The Night* for bass and organ (or piano); for bass, SATB, oboe, clarinet, and strings	CFP
1927;61	193#1	Suite for cello and piano	CFP
1927-72	256	*Hermit Bell-Ringer Of The Tower* for bass, men's chorus, flute, and chimes	PSO
1928;63	137	*O God Our Help In Ages Past* for SATB and organ (or piano)	CFP
1930	362	*Dance Gazhal* for piano	MS
1931	2#2	*Storm On Mt. Wildcat (Fantasy)* for orchestra	MS
1931	119#3	*Mountain Idylls ("Mountain Lullaby")* for piano	AMP
1932	156	*The Moon Has A Face* for medium voice and piano	CFP
1932-72	255	Sonata for cello and piano	PSO
1933	21	Suite for English horn and bassoon	CFP
1933;67	36	*2 Gazhals* for piano	CFP
1934	425	Three Songs for low voice and piano	FMC
1935	3	Trio for violin, cello, and piano	CFP
1935	4	*Missa Brevis* for bass, SATB, strings, and organ	CFP
1935	5	*3 Odes Of Solomon* for medium voice and piano	CFP
1935	10	*3 Preludes And Fugues* for piano	CFP
1935	12	*Sonata Ricercare* for piano	CFP
1935;59	13	*Prelude And Fugue* for bassoon and oboe or flute	CFP
1935	25	*Lament* for clarinet	CFP
1935	26	*Behold, God Is My Help* for SATB and organ/piano	CFP
1935	27	*O Lord God Of Hosts* for SATB, organ or piano, two trumpets, and two trombones ad lib.	CFP
1935	28	*O Lord Rebuke Me Not* for SATB and organ or piano	CFP
1935	29	*Layla* for medium voice and piano	CFP
1935;60	140	*The God Of Glory Thundereth* for tenor or soprano, SATB, and organ or piano	CFP
1936;38	2#1	*Monadnok (Fantasy)* for orchestra	CFP
1936	7	*How I Adore Thee* for medium voice and piano	CFP
1936	8	String Quartet	MS
1936	17#1	Concerto for cello and orchestra	CFP
1936	17#2	Symphony No. 1 *Exile* for orchestra	CFP
1936-67	33	*Love Songs Of Hafiz* for medium voice and piano	MS
1936;52	97	*Quartet 1* for flute, oboe, cello, and harpsichord or piano	MS

1936;54	128	*Prelude And Quadruple Fugue* for orchestra	AMP
1936-59	149	*Hear My Prayer, O Lord* for SSATBB with optional organ or piano	CFP
1937	11	Sonata for violin and piano	MS
1937;61	20#1	*Nocturne* for harp	CFP
1937	22	*Mystic Flute* for piano	CFP
1937	144	*Macedonian Mountain Dance* for piano	CFP
1937-62	144b	*Mountain Dance No. 2* for piano	CFP
1938	24	1. *Yar Nazani* for voice and piano	CFP
		2. *Vaspooragan* for voice and piano	MS
1938;59	142	*Out Of The Depths* for voice and organ or piano; for soprano, SATB, and organ	CFP
1939	31	*2 Shakespeare Sonnets* for voice and piano	MS
1939-43	47b	*Arshalouis (Dawn)* for violin and piano	MS
1940	40a	*Psalm And Fugue* for strings	CFP
1941-62	46	*Let Us Love One Another* for SATB, tenor or baritone ad lib., and organ or piano	CFP
1942	40b	*Alleluia And Fugue* for strings	BB
1942	42	*I Will Rejoice In The Lord* for SATB and organ or piano	CFP
1942;53	135	*October Mountain* for percussion sextet	CFP
1943	43	*12 Armenian Folksongs* for piano	CFP
1943	52#1	*Lousang Kisher (Moonlight Night)* for piano	TP
1944	38	*Mazet Nman Rehani (Thy Hair Is Like A Basil Leaf)* for piano	CFP
1944	44	*Celestial Fantasy* for strings	BB
1944	45	*Armenian Rhapsody No. 1* for percussion and strings	PSO
1944	47a	*Varak* for violin and piano	CFP
1944	48	*Lousadzak (The Coming Of Light)* for piano and strings	PSO
1944	49	*Khrimian Hairig* for trumpet and strings	CFP
1944	50	*Elibris (Dawn God Of Urardu)* for flute and strings	PSO
1944	51	*Armenian Rhapsody No. 2* for strings	BB
1944	56#1	*Chahagir* for viola	BB
1944	56#2	*Yeraz (The Dream)* for violin	M
1944	57#1	*Anahid* for flute, English horn, trumpet, timpani, percussion, and strings	CFP
1944	63	*Greek Rhapsody No. 1* for piano	MS
1944	189	*Armenian Rhapsody No. 3* for strings	CFP
1944	238#4	*Old Dome Of Ararat* for low voice and piano	CFP
1945	39	*Artinis (Urarduan: Sun God)* for piano	CFP
1945	53#2	*Tzaikerk (Evening Song)* for flute, violin, drums, and strings	PSO
1945	54#1	*Invocations To Vahakn* for piano and percussion	FMC
1945	55#1	*Vanandour* for piano	CFP

1945	60	*Mihr* for two pianos	TP
1945-46	65	*Avak, The Healer* for soprano, trumpet, and strings	PSO
1945	w/o#	*Ardent Song* ballet	MS
1946	37	*Vijag* for two pianos	CFP
1946-51	54#2	*Hakhpat* for piano and percussion	MS
1946	55#2	*Farewell To The Mountains* for piano	CFP
1946	62a	*Etchmiadzin* opera	MS
1946	62b	*Prayer of St. Gregory* for trumpet and strings	PSO
1946	66#1	*Kohar* for flute, English horn, timpani, and strings	CFP
1946	66#2	*Agori* for flute, English horn, bassoon, trumpet, timpani, and strings	FMC
1946	67	*Saris* for violin and piano	CFP
1946;59	175	*Lake Of Van Sonata* for piano	CFP
1946	238#2	*Gantznin Orern* for low voice and piano	CFP
1946	239	*The Flute Player Of The Armenian Mountains* for low voice and piano	MS
1947	19	*Angelic Song* for soprano or tenor, horn, and strings	CFP
1947	32#1	*Starlight Of Noon* for voice and piano	CFP
1947	58	*Sharagan And Fugue* for brass quintet	RK
1947	61	*Divertimento* for oboe, clarinet, bassoon, and horn; for four clarinets	CFP
1947	73#2	*Shatakh* for violin and piano	PSO
1947	74	*4 Songs* for voice and piano	CFP
1947;59	176#1	*Madras Sonata* for piano	CFP
1947-51	176#2	*Yenovk (The Troubadour)* for piano	CFP
1947	179	Symphony No. 8 *Arjuna* for orchestra	CFP
1948	14	*Tapor* for band	CFP
1948	15	Suite for band	CFP
1948	57#2	*Vosdan* for flute, trumpet, timpani, and strings	MS
1948	64	*Achtamar* for piano	PSO
1948	71	*Haroutiun (Resurrection)* for trumpet and strings or piano	CFP
1948	75	*Sosi — Forest Of Prophetic Sounds* for violin, piano, horn, timpani, giant tam-tam, and strings	CFP
1948	76	*30th Ode Of Solomon* for baritone, SATB, trumpet, trombone, and strings	CFP
1948	77	*Zartik Parkim* for piano and chamber orchestra	PSO
1948	78	*Artik* for horn and strings or piano	CFP
1948	94	Concerto No. 3 *Diran* for baritone horn or trombone and strings	RK
1948	238#3	*Dulhey, Dulhey* for low voice and piano	CFP
1949	23	Suite for oboe and bassoon	CFP

1949	59	*Is There Survival? (King Vahakn)* ballet suite for orchestra	CFP
1949	81	*Janabar* for violin, trumpet, piano, and strings	PSO
1949	119#2	*Mountain Idylls ("Moon Dance")* for piano	AMP
1949-50	180	Symphony No. 9 *St. Vartan* for orchestra	PSO
1949	238#1	*Gurge Dikran* for low voice and piano	CFP
1950	84	*2 Songs* for voice and piano	CFP
1950	95	*3 Songs* for voice and piano	CFP
1950	99	Suite for violin, piano, and percussion	CFP
1950	112	*Quartet No. 2* for flute, oboe, cello, and piano	MS
1950	147	String Quartet No. 2	MS
1950;51	177	*Shalimar* for piano	CFP
1950	420	Sonata No. 7 *Journey To Sanahin* for harpsichord	FMC
1950	426	*Dream Flame* for low voice and piano	FMC
1951	6#2	*Toccata And Fugue On A Kabarian Theme* for piano	MS
1951	52#7	*Lullaby* for piano	TP
1951	68	*Sing Aloud* for SATB	CFP
1951-66	69	*Sanahin* for organ	CFP
1951	73#1	*Khirgiz Suite* for violin and piano	CFP
1951	85	*Fantasy On An Osseitin Tune* for piano	PSO
1951	86	*Make Haste* for SATB	CFP
1951	87	*4 Motets* for SATB	AMP
1951	88	Concerto No. 1 *Arevakal (Season Of The Sun)* for orchestra	AMP
1951-57	89	Concerto No. 2 for violin and strings	CFP
1951	90	*Upon Enchanted Ground* for flute, cello, harp, and tam-tam	CFP
1951	91	*Khaldis* for 4 trumpets (or any multiple thereof), piano, and percussion	RK
1951-52	93#1	*Talin* for viola and strings	AMP
1951	101	*Hanna* for two clarinets and two pianos	MS
1951	103	*Jhala* for piano	PSO
1951	106	*Gamelan And Jhala* for carillon	CFP
1951	111#2	*Hymn To A Celestial Musician* for piano	PSO
1951;60	187	*From The End Of The Earth* for SATB and organ or piano	CFP
1951	248#1	*Afton Water* operetta	MS
1952	16	*Fantasy* for piano	CFP
1952	92	*Orbit 1* for flute, harp, celeste, and tam-tam	MS
1952	100#2	*Christmas Ode (As On The Night)* for soprano, celesta, and strings	AMP
1952	102	*Orbit 2* for piano; for alto recorder and piano	PSO
1952	104	*Allegro On A Pakistan Lute Tune* for piano	LG

1952	111#1	*Pastoral No. 1* for piano	PSO
1952	248#2	*3 Improvisations* for band	MS
1952-76	293	Symphony No. 30 for orchestra	FMC
1953	98#1	Partita for piano and strings	CFP
1953	98#2	Concerto No. 4 for orchestra	CFP
1953	98#3	Concerto No. 5 for piano and strings	MS
1953	100#4	*Easter Cantata* for soprano, SATB, two oboes, two horns, three trumpets, tam-tam, harp, celesta, and strings	AMP
1953	114	Concerto No. 6 for harmonica or flute or oboe and strings; for harmonica and piano	CFP
1953	115	*Canticle* for soprano, oboe, xylophone, harp, celesta, and strings	CFP
1953	116	Concerto No. 7 for orchestra	AMP
1953	138	*Dawn Hymn* for organ	CFP
1953	139	*O Lady Moon* for soprano or SSA, clarinet, and piano	MM
1953	164#2	*Shepherd Of Israel (Psalm 80)* for tenor cantor, soprano recorder or flute, trumpet ad lib., and string quartet or string orchestra	TP
1953;63	170	Symphony No. 5 for orchestra	CFP
1953	190	Symphony No. 13 for orchestra	CFP
1953	248#3	*The Pitchman* ballet suite for two alto recorders, piano, and celesta; for two flutes and two pianos	MS
1954	122	Duet for violin and harpsichord	CFP
1954	123	*Vision From High Rock* for orchestra	CFP
1954	124	*Glory To God* for soprano, alto, SATB, and orchestra	CFP
1954	125	*The Flowering Peach* theater score	AMP
1954	127	Sonata for harp	CFP
1954	131	*The Brightness Of Our Noon* for SATB	JP
1954	133#1	*The World Beneath The Sea* for saxophone, harp, vibraphone, timpani, and gong	CFP
1954;60	169	*Live In The Sun* for medium voice and celesta (or piano)	CFP
1954;60	181	*Koke No Niwa (Moss Garden)* for English horn or Bb clarinet, two percussion, and harp	CFP
1954	248#4	*The Spook Sonata* theater score for alto saxophone and three pianos	MS
1954	342	Symphony No. 45 for orchestra	MS
1954	412	Concerto No. 9 for piano and strings	MS
1955	100#1	*Ave Maria* for boys' or women's voices, two oboes or trumpets or clarinets, two horns or trombones, and harp or piano	AMP
1955	100#3	*The Beatitudes* for SATB, two oboes, two horns, harp, celesta, and strings	AMP
1955	119#1	*Mountain Idylls ("Moon Lullaby")* piano	AMP

1955	126	*The Stars* for soprano, SATB, English horn, harp, celesta, and strings	CFP
1955	132	Symphony No. 2 *Mysterious Mountain* for orchestra	AMP
1955	129	*Tower Music* for 9 winds	BB
1955	141	*Anabasis* for speaker, soprano, bass, SATB, and orchestra	CFP
1955;65	146	*To The God Who Is In The Fire* for tenor, TTBB, and six percussion	CFP
1956	20#2	*Nocturne* for flute and harp	CFP
1956	82	*Transfiguration* for tenor and SATB	CFP
1956	143	*Ad Lyram* for soprano, alto, tenor, bass, SSAATTBB, and orchestra	CFP
1956	145	Sonata for piano	CFP
1956	148	Symphony No. 3 for orchestra	CFP
1956	150	*7 Greek Folk Dances* for harmonica and strings or piano	CFP
1957	117	Concerto No. 8 for orchestra	CFP
1957	151	*O Goddess Of The Sea* for low voice and piano	CFP
1957	152	*Do You Remember The Last Silence?* for piano	CFP
1957	154	*Persephone* for voice and piano	CFP
1957-58	155	*Meditation On Orpheus* for orchestra	CFP
1957	191	*Poseidon Sonata* for piano	CFP
1958	157	*Magnificat* for soprano, alto, tenor, bass, SATB, and orchestra; for soprano, alto, tenor, SATB, and organ or piano	CFP
1958	158	*Look Toward The Sea* for baritone, SATB, trombone, and organ	CFP
1958	160	*Praise Ye Him, All His Angels* for bass, SATB, and organ or piano	CFP
1958	161	*O For A Shout Of Sacred Joy* for SATB and organ or piano	CFP
1958	162	*Upon Thee Will I Cry* for SATB and organ or piano	CFP
1958;68	163	*In Memory Of An Artist* for strings	CFP
1958	164#1	Sextet for alto recorder, string quartet, and harpsichord	MS
1958	166	Suite for accordion	CFP
1958	167	*Glory To Man* for SAB and organ	CFP
1959	56#4	*Hercules* for soprano and violin	CFP
1959	165	Symphony No. 4 for wind orchestra	CFP
1959	172	*Blue Flame* for soprano, tenor, bass, SATB, and orchestra	CFP
1959	173	Symphony No. 6 *Celestial Gate* for small orchestra	CFP
1959	174	Concerto for accordion and orchestra	CFP
1959	178	Symphony No. 7 *Nanga Parvat* for wind orchestra	CFP
1959	184	Symphony No. 10 *Vahakn* for orchestra	CFP
1959;62	185	*The Burning House* opera	CFP

1959;62	185a	*Overture* for flute and four percussion	CFP
1959	192	*Bardo Sonata* for piano	CFP
1959	213	*Return And Rebuild The Desolate Places* for trumpet and wind orchestra	CFP
1960	32#2	*O World* for male voice, piano, and trombone	CFP
1960	83	*Hymn To Yerevan* for full band	CFP
1960	134	*Immortality* for soprano, SATB, and organ (or piano)	CFP
1960;65	159	Quintet for flute, oboe, clarinet, bassoon, and horn	CFP
1960;64	182	*Fuji* for female voices, flute, harp or piano, and strings	CFP
1960;69	186	Symphony No. 11 *All Men Are Brothers* for orchestra	CFP
1960	188	Symphony No. 12 *Choral* for SATB, flute, two trumpets, timpani, two percussion, harp strings, and ad lib. tape of a mountain waterfall	CFP
1960	188a	*Psalm 23* for SATB and orchestra or organ or piano	CFP
1960	194	Symphony No. 14 *Ararat* for wind orchestra	CFP
1960	195	*Mountain Of Prophecy* for orchestra	CFP
1960	237#1	*Nagooran* for South Indian orchestra	MS
1960	338	*Copernicus* for orchestra	FMC
1961	168	*Child In The Garden* for piano four-hands	CFP
1962	35	*The Lord's Prayer* for SATB and organ or piano	CFP
1962	80	*I Have Seen The Lord* for soprano, SATB, trumpet, and organ or piano	CFP
1962	110	*2 Sonatas* for koto or harp	MS
1962	120	*Sonatina* for piano	CFP
1962	121	Sonata for ryuteki and sho; for flute and organ	CFP
1962	136	*Ko-ola-u* for two pianos	CFP
1962	171	Sonata for hichiriki and sho; for oboe and organ	CFP
1962	183	*Wind Drum* dance drama for unison male or female or mixed voices (or bass or alto solo), solo or group dancer(s), flute, timpani, two percussion, harp, and strings	CFP
1962	183a	*Dance Of The Black-Haired Mountain Storm* for flute and three percussion	CFP
1962	197	*Spirit Of The Avalanche* opera	CFP
1962	198	*Three Visions Of Saint Mesrob* for violin and piano	CFP
1962	199	Symphony No. 15 *Silver Pilgrimage* for orchestra	CFP
1962	200	Sonata No. 1 for trumpet and organ	CFP
1962	201	Trio for violin, viola, and cello	CFP
1962	202	Symphony No. 16 for orchestra	CFP
1963	18	*Variations And Fugue* for orchestra	CFP
1963-64	130	Sonata for two oboes and organ	CFP
1963	133#2	*The World Beneath The Sea* for clarinet, timpani, bells or chimes (or glockenspiel), harp, and double bass	CFP

1963	196	*Pilate* opera	CFP
1963	203	Symphony No. 17 *Symphony for Metal Orchestra* for six flutes, three trombones, and five percussion	CFP
1963	203a	*Bacchanale* for five percussion	CFP
1963	204	*Circe* ballet for orchestra	CFP
1963	204a	Symphony No. 18 *Circe* for orchestra	CFP
1963	205	*Mysterious Horse Before The Gate* for trombone and five percussion	CFP
1963	206	*In The Beginning Was The Word* for alto, bass, SATB, and orchestra	CFP
1963	207	*Meditation On Zeami* for orchestra	CFP
1964	107	*Island Sunrise* for orchestra	CFP
1964	109	*Quintet 2* for string quartet and piano	MS
1964	118	*Sonata No. 1* for flute	CFP
1964	144a	*Macedonian Mountain Dance* for orchestra	CFP
1964	209	*Floating World (Ukiyo)* for orchestra	CFP
1964	210	*Bare November Day* for harpsichord or organ, clavichord, or piano	CFP
1964	211	*Fantasy On Japanese Wood Prints (Hanga Genso)* for xylophone and orchestra	CFP
1964	212	*Dark River And Distant Bell* for harpsichord or piano or clavichord	CFP
1964	237#2	*Nagooran* for cello, timpani, glockenspiel, vibraphones, large chimes, and giant tam-tam	MS
1965	113	*3 Haikus* for piano	CFP
1965	193#2	*Yakamochi* for cello	CFP
1965	214	*5 Visionary Landscapes* for piano	CFP
1965	215	*The Travelers* opera	CFP
1965	216	*Ode To The Temple Of Sound* for orchestra	CFP
1965	218	*The Holy City* for trumpet, chimes or bells in A, harp, and strings	CFP
1965	219	*The Leper King* dance drama	CFP
1966	30	*4 Bagatelles* for string quartet	CFP
1966	105	*Make A Joyful Noise* for baritone or tenor, SATB, two trumpets, two trombones, and organ or piano	CFP
1966	108	Sextet for violin and five percussion	CFP
1966	217	Symphony No. 19 *Vishnu* for orchestra	CFP
1967	41	*Protest And Prayer* for tenor, male chorus, and organ or piano	CFP
1967	70	*5 Fantasies* for brass choir	CFP
1967	72	*Canzona And Fugue* for brass choir	CFP
1967	79	*6 Dances* for brass quintet	CFP

1967	93#2	*I Will Lift Up Mine Eyes* for SATB, boys' chorus ad lib., organ, and harp or piano ad lib.	CFP
1967	153	*Dawn At Laona* for low voice and piano	CFP
1967	220	*Fra Angelico* for orchestra	CFP
1967	221	*Adoration* for voice (or women's chorus with soprano and alto solos; or men's chorus with tenor and bass solos), flute, oboe, clarinet, trumpet, trombone, celesta, chimes, and strings	CFP
1968	96	Suite for piano	CFP
1968	208#1	String Quartet No. 3	MS
1968	222	*Praise The Lord With Psaltery* for SATB and orchestra	CFP
1968	223	Symphony No. 20 *Three Journeys To A Holy City* for full band	CFP
1968	224	*Requiem And Resurrection* for brass ensemble	CFP
1968	225	*Mountains And Rivers Without End* for ten players	CFP
1968	231	*Night Of The Soul (On Shri Raga)* for bass or baritone or men's chorus and three flutes	MS
1968	234	Symphony No. 21 *Etchmiadzin* for two trumpets, timpani, two percussion, and strings	CFP
1968	235	*St. Nerses The Graceful* for three clarinets	MS
1969	6#1	*Toccata And Fugue* for piano	CFP
1969	226	*Vibration Painting* for thirteen strings	CFP
1969	227	*Lady Of Light* for soprano, baritone, SATB, and orchestra	CFP
1969	229#2	*A Rose For Miss Emily* ballet for orchestra	CFP
1970	208#2	String Quartet No. 4	MS
1970	228	*Shambala* for violin, sitar, and orchestra	CFP
1970	229#1	*And God Created Great Whales* for orchestra with tape of whale sounds	CFP
1970	230	*Spirit Of Ink* for three flutes	CFP
1970	232	*2 Consolations* for string quartet	MS
1970	233	*All The World's A Dance Of Snobbery* for piano	MS
1970	236	Symphony No. 22 *City Of Light* for orchestra	CFP
1971	240	*Komachi* for piano	CFP
1971	241#1	*Tsamico No. 1* for piano	MS
1971	241#2	*Tsamico No. 2* for piano	MS
1971	241#3	*Tsamico And Fugue* for piano	MS
1971	242	*4 Songs* for low voice and piano	CFP
1971	243	*Saturn* for soprano, clarinet, and piano	CFP
1971	244	*Island Of The Mysterious Bells* for four harps	MS
1971	245	*The Garden Of Adonis* for flute and harp or piano	CFP
1971	246	*4 Motets* for mixed chorus	CFP
1971	247	*Hermes Stella* for piano	MS

1971	253	*Spirit Cat* for soprano, vibraphone, and marimba	MS
1972	249	Symphony No. 23 *Ani* for large band with antiphonal brass choir ad lib.	CFP
1972	250	*Ruins Of Ani* for four Bb clarinets or any multiple thereof; for strings	MS
1972	251	*Khorhoort Nahadagats (Holy Mystery Of The Martyrs)* for oud or lute or guitar and string orchestra or string quartet	PSO
1972	252#1	*Firdausi* for clarinet, harp, and percussion	FMC
1972	252#2	*Shah Name (Kings Book Of Kings)* film score	MS
1972	252#3	*7 Love Songs Of Saris* for violin and piano	MS
1972	254	*2 Songs* for soprano and piano	MS
1972	258	*3 Madrigals* for SATB	BB
1972	259	*3 Motets* for SATB	BB
1972	269#1	*Though Night Is Dark* for SATB	BMP
1972	341	*Greek Rhapsody No. 2* for orchestra	MS
1973	257	*For The Waters Are Come* for men's chorus	PSO
1973	260	*Dream Of A Myth* ballet for orchestra	MS
1973	261	*Les Baux* for violin and piano	MS
1973	262	Quartet for clarinet, violin, viola, and cello	MS
1973	263	*Night Of A White Cat* for clarinet and piano	MS
1973	264#1	*Tumburu* for violin, cello, and piano	FMC
1973	264#2	*Varuna* for violin, cello, and piano	FMC
1973	265#1	*How Long Wilt Thou Forget Me?* for high soprano and piano or organ	MS
1973	266	Sonata for two bassoons; for cello and bassoon	PSO
1973	267	Concerto for harp and strings	MS
1973	268	*4 Motets* for SATB	AMP
1973	269#2,3	*2 Songs Of Faith* for SATB	BMP
1973	270	Suite for harp	AMP
1973	271	*Pastoral And Fugue* for two flutes	AMP
1973	272	*Dawn On Mt. Tahoma* for string orchestra	MS
1973	273	Symphony No. 24 *Majnun* for tenor, SATB, trumpet, violin, and strings	AMP
1973	274	*3 Sasa Songs* for soprano and piano	MS
1973	275	Symphony No. 25 *Odysseus* for orchestra	PSO
1974	265#2	*Let Not Your Heart Be Troubled* for high soprano and piano or organ	MS
1974	276	*O Lord, Bless Thy Mountains* for 2 pianos tuned in quartertones apart	MS
1974	277	*Fantasy* for double bass or cello and piano	FMC
1974	278#1	*To The Cascade Mountains* film score	MS
1974	278#2	*Ode To The Cascade Mountains* for orchestra	MS
1974	281#2	*Psalm To St. Alban* for horn, two trumpets, and trombone	MS

1975	279	*The Way Of Jesus* for soprano, tenor, bass, SATB, and orchestra	PSO
1975	280	Symphony No. 26 for orchestra	PSO
1975	281#1	*Fanfare To The New Atlantis* for orchestra	MS
1975	282	*A Simple Mass* for soprano, alto, tenor, bass, four-part unison chorus, and organ	AMP
1975	283	*Pericles* opera	MS
1975	308	*Rubiyat* for speaker, accordion, and orchestra	FMC
1976	284	*Ode To Freedom* for violin and orchestra	FMC
1976	285	Symphony No. 27 for orchestra	FMC
1976	286	Symphony No. 28 for orchestra	FMC
1976	287	String Quartet No. 7	FMC
1976	289	Symphony No. 29 for baritone horn and orchestra	FMC
1976	290	Suite for four trumpets and trombone	RK
1976	291	Suite for Eb alto saxophone and guitar	PSO
1976	295	Septet for flute, clarinet, bass clarinet, trumpet, trombone, double bass, and percussion	MS
1976-77	294	Symphony No. 31 for string orchestra	FMC
1977	288	Sonatina *Meditation On Mt. Monadnok* for piano	MS
1977	292	*Glory Sings The Setting Sun* for coloratura soprano, clarinet, and piano	MS
1977	296	Symphony No. 32 *The Broken Wings* for orchestra	FMC
1977	297	Sonata for two clarinets	PSO
1977	298	*How I Love Thy Law* for high soprano, clarinet, and piano	MS
1977	299#1	*Mt. Belknap* for piano	FMC
1977	299#2	*Mt. Ossipee* for piano	FMC
1977	299#3	*Mt. Shasta* for piano	FMC
1977	300	Suite for flute and guitar	FMC
1977	301	*Fred The Cat* for piano	FMC
1977	302	Sonata for oboe and bassoon	PSO
1977	303	*Ananda* for piano	FMC
1977	304	*A Presentiment* for coloratura soprano and piano	FMC
1977	305	*Celestial Canticle* for coloratura soprano and piano	FMC
1977	306	Sonata No. 1 for harpsichord	FMC
1977	307	Symphony No. 33 for orchestra	FMC
1977	310	Symphony No. 34 for bass trombone and strings	FMC
1977	391	*The Spirit's Map* for voice and piano	MS
1977	393	*Dawn On A Mountain Lake* for double bass and piano	MS
1977	398	*Srpouhi* for violin and piano	MS
1978	269#4	*Jesus Meek And Gentle* for SATB and organ	FMC
1978	309	*Sketch Book Of Mr. Purple Poverty* for piano	FMC
1978	311	Symphony No. 35 for two orchestras	FMC

1978	312	Symphony No. 36 for flute and orchestra	FMC
1978	313	Symphony No. 37 for orchestra	FMC
1978	314	Symphony No. 38 for high soprano, flute, trumpet, and strings	FMC
1978	315	*Songs* for high soprano and piano	FMC
1978	316	Sonata No. 1 for guitar	FMC
1978	317	Sonata for flute (bass or alto)	FMC
1978	318	Sonata No. 2 for harpsichord	FMC
1978	319	*Sunset On Mt. Tahoma* for two trumpets, horn, trombone, and organ	FMC
1978	320	*Teach Me Thy Way* for chorus	FMC
1978	321	Symphony No. 39 for guitar and orchestra	FMC
1978	322	Sonata for clarinet and harpsichord	FMC
1978	323	*Tale Of The Sun Goddess Going Into The Stone House* opera	FMC
1979	324	Symphony No. 40 for orchestra	FMC
1979	325	Concerto for guitar and orchestra	FMC
1979	326	Sonata No. 1 for three trumpets and two trombones	FMC
1979	327	*Love Song Vanishing Into Sounds Of Crickets* for piano	FMC
1979	328	Sonata No. 2 for three trumpets and two trombones	FMC
1979	329	Sonata No. 2 for guitar	FMC
1979	330	Symphony No. 41 for orchestra	FMC
1979	331	Trio for three saxophones	FMC
1979	332	Symphony No. 42 for orchestra	FMC
1979	333	*4 Nocturnes* for two saxophones and piano	FMC
1979	334	Symphony No. 43 for oboe, trumpet, timpani, and strings	FMC
1979	336	Sonata No. 3 for harpsichord	FMC
1979	337	*On Christmas Eve A Child Cried Out* for SATB, flute, and harp	FMC
1979	340	*Blue Job Mountain* for piano	FMC
1980	339	Symphony No. 44 for orchestra	FMC
1980	343	*Revelations Of St. Paul* for soprano, tenor, baritone, SATB, and orchestra	FMC
1980	344	Concerto for soprano saxophone and strings	FMC
1980	345	*Catamount* for piano	FMC
1980	346	*Prospect Hill* for piano	FMC
1980	347	Symphony No. 46 *To The Green Mountains* for orchestra	FMC
1980	348	Symphony No. 47 *Walla Walla, Land Of Many Waters* for coloratura soprano and orchestra	FMC
1981	349	Sonata No. 2 *The Divine Fountain* for trumpet and organ	MS

1981	350#1	*Stars Sing Bell Song* for coloratura soprano and Javanese gamelan	MS
1981	350#2	*Pleiades* for Javanese gamelan	MS
1981	351	*Corruption In Office* for piano	MS
1981	352	Sonata for organ	MS
1981	353	*Lalezar* for bass and orchestra	MS
1981	354	*Journey To Arcturus* for piano	MS
1981	355	Symphony No. 48 *Vision Of Andromeda* for orchestra	FMC
1981	356	Symphony No. 49 *Christmas Symphony* for string orchestra	MS
1981	357	Sonata No. 4 *Daddy-Long-Legs* for harpsichord	FMC
1981	358	*Psalm* for brass quartet	FMC
1981	359	*God Is Our Refuge And Strength* for SATB and orchestra or organ and timpani	FMC
1982	335	*Mt. Chocurua* for piano	FMC
1982	360	Symphony No. 50 *Mount St. Helens* for orchestra	CFP
1982	361	Sonata No. 5 for harpsichord	MS
1982	363	*Lake Winnipesaukee* for flute, oboe, cello, two percussion, and piano	MS
1982	364	Symphony No. 51 for trumpet and strings	MS
1982	365	*Shigue* for voice and piano	MS
1982	366	*Hiroshige's Cat Bathing* for piano	FMC
1982	367	*On The Long Total Eclipse Of The Moon July 6, 1982* for piano	MS
1982	368	*Tsugouharu Fujita's Sleeping Cat* for piano	FMC
1982	369	*Lake Sammamish* for piano	MS
1982	370	*Love's Philosophy* for voice and piano	MS
1982	371	*Campuan Sonata* for viola and piano	LCK
1983	372	Symphony No. 52 *Journey To Vega* for orchestra	MS
1983	373	*Prelude And Fugue* for brass quartet	MS
1983	374	*Spirit Of Trees* for guitar and harp	MS
1983	375	Sonata for clarinet and piano	MS
1983	376	*The Waves Unbuild The Wasting Shore* for tenor, SATB, and organ	MS
1983	377	Symphony No. 53 *Star Dawn* for band	MS
1983	378	Symphony No. 54 for orchestra	MS
1983	379	Symphony No. 55 for orchestra	MS
1983	380	Symphony No. 56 for orchestra	MS
1983	381	Symphony No. 57 *Cold Mountain* for tenor or soprano, clarinet, and string orchestra or string quintet	FMC
1983	382	Sonatina for organ	MS
1983	383	*Killer Of Enemies* dance score for flute, clarinet, trumpet, trombone, percussion, violin, and bass	MS

1984	385	*Cantate Domino* for SATB and organ	MS
1984	386	Sonata No. 2 *Invisible Sun* for organ	MS
1984	387	Sonata for alto recorder and harpsichord	MS
1984	392	*Mountain Under The Sea* for Eb alto saxophone, timpani, vibraphone, tam-tam, and harp	MS
1985	384	*Starry Night* for flute, harp, and xylophone	FMC
1985	389	Symphony No. 58 *Symphony Sacra* for soprano, baritone, SATB, flute, horn, trumpet, timpani, chimes, harp, and strings	MS
1985	390	*Cougar Mountain* for piano	MS
1985	394	Concerto No. 2 for guitar and strings	MS
1985	395	Symphony No. 59 for orchestra	FMC
1985	396	Symphony No. 60 *To The Appalachian Mountains* for orchestra	FMC
1986	388	*Lillydale* for piano	MS
1986	397	Symphony No. 61 for orchestra	MS
1986	399	Sonata for piano	MS
1986	400	*A Friendly Mountain* for bass and piano	MS
1986	401	*Bless The Lord* for tenor, SATB, and organ	MS
1986	403	Trio for violin, viola, and cello	MS
1986	404	*Chomulunga* for two trumpets, horn, and trombone	FMC
1987	405	*Mt. Katahdin* for piano	MS
1987	406	Sonata for flute and harp	MS
1987	407	*The Frog Man* chamber opera	MS
1987	408	*God The Reveller* dance score for flute, clarinet, trumpet, trombone, violin, double bass, and percussion	MS
1987	409	Duet for violin and cello	MS
1987	410	*The Aim Was Song* for double chorus, two flutes, and piano	FMC
1987-88	402	Symphony No. 62 *Oh Let Man Not Forget These Words Divine* for baritone, trumpet, and strings	MS
1988	411	Symphony No. 63 *Loon Lake* for orchestra	MS
1988	413	Concerto No. 10 for piano, trumpet, and strings	MS
1988	414	Sonata No. 6 for harpsichord	MS
1988	415	*Lake Samish* for violin, clarinet, and piano	MS
1988	416	*Sno Qualmie* for clarinet, timpani, chimes, harp, and double bass	FMC
1988	417	*Why Is My Verse So Barren Of New Pride?* for baritone and piano	FMC
1989	418	*Out Of Silence* for SATB, trumpet, and string orchestra or string quintet	FMC
1989	419	*Consolation* for piano	FMC
1990	421	Guitar Sonatas Nos. 3, 4, and 5	FMC

1990	422	Sonata for solo viola	FMC
1990	423	Symphony No. 64 *Agiochook* for trumpet and strings	FMC
1990	424	*Hermit Thrush* for organ	FMC
1991	427	Symphony No. 65 *Artsakh* for orchestra	FMC
1992	428	Symphony No. 66 for orchestra	FMC
1992	429	Symphony No. 67 for orchestra	FMC
1992	430	Concerto for oboe and orchestra	MS

DISCOGRAPHY

1950
Zartik Parkim
Dial 6 lp

1953
Concerto No. 1 *Arevakal*
Mercury 40005 lp; 50078 lp (1957)

Quartet 1 for flute, oboe, cello, and harpsichord
New Editions 3 lp

1955
Khaldis, selected piano music
MGM 3160 lp
Heliodor 25027 lp (1966)

The Flowering Peach, Is There Survival?, Orbit No. 1
MGM 3164 lp

1956
Prelude and Quadruple Fugue
Mercury 50106 lp

1957
Suite for violin, percussion, and piano, *Upon Enchanted Ground*
Columbia 5179 lp

Duet for violin and harpsichord
CRI 109 lp

Mountain Idylls
MGM 3181 lp; 3517 lp (1958)

Macedonian Mountain Dance
MGM 3225 lp; 3517 lp (1958)

Talin
MGM 3432 lp

Symphony No. 9
MGM 3453 lp

Kirghiz Suite
MGM 3454 lp; 3517 lp (1958)

Alleluia And Fugue, Anahid, Tower Music
MGM 3504 lp

1958
Kirghiz Suite, Macedonian Mountain Dance, Mountain Idylls, Slumber Song, Siris Dance And Lullaby, String Quartet No. 2, *Celestial Fantasy, Armenian Rhapsody No. 2, Sharagan And Fugue*
MGM 3517 lp

Lousadzak, Concerto No. 2 for violin and strings
MGM 3674 lp
Heliodor 25040 lp (1966)

Symphony No. 2
RCA 2251 lp; 4215 cs (1982); 5733-2 cd (1989)

1959
Concerto No. 7
Louisville 545-4 lp

October Mountain
Urania 134, 1034 lp; 5134 lp (1961)

1960
Meditation On Orpheus
CRI 134 lp
Bay Cities 1004 cd (1989)

7 Greek Folk Dances
Decca 12015, 712015 lp

1961
Magnificat
Louisville 614 lp
Poseidon 1018 lp (1976)

1963
Praise Ye The Lord
MVOX 1112 lp

1964

Fantasy On Japanese Wood Prints (Hanga Genso)
Columbia 9381, 2581 lp; 34537 lp (1977)

Koke No Niwa (Moss Garden)
CRI 186 lp

Symphony No. 4
Mercury 90366, 50366 lp

1965

Sharagan And Fugue
Desto 6401 lp

In The Beginning Was The Word
Methodist Student Movement 100/1 lp

1966

Sonata No. 1 for solo flute
CRI 212 lp

Symphony No. 15
Louisville 662 lp

Allegro On A Pakistan Lute Tune
RCA 7042 lp

1967

Lousadzak
Folkways 3369 lp

1968

Floating World (Ukiyo)
Columbia 7162 lp; 34537 lp (1977)

Ave Maria, Christmas Ode, Easter Cantata
CRI 221 lp

1970

Symphony No. 17, Symphony No. 20
Mark 1112 lp

Symphony No. 11
Poseidon 1001 lp
Crystal 801 cd (1985)

Fra Angelico, Requiem And Resurrection
Poseidon 1002 lp
Crystal 804 cd (1987)

Sonata for trumpet and organ
Redwood 2 lp

1971
And God Created Great Whales
Columbia 30390 lp; 34537 lp (1977)

The Holy City
CRI 259 lp

Symphony No. 7, *Return And Rebuild The Desolate Places*, Symphony No. 14, *Hymn To Yerevan*
Mace 9099 lp

Symphony No. 21, *Armenian Rhapsody No. 3, Mountains And Rivers Without End*
Poseidon 1004 lp
Crystal 804 cd (1987)

Love Songs Of Hafiz, selected songs
Poseidon 1005 lp

Lady Of Light
Poseidon 1006 lp
Crystal 806 cd (1991)

Fantasy For Piano, Symphony No. 6, *6 Dances For Piano*
Poseidon 1007 lp

1972
Symphony No. 4
Cornell University 2 lp

Sonata for harp, Nocturne No. 1 for harp
Klavier 507 lp

Fra Angelico
Orion 7268 lp

4 Songs, *The Flute Player Of The Armenian Mountains*
Poseidon 1008 lp

Distant Lake Of Sighs, selected songs
Poseidon 1009 lp

Saturn
Poseidon 1010 lp

1973
Khaldis, The Spirit Of Ink
Poseidon 1011 lp

Symphony No. 19
Poseidon 1012 lp

Symphony No. 9
Poseidon 1013 lp

1974
Avak, The Healer
Louisville 735 lp

Symphony No. 25
Poseidon 1014 lp

Symphony No. 23
Poseidon lp 1015 lp

1975
Tumburu, Varuna
CRI 326 lp

Symphony No. 2
Golden Crest 402 lp

Symphony No. 24
Poseidon 1016 lp
Crystal 803 cd (1986)

Symphony No. 6, *Prayer Of St. Gregory*
Poseidon 1017 lp
Crystal 801 cd (1985)

1976
Armenian Rhapsody No. 1, Tzaikerk, Prayer Of St. Gregory, Avak, The Healer
Crystal 800 lp; 801 cd (1985)

Meditation On Orpheus
Columbia 33728 lp

1977
Rubiyat, And God Created Great Whales, Meditation On Orpheus, Floating World (Ukiyo), Fantasy On Japanese Wood Prints (Hanga Genso), Island Sunrise
Columbia 34537 lp

Sonata for trumpet and organ (excerpt)
Crystal 362 lp

Island Of The Mysterious Bells
Musical Heritage Society 1844 lp

Talin
Peters International 071 lp

1978
Prayer Of St. Gregory
Avant 1014 lp

Six Dances
Crystal 203 lp

Firdausi
Grenadilla 1008 lp

1979
Mystic Flute, Vanadour, Farewell To The Mountains, Achtamar
Musical Heritage Society 4110 lp

Symphony No. 39
Pandora 3001 lp

1980
Bacchanale, October Mountain
Gale 004 lp

1982
Prayer Of St. Gregory
Afka 4634 lp

Artik
Crystal 507 lp; 802 cd (1986)

1984
The Garden Of Adonis
Bis 143 lp

Artik
Coronet 3122 lp

Celestial Fantasy
Crystal 508 lp; cd (1989)

Armenian Rhapsody No. 2
Crystal 509 lp

1986
Symphony No. 9
Crystal 802 cd

1987
Coy Sweet Love
Positively Armenian 103 lp, cs

4 Songs, *The Flute Player Of The Armenian Mountains*
Positively Armenian 104 lp, cs

3 Visions Of St. Mesrob
Positively Armenian 105 lp, cs

Two Gazhals, 12 Armenian Folksongs, Achtamar, Pastoral No. 1, Hymn To A Celestial Musician, Child In The Garden, 5 Visionary Landscapes, Suite
Positively Armenian 106 lp, cs
Hearts of Space 11024-2 cd

1988
Gazhal #1, Shalimar, Komachi, Love Song Vanishing Into Sounds Of Crickets, Prospect Hill
Fortuna 17062-1 lp, -2 cd, -4 cs

Orbit No. 2, Jhala
Mode 15 cd

1989
Alleluia And Fugue, Elibris, Anahid, Concerto No. 8, And God Created Great Whales
Crystal 810 lp, cd

O Lady Moon
Grenadilla 1073 cs

Symphony No. 2, *Lousadzak*
Musicmasters 60204 cd

O Lady Moon
Spectrum 415 lp

1990
Symphony No. 19, *Requiem And Resurrection*
Crystal 805 cd

Fantasy On Japanese Wood Prints (Hanga Genso)
Etcetera 1085 cd

1991
Invocations To Vahakn
New Albion 036 cd

Lady Of Light, Avak, The Healer
Crystal 806 cd

1992
Dance Gazhal, Slumber Song, Achtamar, Fantasy On An Osseitin Tune, Orbit No. 2, Mountain Dance No. 2, Macedonian Mountain Dance, Mt. Ossipe, Fred The Cat, Prospect Hill, Mt. Chocurua
Koch 3-7195-2H1 cd

BIBLIOGRAPHY

"Shostakovich And His Seventh Symphony." *The Musician*, 47 (September-October 1942).

"Letter To The Editor." *ACA Bulletin*, 7 (1958).

"Composer Speaks." *Music Clubs Magazine*, 39 (November 1959).

"We Start With Music." *American Symphony Orchestra League Newsletter*, 10 (1959).

ANNE LeBARON

photo: Gene Bagnato

ANNE LeBARON / Introduction

ANNE LeBARON was born in Baton Rouge, Louisiana, on May 30, 1953. She received her bachelor's degree in music in 1974 from the University of Alabama, where she studied with Fred Goossen, and her master's degree four years later from the State University of New York at Stony Brook, where her teachers included Bulent Arel and Daria Semegen. As a Fulbright Scholar to Germany in 1980-81, she studied composition with Mauricio Kagel and György Ligeti. In 1983 she lived in Seoul and studied Korean traditional music at the National Classical Music Institute. She also studied composition with Chou Wen-chung, Jack Beeson, and Mario Davidovsky at Columbia University, where she received her Doctor of Musical Arts degree in 1989.

Although trained in piano from childhood, she took up the harp in college, and in 1974 and '76 studied privately with Alice Chalifoux at the Salzedo Harp Colony. LeBaron has since gained an international reputation for her pioneering work in developing extended performance techniques for the harp, as well as for her prowess as an improviser. She has played with numerous improvising musicians, including Derek Bailey, Anthony Braxton, Shelley Hirsch, George Lewis, Fred Frith, Lionel Hampton, Evan Parker, Greg Bendian, Ursula Oppens, Alexander von Schlippenbach, Davey Williams, and LaDonna Smith. She has also written for and performed on harp with two groups, the LeBaron/Smith/Dixon trio and the Anne LeBaron Quintet.

Her compositions range from the hilarious theatrics of *Concerto For Active Frogs* (1975) to the apocalyptic ensemble of *Telluris Theoria Sacra* (1989); from the large orchestral forces of *Strange Attractors* (1987) to intimate chamber pieces such as *Lamentation/Invocation* (1984) and *The Sea And The Honeycomb* (1979); from the Asian-inspired string trio *Noh Reflections* (1986) to her blues-infused opera *The E. & O. Line* (1992; Thulani Davis, librettist). She has also composed for electronic tape alone (*Quadratura Circuli*, 1978; *Eurydice Is Dead*, 1983) as well as in combination with singers and instrumentalists (*Concerto For Active Frogs, The E. & O. Line,* and *Dish,* 1990) and in duets with harp (*Planxty Bowerbird,* 1982; *I Am An American ... My Government Will Reward You,* 1988).

LeBaron has taught theory at the University of Alabama; theory and composition at Stony Brook (where she was also Assistant to the Directors of the Electronic Music Studios); and classical and jazz survey courses at Columbia University. She has lectured and performed at numerous universities throughout the country, including the University of Texas, Bard College, Southwestern University, and Middlebury College.

Among her many grants and awards are the Bearns Prize, three NEA Fellowships, the Creative Artists Public Service Program, a Cary Trust recording grant, Fulbright Full Scholarship, an ASCAP Foundation Grant, the GEDOK International Prize, a BMI Composition Award, a Guggenheim Fellowship, the McCollin Prize, and a Composer Grant from the DC Commission for the Arts and Humanities. Her music has been commissioned by such sources as the Oklahoma Symphony Orchestra, the New York State Council on the Arts, the Strathmore Hall Foundation, the Washington Project for the Arts, and the Fromm Foundation.

LeBaron currently divides her time between her home in Washington, D.C., and an apartment in New York City. I spoke with her at her Manhattan home on October 12, 1992. Despite a running commentary on our conversation from her five-month-old daughter Yvonne, I was able to discuss with the composer her experiences with American universities, her development as a harpist, her work on the final stages of *The E. & O. Line*, and her recent commission to compose a score utilizing several of Harry Partch's instruments.

ANNE LeBARON / Interview

Q: Unlike most of the composers I've spoken to who were born after World War Two, you finished college and went on to get an M.A. at Stony Brook and a Doctorate at Columbia. So you've been through the mill.

LeBARON: Yeah, I've served time more than once.

Q: Was it worth it?

LeBARON: Well, ask me that every year, and my answer might change.

Q: What's your answer this year?

LeBARON: The answer this year is no, it wasn't. I went to get the degree so that I could get a teaching job — I did it for job security. And as it turned out, I haven't wanted to teach since I got the degree — I just started looking for work last year. But that's really why I went through the regimen: to have the doctorate so that I wouldn't have to do jobs that I've done in my life, and which I never want to do again — jobs not related to music, just money gigs.

Q: I take it that your work now as a musician brings in income that you'd originally planned to make by teaching.

LeBARON: It does, with grants like the Guggenheim, and commissions. But you know, there's such uncertainty from one year to the next ... the trade-off for time and freedom.

Q: Was going through the whole route valuable for you as a composer?

LeBARON: In the sense that I wrote pieces that I probably wouldn't have written otherwise. As far as studying with people, yes, that was valuable, and it's given me a solid basis in technique. When I went to study with György Ligeti 12 years ago, he told me — I'll never forget it — "You have all the technique you need. You don't need to go back to the American academic system. They will crush your spirit." To put his warning in context, you should know that Ligeti welcomed me into his class on the basis of a graphic score, *Concerto For Active Frogs*, which is nothing if not spirited.

So, flying back to New York to do the very thing he warned me against, to go back to school — because I was determined to plow ahead and get this doctorate — I was seated on the plane next to a man from India, who read palms. He offered to read mine and predicted, "You will have an ongoing conflict between your head and your heart." And of course, the heart is what Ligeti advised me to protect, while the head kept insisting, "I have to go and finish this academic business." I never, ever forgot his admonition: "They will crush your spirit if you go back." As things turned out, my return to the university scene was sporadic.

In 1978 I started a doctorate at Columbia, and had to leave because I ran out of money. Fortunately, I was offered a job as artist-in-residence in Decatur,

Alabama, and moved South. After a year and a half, a Fulbright Scholarship rescued me from that insular world, and eventually led me to Ligeti in Germany. The following year I had to decide whether to continue at Columbia or enter the new Ph.D. program at SUNY/Stony Brook. Well, Stony Brook offered me a teaching assistantship and Columbia offered nothing; I had no choice and returned to Stony Brook. I spent a year there and then left abruptly. The next year I shuttled between Middlebury, Vermont, where I had access to a Synclavier and Newport, Rhode Island, where the librettist for my opera lived. Meanwhile, my new husband, Edward Eadon, was sent to Korea for the first year of our marriage, and then moved to Montgomery, Alabama, where I joined him. I lasted only six months in Montgomery — stirred things up a bit with a concert that mixed harps and Korean zithers with Salzedo and a central improvisation using audience plants, which I called "Corruption In The Capital." I finally returned to Columbia and resumed the course work toward the doctorate, but was interrupted a couple of times due to subsequent moves — the next being to Alexandria, Virginia, and then to Washington, D.C. So it was in bits and pieces that I finished the degree at Columbia ... the circuitous route made it more palatable.

For my dissertation I first intended to write an opera — I used to call it a blues opera or a jazz opera, but I just call it an opera now. After taking a year to write the required essay and much of the music, it became clear that Columbia simply could not deal with the kind of material I was producing. So the opera was put aside and a chamber work for septet was written instead, *Telluris Theoria Sacra*, which filled the requirements.

I will say that I learned a great deal from every person I studied with at Columbia and at Stony Brook. I don't regret those opportunities at all. But I could never have just gone from one school to the next to the next — it's too structured, and you never get the breathing space to discover what you're all about. So I was lucky in a way, because I had a lot of room to explore on my own, which was basically a serendipitous by-product of economic hardship.

From the beginning I couldn't stand the strict requirements of the university music deparment. I was very rebellious and couldn't put up with any kind of regimentation. When I enrolled at the University of Alabama, an experimental department for highly independent students had just been created, called New College. Students were given freedom to develop their own curriculum, which would culminate in a B.A. degree. When I was accepted into the program, I went away from music entirely for a year and explored other fields like philosophy, religion, everything *but* music. I never knew a person could be a composer because I didn't *know* composers — they were all dead. I barely knew Stravinsky's music. That's how poor the education was in the South. I'd had piano lessons, and I played early-20th-century American music like Charles Griffes. But when I found out that you could actually study to be a composer, and write pieces and have them played, I decided to go back to music. So I arranged a curriculum that closely imitated the music-department requirements. But in New College I didn't have to answer to anybody. The inherent freedom worked beautifully for me — I studied German, I took every course a music student would be required to take, and I graduated.

Q: You wrote *Concerto For Active Frogs* when you were 22 years old. Was that something of a transgression, a young composer producing a humorous graph score?

LEBARON: I wrote this after I graduated from the University of Alabama. I was involved with a group of crazily creative people who were playing music that was definitely ahead of its time — a Southern surrealist aesthetic. We called ourselves the Raudelunas Pataphysical Review.

Q: "Raudelunas"?

LEBARON: It's a made-up word. It can mean anything you want it to mean — Armenian moon worship, for example.

Q: Pataphysics moves in that same direction.

LEBARON: Yeah, we were all Jarry admirers. We were a loosely connected group of amateur and trained musicians, and produced our own shows. We marched in the Alabama Homecoming Parade as the Marching Vegetable Band, right behind the Shriners. I was dragged along in a red wagon, playing the harp, wearing a dress slit all the way up both sides — I'll never forget it. We had brass, accordion, winds, chimes. It was a real band, with everybody disguised as vegetables, in huge papier-mâché costumes. One of our most distinguished members, the Reverend Fred Lane, has several recordings out on Shimmy Disc, including "From The One That Cut You."

Q: So *Concerto For Active Frogs* wasn't thrown in the face of any academic environment; it was more an outgrowth of the kind of people you'd been performing with.

LEBARON: Yes, and it was written for those people to play, with their various abilities in mind. The idea came from a recording I accidentally came across, *Voices In The Night*, a collection of frog vocalizations recorded by Cornell University herpetologists. Each frog was introduced by one of the herpetologists, who had a mean Texas drawl: "Now heah we have hilafahrbodians." And then you'd hear this frog belch. Let me tell you, it was one of the most hilarious recordings I'd ever heard. And all the frogs were utterly different from one another. A few I recognized from having heard them in the South. Others were found in different parts of North America and Mexico. Some sounded drunk, others like they were laughing, and some even sounded physically ill. These were surprisingly human vocalizations, giving me the idea to combine them with human voices in a theatrical setting. I created the piece out of sheer inspiration, after hearing this amazing recording. The first performance of *Concerto For Active Frogs* was part of a live show, "The Raudelunas Pataphysical Review." That show was later released as a recording, on the Say Day-Bew label, with a dissected frog on the cover. The Reverend Fred Lane was the host and star of the show, telling jokes, parodying Sinatra songs like "Volaré" and "Chicago," and insulting the band. He covered his face with Band-aids, and wore a tuxedo with boxer shorts. It was positively demented. I didn't think they'd want *Frogs* on the program because it *was* a serious-music piece (as Fred Lane points out on the record), but everyone said, "Sure, we'll do it." *Frogs* really hasn't changed since then. Even for that first performance, everyone wore green plastic garbage bags. It's been to a lot of places, it's easy to perform, and it makes people feel good. Now that certain species of frogs are mysteriously disappearing from their habitats, I'm planning an evening-length work that will be called *Croak*, and will address contemporary environmental and social issues.

Q: *Concerto For Active Frogs* was your introduction to Ligeti?

LeBARON: Ligeti had the broadest spectrum of musical interests of anyone I studied with — or knew, for that matter. I was especially struck by his passionate, unrelenting curiosity. He never denigrated any composer, although his standards were extremely high. One class was devoted to a discussion of the Scriabin piano sonatas, and another to vocalists such as Ursula Dudziek. Of course, he was a great admirer and champion of Nancarrow, at a time when Conlon Nancarrow was just beginning to be known internationally. He was on the faculty of the Hochschule fur Musik in Hamburg, but held classes for composers in his apartment — his piano was piled high with scores, and there were books lying everywhere. These were always group sessions, as opposed to private lessons. The students included Germans, Canadians — I was the only American that year. There was a small, low table in the middle of the room, brightly lit, used for examining scores that people would bring in. It was like a dissecting table, only the dissection was carried out by the other students, with Ligeti playing the role of moderator. One piece I subjected to this process was my percussion quartet, *Rite Of The Black Sun*, an ambitious, complex score that calls for some 70 instruments. When the recording was played, one of the German composers could hardly contain himself. He protested, "This is awful, immoral music!" So it turned into a kind of verbal slugfest — with probably a lot of misunderstanding going on due to language differences. After that class, Ligeti split us into two smaller groups, because it got out of hand, you know?

At the last class I attended, Ligeti said, "I have this bootleg tape from *Black Orpheus* and I want to play it for you because I think it has musical validity." He put the tape on, and we heard a man and a woman making love on a creaky bed, with congas playing in the background. It was too graphic to be included in the film. We all politely sat there, intently listening to 15 minutes or so of creaks, rattles, squeaks, moans, and shrieks, and select phrases in English. Audio porn! At that time, I was beginning to conceptualize my opera *The E. & O. Line*, imagining train rhythms that turned into instrumental rhythms, and train whistles that turned into human voices. (*The E. & O. Line* is the Orpheus myth told from Eurydice's point of view.) This censored tape from *Black Orpheus* gave me the idea to use the train rhythm, chug-chug-chug, in the scenes where Eurydice and Orpheus are having sex. The Synclavier proved to be the perfect vehicle to create such a simulation. I taped two people getting it on and restructured it into a section of the opera called "Waltz Of The Bedsprings" — the bed hitting the wall is reminiscent of train rhythms, and the squeaking springs are used in ways recalling train whistles. So the *Black Orpheus* tape was a surprising inspiration, and I'll go back and say that Ligeti's openness, that degree of receptivity coming from a composer of his stature, was just remarkable.

Q: Were your studies with Kagel the same sort of situation, where a small group of students met with the composer and went through their scores?

LeBARON: Mauricio Kagel was one of several composers in Germany I had been in contact with, and the Fulbright Commission elected to send me to Cologne, where he taught at the Köln Musikhochschule. I was disappointed in Kagel's manner of teaching — he wasn't at all interested in looking at scores. Kagel's class was large and would meet to develop projects that often included video. My own participation in Kagel's class turned out to be a performance of *Concerto For Active Frogs* which we did with a set, a plastic blue lily pond, and a nude solo frog. The performance elicited a negative reaction that I've not experienced with any other performance of *Frogs*. Suddenly I wasn't taken seriously as a composer — I guess the humor simply didn't translate. There was a group in Cologne that had asked me to write for them, and after some of the players saw *Frogs*, they retracted the invitation.

Q: How did that performance go down with the audience there?

LeBARON: Well, audiences always love this piece because it's funny. But that audience was divided — some got off on it, they enjoyed it, they laughed. Others booed.

Q: It sounds like the typically Germanic misunderstanding that if a work is funny, then it can't be a serious piece.

LeBARON: I think so; I think you've got it right there.

Q: Was *Concerto For Active Frogs* your introduction to working with tape?

LeBARON: Yes, and I have to tell you that making that tape was just the crudest thing you can imagine. Turn on the tape recorder, drop the needle, and fade in and out. There wasn't even any splicing because I didn't learn to splice until Stony Brook. The original tape was a collage made by placing the frogs from the record in a sequence that was theatrically and musically gripping.

Q: So there isn't even any overdubbing on the tape.

LeBARON: No. I've cleaned it up since then, but I haven't recomposed it. The extraneous noise and hiss are gone, so that it doesn't sound as crude as the first version.

Q: It was at Stony Brook that you began composing with tape?

LeBARON: I went to Stony Brook to study electronic music with Bulent Arel and Daria Semegen. (She's now the director of the electronic studios there.) We were taught classical studio technique, such as tape splicing and operating oscillators and envelope generators. The most up-to-date piece of equipment there at the time — this was the late '70s — was a Buchla Series 200 Music Box. That's where I started composing electronic music.

Q: Did you study electronic techniques with Mario Davidovsky at Columbia?

LeBARON: No, I studied composition and wrote for chamber ensembles. I didn't study electronic music at Columbia because the studio was very similar to what we had at Stony Brook. Also, I had started working with the Synclavier in the meantime, and that was the direction that appealed to me.

Q: Is the tape part for *Planxty Bowerbird* completely synthesized?

LeBARON: Ninety-nine percent of it is. Near the end of the piece I took an aggressively plucked, lower wire sound from the harp and fed it into the computer, with minor processing.

The idea was to create the sound of a bowerbird, which I'd never heard. I worked all night in the studio and came home at dawn. Where I lived was next to a patch of woods, and I would go walking in the woods to chill out a little bit, wind down, and those damn birds sounded just like the electronics — or the electronics sounded like the birds. As if they were wired to do what I had been doing. It was eerie. When you work long hours,the electronic sounds stick in your brain, and it was unsettling to hear it migrate up to the trees. I think I was pretty successful at imitating some kind of unknown bird sound.

Q: The image of the bird's courtship rituals, its construction of ornate nests, was what had interested you?

LeBARON: The image greatly appealed to me, but I had started the piece before ever hearing of the bowerbird. A friend sent a clipping from *The New York Times*, which described the bowerbird, and I was enthralled by its peculiar characteristics. Imagine the extraordinary sight of the male bowerbird running around, building the fanciest bower he possibly can to please a potential mate, while she hangs around and watches his efforts, rewarding him if his artistry sufficiently pleases her. The bowerbird concept hovered around for the rest of the creative process. As it turns out, there is a vague analogy between the bowerbird's home decorating and the sonic adornments applied to the harp with the alligator clips and bows.

Q: You also combine electronics and live performers in your song *Dish*.

LEBARON: Dora Ohrenstein commissioned *Dish* for her "Urban Diva" project. Dora was pairing poets with composers, and suggested several poems by Jessica Hagedorn, which were difficult texts to set. I chose two that worked well together for a character portrait. One of them was about male-female interaction in a pick-up setting. I wanted to have a tape running for part of this poem, to embellish and heighten the implications of the sung text. So Dora and I made a couple of forays into Central Park to engage men in conversations — which I planned to tape surreptitiously. We didn't have much luck the first day; in fact, we ran into some trouble! So the next day, I was up front about the taping, and we wound up with some exciting material from one person in particular. Also, Jessica herself and an actor came into the recording studio and they improvised wildly off her lines. So I amassed a large amount of raw material to work with. My desire was to combine words and phrases so that they conveyed the excitement, danger, and hostility which can result from attempting to pick somebody up — but in a way that was texturally integrated with the music. The tape for *Dish* turned out to be related in some ways to the *Frogs* tape, but was created using vastly superior technology. And I added chanting at the end: a friend of mine extemporaneously vocalizing. The mix of the chanting is very subtle. The DX-7 II functioned as an intermediary instrument to bring the tape material — mostly spoken words with a bit of synthesis, and the chant — into the realm of the live performers.

Q: What's the role of electronics in your opera *The E. & O. Line*?

LEBARON: The electronics are there principally to create an otherworldly sonic background that evokes trains and train whistles — train whistles that disintegrate and become human voices or simply splinter off and evaporate, as well as train rhythms that dissolve into the instrumental rhythms. Tape is used about 20 percent of the time, and is almost always combined with live performers.

Q: And that tape is mostly synthesized?

LEBARON: Mostly sampled. The more potent sections of the tape come from samples of trains moving and trains sitting still, spitting steam, and old blues singers and cante flamenco recordings, and the two people moving the bed.

Q: Were any of the opera's singers sampled and used in the tape?

LEBARON: Yes and no. The singer Louise Cloutier provided raw material for some of the tape parts of Eurydice's voice. "When I Lay My Burden Down" is sung by the wife of Fred MacDowell, an extraordinary blues musician from Mississippi.

Q: Have you written all the music for it?

LEBARON: Yes, and I'll finish orchestrating when I know how many instruments we will have for the District Curators workshop in the Spring of '93. I don't care to orchestrate it for the 12 instruments I'd like and then be told we can only have four or five. It's basically finished. It's at the stage were it should be workshopped before it goes into production so it can be tightened and the storyline refined.

Q: Are you committed to working with certain singers, or is that more a question of who's available when performances and workshops are arranged?

LeBARON: Thomas Young will sing the part of Orpheus. I've altered it from a baritone to a tenor part, and he'll be magnificent in the role. I'd like to have Eurydice sung by a pop singer. The three remaining principals will be chosen by audition.

Q: You mentioned earlier that you no longer refer to this piece as a "blues opera." To what extent is the blues involved in the music you've composed?

LeBARON: Orpheus is a blues singer, and at the beginning he sings typical, 12-bar blues. On the whole, the opera reflects the blues; I hesitate to continue calling it a blues opera because such terminology implies that every song is a blues, and there are plenty of other forms in this opera — not to speak of dissonance. But there are some songs that are indeed straightforward blues, others that are extended, more jazzlike, with altered harmonies, and some that are mostly atonal. So it's more like a blues-influenced opera.

Q: What about the notation of the vocal parts? Have you written out all the embellishments and slides, say, in the blues-derived singing, or have you left some of that up to the singers?

LeBARON: This is always such a problem, because you don't know who you're getting unless a singer commits to do a part from the start. Consequently, you don't know how far to go in notating every nuance. For instance, in the demo tape that we recorded two years ago, I had a scat line with every single pitch written out in precise rhythmic notation. A Broadway singer did a fantastic job with it. It's striking, but it doesn't sound very bluesy — a slick, pop aesthetic comes across. On the other hand, Thomas Young took a simple melody and embellished it in ways that could never be adequately notated. He can do this effortlessly because he's absolutely at home in the language. And ideally, one *should* be able to write a blues song without resorting to overly complicated notation, and give it to a singer who can personally contribute to the song. This is what truly interests me, collaborating with singers who are able to bring their life experience into the music.

Q: Which makes it more complicated to find the right singers for the work.

LeBARON: It's terribly difficult. Singers should be given the chance to express themselves in this way, and branch out — Thomas Young being a superb example of someone who can sing complex contemporary opera, straight-ahead blues, and scat like a monster. In my opera, there's one character, Hermes, who has to be able to sing blues, gospel, jazz, and contemporary dissonant harmonies.

Q: And can work comfortably in a countertenor range.

LeBARON: He has to go high; it's a part for a high tenor, yeah. He has to do all that, which is asking for a great deal. There aren't many singers who can manage it.

Q: Plus I take it that all the principals have to be African-American.

LeBARON: In the previous workshops, Louise Cloutier, a French-Canadian, has sung the part of Eurydice. Most people who hear her assume she's African-American. The opera will be set in a sugarcane-cutting camp along the Mississippi delta — of course realistically it has to be a black cast.

Q: The standard opera repertoire has a tradition of ignoring the race of singers. With this opera, the situation isn't so simple.

LeBARON: Some situations don't work in reverse. The style of much of the music and the historical context of our version of the story call for not ignoring race, although at one time I did envision a mixed cast.

Q: Do you see *The E. & O. Line* as something to pitch to the established opera companies?

LeBARON: I would love to have it produced by an established house, but the vast majority are too conservative to touch it. Realism reigns, and my first priority is to get it workshopped with the limited resources we have, so the directors of the more adventurous larger companies can see it. There's more of a possibility that it would be produced in Europe, once the right person gets behind it. The librettist, Thulani Davis, and I were told by a major American opera company that *The E. & O. Line* isn't black enough for them — to give you an example of the agonizing frustration we've experienced in attempting to get a decent production lined up. That comment, ridiculous as it was, generated the decision to no longer describe it as a blues opera — I think it's too misleading. It's not an opera with a series of blues songs. It's something else, a hybrid built on indigenous American folk forms.

Q: I understand you've received a commission to write a piece for Harry Partch's instruments.

LeBARON: I'm so excited about getting to know these instruments. I imagine delving into microtonal scales to be like my experience of seeing tropical fish in their own environment for the first time — a vastly different, stunning, self-contained world to enter into, shaking up one's lifelong perceptions.

Q: Will you combine traditional instruments with Partch's?

LeBARON: Yes. NewBand will be touring with this first piece, so I'm keeping it simple. It's being scored for flute, cello, Surrogate Kithara and one Harmonic

Canon. I'm calling it *Southern Ephemera*. Fragments of old songs like "Wildwood Flower" will waft in and out of microtonal harmonies created by the two Partch instruments.

Q: With Partch, there's a tradition of the musicians being part of a larger theatrical situation, speaking or singing, or being costumed and moving about onstage.

LeBARON: *Southern Ephemera* will eventually become a part of a larger work encompassing more of the instruments. I do envision theatrical elements in the expanded work.

Q: These are renegade instruments in a sense, and can't be approached simply as if they were a string quartet or some other traditional ensemble.

LeBARON: The Surrogate Kithara and the Harmonic Canon are plucked, so I hope to introduce some of the more unusual techniques I've invented for the harp. I'll also stay away from licks that are Partch signatures. In fact, his riffs are probably the most idiomatic ways to play the instruments. In order to discover other ways of creating music on these instruments, it'll be critical to physically work with them.

Q: How long had you been playing the harp prior to your studies with Alice Chalifoux at the Salzedo Colony in 1974 and '76?

LeBARON: About two years prior to that. Originally I was a pianist: I taught myself when I was six years old, on a portable organ from Santa Claus, with those cheesy chord buttons for the left hand. A few years later I suffered through a series of terrible teachers: teenage church pianists, music-store instructors, and the like. We finally located the best teacher in Tuscaloosa, Alabama, a Juilliard graduate. She was one of the most influential people in my life. Her name was Emmett Lewis. She was a spinster who meant business — she projected a hardened warmth. She knew contemporary music, and theory, as well as technique, and I was floating after every lesson. She even had a machine for cutting vinyl records — my first recording-studio experience. I started lessons with her when I was twelve or thirteen, and continued through high school. Then I discovered the harp in college. Every day I would pass a large classroom with a harp — it always looked so lonely, and I thought it could surely use some company. So I asked around to see if anyone on the faculty played it and could teach me. There was a composer who had taught himself to play, and managed to pass along his poor technique to me. (He could knock out a mean version of *Thus Spake Zarathustra*, but couldn't play much else.) One of the Birmingham Symphony harpists heard about my plight and suggested that I come and study with her. I painstakingly relearned the technique, and then rapidly progressed — I definitely had found my instrument. The symphony harpist directed me to a student of Carlos Salzedo's, Marjorie Tyre, and she was wonderful. Out of that background I came to study with the great Alice Chalifoux at the Salzedo Harp Colony in Camden, Maine. The caliber of harpists in residence at the Salzedo Colony — some 30 harpists came from around the world to study with Alice Chalifoux — made for an intensive situation. That's where I really learned solid technique and the literature. Always working on technique. Alice and her niece, Jeanne Chalifoux, who also taught, told me, "You have such a good sense of rhythm. If you work hard, you'll have no problem at all in landing an orchestra job." But I never wanted to be an orchestra harpist, so I left that world for one that had to be invented.

Q: And if you're not going to play harp with an orchestra, things get difficult, because there isn't a large literature for it as a solo or even a featured instrument in chamber ensembles.

LeBARON: Which forced me to make my own way. Before the Chalifoux studies, I was devising unorthodox playing techniques. In Tuscaloosa, a small group of musicians were familiar with recordings of European improvisers — Derek Bailey and Evan Parker, Brötzmann — and we got together at least once a week just to play. We called ourselves Trans Museq, which eventually became a duo with just Davey Williams and LaDonna Smith. That's when I started to improvise on the harp, about halfway through my classical studies.

Q: Is that when you began preparing the harp as well?

LeBARON: Yeah. I used found objects, like an old spring from a screen door. How could I not, with Davey Williams using eggbeaters and electric fish to play his guitar?

Q: Do you now have pretty much the arsenal of implements which you want to use in preparing the harp, or is the field still wide open?

LeBARON: Through extensive experimentation, I've found what works and what doesn't work, and what works in certain contexts and what doesn't. I'm always open to discovery. For instance, I continue to experiment with different weights of paper preparations. Velcro sewing notions offer endless possibilities. I used to go into hardware stores and buy all kinds of implements to try out. But at the same time, I'm simplifying and consolidating. So I generally limit myself to the preparations and bows that I'm most comfortable with and that I really love. I don't use prop preparations anymore just for visual impact; whatever is in the arsenal has to generate sound. So I have a pared-down collection for the extended techniques, yes, but I'm always on the lookout for anything else that might come along. On the other hand, the electronics that interface with the harp are constantly being refined and reworked.

Q: Is the harp part in *Planxty Bowerbird* completely written out?

LeBARON: Yes. I use a steel tuning key, and developed a notation that indicates placement of the tuning key on the string and the resulting pitches, ascending slides to produce descending pitches, and vice versa. The screen-door spring, which is like a textured bow used as a steel slide, requires its own notation, as does the technique of bowing with horsehair bows. Icons representing the implements show what to use and where to use it. By the way, people are always astonished at the thought of bowing a harp, and can't imagine how it's done. Well, you just insert it between the strings! When I demonstrate this to harpists who have never bowed, they're amazed at the ease with which it's done. And I've been surprised by the interest in bowing and other techniques I've developed, because harpists are generally conservative. When I show them how beautifully bowing works on the instrument, it's always gratifying to see how quickly they learn to do it.

Q: How eager are you to have other harpists take up that piece, or the other harp music you've written?

LeBARON: I say the more the merrier! Five or so other harpists have performed *Planxty*, which is the most precisely notated piece for harp in my catalog. By inventing notation for unusual techniques, I believe I'm continuing the process of updating the harp, initiated by Salzedo in the 1930s. Salzedo articulated notations for a number of sound effects, such as the thunder effect, where the low wire strings are struck aggressively and bounce off one another. His notations have been documented, and now serve as a guide for composers writing contemporary music for the harp.

Q: Yet it wasn't the Salzedo literature that got you into the harp in the first place, was it?

LeBARON: It wasn't, no. I played transcriptions — Bach, Satie, Haydn — for weddings, restaurants, and funerals. There are two methods for playing the instrument, the Grandjany school and Salzedo's method. The Salzedo sound is more brilliant and penetrating. Of the two, Salzedo is certainly more my speed. And it just so happened that Alice Chalifoux and Marjorie Tyre were students of Salzedo's, so that's the technique I learned. By playing his works for the harp, I became acquainted with his notational inventions. But the improvisation, yes, came before I was introduced to Salzedo. You can imagine, after a few years of bowing and preparing the harp in total isolation in the early '70s, how exciting it was for me to find out about Salzedo's work.

Q: The *Blue Harp Studies* aren't notated, are they?

LeBARON: Those are not. I was awarded a PASS programming residency, and spent a couple of sessions sampling standard playing along with experimental techniques, then used the remainder of my 40 allotted hours to construct the two pieces. For one of the more striking samples, I placed a broken chain link on two high strings so the contact between the steel and the strings was constant, and slid the link up and down while rapidly plucking a tremolo. I used Soundtools for sketching phrases drawn from the large assortment of sampled sounds we collected. The samples were combined in various configurations on the controller keyboard, and I improvised a few sequences. We laid some tracks using Studio Vision, and three other people — the engineer Alex Noyes, his assistant, and my husband — improvised collectively and individually. I came away with a rich array of sequences and would go home and listen and decide what I thought would work together musically, both in a multitrack sense and in a linear sense. Then in the studio I would carry out the larger architecture of the pieces. Although a lot of thought went into the process, nothing was written down.

I call them *Studies* because I'm writing a harp concerto. My intention was to create a texture that was harplike, but not just your typical plucked-harp sound. They do exist now as pieces in their own right, thanks to the Tellus recording. They also constitute a rough sketch of parts of the harp concerto. For the concerto, I envision the orchestra as a giant multifaceted harp, a cocoonlike backdrop for the solo amplified harp.

Q: Those two *Studies* on the Tellus cd are the only pieces that came out of all that work?

LeBARON: That's right. I wanted to come away with two pieces that hung together, instead of a lot of snippets of this and that. Of course, there's plenty of material that wasn't touched, so I'm sure more music will emerge from my residency there.

Q: What considerations went into writing the harp part for your orchestra piece *Strange Attractors?*

LeBARON: It's a standard, orchestral harp part. I had originally asked for bowed harp, but it's lost without amplification, so I took it out of the score.

Q: You mentioned before how you first heard the Derek Bailey recordings when you were in school. How did your participation in one of his Company recordings come about?

LeBARON: During my Fulbright year in Germany, I got in touch with the improvisers I knew of. I was touring and recording with Candace Natvig and Jon English, her husband, and they lived outside Cologne. Through those performances, I got hooked up with some of the first-generation European improvisers and was invited to play at festivals, in clubs, wherever, and word got around that an improvising harpist was on the loose! I met Derek when he performed in Cologne, and he knew of me from the *Jewels* record, a trio I did with LaDonna Smith and Davey Williams.

Q: Unlike other improvising ensembles you've played with, your quintet is designed to play music you've composed.

LeBARON: After years of free improvisation, I had the desire to work with a group where I had more control. I didn't want it to be five improvisers doing their thing with no structure, but I also wanted musicians who could play free. And I was enthusiastic about writing for this particular combination of instruments: trumpet, tuba, guitar, harp, and percussion. The instrumental concept for the quintet came out of a trio I had with Davey Williams and the horn player Vincent Chancey. I loved the brass with the harp, so I expanded it to trumpet and tuba for the quintet. It's a powerful combination of instruments and personnel, which enables me to blend composition and collaboration.

Q: When you started moving back and forth between the musical scenes of improvisation and composition, did you find yourself in a strange position or was there a lot of awareness among each group as to what the other was doing?

LeBARON: No, there wasn't much mutual awareness — these were two distinct worlds. I'm thinking of Europe and how things were there ten years back. I feel a great affinity with the music of Anthony Braxton, because it's such a unique mix of difficult, cerebral notated music with a built-in freedom. The construction of his languages toward this end is unparalleled.

The reason that improvisation holds such an appeal for me — when it doesn't for most composers; most composers don't even care to hear it — is because it balances the thought processes I use in composing music. My grandmother, who was once the Southeastern women's chess champion, taught me the game as a little girl, and I used to be an avid player of tournament chess. Of course, the game requires advance planning, and my grandmother used to tell me, "If you look long enough, you'll always find a better move." Well, that sensibility worked its way into my composing process. As a slow composer I'm rewriting all the time — and relentlessly looking for that better move. Improvisation appeals to me because it represents the other extreme. Performing, playing free is a balancing act. It keeps the other, more cerebral activity in check, puts it in perspective, and tempers the obsession with forever searching for the best move.

Q: Do you find that there's a misperception in which people think of improvisation as a source of raw material for your composition?

LeBARON: Yes, and I've never dealt with improvisation in that way. In rare cases with the quintet, we'll do something collectively and then I'll write it in if I really like it. But improvisation generally never affects the composed works. Until recently the two have been absolutely distinct for me. I'm beginning to bring them together in some ways. Not that they have to be brought together, but when it happens, there's a wholeness, a sense of reconciliation.

Q: In the West especially, there's a tension about keeping the two areas entirely separate, as though they were mutually exclusive somehow.

LeBARON: We all know they weren't separate when Bach was alive. I do wonder where the turning point might have been, and whether or not the beginnings of jazz contributed to this rift, because improvisation was considered to be part of something more popular and therefore not as highly esteemed. Also with the disintegration of tonality, creative musicians were either exploiting its dissolution or were desperate to codify a new system for composing, and improvisation was anaethema to either goal. And when you consider that academic institutions kept serious contemporary composed music alive for most of our present century, it's clear that internal and external controls were exerted that stifled most divergences from the written note. With composers like Braxton and John Zorn, boundaries have become blurred, the recording industry has become a major player in the picture, and the controls of the past are losing their grip.

Q: Tell me about your studies of Korean music back in 1983.

LEBARON: My husband was sent to Korea five days after we were married. I went to visit him about half a year later, and heard some Korean music, in particular a form called *sanjo*. It's a free, spontaneous improvisation played principally on a plucked zither, the kayagum. The performance was totally entrancing — it was like an Asian version of a smoking blues guitar solo; I'd never heard anything remotely like it in my life except for a smoking blues guitar solo! And I thought, here I am, halfway around the world, and listen to this! When I first told Chou Wen-chung, whom I had studied with at Columbia, that I would be going to Korea, he advised me to seek out traditional Korean music. He said, "I find that it is remarkable in ways that Chinese and Japanese traditional music is not." And he was absolutely right. The Korean people on the whole are very warm, friendly, spontaneous people, and it's all there in the music. When I heard the *sanjo* I knew I had to return to Korea to study the kayagum, especially since it was a plucked instrument. I also wanted to hear more of the vocal music. I returned for the summer of 1982 and lived in the barracks (illegally!) near the DMZ, commuting to Seoul every day and studying the kayagum with descendants of the royal court musicians. I looked up the director of the National Classical Music Institute and said, this is what I want to do, can you help me? And he was so kind and welcoming. He arranged for private lessons, and saw that I was invited to attend recording sessions. Proponents of traditional Korean music are up against a populace that knows little and cares even less about its own musical heritage, due largely to pervasive Western influences. That summer I heard a lot of different vocal music and traditional Korean orchestral music, and made many tapes. It was just extraordinary. My composition *Lamentation/Invocation* comes straight out of that experience.

Q: Was it easy to notate the kind of sound you wanted in that piece, or did that music lead you into some gray areas?

LEBARON: Oh, it's gray. The sounds float around in a sea of microtones; they're not indicated as specific ratios, but instead function as inflections. The instruments in that piece are clarinet, cello, harp, and baritone voice, and at least I had a leg up on the unusual harp notation because I had codified some of it in *Planxty*. There's no improvisation, it's all written out. It was written with all of that sublime Korean music circulating in my brain. The hardest part was notating the elusive vocal slides and nuances.

Q: Those long sustained tones are really tough for singers — almost nobody writes vocal parts like that.

LeBARON: Allen Shearer does a super job on the Mode recording. Other singers who have performed the piece also surpassed the challenges. The part edges on the impossible, but doesn't cross the track.

Q: The Japanese qualities in your string trio *Noh Reflections* must have presented their own set of problems.

LeBARON: I spent a long time on the *Noh Reflections*; that piece gave me a lot of trouble. When you draw from a musical tradition that has developed and refined itself over so many centuries, like the Noh theater, it permeates your entire being. And I'm sure there's residue that finds its way into other pieces, such as the *Blue Harp Studies*.

Q: So many major qualities in your music — the harp preparations and improvisations, the use of animal sounds, your non-traditional notation, your involvement with Eastern music or with jazz or the blues — come from outside your academic training in America. If you were to start teaching here, you'd be more aware of the unique things students need to learn if they're going to compose their own music.

LeBARON: All of the qualities you've mentioned result from my life experience, and the academic training gave me tools to refine what I create out of those experiences. Another balancing act — one quality can easily overtake or overwhelm the other and lead to a "sterile" way of writing or to an "anything goes" philosophy. But you know, walking a tightrope requires patience and risk. The bottom line is: Know thyself — and beware of all the forces conspiring to prevent ever knowing thyself.

COMPOSITIONS

1973	*In The Desert* for soprano, flute, marimba, and temple blocks	GCM
1974	*Three Motion Atmospheres* for brass quintet	NM
1975	*Concerto For Active Frogs* for saxophone, trombone, percussion, male solo voice, mixed chorus, and tape	GCM
1976	*Memnon* for six harps	GCM
1977	*Metamorphosis* for piccolo/flute, oboe, clarinet, horn, trombone, and percussion	GCM
1977	*Light Breaks Where No Sun Shines* for SATB, SAT soli, and two percussionists	NM
1978	*Quadratura Circuli* for tape	GCM

1979	*The Sea And The Honeycomb* for soprano, flute, clarinet, piano, and two percussionists	NM
1980	*Metamorphosis* for chamber ensemble	GCM
1980;87	*Rite Of The Black Sun* for percussion quartet	NM
1982	*Planxty Bowerbird* for harp and tape	NM
1982	*After A Dammit To Hell* for bassoon	NM
1983	*Eurydice Is Dead* for tape	GCM
1984	*Lamentation/Invocation* for baritone, clarinet, cello, and harp	NM
1986	*Noh Reflections* for violin, viola, and cello	NM
1987	*Strange Attractors* for orchestra	NM
1988	*I Am An American ... My Government Will Reward You* for harp, temple bowl, temple bells, and tape	GCM
1989	*Orphans* film score	MS
1989	*Telluris Theoria Sacra* for flute, clarinet, violin, viola, cello, piano, and percussion	NM
1989	*Waltz For Quintet* for flute, violin, viola, cello, and piano	NM
1990	*Bouquet Of A Phantom Orchestra* for the Anne LeBaron Quintet (trumpet, tuba, electric guitar, percussion, and harp)	GCM
1990	*Top Hat On A Locomotive* for the Anne LeBaron Quintet	GCM
1990	*Superstrings And Curved Space* for the Anne LeBaron Quintet	GCM
1990	*Bottom Wash* for the Anne LeBaron Quintet	GCM
1990	*The Celluloid Doll* for tuba, viola, and harp	GCM
1990	*Dish* for soprano, electric violin, percussion, electric bass, piano, synthesizer, and tape	GCM
1991	*The E. & O. Line* electronic blues opera for twelve principals, six-part mixed chorus, and three-part female chorus	GCM
1992	*Tastes Funny, Hunny* for the Anne LeBaron Quintet	GCM

DISCOGRAPHY

1975
Concerto For Active Frogs
Say Day-Bew 1 lp

1983
Dog-Gone Cat Act
Opus One 58 lp

1987
The Sea And The Honeycomb
Opus One 137 lp

1991
"Eurydice Meets Hermes" from *The E. & O. Line*
Word Of Mouth 1004-1 cs, -2 cd

1992
Blue Harp Studies Nos. 1 & 2
Tellus 26 cd

Bouquet Of A Phantom Orchestra, Human Vapor, Superstrings And Curved Space, Bottom Wash, Top Hat On A Locomotive, Loaded Shark
Ear-Rational 1035 cd

Lamentation/Invocation, Rite Of The Black Sun, Planxty Bowerbird, Noh Reflections, Concerto For Active Frogs
Mode 30 cd

collaborations

with Derek Bailey's Company:
Epiphany Incus 46/47 lp (1983)

with Candace Natvig and Jon English:
"Euphorbia," "A Little Left Of Center" Opus One 58 lp (1983)

with LaDonna Smith and Davey Williams:
Jewels Trans Museq 3 lp (1979)

guest artist

with Sven Ake Johansson and Alexander von Schlippenbach:
...Uber Ursache Und Wirkung Der Meinungsverschiedenheiten Beim Turmbau Zu Babel FMP 20/21 lp (1987)

BIBLIOGRAPHY

"In Response." *Perspectives Of New Music*, 20 (Fall-Winter 1980/Spring-Summer 1981).

"Darmstadt 1980." Denys Bouliane, co-author. *Perspectives Of New Music*, 20 (Fall-Winter 1980/Spring-Summer 1981).

photo: Lona Foote

MOONDOG / Introduction

MOONDOG was born Louis Thomas Hardin in Marysville, Kansas, on May 26, 1916. At the age of 16, a dynamite cap exploded in his face, permanently robbing him of his eyesight. He attended the Iowa School for the Blind, where he received his first musical training, and went on to study privately with Burnet Tuthill at the Memphis Conservatory of Music. He came to New York in 1943 and soon gained the friendship of Artur Rodzinski, renowned conductor of the New York Philharmonic. Hardin became a singular exception to Rodzinski's ban on outsiders attending rehearsals of the orchestra. With Rodzinski's departure from the Philharmonic in 1947, however, Hardin discovered his presence was less welcome, especially because of his unconventional ways of dressing.

Hardin adopted the name Moondog that same year, and eventually became a regular fixture on Manhattan's streets, often dressed in full Viking regalia. Despite intermittent lodgings of various kinds (both in the city and upstate), Moondog would spend the next three decades living on the streets of New York. Working there as well: By the '50s he was supporting himself as a street musician, frequently playing on instruments of his own invention, such as the trimbas (triangular drums), yukh (a suspended log struck with rubber mallets), and the oo (a triangular stringed instrument struck with a clave).

Always a prolific composer, Moondog would type out his compositions in Braille and then have them transcribed into conventional notation. (He also produced a good deal of gnomic, witty poetry in the same manner.) His music soon became known for its unusual metric sense, intricate and rigorous canonic procedures, and refined, evocative melodies. But Moondog's music wasn't just composed on the streets; a good deal of it was composed with the streets. Despite the limited location-recording technology of the '50s, he created numerous works in a range of New York City locations, utilizing the sounds of traffic, tugboat whistles, and the surf not just as sound effects or color, but as essential lines in the overall composition. By the end of the '50s, Moondog had released several lps of his striking compositions on the Prestige label, as well as an unexpected project with Martyn Green and Julie Andrews: an lp of nursery rhymes and children's songs — although his quirky rhythms and meters must have confounded more than a few youngsters who wanted to sing along!

Their solution may have been similar to Janis Joplin's when she performed Moondog's 5/4 song, "All Is Loneliness": just sing it in 4/4. Her cover was one more example of how widespread Moondog's music had become by the late '60s, especially with Columbia Records' release of an lp of his orchestral music (much to the delight of the composer, who then took to standing outside the CBS building on Sixth Avenue and 53rd Street).

In 1974, a concert of Moondog's music brought him to Germany, where he decided to remain for a while after the performance. He was on a street in Recklinghausen, wearing his Viking helmet and selling copies of his poetry, when he was spotted by Ilona Goebel. Upon discovering his album of orchestra music, she invited him to live with her family in the town of Oer-Erkenschwick. Today she is his manager, assistant, and publisher of both his scores and writings, through her company Managarm.

I spoke with Moondog by telephone at his home in Germany, on August 23, 1992. Researching this semi-legendary figure of American music had led me to all sorts of versions of his experiences — especially after his move to Germany: His absence form the streets of New York was taken by some people as a sign that he was dead! I wanted to hear his own recollections of his life and work, both on the sidewalks of Manhattan and in the concert halls of Europe, where he has of late found a renaissance of enthusiasm and support for his music.

MOONDOG / Interview

Q: I've read that your father was an itinerant Episcopalian minister, and that he took you out to Indian reservations when you were a boy in Wyoming.

MOONDOG: He was a missionary out there in the cowboy country, and then he went to this convention in the Arapaho reservation. I must have been about 5 or 6 years old then. It was a two-week convention — he was bringing Jesus to the Indians.

Q: But they let you play in one of their ceremonies.

MOONDOG: Yes, Chief Yellow Calf let me sit on his lap and gave me the drumsticks and I beat on the big tomtom when they were doing the Sun Dance.

Q: That must be a very powerful memory.

MOONDOG: It still influences my music.

Q: You've remarked that Swing has its origins in Native American music.

MOONDOG: That four beats to the bar — bom-bom-bom-bom — is strictly in the Swing era, and that's Indian, right out of the Indian drumbeats. And if you hear them sing, their music is full of syncopation. I think their music is very jazzy.

Q: In the '40s, you also played with the Blackfoot Indians in Idaho. How did that come about?

MOONDOG: I was visiting there and they were having their Sun Dance ceremonies: They sing and dance for many hours — a couple of days and nights without eating. I had this little flute and I was standing behind the area where they were performing, and they liked my playing so much they wanted me to come and sit with the singers. Then, when I was staying as a guest in their big teepee, unbeknownst to me somebody rolled a big tomtom in there and then disappeared. I think they wanted me to play on it, so I did.

Q: Are you singing authentic Indian chants in "Wildwood" and "Chant" on your Prestige lps?

MOONDOG: No, it's not authentic. Maybe just a rough comparison to what they do, but it's not authentic.

Q: Was John Wesley Harding really one of your relatives?

MOONDOG: As far as I know.

Q: Being a minister, your father probably wasn't too proud of the lineage.

MOONDOG: Oddly enough, he was proud of it. He was a very great fan of Napoleon too. I guess there must be some aggression in a lot of ministers!

Q: One of your *H'Art Songs* is about John Wesley Harding. In your own way, you've been as much of a maverick as he was.

MOONDOG: Yes, I'm a rebel, but I'm rebelling against the rebels. By the rebels I mean the atonalists and the polytonalists. So I rebel against the rebellion and stay with tonal music.

Q: Was there much music in your life prior to your high-school training at the Iowa School for the Blind?

MOONDOG: In my high school in Missouri I played the drums in the school band. And when I was 6 years old in Wyoming — just after we met the Indians — I used to climb up over a steamer trunk and beat my feet on both sides, and I had a box and I had two sticks, so I made rhythms with them myself.

Q: But you hadn't been thinking of music as a vocation when you were a kid.

MOONDOG: No. I think the blindness made it possible for me to have a musical education which I never could have afforded. I had music teachers who were all conservatory graduates, and I had piano lessons; organ; I played viola in the quartet and violin in the orchestra; I sang in the choir. I studied musical form and harmony, but they didn't teach counterpoint — that I had to teach myself.

Q: And from there you went to the Memphis Conservatory?

MOONDOG: I studied privately with the head of the conservatory — his name was Mr. Tuthill. I studied counterpoint with him, a little bit, but most of it I learned myself by getting books on counterpoint.

Q: Did you take regular lessons at Memphis as well?

MOONDOG: I just came to his house and studied with him privately. He was the head of the conservatory, but I didn't go to any classes, only to him.

Q: When you first came to New York in 1943, were you planning to study with a composer or to start being one?

MOONDOG: I wanted to be where the action was. I knew if I had to make it, I'd have to do it there; that was the focal point. I'd wanted to come to New York for many years, and after I'd been in Memphis for about eight months, I decided the time had finally come to come up there to New York, so I just got on a train and left Memphis. I had been financed by I.L. Meyer who was an art patron, so I came on up to New York and began posing in art schools to make a living. Then I met Artur Rodzinski who was the conductor of the Philharmonic, and he let me come to rehearsals.

Q: Halina Rodzinski recounts in her book that you approached her husband about sitting in on the rehearsal for Mahler's Second Symphony.

MOONDOG: Well, that was the symphony they were rehearsing the week that I was there. It was very interesting: I came to New York early in November, and I took a taxi and came over to Carnegie Hall and got a ticket and I sat in the front row, center. And that was the day that Bruno Walter was taken ill and they had to get a quick substitute; unbeknownst to me, it was Leonard Bernstein. His debut, and I was sitting right behind him; just a few feet ahead of me, it was Bernstein, and I said to myself, "After the first number, I'm going to be the first to applaud, and be heard all over the country." And I was.

The cello soloist in *Don Quixote* was Joseph Schuster, and he was sitting very close to me there, being the soloist. A few days later, I was standing in the entrance to the stage door, and there was an intermission in the rehearsal. Apparently, Joseph Schuster saw me, and he came over to me and said, "I saw you Sunday. Would you like to come to rehearsal?" And I said, "Yes." He said, "Wait a minute," and in a few minutes he came back with Artur Rodzinski who put his arm around my shoulder and said, "Come with me. You can come to my rehearsal." He took me clear to the front of the hall and took me down the center aisle and said, "Sit down now and enjoy yourself." At lunch he took me up to his dressing room. Mrs. Rodzinski had brought some hot soup for him, and that's how I got to meet her. And then Bernstein came in and asked something about the contrabasses. I didn't know who it was, and I said, "Are you a bass player?" And he said, "No, I wish I were." So I got to meet Leonard Bernstein too.

Q: Were you aware that you'd made such a strong impression on Rodzinski, and that it was highly unusual for him to admit an outsider to his rehearsals?

MOONDOG: Yes. He was a very superstitious, spiritual-minded person, and for some reason he got the idea that I resembled the face of Christ. I had a beard and all that, so I think it was partly that, and some kind of intuition that he should be especially nice to me. He was lovely, and I owe a lot to him and his wife.

Q: She's written that he felt you brought him luck.

MOONDOG: Yes, that's the way his mind was working, and I was very grateful to him for whatever he did. In fact, two years ago I went back to New York to do this concert, and I went up to visit Mrs. Rodzinski. She was very friendly, and told me all about what she'd been doing — she wrote a book about her husband and all that.

Q: Was that in a sense the last of your studies, your being able to sit in and listen to the orchestra at work?

MOONDOG: It was a great education to learn orchestration from first hand. And I also had a chance to talk to players about their instruments and their ranges, what the instrument could and couldn't do. It was a first-hand education that was invaluable.

Q: Had you been writing any music for orchestra or large chamber ensembles around that time?

MOONDOG: Not really. I had the opportunity but I wasn't ready for it.

Rodzinski said to me one day, "Louie, do you have anything for orchestra? I'll play it." I didn't have anything. And when I had it, he was dead.

Q: Is it true that eventually you were asked not to come to the rehearsals because of the way you were dressing?

MOONDOG: That's right. I went up one day with some funny clothes on, and he said, "Louie, I want to have a long talk with you." I said, "It won't take very long. You have a freedom in America as long as you don't exercise it." So he said, "Well, do what you want to do," but he sounded very discouraged about me. Then later I heard about this manager of the orchestra, Bruno Zurato; he told one of the violinists to tell me that if I want to come back, I have to wear conventional clothing. But I never did. I cut my own nose off, but I did it for a principle.

Q: Did you find in later years that your appearance was hindering the acceptance of your music?

MOONDOG: A lot of people told me I was standing in my own light, and that they would like to help me in many ways but they couldn't because of how I was dressing. So I paid a price, I can tell you.

Q: I understand Ilona Goebel persuaded you to set those clothes aside.

MOONDOG: Yes, she's the only person that ever was able to do it!

Q: In retrospect, has it really been worth it?

MOONDOG: Well, frankly, it has, you know?

Q: You've gotten more performances now because of that?

MOONDOG: Yes. I think if I'd react as other people do, if I saw somebody doing what I'd been doing, I'd say, "Nothing doing — I can't buy that. It must be some kind of a nut, really — I mean, I can't involve myself with that." That would probably be my own reaction.

When I started changing the way I was dressing, it was a rebellion against organized fashion that dictates what you wear, and insists that you buy something new every year to keep in style, just for profit — that's what was really behind it.

Q: Is there also the sense that, by controlling how people appear, there's a deeper control at work upon how people behave and think?

MOONDOG: Yes, everything — control, control. Big Brother. That's what it is.

Q: I've read that there were particular symbolic meanings attached to some of the Viking garb you've worn, such as the helmet and the spear.

MOONDOG: Well, I always said the spear had a double meaning. It could be used for defense or for attack, and you had a choice to use it to defend yourself or to attack somebody else's liberty.

Q: In your years on the street, did you ever find yourself using it either for defense or attack?

MOONDOG: Oh no. But people would come up and ask me, "What's with the spear?" I'd say, "If you don't get the point, you can climb up and sit on it." And one lady said, "Yeah, but don't twist it"! I used to wear spurs, and a guy comes up: "Moondog, where's your horse?" I said, "Bend over, you'll do." Things like that were happening all the time. Another one says, "Do you have a problem?" I said, "Yes," and I waited a while. "What's your problem?" I said, "You." When you're on the streets, you learn to talk back to them when they come up with those things. One night I was standing on the corner and a girl and her boyfriend came around the corner and she screamed, "Sir Galahad!" I said, "No, Sir Had-a-gal"! That's what you get from standing across the street from the Hilton, you know?

Q: Being on the streets and dressing the way you did may have given some people problems, but doing all that was actually part of your effort to be in the world and be more accessible to people, wasn't it?

MOONDOG: Yes, that's right.

Q: I understand you had a place in upstate New York, near Ithaca.

MOONDOG: Yes, I did have 40 acres up there.

Q: So you could have stayed there if you'd wanted to.

MOONDOG: Well, I couldn't afford to. I had no income at all up there — I just went up there to get away from the city.

Q: How much of your time on the streets were you actually homeless?

MOONDOG: I had a choice. If I kept a hotel room, then I wouldn't have enough money to hire a copyist to copy the music or to go up to my place, because to make a trip up there would cost around $50, including carfare and food for a couple of weeks. I couldn't have the room and the music copying and the trips up there, so I had to make a choice: either keep a room and not go up there, or not have a room and go up there once in a while. So some of the time I would just sleep on the streets to save money. I could have a room all the time, but I wouldn't then be able to do all the other things.

Q: How big a hassle was that life for you? Were you ever assaulted or robbed?

MOONDOG: Yes, I've been kicked when I was sleeping, and pissed on, and abused and robbed sometimes. But never stabbed in the chest — I mean, they could have killed me if they'd wanted to. One night a cop came up to me and said, "Are you all right, Moondog?" And I said, "Yes." He said, "Here's a couple of bucks." He gave me two dollars.

Q: I wanted to know if the police were helpful to you or a hindrance.

MOONDOG: Mostly very nice.

Q: They wouldn't say that you were disturbing the peace?

MOONDOG: Oh yes, some people did call the police, and the police would come and tell me that somebody was complaining about the ticking of the claves — it made quite a loud noise — so I stopped playing the claves. But in general it was very nice. Cabbies even watched out for me, and doormen — if I was staying across the street from some place that had a doorman, they said that they were watching me to see that nobody bothered me. There's a lot of love in New York, really.

Q: How significantly did things change from the '40s to the '70s? Do you think you'd be able to resume that life now?

MOONDOG: From what I hear, I think it would be difficult. They say there's more violence than there ever was before when I was there. And perhaps I'd have more to fear from people who had taken drugs, because they're not responsible for what they do; that's an unknown quantity there, how people react under the influence.

Q: Conditions have changed a lot here since the '70s.

MOONDOG: Well, I spent my apprenticeship there, 30 years on the street. That's enough, I think!

Q: I've read that you adopted the name Moondog back in the late '40s, and that it was a reference to a dog you had in Hurley, Missouri.

MOONDOG: That's right. Some people think that he was a seeing-eye dog, but he wasn't. He was just a dog, half bulldog and half something else. But he was a great pal. He did a lot of howling at the moon. And then years later, in '47, I thought I'd like to have a pen name so I thought of him. But I wasn't original. I found out later that the word "moondog" exists in Alaska amongst the Indians: It's a rainbow that appears over the moon, as opposed to a sundog which is a rainbow that appears over the sun. And in some of the Southern counties, Kentucky and some places, they have a whiskey called Moondog. It's also mentioned in the Norse sagas, the *Edda*, and refers to a giant. And it also refers to the tail of a comet; that's also called a moondog. So it does have quite a history.

I defended the name in court against Allan Freed who was using my name and my record. I had a piece called "Moondog Symphony" which had a howling wolf on it. It was on one of my first 78s, and Allan Freed used it on his radio program as a theme song for his show. I won the case: The judge said that I had worked hard to establish claim to the name, and so they wouldn't let him use it anymore. After the judgment, he got on the radio one night and said, "I cannot use this name anymore because it belongs to somebody else. So from now on the show will be called The Rock & Roll Show."

Q: Is it true that Igor Stravinsky spoke to the judge on your behalf?

MOONDOG: Yes, he called the judge and said, "Take care of this man. He's a serious composer. Do him right."

Q: Had you known prior to that that Stravinsky was interested in your music?

MOONDOG: I didn't know. I was at a rehearsal of the Philharmonic when he was conducting some of his music, but I didn't meet him. But years later I heard that he did that for me. That's quite an honor.

Q: I've read that, in the '51 recording of "Theme," you played all the parts yourself and overdubbed them.

MOONDOG: Yes, I did. I bought a violin, a flute, a baritone horn, and a contrabass and a lot of other things and dubbed them all in. That was overdubbing on very primitive machines. When I recorded for Columbia, my producer Al Brown said, "Why don't you orchestrate that?" So I did.

Q: When did you begin recording your music?

MOONDOG: In 1950 I was playing drums in the doorway of a man named Gabriel Oller who had a shop called Spanish Music Center. When I finished playing a piece, he said, "You're sitting in my doorway. I make records — would you like to make a record?" So I said yes and soon we'd made a series of three 78s. Then I later made an album on my own label but I sold it to Prestige. I had recorded all those things down in the Village and brought it out as an lp, and then a man came to me and said, "I think I can sell this to Prestige." So he went over and talked to Bob Weinstock, and he said he would like to bring it out. That was the first Prestige record and then they did two more. I also did a 10-inch lp on Epic.

Q: Is that the one with the New York Philharmonic string players?

MOONDOG: Yes, right. I had written two suites for three cellos and two violas from the Philharmonic. Then I did the 1969 album on Columbia Masterworks, with a 40-piece orchestra, and the next year I did the madrigal album with my daughter. That's all I did in New York. I came to Europe in '74, and made three cds here, and then the *Elpmas* cd just last year. I introduced there something that I created myself: a 16-part triple canon. I used the marimba mostly on that because it was very reproduceable on the recording equipment; it records well. Some of the samples, like of obocs and bassoons and clarinets, don't sound like those instruments; they sound artificial. But there's something about the percussive quality of the marimba which makes it sound realistic.

Q: *Fog On The Hudson* is one of your 78s?

MOONDOG: That was from a piece that I played on the piano, overdubbing. I got the sound of the foghorns from a man I used to work with, named Tony Schwartz. He gave me that sound and we dubbed them together. I called this piece "Tugboat Toccata."

Q: How difficult was it to overdub at that time?

MOONDOG: They had very primitive machines. To do the dubbing, you had two machines, and you had to play the one recording I did against the one I was going to record.

Q: So it's playing back while you're playing live, and the two are recorded.

MOONDOG: Right, and they mix it. You lose a lot on each take that way; the quality gets worse and worse as you keep overdubbing. That's why it sounded so unclear. But you got an idea that something was happening.

Q: Did the pieces that featured environmental sound happen the same way, with one machine playing the location recording while another machine recorded that along with all the other musicians?

MOONDOG: Some of it was; some was done live on the street, like on the Mars 45. Tony Schwartz had the equipment and he had a car. For electricity, he had some kind of electrical equipment in the car, and so he could come right up to where I was recording — he had a long extension on his microphone cable — and could record on the street.

Q: It's wonderful how the environmental sound sits with the music. It doesn't just add "color," but instead is a part of the total musical sensibility.

MOONDOG: Yes. The orchestra concert I'm doing this month in Switzerland includes "Surf Session" which is something I recorded on Prestige. Here I'll be using a much larger string group, and I'll also be using a recording of the sound of the ocean in the background. We're doing "Fujiyama" also — the 16-part canon I was telling you about — and we'll dub in the sound of thunder and rain at the end.

Q: How did you wind up performing Mother Goose songs with Julie Andrews for Angel Records?

MOONDOG: Well, a certain Ms. Laurence approached me and said she was doing this record, and she wanted to know if I would write the music. So I said yes and wrote the settings to all those Mother Goose rhymes, and then we had a rehearsal with Julie and Martyn Green and Julius Baker who did the flute part. We recorded in '55 and it came out on Angel in '57, I think. Capitol bought that but never brought it out again. I'd like to have it come out again.

Q: It has a delightful section of rhymes about the calendar.

MOONDOG: That was part of the text that they wanted me to set.

Q: I've read that in the '50s you presented the New York Public Library with a calendar you'd prepared, which covered 3,000 years in both Julian and Gregorian computations.

MOONDOG: That's right. It took two weeks to work it out. That's about 1,500 years of Julian and 1,500 years of Gregorian, which goes into the future, of course. The librarian said that of all the mechanical ways of determining time which they've ever had — some were in wheel form and other things — mine was the fastest and easiest to do.

Q: Was Sixth Avenue and the Fifties a congenial neighborhood for you in part because of its proximity to the jazz clubs?

MOONDOG: Yes. I would be playing in that area late at night, and sometimes some of the players from the clubs would come over and listen to my drumbeats for a while. One night Dizzy came by, and another time, Louie Bellson; another time, Duke Ellington. People like that would talk to me. I never did meet Lester Young, but I wrote a piece for him and we did it in my little tournee this summer with the saxophone group I have, called the London Saxophonic. One of the players, Andrew Scott, played it beautifully; I've always had trouble finding tenors who could do it, and he did it very well.

I met Charlie Parker one night, and he said we should do a record together, but the next thing I heard, he was dead. So I wrote this piece, "Bird's Lament." On the record it's too fast; the drummer influenced me to play it faster than I wanted. Now when I play it with the group, it's a little slower.

Q: Didn't you play piano on a bill in Los Angeles with Duke Ellington, in 1948?

MOONDOG: It wasn't a bill. They had an amateur-music contest, and I played a piano solo and won first prize. Then I got word that he wanted to meet me, so the next day or two I went backstage and met him and the band. Then I didn't meet him again until I was back in New York. He came by one night and we talked again — very nice man.

Q: In 1970, you performed at New York's Whitney Museum on a double bill with Charles Mingus. Was there any interaction with him, either prior to that concert or afterwards?

MOONDOG: No, I didn't meet him, but we were on the same bill. I was with the Aeolian Chamber Players and we did some of my pieces, and I did some of my poetry. Very nice audience there.

Q: The Prestige recordings — both in their initial release and now in the cd reissues — turn up in the jazz sections in the stores.

MOONDOG: In Germany, they don't know where to put me. They call it E- and U-music — one is classical and one is pop — and they don't know where to put me. One French reporter said, "It is not pop, it's not rock, it's not jazz, it's not classical, it is just Moondog."

Q: Are you bothered that the music is put in jazz categories when that's not really what it's about?

MOONDOG: It doesn't bother me where they put it, as long as they put it.

Q: Some tracks in the Prestige recordings feature improvised performances.

MOONDOG: I wanted it to sound like that, but actually every note is written down, every note. That's what shocks people: They say, "That can't be written down, it's too free." I say, "Well, that's the point. I want to make it sound free, but every note is written down exactly."

I'm against improvisation because only the composer can improvise; he's the only one that has oversight over all the different parts, what each person is doing. In Sweden, they call a composer a "tone-setter," like a printer setting type — that's the oversight. Players who don't have that knowledge and improvise over a large group of instruments are stepping on everybody's toes here and there; they're lucky if they change chord at the same time. Even Benny Goodman made a lot of terrible contrapuntal mistakes because he was improvising and went his own way, and the other people were being stepped on. But you have to be a master of counterpoint to know this. Even I make mistakes; nobody makes more mistakes than I do. But I analyze every piece, every bar, every note, and any mistakes are eliminated. In a 16-part canon, you have 120 chances of making a mistake. When I analyze, I can't sit down and do it — I fall asleep. So I have to stand up and analyze. Brahms' solution was to stand up when you write.

Q: You've said that your piece *Witch Of Endor* was part of a ballet for Martha Graham.

MOONDOG: Yes, which she never used. She had me come up to her place once, and she said, "I don't know your work." I felt like saying to her, "I don't know yours, either"! Anyway, I wrote this but she never used it. She got William Schuman to do something.

Q: The Prestige recordings feature your playing with dancers at their rehearsals. Were there other choreographers that approached you for music?

MOONDOG: Yes, several times. There were performances by different ballet companies in Switzerland, Germany, Sweden, and France. Last year we got a call from American Ballet Theater. The choreographer had heard the Columbia orchestra album, and he wanted to do a ballet to it. We only had six weeks to get the music together, so we rushed over the music and they did it — called it "Moondance." They said, "Send us the parts and we'll have scores made," and they rushed out to California to start their tournee, and they did "Moondance." They performed it in New York in June, I think.

Q: Louis and Bebe Barron perform a dialogue with you on one of your Prestige lps.

MOONDOG: Yes, on one you hear her voice, and then on another one, where I'm talking about youth and age, that's Louie.

Q: They were real groundbreakers in electronic music.

MOONDOG: Yes, I heard they did something with some kind of outer-space movie.

Q: That's right, *Forbidden Planet*. I'm curious if you had any contact with them regarding electronic music. Did they ever speak to you about it or play some of it for you?

MOONDOG: No, I never got into that. We worked a couple of years together, and then they moved out to the West Coast.

Q: Did Janis Joplin ever get your permission to use "All Is Loneliness"?

MOONDOG: No, she just did it. The piece was written in 5/4 but she sang it in 4/4. She took great liberties, but as long as she called me "a beautiful cat," then I don't mind.

Q: No royalties though, I take it.

MOONDOG: No, I didn't get anything.

Q: Is it true that in the '60s you were playing with Philip Glass and Steve Reich and Terry Riley?

MOONDOG: We used to go up into an old factory building and record some of my madrigals together — just Reich and Glass were there with me. Then I was invited to come over to Riley's house and meet him one night. We never worked together, though.

Q: Do you know what happened to those recordings?

MOONDOG: If they still exist, they would be with Philip Glass.

Q: How did you meet them? Did they just approach you on the street?

MOONDOG: Well, I got to meet Phil Glass because somebody in *The Village Voice* said, "Where are Moondog's friends? He has no place to stay. He has to sleep on the streets." One of the people who called was Phil Glass, and he invited me to stay with him. So I did; I moved down there and stayed with him for about half a year, I guess it was. That's how I got to meet him. Then I met Steve Reich. This is the late '60s — in '68 I moved in with Phil.

Phil Glass is always saying about minimal music, "Moondog is the leader of the pack." We have tonality in common but that's where it ends, because I'm very strict in my counterpoint, and apparently they pay no attention to contrapuntal rules: When it comes to changing and passing notes, they don't know from what, I tell you. I like them personally, but when it comes to counterpoint I'm the most fussy composer that ever lived. One of the papers here said I'm stricter than Bach and Palestrina, which is true: They're full of mistakes.

Q: When you find errors in their work, is their muse nodding or does it seem more that they just don't care about the rules in certain situations?

MOONDOG: There could be different motivations. One might be haste — didn't have time to analyze it. Or possibly they didn't care about the rules. Or they didn't

know — but I can't imagine they didn't know. But even Tallis and Frescobaldi and
Beethoven, Bach, Mozart, they're all full of mistakes. I have to turn the radio off —
I can't stand it, what they're doing to my ears, you know? Unbelievable mistakes,
what they're doing. You'd think the farther back you'd go, the better it would be,
but it's not. Even back in the 14th, 15th centuries, the same mistakes.

Q: Some corruptions could have crept into the scores over the years.

MOONDOG: That is always a possibility, when every note was written by hand
and rewritten and rewritten. But there are too many of them to be that. It's common mistakes and violations of the principle of tone relation going back to
Pythagoras. Well, what can you do? I go my own way.

Q: That's what you can do: Show them how it's done.

MOONDOG: Right. One paper said, "Moondog came to Germany to give
German music refinement"! What a thing to say! I was on television here and I
pointed out where Bach made a mistake in *The Art Of The Fugue*, and I played it
on the piano, the mistake. I heard later that some professor jumped up out of his
chair and said, "Vot, zis American telling us about Bach?" Oh, he was exploding!

I didn't tell them about my German ancestry: My mother's family were all
from Germany.

Q: Is there a Scandinavian background for you as well?

MOONDOG: My father was Norman English, and the Normans of course were
of Viking descent. So it's all the same thing.

Q: To what do you attribute your need for such correctness?

MOONDOG: Well, there's a right and a wrong way to do things. There's two
ways to learn from a master of the past: either you can learn what to do, or you
can learn what not to do. I've learned a lot from Bach; I've learned what I should
do and not what I should not do. Haydn taught Beethoven counterpoint but he
said, "I can't teach this young man anything." Well, I don't know how he could
— he must have taught him a lot of wrong moves in counterpoint, because the
same mistakes are in both.

Q: On one level, what you're involved in is a quest for purity, isn't it?

MOONDOG: Yes — and if you judge the reaction of the people at my tournee,
they're shouting and screaming and stamping their feet. I couldn't believe that a
German audience could react that way. They don't know the rules technically, but
they know them intuitively; they can tell when tones are fitting together properly,
and they react. One lady called and said she wanted a copy of the piece called
"Paris." She said, "Ahh" — that sigh, you know? When you hear that from the people, you know you've reached them. So I have great respect for people who don't
know the technicalities. They can feel it and know when it's right. If you combine

that rightness of counterpoint with melody and with harmony and with rhythm, you've got a winner.

Q: I'm very interested in the work you've done with the overtone series in the last 20 years.

MOONDOG: That's my biggest project in life. Believe it or not, I've discovered that whoever created the universe, whenever, left a message in the first nine overtones — or you can say that the first nine overtones are the message. I just wanted a theme for my *Creation* — I didn't realize that there was anything there. But I discovered in Hamburg that there's a system there. And I discovered that, by using the principle of diminution, I could develop these nine overtones, using a series of diminished sequences of overtone series, and create a pyramidal structure. And in that pyramidal structure, I realized that the secret message was that whoever created the universe is trying to tell us that He's sharing with us the secret structure of the universe. In other words, it proves the principle of contraction and expansion. Hubble was always talking about expansion, but this system in the overtones proves that you can't have one without the other. It also has a lot of other implications, like the two-directionality of time. But scientists that I've approached through the letterbox do not respond. They're either afraid to find out if it's right or wrong, or they're threatened because, if they accept this, it will overturn innumerable theories and conjectures of science.

How could you send a message that would never be destructible? Only in sound waves. Waves are indestructible. Wherever there's a planet that has atmosphere, these overtones could be heard. Apparently, there may be even in our own galaxy some planets that may have an atmosphere, and there may be living creatures there who might be able to discover the message. If this is ever accepted, it's the biggest discovery that was ever made by humanity, because here's a direct message to us — He respects our intelligence enough to think that we should share the knowledge of the inner structure of the universe. And it's there everywhere. Scientists are looking in telescopes and microscopes, and they don't realize that this is here, right here. The secret is all around us, and nobody recognizes it.

Q: Has your work with the overtone series affected your attitude regarding equal temperament?

MOONDOG: I don't really basically accept equal temperament as Bach produced it. When I work with overtones, I'm not talking about equal temperament, because the overtone series has nothing to do with equal temperament. It's all pure tone. I really think it was a big mistake to go in for equal temperament. Every fourth and fifth should be perfect, in perfect tune, and the only way you can use perfect fourths and fifths on a keyboard would be to limit yourself to just a few keys: maybe one or two flats, one or two sharps — that would be it. That's the way it should be. But you make compromises to be able to play music in all 24 keys; then you have to compromise a little. I heard one famous clarinetist say he hates to play

with a piano: "I always have to adjust my intonation to fit this out-of-tune piano."
Bach called it the Well-Tempered Clavichord, I call it Ill-Tempered.

Q: Nevertheless, you've stuck to composing in equal temperament.

MOONDOG: I have. I did a series of piano pieces in every key, in Bach's tradition, but I know it's a compromise.

Q: Have you found that your work with the overtone series has led you to forms
and structures that you otherwise would not have employed?

MOONDOG: Very much so, especially in *The Creation*.

Q: Your long piece "Cosmic Meditation" really is a departure from your other
recorded music.

MOONDOG: Yes, I think there is that element of differentiation there. Right
after the chorus I have all overtones, a little eight-bar introduction. And after that
I have the overtone series, where I produce this little pyramidal structure. And
then after that it's a free thing with overtones, using themes from my *Creation*.
But I want to bring out some really complete ones. They're 81-part canons I call
the *Yin And Yang*. *Yin* would be on one whole cd and *Yang* on another. I've written a series of nine *Yin And Yang* canons. And this would be all using overtones. I
get some reactions here from the critics who say that it's very meditative and
soothing to listen to. The piece on the *Elpmas* cd is just a little thing that we did
in a few minutes; it's not really a complete piece, just a first attempt.

Q: Can you tell me about *Creation*? I understand it was begun in 1971.

MOONDOG: That's when I first got this idea of using the overtone series as a
theme. I left New York in '74 to do some concerts here in Germany, and then I
stayed here. In that same year, '74, in Hamburg, I got the breakthrough on this
structure. From then on I've been refining it and developing it, so that now it's a
complete system. *The Overtone Tree* is one aspect of *Creation*, and it takes about
40 minutes to play it. It's never been performed yet. I have a lot of *Creation* music
based on the Norse *Edda*: a book of songs based on the *Edda*, and I have a lot of
orchestral pieces. I'll be doing some of them from the *Creation* with a big orchestra in Switzerland. We're even using alphorns: I wrote a 16-part triple canon for
alphorns. I've got about four players who can read notes, who also double on
trumpet. We're going to use four if we can get them, and supplement the four
with French horns. We're working on getting a group of sixteen alphorns together. Until then I'll do the sixteen parts on the computer.

Q: Can you tell me about *Cosmos I* and *II*, the 1,000-part canons?

MOONDOG: They're actually a series of eight canons. Each one is 1,250 bars
long, and they all fit together by shifting the bar numbers, so it comes out to
1,000 parts.

Q: You'd actually need a thousand players to perform it?

MOONDOG: That's right. It takes about nine hours.

Q: Could that many players, no matter how skilled, be able to keep together? Isn't it the kind of thing that would sound better if it was played by machines?

MOONDOG: Well, it would be better on a machine. But I didn't write it with any idea of it ever being played — it was just a stunt of mine. What's much more practical is to do a concentration of that thousand-part canon into a hundred-part canon. Then it's playable by an orchestra.

Q: You've commented elsewhere on the value of the sampler in performing canons because of its precision.

MOONDOG: That's right — absolute synch. The sampler was made for this kind of music, and I'm very happy with it. But even so, I always like to work with live musicians whenever possible, even though there is the element of error.

Q: Is the sampler pretty much the only keyboard you're playing these days?

MOONDOG: Yes, that's the only playing I've been doing. On *Elpmas* I did all the keyboards. But when I'm leading with the saxophone group or with the orchestra, I conduct from a drum.

Q: Do you think you'll record any of your own organ or piano playing?

MOONDOG: No, I can't play the organ that well. But I have an organist, Fritz Storfinger, who did the organ on the three cds called "Tonality All The Way." I have a lot of piano music, but I don't really have a concert pianist who's working with me right now.

Q: Storfinger plays the piano very well on your *H'Art Songs*.

MOONDOG: Yes. He doesn't consider himself a pianist, although he's very good.
  We're doing "Do Your Thing" with Stephan Eicher who's a platinum-seller in France; he's got two platinum discs out, and he wants to sing my songs very badly. The only thing is he doesn't read notes. But he wants to sing "Do Your Thing" and he wants to sing "Fujiyama" at this Switzerland concert. He's very keen on getting into classical music. Peter Hoffman started out as a pop singer, and he got into Bayreuth singing Wagner. Stephan Eicher sounds like he wants to get into heavier music now too.

Q: Do you still compose first in Braille?

MOONDOG: Yes, I always work in Braille, and then I dictate the notes to Ilona Goebel. She's invaluable, that person — a marvelous help. She's been my eyes. She's just marvelous.

Q: In what sense is your "Logrundr No. XIX" a portrait of your mother?

MOONDOG: Well, my relation with my mother was very mixed. She was never really close to me but I loved her. She was a very beautiful woman to look at. But when I wrote this piece in Germany in '75, I said, "I'm going to relate that to my mother. There's something about this piece that makes me think about her." So I just called it "Portrait Of My Mother."

You know, I was a black sheep in the family, and she never really took me very seriously. But years later, when she got a copy of my Columbia album with the orchestra, my brother put it on — she was living with him — and she sat there and listened and said, "Did Louis write this?" She couldn't believe it that the black sheep could really, finally do something, you know? So I'm glad she found out that I could do something.

Q: Did your departure for New York also involve a break with the family religion, and thus strain your relation with your parents?

MOONDOG: My father and mother separated long before I came to New York, and they remarried. My brother was raised up by my grandmother mostly, and I was closest to my sister. She began reading philosophy to me when I was 21, and from that time on I broke away from Christianity completely. My sister had a very big influence on me, reading things to me which she thought I should know. In 1933, a year after my blindness, she read a book called *The First Violin*, and something in that book made me want to be a composer, and so from then on composition was the main thing.

Q: In *The H'Art Songs*, there's one song called "Choo Choo Lullaby," which sounds like it also holds some special memories for you.

MOONDOG: That's right, yes. Out in Wyoming we had a store, a trading post, in Fort Bridger, which was nine miles away from the railroad. The railroad station was called Carter, and I use that word "Carter" in there. At the time, Carter was president, so it has a double meaning: Carter, Wyoming, and Carter for President.

And those big engines, you could see them coming, the Union Pacific coming down the track. Enormous engines — I was so little and they'd come thundering by and then they'd stop and you'd get on. God, what a sound, what a sight, to see those big engines coming down at you. A fabulous sound, you know?

For that song, I tried to get the sound of the train whistle by using a chromatic harmonica: I'd blow in to get one sound and blow the other way to get a semitone lower, like it's in the distance — that Doppler effect. I had fun doing that.

Q: In the past, you've described yourself as a "European in exile," saying your heart and soul were in Europe. Now that you've been living there for almost 20 years, has Europe welcomed you in return?

MOONDOG: Yes, I'm making a bigger success here than in the States. It's growing every day. Like yesterday in Zurich there was a two-hour Moondog show, playing my music. Last week we had a 45-minute show playing almost all of the saxophone concert we did in one of our towns here. And I'm getting a lot of promotion in the biggest papers here, like the *Spiegel* and *Die Zeit* — all these big papers and magazines. And innumerable rave reviews. I mean, they seem to love me for some reason. I can't do anything wrong. It's not real.

Q: What about the music video you've been planning to do?

MOONDOG: There are several companies talking about doing it, but it hasn't come up to anything final yet. I'll be on the television with Stephan Eicher, something we filmed in Paris; it'll be out on satellite television in October, I think. That was just for the one number, "Paris."

We have had several television companies recording our saxophone group. One is in Stuttgart, and that was already on television. And Berlin is planning to do something.

Q: Last year in England, there was a series of concerts and seminars in celebration of your 75th birthday. I didn't know there was a following for your music there as well.

MOONDOG: I didn't expect that the people would react like they did in Dartington — that's a very conservative place. Yet the people were really shouting, like at a ball game! And I thought, "Gee, I didn't expect the English to do that."

Q: Your music is obviously feeding people something that they're not getting anywhere else.

MOONDOG: I get that feeling too. I'm filling some kind of a niche. I'm glad I'm in a position to do something about it.

Q: Has there been any feeling over this time of being an American in exile, or do you really feel at home now in Europe?

MOONDOG: My roots are here. I felt that for many years when I was in America, that I really belonged — historically, culturally, and every other way — to Europe. I feel like I like to be close to the things that happened historically, which mean a lot to me.

Q: I read that you went to Beethoven's birthplace and sat at his piano.

MOONDOG: That's right. I played on the piano where he wrote his sonatas. They allowed me to — normally they don't, but in my case they made an exception.

Q: That must have been an amazing experience.

MOONDOG: Oh it was, really. And I was in Mozart's home in Salzburg. The Salzburg association performed my First Symphony there with an orchestra from Czechoslovakia. And they let me stay in a villa there which was reserved for very special guests. They treated us lovely there.

Q: Your performance in Brooklyn at the tenth New Music America was the first time you'd been back to the States in some 15 years, wasn't it?

MOONDOG: Yes, I'd left in '74 and came back in '89. I was very happy at that. And I have tuxedo, will travel, anytime, anywhere — including America.

Q: Is there any chance you might be visiting us again soon?

MOONDOG: Oh, I would be very happy to, but I have to wait for the offers. If I build myself up big enough here, then they'll call their boy home.

Q: What would you speculate has been the effect on your composition of living in Europe all these years?

MOONDOG: Well, I just feel that this is the place to be doing it. If place has any meaning in one's life, then it has a lot of meaning for me. Because to be in the same area where all these things happened, artistically and culturally, which mean so much to me, I feel at home here.

Q: Would you have written something like the nine-hour canons if you had stayed in America?

MOONDOG: Oh, I could have, yes. I could work anywhere. The pieces I wrote on the street were generally short, out of practical reasons, as you can well imagine. If I have a choice, I'd like to work in a place as congenial as it is here. But nothing would stop me from writing.

COMPOSITIONS

symphonies

No. 1 in C Major
No. 2 in A Minor
No. 3 in F Major
No. 4 in D Minor
No. 5 in B-Flat Major
No. 6 in G Minor
No. 7 in E-Flat Major *Infield Symphony*
No. 8 in C Minor
No. 9 in A-Flat Major *The Big Russian*
No. 10 in F Minor *Agnus Mysticus*
No. 11 in D-Flat Major *Portrait Of My Mother*
No. 12 in B-Flat Minor
No. 13 in G-Flat Major *Little Big Horn*
No. 14 in E-Flat Minor
No. 15 in B Major
No. 16 in G-Sharp Minor

No. 17 in E Major *East Is East And West Is West*
No. 18 in C-Sharp Minor
No. 19 in A Major
No. 20 in F-Sharp Minor *Ilon Allein*
No. 21 in D Major *Logue Hill*
No. 22 in B Minor *The Little Russian*
No. 23 in G Major
No. 24 in E Minor
No. 25 in C Major *Creation 1*
No. 26 in A Minor *Surf Session*
No. 27 in F Major *The Northumbrian*
No. 28 in D Minor *The Celtic*
No. 29 in G Major
No. 30 in E Minor *Creation 2*
No. 31 in D-Flat Major *Novette No. 1*
No. 32 in A Minor
No. 33 in A-Flat Major
No. 34 in A Minor *Fachwerk*
No. 35 in C Major *Creation 3*
No. 36 in D Minor *Novette No. 2*
No. 37 in C Major *Shakespeare City*
No. 38 in A Minor *Creation 4*
No. 39 in C Major *Heath On The Heather*
No. 40 in G Minor *Weel, Weel, Dukel*
No. 41 in G Major *Creation 5*
No. 42 in G Minor *The Birds*
No. 43 in A-Flat Major *Novette No. 3*
No. 44 in G Minor *Pentatonic Pastorale*
No. 45 in D Major *The Chromasomatic*
No. 46 in D Minor *Creation 6*
No. 47 in B-Flat Major
No. 48 in F Minor *Novette No. 4*
No. 49 in C Major *Bam Jam*
No. 50 in A Minor *Rodzinski Symphony*
No. 51 in C Major *Notturno No. 1*
No. 52 in G Minor *Notturno No. 2*
No. 53 in G Major *Creation 7*
No. 54 in D Minor
No. 55 in E-Flat Major *Ecologia*
No. 56 in C Minor *The Great White Way*
No. 57 in E-Flat Major *Novette No. 5*
No. 58 in A Minor
No. 59 in C Major

No. 60 in D Minor *Novette No. 6*
No. 61 in Mixolydian Mode *The Overtone Tree*
No. 62 in Dorian Mode *Pythagoras And His Pyramid Of Numbers*
No. 63 in Mixolydian Mode *Creation 9*
No. 64 in A Minor
No. 65 in Phrygian Mode *Callisto*
No. 66 in G Minor
No. 67 in G Major
No. 68 in D Minor
No. 69 in C Major
No. 70 in D Minor
No. 71 in C Major
No. 72 in A Minor
No. 73 in C Major
No. 74 in A Minor *The Sidereal Sea*
No. 75 in C Major
No. 76 in Dorian Mode *Theon Of Smyrna*
No. 77 in Mixolydian Mode *The Two-Directionality Of Time*
No. 78 in C Minor *To The Spirit Of Life*
No. 79 in D Minor *To Archey Proto*
No. 80 in E Minor *Evolevolution*
No. 81 in Mixolydian Mode *Creation 8*

orchestra

Euphony No. 1 in C Major
Mini Sym
The Pentatonic Five
Viking I
Witch Of Endor
Irving Berlin — Always (Portiture)
Leonard Bernstein — There's A Place (Portiture)
Ernest Fuchs — Time Is Money (Portiture)

Symphoniques:
No. 1 *Portrait Of A Monarch*
No. 2 *Smoke Signals*
No. 3 *Ode To Venus*
No. 4 *Dwarf Mountain*
No. 5 *Kobo*
No. 6 *Good For Goodie*
No. 7 *Blue Moon*
No. 8 *Tom-Tom The Piper's Son*
No. 9 *Bird's Lament*

chamber music

Barn Dance
Bird Of Paradise
Bug On A Floating Leaf
Chaconne In C
Cinderella
Dance
Elf Dance
Flip
Fujiyama
Ground In A Flat
Honey Bunny
Kain And Abel
Love Song
Marimba No. 1 "The Rain Forest"
Marimba No. 2 "Seascape Of The Whales"
Marumba
Midgard Serpent
Peace Pipe
Rabbit Hop
Romany Road
Suite Equestria
Tonata In A Minor
Westward Ho!
Wind River Powwow

brass

Battery Park
Ber Jer
Charge Of The Light Brigade
Dirge
Draupner
EEC Song
Esprit De Corps
Fanfarier
Fuchs Fanfare
Galloping Guns
The Georges Three
Ger Eire
Heimdal Fanfare
Helvetian Hundred
Horr The Heroe Hunter

Hugin And Munin
Invocation
Lieutenant Long Knife
Lure Fanfare No. 1
Lure Fanfare No. 2
Napoleon's Retreat
Navigators Of The World
Nurnberg
Old Soldier
Onward And Upward
Pony Express
Ragnarok
Rough Riders
Saxon Hain
Skagarrak
Sitting Bull Custer
Tricorn
Triumphal Entry March
Varus
Verden 782
Waterloo
Wintertour De Force
Yankee Doodle Dixie

strings

As The Earth Turns
Berlin — Jerusalem
Canon In Asia Minor
Chaconne In C
Danse Orientale
Dark Eyes
Drops Of Water
Fantasia
Friska
Frost Flower
Gygg
Log In C Minor
Log In G Major
Love Song
Magic Ring
Speak Of Heaven
String Quartet No. 1 in C Major

String Quartet No. 4 in D Minor
Surf Session
Tryst

saxophone ensemble

Toot Suites:
No. 1 in F Major
No. 2 in G Minor
No. 3 in E-Flat Major
No. 4 in D Minor
No. 5 in F Major
No. 6 in C Minor
No. 7 in B-Flat Major
No. 8 in A Minor
No. 9 in B-Flat Major
No. 10 in C Minor
No. 11 in A-Flat Major
No. 12 in G Minor
No. 13 in B-Flat Major
No. 14 in C Minor
No. 15 in A-Flat Major
No. 16 in G Minor
No. 17 in E-Flat Major
No. 18 in D Minor
No. 19 in F Major
No. 20 in C Minor
No. 21 in B-Flat Major

Bumbo
D For Danny
Dog Trot No. 1
EEC Suite
Heath On The Heather
Mother's Whistler
Novette No. 1
Novette No. 6
Paris
Present For The Prez
Rabbit Hop
Sandalwood No. 1
Sax Max In B-Flat Major
Shakespeare City
Single Foot

Sax Paxes:
No. 1 in F Major *Blast Off*
No. 2 in D Minor *So Long Shorty*
No. 3 in D-Flat Major *Yumpin' Yemeny*
No. 4 in G Minor *Innuendo*

Troikans:
No. 1 in C Major
No. 2 in F Minor
No. 3 in F Major
No. 4 in D Minor
No. 5 in C Major
No. 6 in F Minor
No. 7 in E-Flat Major
No. 8 in D Minor
No. 9 in A-Flat Major
No. 10 in C Minor
No. 11 in E-Flat Major
No. 12 in D Minor
No. 13 in C Major
No. 14 in B-Flat Major
No. 15 in F Major
No. 16 in D Minor

meditation music

Yin And Yang Canons Nos. 1-9
(all 81-part canons in overtones)

Cosmos I in Mixolydian Mode
Cosmos II in Mixolydian Mode
(both 1,000-part canons)

piano

Art Of The Canon, Books I-V
(each book contains 25 pieces in all keys)

Carnival
Encore
Fur Fritz
Fur Ilona
The Great Canon In B-Flat Major
Jazz Book I
Kleine Walzerklange

Mazurka
Prelude And Fugue In D
Santa Fe
Sea Horse
Troubadour Harp Book

organ

Organ Book I Op. 76, Nos. 1-26
Organ Book II Op. 87, Nos. 1-26
Organ Book III Op. 94, Nos. 1-26

Bug On A Floating Leaf Op. 11, No. 4
Crescent Moon March Op. 11, No. 5
Loui Lis Op. 78, No. 16
Mirage Op. 11, No. 3
Oasis Op. 11, No. 1
Organ Duets Op. 88, Nos. 1-9
Sand Lily Op. 11, No. 2
Single Foot Op. 22, No. 3

from *Creation*:
Love Song
Midgard Serpent
Milky Way
Transformata
Wedding March
Wedding Scene
White Giant
World Of Mist

songs

1927	"Oh The Lonetree Bombadiers"
1942	"Electra"
1944	"Lullaby"
1946	"Moon Over Manhattan"
1946	"U.N. Hymn"
1947	"Moondog"
1948	"Jeannie"
1948	"Santa Fe"
1948	"Speak Of Heaven"
1950-70	*Madrigal Books I-X*
1957	"New York"
1970	"Bye Bye Manhattan"

1973	"In Vienna"
1973	"Paris"
1974	"Spruchweisheiten Aus Aller Welt"
1974	"Vocal Rounds"
1977	*H'Art Songs*
1978	*Canons And Couplets*
1979	*Hardin Cards*
1980	*EEC Suite*
1981	*Navigators Of The World*
1983	*Lineare Lieder*
1983	"Acetabularia"
1983	"Archey Proto In My Name"
1984	"Cock A Doodle Doo"
1985	*The Spirit Of Life*
1985	*Levolution Versus Evolution*
1985	"Prince Edward's Isle"
1988	"Cinderella"
1988	"Hnossa"
1988	"Out Of The Mouth"
1989	"Fancy"
1989	"I'm In Love"
1989	"I Plucked A Thorny Rose"
1989	"I Want A Waltz"
1989	"Let Me Love You"
1989	"Mockingbird"
1989	"New Amsterdam"
1989	"Nicole"
1989	"She Was Too Beautiful"
1989	"There's A Rose"
1989	"This One Wish"
1989	"Time Will Heal"
1989	"Waltzing"
1989	"Weeping Willow"
1990	"Out In Wyoming"
1990	"Shakespeare City"
1991	"I Love You More And More"
1992	"Nico Quicko"
1992	"The Only Life Worth Living"
1992	*The Ecologue*

All compositions published by Managarm, Buschstr. 55, 4353 Oer-Erkenschwick, Germany.

DISCOGRAPHY

1952
On The Streets Of New York
Mars A2 ep

1954
Moondog And His Friends
Epic 1002 ep

1956
Moondog
Prestige 7042 lp; 1741-1 lp, -2 cd (1991)

1957
More Moondog
Prestige 7069 lp; 006 cd (1991)

The Story Of Moondog
Prestige 7099 lp; 006 cd (1991)

1958
Tell It Again
Angel 65041 lp

1969
Moondog
Columbia 7335 lp; 44994 cd (1990)

1971
Moondog 2
Columbia 30897 lp; 44994 cd (1990)

1977
Louis T. Hardin (Moondog): Selected Works
Musical Heritage Society 3803 lp

1989
In Europe
Kopf 883 443-907 cd

H'Art Songs
Kopf 883 444-907 cd

A New Sound Of An Old Instrument
Kopf 883 445-907 cd

1991
Elpmas
Kopf 123314 cd

BIBLIOGRAPHY

Moondog Year Book I - VI
(one couplet for each day of the years)

Lotisami
(love poems)

Poetic Impressions
(autobiography in verse)

Thor The Nordoom
(soliloquy in couplet form)

Book Of Novas

The Overtone Tree
(a treatise on a tree)

The Overtone Continuum

Serpentine Sonnets, Book I

‾‾‾‾

All titles published by Managarm, Buschstr. 55, 4353
Oer-Erkenschwick, Germany.

photo: Gene Bagnato

PAULINE OLIVEROS / Introduction

PAULINE OLIVEROS was born in Houston, Texas, on May 30, 1932. As a child, she played piano, French horn, and accordion. After studying accordion with Willard Palmer, she entered the University of Houston as an accordion major in 1949. She also studied composition there with Paul Keopke. She left Houston at the end of her junior year in 1952, deciding to pursue her composition studies in California. She enrolled in San Francisco State College in 1954 and received her B.A. in composition in 1957. She also studied composition from 1954 through '60 with Robert Erickson at the San Francisco Conservatory of Music. In 1957 she began giving improvised performances with Terry Riley and Loren Rush.

In 1960 she formed Sonics with Ramon Sender, a center for concrete and electronic music, which was then part of the San Francisco Conservatory of Music. It became the San Francisco Tape Music Center in 1962, established by Sender and Morton Subotnick while Oliveros was in Europe. In the summer of 1966 she studied electronic music with Hugh LeCaine at the University of Toronto. From there she rejoined the Tape Music Center (which had relocated to Mills College), serving as its Director in 1966-67. From 1967 through '81 she taught electronic music and experimental studies at the University of California at San Diego. She has also been a Visiting Professor at York University in Toronto and at Stanford University.

By the end of the '60s, Oliveros began her groundbreaking series of compositions exploring different aspects of consciousness and meditation, producing her celebrated group of *Sonic Meditations* in 1971 and her series *Deep Listening Pieces* (1970-90). These works in turn led her to create compositions of a ritual and ceremonial nature, such as *Crow Two* (1974) and *Rose Moon* (1974).

Over the years, Oliveros's accordion playing has come to include a range of digital-delay processing with custom performance controls, creating what she has called "The Expanded Accordion." She has performed internationally with her instrument (recently tuned in just intonation), improvising with interactive electronics both as a solo artist and in collaboration with various musicians, including the Deep Listening Band which she formed with Stuart Dempster and Panaiotis in 1988.

Oliveros has received the Pacifica Foundation National Prize, an award from Holland's Gaudeamus Foundation, a Guggenheim Fellowship, and the city of Bonn's Beethoven Prize in 1977. She is currently the Artistic Director of the Pauline Oliveros Foundation in New York State, which seeks to provide administrative and technological suport for innovative artists. Her foundation has received funding from Meet the Composer, Mobius, the National Endowment for the Arts, the New York State Council of the Arts, the Higgins Foundation, the

209

White Light Foundation, and numerous individual contributors.

She is the author of many essays on music, gathered together in the volume *Software For People* (Smith Publications, 1984). She is also the subject of Heidi Von Gunden's book *The Music Of Pauline Oliveros* (Scarecrow Press, 1983). Oliveros has created scores for choreographers Ann Halprin and Merce Cunningham and for the theater collective Mabou Mines. She is a student of T'ai Chi and has a black belt in Shotokan-style karate.

I spoke with Pauline Oliveros at her home in Kingston, New York, on July 20, 1990. Our conversation covered a range of territory, with special emphasis being paid to her unique approach to electronic composition in the '60s, her development as an improviser on the accordion, and the nature of her solo and ceremonial compositions which employ meditation techniques.

PAULINE OLIVEROS / Interview

Q: I'd like to start with your group improvisations of the late '50s, with Terry Riley and Loren Rush. Were you playing accordion in that?

OLIVEROS: I played French horn, but I think I played some accordion. In our very first improvisations, I was playing horn and maybe some auxiliary instruments.

Q: Riley was playing piano?

OLIVEROS: Riley played the piano, Loren played the string bass and the koto, and I played French horn and probably the accordion. But I think I probably felt more challenged by the French horn because it was harder for me to play it in that context. Perhaps I played some accordion too — at this time I'm a little fuzzy. There are tapes of the improvisations at the UCSD library.

Q: I've read that being able to hear those tapes after having played together was very useful for that group's development as improvisers.

OLIVEROS: As far as I'm concerned, the tape recorder was the most revolutionary tool of the time and has continued to be that. To be able to record and get very close feedback on what you do has improved the musicianship of everyone, from the most traditional performers and composers. The sessions that we had were really a revelation. You'd think nothing of it now, but it had great impact at the time because none of us were too much on talking about what we were going to do. We didn't do that, we'd just sit down and play together, and then listen back and then we would talk about it. We were always kind of amazed at what came out.

Q: Any chance of those tapes being released?

OLIVEROS: Well, they're really historical documents. I really don't know. I haven't heard them in 25 years or so. It's been a long time — they might sound really funny and very dated.

Q: I'm curious about the kind of playing you folks were getting into. It wouldn't have been in a jazz style, would it?

OLIVEROS: No, it wasn't that. It was kind of a synthesis of each of our individual styles.

Q: Which you were just beginning to develop at that time.

OLIVEROS: Right, exactly. So you'd hear referential phrases, I'm sure, but the gesture was new.

   Terry and Loren and I did those improvisation sessions actually to accommodate Terry. He had to do a film score in a hurry, so we did some five-minute tracks for him. After that, we just were interested in the idea of playing together, and we did that for a while, maybe for a year, off and on. Then Terry got involved with La Monte Young and they were doing some projects together, and

Loren was off doing whatever he was doing, and I got busy teaching musicians to use improvisation.

Then Ramon Sender and I started doing improvisations together. Ramon and I started Sonics, and that was really the start of the San Francisco Tape Music Center. We did a lot of group improvisations, and then Morton Subotnick joined us. He and Ramon co-founded the San Francisco Tape Music Center — I was away in Europe for a while, and when I came back I became involved again. Up until 1965 we did concerts and always did an improvisation on the concert, in one configuration or another.

Q: Did the French horn move out of the picture by that time?

OLIVEROS: No, it stayed in the picture, and the accordion was in there as much as ever; more perhaps than in those initial sessions with Terry and Loren. I think probably I felt in those early sessions that the piano and the accordion were not necessarily as compatible as the horn and the piano.

Q: What were your feelings as a composer in the '50s toward the accordion? Were you writing pieces for it even then?

OLIVEROS: Oh yes, I composed for it.

Q: Did you ever feel there was something outré about it in a new-music context, or did it always seem perfectly available?

OLIVEROS: It was perfectly — you know, why not? I knew about the stereotype that existed for the accordion, which really came about because of television: In the early days, the public image of the accordion was fixed by Lawrence Welk and Myron Floren. But that was a media image of the accordion.

Q: It certainly wasn't the way you came to that instrument.

OLIVEROS: No, not at all. Of course, in the Midwest there was a lot of stereotypical responses to the accordion because it was used so often in the polka bands and so on. The chairman of the department at UCSD at the time, Will Ogdon, used to be known as the Accordion King of the Midwest, but he never would play the accordion!

Q: It's ironic that the accordion should have an image that would make it seem inappropriate for new music, when so much of your work as an electronic composer is directly related to your music with the accordion. From playing resultant tones in real-time performances of electronic music, to your work now with the expanded accordion, where the two are literally combined, you've always seemed aware of one medium's connection to the other. But was there a time when you regarded electronics as something really divorced from what you'd done before?

OLIVEROS: Well, it wasn't like a foreign thing because of the memories and vocabulary I'd had of electronic sound from early childhood on, which really came from radio. My grandfather had a crystal radio he'd want me to listen to, and he'd be tuning it and it would be full of static and all this funny stuff, and I was really fascinated. My father had a short-wave radio which I used to play with — I liked those whistles in the tunings, and also all the static and interference and what have you. So those sounds were already in my memory bank. My mother bought a Sears, Roebuck wire recorder in the '40s —

Q: What kind of recorder is that?

OLIVEROS: It's a recorder, but you use a spool of wire instead of tape.

Q: And the wire unravels off the spool —

OLIVEROS: I'll say it does! The wire would spill out all over the place. And if it broke, you'd tie a knot in it to keep going. But that was the '40s, and I was already doing some recording and listening to it. Then in 1953, my mother again gave me a tape recorder, bless her heart. She was always interested in the new technology, and that was the opening thing on the market for home use. They weren't available to the public before then, really, except for the wire recorder.

So that tool of recording was present in my life, along with the radio. Then in the end of the '50s I began to think about electronic music, with Mort Subotnick and Ramon. We were all itching to work with the medium. We'd heard some pieces from Germany and France, and some Ussachevsky and Cage. That's how we came to start Sonics and then the San Francisco Tape Music Center, because there wasn't any place where you could do anything. So we put it all together as a kind of cooperative and began to make pieces. It's a long way from where we are now.

Q: It's interesting that you mention the short-wave and crystal radios; there again, you can create and manipulate the sounds in real time.

OLIVEROS: That's right. That's always been important to me, hands-on performance control. Because that's what's fun and what's interesting. I made a lot of tapes — there's a lot of tape music sitting in the closet — but I really wasn't so much interested in that result, as in having done it in real time as a performance. But it wasn't really feasible to drag all that stuff onto the stage. You could do it, but it would mean a lot of schlepping and a lot of problems. So studio insulation prevailed for a while, and a lot of people were caught up and are still in the studio instead of in performance. Some are still enamoured of the studio possibilities — combined with performance maybe, or maybe not. But for me, the live performance is the life of music.

Q: The electronic performances available on recordings, *Bye Bye Butterfly* and *I Of IV*, are both improvisations. Had you mapped out beforehand certain structural things you wanted to accomplish in them?

OLIVEROS: No, I didn't do that. What I did was map out the instrument that I wanted to play these pieces. The design of how they would come into existence was what I mapped, but not the content at all. So it was a kind of performance architecture using tape machines and understanding certain operations in the circuitry which was non-linear. I actually delighted in the notion of a non-linear system for performance, where my reactions to the material would have to be instantaneous. I didn't have time to think about it in rational terms, but had to act in the moment. That's been the key element of my work.

I had been working on this very simple idea of resultant or combination tones, which came from my experience playing the accordion. I've said somewhere that I was staring at those sine-wave generators and seeing that they could go beyond audio range, and somewhere along the line the light bulb went off: "Oh!" My set-up was relatively simple, compared to some of the other things that people did. I used a couple of generators set above audio, in the 30,000-cycle range, or maybe 40,000, amplified the results, and sent it into a tape machine and the delay machine. But I would count on not only the resultants from the oscillators, but also from the bias-oscillator on the tape recorder, which would also get into the act and make a lot of very interesting sounds.

Q: In *I Of IV*, the set-up is also going through a keyboard.

OLIVEROS: That was because I was at the University of Toronto and they had a more sophisticated setup: They had a bank of 12 oscillators. The Tape Music Center was funk — we were lucky if we had three or four oscillators. But at the University of Toronto they had a bank of 12, and each one was on a keyboard, so you could key them in and you could also manipulate the dials. The Hewlett Packard oscillator or Lafayette generator had a big dial on the front, which you'd have to T-U-R-N to sweep the audio range; then there would be a range switch, to switch from times 1 to times 10 to times 100, to get into the different ranges. Well, when I did my combination-tone technique of beating two oscillators together, all you'd have to do is just barely shift the dial and the whole audio range would sweep by. It was like a fine-tuning thing then, and I could get a whole big interaction of all these beating tones. And I'd key them in and out for *I Of IV*.

Q: Was it a discovery process simply to cope with the equipment, or did you have time to work with the setup until you felt you were ready to record a piece?

OLIVEROS: I remember very well about *I Of IV*. I went into the Toronto studio for the first time, and I was just dying to set it up like I had done before at the Tape Music Center. I set everything up and got started, and it took me either a day or the next day — I was there for maybe six weeks, for the summer session; I studied with Hugh LeCaine. It was very soon, maybe the second day, that I got what I wanted and really got into it. I did four tapes that day, so this was one of four.

Reynold Weidenaar was there — he's at NYU and does video and electronic music — and I remember he came in and I was just dying laughing with these sounds. In *I Of IV* there's a very big climactic sweeping sound, and when that happened I was so excited I was dying laughing.

Q: A lot of electronic works of the same time are instantly recognizable as belonging to a specific era, almost in the same sense as hearing ragtime piano. But these pieces of yours still sound new and surprising — that's the novel technique you've described, but it's also the fact that they're being played.

OLIVEROS: I remember a review of *I Of IV* in some magazine, and some guy was talking about it in very positive terms, like you are, but then all of a sudden he said, "Well, it must not be any good, though, because it must have been just thrown together in real time." That kind of attitude still prevails in an academic sense, that you have to construct these pieces very carefully. Well, I do construct them very carefully, but at a very different level.

Q: The instrument is constructed carefully.

OLIVEROS: That's right, the instrument is constructed carefully, so that I can interact with it at a deep level.

Q: The technology itself tends to make people think that they have to construct everything in the music, that the equipment cannot be used directly. To have bypassed that the way you did is amazing.

OLIVEROS: That's always been my direction. Occasionally I've done it otherwise, but I'm much happier with the results when I'm able to have this free-floating interaction with the material.

Q: And again, this approach to electronics seems to be a direct outgrowth of your work with the accordion.

OLIVEROS: Yes, it is. Now even more so, as you've already recognized, with the expanded accordion.

   I remember it was 1967 that I proposed a piece to myself, which was just called simply *Accordion*. What I wanted to do was to play with all these tape delays, but for one reason or another I didn't manage to do it. I was going to do it for a program at the University of Illinois, but it didn't work out and we did some other things instead. I had the idea quite early, but not the means to really do it until later, in the '80s; I got my first digital delay processors and began to work with them in 1983.

Q: The retuning of the accordion in just intonation was later than that?

OLIVEROS: Yes, 1987, I think.

Q: Was that tough?

OLIVEROS: It took 10 days for a master tuner to do it. These are free metal reeds set in wood blocks, and they have to be scratched in the center to flatten them, or filed on the end to sharpen. And you can't hear it in process, like you can tighten a string and hear it; the reed is guess and golly. A tuner has bellows to blow the reed, but he has to go back and forth.

Q: So this accordion's keyboard still has 12 tones to the octave?

OLIVEROS: Here's the way it goes. The right hand is tuned differently from the left hand, but there are six tones in common: B, C, D, E, F, G. Those are in agreement but the rest of the intervals are not. You tune the fifths, and in the right hand it's a seven-limit tuning, so you tune the sevenths and thirds — fifths, sevenths, and thirds. The Eb and Ab are the flattest; Db next; and the Bb is quite nice; the F and Eb seventh are really bluesy — they have a really beautiful sound; the A natural is flat, but sharper than those other steps I was mentioning. If you go C, D, E, F, that's a good tetrachord; C, D, E, F, G is OK; but then when you go A, B, the A is out, it's flat to the tempered system. That's the right hand and it's very melodic; it has really nice tendencies for melody. In the left hand, Db, Eb, Gb, Ab, A natural, Bb all disagree more or less with the right hand.

Q: How much renegotiating was there for you once you started playing the retuned instrument?

OLIVEROS: It took a while to get used to it and to hear how to use it, but it worked for me right away. It was really beautiful just to hear those different colors. There's still plenty of discovery.

There are two sets of the same kind of reed, same range, but they're tuned two cents different, so that you get a kind of vibrato out of that. When you add that in, you can get some very beautiful combinations of beats.

Q: Was the retuning based on certain ideas about the importance of just tunings, or was it more a matter of what you wanted to hear on the accordion?

OLIVEROS: I had been thinking about tuning it in just intonation for some time. The opportunity came up when the Good Sound Band was playing with the Good Sound Foundation, and Loren Rush had two pianos and wanted to tune them, one in five-limit and one in seven-limit. I have a seven-limit right hand and a five-limit left hand, so that I can play with both pianos. And Stu Dempster of course can tune to any system: He's got one of the most precise ears in the universe and can beam right in to any tuning. It's really beautiful.

Shabda Owen is the tuner. He does Terry's tunings and he had worked with La Monte also. It's kind of interesting, isn't it, that from the 1950s we're still interacting with one another and influencing one another, but everybody is their own person. One can go an individual way and come together to make this synthesis, which is a lot of fun.

Q: The retuning of the accordion is also part of your interest in instrument building, which is another constant in your work. I'm referring to the electronic set-ups we've discussed, as well as the "Applebox" pieces from the '50s — which were literally apple crates that were mic'd?

OLIVEROS: Yes, I mic'd the box and put little things on the box and the box would resonate.

Q: The expanded accordion is another kind of instrument building.

OLIVEROS: And it's still growing. I started with two delay processors and then added two more. Now there are eight and I can see it going further. I use foot pedals to control the delay time, which I don't necessarily want to give up; but at Banff in February I had a three-week residency where I worked with a computer programmer and had a program doing that, so I could do foot motions you can't do with your feet — Superfoot! You could go instantaneously without a sweep, which sometimes you liked to have, and just stay there if you want. It could also do some fast oscillation. So the program was really interesting. I had four people playing, and Panaiotis was singing and routing all the signals. Actually, the digital interface was part of a system that he's working on, which is called the Pan Paw. With this foot control you can do all the mouse movements on a Macintosh: One foot can move the cursor and the other foot can do click and drag and double click. We used just the digital interface to control the four lexicon delay processors; they're old ones, not MIDI. I like them and I haven't been able to find any way to replace them yet with any of the current stuff. They have an analog section as well, so you can do modulation. They're very interesting and they sound good — I haven't found anything that sounds any better.

Working with the computer program is in an early stage, but it's a very interesting process. Again, it's a live interaction; the program is going but you interact with it. So it can do some things that you can't do, and it challenges your performance to another level. I expect to keep on going with that.

Q: New music needs new instruments.

OLIVEROS: Yes, it always has, even traditionally. It's just that we're in an accelerated time, an accelerated era, so things are happening faster and so you see instruments coming into existence faster than previous times. There's always been evolution of instruments — if you just look into music history, it's there. Some of the origins of instruments are lost in time and mythology; you get into some pretty weird places if you try to find the origin of the gong, for instance. But old instruments are always being modified. Keyboard instruments have a really interesting development and evolution.

Q: In their tuning as well as in their actual construction.

OLIVEROS: Tuning, social implications — from playing the virginal to playing the piano is quite something, with the pianoforte being a loud instrument and the virginal being very quiet and intimate. There are a lot of reasons to invent instruments.

Q: Do you also take into consideration how readily others can play the new instruments that you're designing?

OLIVEROS: I'm very interested in untrained musicians being able to play as well as professional musicians. In Banff, after this residency we set up the system: I was playing accordion, Panaiotis was singing, Michael Century was playing electric piano, and Trevor Tureski was playing marimba. Then we had a day when people could come in and just play. And some people didn't have any musical training. They sat down and played a sound and heard things coming back, and then played some more, and pretty soon they were playing and they just had a great time. So I think the development of this instrument could be very useful to help children and other people get to music-making really quickly.

Q: A so-called non-musician is someone who isn't trained to use a certain piece of equipment, not someone who is non-musical.

OLIVEROS: That's right, exactly. I'm very interested in the idea of creative music for kids from as early as possible. If kids could do improvisation and creative music-making as well as learning folk songs and traditional music, there would be a very different environment for all of this.

Kids can be artists. They can't be bankers and chemists and all that, but they can be artists, and they could be supported to be artists all the way through their lives, as well as doing other things. It's not just to have another kind of audience development, but it's to have creative expression for all people. And it could happen, it could be available, but it hasn't been a concern of educators. It could be.

Q: In a sense, your working with new instruments puts you in a similar, "untrained musician" position.

OLIVEROS: Yes, I was trying to put myself there. That was interesting for me to do, to try to trick myself into not doing habitual things.

Q: And to discover the real nature of your own musicianship.

OLIVEROS: Right. It's interesting to be in that beginner state, where you're not prejudiced about it, you're not premeditating, you're just open and interacting with what is.

Q: One published excerpt from your dream journals describes a visit to Harry Partch. Did you know him?

OLIVEROS: Yes, I knew Harry well. He lived not far from me and I used to take carrot juice over there once in a while, because I had a juicer.

Q: Your own interest in working with just intonation predated your exposure to his music?

OLIVEROS: The first time I ever came into contact with a justly tuned instrument was in 1953, when I played briefly in his own ensemble for *Oedipus*. That was when he was at Gate 5 in Sausalito.

I didn't last very long in the ensemble. I was a keyboard player, but when I'd look at a note and hit a key — if I hit a C, I was thinking I'd hear a C. I couldn't change my reflexes, so I'd get confused. And Harry was not patient enough to spend the time for me to learn how to do what he wanted. So I just retreated from it. But it was a very amazing experience.

Q: Did that experience lead you to feel you could start designing and building your own instruments, or had those ideas already been there for you?

OLIVEROS: I think those ideas were in the air. Harry's work was certainly part of it, but there were other things. I spent a lot of time with found objects and in junkyards. Downstairs, I still have telephone dial-changers, these long brass things with slots and a phone plug on the end. (This is ancient telephone equipment now.) I clamped those rods to the beams inside a grand piano and bowed them, and they made wailing sounds.

Q: No matter how composers alter their musical materials, they stick to the situation in which the musicians play while the audience listens. You've created pieces that actually utilize the audience, which is a very radical idea. How radically did it affect the way you compose?

OLIVEROS: I understood a very basic thing, and that is that if I listened well and maintained a listening presence, it would transmit to the audience and they'd listen. That's all. And that's a profound thing. It's an all-or-nothing, life/death reality. If you for one moment start thinking about your grocery list, well, you've lost the whole thing.

Q: Did you ever regret the results you got from an audience? Ever feel that they didn't join in the spirit of the piece, or that they did things wrong?

OLIVEROS: If I did, I've forgotten. Most of the time I'm interested in whether or not they're able to overcome their doubts or timidity or blocks, because generally something happens. I've found that people go away thinking about it, and they'll tell me what they thought and how it affected them. So I think, well, something's happening, inside. Whether it manifested as well as it could outside is not so much important as that a concept was exposed and it clicked.

Q: Did you ever get an audience that wouldn't participate?

OLIVEROS: Once. And it wasn't that they wouldn't; they were, but they were waiting for me to do it so they could copy it. I introduced a student group in North Dakota to this — I don't remember which particular meditation we were going to do — but I had forgotten to tell them that I was just going to listen. I've learned over the years how to do this, and that's what I always do now; I put myself in the role of audience because I don't want to influence how they do it at all. But they were waiting for me to initiate this and nothing ever happened. So that was great information, wasn't it?

Q: It got you clearer on how to position the information.

OLIVEROS: Yes. And that's what happens all the time. I get feedback and then restate things. I'm always restating these meditations, and each situation you think, "Well, how am I going to present it?" My presentation of these things has a wide range of conditions and numbers of people, everything from one to 6,000.

Q: Where was 6,000?

OLIVEROS: Michigan Womyn's Music Festival.

Q: That must have been pretty special.

OLIVEROS: Yes, it was. That's the largest group that I've ever dealt with at one time. It was amazing.

Q: What did you do with them?

OLIVEROS: The *Tuning Meditation.* There was just waves of sound. This was outdoors and 6,000 women...!

Q: What persuaded you that audiences were as available to you as musicians and their instruments?

OLIVEROS: I was teaching courses in the nature of music at the University of California. These courses had maybe 100 students or more, and they were not music students, they were general students. The reason I could teach at that university was that I invented whatever I taught; I wasn't fitting into a curriculum, I was helping make a curriculum. We wanted to involve the students in any of the classes that were taught in the practice of making music. So instead of teaching a music-appreciation course, you were teaching them to invent their own: to do improvisation, to do tape music, to do graphic scores, and so on. It was a hands-on course. I made some pieces then for the students to do, and that's how I got started. Then I had a small gathering of women which I worked with at home, once a week, and that's where my *Sonic Meditations* got started. I would compose a meditation for each evening, and we would do a lot of other things — journals, massage, and so forth — working with one another. It went for a couple of years and a lot of material came out of it. Then I did a project at the Center for Music Experiment where we did meditations every day for nine weeks, two hours a day, and had different people come and work with us. A lot came out of that too, knowledge and experience and so on.

Q: When I use the word "meditation" regarding my own practices, I'm referring to the emptying of my mind. You're obviously dealing with more than that in your *Sonic Meditations* or in, say, the score of *Crow Two*, which includes people meditating as part of the performance. How are you using the term?

OLIVEROS: I use it in a lot of different ways. There are different meditational structures and forms — just examine traditional religions for their meditational practices. I'll take two examples, one is yoga and one is Zen. In yoga, the high practitioner is generating large-amplitude alpha waves in a meditative state, and if you introduce a stimulus, there'll be no response; the alpha wave will stay with the same amplitude. If you do the same thing to a Zen practitioner who is just as accomplished in generating high-amplitude alpha, the brain wave changes to beta instantaneously and then goes back. That's a very large difference: The Zen practitioner is balanced between inner and outer, and the yoga shuts down the outside world. These are profound differences in structure. If you analyze these different pieces, the *Sonic Meditations* and *Deep Listening Pieces* (which is another collection of them, about 30 pieces), each one has different uses and different forms. One piece might require a yogiclike state, another one might require a Zenlike state, another one might require going from one to the other. So it's exercising these faculties we have. But the overall use of the term meditation means for me to stay with it, whatever it is.

Q: So that however one is called on to focus the mind, it stays where it's been directed, even if that direction involves changing the nature of the attention; the mind stays focused on what it's doing.

OLIVEROS: Yes, right. So that's a kind of different use of the word, I think. Meditation is just a word, but filling it out is a map of a lot of different things.

Q: What would you say were the most important things you learned as a composer through your work with meditation?

OLIVEROS: Well, what happened was that I learned to compose at a different level. Instead of composing the content, I was composing the outside form and giving people tools to participate in the creative process. And that felt good to me, and it also sharpened my own tools.

Q: Have these experiences led to changes in your musicianship even when you're not involved specifically with meditational techniques?

OLIVEROS: Oh yes, I think so. I think probably the main change is in the expanded listening; the understanding of listening to be my protection, and that it's also my access to not only my own inner development, but also to my interaction with others.

Q: The notion that awareness itself, for performers and listeners, can be adjusted over the course of a piece, that it's another musical parameter available to the composer and not simply a constant, is a real revelation.

OLIVEROS: Well, it was for me!

Q: Had you heard these ideas used musically in other contexts, in religious or ceremonial works from other countries?

OLIVEROS: No, it truly came from my own exploration. And then I began to recognize certain aspects of it in other music, or in my own response to other music.

Q: When you began working in this area in the '70s, it must have been seen by some people as entering into an area that was actually non-musical. Did you ever feel that you had in some sense given up music or moved beyond it?

OLIVEROS: Oh, I didn't feel I had given up music, not at all. But there was a certain atmosphere around with my colleagues and so on, which was like, "What is she doing?" It seemed trivial, maybe, or too simple. But what I found more and more was that the simpler I got, the more complex it was. The process of analysis unfolds layer after layer from the results of some very simple things.

Q: Those complaints of simpleness or triviality leveled against your use of meditation are the same carps one would hear regarding your use of the audience or of untrained musicians.

OLIVEROS: In some of these pieces you can put untrained and professional musicians together and they can advance at their own pace, their own level — there's something for them to do. Take a simple meditation like the *Tuning Meditation*, which says use a long tone on one breath, sing a tone, and then match a tone from someone else as exactly as possible, and then sing a new tone and keep alternating between those two things until you've communicated with everybody you possibly can. Well, all right, those instructions are sort of offhand and very simple, but what happens is, if you're going to sing a tone, first you've got to focus inward and find a tone and then sing it. And then if you're going to match someone else, well you're going to have to listen for it, and then match it. And then you're going to have to go back in, and then you're going to have to decide when you listen again, "have I communicated with that one or with somebody else?" You begin to think about the analysis of that, and it gets very complicated. The result of that is you'll hear a common tone that sort of shifts around at times, then you'll hear something new come in and the direction changes — it's a musical structure which you can pretty well recognize.

Q: What you're describing here is the movement back and forth between focal and global attention, something that you've dealt with extensively both as a composer and in writing about music. These fundamental ideas have implications far beyond music, yet they tend not to be taught or even recognized in the schools.

OLIVEROS: Our education focuses on outer world, finding realization through understanding the outside world. So whatever goes on inside is your own business and don't bother me.

Q: There's also the implication that nothing goes on inside, that one is simply a repository to be filled up with facts and data.

OLIVEROS: That's true. And these are dangerous ideas in terms of the current establishment of education.

Q: I was fascinated by the use of telepathic communication in your music, both between performers and between audience and performers. In *Phantom Fathom*, you attempted to transmit to the dreams of the audience the visual image of an elephant and the aural image of a conch-shell trumpet?

OLIVEROS: Yes.

Q: How'd that turn out?

OLIVEROS: It turned out really interestingly. There were two or three hits on the elephant and also on the trumpet.

Q: How were you able to send them that?

OLIVEROS: I just thought of it. It's not a big deal; you just visualize the elephant and hear the sound.

Q: Would you set aside a certain amount of time each day to do it?

OLIVEROS: Once it's in the channel, it's in.

Q: You only had to do it on your end once?

OLIVEROS: Yes.

Q: Had the audience been requested to do something on their end?

OLIVEROS: Just to pay attention to their dreams.

Q: Nothing beyond that, in terms of trying to tune in to you at a specific time or in a special way?

OLIVEROS: No, nothing like that. Time doesn't work like that in that dream world.

Q: There's obviously information flowing between people on that level all the time, and to use it purposefully to communicate images and feelings is a very powerful idea.

OLIVEROS: Yes, it is. It's one that needs care and consideration and not manipulation; it's the opposite of manipulation and control. It's open reception. And the fear around such a thing has to do with that vulnerable state of receptivity. When we have so many people involved in power and control, you don't really want to be very receptive to that. If you have people who only want to manipulate and control, and don't want to receive and share or be vulnerable, then this can be a very terrifying state to be in, and it needs protection.

Q: You've taught in different universities over the years, but now have left that. Do you have private students?

OLIVEROS: No. I would, probably, if anybody asked me. But I'm not advertising for it.

Q: Is it primarily as a musician that you support yourself?

OLIVEROS: Yes, it's performance, commissions, consulting — piecing it together.... I don't know how I do it! I don't know how I did it for 15 years before I had a job. But I pieced my living together and somehow paid the bills, so now I'm doing that again: piecing it together and wondering how it gets done. I don't know.

Q: It seems that whatever kind of music one makes, if a composer isn't a teacher or a performer, it's very difficult to get by.

OLIVEROS: I couldn't do it without my accordion. That's really true.

Q: All of which makes it all the harder to be a composer.

OLIVEROS: Well, it depends on how you do it. I don't do it the way others do. I'm composing my music in the moment, with my instrument — often. I mean, I also write things. I have a commission now with Susan Marshall's dance company, and I'm working on a tape piece — it has to be on tape. It very likely will represent some departures for me, in doing multitrack work and editing, which I haven't spent much time doing.

Q: How important is it to you to get your earlier theatrical or ceremonial scores performed again? Do you keep trying to get them out, or do you feel that once they're done, they're on their own?

OLIVEROS: Well, I'm just like any other fickle composer: You're always interested in your most recent project. I'm not averse to that, but I prefer that somebody else produce them. I've paid my dues in schlepping and gofering to get them produced.

Pieces Of Eight is hard to put together. Bob Hughes, a San Francisco composer, conductor, and musician, a wonderful person, had played contrabassoon in the original production of *Pieces Of Eight*, and wanted to put that together again. So I said, "Oh. OK, Bob." He started getting into what he had to put together, and it was a real problem. It was hard to do. Some of the things I still had. The Beethoven statue is in the UCSD archive. This woman, Sandra Batzle, made this gorgeous pâpier-mâché bust of Beethoven with eyes that light up. Her husband put the battery for the lights inside the frame, and he did a very cockamamie job of it, because he thought it would be just a throwaway deal, right? And that bust has been all over the place, and the worst problem has been trying to get the lights to work. But her rendering of that was wonderful.

Q: The ceremonial works have their own special performance demands. *Rose Moon* is for an entire cycle of the moon, from when it rises to when it sets.

OLIVEROS: Yes, there have been three-hour performances of that one. It hasn't been done outdoors for the moon; that would be another deal. It could be done without an audience, it could be just done. As far as I'm concerned, I feel like I'm performing it even if there's nobody there. I feel the presence of the environment or whatever it is. I feel presence, so I always perform to that presence.

COMPOSITIONS

1951	*Ode To A Morbid Marble* for piano	MS
1951	*Undertone* for violin and piano	MS
1952	*Song For Horn And Harp And Dance Band*	MS
1952	*Song For Piano*	MS
1953	*Prelude And Fugue* for string quartet	MS
1953	*Fugue For Piano*	MS
1954	*Essay For Piano*	MS
1955	*Trio For Clarinet, Horn, And Bassoon*	MS
1956	*Serenade For Viola And Bassoon*	MS
1957	*Concert Piece For Accordion*	MS
1957	*Three Songs For Soprano And Horn*	MS
1957	*Three Songs For Soprano And Piano*	SP
1958	*Cock A Doodle Dandy* theater music	MS
1958	*4H Club* film score	MS
1958	*Tom Sawyer* theater music	MS
1958	*View From The Bridge* theater music	MS
1959	*18 Children's Pieces For Accordion*	MS
1959	*Horn Etudes* for French horn	MS
1960	*Variations For Sextet* for flute, clarinet, trumpet, French horn, cello, and piano	SP
1961	*Trio For Flute, Piano, And Page Turner*	SP
1961	*Trio For Accordion, Trumpet, And String Bass*	SP
1961	*1000 Acres* for string quartet	MS
1961	*Sound Patterns* for mixed chorus	ET
1961	*Time Perspectives* for four-channel tape	MS
1962	*Lulu* theater music	MS
1963	*Art In Woodcut* film score	MS
1963	*Outline For Flute, Percussion, And String Bass*	MP
1963	*Outline For Septet* for accordion, trombone, trumpet, double bass, piano, and two percussionists	MS
1964	*Fifteen For An Ensemble Of Performers* for instruments, singers, actors, and dancers	MS
1964	*Pieces Of Eight* for flute, oboe, French horn, contrabassoon, bass clarinet, trumpet, trombone, clarinet, and conductor	SP
1964	*Fifteen For Four Dancers*	MS
1964	*Five For Trumpet And Dancer*	MS
1964	*Seven Passages For Elizabeth Harris* for two-channel tape	MS
1964	*Apple Box* for amplified apple box and small objects	MS
1964	*Apple Box Orchestra* for amplified apple box, mallets, and small sound producers	MS
1965	*Rock Symphony* for live electronics and tape-delay system	MS
1965	*Bye Bye Butterfly* for two-channel tape	MS

1965	*Mnemonics I* for two-channel tape	MS
1965	*Mnemonics II* for two-channel tape	MS
1965	*Mnemonics V* for two-channel tape	MS
1965	*Duo For Accordion And Bandoneon With Possible Mynah Bird Obligato, Seesaw Version*	MS
1965	*Candelaio* music for San Francisco Mime Troupe	MS
1965	*Cat O' Nine Tails* theater music	MS
1965	*Covenant* film score	MS
1965	*The Chronicles Of Hell* music for San Francisco Mime Troupe	MS
1965	*The Exception And The Rule* music for San Francisco Mime Troupe	MS
1965	*Before The Music Ends* for two-channel tape	MS
1965	*A Theater Piece* for 15 actors, film, projections, players, and two-channel tape	MS
1965	*George Washington Slept Here Too* for amplified violin, film, projections, players, and two-channel tape	SN
1965	*I've Got You Under My Skin* for solo percussionist and Bat Man	MS
1965	*Light Piece For David Tudor* for electronically modified piano, lights, film, and four-channel tape	MS
1966	*The C(s) For ONCE* for trumpets, flutes, voices, organ, and three tape recorders	BMI
1966	*Big Mother Is Watching You* for two-channel tape	MS
1966	*5000 Miles* for two-channel tape	MS
1966	*Jar Piece* for two-channel tape	MS
1966	*NO MO* for two-channel tape	MS
1966	*I Of IV* for two-channel tape	MS
1966	*II Of IV* for two-channel tape	MS
1966	*The Day I Disconnected The Erase Head And Forgot To Reconnect It* for two-channel tape	SP
1966	*Ultra Sonic Studies In Real Time* for two-channel tape	MS
1966	*The Bath* for dancers and tape-delay system	MS
1966	*Accordion* for amplified accordion with tape-delay system and eight channels	MS
1966	*Hallo* for electronically modified piano, two tape-delay systems, violins, voice, actor, light projections, and dancers	MS
1966	*Participle Dangling In Honor Of Gertrude Stein* for mobile, film, and two-channel tape	MS
1966	*Theater Piece For Trombone Player*	SP
1967	*Lysistrata* theater music	MS
1967	*Circuitry For Percussion And Light*	MS
1967	*Alien Bog* for two-channel tape	MS
1967	*Beautiful Soop* for two-channel tape	MS
1967	*Bog Bog* for two-channel tape	MS
1967	*Bog Road With Bird Call Patch* for two-channel tape	MS

1967	*Engineers Delight* for piccolo, seven conductors (not electronic) for amplification of program sources, four turntables, and modulation	MS
1967	*Mills Bog* for two-channel tape	MS
1968	*"I Hear A Boy Singing ... "*	MS
1968	*O Ha Ah* for mixed chorus	MS
1968	*Some Sound Observations* for two-channel tape	MS
1968	*Double Basses At Twenty Paces* for two basses, their seconds, and a referee with slides and tape	SP
1968	*Evidence For Competing Bimolecular And Termolecular Mechanisms In The Hydrochlorination Of Cyclohexine* theater piece for specialized and unspecialized performers	MS
1968	*Festival House* for orchestra, chorus, mimes, films, and projections	MS
1968	*Night Jar* for viola d'amore, tape, film, and mime	MS
1968	*The Dying Alchemist* for mixed media	MS
1968	*Valentine* for four players with amplification	MS
1969	*In Memoriam Nikola Tesla, Cosmic Engineer* for live electronics	MS
1969	*Events* film score	MS
1969	*Aeolian Partitions* for flute, clarinet, cello, and piano	BCP
1969	*A-OK* for accordion, violins, chorus, conductor, audience, and tape-delay system	PA
1969	*Please Don't Shoot The Piano Player, He Is Doing The Best He Can* for mixed media	MS
1969	*The Indefinite Integral Of Psi Star Psi d Tau = One* for mixed media	SR
1969	*The Dying Alchemist Preview* for trumpet, violin, percussion, narrator, and slides	MS
1969	*The Wheel Of Fortune* for clarinet, slides, monologue, and costumes	MS
1969	*California 99* collaboration	MS
1970-90	*Deep Listening Pieces* for voices and instruments	DLP
1970	*Music For Expo '70* for multichannel tape	MS
1970	*Link* for specialized and nonspecialized performers	MS
1970	*Meditation On The Points Of The Compass* for chorus, percussion, and audience	MP
1970	*Music For T'ai Chi* for accordion, two cellos, and three voices	MS
1970	*To Valerie Solanas And Marilyn Monroe In Recognition Of Their Despair* for orchestra, chorus, organ, electronics, and lights	SP
1970	*Why Don't You Write A Short Piece* for solo performer or group	SN
1971	*Sonic Meditations I-XII* for specialized and nonspecialized musicians	SP
1971	*The Flaming Indian* for tape recorder and microphone	SP

1971	*Bonn Feier* environmental theater piece	SP
1972	*Post Card Theater* for solo performer	MS
1972	*What To Do* for two or more performers	MS
1972	*Sonic Images* for narrator and audience	MS
1972	*Phantom Fathom (II) From The Theater Of The Ancient Trumpeters: A Ceremonial Participation Evening* for any number of performers	MS
1973	*Sonic Meditations XIII-XXV* for specialized and nonspecialized musicians	SP
1974	*A Ceremony Of Sounds* for audience participation	MS
1974	*Crow Two — A Ceremonial Opera* for specialized and nonspecialized performers	MS
1975	*Theater Of Substitution* for solo performer	MS
1975	*Elephant Call* for solo trumpet	MS
1975	*Unnatural Acts Between Consenting Adults*	MS
1975	*Rose Mountain Slow Runner* for voice and accordion	MS
1976	*Cheap Commissions* for composer and individuals	MS
1976	*Twenty-two Cuts From The Red Horse* theater music	MS
1976	*The Pathways Of The Grandmothers* for accordion and voice	MS
1976	*To Those In The Grey Northwestern Rainforests* for unspecified ensemble	Z
1976	*Willowbrook Generations And Reflections* for mixed winds, brasses, and voices (twenty or more) or chorus alone	SP
1977	*Rose Moon* for chorus and marathon runners	SP
1977	*Horse Sings From Cloud* for accordion and voice	MS
1977	*King Kong Sing Along* for chorus	MS
1977	*The Yellow River Map* ceremonial meditation for a large group	MS
1978	*Spiral Mandala* for bass drum with four players, four clarinets, eight tuned glasses, and solo chanter	SP
1978	*The Wheel Of Life* for vocal ensemble	DLP
1979	*Music For Stacked Deck* for four players	DLP
1979	*Double X* for quartet or octet of instruments	MS
1979	*Rock Piece* for any number of performers	MS
1979	*The Klickitat Ride* for chorus and/or instruments and caller	MS
1979	*The Witness* for solo, duo, or any ensemble	DLP
1979	*Crow's Nest (The Tuning Meditation)* installation with film and dance	MS
1979	*El Relicario De Los Animales* for twenty instruments and singer	DLP
1980	*Fwyynghn* theater collaboration	MS
1980	*Angels And Demons* for any number of performers	MS
1980	*Anarchy Waltz* for any number of performers	MS
1980	*MMM, A Lullaby For Daisy Pauline* for audience	MS
1980	*Stacked Deck* theater music	MS
1980	*Traveling Companions* for percussion and dancers	DLP

1981	*Monkey* for children's ensemble	MS
1981	*Tashi Gomang* for orchestra	SP
1981	*Lake CHARGOGGAGOGGMANCHAUGGAGOGGCHAU-BUNABUNBAGAUGG* for any number of performers	MS
1982	*The Wanderer* for accordion ensemble and percussion	DLP
1983	*Gathering Together* for piano eight-hands	DLP
1983	*Earth Ears* for any ensemble	DLP
1983	*The Well And The Gentle* for ensemble	DLP
1983	*The Wheel Of Time* for string quartet	MS
1984	*Tree/Peace* for violin, cello, and piano	SP
1984	*Wings Of Dove* for double wind quintet and two pianos	DLP
1985	*Lion's Eye* for Javanese gamelan and sampler	DLP
1987	*Portraits* for solo or any ensemble	DLP
1988	*Dream Horse Spiel* for voices and sound effects	DLP
1989	*Dream Gates* for solo or ensemble	DLP
1990	*Wind Horse* for mixed chorus	DLP
1990	*All Fours For The Drum Bum* for drum set	DLP
1990	*Contendors* for tape	DLP
1990	*Norwegian Wood* for piano	DLP
1991	*Skin* for accordion	DLP
1991	*Queens Of Space* for mixed ensemble	DLP
1991	*The Future Of Anonymity* for accordion and voice	DLP
1991	*Reflections On The Persian Gulf* for accordion and voice	DLP
1991	*Listening For Life* for tape	DLP
1991	*St. George And The Dragon* for accordion	DLP
1992	*Midnight Operas* for chorus	DLP
1992	*In Memory Of The Future* for solo voice	DLP
1992	*What If* for accordion	DLP
1992	*Seven-up* for voice	DLP
1992	*Phantom* for instruments and voice	DLP
1992	*Metalorgy* for pipes and voice	DLP
1992	*CCCC* for instruments	DLP
1992	*The Ready Made Boomerang* for instruments and voice	DLP
1992	*Inside Outside Space* for accordion and electronics; for instruments and voice	DLP

DISCOGRAPHY

1967
Sound Patterns
CBS Odyssey 32 16 0156, 0155 lp

I Of IV
CBS Odyssey 32 16 0160 lp

1968
Jar Piece
Marathon Music 2111 lp

1969
Outline For Flute, Percussion, And String Bass
Nonesuch 71237 lp

Sound Patterns
Ars Nova Ars Antigua 1005 lp

1973
Trio For Flute, Piano, And Page Turner
Advance FGR-9S lp

1977
Bye Bye Butterfly
Arch 1765 lp

1982
Voice And Accordion
Lovely Music 1901 lp

1984
The Wanderer / Horse Sings From Cloud
Lovely Music 1902 lp

1985
The Gentle, A Love Song
Eigelstein 2025/26 lp, cd

The Well And The Gentle
Hat Hut 2020 lp

1986
Tuning Meditation
Oliveros Foundation cs

The Receptive
Zoar 8 cs

Lullaby For Daisy Pauline
Finnandar 90266-1 lp

Alien Bog (excerpt)
Mills College MC 001 lp

1987
*Two Meditations On Transition And Change: The Beauty Of Sorrow and Tara's
Room*
Oliveros Foundation cs

1988
The Roots Of The Moment (short version)
Hat Hut 0912 cd

The Roots Of The Moment
Hat Hut 6009 cd

La Chambre Obscure, Deep Sea Rendezvous
Hat Hut 6010 cd

1990
Lion's Tale
Centaur 2047 cd

Crone Music
Lovely Music 1903 cd
New Tone 6707 cd (1992) (excerpt)
Nova Era 2002 cd (1993) (excerpt)

Norwegian Wood
EMI 6655 cd

1991
Portrait Of Malcolm
What Next? 0005 cd, cs

collaborations

with the Deep Listening Band:
Deep Listening New Albion 022 cd (1989)
Troglodyte's Delight What Next? 003 cd, cs (1990)
The Ready Made Boomerang New Albion 044 cd (1991)

with Linda Montano, Tom Jarmba, and children:
No More Fear SoundViews Sources cs (1990)

with Gordon Mumma:
Fwyyn Lovely Music 1092 lp (1986)

with Panaiotis:
Dream Horse Spiel Musicworks 45 cs (1990)

BIBLIOGRAPHY

Pauline's Proverbs. Compiled by Rosita. Ed. Linda Montano. Berkeley, California: Serendipity Books, 1976.

Software For People. Baltimore: Smith Publications, 1984.

"Secrets Of An Indian." *Ear Magazine*, 15 (July-August 1990).

"A Conversation." Ione, co-author. *Movement Research*, 6 (Spring & Summer 1993).

photo: Gene Bagnato

TERRY RILEY / Introduction

TERRY RILEY was born in Colfax, California, on June 24, 1935. He began violin lessons at age five and piano lessons at seven. He studied composition with Wendall Otey at San Francisco State University, where he received his B.A. in Music in 1957; and with Seymour Shifrin and William Denny at Berkeley, where he received his M.A. in Music Composition in 1961. During his time at Berkeley, he also studied composition privately with Robert Erickson, and studied ragtime piano with Wally Rose.

In the early '60s, Riley played piano and saxophone in clubs in France and Scandinavia. At the same time, he was composing pieces for tape, and creating music for live instrumentalists with tape-delay systems. Inspired in part by his work with tape delay, Riley began composing *The Keyboard Studies* in 1964, which combined improvisation with repetitive thematic material. Both approaches were also used in a score which he completed the same year, the epoch-making composition *In C* (premiered in 1965 with an ensemble that included composers Pauline Oliveros, Steve Reich, Morton Subotnick, Jon Gibson, and Ramon Sender). Justly famous as the score that launched the worldwide recognition of minimalist music, *In C* has been performed countless times all over the globe.

By the late '60s, Riley was performing internationally as an improviser on soprano saxophone and on electronic keyboards, in music documented on two lps, *Poppy Nogood And The Phantom Band* (1967) and *A Rainbow In Curved Air* (1968). Starting in 1969, he spent two years studying Indian drumming with Phil Ford, Kanai Dutt, and Narayan Rao. In 1970, Riley became a disciple of master singer Pandit Pran Nath, with whom he continues to study North Indian classical vocal music. He has also performed with this celebrated artist as tamboura and vocal accompanist, as well as with other respected Indian musicians, including Krishna Bhatt.

Alerted to the possibilities of composing in just intonation through his friendship with La Monte Young (Riley sang in Young's Theater of Eternal Music in the mid '60s), he began pursuing just tunings in earnest in the '70s, spurred on by his studies of raga singing. Since then, he has performed extensively with justly tuned keyboards, producing such notable works as *The Descending Moonshine Dervishes* (1976) and *The Harp Of New Albion* (1984). By the 1980s, Riley was also performing as a singer in a unique blend of raga and Western stylings. He has continued this personal combination of musics most recently with his group Khayal, with which he tours internationally. In the '80s, Riley also began composing his celebrated series of scores for the Kronos String Quartet, with whom he has also performed on keyboards.

Riley has taught at numerous schools throughout his career, including the Royal Academy of Music in Stockholm, New York University, Cleveland's Institute of Music, Sacramento State College, the Danish Academy of Music in Copenhagen, and the California College of Performing Arts. From 1971 through 1984, he taught North Indian raga as well as composition at Mills College. Among the many awards bestowed on Riley are the Nicola di Lorenzo Prize (which he has won twice), a Cassandra Foundation Grant, a National Endowment for the Arts Award, a DAAD Fellowship in Berlin, and a Guggenheim Fellowship.

Terry Riley currently lives at his ranch in Comptonville, California. I spoke with him on February 1, 1991, at his Manhattan hotel room in between rehearsals for the world premiere of his *Jade Palace Orchestral Dances* (commissioned by Carnegie Hall as part of its centennial celebration). While no conversation with Riley could afford to ignore *In C* or his work with the Kronos Quartet, I also wanted to shed more light on Riley's work as an improviser, his attitudes regarding just intonation, and his studies with Pandit Pran Nath.

TERRY RILEY / Interview

Q: I understand that in the late 1950s, you formed an improvising trio with Loren Rush and Pauline Oliveros because you needed to record a film score in a hurry.

RILEY: Right, yeah. It was done for the sculptor Claire Falkenstein, who lives in Los Angeles and does these huge, beautiful sculptures. She was in San Francisco then, teaching at the California School of Fine Arts. I had met her through a friend and she liked my music and asked me to do a piece for this film she had just made called *Polyester Moon*, which was one of her polyester sculpture pieces. This is about '58 or '59, I think, something like that.

Of course, Pauline and Loren and I had been together in San Francisco State, in a composition class, and we must have been playing together — at least at parties! — during those days. But I think this was the first time that we'd ever tried to do this kind of thing together. I had performed Pauline's music and Loren's music during various times, so I knew them pretty well and we knew each other pretty well. I think we went to KPFA and just sat down and had a session, a one-take type of thing.

Q: And you then went on working in this trio for another year or so, recording yourselves and listening back to the tapes?

RILEY: I don't recall how many times we got together, actually. I do remember the one we made for the film — and, like I said, I do remember a lot of times we used to get together at night and play.

Q: I've read that Loren Rush was playing koto as well as contrabass then.

RILEY: He played koto; he used to play bassoon. Pauline played French horn. I don't think she played accordion on this — she was playing a lot of French horn in those days.

Q: I was intrigued by the presence of the koto — in a way, it anticipates your later work with the group Khayal and its combination of Western and Eastern instruments.

RILEY: This is mainly a California atmosphere, I think. Being on the Pacific rim, musicians have often gotten involved with Asian instruments, even in those days. And of course Loren was very sensitive to where he was living: He used to live in Point Richmond, right on the ocean, and had a house that could have been in Japan at that time. I think his sensibility was going that way.

Q: Looking back, is that trio's music mostly of historic interest today, or do some of those tapes merit being released?

RILEY: I would say that, at that point, I was still very much under the influence of European music: Stockhausen, Nono, even Schoenberg and Webern. I think that all of us since then have developed more into the particular areas that we're interested in. I would classify that more as a student work. We were all young, we were all under certain influences and reflecting those in a way. But it turned out to be kind of an original sound that we got with this trio.

Q: That's what's interesting, because non-jazz group improvisation was still a rarity then. Each performance must have been an attempt to discover and utilize a language.

RILEY: I always liked to improvise. I started out improvising and learned to play the piano at first by ear. I was always more comfortable playing so-called "by ear" than I was playing from notes, and I learned many classical pieces from my older cousin who'd also learned them by ear. I would listen to him play and then do a second-hand version of his version of the Tchaikovsky Piano Concerto or something like that — which we'd even give a different name! It wasn't until I was almost in my teens — I must have been almost in high school — that I started learning pieces from scores. And even then I didn't like to read music; to me, it was very hard to do. So improvising has been my orientation.

Q: In retrospect, did you learn more about composing from that trio than you learned from your classes with Seymour Shifrin?

RILEY: I felt that all my peers during the period I was in college were much more exciting to be around than the teachers. Because they were picking up on more recent developments in music and synthesizing those ideas themselves in their own work. I found everybody in that group of students which I went to school with very interesting — and they still are.

Q: Is it true that the first time you used tape loops was for a dance score in 1960 called *The Five-Legged Stool?*

RILEY: I'd used them before that, but I think that was the first piece that emphasized tape loops.

Q: And was itself a tape piece.

RILEY: It was all tape, yeah. Although one thing I did in those days was play live, record myself, and loop that, and sometimes I would play with that. And some of these pieces were on-going, evolutionary parts of live and looped performances. I remember that at the time I was living in San Francisco and I had this beautiful view of the bay. It was a very romantic little spot, a very old cottage (which has since been torn down) which had a very small garden and a lot of wine bottles outside, and all the tape loops would go out the window of the studio, around the wine bottles, and back into the studio. I had a couple of Wollensack tape recorders (probably borrowed) which I was making these loops on. It was a very primitive form of electronic technology!

Q: You went on to do several pieces for tape after *The Five-Legged Stool*.

RILEY: I really wanted to be involved with live performance. All the tape pieces that I did then usually had some element of live performance in them. That one was done for Ann Halprin's dance; I think it was called *The Four-Legged Stool* when I did it — it started out as *The Three-Legged Stool* and ended up being *Five*. Anyway, in some of the performances I played piano live on the stage when the dancers were there.

Q: I've heard a recording of Chet Baker's group performing with you working a tape-delay system. When was that done?

RILEY: It was done in '63, I believe; it might even have started in '62. I was living in Paris then, and Chet Baker had just come to Paris from Luca, where he had been incarcerated for a little drug episode. (Actually, I think it was about a year he was in jail, maybe more.) I was working with a playwright, Ken Dewey, who used to be here in New York and was tragically killed in a plane accident in 1972. Ken and I worked together many years on theater pieces. But the first time we worked together was in Paris, for the Theater of Nations, and Ken had this brilliant idea to have Chet Baker in this work, playing live with his newly formed quartet. He wanted me to be music director and do something electronically with all this. He also had many of Ann Halprin's dancers and some people from the Living Theater whom he used as actors; also a sculptor, Jerry Walters. Chet Baker was actually asked to be an actor in this thing, with his group. So it was all very integrated onstage; it wasn't music accompanying theater, it was theater with musicians as actors. Which was kind of a new idea and it caused a big riot in France. The French just couldn't understand it at all, and they started arguing with each other during the performance — a typical kind of thing, with fights breaking out.

It was exciting musically for me because that's where I discovered this long-term feedback tape delay, which I used for years, all through the '60s, both in live performance and in the studio. My fascination with that still goes on in some ways.

Q: So that experience was channeled right into your own music, rather than your wanting to pursue similar setups with other jazz or non-jazz musicians.

RILEY: Right. In fact, *In C* is an outgrowth of that. Because after I'd done it electronically, I wanted to see if I could do it, get that kind of feeling, with all acoustic instruments. So I worked on sketches for many pieces and then finally I did *In C*. It was still a kind of improvising; there are choices but they're well defined, specific choices. Before I did it, it was hard for me to figure out what it was I wanted to do. I knew the feeling but I didn't know what kind of technique in writing it or setting it up would be needed, until the idea occurred. And then it came full blown.

Q: That piece is more than 25 years old, and yet I'll still read about "Terry (*In C*) Riley." It seems when composers, especially young ones, produce a major work, no one ever lets them forget it, and they're always being compared to it. Have you ever felt that way with *In C*? Has it become something of a millstone around your neck?

RILEY: Well, there'll be times when I'll be asked to come and do a performance of *In C* even when I'm really doing something else that's more current. But that's the only time I would say that. Actually, I feel very grateful for that piece; it's kind of like my bread and butter in music. It's a gift to me and a gift to the other people who have enjoyed it. So no, I couldn't condemn it in any way — I think it's great. And I still enjoy it. We did a performance for the 25th anniversary of *In C* in San Francisco, which was just absolutely magnificent. That was just a year ago or so, and I think it was the best performance I've ever been in. We even had a trap drummer, George Marsh, playing in it, but it sounds great, symphonic. New Albion is trying to arrange to release it. I'd like to see that happen because it is a very exciting version.

Q: How many different realizations of *In C* have you been involved in?

RILEY: That'd be hard to say. It could be a hundred. It gets performed a lot. The idea that any kind of instruments can play it makes it fun for colleges and even high schools.

Q: Has the attitude of musicians toward the piece changed over the years?

RILEY: Well, I can only cite some extreme examples. Just a few years ago, I was in London with the London Electronic Symphony — they'd asked me to come over. This was close to the 25-year anniversary, and the orchestra actually said things to me like, "This piece can't be done. It doesn't make sense." And I was thinking, "God, after 25 years and so many performances, this is news to me!" But the orchestra had such a row over it that it actually folded soon after, because of the disagreements between the players. So it's still in some ways causing ripples, which surprises me — it's like *The Rite Of Spring* causing ripples in 1940 or 1950.

Q: What about the attitude of audiences? It seems to have always worked with them, hasn't it?

RILEY: I think so. Of course, audiences are always made up of people with different degrees of attention and different abilities to go within themselves or whatever. So audiences seem to have been the same to me since the first performance. The first performance in some ways was the most exciting for me, in terms of the audience, because they really got electrified. It had a great first performance, with a really wonderful cast of performers.

Q: When the Shanghai Film Orchestra did its version of *In C*, on what instrument was the pulse being played?

RILEY: It's been a while, but I think it's either a temple block or a metal bar or metal drum. That's an interesting question, because the Chinese percussionist couldn't play just a steady pulse, ding-ding-ding. He said, "Please, let me play Chinese rhythms." OK, so Chinese rhythms turned out to be like any other rhythms, you know, da-da di-da da-da! He could keep a steady tempo, but when he tried to play a pulse just ding-ding-ding, he couldn't do it; it just was against his every grain of musicianship. I saw how much he was suffering, so I said, "Yeah, play in Chinese traditional rhythms." Then he really loved what he was doing.

Q: That's what I was really curious about, if the liberties taken with that part of *In C* were OK with you.

RILEY: Well, my general nature is always to try to fool around with whatever piece I've done; the next time I perform it, to somehow twist it so that it will come out differently.

Q: Was there any overdubbing used for the recording?

RILEY: No, there's no overdubbing. We did about three or four takes and took the best one of the bunch.

Q: And they never got it over a half hour in length?

RILEY: No. The longest one was 28 minutes. But you know, I had very little time to work with them — I was in Shanghai a week. David Liang, who went over with me as producer and who also has some music on that cd, started out first with the orchestra. He thought he should warm them up because he's Chinese and speaks Chinese. He thought that *In C* was going to be a real culture shock for them because it's very unlike what Chinese musicians do; to have freedom to play what you want is just not something that they're used to experiencing. So he thought he'd start them with his music, and took three or four days to record his music and to prepare them for this. By the time we began recording *In C*, we had only two days. I had to explain everything to them through an interpreter, and the first day went pretty horribly: Everybody was looking at me with totally blank faces, and when they tried to play it.... The next day was our last day — the day after that we were still in Shanghai, but there was a general electricity strike, so there wouldn't be any electricity that day to record with!

So we had to do it in two days, one day of rehearsal and one day of recording. And it actually came out very well. They did finally get the idea that they could actually play these patterns and they wouldn't have to really look at the music after they'd learned it and they could listen to each other and they could really make it swing. They started to understand that it was kinetic, and then they got really turned on and excited. Even when we'd take a break, I'd hear the kids out in the hallway singing and clapping the patterns!

Q: Whose idea was it to do *In C* with a Chinese orchestra?

RILEY: Mine originally. David Liang was hired by Celestial Harmonies to be the liaison. We didn't even know where we were going to do it when we first got the idea. We thought we were going to go to Beijing and do it there. David made several calls to China — he'd worked in China before with different orchestras and he finally decided that this was the orchestra that could do it.

Q: Brian Eno and Jon Hassell collaborated with you on the mixing for that cd. Had you originally planned to bring them in on it?

RILEY: I didn't even know they were going to be involved. When working on a recording, the part I'm least interested in is in the mixing room. I just lose interest after I've recorded. I love the recording part, I like playing, but I've never been one to be tremendously happy mixing and making those kinds of decisions. But Jon loves that and so does Brian. So I looked up Jon as soon as I got to L.A. and said, "I've got this tape we made in China, which I've got to mix for this record." And Jon said, "Yeah, I'll come down if you want help." I said, "Yeah, I'd like your help," because I know Jon is good in the control booth. And Brian just happened to be in town visiting Jon, so he said, "I'll bring Brian along." And that's the way it happened. Brian really got right into it and started setting up the board, and they decided to do all these different things with the mixing, and I sat back and watched them! I think they did a great job.

Q: Were you equally detached from mixing *Salome Dances For Peace*, or was that seen as a chance to create a kind of ideal performance, simply in terms of balancing lines or enhancing harmonics?

RILEY: I was present at all the recording and mixing sessions, but there I think my main concerns at that time were in rewriting the score — I was actually changing passages around and giving them different notes to play. In the studio, we had Judy Sherman, who's a really excellent producer and has great ears for the sound production of a tape. She was hearing things that I wasn't even hearing. I was concentrating on the way they were phrasing things, and in a couple of places I even rewrote a couple of notes — I just said, "Play this instead of that there." What I was really hearing was what I wanted to put into the production, in terms of musical phrasing or dynamics or even changing a few notes around. Judy really oversaw the thing in terms of the kind of sound we were getting in the room — along with David Harrington, who had a lot of ideas about that. We did it at the soundstage at George Lucas' Skywalker Ranch: It's a huge movie soundstage, gigantic. You can make any kind of echo there acoustically, not just electronically, because it's got all these little wings that come in and out of the walls and down from the ceilings. You can create the size of the room that way. We spent a day or two doing that, and once we found the sound of a room we wanted, we stayed with that.

Q: *In C* is frequently referred to as your first notated score, although it's really a set of materials and instructions, not unlike your *Keyboard Studies*. The writing of through-composed scores really begins for you with your works for string quartet in the 1980s, doesn't it?

RILEY: Well, for my student works of the '50s and '60s, I did write out quite a few scores. In 1980, when I started writing for string quartet, I didn't want to do that either. Because of my involvement with Indian classical music, I was thinking — and I still do, to this day — that the greatest music occurs through a kind of ongoing inner process where the musician has nothing to concentrate on but the sound as he's playing; there's no manuscript, there's nothing in front of him but his imagination. I tried to do this with the Kronos Quartet the first time they come up to my ranch. I was going to play with them in the first string quartet, and I'd written out some sketches that were just little fragments of patterns. So I'd play and I'd give them this little piece of paper, and they'd kind of look at it and say, "Well, what do I do with this?" We had a couple of days of just not being able to figure out how to make a piece out of it. So David pulled me aside and said, "Look, what string quartets do best is have the music all written out and really work on it. Then we'll get all this improvisatory feeling you want, after you write us the notes." So with that, I understood what they could do: They could really play well after they had something concrete to put their four personalities into.

Q: Yet your first score for them consisted of musical fragments that could be played in different sequences.

RILEY: The closest we came to that was a piece called *Sunrise Of The Planetary Dream Collector*. It's a little like *In C* in that there are modules, but since the modules are composed together as four string parts, it's more unified.

Q: You've gone on to perform with the Kronos, haven't you?

RILEY: The first concert we ever did together I played and sang with them. Then they decided to play these pieces as solo string-quartet pieces — because they take these things on the road, and also because I think they felt more comfortable with me out of the act! At that point, anyway.

Q: But there is a piano quintet that you did with them.

RILEY: Yes, years later. A piece called *The Crow's Rosary* was the quintet. It was originally going to be for piano in just intonation with string quartet. But when David set up the schedule for performances of the piece, it was a series of one-night stands, and we realized we couldn't do it with piano because there was no time to tune the piano. So I did it with synthesizer.

Q: How did playing in just intonation sit with them?

RILEY: It was very difficult at the beginning, because I chose a tuning which used at least two intervals that aren't played much in common-practice music: the 13th harmonic and the 11th harmonic. And those are a little bit hard; they're something like quartertones but each one is a different sound. So we spent a lot of time just practicing long tones and playing chords. I think we did that for about a year: I'd get together with them, playing the synthesizer, and they'd try to match the tones. There was no music for about a year, only intervals. And we actually set up a couple of residencies together, so we could do that. At the very last minute I wrote the music and they learned it. By that time the tuning was starting to become a little bit familiar to them.

Q: Did you write out your own keyboard part as well?

RILEY: I did in this piece, although I left myself a lot of places to fool around!

Q: Was space also left for them, or did they not want that?

RILEY: I actually created a couple of places in the piece, where I urged them to stretch out, and they did do it and they liked it and developed it a lot. But these were solo parts so they didn't have to do it together.

Q: Has your string-quartet binge of the '80s enabled you to do pretty much what you wanted to do with that medium, or is it something you want to pursue further?

RILEY: I'm writing for string quartet and orchestra right now, a concerto that will feature the Kronos. At this point I'm halfway through, and I'm using them almost as four soloists. That's another way to use the quartet, as individuals against an orchestral palette. I showed David what I'm doing with this and he thinks it's going to be more than one piece. Somewhere down the line I'll probably make another part for it.

Q: The orchestra piece you've just completed, *The Jade Palace Orchestral Dances*, is about 50 minutes long. Were there preconditions to that commission regarding length?

RILEY: I was commissioned to write only a 15-minute work. The length was just something that happened.

Q: Once you'd started *Salome Dances For Peace*, you also realized that it would be much larger than the original commission.

RILEY: Oh yeah. After I'd written the first part, I felt like it was an exposition section of a large symphony or something, where you've introduced all the themes. And I also had other, brand-new materials that I hadn't introduced into it, so I realized I had to make it much longer. I just told David we had to do it, and he went ahead and found the commissions.

Q: The first part of *Salome Dances For Peace* was commissioned by IRCAM. Wasn't that an unlikely source to commission you?

RILEY: Very! I think it came about more through Kronos than through me. I think that they asked Kronos to pick a composer, and maybe weren't really greatly thrilled that they picked me, but stuck by it and went ahead once Kronos decided that I was the one.

Q: Would you have accepted the commission to write an orchestral score if you hadn't been writing for string quartet in the '80s?

RILEY: Probably not.

Q: Would you have gotten that commission if you hadn't written the quartets?

RILEY: No. It was Leonard Slatkin's idea that I write this piece for Carnegie Hall, and he said that because he'd heard what I'd been doing with the later quartets, he felt I was ready to do an orchestra piece. And even with that, I waited a long time to make the decision to do it. I wasn't sure whether I could do it. And I'm still not sure!

Q: Was writing a through-composed orchestral score a compromise for you, or did the challenge of it excite you?

RILEY: A through-composed score was the only option I could resolve into some kind of musical result. I tried to think of ways to make a work like *In C*, which would be some kind of architectural plan for an orchestra to make music without having to go from A to Z. I didn't succeed that way, so I started writing music, as Mozart or anyone else would do. I think that, in the end, the music was great fun to write, to compose it this way and actually work with orchestration and have all these different choices of sound. It was great to do it. But the general problem that you're involved in with orchestras, of getting them to play from their feeling, I think that there still must be a way to do that. If I'm going to continue to write for orchestra, it's something I'd like to try to do at some point, to try to get another idea like *In C*, where you can get an orchestra to play in an inspired way without having to write the whole thing out. It's the solution to a very difficult problem. It's not something that you can say, "I'm going to solve this." Einstein came up with the theory of relativity and spent the rest of his life trying to figure out what it was. I think musicians are often caught in that same situation. They can't come up with a new theory every time they write a piece.

Q: Is your new piece for orchestra in just intonation or equal temperament?

RILEY: It's in equal temperament. But I don't even like to say it's in a temperament, because I don't think those terms really apply with an orchestra. There are so many instruments playing, that what you get is actually a very phased kind of tuning. It doesn't belong to any category, it's just this big wad of sound.

Q: Your work with just intonation began in the '70s?

RILEY: The first time I tuned my electronic organ, was I think in 1972 or '73, something like that.

Q: What impelled you to do that?

RILEY: First of all, I sang with La Monte in '65, and that's when I really got infected by just intonation, when I was singing with the Theater of Eternal Music and hearing how beautiful those intervals were. Then I started studying raga and I realized that all of raga deals with just intervals. There's no equal temperament in raga; they don't even use chords (there's no reason to) and they don't modulate. As I was playing keyboard, a lot more of the feeling of raga started taking over my interest in music. I realized I wasn't using chords then, so why not tune the keyboard in just intonation too? And of course there was *The Well-Tuned Piano*, already composed in 1964, which I was aware of and thought was a beautiful example of keyboard in just intonation.

Q: Your use of retuned keyboards, whether it's the piano of *The Harp Of New Albion* or the electric organ of *Descending Moonshine Dervishes*, generates amazing overtone densities. How much control do you have in their creation? Are you surprised by what you hear as you move through the music?

RILEY: I'm not an acoustician, and I haven't made a big theoretical study of just intonation, although I'm familiar with the intervals and the sounds of the intervals. A lot of the stuff I've done, for instance in *The Harp Of New Albion*, is purely pragmatic: First tune the piano in the theoretical scale, five-limit scale or whatever, and then try to create material from that. But it's all been done by ear. It's just a matter of listening to something — if you like it, it stays; if you don't, it's out. I haven't tried to do it from a study of which overtones should I emphasize or de-emphasize. And with piano you've got this really complex waveform that comes out because of the enharmonicity of strings. You always have something kind of funny going on. It's never as perfect as it would be, for instance, in the voice. To me, the best example of just intonation is the voice against the tamboura. The tamboura is four strings tuned to a very simple resonant relationship, just the fifth degree of the third harmonic, or the fifteenth harmonic. When the voice sings, he can very slightly change the formants in his voice so that different harmonics are emphasized or de-emphasized. You don't have that kind of control with piano, because it's a very complex instrument. So to me, there's nothing like vocal music for just intonation, as far as the real fine controls. A lot of ragas are defined by the emphasis on which kinds of overtones are sounding and how the movement of them is resolved. That's the best form of just intonation, the clearest and the most rewarding to do.

Q: How much of your singing with Khayal is in equal temperament?

RILEY: The piano is tuned in equal temperament, but I don't think the voices and the relationships between the string bass and the voices are. It's an imperfect situation acoustically, like when you're singing with harmonium in Indian classical music: Usually, the harmonium is in equal temperament. What I find interesting to do in Khayal is, when I'm singing, I usually stop playing the piano. I use the piano as interludes, so you've got little riffs where the equal temperament comes in. But when the voices come in, there's a little shift. I don't think I could sing in equal temperament without the piano. I don't know how you would do it!

Q: Is the piano somewhat restrictive for you in Khayal because of its tuning?

RILEY: With electronic keyboards, you can use just intonation very easily. So I think that's where, with Khayal, we'll work more on tunings. Everybody in the ensemble has worked with tunings. One of the things we're doing a lot more with Khayal now is actually introducing ragas with this instrumentation. Because three or four of the players have studied raga with Pandit Pran Nath and have a good feeling for the music. I found I enjoyed singing raga with string bass, just using a string bass and a saxophone as an accompaniment. Well, in India, they use sarangi and harmonium, so why not in America use string bass and saxophone — or another voice? All the great innovations that were made in India were made out of necessity. The sarangi came from Persia; it wasn't in India originally, but now it's a standard.

I find that any kind of tuning is a restriction, because once you set it in that tuning, you're limited to that scale. So if I tune in just intonation, I've got the beautiful intervals that are clear and resonant and full of special feelings. But I can't play chords. So that limitation is there. In equal temperament, I can do any kind of chordal thing, I can change keys and play in any key I want. But I don't have the beautiful resonances. So for me, equal temperament is just another tuning, and I feel that I can use it; it's not something I have to shy away from, like dirty laundry. It's a tuning that does its job really well.

Q: I'd like to get some background on your work as a singer prior to your studies with Pandit Pran Nath. I know that you sang in La Monte Young's *The Tortoise, His Dreams And Journeys* with the Theater of Eternal Music in February of '66. Was that the first time you sang publicly?

RILEY: Except for in choirs, yeah. Or in bars; I used to play barroom piano, which was a big part of my career in the early '60s — and prepared me for what I'm doing now. I was on my way to Europe in 1965, and ended up in New York — somebody offered me a very nice loft just before I was going to get the boat, and so we traded our bus that we were driving for the loft. La Monte was here and I'd worked with La Monte in Berkeley and really loved playing with him and loved his music and his ideas. He was rehearsing with John Cale and Tony Conrad, so I used to drop in and I started sitting in with them, and then La Monte asked me, "Why don't you join the band?" I was going over there every day, and some days we'd rehearse and some days we'd just hang out. I spent a lot of time over there. I always enjoyed improvising and playing with La Monte.

Q: Did you do other vocal performances in those years just before you met Pandit Pran Nath?

RILEY: No. In fact, at that point in my life, before I met Pran Nath, I always sort of thought that singers weren't musicians! You know, because of the tradition of opera singers, I always thought they were the most unmusical. But by studying with him, I've really grown to respect singing so much. Before I met him, I really didn't understand what singing was — or what it could be. After that, I started to really appreciate a lot more people like Ella Fitzgerald and all the great jazz singers. I still haven't developed an appreciation for the bel canto style of voice production, but I can see that the voice itself is one of the most magnificent musical instruments. Pandit Pran Nath opened my ears to that realm of music.

Q: What drew you to study with him?

RILEY: He's a very, very powerful musician. His music is mesmerizing. La Monte introduced me to the first tapes of his music, so I'd been listening to it for years before I met him. Then La Monte brought him out to California in 1970 and he spent time at our house. At that time, he told me, "You must become my disciple." He just said it to me, so I went to La Monte and said, "What does this mean?" And he told me how it was a great opportunity. So I went to India with him right after that. And I was amazed because I had never been with anyone who could produce such incredible music just with their voice. For a while, you thought you were hearing everything you've ever wanted to hear out of music just out of a solo voice. It opened my ears and eyes to a different world that I'd never thought existed.

Q: Can you explain the difference between being a pupil and being a disciple?

RILEY: A disciple is like becoming a family member. Your connection to that person is very close, in the sense that you can demand of each other pretty much anything you could demand of your own mother or father or brother or sister; it's very intimate. And the responsibility towards each other becomes much greater. A student can come and have a lesson and go away and never think about it anymore if he wants. But a disciple has a responsibility to whatever his teacher would ask. And what that disciple would ask of his teacher has to be considered very strongly.

Q: There wasn't any hesitation on your part once he said he wanted you to become his disciple?

RILEY: No. Especially after I was with him a couple of days, I felt there was something very special about being with this person. It was like something I'd felt with only a few people, maybe with someone like La Monte, who's been my lifelong friend. This karmic connection just locked in, and I realized it was meant to be.

Q: And apparently there was a similar recognition process on his part that enabled him to make this offer to you.

RILEY: I think so, yeah. But that was his tradition. His whole training from childhood made him sensitive to that: recognizing people, recognizing their qualities. I think he knew when he came here that his work was going to be here, that he was going to develop a whole body of work here through the musicians he taught and through his own music.

Q: What are your ambitions now as a raga singer?

RILEY: Raga singing is something you do for yourself, for your own soul. It's such a beautiful thing just to practice, that my ambitions in a certain way have all been realized. I'm so happy with having the music to do every day. As far as saying, "I'm going to be a raga singer and sing a concert down in Town Hall," that would be a nice thing to do, but it doesn't have anything to do with my happiness in terms of being a raga singer. Being a raga singer means sitting down in the morning with the tamboura and practicing the ragas.

When I first started, I really thought I wanted to drop everything I'd been doing. At that time, I'd done *A Rainbow In Curved Air* and *In C*, some of my major works. And after I'd gotten into raga singing, I thought, "These are insignificant compared to what this music really has in it" — it's this very old tradition that's so full. And I told him, "I think I'm going to stop doing all my composition and just learn to be a raga singer. This'll be my life — I think I'll stay in India." At that time I didn't want to come back to the United States; I'd been in India six months and I wanted to stay there. And he said, "No, this is not your role in music. You keep composing. Do them both," he said, "side by side."

Q: Can you say what those studies have fed into your composition?

RILEY: Well, I hope what it is is the spiritual bond, the spiritual reinforcement that you get from a very strong other spirit who can empower you, and that somehow empowers your music. That's what I hope it would be — not a specific technique but the ability to get music through inspiration. Which I felt was something I always had, but to become even stronger and be able to instill in that music a very strong spiritual feeling which will then inspire people who listen to it and give them some kind of uplifting experience.

Q: That's also the core of being an improviser, isn't it?

RILEY: Yeah. Looking back on it all, now when I hear anybody — when I hear Miles Davis or John Coltrane — I see that it's all really feeding into this one incredible stream. It doesn't matter where this music originated. There is this wonderful core of... I can't even say it, you know what I mean? It's like it's all coming from the same source. You'll hear it in one turn of a phrase: One second of music will go by and you'll recognize that it's got it. It's got that one thing, so that your life's not the same the next moment after.

Q: More than other traditions of improvisation, raga singing is particularly aware of this sensibility of the performer as a conduit for the music.

RILEY: The raga singer leaves things open a very long time into the event. For instance, it's traditional not to come on the stage saying, "I'm going to sing this raga." What the professional raga singer really wants to do is get out there and have something happen at that moment, which he can then follow. There's some kind of an inspiration that comes when he tunes the tamboura. Sometimes it even happens after he starts singing a raga; another raga will come into his mind, and he can immediately switch gears and that'll be the one. So there's a long time of collecting the energies that he's going to manifest, and then very slowly letting it unfold. But with Western music, often they'll come out and bang, there's a downbeat and you have to be into it right away. It's like you're bringing in something you know. With raga, I think you're leaving yourself open to that unknown a very long time into the performance.

Q: Are you also describing the situation of your own performing?

RILEY: I think that's what I'm really describing! That's the kind of performer I am. One reason I loved raga singing, and why I like La Monte's music and people like that, John Coltrane and Miles Davis, is that Miles could come out on the stage with his horn and sit and look at the audience or not look at them, and the audience falls into such a relaxed place that they're also waiting for this moment to occur: "What is going to happen? What's going to manifest here?" I like those kinds of art experiences, and not to come out with da-da-da-daaa right away. Although that can be great too, if it's the right time for it.

Q: In an interview you gave a couple of years ago, you remarked that your approach to performance has been one of "letting things happen as they grow on the stage," and that you were concerned that working with a group could inhibit this attitude of gambling with the results. Has Khayal proven to be safer in this way, or does that ensemble provide its own uncertainties?

RILEY: Let me answer it this way. I started by playing, at least in this kind of music, with Krishna Bhatt who's a really wonderful sitar player and tabla player. We did a lot of duet concerts. One of the things that I realized I could do was that I could still play as a soloist if I had the right kind of people playing with me. Because Krishna could not only inspire me with his beautiful musicianship, but if I changed course, like I would as a soloist, he was right there. And I found other people who could do that. Zakhir Hussein, this great tabla player, he played with us and he was not only right there, but he was also driving us ahead to places where we never thought that we could be. I think I learned in the '80s what group performance could be. Up until that point, I thought it couldn't be possible. So with Khayal, I think it's getting to that point with those musicians, even though there are four or five of us. From the piano, I direct the general momentum and pace of the piece. But anybody in that group, because they're all very strong musicians, is also capable of influencing the direction. And I think this is what improvising jazz musicans appreciate when they find a group that really works together as well as that. You get very strong people, and everybody has their own particular way of influencing the course of events of that evening. So I'd say now yeah, I think with a group I've gotten into something which I find is just as exciting as anything I ever did as a soloist — maybe even more so.

We're supposed to tour in May in Europe. We want to keep this alive. I want to keep this kind of group playing. A lot of these people I've known over the years, and I think that, in terms of personnel, I could see Khayal open to change and taking different forms; sometimes it may become more vocal. I feel like there's a general group of musicians who could at any time be in it. That's how it's been over the years, even though it wasn't called Khayal then.

Q: I was fascinated by an excerpt I heard of your 1982 vocal work, *The Ethereal Time Shadow*. The first thing I want to know is, is that piece ever going to be released in its entirety?

RILEY: That recording belongs to Sudwest Rundfunk in Germany, and the radio, because it receives money from the German government, was not allowed to let me make a commercial recording of it. You heard it as part of an archive project for Mills College, but that's only an excerpt from a much larger recording, which was one of the best performances I've ever done. Unfortunately, I'm not legally allowed to release any more of that — unless Germany gets taken over by Iraq or something!

Q: Was part of your impulse in creating that work a desire to establish a new kind of vocal music, a special strain of American raga singing?

RILEY: I definitely wanted to introduce singing into my composition and my performance, and I still do. Whenever I get a chance I still want to, because singing is one of my biggest loves now. Because of the nature of singing, because of the nature of the music I'm doing, it's something that's probably going to take a long time to get at the point that I'm trying to reach. Now I'm doing it with Khayal and doing it with other singers. I see it as an ongoing thing, maybe the thing will take a shape as my ideas mature — or don't mature or become more immature!

The recording of *The Ethereal Time Shadow* just happened to catch something that was very important about what different talents I had as a keyboard player and as a singer, and how they should be brought together. In a career, there's always little milestones like that. The next ones I would like to do, though, with more than one voice. In Khayal, I have Molly Holm whom I sing with. Now we're a quintet, and it's starting to get refined a lot more.

Q: The impression I get from your singing is that, for you as a performer, technique takes on a dimension that didn't exist in your saxophone or keyboard playing. If you press a key on a synthesizer, you'll get whatever pitch it's tuned to. But as a singer, you have to create that pitch yourself. Is this one of the challenges you've particularly felt as a singer?

RILEY: There are many challenges with singing. As the critics say, my voice is like Bob Dylan before his morning coffee! I don't have the normal kind of voice which people identify, like Whitney Houston or even Bobby McFerrin or some of the really great singers have. No, I've not got that kind of instrument. Fortunately, I've got the kind of instrument that's very much like the singers of the tradition I'm trying to learn. Abdul Waheed Khansahib was one of the greatest singers of India, and they used to say he sounded like chairs being dragged across the floor. His voice was kind of rough-hewn, but very, very, very full of feeling and emotion, and the quality, the high state he'd taken his singing to as an improvising musician, was unsurpassed. So people don't even think about whether they're listening to a really gorgeous vocal tone; they're really carried away with the music. Westerners I find aren't readily attracted to that so far. I think that there's a certain degree of truth that my voice sounds like Bob Dylan before his morning coffee, and I don't mind actually that it does. What I want to do is to keep developing the art. Because first you have to just keep doing what you're doing. At certain points it's going to break through; at certain points, people just have to bear with it as it develops.

Q: Here in the States especially, we're used to recognizing only certain idioms of singing as demonstrating good technique, and so a lot of what you're doing, the high degree of precision and skill you employ, simply eludes listeners.

RILEY: It's experimental in a certain sense; it's still raw in a certain sense, my practices of a very, very fine and highly evolved tradition and my trying to develop something here. Because we have to do that as musicians. We're Americans, and although I love to sing raga which is an Indian tradition, I think I'll ultimately enjoy my singing more, or I'll make whatever contribution I have to make, more through somehow trying to bring it into my own particular cultural reference. I have to keep trying that, and I think that's what Pran Nath wants us to do too. He wants us to sing raga, but he also realizes that we're born here, and eventually, if his coming here and working with all these people is going to have any meaning at all, they're going to have to bring it into their lives more than just chanting words in Hindi or Urdu. Because eventually that won't mean anything to them anymore. Our own cultural reference will have to take over.

Q: I think that's part of the excitement in *The Ethereal Time Shadow* or *Songs For The Ten Voices Of The Two Prophets*, that something very new musically is taking shape, and we're hearing the very beginning of something unique.

RILEY: As musicians we often don't know what we're doing — we just go on a feeling. At least from my own point of view, I often don't know what I'm doing. Sometimes I feel like I'm working very much in the dark. But I'm working on a feeling that I know to trust. That's essentially what you're doing; you're saying, "I'm on very unfamiliar turf here, but I trust it. I trust my ability to work through it into something." Because once you get into really familiar turf, you start getting a little bit bored anyway. It's when you're in those other places that the exciting breakthroughs happen. With any work that I've ever done, which I feel is worth anything, when I started out working with it, I was really in the dark and I wasn't sure where I was going to come out. So I tend to trust that aspect of music, and that's to me the real high, most beautiful part of it — knowing that you're not the one doing it, that you're actually waiting for something to come through you.

COMPOSITIONS

1957	Trio for violin, clarinet, and piano
1958-59	Two Pieces for piano
1959	*Spectra* for violin, viola, cello, flute, clarinet, and bassoon
1960	*Envelope* for any four instruments
1960	String Quartet
1960	*Concert* for two pianos and tape recorders
1960	*The Five-Legged Stool* dance score
1961	*M...MIX* for tape
1961	String Trio
1963	*The Gift* theater music
1963	*Street Piece Helsinki* theater music
1964	*In A Flat Or Is It B Flat?* for tape
1964	*Shoeshine* for tape
1964	*The Bird Of Paradise* for tape
1964	*I* for tape
1964	*In C* for large ensemble
1965	*Sames* theater music
1965	*Tread On The Trail* for jazz ensemble
1965	*The Keyboard Studies*
1966	*I Can't Stop No* for tape
1966	*Olson III* for chorus and orchestra
1967	*Poppy Nogood And The Phantom Band* for soprano saxophone and tape time-lag accumulation
1968	*A Rainbow In Curved Air* for improvising solo electronic keyboard
1971	*The Persian Surgery Dervishes* for improvising solo electronic keyboard
1972	*Les Yeux Fermés* film score

1973   *Le Secret De La Vie* film score
1973   *Les Metamorphoses Du Regard* film score
1976   *Crossroads* film score
1976   *The Descending Moonshine Dervishes* for improvising solo
         electronic keyboard
1976   *Shri Camel* for improvising solo electronic keyboard
1980   *Remember This Oh Mind* for improvising voice and electronic
         keyboards
1980   *Chorale Of The Blessed Day* for improvising voice and electronic
         keyboards
1980   *Song From The Old Country* for improvising voice and electronic
         keyboards
1981   *Sunrise Of The Planetary Dream Collector* for string quartet
1981   *G Song* for string quartet
1981-82 *The Ethereal Time Shadow* for improvising voice and electronic
         keyboards
1982   *Embroidery* for improvising voice and electronic keyboards
1982   *Eastern Man* for improvising voice and electronic keyboards
1984   *The Medicine Wheel* for voice, keyboards, sitar, and tabla
         (in collaboration with Krishna Bhatt)
1984   *The Emerald Runner* for voice, keyboards, sitar, and tabla
         (in collaboration with Krishna Bhatt)
1984   *No Man's Land* film score
1984   *Winter Man's Dance* and *Mythic Birds Waltz* for string quartet
1984   *The Harp Of New Albion* for piano tuned in just intonation
1984   *Cadenza On The Night Plain* for string quartet
1985-86 *Salome Dances For Peace* for string quartet
1987   *In Winter They Buried The Cocktail Pianist* for mixed ensemble
1987   *The Pipes Of Medb* for saxophone quartet
1988   *3 Songs* for women's chorus
1989   *The Jade Palace Orchestral Dances* for orchestra
1990   *Shades Of White* for mixed instruments and voices
1990   *Reading The Signs* for mixed instruments and voices
1991   *The Sands* for string quartet and orchestra
1991   *June Buddhas* for chorus and orchestra
1992   *The Saint Adolf Ring* theater piece

All compositions published by Celestial Harmonies, PO Box 30122, Tucson, AZ
85751.

DISCOGRAPHY

1966
Reed Streams
Mass Art 131 lp

1968
In C
CBS 7178 lp; cd (1988)

1969
A Rainbow In Curved Air / Poppy Nogood And The Phantom Band
CBS 7315 lp; cd (1988)

1972
Les Yeux Fermés (Happy Ending)
Warner Brothers 46125 lp

The Persian Surgery Dervishes
Shandar 83501 lp

1975
Le Secret De La Vie (Lifespan)
Stip 1011 lp

1980
Shri Camel
CBS 35164 lp, cs; cd (1988)

1982
Descending Moonshine Dervishes
Kuckuck 11047-4 lp, cs
Celestial Harmonies 12047-2 cd (1991)

1983
Songs For The Ten Voices Of The Two Prophets
Kuckuck 11067-4 lp, cs
Celestial Harmonies 12047-2 cd (1991)

1985
No Man's Land
Plainisphare 1267 lp

Sunrise Of The Planetary Dream Collector, G Song, Mythic Birds Waltz, Cadenza On The Night Plain
Gramavision 18-7014-1 lp, -2 cd, -4 cs

1986
The Ethereal Time Shadow (excerpt)
Mills College 001 lp

The Harp Of New Albion
Celestial Harmonies 018/19 lp, cs, cd (1988)

1989
Salome Dances For Peace
Elektra/Nonesuch 79217-2 cd, -4 lp

1990
In C
Celestial Harmonies 7869 cd

In C
Argo 430380 cd

1992
June Buddhas
Music Masters 67089-2 cd

Tread On The Trail
Point Music 434873-2 cd

The Padova Concert
Amiata 0292 cd

collaboration

with John Cale:
Church Of Anthrax Columbia 30131 lp (1970)

photo: Gene Bagnato

NED ROREM / Introduction

NED ROREM was born in Richmond, Indiana, on October 23, 1923. He studied at Chicago's American University with Leo Sowerby and at Northwestern University. In 1943 he took classes at the Curtis Institute with Rosario Scalero, and the following year went to Juilliard, where he studied with Bernard Wagenaar and received his B.A. and M.A. Around this time he also worked as Virgil Thomson's copyist in exchange for $20 per week and orchestration lessons. In 1946 and '47 he was a Fellow in Composition at the Tanglewood Music Center, where he studied with Aaron Copland.

Rorem left for France in 1949, where he studied with Arthur Honegger. After spending time in Morocco, he settled in Paris and became active in the cultural and social life of the city. Through the patronage of Marie Laure, Vicomtesse de Noialles, he was able to produce a steady stream of compositions, most notably for voice and piano, and form valuable friendships with such luminaries as Jean Cocteau, Francis Poulenc, and Georges Auric.

Rorem returned to the States in 1958, and by the mid '60s produced many of his most popular works, orchestral (*Eagles*, 1958; *Lions*, 1963; *Water Music*, 1966), chamber (Flute Trio, 1960; *Lovers*, 1964), and of course, vocal (*Two Poems Of Theodore Roethke*, 1959; *Poems Of Love And The Rain*, 1963). He also composed incidental music for numerous plays and premiered an opera, *Miss Julie* (1965). In 1966 he published excerpts of the diaries he'd kept in Paris; material written in New York was released the following year. Rorem's witty and articulate style, combined with his provocative comments on matters aesthetic, political, and sexual, attracted considerable attention and controversy. Further diary publications would appear in the ensuing years, as well as several volumes of critical essays, all of which would secure for him a literary reputation that, in some circles, has rivalled his renown as a composer.

His abilities as an author have undoubtedly played a part in Rorem's success in writing for voice, in his selection of texts as well as his sensitivity in setting them without sacrificing their integrity and complexities. Combining a tuneful gift with a sure sense of what the voice can do, Rorem has come to be acknowledged as America's premiere composer of art song. But he has also written powerfully for voice with chamber ensemble (*Ariel*, 1971; *Serenade*, 1975) or orchestra (*The Schuyler Songs*, 1987; *Swords And Plowshares*, 1990), as well as for unaccompanied voices (*Pilgrim Strangers*, 1984). Whatever the situation, his vocal writing is prized for its economy, expressiveness, and nuanced sense of theater.

Among the many awards and citations Rorem has received are the George

Gershwin Memorial Prize, the Lili Boulanger Award, a Fulbright Fellowship, the Prix de Biarritz, a Guggenheim Fellowship, an award from the National Institute of Arts and Letters, the ASCAP-Deems Taylor award, the 1976 Pulitzer Prize (for *Air Music*), and the Horblit Award. He also has an honorary Doctorate of Fine Arts from Northwestern University. Rorem has received commissions from numerous sources, including the Ford Foundation, the New York City Opera, the Koussevitzky Foundation, the Atlanta Symphony, and the Lincoln Center Foundation.

Ned Rorem currently teaches at the Curtis Institute, and divides his time between his house in Nantucket and a New York City apartment. I spoke with him at his Manhattan home on December 8, 1990, and again on February 24, 1991. Although he has published several volumes of diaries and had at that time just begun writing his autobiography, he has intentionally written very little about his own music. In speaking with him, I sought to learn more about his earlier, less well known compositions, as well as his more celebrated scores, vocal and instrumental.

NED ROREM / Interview

Q: You've called your *Four Madrigals* of 1947, on texts by Sappho, your "opus one," but I'd like to start a little before then. I read that you did music for two puppet shows earlier that year: *At Noon Upon Two* and *Fire Boy*.

ROREM: *At Noon Upon Two* was on a text of Charles Henri Ford, who's still very much kicking, with puppets designed by the late Kurt Seligmann, a Belgian surrealist. All that came about through John Myers, one of the three editors of *View* magazine. *View* was the American artery of Surrealism published during World War Two by Ford, Myers, and Parker Tyler. The European branch of Surrealism, as founded by Breton, was, of course, notoriously unmusical as well as homophobic, so the *View* contingent was something of an offshoot, certainly an antidote. (Those Europeans, incidentally, hadn't much humor, except perhaps for the filmmaker, Buñuel. I remember with amusement his announcement that, having just made out his will, he had decided to bequeath everything to Nelson Rockefeller. That news rings a cogent bell today when the Guggenheim Foundation is soliciting money from those still-living composers who once held fellowships. What cruel irony, when composers are, by definition, poor, and whose music should be more than enough recompense to the Guggenheim empire!)

Anyway, I got involved with them and wrote background music for a weird playlet about a puppet man looking through a keyhole at two other puppets doing odd things to each other. The score was for flute and piano, with a bit of percussion which I played myself. *Fire Boy* was on a text of Charles Boultenhouse, Parker Tyler's friend. I wrote three songs for it. I've since recycled material from both of these works.

Q: Have you recycled a lot of your music from that time?

ROREM: Not a lot. It might look that way, but that's not really the case. I'm quite prolific, but occasionally I do go back and pillage goodies from second-rate or unrealized things of my youth. Why not? Bach and Handel and Vivaldi and everybody else did. Or I'll take a song out of an unpublished cycle of yore, discard the words, and rearrange it. The Violin Concerto, for example, has a movement that's simply a song without a text.

Q: I was also curious about *That We May Live* from 1946, which is described in your catalog simply as a "pageant."

ROREM: David Diamond was one of the first grown-up composers I befriended when I came to New York. He had been approached to collaborate on a grandiose affair about Israel, of which every aspect was completed except the music. David couldn't do it, so he threw it my way. I got all of $500, which was a lot in 1946 — certainly for me, when I was whatever, 22 or 23. I'm very not-Jewish, except by association; I'm a Midwestern Quaker with a WASP background. But that made no difference to the producers. So I got together with writer Milton

Robertson and his wife Marie Machovsky, a Martha Graham dancer. (At that same time I was working as rehearsal pianist for Martha Graham, so it was all part of the family.) They showed me a lot of horas and other Palestiniana. Robertson provided the script and Bob Schneider produced the thing. I've never seen them since. But I wrote a lot of Hebraic music.

Q: You were actually composing in that style?

ROREM: I tried more then than I would today, for example, because I just sort of did what I was told. Have I salvaged anything? No. But it was a good exercise in orchestration. I hadn't heard any of my own orchestra music before 1946.

Q: That music was for full orchestra?

ROREM: For full orchestra, dancers, speakers, mimes, singers — the whole damned thing. It was a pageant and was first done in Madison Square Garden. Then it was done later in Philadelphia. I remember having to hire a lawyer because they'd promised me another hundred dollars, and I couldn't get it. She got it for me, then charged a hundred-dollar fee.

Q: Regarding your studies at Juilliard, *People* magazine quoted you as saying you "learned nothing."

ROREM: It's unfair to say I learned nothing at Juilliard. After high school, I went to Northwestern for two and a half years. My father, who was an angel, and my mother too, were both very decent about my wanting to be a composer. When I was very young, Father asked me, "Well, how do you expect to make a living?" A very American question. I gave a very un-American answer: "I don't care how I make a living as long as I have enough to eat and can write what I want." He was impressed. Today, even more than then, a child is gauged by how much money he hopes to make, and parents are proud of "my son the doctor." But Father and Mother, although cultured, intelligent, middle-class Chicagoans, were not specifically musically directed; now suddenly they were confronted by a *composer* in the family! That doesn't happen every day. When I quit Northwestern in 1943 to go to the Curtis Institute, that was because Father himself had, in his many travels, presented some of my juvenilia at Curtis and they accepted me right away, which made my parents feel good. But I left Curtis after one year.

Q: I've read that it wasn't a very pleasant time for you.

ROREM: I loved it in many ways — I made dear friends at Curtis. But I didn't see eye to eye with my teacher, Rosario Scalero. He was an unsuccessful composer, though he'd successfully guided both Barber and Menotti, his two prize pupils. He was their sole teacher. But they were a lot younger when they first went to the maestro in the '30s, whereas I was already 19 and had ideas of my own. I strongly feel that young people need to study with, not great teachers necessarily, but someone experienced enough at hearing his own music well played that he needn't be jealous of the student. I left Curtis having learned a lot about the performing world. Some of my best friends today were colleagues at Curtis. Last night I dined with pianist Gary Graffman, who currently runs the school — he was just a little kid at school in those days, four years younger than me. Ironically, now I teach at Curtis, and am writing a Left-Hand Concerto for him.

Father was very annoyed that I went to New York to work as Virgil Thomson's copyist. He cut off my allowance. But Virgil gave me 20 bucks a week for 20 hours copying. I put five dollars in the bank, paid ten dollars rent to my friend Morris Golde, with whom I lived, and had another five left over to get drunk on. A year later, for Father's sake, I went back to school and got a Master's Degree at Juilliard. To get a degree there, as distinct from a diploma, you must take a lot of extra-musical stuff. I passed the musical entrance exams and so didn't take music courses, except piano minor. I took English literature, sociology, a course called hygiene, phys ed, stuff like that. The English teacher was Elbert Lenrow who gave a pretty good course, which included the Greek tragedies in English and the Bible. I'm a literary person, always was, but had never formally studied the classics. Thanks to that I composed my first choruses on Sappho Madrigals, and have never done better.

Q: Were you composing all that time at Juilliard even though you were taking so few music classes?

ROREM: My teacher was Bernard Wagenaar. I liked him as a man but didn't learn much from him, really. I did write my Master's Degree piece called Overture In C, which won the Gershwin Memorial award. I deserved the prize but it didn't. Michel Piastro conducted it in Carnegie Hall, and I got a thousand dollars to boot.

Q: When you won that prize, *The New York Times* reported, "With the money, Mr. Rorem will continue his musical studies in Europe, and it is his intention to devote himself to writing popular music."

ROREM: What does that mean? What month was that?

Q: December of 1948.

ROREM: The Gershwin event was in May of the following year. The Philharmonic played the Overture on May 19. I had planned to go to Europe in '48, because Eugene Istomin and Shirley Gabis were already there, and I was going to meet them. But I got chicken pox. At twenty-three! I convalesced at Mother's and Father's in Philadelphia, and wrote the First Piano Sonata — the "Chicken Pox Sonata." But it was never my intention to write what would then be called popular music. The *Times* could have been misled by just the name Gershwin Award.

I took the thousand dollars and went to France, like everyone else for a few months. In those days, all good Americans went to Paris, as they had after the

First World War. Nobody went to Germany, it was too close to the holocaust, nor to England because it was full of English people. But France was there and everyone, black and white, went to France. I had planned to spend only the summer, but I met somebody, a doctor, who lived in Morocco. By a fluke I stayed on for eight years. The doctor, Guy Ferrand, invited me to spend a month in Morocco. This was in June, and I still had my boat ticket back to New York in September. But when September rolled around, I didn't want to go back. I cashed in the ticket and never returned.

Q: Was Morocco something of a retreat or withdrawal for you, or were you involved in its musical life at that time?

ROREM: Morocco was a perfect spot for two years because I was out of the rat race: There was no competition, no pressure. In Fez, then later in Marrakech, I sort of composed my first everything: I sat down and categorically declared, "I shall now write a symphony" — it was not commissioned — "I shall now write a string quartet." And I wrote things that are just part of the repertory: my Symphony No. 1, my String Quartet No. 1, Piano Sonata No. 2, a Violin Sonata, choral works, piano suites, etcetera. I never wrote "Moroccan music." Well, yes, on two occasions, I did take Moroccan tunes heard on the radio and wove them in an American fabric just for the trick of it. But you'd never guess it. Morocco was the right place at that time. I got a Fulbright around then and went back to Paris to study with Honegger — whom I loved; he was a gentle, intelligent, dying man, and I was the star of his class. But I missed Africa and Guy Ferrand. I told Honegger about my ties in Morocco. He said, "Go on, there's nothing much I can give you now. I'll simply sign your monthly voucher and see that the Fulbright check is sent down there." What a mensch!

So I went back to Morocco. The tension was off there. All I did was compose and live with my friend. I did have an interesting "social" life because every week or two Guy would go off to innoculate tribes full of people who had never seen a city like Fez, where we were living, let alone Paris. I had a new education, learning French thoroughly by going to American movies dubbed in French with Arabic subtitles, reading the papers, and having a lover — lovers are more patient than real people. The best way to learn a language is in bed.

Still, I would go back to Paris every few months to get into trouble, hear concerts, go to parties, sleep around, do things young people do. But I did it with more violence than most. Then I met a woman, La Vicomtesse de Noialles, known to all as Marie Laure, who was rich, famous, powerful, talented, opinionated, with the most beautiful house in Paris. She and I became very close. So I went back and forth over the Mediterranean, then finally settled in Paris for good. But I had come back to France with a backlog of works, most of which were then played in France, mainly because I was there to shepherd the performances. France is the least musical country in the world, and certainly ignores Americans, unless the Americans are there in the flesh.

Q: You've become well known for what you've called your "innate Francophilia."
Yet you've written that Paris in particular is "the least musical of cities," and France
"the most heterosexual of European countries." Either one would take some of the
philia out of anyone's Franco; together, they seem positively damning.

ROREM: Did I write that? Well, such generalities are themselves quite French.
     The music part first. France has produced great musicians, great composers and
great performers, but not a listening public. Now Italians, for example, have a bigger whistling knowledge of their own opera literature than I do or than you do,
and they rise in their seats and sing along. Any Roman barber knows his Rossini or
Verdi inside out. Germans pridefully know their lied, as the Spanish know their
zarzuelas. But the French, who coined the word chauvinism, will say, "Isn't it
beautiful," even as the music is playing. They like to talk about music, more than
they like to listen to it. The French are visual, culinary, sartorial; they know about
food, about dressmaking, about painting. I love the French and have perhaps
earned the right to say all this, though I don't necessarily like it when other people
do. Boulez, for example, had to leave France in order to become a prophet in his
own land. They intellectualize about music. France of course is going downhill
now, culturally. They've got money, or seem to have, but they no longer have creative urgency in any of the arts. Boulez has got France in a stranglehold, with all
that dough from the government and that hole in the ground called IRCAM. With
hindsight, his own music seems now to be quite accessibly Impressionistic, in the
style of the land, but he might not like to hear that.
     As for homosexuality, that's a quaint thing to say. Does it mean anything?
What I must have meant is that any country that's filled with expatriates is
inclined to cater to the sexual needs of those expatriates. France used to be more
broadminded than the U.S.A., and probably still is. But the expatriate milieu is
actually quite small, while the artists' milieu is even smaller. Painters are not on
the whole very gay (likewise musicians). Certainly not in the France of the 1950s.
And the French are a lot more bourgeois than one realizes: They get married, have
children, gain weight, look at television. Italians get married, have children, but
they don't gain weight; they'll spend their last lire not on a bottle of vin rouge but
on a necktie. Again, I'm speaking of the old days. I don't know about today.
Germany was always far more decadent, in the delicious sense of the word, than
France, and overt homosexuality comes with decadence, at least in the eyes of the
right wing. These quips are Gallic generalities. If I once believed them, they no
longer seem very clever.
     There are only two mystiques, or aesthetics, in the whole universe, French and
German. French is superficial in the deepest sense of the word, whereas German is
profound in the shallowest sense of the word. The French are interested in surface: Impressionism. Debussy shows us the glint on a wave during one split-second, and captures the glint forever. Monet shows us the peach-colored tint on a
water lily which will never, never, never come again. The French are also very eco-

nomical. They don't use too many notes, don't double in their orchestration, avoid thickening with schmalz. Germans are the reverse. They dig deep but in one small hole. The four-note motive (on but two pitches) of Beethoven's Fifth Symphony repeats itself until the cows come home. That's neither good nor bad, it's simply a way of thinking.

My attraction toward French culture was instilled long before I ever went to France, and comes partly from being raised in a Quaker Meeting where we didn't have much high camp. No incense, no saints, no gold, no choirs, no *tralala* as the French say. I was fiendishly attracted toward the Catholic church, which made my parents uneasy; they were wary of Catholics and they were probably right.

Q: But they'd let you visit those churches and their services on occasions, as part of your education.

ROREM: Oh sure. But when I came home and started drawing pictures of cruci-fixes and things, they took a dimmer view. They didn't realize that I wasn't inter-ested in the lore of the religion or the holy water per se, so much as in the balletic mystery of it all. In fact, Quakerism has as much mystery, but less veneer.

Q: And today, in pieces of yours such as *Gloria*, it's not the religious idea of the words that's important to you but the poetry and the imagery of the texts.

ROREM: Exactly. Because I am an atheist. There is no God. Yet it's a philosoph-ical necessity for people to have a God. I wish I could believe in Him, but I don't. I do, however, believe in the Belief that has caused great works of art to come about. Of course, there's also a lot of lousy art in the name of the Lord. Just as when I take a bow, thinking myself glamorous on the stage, and am surprised when people say, "Why are you timid and childish when you come out on the stage?," so with my music: I think of it as sensual and heart-on-sleeve, but Poulenc once said, "Be more like us, *mon cher* Ned. Be more French instead of such a Norwegian Quaker." We never "see oursels as ithers see us."

Q: How reciprocated is your Francophilia? Your books haven't been translated into French, have they?

ROREM: No, they haven't. Which miffs me. Nobody knows me in France any-more.

Q: Do they play much of your music there?

ROREM: If they don't, at least I am in good company: The French don't perform anybody's music. They know Cage and Carter. That's all. The last time I was there, in '84, I saw a lot of young people. I didn't like Paris then, but it was still the most excruciatingly beautiful city in the world. You need to be in love to live there.

Q: The idea of your composing a ballet on *The Picture Of Dorian Gray* for a pro-duction supervised by Jean Marais sounds like the perfect convergence of talents. Yet I understand you've buried the score in a trunk somewhere.

ROREM: That's an example of something occurring because I was an American in France. Henri Sauguet, who died just last year at 90, a dear friend of Virgil's, was a friend of mine, too — the wittiest man in the world. He was a disciple of Satie, and on the edge of Les Six. Jean Marais, whom I'd never met, said to him, "We need some music for a ballet we've got in mind," and Sauguet thought that I would be ideal. He was one of those who used to call me "Dorian Gray" when I was in France. Type casting. So I met with Marais, who didn't really know much about music but was a direct and simple guy, considering that he was as famous then as Frank Sinatra. He came to the Hôtel des Saints-Pères where I had a sixth-floor walkup. The telephone man downstairs was all a-twitter when he announced, "*La marais monte.*" Anyway, up came Jean Marais. I was in a room half the size of this, with an adjoining bathroom. On the sofa were pictures that Jean Cocteau had done for me (those on the wall over there). And of course Marais was Cocteau's principle protegé, and he said, "I feel right at home." But he wasn't at home, he seemed nervous. His friend, the American George Reich, danced at the Opéra Comique, whose chief choreographer Paul Goubé dreamed up the idea of doing *Dorian Gray* with Jean Marais as the painting and George as the living, ageless Dorian. So they got me for the music.

I'd written for modern dance, but never for ballet, and certainly not in France. It was about 40 minutes, and scheduled to be premiered in Barcelona. The man who commissioned it, Alberto Puig, paid for the whole mess of people, orchestra and all, to come to Barcelona and do a one-night stand in May of '52. What a bomb! Julius Katchen had previously played my Second Sonata in Barcelona without my being there, so the Spanish knew my name, thank God. I went back to Barcelona in 1964, when Steinberg did my Third Symphony there. By then the *Dorian* fiasco was forgotten. But I recall Marais with pleasure, and still see him occasionally.

Q: Had you stayed in France, could you have carved out more of a career for yourself in terms of commissions and performances?

ROREM: Probably not. I wouldn't have stayed if it hadn't been for Marie Laure. My life was hardly a typical American life: I lived with the richest woman in France. Private patronage is a thing of the past, yet for me then there was still a touch of Proust's *avant guerre* dribbling in. Every day for lunch she would have worthwhile people, Cocteau, Balthus, Poulenc, the Aurics, Dora Maar. Well, not *every* day. I did not lead an idle life; I worked hard. I thought of the physical ease as, in a way, a scholarship. I'm alcoholic, though it's no longer a problem because I now just don't drink — it's been 22 years. But I would play as hard as I worked, and I would go from Hyères in the south of France, where she lived, to Cannes to get drunk and screw around. Well, I'm still alive to tell the story. Anyone today living the life I lived then would not survive, for various reasons, not just health: You'd get killed. Life in bars and streets was less dangerous in those days. Partly because of her — not to mention lovers — I stayed in France. But finally I told myself, I'm American, my problems were born in America and can only be solved in America.

Q: Musical problems?

ROREM: The whole concept of what it means to be a composer in our world.

I had a relationship that ended badly in 1957, which is when I returned to residence in New York. Here, I started earning my living as a composer, and have been doing so ever since — knock wood.

Q: Back in the '70s, John Gruen wrote that you were one of the few people who supports himself as a composer.

ROREM: I support myself, yes, but humbly. I've never been a whore though I sometimes wish I could be. I'm too lazy to write the kind of music I don't want to write, music that's in style, serial one year, minimal the next. To write a musical and make big money — or even to have a flop — you have to know people that I'm not interested in knowing, like producers, backers, collaborators, cash-minded Broadway types. If I do live off commissions, it's not a grand life, and with no guarantee for what will happen after two years from now. But I do exactly what I want.

Q: I had thought that it was the money from writing prose which made the difference for you financially.

ROREM: No. When I published my first book I was already 40 and had lived as a professional musician 20 years before that. Since then I've led a schizophrenic life, or rather two parallel lives. People who read my books often don't realize I write music, and people that invite me to music schools to do a stint often don't realize I write books. What I earn from prose is less steady than from music. I'm a composer who also writes, not a writer who also composes.

What a composer gets, even the best known composers — and there aren't that many — to write a symphony is a tenth of what, say, Phillip Roth gets to write a novel. And I'm still talking about high art, not about Harold Robbins, much less Mick Jagger or that whole world of pop, where they make billions. Even a Pavarotti earns from a one-night what a composer earns from a whole opera which can be several years' labor.

Money is always a concern, just to pay the bills. What I get from teaching is negligible; what I get from prose and royalties and so forth is negligible. I have an advance for an autobiography from Simon & Schuster, but it's not all that much. It'll keep me alive for a year and a half.

Q: You've gotten money in the past from the NEA, both as a composer and as a writer. Have you had any dealings with them since they've started policing the work they partially support?

ROREM: I've signed various petitions that are against the dumbness of it all.

Q: Does that put you on an NEA shit list?

ROREM: I don't care at this point. I've had two or three (or four or five, I forget) grants, both as composer and author, directly from the NEA, and I appreciate these grants. But now, and not just because of Helms, the bottom seems to be falling out of the NEA.

I'm not a pornographer, though I'm not against it. It's amusing to hear people talk about their "tax dollars" because it's not dollars, but pennies that go to the arts in the USA. In Australia, which hardly has the money that America has, citizens pay the equivalent of eight tax dollars a year for the arts. The NEA has done a lot of good, yes. But they're inclined to push populist art without making a definition, and there is a difference in kind between me or Wuorinen and school children or street mimes. That doesn't mean I'm any better. Also, pop music can look elsewhere for money, because it's inherently a more lucrative thing.

It's rather healthy, all the flap. The Mapplethorpe pictures are perfectly beautiful. How embarrassing — what the French must be thinking of all this about fundamentalist fuss! But for all I know, they're doing it now too. The French can be evil and mindless, but in different ways. They have people like Le Pen, a real fascist, anti-Semitic, and who has 15% of the vote or something like that in France. But I doubt that he's concerned with cultural pollution.

Q: In *The New York Diary* you commented on the difficulty of writing your Flute Trio.

ROREM: It's hard to write music. Writing anything is hard. The last movement of the Flute Trio, I remember, was hard because it's fast. It's easier to write slow music. You can sometimes improvise or even compose it at the speed it takes to hear it; whereas with fast music, it can take a month to set down 30 pages that last one minute. This has to do with gauging and perspective and distancing and so forth, and not just mooning around and being inspired. You can't be inspired for much more than an hour at a time anyway, and some pieces take weeks, months, years.

Also, as I remember, there's only a small amount of information in that last movement. Which meant using that information upside down and backwards with the age-old devices of elongation and diminution, then trying to make it all theatrical, make it have contrast, and still hold together.

Q: You wrote almost no chamber music for a long stretch after the Flute Trio. There's *Lovers* and several scores of incidental music for the theater, but it's only in the last 20 years that you've produced a real body of chamber pieces.

ROREM: Chamber pieces without voice.

Q: Yes, precisely.

ROREM: Because there are a lot of chamber pieces with voice: trios, quintets, quartets.

Lovers is ten movements and lasts the same amount of time as the Flute Trio, which has only four. The Trio was a question of development; *Lovers* was a ques-

tion of using one inspiration and shutting up after it had been expressed —
there's a movement in *Lovers* that's only eight measures long.

Q: That form of a series of images is a congenial way for you to work.

ROREM: It was. I'd like to get out of that rut. I'm writing a piece now, the
piano concerto for the left hand, which I think will have only eight movements!
But the piano trio *Spring Music* has only five, and the string quartet which I've
just finished has five.

Q: I'm very interested about that piece, because it's been 40 years since your
Second String Quartet.

ROREM: Will I ever write another one? The First Quartet doesn't count; there
are only two quartets, but the Second Quartet was printed so quickly, and with
that title, that I couldn't change it to "First Quartet."

When dealing with the human voice, I have a text and so I know where I'm
going before I start. Without a text, I flounder more. I have to decide where I'm
going according to some sort of imagined scenario. I'm a bit at a loss if I don't
have a voice, which means in a way that I have to work harder. Maybe, as a
result, the piece will be a better piece or at least better crafted. Then again, it's
not for me to say.

Q: Did it seem a bit much to be working on both a piano trio and then a string
quartet, after not having done either for so long?

ROREM: And the Trio was written right after *The Auden Poems*, which is for trio
plus voice. However, that's a radically different thing. With a trio plus voice, you
think orchestrally. And the voice is the star — even if you don't want it to be, it
has to be. That's the nature of the beast.

I didn't want to write a quartet. But then, when it was the Guarneri that
would play it, I decided I should.

Q: You felt reservations just about the genre itself?

ROREM: Well, about getting ideas for this abstract combination — until I put
aside the worn-out notion that the string quartet is the most profound and intimate of combinations. Why can't a person write silly music for quartet? Why
can't they write French music or light music or gorgeous music? Why must it
always be so belabored? So I composed what I wanted to, and think it's a pretty
good piece as far as structure is concerned. I don't know yet if it comes to life (it
won't be played till next June), but I'm not ashamed of it. Yes, it is more complex
perhaps than other pieces of mine, but certainly Milton Babbitt wouldn't hear it
that way. One of the five movements already existed in the multisectioned
Remembering Tommy, which is not as a whole an entirely successful work. I
rearranged the movement for string quartet, which meant a fifth of my work was
done! It's exquisitely tonal, and the rest of the music is less so. In the Piano Trio,

the next-to-the-last movement was written two years ago as a four-hand piece for the birthday of Shirley Perle, but the rest of it is all original.

Q: Did writing chamber music pick up for you in the '70s mostly because of commissions? They can run in cycles for a composer.

ROREM: I usually get commissioned to write what I want to write anyway, because people know what they want from me. But some time ago, I would get more commissions than I wanted to write pieces for voice and orchestra. Once pieces of that genre get premiered they're seldom heard again, so I didn't want to write yet another piece for voice and orchestra.

I got commissioned to write *Night Music* for violin and piano right after finishing *Day Music* for violin and piano. I didn't want to accept because I now had other things in mind.

Q: Yet you went ahead and made it a companion piece to *Day Music*.

ROREM: They nourish each other. In one way, it was difficult because I was stale on the idea; in another way it was easy because I wasn't stale — the idea still churned.

I also wrote two concertos, the Organ Concerto and the Violin Concerto, at the same time, and used the same device in each of them. Things come in pairs. Just like I wrote the saxophone suite, *Picnic on the Marne*, and the cello suite called *Dances* at the same time. I tend to have any piece I write feed off the previous piece. But the third piece doesn't feed off the first: They go one-two, two-three, three-four, four-five, five-six, like that. And then sometimes six-one: I'll steal something from before.

Q: You've produced a good deal of orchestral music, but the last time you wrote a symphony for full orchestra was in the late '50s. Do you think symphony-writing per se is old hat?

ROREM: I called pieces symphonies to impress my mother and father — "symphony" means you're grown up. I now have a student from Scotland, David Horne is his name, who wrote a two-movement orchestra piece and wondered what to name it. I said to call it symphony. Instead of those currently "in" titles like "And The River Flows Through The Jade Nightmare" or "The Easter Eggs Of Fate," just call it symphony. Symphony applies to anything now. It always did. Between a Tchaikovsky symphony and a Haydn symphony, there is a gulf. And *Francesca da Rimini* could as easily be called a symphony.

Of the four symphonies I've written, none is a symphony in the sense that their first movement is in sonata-allegro form. But they all deserve the title because they're all big-scale, multimovemented affairs with cyclic use of material. Including the *String Symphony*. But I don't know if I'll ever write another one. I try not to disqualify any species per se; just about whether the species is done well or isn't done well.

Q: Was the *String Symphony* commissioned as a symphony?

ROREM: The orchestra in Georgia wanted me to write a piece for voice and orchestra, and I said no way. (That's the first time I've ever used that phrase!) I had just written *After Long Silence*, a very pretty suite for voice, strings, and oboe. I wanted to write a straight, big orchestra piece, and then thought that just strings, which I've never done for that size, would be fun. I also definitely had Robert Shaw and his orchestra in mind, and tried to write a piece that would impress Shaw because I worshipped him when I was a post-adolescent.

Q: And part of the way to impress him was to do the piece as a symphony?

ROREM: I wanted to write what I wanted to write, but I didn't want to lose him by being huffy about not writing what he wanted. I said, "Please, I've just finished that. Can't I write something not with voice?" I might have done it if he'd wanted a choral piece; but I don't remember that he did.

The two big choral pieces, the *American Oratorio* and *Good-bye My Fancy*, are both symphonies. Especially the second one because it's a three-movement structure. I might do another piece like that and call it a symphony.

Q: Your projected orchestral piece *Whales* I understand was intended to form a triptych with *Eagles* and *Lions*.

ROREM: Actually, I wrote three big gorgeous pages and orchestrated them and copied them. That's a long, long time ago, in the early '60s. After I wrote *Lions* and *Eagles* and thought about *Whales*, both Crumb and Hovhaness came up with whale pieces, so I lost interest. Which is understandable: We were all three barking up the same tree. An underwater tree, of course.

Q: Were you at all interested in the actual whale's sound? That's a common thread in both the Crumb and Hovhaness works.

ROREM: No, I wouldn't have done that. I did it once, with the music for the original stage production of *Suddenly Last Summer*. When Sebastian's mother is talking about the gulls that swoop down and eat baby turtles, I wrote some long, quivering, ominous phrases to back her up, and in the studio we superimposed the screeches of real gulls, which was effective enough I suppose.

Q: Would *Whales* have had a dream as its basis, as *Lions* did?

ROREM: No, I was going to base it — as I'd based *Eagles* — quite literally on a pre-existing poem. In fact, the only time I've ever written illustrative program music has been in the tone poem based on Whitman's "The Dalliance Of The Eagles." Every one of those ten long lines I parsed ahead of time and said, "I will represent this first line in music this way; the second line that way; the third line; the fourth line; and so on." If you read the poem, the music inevitably — dare I say literally? — reflects each verse. The verse became an excuse to write music, the way another person would use sonata form. I don't really believe that nonvocal music represents anything beyond itself; or if it does, we can't pinpoint it. But such is music's flexible power, that whatever its composer says, in words, about it, is likely to be visually conjured up by the listener. This was true with *Lions* — I'd based that on a dream. But *Sunday Morning* isn't really based on Wallace Stevens' poem. The titles were tacked on after the fact. Thanks to program notes, listeners "see" the sea when they hear *La Mer*. But if Debussy had named his tone poem *Abbatoirs*, listeners would "see" slaughterhouses while hearing the identical score.

The solo cello suite *After Reading Shakespeare* is in nine movements, each with an epigraph from the bard. I had those pretty much in mind while working. But those are intellectual statements made by man on the state of man, whereas *Eagles* is about animals. It's easier to think up musical reflections of animal behavior than a musical reflection of King Lear at his own death. It's easier at least for me to get a musical idea from a depiction of nature than from a human outcry.

Q: Is *A Quaker Reader* something of an exception to that?

ROREM: Yes. The epigraphs for those eleven pieces stood before the fact. Certainly in "Mary Dyer did hang as a flag ...": There's a trill at the beginning on the pedals, like the jiggling feet of a person just hanged. In a scene from Sartre's filmed version of *The Crucible*, they hang a bunch of witches: The camera goes to their feet. We don't see their necks cracking or eyes bulging, we see their feet shuddering. Hence the pedal point at the opening of my music — an image I would never have gotten if I hadn't seen that movie.

I don't like to intellectualize music. But the older I get the more useful it seems. I would have turned up my nose 20 years ago at thus describing music visually to a performer.

Q: Do you find there are common misconceptions among performers when they first approach your music?

ROREM: Since I compose mostly on commission, I usually know who I'm going to get before I get them. Nor is my music problematical in the sense that, say, Elliott Carter's music is. You can pretty much get the point of what I'm after just reading through it. So when I show up at a final rehearsal, all I'll say is: faster or slower or louder or softer. I seldom say, "more something else." When a group like the Beaux Arts Trio, who are used to playing standard repertory, play a new piece, they approach it as though it were real music rather than "something contemporary." They practice and then we talk. They'll sometimes put in interpretive things, a tinge of vibrato or a twist of rubato, which I might not have thought of. I'm always vaguely flattered when people "interpret" my music. But of course, I've lived among singers for so long, and as performers they have the broadest gamut of approach. With a female as opposed to a male interpreting the same song, the approach is by definition wider than two oboists or two pianists playing the same thing. When I teach a class of singers, I am more lenient about even the speed of a given song if a bass sings it or if a soprano sings it. With your eyes closed, there's a big difference between a bass and a soprano, but none between a male and female drummer. Sopranos can demand and get equal pay, which women instrumentalists cannot.

Q: I was wondering if perhaps, precisely because your music isn't like Elliott Carter's, musicians might assume it's simpler than it really is, or that what's happening is more on the surface than it really is.

ROREM: I've nothing to add — I mean, you've said it.

A good musician gets the point, so that nothing you say is really necessary, while a bad musician never gets the point, so nothing you say can help. Sometimes you'll hear a piece played so wrong, usually by people who don't have much métier. All I can do as a composer is try to spark enthusiasm — especially if I'm enthusiastic. That helps. People like to be flattered. If I'm not enthusiastic, they can't help but know.

Q: I'm familiar with your comments about Billie Holiday's phrasing and nuance in your own development as a songwriter. What I'm curious about is your remark that Count Basie's piano playing still shapes the way you approach composing for piano. Was that a bit of an overstatement, in retrospect?

ROREM: It's certainly true of Billie. I loved her. Still do. Her name is sacred to me.

Q: You knew her, didn't you?

ROREM: Well, sort of. In Chicago, when "Strange Fruit" first came out in 1938 we all went to see her at the Panther Room. It was magical, it was theater, it was grown up. She smelled good, she looked good, with that gardenia in her hair, she drank mintlike drinks and wore satin clothes and long red earrings, and sang those unbelievably sad songs — almost always by white people, standard repertory, as distinct from Bessie Smith, who did the blues. It wasn't the tune but her way with the tune that influenced me.

I'm American and no American of my generation was unaffected by jazz, even Elliott Carter — or so he claims.

Q: Could you describe how the way in which you notate or even conceive the piano writing for your songs has been affected by your work as an accompanist — I mean, as a pianist?

ROREM: Accompanist is a good word.

Q: Is it? It makes me a little bit nervous.

ROREM: It's a good word if you clarify that the singer too is an accompanist — accompanying the piano. The two accompany each other through the adventure of the song.

I've always been a pianist — it's my only instrument, my sole point of reference. The fact that sometimes I do and sometimes I don't play my own music in public might affect some pieces. If I'm composing, say, a chamber music piece that includes piano, for somebody else, I don't conceive for my hands. Last summer I wrote a piece for trio plus voice, knowing I was going to play it myself. I fashioned the patterns according to my performing ease. When I've had to learn certain pieces by myself but not written for myself, I learn them as though I were learning somebody else's music.

Q: You mentioned the element of theater in Billie Holiday's singing. You've written that Marc Blitzstein helped show you how the theater was integral even to what you called "remote forms like recital songs."

ROREM: All art is theater. Any art that exists in time — like drama, or music — is theater. People pay to sit still and experience something. That is theater. Song is theater. Last night, while coaching a baritone, I said to him, "This is not real life, it's a concentration of life. You are a singer, you have to look at the audience, from you to them. You can't hide behind your instrument as a violinist does, or a pianist. Your face will be scrutinized, it's part of the show. If you lift your eyebrow ever so slightly, it must mean something." If Billie Holiday closed her eyes, it's because she had to. It was the tiny gesture that made mountains crumble. A song is a miniature opera. A song that lasts for one minute is still an event that goes from A to Z.

Q: I'm curious about your 1965 opera *Miss Julie* and its revision in 1979. Was that mostly a matter of cutting and tightening, or did it involve some real rewriting?

ROREM: It was originally a two-act opera, two hours long. The librettist, Kenward Elmslie, and I did the sensible thing and went back to Strindberg's version, which was one act. Intermissions are always dangerous. We cut the chorus, and squeezed the opera into an hour and 35 minutes, which was also much less expensive.

Q: The Painted Smiles LP of highlights from the '79 performance made a big impression on me, not the least reason being I could understand almost everything that was sung. That isn't true of a lot of recordings of your songs — with the exception of most of Donald Gramm's performances.

ROREM: He's irreplaceable. I miss him.

Q: He comes right through — it's just amazing. And it makes me wonder to what extent intelligibility and the communication of words contribute to the theatrical sense you've been describing.

ROREM: It's maximal. All singers should forget about their voice 99% and think about the words 99%. The great ones, like Donald Gramm, when teaching classes for singers, don't talk about diphthongs, they talk about verse. Phyllis Curtin says, "I think about what the poem means. It's got to mean something to me. Whether

I like the poem or not, I have to pretend that I do, because I impart the poem to the audience through the music." Donald said, "I know I have the greatest voice in the world, so I forget about that and think mostly about the text. But I don't psychoanalyze it." A man inherently has better diction than a woman because he sings in the spoken range more than a woman does.

Q: In your notes to *Pippa's Song*, you said that because the coloratura register was so high, for once it was your fault, not the singer's, that the words couldn't be readily understood.

ROREM: I wouldn't perhaps set it that way today. When I take a liberty with prosody, I have a reason. I don't repeat words which the poet has not repeated, but I will do a melismatic thing, as in *Pippa's Song*. Or I'll decide the words don't make much difference since everybody knows them anyway, or at this particular point the tune's more important than the text, and so forth. I don't do this out of inspiration, but out of calculation.

In *The Schuyler Songs*, "It — the war — goes on" is said twice because Jimmy Schuyler repeated the words. I'm always amazed when somebody like Benjamin Britten, who's no fool and knew a thing or two about word setting, would not only repeat words but functionless words, like "the." In his operas, that's OK, because the character might be someone who stutters. But on poems of Michelangelo or Thomas Hardy, I don't know why he does it. There's always an alternative whereby a composer can keep his notes and eat them too.

Q: You've set texts in other languages than English. Is it true that you've promised yourself not to set French anymore?

ROREM: America has for generations been the leading country in the world, so far as prosperity and business and munitions are concerned. Nevertheless, we've always had a vague inferiority complex about the arts, which is why we still hire European conductors; which is why most of the opera that is done is still done in the language it was written in, with or without supertitles; which is why composers of vocal music (I mean just songs, not opera), of whom there are fewer and fewer, will as often as not write music in languages not their own. And why singers learn to sing (usually badly) in every language except their own. If I and my brothers and sisters don't create an American song literature, no one's going to do it for us. Certainly there's no Frenchman setting only words in American to music, the way George Crumb so madly sets Lorca rather than letting the Spanish do it. We've got a huge literature of first-rate poetry in the American language, from both the 20th and 19th centuries, just as legitimate as any other language, and it's a waste not to use it. I'm still surprised when song composers of all persuasions in America will still write in mostly other languages.

Yes, I too have written in other languages, mainly on commission. In a way I've earned the right to do it because I've set hundreds of different poets and prosifiers in English. I did two poems of Plato in old Greek because a young person in the early '60s wrote me a letter and said he would give me a hundred dollars apiece if I would do so — as a birthday gift for his lover. The idea touched me. I did a mass in Latin, as a phonetic experiment, because nobody knows how Latin goes anyway. I did many songs in French in the '50s, but I was after all living in France, and it was a second language. And I've set some Italian poems that have never been published or even sung, during the winter that I lived in Rome. The trouble with all that is, if a Frenchman is going to stoop to singing something by an American, he's at least going to try to sing something in English; and if an American singer's going to stoop to singing something by an American, he's not going to want to sing French songs by that American. So the songs never get performed.

It's important to stress the evil of Americans writing in foreign languages. I feel even moralistic about it, as I feel moralistic about repeating words that the poet hasn't repeated. Song in English should come from pride in our own tongue, the way the Germans and French have pride, the way the Italians have it, the way even the English have it, but which we don't. Not repeating words: that has to do with respect for the poem.

Q: I was very interested to read that you'd received some flak for writing *Ariel*, your piece for voice, clarinet, and piano, on the basis that a man shouldn't be setting poems by Sylvia Plath.

ROREM: That was at the beginning of the women's movement. Robin Morgan was more hyperthyroid in 1971 than she is now 20 years later. I recall being shocked when she, a close friend, told me, "Keep your hands off Plath, she belongs to our sisters," because poetry doesn't belong to anyone, including the poet, once it's written. When I composed *Women's Voices* for Joyce Mathis, a black soprano who commissioned me, I set to music all women's poems. But I didn't take any black women, for the simple reason that there's no black in me. All the female black poetry — most black poetry, period — in 1975 (and for all I know today) is about the condition of being black, a condition which I'm very, very, very, very sympathetic to, but cannot identify with, except intellectually. On the other hand, there's a lot of woman in me, and half of my ancestors are women. And I know as much about women in my way as Robin Morgan and the feminists do.

Q: In the Plath poems you set, the persona is female but there's nothing she describes which is so unique to being female that those images couldn't be appreciated by a man or used by a man.

ROREM: However, time has passed and I don't know whether I would use them today. The interesting thing is not whether I have the right, but whether Robin Morgan or her clan can tell whether a woman or a man had done the settings, if they didn't know beforehand. Women composers are not as worried as they used to be. "No one's going to call me a woman composer," they would seem to declare, and write music that was far more butch than any man's. All that's changed today. There's a wider space between a good and a bad composer than between a male and a female composer.

Q: Has *Ariel* been performed as much as your other cycles?

ROREM: Well, things go in ... cycles. One teacher, say, will get ahold of the piece and assign it to a lot of students; or one singer will hear it and then decide to perform it on tour; or the shove will come from a clarinetist, because it's a showy piece. If I go to a college or something like that, they might get a soprano and a clarinetist on the faculty to do it with the pianist. And I've heard it done very well indeed by lots of different kinds of people. I would just as soon hear a man sing it if he wanted to.

Q: I wanted to ask you about that.

ROREM: Music is above sex. It can be about sex, but it isn't sex; it represents sex. Therefore, a woman playing a man's role in the Strauss or Mozart operas, once you get used to it, you don't question it. When black Leontyne does white Tosca, you get used to it in about a minute. When men do women's roles, we're not used to it, so it strikes us as either funny or macabre (as when *The Maids* of Genet, which was written to be performed by men in drag, was done that way as a ballet by Herbert Ross — it's frightening). A lot of people don't agree, but I think that a man can sing a woman's songs and vice versa — providing that the voice can adapt itself without too much transposition. A woman once asked me if she could do *War Scenes*, and I said, why not? It's her world too; the war effects her just as much.

Q: There's a wonderful observation you made about William Flanagan's music: "In refusing to conform to the non-conformists, he presents himself as the most avant of the avant-garde."

ROREM: He was still alive when I wrote that. I wouldn't say it now.

Q: Would you write that about your music?

ROREM: I don't write about my own music.

Q: I've noticed!

ROREM: I'm not interested in what composers say about their own music. Composers can't really know anything about their own music from the outside in. I may be astute about other people's music, and say things that need saying, and I love writing about music that I love, rather than music I hate. But my own music must sing for its supper all alone.

Q: I'm interested in this idea of conservatism as a form of rebellion. Were you thinking also of your own music when you wrote that about his?

ROREM: I might have been sympathetic to Bill because musically we were two of a kind. I was more publically successful than Bill and a lot more prolific. He didn't resent that, although he did try to imitate my devices. But he wasn't me so it didn't work. I don't mean imitate the music, but the life I led. His metabolism was different from mine.

I write what I write. I survived a long, long period when my music was not in fashion. As I said before, I'd like to be a whore but can't. I'm too lazy. Never during that period from 1955 until 1980, did I write a piece of the kind everyone else was writing, willfully ugly, which nobody liked anyway. Copland did it, but I knew his heart wasn't in it. Plus, all the other younger people. It's easy to hide behind such music, because you can't tell the good from the bad. When the revolution came and my music became fashionable again, I felt like the Prodigal Son's brother who had always been a good boy.

Probably I'm a contradictory type, as I try to see the outside world seeing me. On the one hand, I'm a conservative because I write tonal music, and *au fond* I feel that all music is tonal. Yet I'm radical by being a gay atheist. Then again I'm a monarchist in a way, an aristocrat — I don't think everyone's equal. I despise William Buckley politically, but concur with much that he believes in artistically. And I am many things that he detests.

Q: You've made a very interesting distinction between what you've called conservative and reactionary music, that reactionary music uses traditional devices unchanged, whereas conservative music uses traditional devices freshly. Have you ever written reactionary music, do you think, looking back?

ROREM: Not on purpose. I might have. But first of all, that's my definition. Nor can freshness be willed into being.

Originality per se is not a very important virtue. Anyone can be original. Anyone can do something nobody else has done, but that's not necessarily going to make what you do any good. Nothing comes from nothing, everybody is influenced. People who don't know what their influences are are the innocent reactionaries, because they go blithely along with their postcard pieces unaware that they've stolen them intact from somebody who does it better. A true musician knows that he is stealing, and tries to cover his traces. The act of covering the traces is the act of creation.

Q: You've commented many times about the distinction between the art of composition and the craft of orchestration.

ROREM: Now I wouldn't even say the art of composition. It too is a craft. When talking to lay people or to the National Endowment for the Arts, I may talk about the "artist," the "creator," and all of that nonsense, because they should think the artist is somebody special. And he is! He should be offered barrels of rubies and not have to give anything in return — except his own gifts. He should be allowed to be a bastard, and most people are — not bastards, really, but yet no better than they should be, since the beginning of time. I can teach anyone to write a perfect song.

Because it's a craft. But whether the song bleeds and breathes is up to God — the God I don't believe in. It's up to whatever art is.

Now, I wouldn't say that to everybody. I'm of two minds. I do think that before the Industrial Revolution, music was considered a craft. Would that it could be taken seriously as a craft today! It's only taken seriously by people who put composers on a pedestal but starve them to death. In fact, composers don't exist at all today — as opposed to painters or authors. A composer does not exist in the ken of cultured intellectuals who know Kafka and Kierkegaard and painting of the past and present; when it comes to the music of the present, it's pop music. What I'm doing, and the other people in your book, is very, very peripheral to the general consciousness — with a few exceptions. Philip Glass is an exception, but his audience is not essentially a musical audience; it's a yuppie audience. Steve Reich's the same: Fred Waring without the tunes.

Q: I'm interested in your attitude about writing orchestral music. How separate are the two things, composing for orchestra and then orchestrating what you've composed?

ROREM: When a composer is writing an orchestra piece, he has the orchestra constantly in mind. When he gets an idea for an instrumental piece, he's not just "getting an idea," but an idea for English horn or four horns or strings or guitar or whatever. Most of my orchestra music was originally conceived for the orchestra. One can tell, in the final analysis, what was originally conceived for the orchestra. (Chopin's and Schumann's symphonic music reeks of the keyboard.) But sometimes I've taken pieces from the past — inevitably small ones — and out of perversity revamped them for a different medium.

Does this inhibit inspiration? Inspiration's an outsider word. All composers are inspired: Their main problem is how to hone the impulse into something communicable. The greatest artists have no more than about five inspirations in their whole life. These come like flashes in the night: The sky is aflame and suddenly you see, as through mescaline, some sort of truth for a few seconds — you couldn't live longer with such brightness without going mad. You spend the next few years trying to recover that flash in various sizes and shapes and mediums. Then along comes another inspiration — or not. But even without these flashes, I don't think composers necessarily get "better." Is the late Beethoven or late Ravel or late Chopin any better than the early? But in Beethoven's case (not Ravel's or Chopin's) there *is* a change in grammar. People don't see themselves, which is why I don't write about my own music — at least not inspirationally. I do know that after I started publishing books, and realizing that total strangers were going to be reading such madness, I got a new sense of responsibility about my prose. I've tried to make it less self-centered. My music got tougher as the prose got sharper. Maybe. In any case the two crafts are unrelated — I'm schizoid.

Q: The image of your work is that the music expresses your sense of order, control, and balance, whereas the writing, particularly the *Diaries*, is wild and uninhibited and expresses the appetites. Yet your writing, whatever the subject matter, is always disciplined, controlled, and discreet, never sensual or erotic, whereas the music, especially for orchestra, is filled with sensuality and the visceral, and is extremely volatile and changeable.

ROREM: That's you talking.

Q: You don't see those qualities.

ROREM: It doesn't make any difference whether I see them or not. The important thing is that you see them. I'm making them for you. To say I agree with you, that's sheer vanity. I should say only that I'm very interested in what you're saying. Which I am.

Q: This impression makes me think of what Poulenc had said to you, that the orchestra was your true nature.

ROREM: When I told Virgil Thomson that Poulenc had said that out of jealousy, so I wouldn't write songs, Virgil was shocked by such arrogance. But I was probably right.

Q: Perhaps Poulenc was implying that the texts of the songs provide a mask or persona, whereas the natural expressiveness that's at the heart of your music functions more on its own when you write for orchestra, regardless of any programmatic ideas the composition may have.

ROREM: But that's involuntary. Even with prose, when I'm writing about something beyond my navel — an obituary, a précis of an opera, a historic souvenir — I hope it comes across that way. When writing about someone I never knew, like Ravel, I don't know how other people read it, but I try to include intelligent and original information. I don't know if I put information in my music, because I don't know what information means in music. Do I give the impression of being conceited? I'm not. I think I know my worth, and that there are certain things, however small, I can do that nobody else can do. If I didn't believe that I would stop. But I don't know how important these things are. Then again, I don't know how important anything is. I don't know how important George Bush is, and he runs the world; or how important Michael Jackson or John Cage are, who are disproportionately famous. No one knows the future, but I persevere, mainly because I need to keep living. I do love my work, though the driving urge is not what it was in adolescence. Self-doubt looms always. Is it for everybody? Even if it were, does that mean it's going to be any good?

COMPOSITIONS

1943	*Four-Hand Piano Sonata*	MS
1943	*The Seventieth Psalm* for mixed chorus and wind ensemble	B&H
1944	*Doll's Boy* for voice and piano	B&H
1944	*Overture For G.I.'s* for band	MS
1944	*Song Of Chaucer* for voice and piano	MS
1945	*Dawn Angel* for voice and piano	MS
1945	*Lost In Fear* ballet with piano accompaniment	MS
1945	*A Psalm Of Praise* for voice and piano	AMP
1945	*A Song Of David* for voice and piano	AMP
1946	*Absalom* for voice and piano	B&H
1946	*Alleluia* for voice and piano	B&H
1946	*Cain And Abel* opera (unorchestrated)	MS
1946	*Concertino Da Camera* for harpsichord and seven instruments	MS
1946	*Fantasy And Toccata* for organ	B&H
1946	*The Long Home* for chorus and orchestra	MS
1946	*On A Singing Girl* for voice and piano	B&H
1946	*Seven Little Prayers* for voice and piano	MS
1946	*Spring And Fall* for voice and piano	TP
1946	*That We May Live* pageant	MS
1947	*At Noon Upon Two* puppet show	MS
1947	*Catullus: On The Burial Of His Brother* for voice and piano	B&H
1947	*Fire Boy* puppet show for voice and piano	MS
1947	*Four Madrigals* for mixed chorus a capella	TP
1947	*The Lordly Hudson* for voice and piano	TP
1947	*Mongolian Idiot* for voice and piano	MS
1947	*Mourning Scene From Samuel* for voice and string quartet	CFP
1947	*A Sermon On Miracles* for unison chorus, solo voice, and strings; for voice and piano	B&H
1947	*Spring* for voice and piano	B&H
1947	String Quartet No. 1 (withdrawn)	MS
1947	*Three Blues Of Paul Goodman* for voice and piano	ROP
1948	Concerto No. 1 For Piano (withdrawn)	MS
1948	*Death Of The Black Knight* ballet	MS
1948	*Dusk* incidental music	MS
1948	*Echo's Song* for voice and piano	B&H
1948	*Hippolytus* incidental music	MS
1948	*A Quiet Afternoon* for piano	PSO
1948	*Requiem* for voice and piano	PSO
1948	Sonata No. 1 for piano	CFP
1948	*Three Incantations* for voice and piano	B&H
1948	*Toccata* for piano	CFP

1948	*Two Poems Of Edith Sitwell* for voice and piano	B&H
1949	*Barcarolles* for piano	CFP
1949	*Cock-A-Doodle* incidental music	MS
1949	*Little Elegy* for voice and piano	B&H
1949	*Mountain Song* for flute and piano	PSO
1949	Overture In C for orchestra	MS
1949	*Penny Arcade* for voice and piano	MS
1949	*Rain In Spring* for voice and piano	B&H
1949	*Seconde Sonate Pour Piano*	GB
	(revised 1950: Sonata No. 2 for piano)	TP
1949	*The Silver Swan* for voice and piano	PSO
1949	Sonata For Violin And Piano	CFP
1949	Suite For Two Pianos	MS
1949	*What If Some Little Pain* for voice and piano	B&H
1950	Concerto No. 2 for piano and orchestra	PSO
1950	*Flight For Heaven* for bass-baritone and piano	TP
1950	*Lullaby Of The Woman Of The Mountain* for voice and piano	B&H
1950	*Pastorale* for organ	PSO
1950	*Philomel* for voice and piano	B&H
1950	*Sicilienne* for two pianos	PSO
1950	*Six Irish Poems* for voice and orchestra	PSO
1950	String Quartet No. 2	PSO
1950	Symphony No. 1	PSO
1951	*Another Sleep* for voice and piano	MS
1951	*Ballet For Jerry*	MS
1951	*The Call* for voice and piano	TP
1951	*Cycle Of Holy Songs* for voice and piano	PSO
1951	*From An Unknown Past* for mixed chorus or voice and piano	PSO
1951	*Love In A Life* for voice and piano	B&H
1951	*Melos* ballet	MS
1951	*The Nightingale* for voice and piano	B&H
1951	*To A Young Girl* song for voice and piano	B&H
1951	*To A Young Girl* song cycle for voice and piano	MS
1951	*Whiskey, Drink Divine* for voice and piano	MS
1952	*An Angel Speaks To The Shepherds* for voice and piano	PSO
1952	*A Childhood Miracle* opera for six singers and thirteen instruments	PSO
1952	*A Christmas Carol* for voice and piano	TP
1952	*Dorian Gray* ballet	MS
1952	*The Mild Mother* for unison chorus	ECS
1952	*The Resurrection* for voice and piano	PSO
1953	*Boy With A Baseball Glove* for voice and piano	MS
1953	*The Corinthians* for chorus and organ	CFP
1953	*Design* for orchestra	B&H

1953	*Eclogues* for voice and piano	MS
1953	*A Far Island* for mixed chorus	TP
1953	*Five Prayers For The Young* for SSA	TP
1953	*Gentle Visitations* for SSA	TP
1953	*I Feel Death* for TTB	B&H
1953	*Jack L'Eventreur* for high voice and piano	B&H
1953	*Love* for voice and piano	B&H
1953	*The Midnight Sun* for voice and piano	ECS
1953	*Poèmes Pour La Paix* for medium voice and piano	B&H
1953	*Sally's Smile* for voice and piano	CFP
1953	*Six Songs For High Voice* for voice and piano	CFP
1953	*The Tulip Tree* for voice and piano	ECS
1954	*Anacreontiche* for voice and piano	MS
1954	*Four Dialogues* for two voices and two pianos	B&H
1954	Sonata No. 3 for piano	CFP
1954	*Three Poems Of Demetrios Capetanakis* for medium voice and piano	B&H
1955	*All Glorious God* for mixed chorus	CFP
1955	*Burlesque* for piano	MS
1955	*Christ The Lord Is Ris'n Today* for mixed chorus	CFP
1955	*Poem For F* for voice and piano	MS
1955	*The Poet's Requiem* for orchestra, soprano solo, and mixed chorus	B&H
1955	*Sing My Soul* for mixed chorus	CFP
1955	*The Young Disciple* incidental music	MS
1956	*The Robbers* melodrama in one scene for three male voices and thirteen instruments	B&H
1956	Symphony No. 2	B&H
1956	*Three Poems Of Paul Goodman* for voice and piano	B&H
1957	*Conversation* for voice and piano	B&H
1957	*Five Poems Of Walt Whitman* for voice and piano	B&H
1957	*Fourteen Songs On American Poetry* for voice and piano	CFP
1957	*The Lord's Prayer* for voice and piano	CFP
1957	*Settings For Whitman* for spoken voice	MS
1957	*Sinfonia* for wind symphony orchestra	CFP
1957	*To You* for voice and piano	TP
1957	*Visits To St. Elizabeth's (Bedlam)* for voice and piano	B&H
1958	*Eagles* for orchestra	B&H
1958	*Pilgrims* for string orchestra	B&H
1958	*Slow Waltz* for piano	MS
1958	*Suddenly Last Summer* incidental music	MS
1958	Symphony No. 3	B&H
1958	*The Ticklish Acrobat* musical comedy	MS
1959	*The Cave At Machpelah* incidental music	MS

1959	*Early Voyagers* ballet	MS
1959	*Last Day* opera in nine minutes for male voice and six instruments	MS
1959	*Mamba's Daughters* unfinished opera	MS
1959	*Miracles Of Christmas* for mixed chorus and organ	B&H
1959	*Two Poems Of Theodore Roethke* for voice and piano	B&H
1960	*Eleven Studies For Eleven Players*	B&H
1960	*Motel* incidental music	MS
1960	*Polish Songs,* Op. 74	
	(Chopin, arranged by NR for piano)	MS
1960	*Prayers And Responses* for mixed chorus	B&H
1960	Trio for flute, cello, and piano	CFP
1961	*The Anniversary* unfinished opera	MS
1961	*Ideas* for orchestra	B&H
1961	*King Midas* cantata for voices and piano	B&H
1961	*Virelai* for mixed chorus	B&H
1962	*Caligula* incidental music	MS
1962	*Two Psalms And A Proverb* for mixed chorus and five strings	ECS
1963	*Color Of Darkness* incidental music	MS
1963	*For Poulenc* for voice and piano	ECS
1963	*Four Poems Of Tennyson* for voice and piano	B&H
1963	*The Lady Of The Camellias* incidental music	MS
1963	*Lift Up Your Heads (The Ascension)* for mixed chorus, wind	
	ensemble, and timpani	B&H
1963	*Lions* for orchestra	B&H
1963	*Poems Of Love And The Rain* for mezzo-soprano and piano	B&H
1964	*Laudemus Tempus Actum* for mixed chorus and orchestra or	
	piano	B&H
1964	*Lovers* for harpsichord, oboe, cello, and percussion	B&H
1964	*The Milk Train Doesn't Stop Here Anymore* incidental music	MS
1964	*Two Poems Of Plato* for voice and piano	MS
1965	*Excursions* ballet	MS
1965	*Miss Julie* opera in one act	B&H
1966	*Feed My Sheep* for voice and piano	MS
1966	*Hearing* for voice and piano	B&H
1966	*Letters From Paris* for mixed chorus and small orchestra	B&H
1966	*Water Music* for clarinet, violin, and orchestra	B&H
1967	*A Birthday Suite* for piano four-hands	MS
1967	*He Shall Rule From Sea To Sea* for mixed chorus and organ	B&H
1968	*Bertha* opera in one act for singers and piano	B&H
1968	*Some Trees* for three solo voices and piano	B&H
1968	*Spiders* for harpsichord	B&H
1968	*Three Sisters Who Are Not Sisters* opera in three scenes for five	
	solo singers	B&H

1969	Piano Concerto In Six Movements	B&H
1969	*Two Holy Songs* for mixed chorus and keyboard	PSO
1969	*War Scenes* for voice and piano	B&H
1970	*Fables* five very short operas with piano	B&H
1970	*Gloria* for two voices and piano	B&H
1970	*Praises For The Nativity* for four solo voices (SATB), mixed chorus, and organ	B&H
1970	*Three Slow Pieces* (1950, 1959, 1970) for cello and piano	B&H
1971	*Ariel* for soprano, clarinet, and piano	B&H
1971	*Canticle Of The Lamb* for mixed chorus	B&H
1971	*Canticles, Set I* for mixed chorus	B&H
1971	*Day Music* for violin and piano	B&H
1971	*The Nephew* incidental music	MS
1971	*Panic In Needle Park* film score	MS
1972	*Canticles, Set II* for mixed chorus	B&H
1972	*Last Poems Of Wallace Stevens* for voice, cello, and piano	B&H
1972	*Night Music* for violin and piano	B&H
1972	*The Serpent* for voice and piano	B&H
1973	*Four Hymns* for mixed chorus, unison voices, and keyboard	B&H
1973	*In Time Of Pestilence* for mixed chorus	B&H
1973	*Little Prayers* for soprano and baritone solos, mixed chorus, and orchestra	B&H
1973	*Missa Brevis* for four solo voices (SATB) and mixed chorus a capella	B&H
1973	*Prayer To Jesus* for mixed chorus and keyboard	B&H
1973	*Solemn Prelude* for seven brass instruments	MS
1973	*Three Motets* for mixed chorus and organ	B&H
1973	*Three Prayers* for mixed chorus a capella	B&H
1974	*Air Music* for orchestra	B&H
1974	*To Jane* for voice and piano	B&H
1974	*Where We Came* for voice and piano	B&H
1975	*Assembly And Fall* for orchestra	B&H
1975	*Book Of Hours* for flute and harp	B&H
1975	*Eight Etudes* for piano	B&H
1975	*Serenade* for voice, violin, viola, and piano	B&H
1976	*Hearing* opera in five scenes	B&H
1976	*A Journey* for voice and piano	B&H
1976	*A Quaker Reader* for organ	B&H
1976	*Sky Music* for harp	B&H
1976	*Women's Voices* for soprano and piano	B&H
1977	*Romeo And Juliet* for flute and guitar	B&H
1977	*Sunday Morning* for orchestra	B&H
1977	*Surge Illuminare* (*Arise, Shine*) for mixed chorus and organ	B&H

1978	*Three Choruses For Christmas* for mixed chorus a capella	B&H
1979	*The Nantucket Songs* for voice and piano	B&H
1979	*Remembering Tommy* for cello, piano, and orchestra	B&H
1980	*After Reading Shakespeare* for cello	B&H
1980	*Back To Life* for countertenor and double bass	B&H
1980	*The Santa Fe Songs* for voice, violin, viola, cello, and piano	B&H
1980	Suite For Guitar	B&H
1981	*Give All To Love* for two-part mixed chorus and piano	B&H
1981	*Views From The Oldest House* for organ	B&H
1981	*Winter Pages* for clarinet, bassoon, violin, cello, and piano	B&H
1982	*After Long Silence* for voice, oboe, and string ensemble	B&H
1982	*Jeannie With The Light Brown Hair* (Foster, arranged by NR for voice and piano)	B&H
1982	*Little Lamb Who Made Thee?* for mixed chorus and organ	B&H
1982	*Praise The Lord, O My Soul* for mixed chorus and keyboard	B&H
1982	*Three Calamus Poems* for voice and piano	B&H
1983	*Mercy And Truth Are Met* for mixed chorus and keyboard	B&H
1983	*Dances* for cello and piano	B&H
1983	*A Whitman Cantata* for men's chorus, twelve brass, and timpani	B&H
1984	*An American Oratorio* for tenor solo, mixed chorus, and orchestra	B&H
1984	*Picnic On The Marne* for alto saxophone and piano	B&H
1984	*Pilgrim Strangers* for six solo male voices	B&H
1985	*The End Of Summer* for clarinet, violin, and piano	B&H
1985	Organ Concerto	B&H
1985	*Septet: Scenes From Childhood* for oboe, horn, piano, and string quartet	B&H
1985	*String Symphony*	B&H
1985	Violin Concerto	B&H
1986	*Frolic* for orchestra	B&H
1986	*Homer* for mixed chorus and eight instruments	B&H
1986	*Seven Motets For The Church Year* for mixed chorus	B&H
1986	*Song & Dance* for piano	B&H
1987	*The Death Of Moses* for mixed chorus and organ	B&H
1987	*Five Armenian Love Songs* for mixed chorus	B&H
1987	*The Schuyler Songs* for voice and orchestra	B&H
1987	*Te Deum* for mixed chorus, two trumpets, two trombones, and organ	B&H
1987	*Three Poems Of Baudelaire* for mixed chorus	B&H
1987	*What Is Pink?* for three-part treble chorus and piano	B&H
1988	*Bright Music* for flute, two violins, cello, and piano	B&H
1988	*Fanfare And Flourish* for organ and four brass	B&H
1988	*Fantasy And Polka* for orchestra	B&H

1988	*Goodbye My Fancy* for mixed chorus, soprano and bass soloists, and orchestra	B&H
1988	*Lead Kindly Light* for mixed chorus a capella	B&H
1988	*Love Alone* for men's chorus and piano four-hands	B&H
1988	*A Quaker Reader* for chamber orchestra	B&H
1989	*Anna La Bonne* scene for voice and piano	B&H
1989	*Are You The New Person?* for voice and piano	B&H
1989	*The Auden Poems* for tenor, violin, cello, and piano	B&H
1989	*Breathe On Me* for mixed chorus	B&H
1989	*Diversions* for brass quintet	B&H
1989	*For Shirley* for piano four-hands	MS
1989	*Full Of Life Now* for voice and piano	B&H
1989	*Organbook I*	B&H
1989	*Organbook II*	B&H
1989	*Organbook III*	B&H
1990	*Spring Music* for violin, cello, and piano	B&H
1990	*Swords And Plowshares* for four solo voices and orchestra	B&H
1991	Third String Quartet	B&H
1991	Concerto For Piano (Left Hand) and Orchestra	B&H
1991	*Choral Alleluias* for SATB	B&H
1991	*We Are The Musicmakers* for SATB and piano	B&H
1991	*Their Lonely Betters* for voice and piano	B&H
1992	*A Dream Of Nightingales* for voice and piano	B&H
1992	Concerto For English Horn	B&H
1992	*Triptych* for chamber orchestra	B&H
1992	*Spirit Divine* for SATB and organ	B&H
1992	*O God My Heart Is Ready (Psalm 108)* for SATB and organ	B&H
1992	*Christ Is Made The Sure Foundation* for SATB and organ	B&H

DISCOGRAPHY

1952
Piano Sonata No. 2
London 759 lp

1959
Design
Louisville 57-5 lp

1963
Barcarolles
Epic 1262 lp, 3862 lp

1964
The Call, A Christmas Carol, Cycle Of Holy Songs, Early In The Morning, Echo's Song, Upon Julia's Clothes, To The Willow Tree, I Am Rose, The Lordly Hudson, Lullaby Of The Woman Of The Mountain, My Papa's Waltz, The Nightingale, O You Whom I Often And Silently Come, Rain In Spring, Requiem, Root Cellar, Sally's Smile, See How They Love Me, The Silver Swan, Snake, Pippa's Song, In A Gondola, Song For A Girl, Spring, Spring And Fall, Such Beauty As Hurts To Behold, To You, Visits To St. Elizabeth's, What If Some Little Pain, Youth, Day, Old Age, And Night
Columbia 5961 lp, 6561 lp
Odyssey 32 16 0274 lp (1968)
New World 229 lp (1978) (selections)

Eleven Studies For Eleven Players
Louisville 644 lp

Two Psalms And A Proverb
Cambridge 414 lp, 1416 lp

Visits To St. Elizabeth's, Alleluia
Desto 411-12 lp, 6411-12 lp

1965
Lovers (excerpt)
Decca 101108 / 710,108 lp
Serenus 12056 lp (1975)

Poems Of Love And The Rain, Piano Sonata No. 2
CRI 202 lp

1968
Ideas (excerpt), *Water Music*, Trio for flute, cello, and piano
Desto 6462 lp

Trio for flute, cello, and piano
Westminster 17147 lp; 8239 lp (1973)

1969
Poems Of Love And The Rain, Four Madrigals, From An Unknown Past
Desto 6480 lp
Phoenix 108 cd (1991)

Some Trees, Little Elegy, Night Crow, The Tulip Tree, Look Down, Fair Moon, What Sparks And Wiry Cries, For Poulenc
CRI 238 cs, lp

1970
War Scenes, As Adam Early In The Morning, O You Whom I Often And Silently Come, Look Down, Fair Moon, Gliding O'er All, Four Dialogues

Desto 7101 lp
Phoenix 116 cd (1991)

1971
Symphony No. 3
Turnabout Vox 34447 lp

1972
Lions
Orion 7268 lp

1973
Ariel, Gloria
Desto 7147 lp

Day Music
Desto 7151 lp
Phoenix 123 cd (1991)

1974
A Christmas Carol, Guilt, For Susan, Clouds, What Sparks And Wiry Cries
Duke University Press 7306 lp

Night Music
Desto 7174 lp
Phoenix 123 cd (1991)

Piano Concerto In Six Movements
Louisville 733 lp
Albany 047 cd (1991)

1975
King Midas
Desto 6443 lp

Sing My Soul
Orion 75205 lp

1977
Book Of Hours
CRI 362 lp

1978
Blessed Art Thou, Canticle Of The Lamb, He Shall Rule From Sea To Sea, Lift Up Your Heads, Love Divine, All Loves Excelling, Virelai
Boosey & Hawkes 5001 lp

Romeo And Juliet
CRI 394

A Quaker Reader
CRI 396 lp

Visits To St. Elizabeth's
Musique Circle 45567 lp

1979
Miss Julie (excerpts)
Painted Smiles 1338 lp

Missa Brevis
Vox 5354 lp

1980
Mourning Scene From Samuel
New World 305 lp

A Quaker Reader (excerpts)
Gothic 87904 lp

Serenade On Five English Poems
Grenadilla 1031 lp

Suite For Guitar
Coronet 3115 lp

Three Motets On Poems Of Gerard Manly Hopkins
Gamut 7501 lp

1981
Piano Sonata No. 1
Opus One 73 lp

1982
After Reading Shakespeare
Grenadilla 1065 lp

1983
Last Poems Of Wallace Stevens
Leonarda 116 lp

The Nantucket Songs, Women's Voices
CRI 485 lp

1984
Alleluia, Two Poems Of Edith Sitwell, Root Cellar, Snake, The Serpent, Poems Of Tennyson, Conversation, Visits To St. Elizabeth's, Rain In Spring, For Susan, Such Beauty As Hurts To Behold, Clouds, Sally's Smile, What Sparks And Wiry Cries, The Lordly Hudson, The Nightingale, A Christmas Carol, Sometimes With One I Love, O

You Whom I Often And Silently Come, I Am Rose, A Journey, Let's Take A Walk, See How They Love Me, Early In The Morning
GSS 104 lp

Two Poems Of Theodore Roethke
Orion 84476 lp

1985
Romeo And Juliet, Piano Sonata No. 2, *Nantucket Songs, Some Trees*
CRI 607 cs

1986
Sinfonia
American Wind Symphony Orchestra 106 lp

Spiders
CRI 5343 lp

1987
After Long Silence
Spacio 2079 lp

Air Music, Eagles
Louisville 787 lp
Albany 047 cd (1991)

Give All To Love, Hearing, Letters From Paris
GSS 106 lp

1988
String Symphony, Sunday Morning, Eagles
New World 353-1 lp, -2 cd

Interlude
Elektra Nonesuch 79178-2 cd

1989
A Quaker Reader, Views From The Oldest House
Delos 3076 cd

3 Motets
Gothic 78932 cd

1990
3 Motets, Praise The Lord, O My Soul, Sing My Soul
Gothic 78932 cd

1991
The End Of Summer
Crystal 742 cd

Pilgrim Strangers
Chanticleer 8804 cd

Violin Concerto
Deutsche Grammophon 429 231-2 cd

1992
Bright Music, Winter Pages
New World 80146-2 cd

BIBLIOGRAPHY

The Paris Diary Of Ned Rorem. New York: George Braziller, 1966; reprinted in *The Paris And New York Diaries Of Ned Rorem 1951-1961.* San Francisco: North Point Press, 1983.

Music From The Inside Out. New York: George Braziller, 1967.

The New York Diary. New York: George Braziller, 1967; reprinted in *The Paris And New York Diaries Of Ned Rorem 1951-1961.* San Francisco: North Point Press, 1983.

Music And People. New York: George Braziller, 1968.

Critical Affairs — A Composer's Journal. New York: George Braziller, 1970.

Pure Contraption — A Composer's Essays. New York: Holt, Rinehart & Winston, 1973.

The Final Diary, 1961-1972. New York: Holt, Rinehart & Winston, 1974; reprinted as *The Later Diaries Of Ned Rorem, 1961-1972.* San Francisco: North Point Press, 1983.

An Absolute Gift: A New Diary. New York: Simon & Schuster, 1977.

Setting The Tone: Essays And A Diary. New York: Coward, McCann, Inc., 1983.

Paul's Blues. New York: Red Ozier Press, 1984.

The Nantucket Diary Of Ned Rorem, 1973-1985. San Francisco: North Point Press, 1987.

Settling The Score. New York: Harcourt, Brace, Jovanovich, 1988.

Knowing When To Stop. New York: Simon & Schuster, 1993.

photo: Gene Bagnato

LAURIE SPIEGEL / Introduction

LAURIE SPIEGEL was born on September 20, 1945, in Chicago, Illinois. After having attended classes in Illinois at Shimer College, she studied at Oxford University from 1966 to '68, and then received her B.A. in Social Sciences from Shimer. While in London, she also studied classic guitar, theory, and composition privately with J.W. Duarte. Returning to the States, she studied guitar with Oscar Ghiglia at Juilliard from 1969 to '72, and Renaissance and Baroque lute with Suzanne Bloch and Fritz Rikko; she was also studying privately with Michael Czajkowski and Alexander Bellow, and took composition lessons from Vincent Persichetti and Hall Overton. From 1972 to '75 she studied composition with Jacob Druckman, and computer composition with Emmanuel Ghent. As a resident visitor at Bell Labs from 1973 to '74, she worked in computer music with Ghent and Max Mathews, and in computer graphics with Kenneth Knowlton. In 1975, she received her M.A. from Brooklyn College.

Spiegel has composed electronic music since her first encounter in the late '60s with Morton Subotnick's original Buchla Synthesizer at the NYU Composers Workshop. Using the GROOVE system at Bell Labs, she created numerous works, including *Appalachian Grove, The Unquestioned Answer* (both 1974), *Drums*, and *The Expanding Universe* (both 1975). Today, she is at the forefront of developments in computer technologies, expanding the compositional and performance capabilities of computers through the many innovations she has devised. She helped design the AlphaSyntauri synthesizer for use with Apple II microcomputers, as well as the McLeyvier synthesizer. *Music Mouse*, her unique Macintosh software, has been a major breakthrough in the performance of realtime computer music, without reliance on an instrumental keyboard or acoustic or sampled sounds. Her 1991 cd *Unseen Worlds* includes seven improvisations which she created with *Music Mouse*.

She has written numerous soundtracks for films and videos, and has created her own videos as well, including *Voyages* (1978) and *A Living Painting* (1979), in which changing abstract shapes create what she terms "visual music." She has also collaborated on video projects with Nam June Paik, Bill and Louise Etra, and Tom DeWitt. Spiegel's music has served as scores for many choreographers, including Elliot Feld, Kathryn Posin, and Alvin Ailey. Her realization of *Kepler's "Harmony Of The Planets"* was chosen as the opening track of NASA's "Sounds Of Earth" recording which was sent into space on the Voyager Spacecraft in 1977.

Spiegel has received grants and awards from the Rockefeller Foundation, the

Creative Artists Public Service Program, ASCAP, Meet The Composer, and the Experimental Television Lab at WNET in New York, where she was artist-in-residence in 1976. She has been assistant to the director of electronic music at the Aspen Music Festival; guitar and electronic music teacher at Bucks Count Community College; composition teacher and director of the electronic music studio at Cooper Union; and director of the computer music studio at New York University. Since the '80s, she has worked as a freelance computer consultant to various major corporations.

I spoke with Laurie Spiegel at her Manhattan home on December 24, 1992. Along with learning more about her involvement with different electronic-music systems, from the Buchla synthesizer to the computer, I was eager to discuss with her the impact of her *Music Mouse*, for both her own composition and the music made with it by others, as well as her experiences in attempting to copyright her innovative software.

LAURIE SPIEGEL / Interview

Q: How does someone who left high school and taught herself to read music notation wind up getting her B.A. and M.A.?

SPIEGEL: I went to a great college called Shimer in western Illinois, which took me without requiring me to finish high school. It was an experimental offshoot of the University of Chicago, which gave you no usable skills whatsoever, but gave you a great basic education in thinking. My B.A. was in the Social Sciences, so my M.A. in music took a long time to get, because I had to go back and fill in a lot of missing music education. But I'd played music by ear since childhood, so a lot of the theory was, effectively, just learning the names of things that I already knew by sound.

Q: Through playing the guitar?

SPIEGEL: Mostly. When I was 14, in Chicago, I got myself a Harmony guitar, stamped "factory reject," cheap. My grandmother from Lithuania played mandolin and had given me a mandolin when I was maybe nine or ten. I kept it like a secret under my bed, and I would take it out at night and play sad melodies against a drone string. I got into making up music as sort of a private way to express — to deal with — my emotions from being a kid in a difficult family. At some point, my mother gave me a harmonica which I liked a lot too. But I didn't have childhood piano lessons. I'd been improvising and playing guitar, mandolin occasionally, and then added banjo because there were always too many guitar players. In the early '60s, folk music was in and was genuine. By the mid '60s, I'd reached a point where playing music and some other things in my life kind of dead-ended. I'd dropped out of college, and was living in a house trailer in western Illinois, near the Mississippi River, with no electricity — just a kerosene lamp — and no running water, no phone, no TV or FM radio. There wasn't much else to do but read and write and play music, and I felt I was just playing the same stuff over and over. So I decided I'd teach myself to read notes; and also to go back to school. I haven't been in a rut since.

Q: You used Bach scores as your guide?

SPIEGEL: I got a copy of Bach's Two- and Three-Part Inventions and tried working them out on my guitar.

Q: At that time, were you thinking at all about electronic music? Had you heard anything then?

SPIEGEL: No. I hadn't heard — and didn't know about — electronic music, or hardly any 20th-century-composed music either, really. I had messed around with tape recorders since I was little though. My father was extremely fond of gadgets. He built things with pulleys and gear-wheels, and had a sequence of small businesses building things like parade floats. He was sort of an inventor, and had some patents for pump designs from when he was trying to build small fountains. He taught me to solder when I was nine or ten — I think it was the only thing we did together during my whole chldhood — and talked me through building a crystal radio. We had always had wire or tape recorders, and I discovered pretty young that if I cut the tape with scissors and got a piece of adhesive tape out of the medicine chest, I could tape the pieces back together in a different order. So I discovered splicing by myself, without knowing the word, and messed around with tape a bit.

But starting when I was 7, I thought of myself mainly as a writer. I knew I had to be some kind of artist — my subjective experience was too different from how it was "supposed" to be, from what the grown-ups told us kids was happening. I felt a real need to tell things like they were, like they felt; a need for emotional honesty, which I hope comes across in my music.

When I was 17, they said, "What do you want to be when you grow up? Where do you want to go to college?" When I said, "I want to study music," they said, "You can't do that — you're 17 and you don't read music and you've never studied it. Next subject?" Of course, at that time, the placement exams they gave us in high school were segregated for girls and boys, and everything I wanted to be was for the boys: They got doctor, we got nurse; they got writer, we got librarian; they got scientist, we got lab technician — all like that, right down the line. Later, when I was in England studying at Oxford, I took classic-guitar lessons from Jack Duarte in London. He also turned out to be a composer, which was great. He taught me a good bit of theory as well. I'd begun writing down some of my improvisations when I started being able to read notes; just trying to get down things I'd made up so I wouldn't forget them. He pointed out to me that that was called "composing," and that if I wanted to pursue it seriously as a thing in itself, in addition to just playing, then I should do the same thing as with playing, namely just do it every day. It didn't matter if I threw it out, just that I get in the practice of doing it a lot. That stood me in good stead later, when I was composing on deadlines for films; though I tend to work in binges, I know how to make myself work. The thing about composing was, I'd never met anyone who did it. It was not something that people did. I knew writers and artists, but I didn't meet composers. There was all this incredible music which had somehow once been composed — case closed.

At Oxford I discovered that if I sat in a corner and played my guitar and just made up things, people liked to have me around a lot more than if I was all excited about ancient Greek philosophers, or really furious with what the logical positivists were doing to Kant — one of my absolute favorites. People seemed to like me better if I just played music. I think being intellectual was considered a man's thing still. They didn't even allow women Rhodes Scholars till 1976; I was there on a special undergrad program. I still thought of myself as a writer till about age 23, when music really just took me over. Then I realized I had to give it a chance, that if I didn't give music a year, I'd regret all my life not having tried to see where it might go, because I loved it best.

Q: Was Oxford part of that effort to give music a chance?

SPIEGEL: No. Part of it was coming home to Chicago after two years at Oxford, with my new Social Sciences degree, landing in the middle of the 1968 Democratic convention, with tear gas and tanks all over the place, then moving to New York and getting involved in political activism to the point of utter disillusionment, which a lot of us felt that year, '68, '69. I realized I had more hope of making a positive difference in this world by just touching people inside with music than through politics. Also I discovered that, despite being allegedly bright and even "Oxford educated" and all, that the only work I could get was as an underpaid, overworked secretary or file clerk. Things were a lot more sexist back then. I did try applying to IBM to train as a programmer, but they said that I didn't have what it took; I think they took one look at me and decided I didn't fit their stereotype of what a programmer should be as a human being. I had no problem learning to program later, once I got access to computers. Anyway, that first year in New York was pretty miserable. I wasn't able to make contact with anyone with similar cultural interests, and I couldn't get any work that was above the drone level.

Q: When did you start going to Juilliard?

SPIEGEL: I had a roommate at one point who was just starting at the Manhattan School of Music. She was a pianist and I didn't think she was that great in terms of musicality, and I thought, "Well, if she's good enough to get to study music, maybe I can too." Ultimately, I did get a Masters in Composition, though it's never been much use to me. But some people like to know I have it, like when I've taught music at colleges.

Q: Living with this person prompted you to apply to Juilliard?

SPIEGEL: Yeah, but I didn't really apply at first. You could just start taking courses through the extension division, and if you did well, they couldn't get rid of you. They had to let you more and more into the regular division, even graduate courses. And then I just kind of got adopted. Persichetti would keep giving me lessons; he'd see me in the hall and say, "You've got five minutes? Come into my office and show me what you're working on," and he'd give me these little lessons. And for many years after I left there, he'd phone me once in a while to ask how my composing was going — he cared. And then I studied for several years with Jake Druckman, and was his assistant privately, proofreading orchestral parts, typing up his ASCAP reports, doing sound checks, tape editing for him, those things.

Q: At Juilliard, had you wanted to compose, or was it more a matter of getting involved in music at all sorts of levels?

SPIEGEL: I'm not even really sure. It was still beyond my wildest dreams to become a musician of any kind. I loved music and was playing a lot, and I wanted to learn: I wanted more technique, history, theoretical understanding. Thinking of myself as a composer happened *ex post facto*, years later. I played classic guitar, but soon realized that the pieces I liked most were all transcribed from lute. So I switched to the lute and started getting little gigs — like being onstage lutenist in Jacobean revenge tragedies.

The Juilliard drama division was great but the music division was very uptight. You had kids with incredible chops who couldn't play a note of their own free will; it had to all be written out by someone else for them to read, sort of like knowing how to talk but not being able to just express yourself in words, not being able to speak without a script someone else had written. I couldn't believe it, because my own musical experience had been almost entirely self-expression, communication, and folk music — music by ear. I mean, where I came from, Dylan was considered too commercial at first! I'm originally from the south side of Chicago, 49th and Woodlawn, and blues was in a way an ultimate thing. I never got involved in jazz. Blues always felt much purer to me, much stronger, deeper, less about virtuosity, technique, theory, novelty.

By the end of that first year at Juilliard, I had aced the basic ear-training and theory courses, and taken some graduate seminars and coaching in Renaissance and Baroque ornamentation and continuo realization on the lute. I had also been introduced by my ear-training teacher Mike Czajkowski to the Buchla synthesizer at NYU — what was left of Mort Subotnick's old Intermedia Program, and I fell madly in love with electronic music.

Q: What prompted him to bring you to that?

SPIEGEL: I started showing him some of my compositions, and he said, "You know, there's something that I think you might really like. Why don't you just come downtown with me some time when I'm going to the studio?" He took me to Mort's studio, which was at that time over the Bleecker Street Cinema, but I didn't really start working with the Buchla instrument till it moved to the NYU Composers Workshop, which was underneath the Fillmore East, on East 7th Street. It was a basement studio with water bugs — when you plugged patchcords in, you had to be careful not to squish anything lurking inside!

Then there was an immediate link-up with video people from The Kitchen: We were painting the cabinets in the new studio blue to store tapes in one day when the video artists Woody and Steina Vasulka came in, and Woody said — really dramatically — in this gruff Czech accent, "Ve vant your ekvipment for our experiments!" So I rapidly got involved and met a lot of people at The Kitchen, when it was still at the old Mercer Arts Center, before the building collapsed. I had music in two of The Kitchen's first four concerts. Rhys Chatham, Eliane Radigue, and I had teamed up to tackle learning the Buchla, and we became good friends. So when Rhys started the music series at The Kitchen in '71, I was one of the people he could count on to throw in enough music during that first month to help launch it. I was still studying at Juilliard, which was uptight and had nothing to do with the real world, so "downtown music" was a good counterbalance — a lot more relaxed and fun, more people-oriented and open-minded.

So by the end of that one year I gave myself to try music, I was studying, performing, composing, and had a job setting up a studio and teaching one of the first college-level courses in electronic music in the country, in Bucks County, Pennsylvania — I went there one or two days a week, teaching electronic composition and classic guitar. I also got a job as staff composer for a small film-production company called Spectra Films. It did mostly educational and kids' stuff, but was run by Fred Pressberger, an old Viennese Jewish filmmaker who'd been apprenticed to Fritz Lang when he was young. He taught me a tremendous amount about scoring films, where to put music, how and when to bring it in and out or go emotionally contrary to the action with it. These weren't exactly major films, but I scored six of the Babar stories and other stuff I liked too.

Q: Those jobs pretty much paid your tuition at Juilliard?

SPIEGEL: They did, and my rent, amply. Rents were a lot cheaper then; tuition was high.

Anyway, by the end of that trial year I'd allowed myself, I was making more money, learning a lot, and having a much better time by being a musician — versus coming from Oxford's philosophy, history, and all, plus England's fantastic '60s counter-culture, into dead-end sexist typing jobs. It was clear I should stick with music.

Q: When Michael Czajkowski took you to the Buchla synthesizer, that wasn't part of anything Juilliard was doing to expose you to electronic music — he'd been working with that instrument himself.

SPIEGEL: Yeah, he'd worked very closely with Mort Subotnick. When Mort gave up the Bleecker Street studio and went out to Cal Arts, Mike took it over and ran it as the NYU Composers Workshop, which composers joined to get six hours a week or so of studio time, depending on how many people the time had to be split between. Also, sometimes, Jake Druckman would let me use his time at the Columbia-Princeton Studio, so I got to know Vladimir Ussachevsky very well, and Otto Luening and Pril Smiley and later Alice Shields a bit. So I had what might be viewed as a totally multiplexed musical life, because I was in Juilliard, the NYU studio, the downtown avant-garde — the Kitchen crowd, where people wanted something either sonically involving or just nice to hear, and even beauty was OK. I also did music for plays and experimental video artists too — plus playing early music on lute, teaching music at a community college in the country — and the soundtrack job, where basically I worked like an illustrator, and style didn't even matter most of the time, as long as my music helped the emotions get felt.

Q: Were those electronic scores?

SPIEGEL: It took me a couple of tracks to sell them on electronic scores. But I had to do a variety of styles, including traditional instrumental writing — I was studying it at Juilliard anyway. But the soundtracks' conceptual content didn't matter; if I felt like writing invertible counterpoint, I did — as an in-joke for myself; nobody was going to notice it. What mattered was the emotion.

Juilliard was never post-Webernite serialist conceptual like Columbia was; it was much more atonal expressionist. Being a conservatory, Juilliard was spared the integration into an academic atmosphere which put so many university-based music departments right down the hall from the math or physics department, so composers would begin to feel they had to be able to prove why they wrote every note, like in other fields. Juilliard had lots of musicians from all over the world, just about killing each other to play Rachmaninoff concertos. It had some very fine musicians on faculty, who really loved music. Unfortunately, it was a very competitive atmosphere. And unlike the downtown avant-garde or soundtracks or folk music, Juilliard was still biased toward complicated, dense atonal stuff — still very European-dominated, aesthetically. Also unbelievably apolitical: The year of the Kent State shootings, everybody just wanted to practice for faster trills. Every other college was up in arms demonstrating, but not Juilliard — except Noah Creshevsky organized a performance of *In C* as a protest at one point.

Q: Is it true that Elliott Carter wouldn't let you play your electronic pieces for the composition jury at Juilliard?

SPIEGEL: True. That was one of my lowest moments. It was not considered "real music" — nothing was admissable but my written scores, and I didn't really have that much written music to show, because I'd started composing late, and once I hit the synthesizers, I just fell in love with working directly with their sounds, and all the things I could do with them. My written music was also more traditional. I got highly mixed comments from various Juilliard faculty, some of whom were my teachers and some not. One teacher told me that the fact that I'd written a piece in E Minor didn't mean for sure that I didn't have any musical imagination, but it wasn't a good sign — though I'd thought it a pretty natural thing for any guitarist to do. Once I brought in a piece that was six pages long and said, "I'm having trouble with this transition here; it just doesn't feel right," and I got this sexist answer, "This is fantastic! Do you realize how few girls can actually finish writing six whole pages of music?" — which was no help at all. It was OK if Xenakis came and lectured us and played his electronic music. But Elliott Carter gave me a really hard time. He probably wouldn't even remember it, but it was one of those things where I walked out of the room and just cried. He hadn't let any of what I considered my best work be heard.

Q: Because they were tapes of electronic music rather than scores for traditional instruments.

SPIEGEL: Right, though I did have graphical scores for some of them. The whole thing seemed oriented toward the minutiae of traditional notation, and demonstrating mastery of it, not about musicality in sound.

Q: It was also about trying to aspire to become like them.

SPIEGEL: For Elliott Carter particularly that was true. It wasn't true for Vincent Persichetti, who really did his best to help you be yourself, and who had among his students Phil Glass, Steve Reich, and Jake Druckman. He really cared about helping you do what you wanted to do, which is what I've always tried to do with my students. The thing is to give them the moral support and psychological guidance to be themselves, and the technique to do what they want, and to help them find their sensitivities and work with them on their problems. It's for them.

Of course now it's inconceivable that any music department, even at the high-school level, would refuse to accept electronic work as music. But I was at Juilliard from '69 to '72, and it was different then. But I did have my own balance, because I could use electronics downtown and in my soundtracks. It got even better balanced when I went to Bell Labs, where they had computer-controlled analog sound equipment. After four years with analog synthesizers, it felt like the same kind of dead end as back in the house trailer, in '65, on guitar. I needed memory, storage, and to be able to use more complex logic and go back to the same piece over and over to refine it, the same way I'd needed to learn notation back then.

I'd met Max Mathews and Emmanuel Ghent at The Kitchen where we'd all done concerts. They'd heard some of my electronic music, and I'd heard and been very impressed particularly by what Manny was doing. Bell Labs was wonderful; it wasn't a music department or art scene. It was an acoustic and behavioral research center, without aesthetic biases. A lot of scientists there loved and cared about music, but without having vested interests in any particular new-music faction. It may also have been the only computer music studio at that time that I — as a woman — would have been let into. Computers and composition were still both very male-dominated fields. If I'd managed to get into an academic studio, and could handle its aesthetic biases, I'd probably have been relegated to maintaining the studio log and bringing people coffee — the way Pril Smiley and Alice Shields really never got due credit for their work keeping the Columbia-Princeton Center going all those years.

Q: Were you still working with Jacob Druckman during the time you were at Bell Labs?

SPIEGEL: Yeah, they overlapped. After Jake won the Pulitzer, Brooklyn College coincidentally decided to upgrade its music department to conservatory level, and they offered to double his salary, I believe, if he'd go teach there. Juilliard, where he had been since he was a student, didn't really appreciate him or treat him that well, even after he won the Pulitzer, so he decided it was time for a change and took the offer. I was already working as Jake's private assistant, and Brooklyn made me an excellent offer too, so I went with him, and finished my Master's Degree there. They gave me free tuition plus a monthly graduate fellowship that was several times my rent.

There I met Wiley Hitchcock and got a research fellowship with the Institute for Studies in American Music. I took trips to the North Carolina mountains and taped banjo and fiddle tunes. I did lots of research on pre-Civil War American music, for projects that Wiley and also Richard Crawford were doing; also research for the 1974 ISAM-Yale Ives Conference. Wiley helped get me back to folk music's directness and freedom to be itself — like the way shape-note music enjoys parallel fifths, which were taboo at Juilliard. Brooklyn also let me do independent study, and gave me credits for work I did at Bell Labs, whereas Juilliard rejected that entire range of my work as non-musical. So I got the Masters at Brooklyn in 1975.

Q: That same year, Jacob Druckman said, "There's really nothing more horrible, more 1984-ish, than being present at a concert where there's nothing onstage except two loudspeakers." Did his attitudes toward electronic music play a role in your approach to it?

SPIEGEL: No. We were very different from each other on that. It has a lot to do with my having come from the Midwest, and having lived for several years in a very small town where you couldn't even get FM reception. Music was something you and your friends did, alone or together, playing it or listening to records. Concerts were foreign, distant ritual-like things you read about, for people in urban in-groups. For me, pretty much all along, the loudspeaker and the home were music's fundamentals, where music belonged and felt right. Also, it was obvious to me pretty early that concerts just were no longer the most efficient way to get a musical experience to the largest number of people — the purpose they'd developed for. I loved the actual sound and process of electronic music. I think Jake felt electronic sounds as different sorts of weird beings he could put into dramatic relationships with human musicians onstage: In *Animus I*, the speakers virtually attack the soloist. By the time he did the one for Jan DeGaetani, of course, the speakers were more supportive. But his music was essentially concert-oriented and mine wasn't.

I never wanted to do concerts. I wanted to do records and radio, and to write easy pieces with lots of emotional depth for people to read and play at home, for their own enjoyment and to express their feelings. That's my philosophy in my computer software too, to try to make it easier for more people to express themselves in musical sound, people who'd love to play music but didn't get music lessons as kids or for whatever reason believed they couldn't, who — unlike me — gave up. For me, home was always the most import place for deep musical experience. Loudspeakers on stage seemed only a hair more artificial than music being onstage in the first place.

I felt very frustrated doing little electronic concerts in little SoHo galleries for little artist audiences, even friendly ones. I wasn't reaching the people I wanted to reach: people like me when I lived very isolated in the middle of a bunch of cornfields and needed music to tell me I wasn't alone in my internal experience and emotions. Those are the people I wanted to create for. As an artistic voice, just like when I was seven, I wanted to bring into shared experience all that private scary stuff you think no one else feels, which overwhelms you when you're alone. I wanted to touch people deeply and ring true. I wasn't out to make history or change. To me, doing concerts was mainly a way to get well enough known that I could make records, get published, do broadcasts, and start really getting music out to people. It didn't work. Doing concerts just got me more concert offers till I gave up on it.

Q: Was your involvement with computers at Bell Labs comparable to your encounter with the Buchla synthesizer? Was there that same sense of having found your instrument?

SPIEGEL: Yes, but differently — more indirect and initially frustrating — because first I had to learn to program. Max Mathews told me, only a couple years ago, that when I started there, he didn't realize I didn't know how to program. I must have picked it up really fast.

Q: You didn't tell him?

SPIEGEL: Well, I thought I had. But maybe we each just assumed different things. He'd said, "Nobody'll tech for you here. You'll have to do your own." And I said, "That's fine." Then I worked through all the examples in a standard FORTRAN textbook, and also worked with Manny Ghent, helping him debug, and I watched the logic. At that point, it was DAP 24-bit assembly language and FORTRAN IV. It's a different universe out there in computer space now, verbally; I still have stuff on punch cards. Bell Labs was state of the art, but for those days. We're talking about music made on room-sized 32k computers, with 8k of core the size of a refrigerator-freezer combination. If one balked, you'd kick it to make it work again. You could pull out a memory card, go down the hall, stick it into another computer, and it would still have the data on it, it was that slow. When we got washing-machine-sized one-megabyte disc drives, people were walking around saying, "How are we ever going to write programs that will fill up a whole megabyte of storage? It's so much room!" That sounds silly now, and modern programs are more complex, but programmers have also gotten sloppier too. It's ungodly the size of the programs we see these days, and how much hardware speed it takes to run them — too many layers between you and the actual machine to be able to see its untried potentials. I really enjoy the aesthetics of programming: efficient, fast, tight code is beautiful; I'm an oldtimer, I've programmed for decades by now.

Other composers working with synthesizers wanted smaller, lighter instruments to take on the road for live concerts. But I was after greater compositional power and control, and the ability to design more complex logic, realtime interactive logic — the spontaneity of direct improvised expression, but not playing notes. I wanted to play levels and aspects and kinds of music that never even could be written down before, non-realtime, or described. That level of interactive power was unfortunately not possible many places, nor portable till much later: the era of MIDI, which — despite its limits — actually let me write a program like *Music Mouse*, which is an intelligent instrument, and have it go to 20,000 people, mostly to use at home. We were able to make intelligent instruments way back in the early '70s, by controlling analog synthesis equipment with a digital computer 300 feet away, over trunk cables. You kept having to go back and forth to repatch and calibrate — walking miles and miles and miles in a session! And then your shift would be over and the next user would repatch and calibrate everything differently.

Q: At Bell Labs, you created *Kepler's "Harmony Of The Planets"* which NASA included on a recording on the Voyager spacecraft in 1977. Where is it in space now, do you know?

SPIEGEL: Two Voyagers went up. One of them is actually outside the solar system and has sent back pictures of the solar system taken from outside it. I'm not sure where the second one is, but it's quite some distance on a different path. The *Kepler* being on them was a wonderful thing to have happen. Even Max was very excited that something done in the Lab was on that golden disk.

Q: It's actually on an lp?

SPIEGEL: They made a gold lp, yeah. That was the best recording technology then. But what's really astounding is that the computers onboard those Voyagers — which were basically about Apple II-level technology — are still running and were programmed well enough to be reprogrammable from Earth as new ideas and procedures and software knowledge evolved. They continue to function — no one's heading out in a space shuttle to reboot a Voyager spacecraft computer that crashed. They were done right in a way that's almost unimaginable now, considering the state of today's technology.

Q: How did your involvement in this project come about?

SPIEGEL: There was a good deal of press after the first public presentations of the *Kepler* piece. Ann Druyan and Timothy Ferris thought it was something that would fit right in and brought it to Carl Sagan's attention, and they chose it as the first cut of the "Sounds of Earth" section of the Voyager record. It took me several months' work, but was at a time when I guess I needed a break from innovating, exploring; I needed work that was more cut and dry. It was a fairly straightforward translation of planetary motion into sound, as conceived by an early-17th-century astronomer — Kepler's instructions for how man could hear, as music, the harmony which God had composed into the cosmos. It was good to do it. Things had gotten very busy and overloaded for me. I'd also been working on computer-generated video at Bell Labs. When you went those 300 feet between the analog and digital audio labs, you passed by this other lab that had these images growing on a display screen. It was irresistible — inevitable to make contact, which turned into a long, fruitful collaboration and friendship with Ken Knowlton, a great writer of both computer languages and evolutionary algorithms for images. I learned a tremendous amount from him. In 1974, I wrote what's now called a "paint" program but which I called a "drawing" program then, using a Rand tablet and lots of other input devices. We didn't even have a real frame buffer yet; lots of little probes stuck out of the back of one of the computer's core units and went into the back of this video monitor. The computer could open the shutter on a camera, then put up on the video screen all the pixels that should be green, then all the red ones, then the blue, then close the shutter and compute the next frame for the next ten minutes or so.

I thought, "Wow! This has got to go realtime and become a visual musical instrument!" But first it took months getting recordable NTSC video out. Then I took the GROOVE music software — meant for composing patterns of change over time, and got it to output image parameters in realtime on that other lab's computer. During this period I also got very involved in the Experimental TV Lab at WNET, doing soundtracks and also as a Video Artist in Residence.

By '78-9, I could do my first video pieces with my hybrid system at Bell: *A Living Painting* and one called *Voyages*, which used the same software for both music and image, but recorded at two different times on two different computers in two different rooms. I'd made it so I could record my drawing motions in real time, overdub additional drawing passes, use algorithmic logic to elaborate textures on them, and edit it all too. Max thought I was crazy at first, but after seeing me working on this for about three years, he came in one day and said, "You know, I think maybe you're really onto something here." I called the system VAMPIRE, for "Video And Music Program for Interactive Realtime Exploration," and also because I wrote and used it mostly at night.

Unfortunately, soon after, we lost everything. There was the AT&T divestiture, and they went over to UNIX-based time-sharing systems, from dedicated computers, which precluded realtime work.

Q: And so Bell Labs ended for you around 1979?

SPIEGEL: Yeah. It all broke up — for us all in those labs — at the end of the '70s. A lot of people left. It became a different kind of place.

Q: In 1981, you told the First International Congress of Women in Music that there were a lot of musically adept people in the computer field, who were outside the new-music scene because "they didn't like the atonal music or art-world politics." Were you also describing your own situation?

SPIEGEL: Yeah. I'd already published my "Open Letter in the Wake of New Music New York" in *Ear Magazine*, about why I'd become as disillusioned with the downtown music scene as with the uptown one. My subsequent article — published in *Ear*, then rewritten for the *New Music America '81 Catalog* — went a lot further and even accused the new-music concert establishment of having a vested interest in keeping us from reaching wider non-concert audiences through the use of newer media, which might make our work self-supporting without them. After that I got very few concert offers ever again.

By that point, I was already involved with the Apple II computer. At first, I saw these little micros, and thought, "This is a joke. How can you program something where there are no flashing lights so you can't even read the binary numbers in the registers? You can't even get at the actual computer inside, only at a keyboard. And it's so tiny." But then Jef Raskin brought me this prototype 48k Apple II, and later, Steve Wozniak looked me straight in the eye and said, "Laurie, do music with it! That's what I built it for!" — because Woz loves music, despite his "Us" Festival not being the greatest success, and Jef Raskin is a fantastic musician. There was a lot of love of music at Apple when it was still only about four people. The Apple II put me in touch with a grassroots personal-computer movement.

Before micros were considered viable for business use and got really commercialized, it really was a counter-culture movement — about putting into the hands of the people a power which only the banks, utility companies, government, and military — "Big Brother" — had had till then. That's where the old scary stereotypes of computers came from: their early owners and how they'd used them. Notably, ironically, that AT&T divestiture that clobbered our lab was all about this kind of thing. AT&T was about the only information carrier which did not in any way try to control the information content its channels carried — it just provided signal connection as multidirectionally and cheaply as it could, but it was barred from digital stuff till that divestiture trade-off; that's why the French have a computer terminal in every household's phone now but we don't yet.

So I got involved with these little computers and got excited, breaking out of a New York ghetto into a big grassroots thing, working on software for lots of people to use, putting out pieces on floppy disk, or distributing sounds by modem. But as soon as I started working with micros, nobody wanted to hear my studio compositions any more. If I couldn't play it live, they didn't want to hear it. And there'd never been much interest by performers in my instrumental works; people wanted the electronic ones, and now they only wanted them if I played them live.

I'm a composer; I can't do my best work if I'm limited to what I can schlep around or play live. I need my studio, I need more equipment, and to be able to take my time and do things over. Back in the early '70s, I was relieved when things worked out well for me as a composer, so I wouldn't have to be a performer. Though I'd always wanted to play music, and to learn to play better, I'd never really wanted to perform. I was always nervous and unable to sleep before, and depressed after, a performance — though I can get up on a stage and generate energy, and no one knows I'm scared stiff. But concerts had just been a way to get well enough known to get to do records and other media which put music into people's homes. That's where the real musical action is, where people live their lives and deal with their emotions and those scary subjective non-verbal experiences that society, by consensus, pretends don't exist, and which they hate artists to bring out in the open. Home is where people are often alone and need music.

I didn't want to go around like a trained monkey, playing a microcomputer live, being a novelty, or let concert producers exploit me — one told me, if I'd play on this series, he could kill two birds with one stone, getting both a woman composer and a computer on the series in one shot. I wanted to be able to do my best work, in my full studio, at leisure. Coincidentally, I'd just published those critiques of the alternative performance scene about the same time people started requiring that I play my Apple II live. So the '80s were pretty dead for my music: I wasn't performing, instrumentalists didn't play my scores, and so almost no one heard my music. I spent the '80s mainly involved in technology and software, studying and trying more new ways to create, and exploring logic-based intelligence that would let me go further musically, and enable even beginners to have satisfying musical self-expression. Late '85 into '86, I wrote *Music Mouse* for both of these ends.

Q: At that same 1981 Congress, you also remarked, "If you could get to work with the sound with the same kind of freedom that you have with a piece of paper, then that would be very good — but we're not there yet." With *Music Mouse* and other programs you've developed, have we gotten closer?

SPIEGEL: Closer, but still nowhere near. *Music Mouse* is really direct, but that's different — an instrument for computer-assisted improvisation — though a composing tool, too, since playing and improvising are often part of the composing process. *Music Mouse* has its own constraints, which I chose to fit to my own aesthetic, my own musicality. This turned out to be rather controversial. People expected creative tools to be general purpose and neutral, like word processors, which don't bias your style or content. But an intelligent musical instrument — any instrument, actually: a flute versus a piano for example — has its own unique aesthetic realm and musical biases, and especially a new one made by a composer for her own use foremost.

Otherwise, mainly no. Most software is nowhere near as direct or immediate as a pencil. A keyboard has its own problems as a computer data-entry tool: You have to select each note, and its duration, articulation, dynamic, and instrument in a separate act, changing data-entry modes then waiting for the screen to redraw between them. If you decide to make some change — say, from two eighth notes to a dotted eight sixteenth — that's a bunch of operations, often even requiring replacing or rebeaming the notes. With a pencil, a quick little dash and a dot give you that dotted eight sixteenth, and the difference between write and erase is just which way you turn your hand. You have random access to everything on a big page where you can see a lot more context, and can scribble verbal notes, draw curves, or use your private shorthand of symbols. Also, a pencil isn't modal: You can specify instrument, duration, and pitch in a single gesture. Notation is a genuine, natural, evolving human language, and connotation and meaning change with context and style; I still haven't seen notation-playing software that even really knows what to do at a fermata.

I always wanted electronic music for its wonderful new possibilities, for what was different, unique about it, not to simulate the old ways. It can't really do that anyway. Doubling an oboe with a flute, to mask and make a sound a bit less bright — these kinds of things don't reproduce in computer simulation; and anyway, why bother when the real thing already exists? When electronic sounds try to simulate instruments, they may sound reasonably good when solo, but they don't blend the same, or change timbre the same over their registers or with loudness. It's stupid to use a whole new world as a simulator for one we've already got. But that seems to happen in the first stage of every new technology introduced: It's used first to simulate preceding successful technologies. I'm not sure why. Lack of imagination? Not really seeing the Thing In Itself?

There is a ton of software I'd like to write, but it's much harder for one person to develop software now. Lots of things have been standardized in complex, hard-to-work-with ways that limit the freedoms I'm after by their assumptions. There's a lot of benefit to standardization, but I think it's too early to have had so much of it done. More musical needs have to be understood and technological possibilities known. But the whole MIDI era is one standardization.

In 1983, before I'd heard of MIDI, I tried designing a standard digital representation for music, for telecommunications, under a Canadian Department of Communications grant — you couldn't get funding for this stuff here. It was a project with British Columbia Telephone and Microtel Pacific Research to do highly intelligent, logic-based music-encoder/decoders to network by phone, to send music or even play live with people far away, and eventually to publish by phone. It was like MIDI in some ways, but I think a lot less limiting — with lots of descriptors for process, relationship, structure, for testing conditions, adapting to context; it wasn't just a note-level alphabet. Then just when we had a working prototype and first ANSI standard draft, suddenly there was MIDI. It beat us to the punch. You had to use it; everything on the market was overnight designed for it.

MIDI wasn't done as a proper ANSI standard. That requires several rounds of publishing and getting feedback from potential users before a standard is ratified. MIDI was designed by a small group of manufacturers and engineers behind closed doors. They didn't consult musicians or experienced computer musicians like me or Max Mathews, who'd tried many digital representations of music over the years. I don't think they cared about what was best for music or musicians, or tried to avoid creative limits. MIDI was simple, cheap, and foisted on us as a *fait accompli*. Here it is, standard and set, music's new language, its notation for the computer age.

Now of course, they've tried to compensate for its lacking basic stuff they'd never thought of, like being able to change the definition of an instrument as an integral part of a piece as it unfolds. They'd just assumed you'd only compose for unchanging, predesigned instruments, like for traditional wood or metal ones. Also, the information flow is one-way. Not making MIDI full duplex was idiotic

— your computer sends notes to your synthesizer to play, but the synthesizer can't tell the computer when the notes have faded to silence or send back any other information. So many things were poorly thought out that it's really good that MIDI was kept low-level and simple, so it didn't do more damage. But there are now six different ways to trigger a note; it's not really very standard after all; it's been stretched and stretched to try to fit real music.

I tend to be led by visions of possibilities, rather than "here's something — what can I do with it?" But the way most music software is designed today, the compositional process is reduced more and more to a capture-and-edit rather than an envision-and-realize process, where music starts inside you and then finds its way to becoming audible, as you pin it down to a zillion specifics. In that process, computers can be helpful in ways that haven't been getting attention. Capture-and-edit is very easy; it doesn't require much understanding of music's methods or of the psychology of creation, or the ability to focus imagination. Commercial software companies look at finished scores and ask "How can we make a screen that looks like this and can be edited?" instead of "How was what's written here arrived at? What processes went on?" So there's lots of software out for essentially, pre-chordal, pre-orchestral, Notre Dame-school technique: You're expected to enter, or record, a bass line from the start of a piece to the end, then go back and put in drums from start to end, then go back and do the other lines. You don't think like that if you're through-composing, dealing with the whole content of each moment while feeling your way to the next. This overdub model is ok for, say, a simple strophic song form with repeating rhythm and chords. But you have to have the entire harmonic progression memorized or written down on paper, in which case either it's pretty simple or you're composing on paper or working it out in your head first anyway. The computer isn't really helping you compose; its mainly just a performer or copyist.

I've tried overdub composing, on tape and with my own and others' software. That's why most of my software, including *Music Mouse*, lets you deal simultaneously with all the parameters across a moment. You have several voices, which can have doublings, and as many touchable controls as a computer has inputs — for timbral and compositional parameters like transposition, inversion, relative motion in different ways, type of harmony and a lot more. *Music Mouse* is my personal choice of a group of controls that work well together for me. It's enough to keep your hands full, so I automated some stuff by logic, like harmonization. It's not just scale templates, stencils. I put a tremendous amount of thought into things like providing smooth transitions if you go from any octotonic chord to a diatonic one. I made the best compromises I could, to get the most musical output, but for my own taste, not trying for some universal aesthetic. So it's biased toward step-wise motion rather than large leaps, to sound traditionally melodic even when atonal. I chose to automate some things so you'd be free to play a larger number of variables altogether; you're playing all the orchestration in real time, plus all the notes. I want to work on the level of playing a full symphony orchestra plus chorus as a single live instrument. Before computers, the closest we got was the organ, where if you had both hands full of keys, you had to drop notes to change stops, and that's abrupt change, not timbral dissolve.

Bach would have loved these things, and I think he'd have been frustrated with the same aspects of the standardization which frustrate me. It's like they looked at an orchestra score and said, "This looks like a multitrack tape. I guess people do it the same way," then made it really hard to move between instrumental staves, but easy to move along one staff because it's like one track on tape. A lot of commercial software is based on unresearched assumptions about how people compose and orchestrate.

There's a tremendous need for composers to be more involved in the design of their own tools. I've chronically lacked enough composing time in large part because I didn't have adequate tools for many things I wanted to do musically. I've spent astronomical time writing software but still have light-years to go. But I have to compose how I want — not fitted into some format derived from a reverse-engineered finished score. I don't conceptualize musical time the way these current standards do, or the relationship of orchestration to pitch-time content either. You have to work around these things, and the way each brand of computer or synthesizer has set up its own control interface. My software is out for Macintosh, Amiga, and Atari, and they all have different jargons for basically the same graphic metaphor. Music has an incredible thousand-year accumulation of vocabulary for process and relationship; but you can't use it to communicate with your computer.

Q: Has the copyright for *Music Mouse* been resolved yet?

SPIEGEL: According to the Copyright Office, it has — finally — after more than five years of correspondence and phone calls. But it hasn't really been satisfactorily resolved because they've ignored the problems. The whole copyright system is based on the idea of one single composer creating something finite and fixed in form, then profiting from the rights to it. But now that artistic information can exist as software and is malleable, it's traveling around like folk songs, with everyone in its movement path able to change it a bit in some way for their own use, and then pass it on. Someone tries to circulate their visual art on a disc, and someone else might change the colors or draw over part of it and circulate that. Every time someone plays a MIDI file in a different studio, it will sound different; they'll have different synthesizer sounds and do a different mix, and maybe add or change parts. In the 20th century, composing has become more collaborative: rock groups, jazz bands, various kinds of improv groups. In the early days of compositional algorithms, you wrote a piece of software for your own use as a composer, to do a particular piece or a set of pieces. (Three of the four pieces on *The Expanding Universe* used the same algorithmic program, with different parameters.) Now, if one person writes an algorithm which generates music, a different person might use it, as with *Music Mouse*. I consider this a form of remote compositional collaboration. But the Copyright Office ruled in a way that failed to recognize the creative decision-making input of the computer program's author as a creative contribution to the final piece; they didn't go for a double-composer model when one of the creative decision-makers was a piece of software — or really, that software's author.

The entire set of divisions of labor in the creation of intellectual property is rapidly becoming so different from the old model embodied in the copyright law that at some point they'll have to deal with it. With the current law, *Music Mouse* had to be one of three things. Was it: One, a musical composition — open-form like Earle Brown or Pauline Oliveros do, a Laurie Spiegel composition? It was written up in many places as, "If you like Laurie's music, this will be a good program for you, but if not, you'll be aesthetically limited in ways you won't like," or "Its music's always got Spiegel's personal stamp on it," or even "This is a Laurie Spiegel composition put out as a computer program." Or was it Thing Two, the same catagory as literature — to copyright the text of the actual computer program as a written text. This also stretches the limits, because if you wrote a program in PASCAL which acted exactly like my C language one, it wouldn't look at all the same on paper; it would be a completely different text, not necessarily even a translation. Usually they register computer software as text, and that's what they finally ruled *Music Mouse* was.

Q: Their decision was to copyright *Music Mouse* as a text, the same way a novel is a text?

SPIEGEL: Yeah. The third category, the one I'd originally applied in, and where I thought it belonged, was audiovisual works. That category started out with film and video, and was therefore incredibly biased toward fixed, recognizable, visual content, really underplaying the audio part of "audiovisual." This category had already been stretched to include video games, and there were already precedents acknowledging that the creator had some rights in works using output from them: If you turn on your VCR and flip TV channels, copyrights in all the stuff you tape still belong to the producers of what you taped; and if you videotape a Pac Man or Nintendo session, copyright to the game images on your tape still belongs to the games' creators, even though the images will be sequenced differently for different runs of a game. Now that's more like an Earle Brown piece or a jazz player's variation on a standard tune. That was the existing category I thought fit *Music Mouse* best; if you made an original work with it, there'd still be acknowledgement of some creative content determined by the composer who wrote the software — who told the computer just how to turn a mouse move into four-part harmony — versus giving complete rights to the music to whoever just moves the mouse. It's remote collaboration, sharing the creative process; I may never meet the end user, but it nonetheless is a collaboration when they decide that *Music Mouse* puts out stuff that goes the aesthetic direction they want to go and they use it. They come up with their own sounds and their own final music, but there's some of me in there too. It's a new variation on the idea of "variations on the theme." There may be very little of me in when they get done, but it's still been formed quite differently from whatever they'd have composed without it. It's like a word processor which, if you were writing a play, would guide the dialogue or plot.

I really wanted to get the Copyright Office to acknowledge a need for a new class of works, which I suggested calling "generative works": intellectual property which generates other intellectual property, or at least contributes significantly to its nature or content, whether music, art, or text. This will increasingly happen layer on layer: Somebody uses a program written by someone else, and it generates notes; then they run the notes through a program someone else wrote, which has its own editing logic or embellishes or adds style characteristics; then they record that, using sounds someone else sampled from yet another person's recordings or synthesized sounds someone else designed. The traditional divisions of labor for music just don't hold; you don't have just one composer in total control, then relatively passive performers, and audience. You've got combined authorship. Different people create sounds, software that can modify or edit music by specified aesthetic criteria, people writing algorithmic generators which churn out material anyone can sculpt, mold, orchestrate, and change as they please. Also, you've got recording-studio engineers who, really in many ways, assume a conductor's role — or way beyond in cases of producers like Brian Eno, who really uses the studio as a musical instrument in itself and a musician as raw material. The old model doesn't fit, and so we see increasing unfairness to artists who aren't being rewarded for their creative work due to an antiquated intellectual-property-rights system that's simply failed to keep up with what's really going on. The creative processes that go into a work are much more widely distributed, decentralized, and spread out among different people than ever before. New technology requires new, more varied, technical skills, and music's always been a very technical art.

Also, just as in folk music or jazz, much computer-based music may never exist as finished, finite pieces that can be held as private property; there may simply need to be a new socioeconomic model to accommodate communal repertoire, cultural common property, music that branches into variants, like folk songs do as they change over time and place. Some branches off of a piece of music data might be dead ends, once made, but some may become great landmark works, heard everywhere. Remember what Bach did with those simple folk chorale tunes? Or his transcendent transcriptions of how he heard others' works? Was he their sole author? No. How would his creative contribution be classified, rewarded, under our laws?

As the number of people who affect the content of that kind of ever-changing communal music grows, it becomes impossible to analyze the creative content in percentage shares or quantify the value of any one individual's contribution. Linking a person's remuneration for creativity to their ownership of some Thing they've made may be an obsolete way to support creative work. The idea of music as private property just doesn't fit all music. Another economic support system, altogether different from the intellectual property idea, is needed.

The judgment to copyright *Music Mouse* as text just ignores such questions. But there is no way to absolutely identify a *Music Mouse* piece; they're all different, and its output can be processed and edited in infinite ways later. I never claimed it was a composition; I always called it an instrument. But it is "intelligent" and makes decisions for you to the point where someone who's, say, a filmmaker or a choreographer is able to do music for their own works. It's an enabler. If I make five bucks off one copy sold, and its buyer can then land a big film-score job, though all they ever did before was sound effects — is that economically fair? Their job resulted from my 15 years' work on interactive composition, my personal investment in research and development. It's an instrument, but an active collaborator. *Status quo,* all royalties go to whoever finalizes a fixed-form sound composition, regardless of how many different people's creative decision-making may have gone into it. Not fair. Not realistic. Not supportive to creativity the way it's being done now.

Q: Has this experience soured you on developing other kinds of software for the marketplace?

SPIEGEL: The problems of getting distribution and providing technical support and database maintenance and such stuff have soured me enough that I'm not sure whether I'd want to do another program commercially, versus shareware or public domain. Public domain is attractive in some ways: You won't get anything back, but then people don't expect as much from you. It gets rid of all the problems of considering such creative works as "property." You have a lot more freedom — no drags like marketing, contracts, accounting, inventory. You can just upload onto a network, go on to other things, and people can like it or lump it. No one will demand their money back because it doesn't do something other software does. You still get feedback — like "I touched the mouse and this sound came right out and made me jump; it shouldn't have done it; I hadn't started anything yet. It's doing stuff all on its own!" Ussachevsky's first reaction to *Music Mouse* — and I'm still not sure what he meant, though he clearly liked it — was "Thank God Stravinsky didn't live to see this!"

I honestly don't know. I'm very disheartened with the distribution systems for both music and software — that's the real problem. We're in a transitional period where information, which should be able to travel freely and cheaply as electronic or optic data, is still being distributed as manufactured objects, which keeps costs high to support a bunch of middlemen who control the means of object production, as though we were still in the kind of 19th-century economy Marx dealt with so brilliantly. We're locking informational value into a manufactured-commodity economic model, and thereby putting it through all the same bottlenecks: record companies, sales projections, profit thresholds — there are sales volumes below which it's not profitable to manufacture, package, warehouse, and ship music or software objects. To have to guarantee thousands of sales because data's being handled as objects is insane for digital information. Ways to distribute cheaply through wires or even air already exist. Profit thresholds for manufacture mean that minority creators can't get works into the marketplace or to their audiences.

And those who want their stuff can't get it at all till a lot more people want it too. That's why I had to do concerts to build demand before I could do records.

Q: How much of this is simply the glacial slowness of bureaucrats in adapting to social and technological change, and how much is it a deliberate attempt to centralize and control the flow of information?

SPIEGEL: I think there's a lot of the latter, but not necessarily deliberate. It's more like inertia. Old paradigms and habits die hard. But the liberation of information from objects involves questions no one's answered; like how do you attribute value to information? Clearly, the informational value of a bunch of random digital garbage is different from that of the same number of bytes containing *The Art Of The Fugue* or a concise composing algorithm which can churn out an infinite amount of music. "$e = mc^2$" is just 7 bytes long, but its value's awesome. One of what I call Spiegel's laws, in this book on informational economics — which I've been not quite getting back to writing ever since Oxford — is that information tends to go where it's wanted and resists going where it's not wanted. (That's, of course, without the drag effect when information's forced to haul objects around with it.) The laws by which information gains and loses value haven't been explored. In Marx's terms, information has both use value and exchange value; but it also has other valuation properties. It can become obsolete. It has truth value, or a true-false quotient which can be perceived to change, and affects its value, though false info can have very high use value too. It loses value as it becomes more redundant — that's plain old supply and demand: Scarce information is very valuable. Then there's the question of control of access to it, ownership, secrecy, and things like our distribution bottlenecks — you know — record companies, publishers, broadcasters, libraries, data networks.

So besides not having criteria for determining information's value, we also don't understand much about the value of information-access control. And there are lots more questions: how context-sensitive information's value is, and questions like meaningfulness, which even Claude Shannon's brilliant information theory didn't touch. Information theory per Shannon and John Pierce, incidentally, is one of my great inspirations; it's been used in a lot of my algorithmic pieces — not *Music Mouse* but other works. People put too much emphasis on *Music Mouse* because it's the only music program seen by the public. But I've written many others, some heavily influenced by Shannon's work, which was about optimizing communication, and gave me a way to impose dramatic emotional form onto algorithmic output. I've heard a lot of algorithmic music that's dramatically pretty flat. In contrast, I learned early how to vary informational entropy (that's essentially the ratio of the predictable to the unexpected) throughout a piece, to make drama and emotion by playing off of expectations. It's a variable I like to play live.

When you try to talk about changing how we attribute value to information, to creating, lawyers or the Copyright Office people just go pale and run back to the old ways, because, my God what do we do? They're not getting paid to do that level of thinking. I've talked to ASCAP and BMI house counsels and been told things like: When Muzak or some other zillion-dollar business starts using other people's algorithms to generate music, then there'll be enough bucks to bother with these questions, but not till then. "Then" may be too late. Maybe four years after I sent my copyright application for *Music Mouse* to Washington, the people I was dealing with said, "When this first came in, it was one of a kind and we put it aside as minor. But now we have a whole pile of stuff raising similar questions, and they keep coming in!"

Virtual Reality's another example of a technology where people not only forgot its history and evolution, they also don't want to think about its implications or full potential; so they make false analogies back to mid-'60s LSD, which has nothing whatsoever to do with it. VR requires new thinking, questioning. The Big Powers — rights handlers, manufacturers — are scared we might have to scrap the old economics of creation, and go to a different structure, to change concepts like ownership of works or works as finite, unchanging things. We actual creators have less to lose if there's change. The current system just doesn't pay us. But we're still getting new travesties on the books, like this DAT-tax bill that just passed, which essentially taxes creative artists for making digital copies of their own works to distribute to fewer people than could support pressing a cd, with the tax revenue from the blank DAT tape going to the big record companies which make cds. It's unfair, illogical; it blatantly puts the cost of supporting the *status quo* on the backs of the artists who suffer from it.

Q: With the seven improvised pieces made using *Music Mouse* on your cd *Unseen Worlds*, did you feel that this was exactly what *Music Mouse* is supposed to do, or was there more a sense that you've barely scratched the surface of its potential?

SPIEGEL: Those were just things I felt like doing at the seven moments when I did those seven movements. That is what the program's for, but there's plenty of other music it could do. I did edit them a bit digitally on hard disc, and do some digital signal processing, and I even went in and took out a note here or there. There are still things in them that bother me, where I'd like to have crossfaded to a different eq and back out or something, because there's a limit to how much you can control in real time. Also, in one place, a friend accidentally punched a 22-second drop-out into the master of one piece. I fixed it pretty smoothly — I don't know what prize I'd award to someone who found the place where I patched that up. Things like that happen and you just have to deal with them; but mostly they all just came out as they are on the cd. I do some thinking first, some planning; I don't just sit down and play. I have to decide the orchestration and starting setup, and think about the processes available to me. As with analog synthesizers, I don't start pieces with everything running full blast. First I check out all the parameters that can be run full blast in a given orchestrational setup, with *Music Mouse* as an interface, and what variables I can move, then I go back and pick a starting place, one that's simple and held back, so I have lots of room to expand in every dimension where I can move, so I can make buildups, climaxes, overloads, tensions to resolve. There's a lot of pre-composition in that kind of improvisation. You have to know your instrument really well, and I like to try to make a different instrument, in some way, for each piece.

Q: There's certainly a wide variety among those seven pieces.

SPIEGEL: Though they're all the same technique — a pretty simple setup: A 1986 Yamaha TX816 synthesizer (now obsolete), and Eventide digital signal-processing units I love dearly. Eventide's a company I've consulted for on and off in various ways, and have known well as good friends since the mid '70s.

Q: These pieces get into a strange rhythmic quality. You can feel that they're being played, but not in the moment-to-moment sound. It's the larger sense of gesture and compositional change which has the sense of a live musician.

SPIEGEL: Well, the instrument's meant to be played on the composition level, not so much on the note level. Or maybe that's from exploring each sonic space first, so I can start low, knowing in advance the directions I can go. This is something I discovered working with the Buchla and other analog synthesizers in the late '60s. You could set up a dense patch with a zillion things going on, and then take down one element at a time till it got very simple, maybe just a single steady sound. Then, in playing the piece, you knew what you could build toward, and could go several minutes, by bringing back up, introducing, all the stuff you'd pulled down. It's like you've clearly envisioned the finished sculpture buried in a rough rock before you pick up your chisel to reveal it more and more as you go. When you get something really intense going, you don't just say, "This is fantastic!" and push "Record." You think, "In what order do I want to reveal its different aspects? How do I want to build to this over time?" I also work at the harmony of the climaxes; harmonic cadences are very important to me still, synchronizing harmony and density with dynamics and timbre in climaxes. There's a lot of preparatory thinking and feeling out; it's not just spontaneous. I think most people who improvise have their own bag of tricks or pet processes; they don't start from absolute nothing each time. Preparation makes it easier to feel and act spontaneously, moment to moment, during the actual recording run. My feel for form is one of the things that always separated me from the minimalists, and made me slip through the category cracks. I tried and tried in the early '70s to do drone music, but friends like Rhys kept telling me, "Laurie, you just don't have it — this is still moving too fast. Slow down and try again." I tried but I just couldn't. I come out of an unabashed love of many great masterworks of previous eras.

Q: Especially the Renaissance and the Baroque.

SPIEGEL: And the Romantic too — I also come out of Chopin and Beethoven and Schumann and Brahms. I love Shostakovich tremendously. But Bach above all. And some earlier ones: Dowland I think is very much underestimated; Machaut is fantastic — but then people do know that, if they know early music at all. Folk music and early European music both tend to be more process-oriented than form-oriented. You see the changeover right when Bach was culminating the processes of imitative counterpoint in *The Art Of The Fugue*, while the young Mozart and Mannheim school guys were working on sonata form and rondo and all those other fill-in-the-blanks forms. When a climax happens in pre- or non-classical — process-oriented — music, it builds more organically and naturally, because it's not an obligatory climax, like before a sonata's bridge back to its original key to recap its first and second themes. It's something that just happened at some arbitrary point, when it hit you to bring back the subject in inversion, augmented, in the bass, and you felt a chill go up your spine.

I got into composing grown up, after my values and preferences had already been formed by listening. For many years I thought starting composing so late was a horrible disadvantage, but it turned to be a real plus instead. I'd spent the first 23 years of my life not seeing myself as a composer at all, free to listen to music with no vested ego interest in any particular type of it, just enjoying it and finding out what I liked and what moved me, and getting my values clear. Then when I set about learning enough technique to be able to create music to fit my values, it was natural — in fact necessary — to explore, even invent, alternative techniques, because I was so far behind, age-wise, on traditional techniques. Starting composing late, I needed to find ways around my ignorance and lack of practice, in order to express in sound what I needed to, artistically. I didn't have time to just go the slow traditional route of writing down a zillion notes on paper then waiting up to 40 years to hear them. I needed ways to do music that could be heard now, so I could learn faster and really communicate in sound. New techniques bought me time; I could work professionally in music while still studying hard to get some mastery of notation, keyboard, and traditional skills. I didn't get into the avant-garde by trying to get even with — or rebel against — some childhood piano teacher who'd forced me to do music some artificial proper way. I ended up being called avant-garde, an innovator, as a spin-off.

Q: Regarding the rhythmic nature of your pieces, it seems to me that what's coming out is not so much the physical rhythms of a performing musician, but more the rhythms of nature, the larger cycles of natural processes.

SPIEGEL: That's beautiful. Thanks. One thing music notation developed for was to fill the need to synchronize ever larger numbers of musicians, and those metric synch pulses became increasingly dominant over time. Early in notated music, rhythm was very free, as in melismatic trope. The Renaissance was still extraordinarily diverse, rhythmically. By the Baroque, musical time felt a good bit more regulated, and by the Classical, it was uniform enough to feel boringly predictable at times. Then in the 19th century they began trying to break free; you find more rubato and tempo shifts and like that. In our own time you see the level of contrivance of Elliott Carter's metric modulation, which extended the notational system to give more precise control of tempo change, but which also let the whole sense of spontaneity music was trying to get back to somehow fall by the wayside. Graphical scoring, like Jake Druckman's, gave more rhythmic freedom, but often things went by too dense and fast to hear it.

When I played the guitar in my teens, or the mandolin I kept under my bed when I was younger, I never played against a metronome; I didn't read; I wasn't exposed to the tyranny of the bar line, which is like the tyranny of the clock. I just practiced self-expression. The music I've been concerned with is just for and of individuals, for personal expression and direct person-to-person communication. Maybe that's why I never really got into chamber music or works for tape plus live players. Scripting interactions between players wasn't really of interest to me. I try to make very direct communication to listeners, and also to find ways to enhance other people's self-expression — like software with built-in expertise. Or I write pieces for reading at home — though I've also loved it the few times performers have played my written stuff onstage. I enjoy sight-reading a lot; I never bother to memorize anything, I just like to read and read. I like to write for people who enjoy doing this too, though it never gets published or to them. I'm very content-oriented, but I also love form and structure — otherwise I wouldn't love programming computers or Bach so much. I structured *Unseen Worlds* as a Hegelian dialectic: The thesis is intuitive, spontaneous, expressive stuff; the antithesis is precomposed, algorithmic, totally procedural and predefined; then the synthesis — the last work on the cd, *Passage* — is composition: some un-analyzable hodge-podge melding of those two extremes, different for every composer and at every moment while you do it.

Q: The procedural, composed pieces are the most familiar rhythmically, while the played, spontaneous pieces take rhythm into a very different area.

SPIEGEL: It's easy to predefine, to precompose, what sounds familiar, normal. It's the unfamiliar that needs the spontaneity of the moment — the freedom not to feel compelled to move a sound till it feels right, or when into something, to just keep going, to keep following it, moment to moment.

I have problems with most commercial music programs. They want to think of time in beats or ticks — though I did compose *Passage* in a sequencer. I never look at bar lines — I have to look past and through them. I felt immediately locked out as soon as I tried to use the notation program *Finale* — a widely used Macintosh notation program, because its basic unit of music is the bar. When I booted it, I wanted to write unbarred music, an unmeasured prelude for a harpsichord commision a couple years back, and I couldn't get out of the bars! They had me behind bars! You were forced to think in them. It was useless, an impediment. I went back to pencil.

When you're sitting out on the back porch with your guitar, after your parents have had some big fight, and you feel down and just play your guitar — that's where my music really comes from. You try to deal with the emotions you feel at each moment, feeling for the right next sounds. Sometimes you'll fall into something which will just catch and move rhythmically a while, but it's basically moment-to-moment. If you're making music for people to listen to instead, like a tape piece or cd, you're making an experience for them, and it needs to build and to take them somewhere, to move organically, naturally, through changes of view and perspective and color and feel, and through tensions and releases which give it form. It's one thing to improvise just to deal with your own feelings; it's another to honor and keep the trust of listeners who've opened themselves up, in their homes, and let something you've made take them over. It has to be right, trustable, safe, so they can let go and feel it as deeply as they can. You can't lay on them anything artificial, extraneous, harsh, or hurtful that would make them close off, pull back.

What you asked about rhythm relates to style. I guess I always wanted to transcend style. It was in the way — full of associations, connotations. If you're doing this or that style of music, you'll automatically turn off a whole bunch of people, be typecast — though you can also turn off everybody by not being in anyone's favorite style! I guess I just never needed to fall back on standard styles or forms, just to be open to where it feels like the music wants to go. That's key, that IT wants to go somewhere, all by itself — you just let it take over. Composing isn't really something you do by will, it's something that you let happen to you. If you try to coerce it into preconceptions, it can be very hypocritical and very shallow. You have to let music be itself, just open your sensitivities as much as you can to find a way to make it hearable; then, hopefully, some people, at least a few, will hear it with the same mind-set.

Even back in the folk-music days, I never was good about keeping steady rhythms or playing things straight. I'd always start improvising on tunes and go off, and I'd feel frustrated if I didn't get to do so. It's as fluid as electronic information, music. I suppose starting out in folk music did influence my thinking on fixed, predefined pieces, which always seemed just a subset of music, and also started me out thinking of music as process more than product.

Q: How interested are you now in composing music away from electronics?

SPIEGEL: Very — and I always have been. I've just been discouraged because there hasn't been much interest. Mostly, I like writing solo pieces for people to just read and play for themselves. But Joe Kubera's been good enough to perform some of my piano pieces in concerts a few times, and that's been wonderful. He premiered four pieces at Merkin Hall in early '91, and Barbara Cadranel played my harpsichord piece around then too. So some of my keyboard stuff got heard. There haven't been more than a couple of performances my whole life of any of my classic-guitar pieces, though that was my own personal, native instrument, the one I learned music on and wrote for first. In many ways, I have more freedom with the electronic stuff, and I love it, but it's all that anyone seems to want from me. I've got notebooks full of staff-paper pieces, which by and large have never been heard by anyone. I did have a piece, *Hearing Things*, for a 27-piece chamber orchestra, performed — once. Other than that, there's been very little interest, though there's been positive response. My *History Of Music In One Movement* for solo piano has been performed maybe three times. It got boo'd as reactionary once, but people like John Cage loved it! In eight minutes it evolves through all the historical styles, without a single actual quote. It was incredible fun to write; I got to let myself feel each period of history, and its need to break out into the next period's style, to experience all those transitions from the inside.

People have this image of me as some "out there" visionary. But I'd be pleased if any of my music, in any medium, were just in print, publicly available. I have nothing out, nothing. Scarlet Records went out of business three months after releasing *Unseen Worlds*. The old lps are all out of print, and nobody's got a record player anymore anyway. My written music just sits in file folders and notebooks and my tapes sit in boxes. Ironically, there are literally tens of thousands of copies of *Music Mouse* out there.

Q: Has any of the work done with it gotten back to you?

SPIEGEL: Oh yeah, I get stuff from users a lot. Although it totally ate me up time-wise, a really wonderful support network came out of it, spanning people doing all different kinds and styles of music. I've got a whole box of tapes sent me by *Music Mouse* users.

Q: Were you startled by anything you heard them doing, which you wouldn't have anticipated would be done that way?

SPIEGEL: Rarely. But sometimes, though there's more redundancy than I expected. The first time I heard it used with a drum machine, it totally knocked me out. It never, ever, would have occurred to me to try that; every pitch was mapped to a different percussion sound: To get an ostinato going you hit "a" for automate, and it starts generating patterns — that's been called its "instant Phil Glass mode." Trimpin played his 127 computer-controlled wooden shoes with it. That's certainly not one I'd ever come up with! And it's been used to run theatrical lighting, too. Tom DeWitt did a videocamera interface, so a dancer or someone in front of the camera could play music by just moving around; they'd be the mouse, and the music would follow them moving around. People have done lots of neat things with it, but it's an old thing by now — I wrote it in '85, '86. The best surprises were how valuable it turned out to be in music therapy, in hospitals and prisons, and for an incredible number of people who'd never played music before they got it but always wanted to — including disabled people who couldn't otherwise play music at all. I made it for myself at first, but then so many people started asking for copies that I had to start selling it. So these results were all unexpected.

It's pretty appalling that you can spend as much time and effort as I have composing music in this society, and have absolutely nothing available, and very few copies of anything that ever was available ever got sold, since they were never really marketed or promoted. Composing really doesn't sustain itself economically, unless you teach it or sell your time to TV and film. But you can write one simple piece of software that's just a reasonably well-thought-out, fairly obvious idea nobody's done before, and live on it for five years. It's crazy! One answer is that people's hunger to be able to make music is much greater than their appetite for new stuff to hear. A lot more people want to make music than know how to. Another answer is just that technology and software aren't called "arts," so the "intellectual property" is considered valuable — and you should be remunerated for creating, whereas music is something you should be punished for — being so self-indulgent as to be a parasite off of society by making it. It's OK to watch stupid old movies on television, but you should suffer if you use the same amount of time to write music instead. There's something wrong with this picture.

COMPOSITIONS

1967-70 *Five Easy Pieces* for classic guitar
1969-72 *Four Movements For Classic Guitar*
1970 *Passacaglia* for classic guitar
1971 *A Deploration* for flute and guitar; version for flute and vibraphone
1971 *Three Motets In Sixteenth Century Style* for voices
1971 *Three English Gardens: Afternoon, Evening, And Night* Buchla synthesizer
1971 *Orchestras* Buchla synthesizer
1971 *A Tombeau* Buchla synthesizer
1971 *Sojourn* Buchla synthesizer
1971 *Before Completion* Buchla synthesizer
1971 *Mines* Buchla synthesizer
1971 *Harmonic Spheres* Buchla synthesizer
1972 *An Earlier Time* for classic guitar; computer realization on Apple II with Mountain Hardware Boards 1979
1972 *Raga* Electrocomp synthesizer
1972 *Sediment* Electrocomp synthesizer
1972 *The Clinic* Electrocomp, incidental music for theater
1972 *The House Of Bernarda Alba* Electrocomp, incidental music for theater
1972 *A Prelude And A Ponderous Passacaglia* for classic guitar (Apple II realization of *Prelude* created 1979 was retitled *Destiny*)
1972 *The Library Of Babel* Electrocomp, incidental music for theater
1972 *The Devils* Electrocomp, incidental music for theater
1972 *White Devil* Electrocomp, incidental music for theater
1972 *Return To Zero* Moog modular synthesizer
1973 *Sunsets* electronic music
1973 *Introit* musique concrète

1973	*Two Fanfares* Buchla synthesizer
1973	*Etude* for classic guitar
1973	*Purification* electronic music
1974	*A Tablature Study* for classic guitar
1974	*Water Music* musique concrète
1974	*A Meditation* analog electronics
1974	*Appalachian Grove* GROOVE system (computer-controlled analog synthesis)
1974	*The Unquestioned Answer* GROOVE system versions for piano; for harp with synchronous live computer graphics 1981
1974	*The Orient Express* GROOVE system
1974	*Pentachrome* GROOVE system
1974;76	*Patchwork* GROOVE system
1974	*War Mime* Electrocomp and musique concrète, video soundtrack
1974	*War Walls* Electrocomp and musique concrète, video soundtrack
1974	*Zierot The Fool* Electrocomp, video soundtrack
1974	*Studies For Philharmonia* audio-controlled video synthesis collaboration with Tom DeWitt, Phil Edelstein, Electrocomp, and others
1974	*Cathode Ray Theater* Electrocomp synthesizer, video soundtrack
1975	*The Expanding Universe* GROOVE system
1975	*Das Ring* computer-controlled audio and video synthesis collaboration with Bill Etra, GROOVE, and Rutt-Etra synthesizer
1975	*Emma* film score
1975	*A Study* for classic guitar
1975	*Raster's Muse* video soundtrack
1975	*Just A Day In The Life...* video soundtrack
1975	*Drums* GROOVE system
1975	*Clockworks* GROOVE system
1975	*Old Wave* GROOVE system
1975	*Waves* dance score for nine instruments and GROOVE-generated tape
1975	*Music For Dance* GROOVE system, dance-video score/soundtrack
1976;90	*à la recherche du temps perdu* for piano
1976	*Narcissicon* video soundtrack
1976	*A Voyage* GROOVE system
1976	*East River* GROOVE system, dance score
1976	*Music For A Garden Of Electronic Delights* musique concrète
1976	*A Folk Study* GROOVE system
1977	*Escalante* dance score
1977	*Kepler's "Harmony Of The Planets"* computer realization of Kepler treatise
1977	*Guadalcanal Requiem* GROOVE, concrète, cello, mixed media, video score
1977	*Concerto For Self-Accompanying Digital Synthesizer* C language,

Hal Alles realtime digital synthesizer

1977   *Five Short Visits To Different Worlds* various analog and digital media

1977   *Evolutions* VAMPIRE system, computer-generated music and images, videotape

1978   *An Acceleration* GROOVE (algorithm for perception illusion of continuous acceleration done in collaboration with Dr. Kenneth Knowlton, Bell Labs)

1978   *A Short Canon* for classic guitar or piano

1978   *Voyages* VAMPIRE system, computer-cogenerated music and video

1978   *Zierot In Outta Space* mixed analog electronics, concrète sounds, and banjo, video soundtrack

1979   *After Dowland* for classic guitar

1979   *After Sor* (or *Guitar Study*) for classic guitar

1979;90 *A Prelude* for classic guitar
versions for piano; string quartet; saxophone and synthesizer

1979   *Song Without Words* for Theremin and classic guitar
version for mandolin and classic guitar 1986

1979   *An Isorhythmic Double Canon* versions for piano; string quartet

1979   *A Living Painting* VAMPIRE system, silent visual study, videotape

1979   *Voices Within: A Requiem* Electrocomp and classic tape techniques

1979   *Time Clock* for piano computer realization on Apple II with Mountain Hardware synthesis boards

1979   *Contraries* for piano
computer realization on Apple II with Mountain Hardware boards

1979   *Destiny* computer realization of classic-guitar work

1979   *After Dowland* computer realization of classic-guitar work

1980;90 *An Album Leaf* for piano

1980   *Two Nocturnes* electronics and tape manipulation

1980   *Modes* Apple II computer with ALF system and Eventide HM80

1980   *The Phantom Wolf* Electrocomp synthesizer, lute, guitar, banjo, harmonica, bamboo flute, film score

1980   *A Quadruple Canon* Apple II computer with ALF system and Eventide HM80

1980   *A History Of Music In One Movement* for piano
version for Apple II computer 1981

1980   *A Canon* for chamber ensemble with Apple II

1980   *Phantoms* for chamber ensemble with analog electronic tape (Electrocomp)

1981   *Winter Energy* for piano

1981   *A Paraphrase* for piano

1981   *After Clementi* for piano

1981   *Nomads* Apple II computer with ALF system and Eventide HM80

1981   *A Harmonic Algorithm* Apple II with Mountain Hardware boards

1981	*Three Chromatic Retrogrades* for piano
	#3 arranged for string quartet 1984
1982	*Unicorn* Apple II with AlphaSyntauri system, film score
1982	*Progression* computer-generated music
1982	*A Fantasy* for piano
1982;90	*Fughetta* for piano
1982	*A Cosmos* computer-generated music
1982	*Three Movements On Descending Scales* for piano
1982	*Two Short Cyclic Scores* for piano
1982	*A Modal Retrograde* for piano
	version for string quartet 1984
1982	*A Twelve Tone Blues* canon in retrograde inversion for piano
1982	[untitled, based on *Winter Energy* above] for piano
1982-83	*Three Modal Pieces: A Cosmos, A Legend, A Myth* McLeyvier
	computer-controlled analog synthesis
1983	*Hearing Things* for chamber orchestra
1983	*Idea Pieces* various computer systems
1983	*Harmonic Rhythms* McLeyvier
1983	*Immersion* McLeyvier
1983	*Precious Metal Variations* film score
1983	[two untitled short movements] for classic guitar
1983	[untitled short movement] for two classic guitars
1983	*Precious Metal Variations* McLeyvier, film score
1984	*Point* McLeyvier, film score
1984	*Over Time* McLeyvier, dance score
1984	*A Cyclic Score* for piano or two solo-line instruments
1984	*A Stream* for mandolin
1985	*Gravity's Joke* McLeyvier, dance score
1985	*Rain Pieces* McLeyvier, dance score
1985-86	*Music Mouse –An Intelligent Instrument* interactive generative musical process for Apple Macintosh, Commodore Amiga, Atari ST personal computers
1985;86	*A Prelude And A Counterpoint* for piano
1986	*Dissipative Fantasies* McLeyvier, film score
1986	*Music Mouse Demonstration Music* twelve computer-assisted improvisations
1986	Music for *Signals* Music Mouse, MIDI, FM synthesis, digital signal processing, dance score
1986	*Cavis Muris* Music Mouse, MIDI, FM, DSP
1987	*Lyric For MIDI Guitar* for classic guitar with computer interface
1987	*An Arpeggio Study* Emu Emulator II plus computer editing
1987	*Passage* Macintosh and Amiga computers, MIDI, FM, signal processing

1988	*Motives* open-form listener-variable algorithmic MIDI piece, Macintosh
1988	*Dryads* mixed computer techniques, MIDI, FM, DSP, film score
1988	*Returning East* for piano
1988	*After the Mountains* for piano
1988	*Finding Voice* Music Mouse, MIDI, FM, DSP
1989	*Three Sonic Spaces* Music Mouse, MIDI, FM, signal processing and editing
1990	*Fantasy On A Theme From Duarte's "English Suite"* for classic guitar
1990	*The Hollows* Music Mouse, MIDI, FM, digital processing and editing
1990	*Sound Zones* Music Mouse, MIDI, FM, digital processing and editing
1990	*Riding The Storm* Music Mouse, MIDI, FM, digital processing and editing
1990	*Two Archetypes: Hall Of Mirrors, Hurricane's Eye* Music Mouse, MIDI, FM, digital processing and editing
1990	*Two Intellectual Interludes (Data And Process): A Strand Of Life ("Viroid")* and *From A Harmonic Algorithm* C language, Macintosh, MIDI, FM synthesis
1990	*Three Movements For Harpsichord* for French double harpsichord (slightly revised 1991 and retitled *Prelude, Ayre, And Toccata*)
1990	*Continuous Transformations* Macintosh, mixed synthesis and signal processing techniques, soundtrack for computer-generated film
1990	*A Volume Of Three Dimensional Julia Sets* mixed synthesis, sampling, and signal processing techniques, soundtrack for computer-animated video
1990	*A Musette* for harpsichord, piano, or other keyboard

All compositions published by Laurie Spiegel Publishing. Inquiries about scores should be sent to Deep Listening Publications, 156 Hunter Street, Kingston, NY 12401.

Inquiries regarding Laurie Spiegel's software should be directed to Aesthetic Engineering, 175 Duane Street, New York, NY 10013.

DISCOGRAPHY

1977
Appalachian Grove (excerpt)
1750 Arch 1765 lp

1980
Patchwork, Old Wave, Pentachrome, The Expanding Universe
Philo 9003 lp

1981
[untitled]
Just Another Asshole #5 lp

1983
Drums, Voices Within
Capriccio 1002 lp

1991
*Three Sonic Spaces, Finding Voice, The Hollows, Two Archetypes, Sound Zones,
Riding The Storm, A Strand Of Life ("Viroid"), From A Harmonic Algorithm*
(excerpt), *Passage*
Scarlet 88802-2 cd, -4 cs
Aesthetic Engineering 11001-2 cd (1993)

1992
Kepler's "Harmony Of The Planets" (excerpt)
Warner New Media 14021 cd

1993
Cavis Muris
CDCM Vol. 14 Centaur cd

BIBLIOGRAPHY

"A Dialog With Laurie Spiegel." *Ear Magazine*, 2 (November 1976).

"A Pitch-To-Color Translation." *Ear Magazine*, 3 (March 1977).

"Visualize Music." *Ear Magazine*, 3 (Summer 1977).

"Three Short Poems And Two Observations." *Ear Magazine*, 4 (March 1978).

"Can Nothing Be Controversial Anymore?" *Ear Magazine*, 4 (May 1978).

"An Open Letter In The Wake Of New Music New York." *Ear Magazine*, 5
(November-December 1979).

"In Response." *Perspectives Of New Music*, 20 (Fall-Winter 1980/Spring-Summer
1981).

"The AlphaSyntauri: A Keyboard-Based Digital Playing And Recording System
With Microcomputer Interface." C. Kellner and E.V.B. Lapham, co-authors. *67th
Convention Of The Audio Engineering Society* (November 1980).

"A Non-Performance Viewpoint." *Ear Magazine*, 6 (November-December 1980); reprinted in *New Music America 1981 Festival Catalog.*

"Comments On Common Complaints: Notes On Feminists In Music." *Ear Magazine East*, 6 (April-May 1981); reprinted in *Ear Magazine*, 15 (July-August 1990).

"Apple Music: A Musician's Viewpoint." *NIBBLE - The Reference For Personal Computing* (May 1981).

"Macro Music From Micros: A Different Animal." *Creative Computing Magazine*, 7 (May 1981).

"Coming to Terms With Computer Music: A Glossary." *Personal Computing*, 5 (July 1981); reprinted in *BAUD*, 2 (August 1981).

"Manipulations Of Musical Patterns." *Proceedings Of The Symposium On Small Computers And The Arts*, IEEE (October 1981).

"Music And Media." *Ear Magazine East*, 7 (February-March 1982).

"Sonic Set Theory." *Proceedings Of The Symposium On Small Computers And The Arts*, IEEE (Oct. 1982).

"Jon Appleton's 'Four Fantasies For Synclavier.'" *Computer Music Journal*, 7 (Summer 1983).

"McLeyvier Corrections and Update." *Computer Music Journal*, 7 (Summer 1983).

"State-Of-The-Art Questions." *Proceedings Of The Symposium On Small Computers And The Arts*, IEEE (October 1983).

"A Preface." *Ear Magazine*, 9 (May-June 1984).

"On The Standardization Of Musical Editing Systems." *Computer Music Journal*, 8 (Winter 1984).

"Causal Chain Challenged." *Science News*, 128 (August 17, 1985).

"Proposal Of Types Of Holdings For An Electro-Acoustic Music Archive." *Journal Of The Society For Electro-Acoustic Music In The United States*, 1 (October 1986).

"MIDI Software Classifications." *Bulletin Of The International MIDI Association*, 3 (November 1986).

"Regarding The Historical Public Availability Of Intelligent Instruments." *Computer Music Journal*, 11 (Fall 1987).

"Invasion From SBACE." *Ear Magazine*, 13 (May 1988).

"Old Fashioned Composing From The Inside Out." *Proceedings Of The 8th Symposium On Small Computers In The Arts* (November 1988).

"Laurie Spiegel Responds." *Computer Music Journal*, 12 (Winter 1988).

"Distinctions Between Terms: Random, Algorithmic, And Intelligent." *Active Sensing*, 1 (Fall 1989).

"What's New? Not Enough." *New York Times*, second section (July 15, 1990).

"Tape Music (Or Studio Composition): Performance Problems." *Array*, 10 (Fall 1990).

"Put A MIDI Service Technician In Your Computer." Craig Anderton, co-author. *Electronic Musician*, 6 (December 1990).

"An Open Letter On Women In Computer Music, Etc., Re: Writings In *CMA Array*, Vol. 11, No. 2." *ICMA Array*, 11 (Summer 1991).

"In Response To 'Visions Of Information.'" *Apple Direct*, 3 (July 1991).

"DAT Formatting Protocol, Another Point Of View." *Journal SEAMUS*, 6 (November 1991).

"Music: Who Makes it? Who Just Takes It?" *Electronic Musician*, 8 (January 1992).

"Getting History Straight." *Keyboard Magazine*, 8 (March 1992).

"Regarding 'Performance With Active Instruments.'" *Computer Music Journal*, 16 (Fall 1992).

MORTON SUBOTNICK

photo: Gene Bagnato

MORTON SUBOTNICK / Introduction

MORTON SUBOTNICK was born in Los Angeles, California, on April 14, 1933. At age 12 he studied harmony and composition with Nicholas Rossi. He received his B.A. from the University of Denver, majoring in English literature while playing clarinet in the Denver Symphony Orchestra. After serving a stint in the Army, he attended Mills College, where he studied composition with Leon Kirchner and Darius Milhaud and received his M.A. In the late '50s, he was Music Director of the Ann Halprin Dance Company, and began composing his first electronic pieces: *musique concrète* for theatrical productions and documentaries. In 1962 he co-founded the San Francisco Tape Music Center with Ramon Sender.

By 1965, Subotnick was in New York City, working as Music Director of the Repertory Theater at Lincoln Center as well as artist-in-residence at the New York University School of the Arts. Soon after he was supplying electronic music for the Electric Circus. At this time Subotnick was commissioned by Nonesuch Records to compose an electronic work specifically for lp: the landmark *Silver Apples Of The Moon* (1967). A series of electronic pieces on record followed, including *The Wild Bull* (1968), *Touch* (1969), *Sidewinder* (1971), and *Four Butterflies* (1973).

In the late '70s, Subotnick began composing scores that combined live musicians with what he termed an electronic "ghost score." In this procedure, there are no pre-recorded electronic sounds; instead, live sound produced by the musician is picked up by microphones, modified, and played back during the performance over loudspeakers. The ghost-score sounds are produced by a tape recorder with outputs that are attached to a box containing various modules: stereo-location processor, ring modulator, frequency shifter, voltage-control amplifier, and modules for changing audio signals into control signals. Compositions in this series include *Liquid Strata* (1977), *The Wild Beasts* (1978), and *Axolotl* (1981).

Since the '80s, Subotnick has developed other methods of interactive electronics for live performance with instrumentalists, including *A Desert Flowers* (1989), in which the conductor's baton controls the electronics, and the "smart tape recorder" computer of *The Key To Songs* (1992). At the time of our interview, he was completing the first work conceived specifically for cd-rom, *Five Scenes For An Imaginary Ballet* (1992).

Among Subotnick's numerous grants and awards are six from the National Endowment for the Arts (Music Composition, Inter-Arts, Opera, and Media programs), Meet The Composer and ASCAP awards, a Guggenheim Fellowship, two Rockefeller Foundation grants, the American Academy of Arts and Letters

Composer Award, and the Brandeis Award. He has taught at Mills College, University of Maryland, University of Pittsburgh, and Yale. He has had residencies at DAAD in Berlin and at MIT. He is currently on the faculty of the California Institute of the Arts, where he heads the Composition program and is a co-director of the Center for Experiments in Art, Information, and Technology.

I spoke with Morton Subotnick at my home in New York City on March 20, 1992, and then on two subsequent occasions that year, on July 23 and October 13, by phone in his home in Santa Fe, New Mexico. Discussing Subotnick's music with the composer is virtually a crash course on the history of electronic composition in America, from its beginnings to the most recent developments in computer and cd technology. I was also interested in learning more about Subotnick's days with the Electric Circus, his various solutions to combining electronics with live performers, and his long-term involvement with theater.

MORTON SUBOTNICK / Interview

Q: I understand that your first electronic pieces were actually *musique concrète*, not synthesized works: incidental music for *King Lear* and *The Balcony*. Had you already been interested in synthesis by then, but just didn't have access to the technology?

SUBOTNICK: Well, that was 1957, 1958, and the technology almost didn't exist. There were some oscillators, but I actually could not afford it — they were very expensive. But partly it just wasn't there; there was nothing like a synthesizer. In the *King Lear* score, I used a Wurlitzer electric piano as one of the sound sources. There wasn't much manipulation you could do, just forwards and backwards; there wasn't much in the way of EQ. Everything you used was basically test equipment; there was no consumer market for it, so everything was just enormously expensive. In the late '50s, an oscillator — Hewlett Packard was the main oscillator — was $400 or $500. That's one oscillator to make one sound. Whatever filtering and equalization and so forth were all very high-end, expensive equipment. To build a simple studio that would have maybe two tape recorders and three or four oscillators and whatever minimal mixing would have been about $40,000 — in 1950s money. It's hard to imagine, because you're still talking tube technology. Making a tube, compared to a little resistor or diode or the transistor which came in at that point, was just enormously expensive.

The first studios I guess were around 1954, 1955, so we're talking about almost the very beginning. There was some movement, some things were happening before, but I think the Cologne studio was around 1954 or '55, and the Columbia-Princeton studio around the same time. We were aware of that. I actually didn't know that they had started only a few years before, but I knew they existed, and we knew the music, basically the only music that did exist. I was a graduate student at Mills; Terry Riley was at Berkeley; La Monte Young was there a couple of years later, I guess; and there were several others around at that time. I'd been in the Army in San Francisco during the Korean War, and that's how I ended up there. I'm not sure of the exact date, but it was around then — I graduated in '59, so this was '57, '58, somewhere in that range. And we were aware of all of the stuff that was going on. But I really was interested in the theater. I worked with the Ann Halprin dance company and became Music Director for the Actors Workshop which eventually became the Lincoln Center Repertory Theater. It seemed to me, for the work I was doing in the theater and with Ann, that *musique concrète* was the more meaningful thing to do: changing the concept of sound effects into art in itself.

Q: More meaningful than writing for regular instruments?

SUBOTNICK: More meaningful than regular instruments, but also more meaningful than electronic sound. At that time, electronic sound was pure sine tones or square waves or sawtooths — it wasn't a complex sound of some sort. I remember I did a series of film scores, *Computer And The Mind Of Man.* There were six of them, and the first three I did with garbage cans; my main instrument was a huge gas tank that must have been from a bus. I filled it with different amounts of water and hung it in the basement studio that I had. And by hitting it in different places, it made all these wonderful sounds. I also close-mic'd coil springs from streetcars.

Q: You recorded those sounds on tape, and then manipulated the tape for the scores?

SUBOTNICK: Actually, I didn't do a lot of manipulation. I had an old, broken-down piano and other things, and I hung them through the basement. I made a path for myself with a microphone at one end, and I would rehearse these action pieces: I would fly through the space, hitting this and that, and then turn the tape recorder off at the other end. Then I'd figure out another pass. I think I had two tape recorders, one at either end of the room. When I'd get to the end of the room or when I'd made a circle, I would turn it off — I don't remember exactly how I did it. I think I made $200 a score, so I had $600 after the first three, and I bought my first oscillators. I did the next score with the oscillators, and then they called me and said, "This is nice but it's not really computerlike, like your first ones"! And it's true, because those oscillators sounded like a bad oboe! So I ended up having to do all of those scores on that equipment.

Q: Executing the music in that way, as an exercise of moving through space, is a form of theater too, isn't it?

SUBOTNICK: Yes. It was performance-oriented, and I always felt very close to that. Even later, when I did *Silver Apples Of The Moon,* I was always performing onto the tape — in that case it wasn't tape, but there was always a performance element. I was not really interested in the kind of formal procedures with tape music, which were going on in other places — arithmetic series and things like that. I was really interested in direct contact with the medium, whatever it was.

Q: Is it true that your combination of electronics and theater got you kicked out of the San Francisco Conservatory?

SUBOTNICK: Well, yeah. What happened was that Ramon Sender along with Pauline Oliveros had started a studio at the San Francisco Conservatory — I don't remember the year. I had started my studio in my basement. They started a series called Sonics and that first year I met them. We joined forces and started to combine equipment. The final performance of the Sonics series was a fairly wild evening by anyone's standards. It was a smell opera with the Ann Halprin company: They moved through the audience and had conversations with members of the audience, and on the basis of the personalities would concoct a perfume and spray them. The place was really quite odiferous! One of us — I don't remember which — had found a tape in an alleyway, and we sealed it and played it for the first time that night. None of us had heard it before. It turned out to be a Sunday-morning psychodrama from a church, about a young woman who'd had a baby out of wedlock. And we had silent television on and a couple of other things, light projections, all going simultaneously. It went on and on. That was the evening we did the piece with tropical fish: There were staffs on four sides of the fishbowl, and Pauline and Ramon and Loren Rush and myself each sat in front of a side of this thing. We each had an instrument, and as the fish moved through it, that was our score which we played! In the review the next day, the headline was "Concert Literally Stinks"!

And that's when we formed the San Francisco Tape Music Center. They were more in the form of performance-oriented happenings around that time, towards the end of the '50s and the beginning of the '60s. At the same time I was working with Ann Halprin on *The Five-Legged Stool.*

Q: Terry Riley also did a *Five-Legged Stool* for her.

SUBOTNICK: Right. He'd started but then went to Paris, so I took over. My *Five-Legged Stool* had almost no music in it; there were occasional isolated sounds. I'd actually gotten more involved in staging — I wasn't just the composer; we'd gotten involved in every aspect of it. And then I did *Parades And Changes* from there, which took up the next three to four years to do. It was similar, although part of the score turned out to be *Silver Apples Of The Moon*; I was working on it during that period — took me a long time.

Q: I'm curious how your training in clarinet and composition and theory prepared you for the work you've been describing.

SUBOTNICK: It didn't at all! Except for the performance side: I was a performer from the time I was a little boy. I was playing in public when I was quite young, and was a professional clarinetist by the time I got out of high school. My first job was with the Denver Symphony Orchestra, when I was, I guess, not even 18. I had studied all the traditional compositional skills in junior high and high school, so when I went to USC and took their placement exams in theory, I placed out of all of that stuff, the first day of school. I went to USC that first semester in February, I guess I was 17, and that spring was offered a job in the Denver Symphony and left school. I played the summer season and the whole next season until I got drafted.

Q: Had you heard any electronic music by then?

SUBOTNICK: Well, that was 1951, there wasn't any electronic music that I know of. I was very fortunate in high school in Los Angeles: The music teacher was a very fine pianist, and he took me to the Monday evening concerts, so I got to hear Schoenberg and Stravinsky — even at one point wrote a letter to Henry Cowell who was working on the Ives biography at the time. So I knew this kind of stuff in high school, but if my memory is correct, I think there were just one or two recordings of Webern at the time; very few of Schoenberg; some Berg. The first recordings of the Bartók string quartets had just come out a few years before. There just wasn't much around.

When I went to Denver at the end of '51, the beginning of '52 — something like that — I met Jim Tenney and Stan Brakhage. We were all getting out of high school around the same time and hung out together and learned together what was going on in the various arts. That was sort of the beginning of my avant-garde side — although in high school I wrote a piece for the school orchestra and chorus which they refused to do because it was too out there! So I guess I was fairly out there all the time. But there was no real preparation from that standpoint. As a matter of fact, in the early '60s, Ramon and I tried to design what we thought was going to be the composer's palette, using transistors — we were trying to find an engineer who could do this. We had this vision of what turned out to be a synthesizer, only there wasn't one at that moment. We called it the Black Box: a home palette for composers. We figured that, for $400 to $500, someone could have this thing and turn the knobs and in effect draw the music and make what they wanted. I bought the Navy book on electronics and realized that I didn't know anything about electricity, so I had to go back and pick up the Navy book on electricity in order to get to electronics — all the terms just didn't mean anything to me! That was real hard work — I remember having a headache a lot!

Q: Was there any useful input in this area from your studies at Mills with Leon Kirchner or Darius Milhaud?

SUBOTNICK: No, not at all, not in that area. The only electronic music Kirchner did was the thing I did for him, the string quartet. He came to my studio in New York and stayed with us for about a week or so. I set up the studio for him. He also used tape in *Lily* — I didn't have anything to do with that, but the studio he used was the studio I'd set up at Harvard. But Kirchner was very important to me, in terms of energizing certain aspects of my musical life. In fact, he was the one who got me with the Actors Workshop: They had asked him for the name of a young composer and he got me over there. There was that kind of spirit.

Milhaud was actually the moving force for our taking the center to Mills: The Tape Center in San Francisco had a long, long flight of stairs, and he was never able to go there. He'd really wanted to touch base with this, and I think he did a little piece, I'm not really sure — I was gone by then. But there was really no input at that point. Musically there was a lot. We'd have tea together with Milhaud, and he would go through life in Paris in the '20s — we got a lot of information about that — and we'd exchange information about the latest stuff at what would become the Tape Center. But otherwise we were really out on our own — there wasn't much there. It was really a wide open world at that moment. It's hard to imagine at this point.

Q: It's been suggested that your work with Don Buchla and the visual artist

Anthony Martin, using slides and light projected through liquids, had a big influence on the rock performances of the psychedelic era. You were doing that sort of work in the mid '60s?

SUBOTNICK: The first one was '62. I think it may have been the first public performance using a light show, but you know, someone will always beat you to it and say they were first. But it was early, that's for sure. Lee Romero was with the San Francisco Mime Troupe — Steve Reich was writing for them. Lee did these light shows in his living room, and I got the idea to use it in a piece based on a Petrarch sonnet. It used a light show and a set; there was a dancer, a viola, a grand piano with a quotation from Liszt, and a moon that was projected over the piano. It was my ode to Romanticism. In its first version, it was a full-evening work, and we ran it at the Tape Center for four or five weeks — people kept coming. The first performance had Lee doing the light show, but he was very shy and didn't want to be involved with the public anymore, so Tony Martin took over and from that point on did the whole thing. That couldn't have been later than '63. It was a fairly big event in our circle at that time. I had done one in '61, which had used lights but not a light show, and this was my next attempt. In 1961 I did a piece called *Sound Blocks* which actually paved everything I was going to do and am still doing; this Petrarch thing was the next step on the way. The first *Misfortunes Of The Immortals* — I'm working on a new one — with the Dorian Quintet was definitely an outgrowth of that. Now I'm moving closer and closer to catching what I was trying to do at that point. I've never let go, I've been at it all this time, trying to hang in there and figure out what it's all about for me and what it's doing.

The Trips Festival in San Francisco, which I believe was either '64 or '65, moved everything over. Bill Graham went to the Trips Festival and from there started Fillmore West. So actually my work preceded all that by a year or two. So when it started, I was already around everybody. But I did not get into the rock scene until 1967, when I was involved in the start of the Electric Circus in New York. And I didn't do that on purpose; I did that accidentally, in a way. When they started the Fillmore West, the technology was all in place; it was obvious to them that what we were doing was what they needed. So Tony and Buchla went and took the light show to the Fillmore West. I think Tony actually toured with the Jefferson Airplane for a while. (I don't know that for sure — it's hard to remember all this.) Anyway, he was doing the light shows at the Fillmore West, and we'd all go and sit up in the light booth and wiggle plates here and there. And it was quite a scene, obviously. But it was not really my thing; I was not too involved in it and I didn't really care that much about it.

When I got to New York — because of the Lincoln Center Repertory Theater — I had a studio above the Bleecker Street Cinema, and these guys who wanted to start the Electric Circus were steered to me. (I forget their names; one guy was from the William Morris Agency. They'd hired a young guy and gave him

$20,000 a year to spy on hippies to find out what they liked and what they did so they could develop products and shows! It was quite a funny scene!) I'm not positive about this — this is how I remember it, but whether it's true or not, I don't know. I think Stewart Brandt had coined the term "Electric Circus"; all these guys were into copyrighting and patenting, and I think that name was copyrighted and these guys bought it from him. But they didn't know what it was; they had this idea of a discotheque that was an electric circus, but they didn't quite know what this thing was, so they were steered to me, thinking I could tell them what an electric circus was. So they paid me I think $200 to tell them what an electric circus was, and I did it so well that they gave me $200 a day to go to these places and set up and do this thing. Well, that was a lot of money for me. Then it turned out that I was fundraising, and so I said, "Look, this is ridiculous. You're getting hundreds of thousands of dollars and I'm getting $200, this doesn't even make sense." So they said OK and we did a contract that I would get $4,000 a year for as long as the Electric Circus ran, and I didn't have to do anything once it got going except these things, so I did them for a while.

Q: Electronic sound as well as lights and projections?

SUBOTNICK: Electronic sound — I made pieces and had strobe lights going with the pieces — and I would describe, verbally, what an electric circus could be. So they got their money and opened the Electric Circus. We used *Silver Apples Of The Moon* as the opening for the Electric Circus, and the Kennedys and all these people came that night. Then we did the Electric Christmas at Carnegie Hall. Right after that there was supposed to be a nationwide tour of the Electric Christmas, and I somehow found out that these guys were getting money from places like the Coffee Council of America: hundreds of thousands of dollars in order to serve nothing but coffee drinks, because teenagers weren't drinking enough coffee. All this kind of stuff, and I got real sick so I quit; I didn't collect my money anymore and didn't do the tour. That was the end of my experience with that. But all that had its seeds in that early period, '61, '62, '63, when we were putting all this stuff together.

Q: Did you create *Silver Apples Of The Moon* because of the commission from Nonesuch, or had you been working on a piece which turned into that work once their offer came along?

SUBOTNICK: First of all, the Buchla synthesizer came into being full-fledged only in '64, '65; we were working on it for several years, but the actual instrument was really finished then. And there was nothing else. The Moog was a series of component parts: a keyboard (I think there was a keyboard), a couple of oscillators, an envelope generator. But it wasn't an entire setup. The Buchla was probably the first total home-studio synthesizer in the normal sense of the word. I went to New York and I was working on this piece with it; I didn't know what the piece was, just that I was working on my first piece. And I'd just work eight, ten hours a day, five or six days a week, until it began to make sense to me in some way. Out of that came the music for those years: the music for *Parades And Changes* for Ann Halprin; all the music for the Electric Circus — they had pieces to dance to, and I chose all the pieces, and then had interludes between them and then there'd be a show. The first few months of the Electric Circus were quite remarkable: You'd be dancing and the room would get dark and then all of a sudden a whole side of the room would come up with purple and black light, and there'd be a fire-eater and music — maybe four or five or six minutes of no dancing, just images of people flying across the ceiling. The whole evening was developed to reach this peak of things: You would see 25 people in black light, suddenly eating bananas, just standing there one after another, and then they'd disappear. It was really quite remarkable. Then they got nervous and wanted people to dance all the time, so they got rid of all the interludes and all the other stuff. So the music during those two years was for everything; it was the music I was turning out as a result of learning what this was all about. In the meantime, I got the commission from Nonesuch, so the end result of that two-and-a-half years of exploring was *Silver Apples Of The Moon*. And then the next year *The Wild Bull*, which was a continuation of that work. It was just continuous work, and at the end there was a piece somehow.

Q: *Silver Apples Of The Moon* was the first time an electronic score was commissioned for release on recording. Had you attracted Nonesuch's attention through your work at the Electric Circus?

SUBOTNICK: Probably. I really don't know, but that would be my guess. I seem to have been fairly well known. After *Silver Apples*, a rock group called themselves Silver Apples and invited me to their opening. People like the Mothers of Invention — not Zappa but the other people — would pop by. People from the Velvet Underground and the Warhol movies would be regulars; they'd come by at night and I'd be working, and they'd pop in to see what was going on. There wasn't much going at that time, so I guess I was sort of a phenomenon that people paid attention to. And one night this guy appeared. Tony and I had done some concerts by then, and I'd been giving lectures on the ethics and moral qualities of the recording industry and of what a recording ought to be. You also have to understand that this was the time of stereo and hi-fi — it just appeared. Long-playing records had been around only for a short time at that point. So the whole nature of it was undefined. A Brahms symphony on a 78 didn't mean anything; they were black-and-white snapshots. So I gave this series of lectures on how the world would rise up and forbid high-fidelity recordings of anything that ought to have been done live, and that the record companies would respond by understanding that it was immoral and unethical to record things that ought to be live, and instead relegate all of that to 78s, the black-and-white snapshot, and then move to creating a new medium, a new art form, by commissioning works for the record industry. And I said, "The record companies will eventually see this and start coming, and this will be a new art form." I'd been going around doing these little talks to pick up some extra money for the better part of a year, and one night this guy appeared at my studio on Bleecker Street. We didn't have any locks on the doors, so he just walked in. He gave me this big speech about the record and commissioning. He had on a suit and I thought he was some guy who'd been at a lecture and decided to play a prank — this is like two o'clock in the morning. He said he was the head of Nonesuch Records. I'd never heard of Nonesuch Records, so I sent him on his way — after I gave him a real talking to about coming in and bothering me. That morning at about six, I saw my kids off to school, got back home, and had some coffee. I put on a Bach Brandenburg Concerto, to sort of wash my brain free, as I always did in the morning, and lo and behold it's Nonesuch Records! I was dumfounded — I'd been doing these lectures and now I'd had the opportunity to do this, and I'd kicked the guy out of my studio! I frantically tried to contact Nonesuch Records but there was no phone number: They were part of Elektra and didn't have a number of their own; they were a tiny office in the building. This guy was the head of Elektra Asylum — Jack Holzman was his name. But I didn't know they were part of Elektra Asylum — I guess I could have looked more carefully — and I never did find them. That night he showed up again. Before, he had offered me $500 as an advance on royalties. And he said, "Before you say anything, before you kick me out again, we thought it over and we're going to offer you $1,000." And I said, "Great, I'll take it"!

Q: What you were describing about the ethics of the recording industry actually did take place, only it happened in rock music.

SUBOTNICK: That's right, it started with the Beach Boys and "Good Vibrations." It really did happen. My basic vision was correct. Classical music never did understand it but the commercial people did. That's why those were the people who were visiting my studio: As soon as they saw me doing this, they understood immediately what it meant. It didn't mean that to me because I was looking at something else. And my whole life from that point on has been spent in the crack between those two worlds. My mind in the one direction which the classical world couldn't deal with, but the rock world and the commercial world could deal with, although it wasn't theirs either.

Q: Earlier, you had mentioned the importance of the aspect of performance in making your music. How did this shape your approach to composing strictly for tape?

SUBOTNICK: I'd given up live performance on the clarinet in '64 when I moved to New York. I had been doing basically classical music: Brahms quintet, Mozart quintet, chamber music, and concertos. I was an extra with the San Francisco Symphony and had a fairly big reputation as a clarinetist at the time. I was a very good performer and I enjoyed it, but I felt that that side of the performance area was almost in competition with my insides. I was at a point where I wasn't writing classical music in the normal sense of the term; I was already in a place that was not accepted by the classical world. And at the same time I was totally accepted as a performer. It was a very complicated thing for me to deal with, so I gave up the clarinet to devote myself to this other thing. Also, there was so much to do, so much to learn, and I wanted to just immerse myself in it. It wasn't like a job where you go off and write a piece; it was my life that I really wanted to do. But the instinct, the feeling of performance, of molding things and shaping things, was part of me from the time I was seven years old. One of the things that attracted me to the medium was the ability to sit in my studio and mold it and listen to it and come back to it. So that part of it I maintained. There are two sides to this, and that was one. The other side was aiming toward theater and music as a big single thing, not just theater with music. Those two things really occupied my thinking.

I developed ways early on of being able to sing and use the Buchla touch plates to produce what I called energy melodies and shapes. Basically, what I did was warble an energy shape — loud to soft — and my fingers would do the same by pressing different ways. Using my voice and two or three fingers of each hand, I'd end up with four or five energy shapes simultaneously. These were recorded using sine tones and filters so that they'd be different pitches on a single track of two tracks. When they came back, these shapes could be converted into control voltages. I had these envelope followers made for me by Buchla and they would convert what I had done into pure voltage. Then I could take a segment of it and decide that the shape which went slightly up and then quickly down and then gradually up again in a period of three seconds would be the shape of a melody. I would apply it then to a pulse generator and I would tune the knobs so I would get like 14 pitches in that shape, which would go up and down and up. Then I could play with that, just by listening to it over until I got exactly the right melody, and make it move in space, change its timbre, do all of these things out of real time even though the performance was in real time. Instead of splicing things together, I would take the whole thing and cut it up into little bits and fine-tune them. I had a number of sequencers that were being run by these energy shapes, and I could just sit back and listen and just keep tuning. Sometimes it would be months before I would actually commit it to tape; I'd just listen to a segment over and over again until it came just the way I wanted it.

Q: Composing electronic music has given you a unique opportunity to work with space, both the movement of sound in space and the creation of a sense of space for the listener — altering the sound to make it seem to exist someplace that's huge, say, or someplace very intimate. Has your attitude toward working with this parameter changed over the years?

SUBOTNICK: That to me was finally the essence of what the whole medium was. In '69 I did *Touch* for Columbia Records, which was their first quadrophonic recording for the home. It's a really dynamite quad piece, because it spins around and does all that stuff. And I still think that, in the home, there is a place for that kind of experience. But it became clear that, without the proper equipment, this wasn't going to work, so I began to think instead of two-dimensional canvases where the sound came to you but never went beyond you; it went beyond the wall and used the left-to-right space. I began to think of the later pieces in that sense, so the energy melodies had this spatial thing: They would move and place themselves forward and back and from side to side.

It's still problematic; I don't know the answer to it. It's an area that I've dealt with in a number of different ways. But I think you're quite right, I think it's one of the special domains of this medium, and I don't think we've really understood what it quite means yet.

Q: With public performances, you've been able to set up more elaborate speaker arrangements for the music.

SUBOTNICK: I did up until the beginning of the '80s, up through *The Double Life Of Amphibians* which was for the Olympics at Los Angeles and used speakers around the auditorium. Since then, I've moved to the proscenium again. And it has to do with content. I would never use surround sound with a dancer on the stage, because the focus should be to the dancer and behind, but never behind you; that dancer should be the edge of the universe in some way. So I've been very careful about how that works — all the way back to Ann Halprin, where there were very few sounds sometimes because the dancer had to be the most important thing in the world at that point. With a symphony orchestra or a string quartet, the chamber group should always be the focus. I've coined the term "a theater of sound," and these people, the chamber musicians in the pieces I do for them, are the Ophelias on the stage. The music should never diminish them; it should always make them bigger than life, not smaller than life.

With *Jacob's Room*, the work that I'm hoping will get premiered next year, I've got a notion — and I don't know how it's going to be worked out yet — that we might all be in Jacob's mind in this piece. The dream is on the stage, and I may actually place the voice of Jacob in the audience. I'm not really sure of this yet; I'm working on this, I'm playing with it. I don't know exactly how it's going to work. The point of it is that there are times when the use of space becomes contextual, and it needs space in order to work. If it doesn't, then it becomes a trick and actually detracts. I'm not really interested in trains going around the auditorium — I like it, and I would go anywhere to hear a train go around an auditorium, but that's not what I'm interested in doing.

So from that standpoint the whole medium is very important; how space is used is terribly important. You do have the opportunity to do a lot of things. I don't always do them because they don't fit the message that is there at that moment.

Q: Regarding your pieces for musicians with ghost electronics, particularly the works for solo instrumentalist: Has it been difficult to get the proper balance between the instrument and the amplifier? Are we hearing a duet or a single sound source?

SUBOTNICK: My vision of it is that we hear a single sound, that we don't know the difference.

Q: That's certainly the case with the recordings of these pieces. What about in live performances?

SUBOTNICK: When it's in my hands, it always sounds like it does on the lp. But they get done quite a bit, and obviously I'm not always there. My guess from what I've heard, the recordings that people send me, is that the musicians want to be heard. They don't have the idea that they are being heard; they have the idea that they're not heard the way they're playing and they want to get out front. I think, for a while there anyway, that the electronics were acting as a backdrop rather than as part of the fabric. I had imagined the ghost pieces as a fabric, sort of like an architectonic space where the sound becomes a function of whether there's oxygen or helium, say; whether there's sand or hollow walls or water — that different physical mediums will effect how sound is heard, so that you were playing the piano in a world where there was no cause and effect, and suddenly half the room becomes absorbent and the other half becomes reverberent, or the room changes from helium to some other mixture so that the pitches actually weave and change. That was the sense I had of these pieces: where the physical nature of the stage, acoustically, is changing, so that we have the sense that the stage isn't what we expected. My first image was of the old Hollywood movie where the composer's the pianist and the building is burning down while he's playing his last concerto! For me, it's antithetical, it doesn't mean anything, if you hear the player and it's normal. That's impossible in this world that I've created. The idea is that it is just the piano, but the piano is doing what a piano can't do, which is changing pitch and changing quality throughout the piece. The pieces are all about that kind of change. My guess is that they're not done that way often; I don't know.

My recordings of these pieces always pose a dilemma for me, having been a preacher about not doing things on record that should have been done live, so I never know what I'm doing with that anymore — it's always a problem for me. I try to make the records so that they're special as a record and you will never hear it that way again. But that's confusing to people because they go to the auditorium and they hear something else; it's not quite the same. But the blend is what I expect.

Q: How quickly do you want to have the soloist practicing with the ghost electronics?

SUBOTNICK: As late as possible. Like the man in the burning building, they have to know what they're doing but they should be unaware of the result, so that they are playing masterfully without being affected by the result. The ideal would be that they never played with it before, but that's almost impossible because you've got to do something with it. But my recommendation is always to do it as late as possible; to make the piece project as a piece, so that's what you feel when you're doing it, and never to have monitors, so the speakers are in front of you and you're very unaware of the total result.

Q: So you're not really trying to change the musician's relationship with the instrument.

SUBOTNICK: Not in these pieces, no.

Q: It's the audience's relationship with the instrument which you're altering.

SUBOTNICK: That's right. They started off being quad pieces, but after the first one I got rid of the quad and made it the proscenium, because it's this world we're looking into; it's not our world, it's this person who's in this world and is unaware of what we're hearing.

Q: Did you ever ghost an orchestra?

SUBOTNICK: Yes. That was before the ghost pieces. I did a piece for the Los Angeles Philharmonic, called *Two Butterflies* — it must have been 1974 — and it had 12 violins with contact mics and whisper mutes. The orchestra was divided up into small groups. It looked like a regular orchestra, but I divided them into groups and had lots of microphones on little tiny groups; I don't remember how many, but there were lots of microphones. They did things like whisper and make all kinds of little sounds, and the instruments with the contact mics were controlling the amplification of the different groups, so that I could blend this group with that group, and bring another group out with a pizzicato. So there were literally two compositions going on simultaneously: the normal composition that they were playing (well, it wasn't very normal!) and the amplified version that these string players were controlling. And there was this special box that was made for it, which was full of voltage-control amplifiers, so that the conductor could make a downbeat and there could be one violin with a pluck on the downbeat, another one making a crescendo, another one making a decrescendo, and you could have three groups amplified differently as a result of that. Then I did a second one for the bicentennial called *Before The Butterfly.* That used the same technique except that there were five soloists who were amplified by the 12 strings instead of the whole orchestra.

Q: Is this the same thing that's happening in *Ascent Into Air*, where the cellists are controlling the electronics?

SUBOTNICK: *Ascent Into Air* was the switchover from the ghost pieces. The ghost was originally my voice, with the electronics controlling the live performer. What the cellists did here was a live ghosting of electronics: Their performance was controlling the sound of electronics, which is the other way of the ghost pieces.

Q: It's fascinating the different solutions to combining electronics and orchestra which you've developed over the years, from *Lamination* where a tape plays along with the orchestra, to *A Desert Flowers* where the conductor's baton controls the electronic sound.

SUBOTNICK: *A Desert Flowers* is what *Lamination* wanted to be but couldn't be. I called it parallel synthesis, where instead of altering the sound of the instrument, you add a sound to the instrument simultaneously, which glues to the instrument's sound. In an orchestration, you would blend an oboe with a muted trumpet and cross-fade them to get a new sound out of them. This is now an electronic sound made of organic sounds and synthesized sounds which are glued to the oboe and the trumpet, altering both as a result. That's what *Lamination* meant, that you were laminating the two. But in *Lamination*, the conductor and the orchestra had to follow the tape. With *A Desert Flowers*, the sounds are flowing with the group. It just works amazingly well. I was very modest in my use of that, but now that I know it really works, I'm going to explore it much further. It's an amazing quality. People aren't aware most of the time of what they're hearing; they just have no idea what they're hearing. That's really what this is all about, coming in and out of an experience. You don't say, "Oh wow, listen to that great electronic thing over there and this great trumpet over here." It's like the whole thing blossoms into something you haven't ever seen before, like an exotic flower.

Q: The conductor in the recording of *The Key To Songs* is also designated as being the computer operator for the piece. Is this a similar situation to *A Desert Flowers*?

SUBOTNICK: No. It's hard to imagine, but *The Key To Songs* was done when the Macintosh was still a baby computer — what I can do now, you couldn't do then. It was written with the idea that the trilogy would end up with major inter-action, which it did. But *The Key To Songs* is primarily a motor piece and doesn't require much interaction. What the computer operator in *The Key To Songs* does is start the computer. The computer automatically stops itself at the right place — it's like a smart tape recorder — lines itself up with the next place, and is ready to go. All you do is press a key, and it does everything else for you. During rehearsals, you can access any measure in the piece and change the tempo and remix the mixer from the computer keyboard. So for rehearsal purposes, it's an extremely smart tape recorder. It's interactive by traditional standards these days, but not by my standards; it's a very low-level interaction. The next piece, *And The Butterflies Begin To Sing*, has more, and the third one, *All My Hummingbirds Have Alibis*, is totally interactive; there are no sequences running at all, and everything is responding to what the players are doing.

A Desert Flowers was one step further, and then *All My Hummingbirds Have Alibis* was one step further than that. What we're working on now is a body suit; Mark Coniglio is working on that, it's really his. But what I'd like to do is convert the upper part of it, the torso and the arms, and figure out software so that a conductor can conduct freely and do expressive things with both hands, and the computer would know everything that the conductor's doing and would be able to respond.

Q: As opposed to responding only to the movements of the baton.

SUBOTNICK: Right. Which is what happened in *A Desert Flowers* — very successfully, but still, there's a long way to go to the next step.

Q: So the conductor would actually suit up in this outfit?

SUBOTNICK: It probably wouldn't be a shirt; it would probably be two sleeves. And then the conductor would rehearse with the computer alone, at the very beginning, and the computer would learn that this kind of a gesture at this point in the piece is 4/4, and that that gesture is a cue to the oboe, and so forth. And then gradually, through rehearsals with the orchestra and the conductor and a computer operator, the computer would say, "I expected you to do this tempo change, but you did that one instead. Do you want me to reschedule or go back to the original or go somewhere in between? Are you searching for a new tempo, and if so, I'll just average out until you find what you're doing." And it gradually will be able to anticipate what the conductor is doing. That's not very far off; I'm hoping by a year from September to be able to have the first version of it, and by the year after I'll be able to put it into a piece.

Q: *Place* for orchestra and the string-quartet-and-voice version of *Jacob's Room* are really the only pieces without electronics which you've composed since the early '60s. Do you try to avoid composing strictly instrumental music?

SUBOTNICK: I'm not very interested in it. *Place* was fine when we performed it with the Oregon Symphony, but I felt it needed some revision. It just wasn't interesting to me. There was a point in my life in the late '60s when I was at a crossroads. I know I could have earned a lot of money — I had the potential at that point because of where I was, who I was, and what I was doing; I was offered a number of things that would have led me into a commercial career that could have made me ... not wealthy like Ross Perot, but well-off. But I didn't choose that. I chose to go on another road, and I was lucky in a way that I could choose it, and know why I was choosing it. And I chose it because I wanted in my lifetime to spend as many hours and minutes of my life doing the things that were the most meaningful and the most rewarding internally for me. Writing commercial stuff was not, and I feel the same way about strictly instrumental music. I really love working with media; I love the challenge and the complexity and the immediacy of it. On the other hand, I don't feel that I have that much to offer, myself, to the rest of the world in strictly instrumental music. In a way, I gave it up when I gave up playing the clarinet.

Q: What's great is that you've still been able to compose so much music for concert instruments, but within this new context.

SUBOTNICK: I like working with instruments, but in this new context, not as a strictly instrumental work. I'm very media-conscious, so that if you don't use the medium, the music has to be different. If you're writing a string quartet, the music has to be different than it is if you're extending the instrument or extending the medium by using technology.

Q: Does having your electronic pieces available on compact disc instead of lp seem to you a significant improvement?

SUBOTNICK: Oh yeah, I just love it. I love the size of it, I love the sound of it. It doesn't always sound good, but I think that's just because we don't know how to do it yet.

Q: I was interested to see that *Return* was ADD instead of DDD, so you're still working with tape at least initially.

SUBOTNICK: DAT machines just came into being a couple of hours ago! I did that for the return of Halley's Comet, so I didn't have access to anything then. Also that was a multichannel work done for observatories and planetariums, which was reduced to two-track for the recording. I'm working on my new one with Michael Hoenig, and he wants to master it eventually on analog tape. There are people who sort of have this thing about analog tape. I don't, really.

Q: There are sections of *Return* on the lp release which were deleted from the cd version.

SUBOTNICK: The recording was the exact thing people heard in the planetarium, and the idea was that those records would be available in the planetariums, so people could buy a record and take it home. As it turned out, the record came out after the comet was gone — it took them too long to get it out. But for the experience with the sky show, the extra material made a lot of sense. If you're just listening to it, I felt they were redundant; some of the direct references to medieval times were not musically as interesting to me, so I made the cuts on that basis.

Q: From the late '60s to the late '70s, you created at least seven major pieces for solo tape. But since then, *Return* has been the only one you've made.

SUBOTNICK: Right, and I don't consider that a tape piece in the normal sense of the word. Actually, in the normal sense of the word, it is a tape piece, but in my sense of the word, it isn't. My view of a tape piece, the way I've approached a tape piece, was to build something from scratch in my studio, and not really know where it's going to go — just let it grow out of the work in my studio. But *Return* was almost like a movie score — it was conceived for planetariums. I'd mapped out *Return* and said there'd be this here and that there, and then I went about doing it. Like what you would do when you're writing a string quartet: I had a clear picture of what it had to be, and then I wrote it and I produced it and it came out. It's true, it was on tape, but it doesn't resemble anything like what my tape pieces resemble, because they ordinarily grow from little tiny kernels that I start in my studio. When I was doing them, I would just start working in my studio. It was my life for seven months or ten months or three months or whatever it was. And at the end of that period, what came out was it. Like a painter getting ready to do a show: You lock yourself in your studio, and you do four months of painting, and at the end of that time, you show it. That's the way I felt about this, that it's a studio art. And I still feel that way about it.

Q: Was it mostly a matter of commissions, or had you decided that you wanted to stop creating tape pieces for a while?

SUBOTNICK: In '61, I had finished a piece called *Sound Blocks* and had it performed. That piece had a person in the middle of the space, who spoke at the end; there were four loudspeakers, four musicians, lighting, and tape. That was my breakaway piece. (It just exists in manuscript form.) It was very successful, and I felt that this is what I wanted to do, so I set myself a task: At some point in the next several years, I wanted to make a piece like this but with better control over all the media. So I started with the electronics and I worked, and it took me until '75 or '76, when I did *Until Spring*, to get the sense that I really understood what a tape piece was. The ghost pieces and all the instrumental works that have gone since, were my ability to deal with instruments. In the meantime, I've gone back to the lighting, and I have *Jacob's Room, Hungers*, and a couple of other pieces that I'm doing. So I'm beginning now to get a sense of the use of light and image. I'm hoping now, within the next five years, to be able to accomplish the piece that I started out to do in 1961! I actually set these tasks — I didn't care how long they took — so I could feel that I knew what the medium meant to me. But because of the cd-rom, I am getting back to a new medium. I feel like I'm right back to *Silver Apples Of The Moon* with it; it's a whole new thing that's energized me in my studio. It's very exciting.

For me, the new medium is the cd-rom and its children which will come after. The cd-rom connects with a computer, so you can interact with it in a number of different ways, which you can't do with a normal cd. And you can use the computer screen for graphic readout. Eventually, you won't need a separate computer; there'll be smart-enough and big-enough cd players that will hook up with your tv screen, which will be able to do this. Right now, it's a fairly elaborate set-up, because you need a computer and a cd-rom. Eventually, they'll all converge into a single medium, along with the laser-disc players.

Q: To what extent does the cd-rom interact with the computer?

SUBOTNICK: The distribution and dissemination of music (fine-art music, in any case) has been recordings; "sheet music," as they call it; music education; and books and articles about music. The potential — and my gut feeling is that this will really happen — is that all of these, the music, the scores, and everything about the music, including some form of music education, will merge into an industry in which these will all exist within one item that will look like the cd-rom. (It probably won't be, physically, the cd-rom, but it'll look like the cd-rom.) And in one form or another this will exist for every single piece of music. I've been given the opportunity to do what I believe is the first example of this for a work which was intended especially for the cd-rom, *Five Scenes For An Imaginary Ballet.* The *Five Scenes* was actually conceived for the cd-rom and has no other existence. *All My Hummingbirds Have Alibis,* which is also an imaginary ballet, is an earlier work which we've also recorded for the cd-rom, and it represents an example, from my standpoint, of how the recording industry and the music industry will work. I feel very fortunate. When I did *Silver Apples,* it was the first electronic commission for a recording — or at least, that's what we all understand it was; someone may dig up something else at some point, but up until now, that seems to be it! This may well be the first for this new aspect of the medium, and I feel real happy about that, that it's something I've been able to deal with twice. There's a continuity for me.

All My Hummingbirds Have Alibis is based on a collage book by Max Ernst. So when you come up with the piece on the cd-rom, you have a lot of choices. One of the choices is to simply play the music. You can start anywhere you want in the piece, any measure you want, and you can play a single section or the entire work from that section to the end or from the beginning to the end. You can do this kind of thing on a cd anyway, you can pick out places to play. However, you then can make three choices. One is, shall I have on the screen the Max Ernst images for these scenes — and it will then change the images as the scenes progress. Or you can choose to follow the score, in which case the score will turn pages for you as you go. (If you prefer to read a score in paper, you can print it out.) You can also flip the pages of the score without any music going, and say, "Let's listen to this" and click on it, and get the music for that page or that measure. Or if you don't read music — or even if you do — you can choose a written narrative that describes in somewhat poetic terms, not technical terms, the nature of the music, what it's doing: "The cello just entered...." It's something easy to read, which gives you a verbal guide to what's going on. And it progresses as the piece goes. Now, at any point during the progress of it, you can switch between any of those modes. So if you're watching the narrative, you can click at any point and it will immediately access the measure you're in on the score. And vice versa, you can just go in and out of this thing. This alone is an incredible break-through in terms of active listening and participating.

Then you might ask the question, "What's the background of the piece?" So there are very intensive program notes which are quite deep — they go into the biography of Ernst and the biography of me — and there you can go all the way down to the full listing of my works. You can go much further than you could with liner notes, because you've got an infinite number of pages to deal with there.

You could also ask the question, "How was this piece put together?" So there's a section about the music. You click on that, and it tells you everything: how the harmonic structure was literally created; the rhythmic structure; how the computer interacts with it, what kind of language the computer needs to be able to understand it; the text and how it was accessed. And at every point along the way there are musical examples: You click on it and you get the measure from the music which describes what's going on; it gives you a reading of what went on at that point. You can also go into the technology — there's a section on how MIDI works, where the programmer Mark Coniglio talks to the listener. And there are animated references as he talks: Things on the screen demonstrate what he's talking about. And nested within that are examples that you can try out yourself. For instance, you can create a sequence and record it and then play it back to understand how sequences work. It's totally interactive, and there's a section on the program language INTERACTOR, which is also spoken through, where you can access words: You can go and it'll play different words for you and how they were processed, and you can hear the difference between them. Then there's a whole section on the recording process, with Michael Hoenig, the recording engineer, talking about how he recorded it — and again, there are images and demonstrations and things you can access.

Q: Physically, the cd-rom is a regular cd? All that other information exists on the same disc along with the music?

SUBOTNICK: That's right, it's still a cd. The cd-rom was really invented for an encyclopedia-type information thing. People bought cd-rom in the first place to have a cd that would have Encyclopaedia Britannica on it. Now we have audio and computer information on it. And because the computer is involved, we can also become interactive with it — this is what's so remarkable about it.

I'm on the edge of a new medium. It's not magnificently different like the difference between Noh plays and Shakespeare, but it's as significant in difference as, say, Chopin preludes and Beethoven symphonies — there's an intimacy here that's involved. For the *Five Scenes*, the work that's especially created for it, I animated an image from Max Ernst, but not "animated" in the sense that it comes to life. Rather, I animated the viewing, so that you see parts of it or the whole thing as the music goes — I direct your eye through the image. Also, the language comes on so that instead of there being simply a sentence or a phrase on the screen, it flows on; it actually causes a reading, as if it's speaking to you, rather than it just being there and you reading it. For instance, one of the earliest phrases in the work is "Rise, dear child. Follow me." You hear a male voice say, "Rise," and the "S" swishes around the room. Then he says, "dear child," and then, in the same pacing on the screen, "Follow me" comes up. So you move from your ears' perception of words to your eyes' perception of words. The transfer is so timed that you become totally integrated with the screen in that sense. The loudspeakers should be placed more or less at either side of the monitor — this allows you to hear the music in three dimensions. The sound moves behind you and in front of you, but only if you're sitting in that one place, in front of the screen in your viewing position. If you're not in that field, you're not going to hear this. So not more than one or two people could experience this at a time. There's no way you can get this experience except close to your screen because you're directly involved with it.

You can also stop it and say, "What the hell's going on here?" and click, and an annotated version of the same thing pops up: The same thing happens, except there's a dialogue on the screen which says, "The 'S' which transformed is about to move around the space, and then the words are going to come on, paced exactly with what you've just heard, so you go from your ear to your eye in reading." It explains what the intention was, what's going on. Then you can move back to the regular piece again.

Well, you get the idea. It's a very rich experience, and I am extremely excited about it — as you can tell! To be involved at this level, at the very beginning, it's just been very exciting for me.

Q: Will the cd-rom be significantly more expensive than a regular cd?

SUBOTNICK: Yeah, it'll probably be in the $40 to $50 bracket. I think it'll always be that much more because of what you're getting. When you consider if you had to buy a book on MIDI; the Max Ernst drawings; plus the whole score — if you went out to buy the score, you'd have to pay $25 or $30. And there are also four oral essays of my own where I talk to the listener or viewer about composing in the 20th century, my views on Max Ernst and Surrealism, the cd-rom as a medium, and one other I that can't remember right now. You're talking about an enormous amount of information. It's interesting because, economically, if this does becomes a single industry, it's going to play havoc on legal things; publishers will probably fold unless they get into it — I don't know what would happen. But whoever is going to do this can produce the whole thing at just a little bit more than what any one of those things would have cost — and be able to sell it at a much higher rate than any one of those things can sell at this point, and have a much wider audience than either fine-art music, or the score, or the books about music, because you have all of those tied together into one. It's really remarkable.

Q: You've remarked elsewhere that you were able to step into the new MIDI technology with ideas that hadn't been tested, because you'd already been thinking along those lines for the last 20 years. How close had you come to predicting what MIDI would be before it actually arrived?

SUBOTNICK: Close to 100 percent. There are two aspects to MIDI. One is mind-blowing and has nothing to do with what I or anyone else could have envisioned (or maybe someone else could have!), and that is the very fact that it's a common code which anyone can use. That's separate; I'm not talking about the fact that it's MIDI and that anybody can use it, whether they have an IBM or a Macintosh. That's sociologically and economically and politically a mind-blower;

that's really wonderful. But what MIDI does is I think what you were talking about, and there what you're dealing with is basically the ability to encode some kind of information, translated through a neutral zone which is this code, and pass it on and be able to translate it into anything you want to translate it into later. In the late '60s, there was no MIDI, of course; there was no digital synthesizer. But I was using my voice and finger-pressure, recording them onto tape, and then translating them back through envelope followers and turning them into control voltages. This process is exactly what MIDI does; that is the process. The reason I said that when MIDI came I actually already knew things that other people using MIDI were going to discover only after working in it was because I already knew what it meant to interface yourself with your computer and try to create a piece of music. It meant that you needed all kinds of things, some of which don't exist yet and some of which aren't complete — we're getting there, but we're not quite there yet. But as soon as you start doing it, we really have a finite number of things that we can really, importantly wish to do: You want to be able to transmit and edit pitch information, you want to be able to be spontaneous with it, you want to be able to be exact with it, and at any time you want — and with all the other information as well. That's what my book *Parametric Counterpoint* was about; it was breaking down music into all of its component parts, to show how each affects something else, and that we need to be in control of each one of them. Because if you change any one of them, it alters the meaning of what you're trying to do. Basically, what you're after is a system that allows you to do that, and MIDI and the newest synthesizers are fast moving toward that. Most people treat them like musical instruments — MIDI stands for "Musical Instrument Digital Interface" — which is a misnomer in terms of what the potential really is. It's not being an instrument which is the real potential, although that's part of it; it's the ability to get in and do the kinds of things which people are now discovering they can do, which I was trying to do in the late '60s, that is, to be expressive at one level, like with your voice, and translate it into many other levels, and to control all aspects of that expressiveness.

We're documenting this in the cd-rom. When we recorded *All My Hummingbirds Have Alibis*, we recorded the pianist on a MIDI keyboard rather than on a real piano, and the mallet player on a MIDI mallet instrument rather than on a real mallet instrument, so that the other two instruments, the flute and the cello, are the only things that were mic'd. Nothing was on tape except the flute and the cello, so they were totally isolated, there was no other sound. We had a parallel MIDI track that had the performances of everything else, including what the interaction of the computer was doing — but they weren't in audio, they were only in MIDI. Then I could restructure the performance: for instance, get better crescendos. I could feed my own interpretations into the pianist's and mallet player's parts to get them to idealize what it is that I wanted, but from their performance — I didn't make a computer out of them, their timing remained the same. But if they made a gross error, I could fix it; or if they didn't quite get the amount of accent which I wanted, I could fix that. And then I could route that back to my own disclavier, and we recorded the disclavier played by Gloria Chang seven months before in a recording studio, put it back onto that, and mixed it in. So we had real piano, and the same thing with the mallet part. And we were able to take ages to perfect each sound. It's exactly what I was doing in '68, except it's so much better now — you can really do it now, whereas you could only barely do it then. I dreamed of doing it and I did it the best I could, but it wasn't really exact; it didn't stay there from one day to the next. Now I can literally work for eight hours, go off to dinner, come back, and take up from where I left off, and it'll be there. In the old days, you had to go with whatever degree of change had occurred in the time you'd left.

Q: Can you tell me more about your book on electronic music?

SUBOTNICK: I actually pretty much finished it. I called it *Until Spring: A Study Of Parametric Counterpoint*. It didn't get published because MCA went out of the publishing business. I never went to another publisher, so it's still sitting in manuscript form. It wasn't really ready to go, and would probably have to be updated at this point, but I don't have the time. It was for me the end of something, and I think it would be really interesting to younger people right now. It wasn't just for electronic music, although I oriented it in that direction. It had to do with the idea — which is easy to understand with modular synthesis — that things like a melodic contour could be understood in terms of energy shape. So I reduced everything to energy shapes. There were energy melodies which could be in the form of crescendo/diminuendo; loudness and softness; timbral change; the location of a sound in space; pitch changes. It was a way to organize your thinking, and do exercises on a single note: You could actually have parametric counterpoint. *Until Spring* was a piece where I sort of mastered that for myself, and that was the reason I called the book that.

Now I've been working on a children's composition program with the computer. The impetus of it was that kids can't really do creative things compositionally; they can improvise at the piano and do things like that, but they can't restructure things, they can't think composerly, because they don't have any tools to do it with. Whereas they can do it with fingerpaints: Some kids just paint, but other kids plan the page and then make it. My daughter had done paintings when she was three or four or five years old, which would go on for days: She'd say, "Well, you know, there's going to be something here." And my son now does the same thing. I'm sure a lot of kids do that, but they can't do that with music. So this program was designed to be able to let a kid get away from the page and think about it and then go back to it. It's been working extremely well, and it's turning into a program where the music that they make gives them an ear-training course: an entire course on music theory and analysis and comparative music. It'll take what they do, and they can listen to a little piece of Mozart, and it will change the Mozart into their syntax, or change their syntax into Mozart's syntax without changing their music itself. They can get a feel for how music is made. I'm hoping to publish it as a cd-rom, but it's going to be published in one form or another as an interactive medium and be available by next fall.

Q: Your pieces for tape which were released on lp, such as *The Wild Bull* and *Touch*, were in a sense partially formed by the medium itself: They'd be 30 to 40 minutes long, and have two sections corresponding to the two sides of the record. Would you have made those pieces pretty much in those forms regardless of the nature of lps?

SUBOTNICK: No, I made the pieces specifically for the records: They had two sides, two parts. I even had a kind of spiritual sense about what the two parts were; I felt that the two parts were male and female, and when you turned the record over from one side to another, no matter where you started, you would get the other side of the music. In *Touch*, for instance — this is superficial, but it was part of it — it was slow-fast-slow, basically, in the larger sense, on one side, and fast-slow-fast on the other side. There was some kind of inversion always taking place. I was very caught by the medium itself.

When I started, I thought of the record as a very finite medium, and I really did believe that people would not want to listen to symphonies in their living room because it really is a loss of something if that's the only way you know that music. But I was really wrong! People did want to listen in their living rooms, and the real music that got done for records, which became identified with them, was popular music, rock & roll and all that. Then the whole record medium got to be more high fidelity and more high fidelity, and the whole concept was to make the record player more real and more real. A kind of virtual-reality living room began to take place, so that you were not any longer in your living room but were somewhere else. As that happened, the kind of intimacy of the record as a medium disappeared for me; it wasn't an art form any longer, it was a hybrid, it was something that signified some other world somewhere else. It wasn't your world, it was the symphony orchestra on the stage, not in your living room — that's why people listened. The rock & roll people were the only ones that used the medium, but even there it duplicated what you got in a big auditorium: It was this electrified experience. It wasn't really personal to your living room or to your listening situation. And the cd has only extended that: It becomes an infinite surface — you don't have to turn the record over — but basically, nothing has changed except that it's become even more high fidelity and more virtual reality. The cd-rom represents a different situation because as soon as you have to fix your eyes, you can't move around, you can't leave the thing. So you're drawn to the object itself, and the object now truly becomes a medium in the sense that a medium can become an art object, in that you have something to focus on; it's not just ambient sound in the room. If it were projecting light in your room, for instance, it would be more like what the record became. But as long as you must focus, it becomes like an object of art, and that really interests me because it now brings us back to that intimacy. It's re-energized my interest in the medium.

Q: How far along is *And To All A Theatrical Death?*

SUBOTNICK: I haven't actually physically started it, but I've got a lot of mapping in my mind. When I get into working on a piece I just do nothing but that, and I'm not at that stage with it yet — I still have work to do on *Jacob's Room.* But it's conceptualized; it's down to the point where I think I can actually do nothing but just work on that in a couple of months.

Q: The idea of a dancer being absorbed by a hologram sounds like an amazing moment.

SUBOTNICK: There's a male and a female angel, and they control the entire environment with their hands and their bodies. Through a hologram they've found a member of the human species, and they're bringing that to us, the audience of angels, and it's Joan LaBarbara in a wheelchair. They're giving us a sample of what it was like to be a human, and her life is poignant and dramatic and moving and touching. These angels are exotic and beautiful; everything they do is with ease. But by the end of the evening, you discover that you don't really have any feeling for them; you only feel for this creature in the wheelchair. And it turns out at the end that they are probably robots — you don't know for sure. They are probably the personification of technology. So the piece is about technology. The whole piece is called *The Misfortune Of The Immortals* — it's the second version of that other piece. It deals with the question of what do we do when we distance ourselves from the action? A person who doesn't do their own correspondence; a person who doesn't wash their own dishes; all the way to the person who doesn't live their own life. And we move through the technology, because it can do this for us, to the point where we don't actually touch the thing itself. And what happens to us? What do we actually become? It's not an answer, but it is the question that this piece deals with.

COMPOSITIONS

1956	*Prelude No. 1 (The Blind Owl)* for piano	MS
1956	*Prelude No. 2 (The Feast)* for piano	MS
1958	*Mr. And Mrs. Discobolos* for clarinet, violin, cello, narrator, mime, and tape	MS
1959	*Serenade No. 1* for clarinet, flute, vibraphone, cello, piano, and mandolin	MS
1960	*The Balcony* theater score for tape	MS
1960	*King Lear* theater score for tape	MS
1961	*Serenade No. 2* for clarinet, horn, piano, and percussion	MS

1961	*Sound Blocks* an heroic vision for violin, cello, xylophone, marimba, tape, lights, and narrator	MS
1961-63	*Mandolin* for viola, tape, and film	EAM
1962	*Prelude No. 3* for piano and tape	MCA
1963	*The Five-Legged Stool* dance score for tape	MS
1963	*Play! No. 1* for woodwind quintet, piano, tape, and 16-mm film	MCA
1963;76	*Ten* for ten instruments	EAM
1964	*Galileo* theater score for tape	MS
1964	*Play! No. 2* for orchestra, conductor, and tape	MCA
1965	*The Caucasian Chalk Circle* theater score for male narrator-singer, three female singers, percussion, mandolin, and accordion	MS
1965	*Play! No. 3* for pianist/mime, tape, and 16-mm film	EAM
1965	*Play! No. 4* for soprano, vibraphone, cello, four game players, two game conductors, and two 16-mm films	EAM
1965-66	*Danton's Death* theater score for tape	MS
1966	*Prelude No. 4* for piano and tape	MCA
1967	*Silver Apples Of The Moon* for tape	EAM
1967	*Lamination* for orchestra and electronic sounds	MCA
1967	*Parades And Changes* dance score for tape	MS
1968	*Reality I/II* for tape	MS
1968	*Serenade No. 3* for four players and tape	BCP
1968	*The Wild Bull* for tape	EAM
1969	*Touch* for tape	EAM
1971	*Sidewinder* for tape	EAM
1973	*Four Butterflies* for tape	EAM
1974	*Two Butterflies* for amplified orchestra	EAM
1975	*Before The Butterfly* for orchestra and seven amplified instruments	EAM
1975	*Until Spring* for tape	EAM
1977	*Liquid Strata* for piano and electronic ghost score	EAM
1977	*Two Life Histories* for clarinet, male voice, and electronic ghost score	EAM
1978	*The Last Dream Of The Beast* for female voice and electronic ghost score	MS
1978	*Parallel Lines* for piccolo, electronic ghost score, and nine players	EAM
1978	*Passages Of The Beast* for clarinet and electronic ghost score	EAM
1978	*A Sky Of Cloudless Sulphur* for tape	EAM
1978	*The Wild Beasts* for trombone, piano, and electronic ghost score	EAM
1979	*After The Butterfly* for trumpet, electronic ghost score, and seven players	EAM
1979	*Place* for orchestra	EAM
1980	*The First Dream Of Light* for tuba and electronic ghost score	EAM

1981	*Ascent Into Air* for chamber ensemble and computer	EAM
1981	*Axolotl* for cello and electronic ghost score	EAM
1981	*A Fluttering Of Wings* for string quartet with or without electronic ghost score	EAM
1982	*An Arsenal Of Defense* for viola and electronic ghost score	EAM
1982	*Axolotl* for cello, electronic ghost score, and chamber orchestra	EAM
1982	*The Last Dream Of The Beast* for soprano, electronic ghost score, and chamber orchestra	MS
1982	*Liquid Strata* for piano, electronic ghost score, and orchestra	MS
1983	*Trembling* for violin, piano, tape, and electronic ghost score	EAM
1984	*Jacob's Room* for string quartet and voice	MS
1985	*The Key To Songs* for chamber ensemble and computer	EAM
1986	*Return* for computer-controlled digital synthesizer	EAM
1986	*Jacob's Room* for voice, cello, and computer-controlled digital synthesizer	MS
1986-87	*Hungers* opera	EAM
1987	*In Two Worlds* for alto saxophone, electronic wind controller, and orchestra; for alto saxophone and computer	EAM
1988	*And The Butterflies Begin To Sing* for chamber ensemble and computer	EAM
1988-89	*A Desert Flowers* for orchestra, computer, and MIDI baton	EAM
1991	*All My Hummingbirds Have Alibis* for flute, violin, cello, keyboard, mallets, and computer	EAM
1992	*The Key To Songs* for two pianos, orchestra, and computer	EAM
1992	*Five Scenes For An Imaginary Ballet* for cd-rom	MS
1992	*Jacob's Room* opera for two characters, cello, video, lights, and computer sound	EAM

DISCOGRAPHY

1967
Silver Apples Of The Moon
Nonesuch 71174 lp; cs (1987)
Wergo cd (1993)

1968
The Wild Bull
Nonesuch 71208 lp
Wergo cd (1993)

Electronic Prelude, Four Electronic Interludes
Columbia 7176 lp

1970
Touch
Columbia 7316 lp

1971
Lamination
Turnabout-Vox 34428 lp

1973
Sidewinder
Columbia 30683 lp

Prelude No. 4
Avant 1008 lp

1974
4 Butterflies
Columbia 32741 lp

1976
Until Spring
Columbia Odyssey 34158 lp

1979
Liquid Strata
Townhall 24 lp; cd (1993)

1980
A Sky Of Cloudless Sulphur, After The Butterfly
Nonesuch 78001 lp, cs

1982
The First Dream Of Light
Crystal 398 lp

Axolotl, The Wild Beasts
Nonesuch 78012 lp, cs

1983
Parallel Lines
CRI 458 lp

1984
Ascent Into Air, A Fluttering Of Wings
Nonesuch 78020-1 lp, -4 cs

Passages Of The Beast
Owl 30 lp

1985
The Last Dream Of The Beast
Nonesuch 78029 lp, cs

1986
Return
New Albion 010 lp; 012 cd, cs

The Key To Songs
New Albion 012 cd, cs
Mills College MC 001 lp (excerpt)

1987
The Double Life Of Amphibians (excerpt)
IRCAM 0001 lp

1988
An Arsenal Of Defense
CRI 6017 cs

1989
Touch, Jacob's Room
Wergo 2014-50 cd

1992
In Two Worlds
NEUMA 450-80 cd

All My Hummingbirds Have Alibis, Five Scenes For An Imaginary Ballet
Voyager LS36 Macintosh cd-rom

1993
Trembling
CDCM Vol. 13 Centaur cd

BIBLIOGRAPHY

"Pauline Oliveros: Trio." *Perspectives Of New Music,* 2 (Fall 1963-Spring 1964).

"Extending The Stuff Music Is Made Of." *Music Educators Journal,* 55 (November 1968).

SUN RA

photo: Gene Bagnato

SUN RA / Introduction

SUN RA was born Herman "Sonny" Blount in Birmingham, Alabama, on May 22, 1914. Of course, that information has never been confirmed: Sun Ra has long insisted that his planet of origin is Saturn, not Earth. Like the poet Dante, another traveler of the cosmos, he has admitted to being born under the sign of Gemini, while leaving his actual birthdate a mystery. But mystery has long been the essence of Sun Ra's music as well as his persona — twin creations of one of America's most original and provocative composers.

As a child, his parents took him to hear the great blues singers of the '20s, including Bessie Smith and Ethel Waters. He also showed an early enthusiasm for the records of Fletcher Henderson. While in high school he formed his own band and toured the South in the early '30s. By the late '40s, he was playing piano and providing arrangements for Henderson's band at the Club DeLisa in Chicago. Around this time, he also performed with Stuff Smith and Coleman Hawkins, and recorded with Yusef Lateef and Eugene Wright.

Remaining in Chicago, Sun Ra was leading his own groups by the early '50s. Bringing together his studies of the Bible, Egyptology, and outer space into a dynamic personal philosophy, he began using the name Sun Ra and dubbed his big band the Arkestra. In 1956 he released his first Arkestra lp, *Jazz by Sun Ra* (later reissued as *Sun Song*). Shortly thereafter he formed his own record label, Saturn, on which he has continued to press and release his own recordings, documenting his music throughout the decades, while also making recordings for numerous labels in America and Europe.

Sun Ra and his musicians settled in New York City in 1961, and remained there for most of the decade, performing regularly at a small East Village club called Slug's. The Arkestra sets there established the band's standards for years to come: The musicians dressed in colorful, glittering costumes, and often marched around the audience while playing or singing; performances would be supplemented by dancers and light shows; and the sets themselves became unpredictable excursions over the history of African-American music, embracing its past (straight-ahead arrangements of classics by Jelly Roll Morton, Henderson, and Duke Ellington), present (Sun Ra's driving hard-bop originals), and future (roof-raising collective free improvisations). Many of the Arkestra musicians became adept multi-instrumentalists, and the band's percussion section grew to include a vast array of exotic and original instruments. Above all there was Sun Ra himself, reciting his poetry, lecturing, leading the band, singing, performing inspired solos or invisible accompaniments, as needed, at the piano or his many synthesizers.

(Long devoted to electric keyboards, he has played a range new instruments, including one of the first Moog synthesizers.)

In 1968 Sun Ra and the Arkestra relocated to Philadelphia, where they continue to reside. Their base of operations is a large house that is home to Sun Ra and many core members of the group, as well as temporary lodgings for other, more transient musicians of his band. Run by Sun Ra with a strict sense of discipline and commitment to their work, this arrangement has permitted the band to survive lean financial times, making it the only original, performing big band still active after 40 years. Perhaps the greatest tribute to Sun Ra's abilities as a composer — as well as his charisma as a leader — is his ability to keep gifted musicians with him even when they could become better recognized (and recompensed) elsewhere. Tenor saxophonist John Gilmore has played with Sun Ra since 1953; altoist Marshall Allen and baritonist Pat Patrick (who passed away in 1992) joined up the following year. Other long-term Arkestra musicians include bassoonist James Jackson, singer June Tyson (who passed away in 1992), and trumpeter Michael Ray. Over the years, many distinguished musicians have played in the Arkestra, such as Clifford Jarvis, Marion Brown, Pharoah Sanders, Julian Prester, Robin Eubanks, Ahmed Abdullah, Vincent Chancey, Don Cherry, Ronnie Boykins, Billy Bang, Charles Davis, and Elo Omoe.

Today, the Arkestra continues to perform internationally, despite the heart trouble that has recently confined Sun Ra to a wheelchair. On September 1, 1990, only a few weeks before his illness, I spoke with the composer at his hotel room in Cambridge, Massachusetts, in between his series of performances there with the Arkestra. Although plainly exhausted from his crushing schedule, he seemed pleased to treat me to his provocative, visionary ideas about music, race, and space.

SUN RA / Interview

Q: Your work with the Arkestra has sought to bring an awareness of space to people, and of the potential for change within ourselves. Looking back over the years, how would you evaluate your success?

SUN RA: Well, actually I was trying to be a success at playing a low profile. Since this planet has a habit of assassinating leaders, mistreating them, I didn't want to be no leader. I decided I didn't want be it at all — bypass it.

Q: Nevertheless, you've become one, haven't you?

SUN RA: I already was one; I'm a natural leader. But judging from what they did to leaders, including God's son, who wants to be a leader? Not me. They say they crucified him, so what chance would I have?

I went to Africa, and they had headlines: "Africa kills its leaders." Headlines in the paper, in Nigeria. I saw that: "Africa kills its leaders." Now, why'd they put something like that in the paper unless it's true?

Q: They're trying to warn leaders to stay away, perhaps.

SUN RA: And that's the problem, we don't have any in Africa.

Q: Why do people reject the presence of a leader?

SUN RA: Because they talking about freedom. Freedom means you don't have leaders. Equality means you don't need a leader, everybody's a leader. And that is a lie, because not everybody could be President of the United States. If freedom was true, and you had a free democracy, you'd go out in the street and get any man and put him up there, any woman, any child — don't worry about the age, everybody's equal. You put them right in the White House, take Bush's place, because they're all equal. But then they got political problems, because the rest of the nation's not going to recognize them; they're not going to do it. So then what you've got's a problem. You put somebody up there from the people, doesn't matter the people, they haven't been to school, who don't have no background — they will not be accepted by the rest of the nations. So the rest of the nations don't believe in democracy. So if you're alone on the planet, yes. But you're not alone. You still got kings and queens, prophets and emperors and everything, and they not gonna recognize a common man; they not gonna do it.

So then you have to be realistic and see that it's a fantasy. It most certainly is. And maybe some intellectuals might have felt that humanity's problems were solved, but they were quite wrong. They were quite wrong. And the world has to recognize, not everybody can be a scientist; not everybody can sit down and plot for to send something outside the solar system; not everybody can deal with chemicals and atomic fission and all. They can't do it. Some mathematical things, the average man cannot even talk about; it'll go so far, he will stop. So then, if they're not equal in scientific things, they're not equal in anything.

And then you have to have something to go by, so if you go out there in the forest, you won't find no two animals alike; you won't find no two leaves alike; you won't find two blades of grass alike; you won't find two stones alike. In all of nature, you cannot find any two things exactly alike. So then, what are they talking about? They talking about some man-made doctrine, trying to do something for humanity, but making a most dreadful mistake, because they don't have the truth on their side.

Q: What creates this hunger for equality, if it's an illusion?

SUN RA: Somebody's taking advantage of man, and using some nice words on him to cause this confusion. That's what's happening. It's not God, it's not the Devil either. Some superior intelligences are using words like "equality," "democracy," "truth," "liberty." They're using words that are really supposed to be nice, but the words are traps. They been doing it a long time, and they think man never will wake up to the fact that they are doing it. 'Cause see man blames it on God and he blames it on Satan — they taught him that. 'Cause they never want him to research to find out what's happening to him. They thought he never would wake up, and not one person in human form would ever wake up and say, "Well, no, that doesn't fit. Why would God do that to people? And why would Satan take the time to be bothered with something as insignificant as a man?" No, it doesn't make sense. What would he want with him? He can't use them, since they only use but five percent of their brain, won't want nobody like that. Satan's supposed to be very intelligent — what would he want with a man that's here today and gone tomorrow? No, it doesn't fit. And why would God want to impose things on man, when actually He doesn't have to. He could enlighten him, take him off this particular sphere, and teach him something. But of course, man doesn't think like that. He say, "God loves everybody," then he turns around and he says, "Everything happens for the best," and he stops right there. He never says, "This is most dreadful; this is not love; this is something else. Something is wrong between me and God or somebody; somebody is not fitting." He never says that. He's willing to accept it and say, "Well, that's it."

Q: So words such as "equality" and "freedom" get thrown around, but ideas of discipline and precision tend not to be offered to people as something to achieve in our lives.

SUN RA: Oh yes, it is. In that so-called good book, it said definitely, "A man cannot learn without discipline." So that is your key. It says that: "A man cannot learn without discipline." Then it comes pointedly and says, "Take care this liberty of yours does not become a stumbling block." It says that. And then it deals with righteousness, right in that so-called good book, and it says, "Why be righteous overmuch? Why should you destroy yourself?" So it warns against righteousness, you see. It warns against liberty. It warns against freedom too: It says, "Free among the dead like one that is slain." The book's got freedom over there equated with death. It's right in the book. And furthermore, the book say, "I proclamate a freedom for you. Freedom through the sword" — that's war — "freedom through the famine" — that's children starving in Africa — "freedom through the pestilence" — AIDS and diseases. It's got it in that; it's got God saying, "I proclamate a freedom for you." And that's what freedom is: the sword, the famine, and the pestilence.

They say, "Believe and be saved." But they don't believe that. So therefore, they don't believe equations. If they believed that Bible, they'd say, "Oh well, we better not deal with the word 'freedom'; we better not deal with trusting in God, either. We can't trust Him." They got to change and go by the equations, what the book said. The book says, "Our Lord God, You have greatly deceived these people; tell them they have peace and the sword reached to their very soul." That's what the book said. And it's got something else in there too, about "God will send them a strong delusion, in order they might believe a lie." It tells them God will send them a strong delusion. How they gonna trust God, when He gonna send a delusion? How they gonna trust God, when the prophet cried when he saw what would happen to people? And when the prophet looked in the future and said, if these things continue to happen, "there will no flesh be saved on the planet Earth." And that's what the prophet told God.

Q: And we're heading that way, do you feel?

SUN RA: It's right in the Bible. That's what he told Him. He cried and said, "No flesh will be saved." What is gonna be done in the future? Now of course, preachers got that. They talking about God is love and somebody will come and save and all that. But they should read the book carefully: It had a prophet crying when he saw the future. He saw all this. He saw everything that's happening today, and cried. And told God, "Our Lord God, You have greatly deceived these people." Now, people are teaching that Satan is the deceiver, but the Bible said God is.

Furthermore, the Bible says that the reason you got confusion on this planet is that God confused the language of the world in order so that man could not become unified. That's what it said, at the Tower of Babel. Now, if they believe the book, they should blame God for their troubles. And they have to find out, what can they do about it? In other words, they saying, "Your arms too short to box with God." But you better do something.

Q: Can music show people a way to better themselves?

SUN RA: It's the only way you can talk to God now: through sound. You got to talk in pure language. The other languages are confused; every language is confused. Everything is confused except sound, purity of sound. So you find some pure musicians playing pure sounds, you can reach God. Because the Bible's got God saying, "I hate your music." Now, nobody says nothing about that, but it's got God saying, "I hate your music. I hate your New Moon festivals. I hate your solemn assemblies" — that's the church. So they go on and they still saying, God is love, and they won't pay any attention to what that book is saying. And it's supposed to be the word of God.

So then you might say, "Well, that's far-fetched to say that that is true." Then you have to look and see — has there been any indication that God hates the music people are playing? Now notice, it said, "I hate your solemn assemblies" — that's the church. There's an indication that it's true, 'cause down in Atlanta, Georgia, Rev. King's mother was playing a sacred song, singing to God, and a black man stood up and said, "I am God. I hate your music," and shot and killed her. Right here in America. Now, they let that pass by and didn't see the meaning of that. The man stood up and said, "I am God. I hate your music" — the same thing the Bible is saying — and shot her and killed her in the church, while she was playing a sacred song. Now, they should actually judge a tree by the fruit. Nobody said anything about that. How could somebody be singing to God, praising God in the church, playing music to Him, singing about Him, and He has somebody stand up and say, "I hate your music. I am God," and shoot and kill her? You mean to tell me man is so stupid that these people didn't see that that was a sign from God, trying to wake them up, saying "Yes, I don't like what you're doing. Don't sing those songs to me. I hate your solemn assemblies. I don't wanna hear them sad songs. Don't sing nothing like that to me." That's what he meant to them.

It's quite true. There is a God. The trouble is, there is one. If there wasn't, people would get along very well indeed. But there is one, and unfortunately, they don't have no diplomatic relationships with Him. At one time, the church could reach Him but no, not now. Because He has proclaimed, through this Jesus, He proclaimed this planet to be the kingdom of Heaven. This is Heaven, right here. He said, "The kingdom of Heaven is near at hand"; he meant, this planet is now no longer Earth, it's the kingdom of Heaven. It's Heaven number three. And that is true, and the Bible says that: Heaven number three. It say, "Somebody was caught up in the spirit on Heaven number three." That's this planet. So if you've got a number-three Heaven, you've got a number four and number five and number six; you got a number-one Heaven. This is number three because this planet is three from the Sun. It is the Heaven number three. It is the haven, you see, like you got outer space; this is the space port, ships land here, it's a haven. So it's Haven number three. "Heaven" is a double word: You take the e out, and you've got "haven." You can take the e out, you don't need the e in there. You take the e out and you've got "haven," meaning home. And this is home for a ship. Ships are berthed here. They come in to port, and this is a space port for those from outer space. To them, they call this a space port. 'Cause you see, space is just like the sea; it's a space sea. Like you got the water sea, you got the space sea too. Now, people have to be rescued on this planet to something else so fantastic, it's unbelievable. But this planet, they have to evolute. They have to. If they stay like they are, they gonna get destroyed. It's time for change. They have to change.

Q: Can the music help them do that?

SUN RA: It's the only thing that can reach people. Music is a universal language, so you can speak to them too. 'Cause their languages are different, and their frequencies are different. But music don't care nothing about no frequencies, it covers all frequencies and all planes. It's eternal. It goes on up and it keeps on going. That's what sound does, it keeps on going. It does not stop here; it does not stop in a room. It goes out there and keeps on going. Well then, people out there, other beings, they'll hear it. They'll hear it. It'll reach a point where, if they don't hear it, they will feel it. They have to. So then you can reach any type of being with music. It's the only thing that's left. But this planet has regarded musicians as a luxury, entertainment as a luxury, when actually it's a necessity. It is a vital necessity at this point. In fact, in the Bible, where it's talking about the end of time, it does say, when you see all these troubles and everything, rejoice, have a good time. Folks are supposed to be partying 24 hours a day now, because it's the end of the age. And it tells them to do that, be glad that the age is over.

Q: Do you think that today people understand what you're saying through your music better than they understood 10 years, 20 years ago?

SUN RA: Well, I mean, it depends whether I let them. 'Cause I want a low profile. So I didn't put out the music that maybe they could understand. You know, like music is a language, so they got to have the grammar; they got to have the principles of the grammar of it. It's just like any other language. You might speak the language, but you need the grammar. You don't really know the language unless you got the basic keys to it. You start at the bottom. Now, if they had the basics of what I represent, or knew what I've experienced in so-called life, they would feel the music more. But since I never sought to be famous or nothing like that, I'm really trying to keep from being part of humanity, 'cause I don't like what's happening to them. And I never wanted to be like them, 'cause I knew where it's all headed. I knew it was gonna be just like they are now. I could see that as a child, and I didn't want to be part of this. I knew everything about people: where they were headed and why they was gonna get there. I knew that. And I knew they could stop it too. So I just stepped back. I watched my so-called generation be a complete failure, because they believed the status quo and they believed what they were doing was right. But I watched them as they died and as they left the planet. They didn't know what I was thinking, but I was thinking that beauty and music and sincerity is the answer. That's what I was thinking. And I was seeing people neglect that with their children, I saw that. I saw them bypass jazz and other forms of art and culture, I saw that. And I saw that their children was gonna be left with no way to turn, I saw that. Because they were neglecting some basic things that their children were gonna need in this age. So I stepped back. I didn't offer what I had to offer. Just now and then I put something out there. But my basic thing, I kept it. Because I realized if I put it out there, commercial folks were gonna use me and take advantage of me, and then take what I had and give it to someone and let them put it out and fool the world, like they was creating instead of me, I saw that. And therefore I stepped back. I didn't put what I could have put out there, and just waited until they would not have any creativity. That's now. 'Cause they didn't have me to steal from. And I planned it like that. I got all the creative ideas and everything, and they don't have any. So it's too late for them to steal now, 'cause I'm too far advanced. And they might not like me, or they might not approve of what I did, but I did it deliberately. I wanted to bypass the planet 'cause they were trying to bypass me. So I helped them; I helped them to bypass me.

Q: So the recordings you've released and the performances you've given are just a fraction of what you could have shown people.

SUN RA: Just a small fragment. With a lot of empty space and narrow voids in that. And they were planned perfectly by me. You hear the first track; the next track I put out nullified the first one and it would brush out of their minds. So they never even heard the album. My music is fixed up with nullification; by the time they get to the end, the only song that would remain would be the last song they played. And they'd get another lp and they'd put that on, it's gonna nullify that last one. I planned it perfectly. So therefore, they never have heard the music. The only way they could possibly hear it is to play each track separately — don't play nothing else, 'cause if they do, they get nullification and they will not hear that song. In fact, if they keep on playing the album, they'll go to sleep. I planned it like that. And the whole album'll play, and they'll wake up and say, "Oh, I went to sleep." Went to sleep and they didn't hear it. I planned it like that. 'Cause I'm a scientist, you see. I knew exactly what I was doing. 'Cause I didn't trust them. I paid them back for what they've done to other leaders.

Q: Will some of the material you've held back be released later?

SUN RA: I'm getting calls now every day about releasing it. See, the truth has to be told now. A fellow came to me and told me he was working in a music store when he was young, at a stage just reaching manhood. He said that one day they took all my records in this record store and put them in the garbage can. He said he hadn't been noticing really; the records was selling but he hadn't heard them. But when he saw that, he got curious. So he went and got the records out of the garbage can, took them home, and he played them. He said he became a Sun Ra fan, and he realized the value of the music. And he said, when he got grown, he was going to see that the world heard that music and put it back out there. He told me that in California. Now see, all along I didn't know that. It was commercial folks or something, they didn't want people to hear the music, and went that far: Take all of them off the shelves and put them in the garbage can, even though they were selling. He told me that. Well, it proved that I was right about forces that be trying to stop creative people. I was right. He's called me up several times, and I was telling him the other day, "Well, I have to keep on moving. I can't bring the past back or nothing like that. I have my plans what I've got to do. Since the commercial folks bypass me, I plan to put that out, but I'm gonna put it out only in occult stores, because they've got all these occult books and they don't have no music. So I'll put it over in there. And that means that people who are researching, who are sincere, they will hear the music. The others will have to go to the occult bookstore and get the music." He said, "You'd do that?" I said, "Oh yes, I'll do that. 'Cause I'm fighting the battle. I don't know why I have to fight it, but if they want to fight, they got a master strategist." I'll put records in the occult stores. Since some forces don't want it to be out there, I help them. The best way to defeat an enemy is help them to defeat you. Then they can't possibly stop you, 'cause you're helping them. Let them help me help them to fight against me. So actually we're in unity. I'm helping them.

Q: When the term "Saturn" turns up in an occult bookstore, people know the implications about discipline and responsibility.

SUN RA: Of course they do, 'cause they're studying things about magic and everything else over in there. So if they had the music, they would have more communication with spirits and more communication with outer space and other things. The music would be the bridge to other dimensions. They need the music. And so I say, well OK, I'll put it over in occult stores. Now, none of the commercial record companies can do that. So then I'll be out of their way. I help them to defeat me by simply getting out of the way; put it over there. And my records will be over there, selling to the people who deserve it. And I won't be trying to convince nobody to listen to me — no, I'm not egotistical. I'm here to do a job, so I have to plan how to defeat this; the best strategy to defeat me, use the Bible and everything to shut people up. But I know the book — they don't know the book. I use the book on them. I just haven't used it. I was waiting for them to have pureness in heart and do what's right. If they don't want to do what's right, I'll show them what to do that's right by me doing completely wrong. I'll set up humanity for to push the button on them, and then tell them, "All right, now you have a choice. You listen to me or be eliminated off the planet." And I don't need no atomic bomb, I don't need no poison gas. All I have to do is speak certain words backwards, and you're through. And tell them that, and say you can believe it if you want to, or not — I don't really care. 'Cause if you're my enemies, getting rid of you would be very nice; just leave me and the Creator. We're good friends; I have an eternal friend. Man is not eternal, so you can't depend on nobody. They're here today and gone tomorrow. What would I want with friends like that? But the Creator is eternal; He'll be here always. And that's a nice friend to have.

Q: It seems as though people are already working hard to wipe themselves out, without your having to intervene.

SUN RA: Well, they got help. It's not coming from God. They got a third thing

that's supervising them to their destruction. It's not God and it's not Satan — the
other force taught man that, to keep him from ever researching. He's so satisfied,
that he thinks Satan is doing this and God is doing this, and he never wake up
saying, "I'm gonna investigate why my condition is like it is." Because why should
he, since there were two things, God and Satan. He never thought about the third
thing. And the third thing taught him all about God and Satan; the third thing
sent the sacred books and everything, to keep him brainwashed, forever, to set
him up for destruction. And the third thing sent him all these inventions he's got,
where he can just go on and be self-destructive — they don't care. If he don't
show some semblance of intelligence — they're very advanced intellectually and
otherwise, and they know some things that actually would almost run a man crazy
thinking about it happening. They know some things; they're superior beings, you
see. I read the other day about a being showed up to some people, told them he
was from another frequency, and that, because he is from another frequency, they
were on a different density from him, but he's still real. He said, "I'm gonna show
you I'm real. I'm gonna walk through you," and he walked through them. He
showed them he was a different density but in the same place they were. And so
he walked through them. Then he said, "Now I'm gonna touch you to show that
I'm real." So he touched them; he touched somebody's arm, a girl's arm, and he
touched her so strongly that he put a bruise on her arm. He said, "I just want to
show you that I'm real." And then he melted into a pool of water or something,
right before their eyes, and the pool evaporated. He showed them: just boom,
there he was. He showed them. So then they were researching those psychic
things, and he came, and he showed them that he was real. Now, it wasn't what
you call a ghost. It was just a being that was moving on a different frequency. Like
that TV: You see, you turn it on, here comes something on the TV. Then, you
switch the dial, and — the same air and everything, everything is out there — and
you searching for a channel or frequency, then you got something else. Life is like
that, just like that TV. So you get different frequencies. Therefore, you can't say
"equality," because every person got a different frequency — like he got different
fingerprints, different frequencies.

Q: And frequency is sound — vibration.

SUN RA: Yes, that's what it is, the voice. Frequency is voice cause it makes a
sound. That's life. Without frequency, no movement.

Q: That's how even the statues can have sound, because they're vibrating.

SUN RA: Oh, yeah. Each statue makes a sound. I saw a picture called *Unheard
Melodies*, and that should be in every school. They were investigating something
with some statues from ancient days, and they proved that each statue made a different sound from the other. And they did it because when the wind came by, the
wind made a sound: Pfeewww. And this statue made a sound, the same sound
every time. So that means that people who are worshipping some kind of statue,

they are being frequencized, you might say. They keep on standing in front of that statue and the vibrations are coming at them, and they're being made into the frequencies of their statue, whether it's Buddha, Jesus Christ, whatsoever. They before that image, and being before that image can really do something to them. And that's how delicate the situation is. We like in a magic kingdom, magic. I mean the whole thing is like magic. They have to get to the point to see that the greatest magician in all the universe is the Creator. 'Cause He made all of this up out of nothing. And only a magician can do that. He made it out of nothing. And even today, things have been patterned by a magician. You take that Israel over there. They are following the path of a magician named Moses. And they doing what they do over there because of what he said. When he told them, "Go out and kill the nations," that's why they over there messing with the Palestinians, 'cause they following him. He told them, "These other nations ain't no good, get rid of them. The Lord wants you to kill them. And go out and kill them in the name of the Lord." That's what Moses taught. That's the reason Hitler tried to kill all the Jews. He saw that; he saw that everybody who was a gentile was in danger of getting wiped out if the Jews ever had power, because he got the book that says so. It doesn't make no difference whether the book is true or not; nevertheless, they were taught that. And whether they realize it or not, they still follow it — they have to — what they say is God's word. And they be busy trying to do that, killing people in the name of God. And that's what that Jesus came to say: "There'll come a day when those who say they're worshipping God will kill you." Right in the book: "There'll come a day when those who say they're worshipping God will kill you." And therefore, you're going to have persecution and all that with warring people. Well, he wasn't really a man you know — another type of being, a different type of being. So then it made no difference about him being killed or whatever it was, since he wasn't a man, the grave could not hold him, 'cause he was real and not real. He was in a different frequency; one of them beings, definitely.

Q: And people cast him out because —

SUN RA: Because he wanted them to do it. He most certainly wanted them to do exactly what they did. That's the only way he could trick them into the condition we in today. He wanted them to get in this condition because they angered him. And he had all this power, so he planned how to get even with them. So he went acting meek and humble, rode a jackass and everything, show us humility, and they put out palm leaves — Palm Sunday — and they honored him, "Hail to the King." Turned it all down and went to the cross instead. Now, man shouldn't be so stupid that he shouldn't ask, "Why would he do that?" He had the world at his command; healed the sick and raised the dead; people are honoring him, "Hail to the King." Turned all that down and go and get on the cross instead. And Pilate asked him, "What is truth?" Refused to answer; didn't defend himself. No, uh-uh: Something is wrong. That means he wanted that; he wanted them to do exactly what they did. He said, "It is not proper for a prophet to die outside of Jerusalem. So kill me." Now, why he gonna do something like that, unless he's telling them, "Now if you go and you be against me, you gonna be in trouble. I would have helped you, if you'd only listened to me. But since you're not gonna listen to me, you'll be scattered abroad, you'll have wars and rumors of wars, you'll have earthquakes and everything; you'll have all kinds of disaster happen to you." He told them that. And lo and behold, all these wars, rumors of wars, floods, earthquakes — every word he said came true. He wanted them to do that. He's been following a ritual. He's setting up something. "I'm the alpha and omega" — that's what fraternities use. He was establishing the Alpha Omega Fraternity, and everybody in the Christian church is in the Alpha Omega Fraternity, and don't know it 'cause of Greek testaments, you know. And all fraternities are based on the Greek: alpha, omega. Alpha, omega is the Christian church. It's not a church at all — it's a secret society, it's a fraternity, it's a brotherhood thing. It most certainly is. And if people have been listening — for instance, like I heard a black woman saying — they was in one of them churches on the radio — she was singing and all that, they was shouting and singing. All at once, she said, "Brother Jesus!" I heard that. I'm always listening to what people say. She said, "Brother Jesus!" Now see, there the fraternity is again. Why she calling Jesus her brother? Fraternity. She might not even know what she was saying. But there's a Creator there, and now and then he throws something over, right on people. Like I told you about that shooting, Reverend King's mother, and he said, "I am God." And He be testing people out. People waiting for Judgment Day — it's always Test Day, Examination Day. These people are constantly being examined, 24 hours a day.

Q: Are people examining themselves, as well as being examined?

SUN RA: Oh, no. They quite complacent, say God will take care of them. And they being taught that, so that makes them very complacent, since God will take care of them. And of course, these forces got it fixed up where it seems that God is taking care of them — well, they have to try and make the book look like it's real. So then they do make it true that God takes care of them. Right in the cemetery, they got caretakers: They take care of them that way. That's what they call the folks who be digging the graves there, caretakers; the ones who take care of the grass and take care of the funeral, caretakers. So God will take care of them, right over there in the cemetery. Then you got a book called *God's Little Acre*. Now, if you look in the dictionary and see what does that mean, it'll say, "cemetery." God's little acre. So it's saying the only thing that God owns is the cemetery. 'Cause they had a play about that, *God's Little Acre*. In the early days, the cemetery was always in the churchyard. You go to an old church, and the cemetery's in the churchyard. That's God's little acre. So someone fixed it up where God's little acre is the cemetery. They have to wake up now and see that they're involved with something that's very dreadful, namely G-O-D. Worse thing could possibly be is that. And really, it's not that he's the enemy of man, he's just the most terrible figure. G-O-D, it's awful. You take in New York City, one Jewish newspaper never writes the word "God" out; they put "G-dash-D." They don't write G-O-D; that's so terrible, they don't write it. They know something. They put G-dash-D for God; they never write G-O-D. They put G-dash-D for God in New York City. Now I don't know whether they doing it anywhere else, but I have a scientific mind and I observe every little thing. Things I see, it records on my mind.

Q: Because the world is full of signs and evidence of what's going on.

SUN RA: Of course it is. It's all around, these signs. For instance, in Europe we'd pass by railroad stations and I kept on seeing, "EXPRESS G-O-D-S." I say, "You know what? That means 'goods.'" In America, it would mean "gods," but in Europe, G-O-D-S means goods. So then, express good/God. I say, now that's a trick word there. Because why? Because there are people who get ahold of the name of God, they wanted to name a good. And of course, it's quite appropriate: They're really good-for-nothing. See, so they come now where they're good-for-nothings. So it's a trick for them to be good, 'cause they good for nothing. They don't get nothing for being good. And I seen a lot of leaders come up that was very good, but they always good for nothing — that includes Reverend King and the rest of them. They didn't get nothing for being good. They were good-for-nothings. See, I go and say that to people, they get quite upset, but they were good-for-nothings. They didn't get nothing for being good.

Then you come to the question of black people in America. There's something took control of them and used them, used them as a trick bait for a nation, deliberately put them in the midst of a nation to see how it would treat them: testing their hearts out. They're a big Test Day for America. So I tried to figure out, well, why there was slavery and all that. And why did they come in the Commerce Department and not in the State Department? All the rest of the nations here came through here in the State Department, all except black people — they came through the Commerce Department. Now, Commerce Department is for goods. It's for items of commerce, and that's goods, you see, items. They came in the Item Department, into the Goods Department. But since goods means gods, they came in America through the Gods Department. They did not come in through the Human Department and the Man Department. They came in as gods into this country. Now, it makes it very serious, and that explains why they didn't have no last names, because kings and queens do not have last names, just one name. And they had one name — Mary and James and John — they did not have a last name. 'Cause gods and kings and queens don't have no last name. So something used them and put them in this kingdom as kings and queens, and didn't have no last names. So then as time went on, they began to get some white people's names and used that. And that's the way they got their names; they just took the names. They had their names of Mary and John and Jim and all that, but then, for last names, they didn't have no last names, so they figured white people had last names, so they took the names of the plantation owners and the white person who'd help, and took their names, and used it. And use it today. That's why I don't use no name except Ra because I saw that, and I'm not going to go and take somebody else's name; I'm not going to do that. I got my name, the Creator gave me my name. And I could really do it scientifically; I did it scientifically, and according to the book, which does say "God is the father of the fatherless." I don't say God is my father 'cause I don't have no earth father, he's not on the planet. So therefore, if God is the father of the fatherless, since I'm fatherless, then God is my father. Of course, I haven't said that before 'cause they think they're so smart. But I don't have the name Ra for nothing. Because you know, the Bible does say — well, if you go all the way back to ancient Egypt, it does say that Ra is the father of the gods, not man; he had nothing to do with him. The ancient Egyptians did not call themselves man. In fact, they taught that the worst thing you could possibly do is fall down to the level of calling yourself a man, and they taught against it. And it got right over in this Bible, which does say, "Man is filthy and abominable. Man is like the beast that perishes. Man that is born of woman is few of days and full of trouble." It talks against man. So now who wants to be filthy and abominable? Who wants to be like the beast that perishes? So to call himself a man, that's what's coming. Because man is in trouble because why? To say that man is like the beast that perishes, and then turn around and say man is made in the image of God, is really calling God a beast. And I'm sure God don't like that; that that's all they think about Him, gonna call Him a beast, and say man is made in the image of God and then turn around and say man is like the beast that perishes, they calling God a beast. And now some books, if you study India and other places, they say that. I saw one. It said, a beast said, "Think not that I came to bring peace. I came to bring a sword." Now that's what Jesus said. They said a beast said it. They called him — right in the book — the beast said, "I'm alpha and omega, the beginning and the end." They're talking about Jesus. So then, they got him as the beast.

Q: In Revelations, the Anti-Christ is called a beast.

SUN RA: Well, the Anti-Christ, that would be the salvation of man. Definitely. That's his only hope now, Anti-Christ. 'Cause in the lost books of the Bible, it does say it: "In the kingdom of Christ, there shall be evil and filthy days." That's where we are now. It said that, but they took that out of the Bible. But it does say, "In the kingdom of Christ, there shall be evil and filthy days." Right in the book. But of course, they don't have that book. 'Cause they haven't studied. I've made research on humanity to see why they in this condition. And I have been taught by outer-space beings and the Creator the real truth, and I got it. I can't back away from it and say it is not true. It is true. I'm not dealing with faith and hope; I'm dealing with wisdom. I'm not even dealing with knowledge; I'm dealing with the unknown and ignorance. 'Cause I'm ignorant: I don't know what's happening here. I'm just a student of things, and I learn everyday. And I got so much to learn, it's amazing. I'm just getting started learning things, about music and other things, to what to do with it. To have talent is all right, but what you gonna do with it? Lotta people got talent, but they're here today and gone tomorrow, they're not able to do anything with it, they don't stay here long enough to do it. The water in the river evaporates every day. People are the same, they evaporate: They here one day, the next day they evaporate and go somewhere. So then the water is eternal; it evaporates and goes somewhere else. That's nature.

Q: The same with sound: It travels on out to somewhere else.

SUN RA: Yeah. Now you got someone saying the echoes seem like the real thing. But it's just the echo. This planet, it's a big test.

Now I got a record that I should put out, I'm thinking about it. But I don't want to be a religious figure, you might say, and get involved. People need help so badly. If I put this record out, it'll make everybody look at me and listen.

Q: Which one is this?

SUN RA: Well, it's a record called *Music From The Private Library Of God.* That record. Now, in this record, I'm talking and I'm saying, "God says He don't want you anymore. You failed the test. You know the rest." That's just what I'm saying: "You failed the test. God says you failed the test. You know the rest." And that's very simple, isn't it? And I won't have to tell them the rest, they already know. And it's very simple, even a child will understand that. "God says you failed the test. You know the rest."

Q: Why do you hesitate to release this album?

SUN RA: Because even the church'll turn around and look at me as some kind of a leader, to teach them. And of course I know the answers, but it would completely disrupt the church — disrupt governments, the schools, everything.

Q: Is that bad?

SUN RA: Of course it is. It's the real truth.

Then, to amplify: I went to Istanbul, Turkey, and we played a concert there, and some people came up and gave me a book called *The Book Of Information.* Said, "Brother Ra, this is for you," and this book happened to be dictated to them from outer space — took it from the satellite, into computers, dictated. And it's a book of about 40 chapters or thereabout. It's in English. And they said, "This is not a book of the 20th century; this is a book of the 21st century." And the book goes on up to the 31st century, talking about the future and things that man will have to do to survive. It's most remarkable. It's most remarkable. It is more profound than science fiction; it's talking things that I ain't never read in no science fiction. It talk about universes, so many universes out there that's millions of light-years apart from one another, that don't know nothing about each other out there. Space ends they say, you got that out there; that God put them out there, millions of light years apart, like islands of universes. And they said that God in a sense is a mystery to them. All they know is, out there in space — you got all this empty space, you see — all at once you had big bang: Bang! And God has created a whole universe. Not like they say here, one day creates that, no: The whole thing, you see, there it is, bam! right before your eyes. An entire universe, not just one little planet or one star; the whole thing. They call it the Big Bang. Say they don't know how He does it, but He does it. I mean everything: The trees, the flowers, everything is there in one split second. That's how it is, that's what it said. They don't know words to describe God. He does that. Down here they talk about He went to sleep on the seventh day. He out there making universes in one split second.

So see they got to stop and consider what God is. That's somebody to be afraid of, really. Got all that power. Ain't nobody to tell Him, "Don't!"; nobody to spank Him and say, "You shouldn't do that." Nobody. He does what He wants to do. Now, that's why people got to look good at this Moses and Pharaoh thing, and see what did they tell each other. So then you got Moses talking about God's chosen people and all that. You got Pharaoh saying, "I and my people are wicked; the Lord is righteous." And Pharaoh said, "In comparison to God, all of us — me and my people — are wicked." That's what he said. Well, the world has to look at that. Moses talking about his people are superior to other people, and gentiles got to die and all; Pharaoh was saying, he and his people are wicked, all of them; took the whole kingdom and made all of them wicked. That's what Pharaoh did. And then it comes down to this Bible they got, where it's being said in there, "In the last days, God will raise Pharaoh up from the earth." It's talking about Pharaoh, it ain't talking about Moses, it ain't talking about Jesus. It say, "In the last days, God will raise Pharaoh up from the earth, in order that he might declare His name to the nations." That's right, that's what they got God saying in the Christian Bible. He'll raise Pharaoh up from the earth, in order that he might declare the name of God to the world. And people got the book and they don't read it. Not Abraham, Isaac, or Jacob; gonna raise Pharaoh. So Pharaoh must be all right with God. You know, the word "Pharaoh" means "the living God," too, in ancient Egyptian; it means the living God. That's right. The definite article in there, that is P-H. Like they say T-H-E, the; back then, it was P-H. And that's the first part of Pharaoh, P-H. So the world's got to face that. And they got to unravel this puzzle. Because if the living God means Pharaoh, then when they got in the Christian religion Christ asking Peter — which means "interpreter": inter-preter, Peter — "Who do you say I am?" And Peter said, "You are the son of Pharaoh." But of course, in this book, they got, "You are the son of the living God." But Pharaoh means the living God.

So you see, people should wake up. Something is going on. And they sit there and look at these movies, it's very instructive. TV's instructive. Radio is instructive. And you got a lot of things that are trivial and ridiculous, but you got some things out there that are sincere and life-giving; even better than life being given. You got it out there. Everything is here.

DISCOGRAPHY

Deep Purple (1953-54; '55)
El Saturn 485 lp (1973)
Evidence 22014 cd (1991) (Side A only)

Jazz by Sun Ra (1956)
Transition j-10 lp (1957)
reissued as *Sun Song*
Delmark 411 lp (1967); cd, cs (1990)

We Travel The Spaceways (1956; '58-9; '59-60)
El Saturn 409 lp
Evidence 22038 cd (1992)

Sun Ra Visits Planet Earth (1956; '58)
El Saturn 207 lp
Evidence 22039 cd (1992)

Sound Of Joy (1957)
Transition lp (1957)
Delmark 414 lp (1968); cd (1990)

Jazz In Silhouette (1958)
El Saturn 205 lp
Impulse 9265 lp (1975)
Evidence 22012 cd (1991)

Sound Sun Pleasure (1958-60)
El Saturn 512 lp
Evidence 22014 cd (1991)

Interstellar Low Ways (1960)
El Saturn 203 lp
Evidence 22039 cd (1992)

Bad And Beautiful (1961)
El Saturn 532 lp
Impulse 9276 lp (1975)
Evidence 22038 cd (1992)

Art Forms Of Dimensions Tomorrow (1961-62)
El Saturn 404 lp
Evidence 22036 cd (1992)

We Are In The Future (1961-69)
Savoy Jazz 1141 lp (1984)

Cosmic Tones For Mental Health (1963)
El Saturn 408 lp (1972)
Evidence 22036 cd (1992)

Other Planes Of There (1964)
El Saturn 206 lp
Evidence 22037 cd (1992)

Magic City
El Saturn B-711 lp (1965)
Impulse 9243 lp (1974)

The Heliocentric Worlds Of Sun Ra, Vol. 1 (1965)
ESP 1014 lp (1965); -2 cd (1991)
reissued as *Cosmic Equation*
Magic Music 30011 cd (1990)

The Heliocentric Worlds Of Sun Ra, Vol. 2 (1965)
ESP 1017 lp (1966); -2 cd (1991)
reissued as *The Sun Myth*
Magic Music 30012 cd (1990)

Nothing Is (1966)
ESP 1045 lp (1967); -2 cd (1991)
reissued as *Dancing Shadows*
Magic Music 30013 cd (1990)

Monorails And Satellites (1966)
El Saturn 509 lp
Evidence 22013 cd (1991)

Pictures Of Infinity (1968)
Black Lion 106 lp (1974)

Holiday For Soul Dance (1968-69)
El Saturn 508 lp
Evidence 22011 cd (1991)

Out There A Minute (1968-69)
Blast First 42 lp, 71427-2 cd, -4 cs (1989)

My Brother The Wind, Volume 2 (1969-70)
El Saturn 523 lp
Evidence 22040 cd (1992)

Nuits De La Fondation Maeght (1970)
Recommended 11 lp (1981)

It's After The End Of The World (1970)
MPS BASF 20748 lp (1972)

The Solar Myth Approach, Vol. 1 (1970-71)
Affinity 4 lp (1980); 760 cd (1990)

Space Is The Place (1972)
Blue Thumb 41 lp (1973)

Live At Montreux (1976)
Inner City 1039 lp (1978)

Cosmos (1976)
Inner City 1020 lp (1977)

Solo Piano, Volume 1 (1977)
Improvising Artists 850 lp (1978); -2 cd (1992)

St. Louis Blues (1977)
IAI 858 lp (1979)

Unity (1977)
Horo 19-20 lp (1978)

New Steps (1978)
Horo 25-26 lp (1978)

The Rose Hue Mansions Of The Sun
Saturn 91780 lp (1980)

Aurora Borealis (1980)
Saturn 10480 lp

Sunrise In Different Dimensions (1980)
Hat Hut 17 lp (1983)

Strange Celestial Road
Rounder 3035 lp (1980); cd, cs (1987)

Nuclear War (1982)
Y Records Ra-1 lp (1982)

Love In Outer Space (1983)
Leo 154 cd (1992)

Stars That Shine Darkly
Saturn 10-11-85 lp (1985)

Stars That Shine Darkly.... (Part 2)
Saturn 9-1213-85 lp (1985)

Cosmo Sun Connection
Saturn/Recommended lp (1985)

A Night In East Berlin (1986)
Leo 149 lp, cd (1987)

Reflections In Blue (1986)
Black Saint 101-1 lp, -2 cd, -4 cs (1987)

Hours After (1986)
Black Saint 120 111-1 lp, -2 cd, -4 cs (1989)

Blue Delight (1988)
A&M 5260 lp, cd, cs (1989)

Purple Night (1989)
A&M 5234-2 cd, -4 cs (1990)

Live London 1990 (1990)
Blast First 60 cd (1990)

Mayan Temples (1990)
Black Saint 120 121-1 lp, -2 cd (1990)

Destination Unknown (1992)
Enja 7071-2 cd (1992)

collaborations

With John Cage:
John Cage Meets Sun Ra (1986)
Meltdown MPA-1 lp (1987)

with Walter Dickerson:
Visions (1978)
Steeple Chase 1126 lp, cs (1979); 31126 cd (1988)

BIBLIOGRAPHY

Different volumes of Sun Ra's poetry have been published under the title *The Immeasurable Equation*. For information, write to Saturn Research, P.O. Box 7124, Chicago, IL 60607.

SUN RA: IN MEMORIAM

On May 30, 1993, Sun Ra died at Baptist Medical Center-Princeton in Birmingham, Alabama. Having spent his life traveling the country, the globe, and the spaceways, he left the planet from the city where, some 80 years earlier, he had first arrived.

In that lifetime, Sun Ra produced one of the richest and most inspirational bodies of work in American music. Fortunately, he took special care to document his work, and as those 40-years-worth of recordings are sifted through and made available, we can expect to discover new depths and vistas to his art — he's clearly destined to cast a long shadow on the music of the 21st century. Here and now, however, I simply want to point out that Sun Ra created that legacy with very little of the support or recognition lavished upon others. In a civilized society, an artist who had so continuously demonstrated his abilities and his commitment, and who in his eighth decade was working harder — and better — than ever, would have been regarded as a national treasure, and treated accordingly. But then, obviously, a civilized society couldn't produce Sun Ra.

That's assuming he was a product of this planet which he and the Arkestra graced with his music. Such an assumption, however logical it may sound, isn't the only way to approach his work — and it certainly isn't how he wanted to be considered as an individual. Both the man and his music were "here to go," as Brion Gysin would say: avatars of an existence beyond the egocentric drives that we're conditioned to identify with and to cherish.

We're taught that a fine line separates the ridiculous from the sublime. Sun Ra saw two lines: =. With that immeasurable equation, he could reconceive five-and-dime consumerism into mythic art before anyone was thinking about pop, postmodernism, or punk. It showed him how naturally he could go from composing "The Magic City" to covering "Holiday For Strings." It described for him the efficacy of lecturing and reciting his poetry while wearing a lampshade or an upside-down coat hanger on his head.

But if you truly believe in spectacle and surprise, if you hold no contempt for any of the most familiar commodities, if you feel no fear whatsoever at the prospect of being considered foolish, then you can't expect people to know who you are or what you're doing. In this book, Sun Ra speaks frankly about his keeping a low profile so that humanity could bypass him. The rhetoric of discipline, myth, and interplanetary travel, the bargain-basement glitter and glitz, the sight of veteran musicians frolicking like children up and down the aisles of their performance space — these are the tactics of invisibility. A country as uptight and judgmental as America can respond to such behavior — particularly from a child of its former slave class — only with its eyes, ears, and mouth sealed tight. That's why there are so many histories, encyclopedias, and critical anthologies on jazz which fail to mention Sun Ra's name; and surveys of the development of electronic music which totally ignore his groundbreaking work; and eminent commentators on performance art or multimedia or music theater, who don't even know who Sun Ra is — or rather, was.

No, I'm sorry: is.

The sets of Sun Ra and his Arkestra were exercises in the poetics of joy — another cloak of invisibility, because joy is so rare in our music and in our lives that many people can't recognize it even when they're feeling it. But joy, if you've been listening, doesn't end just because the music has stopped.

photo: Lona Foote

JAMES TENNEY / Introduction

JAMES TENNEY was born in Silver City, New Mexico, on August 10, 1934. He attended the University of Denver from 1952 to '54, and Juilliard from 1954 to '55, where he was a piano major, studying with Eduard Steuermann. In 1955 and '56, he also studied composition privately with Chou Wen-chung in New York City. He attended Bennington College in Vermont from 1956 to '58, where he studied piano and composition with Lionel Nowak, and conducting with Paul Boepple and Henry Brant. During this time, he also studied composition privately with Carl Ruggles. After Tenney received his B.A. from Bennington in 1958, he attended the University of Illinois in Urbana from 1959 to '61, where he studied composition with Kenneth Gaburo, electronic music with Lejaren Hiller, and conducting with Bernard Goodman; he also held assistantships there with Hiller and Harry Partch. After Tenney received his M.A. from the University of Illinois in 1961, he returned to New York City where he studied composition privately with Edgard Varèse from 1961 to '65, and piano with Dorothy Taubman from 1968 to '70.

Tenney was Associate Member of the Technical Staff at Bell Telephone Laboratories in Murray Hill, New Jersey, from 1961 to '64. There he created a series of landmark electronic works, including *Phases* (1963) and *Ergodos II* (1964), while developing programs for computer-generated sound and composition. He also developed electronic and computer music systems at Yale University and the Polytechnic Institute of Brooklyn.

As both pianist and conductor, Tenney has long been active in the performance of 20th-century American music. He was co-founder of the Tone Roads Chamber Ensemble in New York City (1963-70), and has performed with the ensembles of John Cage, Harry Partch, the Fluxus composers, Steve Reich, and Philip Glass.

Tenney was Research Associate in the Theory of Music at Yale University in New Haven, Connecticut, from 1964 to '66. In New York City, he was lecturer at The New School for Social Research from 1965-66, and at the School of Visual Arts from 1968-69; from 1966 to '70, he was Visiting Associate Professor at the Polytechnic Institute of Brooklyn. Tenney has also taught one-term appointments as Visiting Lecturer at the University of South Florida, Tampa; California State College at Dominguez Hills; the University of California at Santa Barbara; and Stanford University. He taught composition at the California Institute of the Arts, Valencia, from 1970 to '75, and was Visiting Associate Professor of Music at the University of California at Santa Cruz from 1975 to

'76. Currently, he is Professor of Music at York University in Toronto, Ontario.

As theorist, Tenney has written numerous books and essays, including *META +HODOS* (1961), "John Cage And The Theory Of Harmony" (1984), and *A History of 'Consonance' And 'Dissonance'* (1988). He is the subject of *Soundings 13: "The Music Of James Tenney,"* which includes some of his essays and scores, as well as information on Tenney's earlier music. He has received grants from the National Science Foundation, the National Endowment for the Arts and Music, the Ontario Arts Council, the American Academy and Institute of Arts and Letters, the Canada Council, and the Fromm Foundation.

I spoke to James Tenney by telephone in his home in Toronto on August 6 and 12, 1992. Although I was eager to learn more about his association with many of America's great composers, I was concerned that his own composition and ideas have been too long ignored in part because of his connection with the masters of preceding generations. So I was particularly interested to speak with him about electronic music, just intonation, and the role of the harmonic series as a compositional tool.

JAMES TENNEY / Interview

Q: Can you tell me when you first learned about the harmonic series?

TENNEY: In school. I had a teacher at Bennington College in 1956, who gave a course in musical acoustics. He was the conductor of the Dessoff Choirs in New York, a Swiss musician named Paul Boepple — wonderful musician. His course in musical acoustics included the harmonic series. That was also my introduction to some questions about tuning systems.

Q: Wasn't it unusual at that time for him to have gone into the harmonic series?

TENNEY: Yes, that's right. And whatever I gained from him was very much amplified and extended by my courses with Lejaren Hiller, when I was doing graduate work at the University of Illinois.

Q: Did the subject recur then strictly in terms of acoustics, or was there already the idea of composition?

TENNEY: No, it was just a question of musical acoustics. The idea of using it in composition I think I may have originated myself; I can't think of any precedent for it.

Q: Did it seem to offer compositional possibilities when you studied it at Bennington?

TENNEY: No, not really. In fact, I didn't really begin to use it as a structural, compositional idea until 1972, I think, which is 15 years later.

Q: What helped you realize that the harmonic series could be useful in composition?

TENNEY: That's really hard for me to reconstruct. I wrote two pieces that year, 1972, which used it: a piece for orchestra called *Clang* and a piece for string quintet called *Quintext*. In both of them I used the harmonic series in this compositional way. I can't frankly remember how that came to me — I think it had to do with looking for some new way to integrate a composition. And I've always been fascinated by the sheer acoustical and psychoacoustical fact involved there, that the auditory system integrates what, from an acoustical standpoint, is a complex set of frequencies. For one reason or another — and this is an extremely important theoretical question as far as harmony is concerned — the auditory system is able to integrate that complex set into a singular percept. And I think it's quite possible that just thinking about that, I began to think of it as a possibility for compositional integration. The whole interplay between multiplicity and singularity, complexity and simplicity, began to interest me. Of course, this is not a new goal in music; it's an old notion of variety within unity. I can think of Schoenberg as an example of someone who talked about that. But it goes back at least a hundred years earlier, in terms of aesthetic and theoretical ideas about what the composer is up to.

Q: Have you found over the years that the harmonic series has been most important for you in terms of tuning or in terms of structural forms?

TENNEY: Well, the harmonic series as such I would say is connected to both of those issues. But let me clarify something here. I agree with Partch in his opinion (or in his assertion; it's stronger than an opinion!) that the question of just intonation does not have to do with the harmonic series. He had to do it that way because it would have made big theoretical problems with his U-tonality, the undertone relationships. So he had to say that it's not because these intervals are in the harmonic series. Well, I agree with that for other reasons. I've come to the conclusion that it's not because they're in the harmonic series and somehow we recognize them as natural, that they have the potential importance that they have. I have a different viewpoint about that. However, the harmonic series is physically the paradigm of that set of important relationships. We can find them there; it's a very useful tool for teaching and demonstration. But in terms of the theoretical aspect of it, I think Partch was right — which means that Rameau was wrong. Whoever has taken the position that somehow, because it's there in the harmonic series, we're imitating nature when we play with it — well, just immediately, the minor triad throws that theoretical position into disarray. However, the fact that the auditory system does integrate that set of pitches (in certain circumstances, anyway) into a singular percept is fascinating and useful, musically, in that it opened up a number of possibilities for large-scale form and/or a process of going toward or away from simplicity, which turned out to be very useful compositionally.

Q: As you've worked with the harmonic series over the years, has it taken you into areas you would not have anticipated?

TENNEY: Some of my work, and often the pieces that are harmonic-series related, have a minimalist character which they might not have without it. Even though I'm a friend of Steve Reich and Phil Glass and all, and was active in that scene which was developing in New York in the '60s, manifestations of minimalism in my own work were infrequent. A piece that I did called *For Ann (rising)* is minimalist in a more generic sense than works of Steve Reich or Phil Glass. But the idea seems to lend itself to what Steve calls "gradual process"; often the pieces that are related to the harmonic series can also be seen as gradual-process pieces.

Q: Such as *Saxony* or *Voice(s)*.

TENNEY: Yes, or *Clang* or *Quintext V*.

Q: You're using the term minimalist here to signify gradual-process compositions. I've found that it's also a useful term for music which, whether it employs gradual processes or repeating patterns or a singular event or whatever, is essentially nondramatic.

TENNEY: Yes, I know what you mean, and that attitude was very important to me for a long time. And in fact it's interesting that that's one of the things that the minimalists — whether they would like to hear this or not — have in common with John Cage.

Q: For New Music America's 1984 brochure, you wrote an essay called "Reflections After Bridge." I take it that the title refers to your score *Bridge* for two pianos, eight hands.

TENNEY: Yes.

Q: Elsewhere, you've spoken about how that work implies a bridge or *rapprochement* between the ideas of John Cage and Harry Partch — which is also the thrust of that essay. Do you think these two streams in recent years have come closer together, in either your own or other people's music?

TENNEY: I feel that, in my own work, there's absolutely no boundary. And that piece was partly intended as a demonstration of that. Although that attitude goes back a long way: the attitude that these various currents are not mutually exclusive, and that a composer ought to be able to move much more freely in the entire field than the labels and the stylistic categories seem to suggest. I've got a piece, for example, called *Chromatic Canon* for two pianos, which I dedicated to Steve Reich. It was performed in New York last year and Steve was there to hear it, sitting with me in the audience. Afterwards, we left and he said something like, "You've put me in bed with Schoenberg!" I think he meant that it seemed like a very unlikely marriage, right? But that's my whole point. And I think he was pleased by that — he said he liked the piece.

The whole idea is that music is music, you know? I like Ives' attitude about this stuff, his statement about eclecticism being every composer's duty. What he's saying is that we should feel free to do whatever. That's not part of the European sensibility, I would say; the European sensibility was exemplified by Schoenberg, who felt so strongly when he went into an atonal harmonic style, that he had to purge the music of anything that might suggest tonality, that they somehow couldn't be there together. Ives to me demonstrates that that isn't necessarily so, and that they can coexist. But it takes a very Whitmanesque large embrace to accommodate that!

Q: Have you had any feedback from John Cage regarding these ideas?

TENNEY: Yes. He heard my piece called *Critical Band* in Florida, at the New Music America concert there, and called me on the phone afterwards to say how much he liked it. And he said, "Well, if that's harmony, I'm all for it!" I was very, very gratified by that.

Q: Is it true that, when you were working with Partch's ensemble at the University of Illinois, you actually got into trouble with him because of your interest in Cage's music?

TENNEY: Well, I was not just working with the ensemble; I actually had an assistantship working for him personally in his studio. And I annoyed him. I didn't realize I was doing this, but it irritated him no end that I was continually bringing up the names of other composers and asking him what he thought of them. And if I liked them and he didn't, I guess I argued with him or something. Anyway, he finally fired me from this position as his assistant. When I went to see him to try to dissuade him from that, he told me he wouldn't budge. I asked why and he called me arrogant. And I suspect I probably was, partly through just sheer naiveté and not being too tactful. And that was the end of that. Of course, that experience was a very profound one, and I studied his book during that time. The personality clash didn't have anything to do with my interest in his ideas. It took a while for these ideas to percolate, but ten or twelve years later, it did happen.

Q: Were you able to build some kind of bridge with Partch in his final years?

TENNEY: No, I was never able to do that. And I feel kind of badly about that, but he became more and more difficult to communicate with.

Q: Have you had any positive feedback from his followers in recent years?

TENNEY: I feel like I have a good relationship with people like Danlee Mitchell and Dean Drummond and David Dunn. I think they see me as not in any sense antagonistic to Partch, but just the opposite. They know that I value Partch's work very highly, and the fact that we couldn't get along for more than six months is kind of irrelevant now.

Q: Does the retuning of both pianos for *Bridge* hinder performances of the piece?

TENNEY: Yes, it does.

Q: That introduces the whole issue of writing for conventional instruments in alternate tunings. How serious a dilemma has that been?

TENNEY: As I see it, you have only three options here. One is to work with conventional instruments and new tunings for them, and you encounter one set of problems. Another is to do what Partch did, build your own instruments, and you obviously encounter another set of problems. The third is opened up by electronics and computer technology, and that's probably the smoothest sailing; it doesn't in itself entail problems, I guess. But it lacks something of the immediacy of acoustical instruments and that live performing situation. I have not done anything electronically with tuning. I might, one of these days; it's not a hard-and-fast thing. But I've not been strongly attracted to it, partly because I have a feeling that there's a kind of evolutionary process involved; all of us experimenting with things like this are involved in the evolution of human hearing. The effect of writing for live players who have to struggle with their instruments, who have to struggle with problems of retuning pianos, for example, and learning these things again — I just feel like the roots go deeper this way. In a way, electronics is too easy. There's much less in the way of actual change of musical consciousness. I want it to be understood that I in no way object to anybody's working electronically this way. It's just to try to explain why I haven't done it. I tend to be more interested in the challenge of dealing with conventional instruments and live players in an acoustical situation. It's been really interesting to me to work with ensembles on some of these pieces. Initially the players are very skeptical: They look at the score and say (or at least think to themselves) something like, "Well, why doesn't he get a machine to do this? This is too much to ask us — human beings can't do this." I've had several experiences now that convince me, first of all, that they can learn — in a matter of minutes or hours, in a coached situation. And my experience with that has always been their delight at that fact; their discovery that they can hear more than they thought they could hear, that they can make distinctions that they didn't realize they could make. That was my experience with the Relâche ensemble in Philadelphia, with the Recherche ensemble at Darmstadt a couple of years ago, and with the group of players that did *Voice(s)* here in Toronto.

Q: Did the composition of *Voice(s)* lead you to add the postscript to *Saxony*, in which that score can be performed by other instrumental groups, even with alternate fundamentals for the tunings?

TENNEY: Not *Voice(s)*. Shortly after I wrote *Saxony*, the situation arose at those New York concerts of my work which Steve Reich produced in 1979, where there was the possibility of doing a version for three players. Tape delay is used in that piece, and as in almost every piece where I've used tape delay, the motivation for using it is basically to thicken the texture — I sometimes call it the poor man's orchestra. It's obvious that I can thicken the texture by having more players following the same formal plan as well. So right away there was a version for three players. Then I began thinking about it, and I kind of generalized it. I have somewhere in my papers a kind of Ur-version of it which has never been published. It doesn't specify instrumentation or actual pitches, it's just the basic concept that could be arranged for any group.

Delay is a big practical problem in general, of course, because it's so sensitive, so touchy, it can build up room resonances — all kinds of things can go wrong. As many times as I've written pieces that call for delay, I have vowed never to use it again, and I always break my vow! But it's so difficult to handle. Digital delays now have already overcome part of the problem. The old form of delay was two tape recorders with a tape running from one to the next, and this is just extraordinarily vulnerable to problems. But digital delay gets rid of a lot of those problems, and eventually the technology will be such that it'll be trouble-free. So I guess I don't regret having done it, but I must say that whenever I've had to perform one of these things, I've been on pins and needles for the whole time.

Q: Regarding the use of improvisation in *Saxony* and *Voice(s)*: Are you indicating that it doesn't really matter what the instrumentalists play, as long as they use the pitches designated for the different sections of the work, or are you specifically concerned that the players should be improvising rather than playing parts you could have written out?

TENNEY: The first, not the second. I've never really been interested in improvisation as an expressive activity on the part of the player. In my work, improvisation is creative, but in a much more modest way. That is, just as it is in playing a piece by Cage from the late '50s, say, where lots of decisions about all kinds of parameters are left up to the performer — again, Cage is not interested in the performer's self-expression. I'm not either — at least, to begin with, I'm not. There's another level at which certainly one performer may realize one of my pieces in a way that pleases me a lot more than another. But somehow it's different; it's a different criterion of success. It's hard for me to pin this down. It's not self-expression, but one performer may accomplish the task much more interestingly than another.

Q: Are those two pieces, along with *In The Aeolian Mode*, the only works of yours which offer these latitudes?

TENNEY: *Clang* involves that too. It was in that piece that I first started using the notation of what I call "available pitches." It will probably never be played while I'm alive; it's one of those things which runs so against the grain of the habits of orchestral players, that I have the feeling that it will never happen. Which is too bad. It was given a reading by the L.A. Philharmonic, in a special program: They had gotten a grant to have some pairings of young conductors and young composers, to do readings. The conductor that had been asked by them was Lawrence Smith, who was teaching at Cal Arts at the same time I was, and he came to me one day and said, "Have you got a piece for orchestra?" I'd been thinking about one, but I hadn't actually done it. I said, "Well, no, but I will in a week!" So I composed that piece and it was actually given a reading. And I heard it, so I know it's a good piece, but I don't know if anybody else is ever going to hear it.

Q: Both of your *Collage* tape pieces use rock music. Does that involvement hold over in your scores for multiple electric guitars, the *Septet* and *"Water On The Mountain — Fire In Heaven,"* or are you really interested in something else when you use those instruments?

TENNEY: Well, I have an interest in that. *Septet* can even seem to be a little bit reminiscent of it because of the strong rhythmic drive. But the other piece is entirely different: It's very abstract, and it was done with the same program — just with different input settings — that was used to do the piece for six harps, *Changes*. In *"Water On The Mountain — Fire In Heaven"* the electric guitars are being used much more purely, without that sense of connection with rock. Although I know it's unavoidable in a live performance; there is going to necessarily be that connection, and that's fine with me. But the sound is much more abstract.

Q: I've read that you considered scoring that work for unamplified guitars.

TENNEY: I don't remember now, but I think the final version of the instructions in the score is that it can be done either way; just six instruments of the same timbre. I think it would be kind of neat to hear it on six classical guitars.

Q: Is that a harmonic-series work as well? Did you retune the guitars the same way you did with the *Septet?*

TENNEY: No, the guitars are retuned the way the harps are retuned in *Changes*, which is in sixths of a semitone. It's not a harmonic-series piece, but it's based on a harmonic system. The tuning is a tempered tuning but with 72 pitches in the octave. And the reason I chose that is it provides extremely good approximations of all the important just intervals up through the eleven limit. But it's practical on a tempered instrument. In *"Water On The Mountain — Fire In Heaven,"* each guitar is, within itself, tuned normally, but at a sixth of a semitone above or below the next guitar.

Q: What prompted you to undertake the research that resulted in your book, *A History of 'Consonance' And 'Dissonance'*?

TENNEY: All along I've been interested in certain theoretical questions, going all the way back to *META∕HODOS* which was written in 1961. But in the early '70s, I got more and more interested in the problem of the theory of harmony, and decided at a certain point to attack it, in effect; to undertake to do something in that area. I hadn't touched harmony in *META∕HODOS* or anything earlier. I'd left it alone, always with a sense of postponing it, that one of these days I would want to try to deal with it. So when I finally did begin, one of the aspects of that larger question of harmony was of course the old question about consonance and dissonance. There's a big literature there of theoretical ideas and opinions and actual psychological results and psychoacoustic experiments and so forth. When I began to get into that literature, I saw that there were these incompatible schools of thought, these strange discrepancies between not only the definitions of those terms but even the correlations of different intervals. And I thought, "This is very curious. What the hell's going on here?" The more I read and thought about it, the more I began to suspect that the semantic and theoretical disagreements must be based on something, and that it was likely to have to do with the historical development of these things. So I thought I would take a little detour here, take a couple of weeks off and just study the history. Well, a year and a half later, I found that I had gone into the history of music theory in a way that I never thought I would, and found it quite interesting. And essentially answered the question, as far as I'm concerned, that the disagreements are based on actual different conceptions of what those terms mean; conceptions always related to musical practice at a given time. At the end of the book, I compare it to Thomas Kuhn's notion of "paradigms" in scientific history, and as these paradigms changed, the terms didn't.

But this was never made explicit, it was never made clear, and so these absurd arguments would develop about whether the fourth was a dissonance or not. And of course, in one period, given one set of criteria and one musical context, it was a dissonance; in another situation, it clearly is not. So it clarified the whole thing for me, anyway, and I could let it go then. It took a long time.

Q: Were you able to funnel any of that research in a concrete way into your own composition?

TENNEY: No, not really. It didn't affect my composing in any way that I could see. All it would affect, I guess, would be how I might describe what I'm doing. Essentially, the consonance/dissonance concepts that are the most relevant to contemporary music are what I call CDC-2 and CDC-5: the one that first develops with polyphony, and the one that Helmholtz was talking about. They're closely related to each other, and when we talk about the dissonance in Varèse, I believe that's the primary sense of it. We're not talking about Rameau's sense of it or Dufay's sense of it.

Q: Is it true that your having heard Varèse's *Déserts* and *Poème Électronique* was the impetus for your own work in electronic music?

TENNEY: The answer's probably yes, although I must have read little essays or articles that Varèse had written, which talked about electronics, maybe even before I actually heard those pieces. But I heard those pieces as soon as one could, almost right after they were done, and they were very important to me.

Q: Were they the first electronic music you'd heard?

TENNEY: Yes, I think so. *Déserts* was completed I think in 1954, which was when I moved to New York. The *Poème Électronique* is I believe 1957 or '58. So that music I heard in New York.

Q: But you had not actually been studying with Varèse then.

TENNEY: No, it was before I would say that I was studying with him — although I had met him through a friend of mine, a filmmaker named Stan Brakhage. He had made a film using a recording of a piece of Varèse's, and he wanted to go see Varèse to get his permission to use it, which he got. Stan was my roommate in the first few months when I moved to New York, and he took me with him, and we both met Varèse then.

Q: That must have been really special.

TENNEY: It was great. That's how I met Cage, too, the first time.

Q: Through Brakhage?

TENNEY: Yes, the very same situation.

Q: Had you heard their music prior to those meetings?

TENNEY: Yes. Through the Varèse Record, so-called now, with Frederick Waldman conducting, which I had very soon after it was out — that was 1951 or something. I had a recording of Cage's *Sonatas And Interludes*. In fact, I heard Cage himself perform them in Denver in about 1951 or '52. So I knew the music and it was already very important to me.

Q: Was there the feeling that electronic music was going to be the music of the future, and therefore you wanted to climb aboard, or was there more the sense that this was something you wanted to investigate for your own personal interests?

TENNEY: Well, both. At the time, there was a sort of idealistic vision that Varèse had already articulated in the '20s. I was aware of that, and it felt like, yes, in some ways, this is the future. So I was hungry to get involved with it as soon as I could, or in any way that I could. In fact, it didn't actually become feasible until I went to Illinois in '59 — and that's a long time after I'd become interested in it.

Q: There wasn't any place you could go at that time in pursuit of this interest, even working only with tape, except for the University of Illinois?

TENNEY: Well, there was the Columbia studio but it was a pretty closed shop. Some hayseed out of Denver like me wasn't going to just waltz in there and say, "Hey, I'd like to use your equipment"! So my first opportunity to do anything was when Hiller started that studio at Illinois.

Q: Richard Maxfield had just started teaching electronic music at the New School in New York City in 1959.

TENNEY: I don't know how early Richard started. Somebody really needs to research that because Maxfield was very important and he's very much a forgotten figure. But I didn't meet him until the '60s; I didn't become aware of his work until then. I hadn't heard of him in this earlier period.

Q: Working at Illinois meant composing exclusively with tape, didn't it — it wasn't possible to work directly with synthesis yet.

TENNEY: Well, not for me — synthesis techniques were so primitive in that studio. It was very difficult to make a piece using synthetic sounds because essentially what we had were a few Lafayette sine- and square-wave generators. You turned the dial to set the frequency and then you turned it on. We didn't have gates, we didn't have voltage control — we had nothing that everyone takes for granted in analog synthesis ever since Buchla and Moog created their synthesizers. This was before what you could even call synthesizers. The only thing that I was able to do which was of any interest to me was a variety of *musique concrète*.

Q: Were the *Improvisations for Medea* and *Collage #1 ("Blue Suede")* the only pieces you were able to do there, or had you worked on other tape compositions at Illinois?

TENNEY: I worked on another piece, where I was attempting to work with synthesized tones and play with timbre, but I didn't like it. I didn't like those sounds, finally — there wasn't enough of a way to loosen them up, they just sounded mechanical to me. So it was rather a frustrating time, that first year or two at Illinois, because I kept trying to do something with very little success, until I moved in the direction of concrete sounds. It wasn't until the computer-synthesis program became available that I felt I could really work with purely synthetic sound.

Q: Learning about the developments at Bell Labs made you feel there was a potential in the medium, which had been eluding you up until then?

TENNEY: Right. When I read Max Mathews' article in the *Bell Systems Journal*, I said, "That's the medium for me."

Q: And once you were at Bell Labs, you composed a whole series of electronic pieces. I've read that you would play that music for Carl Ruggles, to get his feedback on them.

TENNEY: That's right.

Q: I'm intrigued by that, because despite his having been friends with Varèse, that kind of music seems so far removed from his own interests. Did he really have an ear for what you were trying to do?

TENNEY: I think so. He was trying very hard to be sympathetic, and trying very hard to understand what was happening. I think it was kind of exciting for him to be able to feel that he was in touch with this radical new stuff. Here I was, doing the latest thing and playing it for him, and he was enjoying that. I believe it made him feel more up to date. And it was wonderful because he knew how much I loved his music, so he could see in me no problem with stylistic discrepancies, and he sort of adopted the same attitude. He was very supportive of not only my electronic music but also my instrumental music at the time — which was not really like his at all. And I think he cherished his earlier contact with Varèse, even though they weren't always on the best of terms. He was proud of that contact.

Q: Are you referring to these sessions when you cite him as one of your teachers, or was that more true of the preceding years when you were at Bennington?

TENNEY: That began when I was a student at Bennington, but it was not a formal thing. Ruggles lived in the little town of Arlington which was about fifteen miles north, and he wasn't really teaching, formally. But I spent so much time with him, going over his music with him and showing him mine and getting his opinions about it, that I have no qualms about saying I studied with him, even though they were not what you would call composition lessons.

Essentially, that was my relationship with Varèse too. It was never something like, "OK, come next Wednesday afternoon for a composition lesson." I would call him up and say, "Can I come and see you and bring some music and talk with you?" And we would arrange a time and spend a couple of hours.

Q: Did you play your electronic music for Varèse as well?

TENNEY: Oh yes. I don't remember if I played for him the music I had done at Illinois; probably I did, but I just don't remember that. What I do remember more clearly is how interested Varèse was in the computer-music technology, because he had that history of his efforts to arrange some kind of collaboration with the acoustician at Bell, Harvey Fletcher, and nothing had ever come of it. Here he saw that finally something like this was happening, and it was very exciting to him. So he was very interested in the music.

Q: I've read that, after composing a series of computer-music pieces, you created a computer-generated roll for player piano in 1964. To have gone from the most sophisticated music-making technology to such a neglected, folk machinery is really wild.

TENNEY: Yes, that irony appealed to me. But how it came about was quite by accident. An engineer at Bell Labs stopped by one day, and we were talking about computer music. He said, "Have you ever done anything for player piano?" and I said, "No." It turns out, he was sort of a hobbyist, and I guess he owned player pianos and knew where to get blank rolls and had tools to punch them and so forth. He said, "Why don't you do a piece for player piano? I'll punch the roll for you." So I said, "That sounds really interesting," and I wrote a program to generate such a piece. Then I marked the roll in pencil where it needed to be punched, and turned it over to him to punch. He had it for a while and didn't get to it right away, and then he moved; he left Bell Labs and he went to Illinois, I think. I didn't hear from him again for about five years, and then I got a letter from him which said, "I was going through a stack of old papers that were filed away in a box, and I found your player-piano roll. What would you like me to do with it?" I said, "Well, send it to me, for heaven's sake, I want it!" So he sent it and here it was — I didn't have a player piano and he wasn't around. I was in New York and I thought, "What can I do now?" I looked in the telephone book, found the Aeolian Piano Company on 57th Street, and put my roll under my arm and took the subway up to 57th Street.

I went into this great big showroom on the ground floor, with player pianos all over the place. The salesman came up to me and I said, "I have a player-piano roll and nowhere to play it. Could you play it for me on one of your pianos?" He said, "Sure," and he took the roll, went over to a little spinet player piano, put it on, and flipped the switch to start it. It got about three seconds into the piece and he turned it off and said, "You've done something wrong"! I knew where he was coming from, but I said, "Well, what have I done wrong?" He said, "I don't know, but it's just not right"! I said, "Is there anybody here who could tell me what I've done wrong?" And he said, "Well, there's a guy up on the sixth floor, who might be able to help you." So I took the elevator up to the sixth floor which I think was the top floor of the building. It was a big loft area; most of it was probably accounting secretaries, typing. But off in a corner was a little workshop area, and inside there was an old black man named Lawrence J. Cook. He'd been there since the '20s, and he knew player pianos inside out; he was the repairman for them. Well, I went through my same spiel, and he said, "Sure," and he put it on, ran it, and didn't bat an eye! And that was how I heard it for the first time.

I asked him if I could bring it back with a tape recorder and record it, and he said yes. So I came back in the next day or two. The piano he was playing it on had the roller mechanism that ran both on an electric motor, and on foot pedals that you pumped in the old-fashioned way, like on a harmonium. He said, "Would you like it on the electric or with the pedals?" The electric motor was kind of noisy, so I said, "I'd like to try it with the pedals." And he said, "OK, I'll pedal it for you." He did that and it was wonderful to watch, because this piece involves changes of texture from one note at a time to areas where there's an aggregate of I think 65 notes, playing almost simultaneously. And he pedaled it, steadying himself by holding onto the two wooden ends beyond the keyboard. He'd watch that roll come through, and when there was a thin texture he would slow down the pedaling so that he wasn't pumping so much air, and when he saw these big clusters coming, he would start pedaling harder. So I got a real "interpretation" of my roll, which was just beautiful.

Q: You weren't familiar with Conlon Nancarrow's music at that time, were you?

TENNEY: Right, I hadn't heard of Nancarrow until Columbia came out with that first record.

Q: Is it true that for your second work for player piano, *Spectral CANON*, Nancarrow actually punched the roll for you?

TENNEY: That's right. He has this special machine that he had designed; I believe it was based on the design of the machine that Lawrence Cook had in his shop. When I told Conlon that I was working on this piece, he said, "You mark the roll and send it down to me, and I'll punch it on my machine."

Q: Had you been able to play that earlier piece for him?

TENNEY: Let's see. First I met him when I visited Mexico City once, and then — this is about '72 or '73 — when I went back home, I sent him a tape of the first player-piano piece. And he said he liked it.

Q: We were talking before about the harmonic series and your inspiration to use it compositionally. In your first work with computers, there again you used the machines not only to synthesize sounds, but also to generate compositional material. That was fairly unusual at that time.

TENNEY: There was the rather didactic *Illiac Suite* by Hiller (my teacher at Illinois) and Isaacson. Beyond that, I think Xenakis was the only other person that I was aware of who was trying to do that sort of thing.

Q: And that use of the computer has been the real holdover for you, even after you stopped making electronic pieces.

TENNEY: There's one point that needs to be clarified. I actually did not use the computer for quite a few years. So that my recent work with the computer constitutes a kind of return to that, after having left it for quite a while. *Bridge* was the piece that represented that return.

Q: So it would be fair to say that, at the far end of your work with electronic music, you really felt the need to make a break with it all together.

TENNEY: Yeah, right after *For Ann (rising)*.

Q: That piece was where you jumped off the train.

TENNEY: That's right. Except that I had no such intention in the making of the piece. It just happened that way. There's a lot of sheer coincidence involved, in that it was done just shortly before I left New York and moved to California and everything changed. Although the title of it has to do with a recent marriage and a new family developing; it was, I suppose, symbolic of the fact that things were changing for me. But I really didn't think of that in making the piece. It was just something I was interested to try to do.

Q: But after that work, you pretty much felt you'd reached a plateau in terms of what you could do with electronic music?

TENNEY: For the moment, yes. But then what happened was I moved to California for a teaching job at Cal Arts. What they had there was analog-synthesis equipment which I had never really worked with. I'm not a knob-turner, and if you're not a knob-turner, analog synthesis is not very comfortable. After my frustrations at Illinois, and the fact that I got into the computer work so early, the analog systems just weren't for me. But I found at Cal Arts that I was surrounded by fantastic performers — really good players — so I started writing music for acoustical instruments again.

Q: Looking back, would you say your experience working at Bell Labs was one more of frustration than satisfaction?

TENNEY: Not really, it wasn't the frustration. I'll tell you how I've always felt about it. I devoted almost exactly a decade of my life exclusively to electronic and computer music: The first piece, *Collage #1 ("Blue Suede")* was April '61, and the last piece was March '69, *For Ann (rising)*. But I was involved at such a ground level in the medium that I was always having to deal with development problems. It wasn't like, here's a studio, the equipment works, you come in and use it. At Bell Labs, something was working, but I was actually brought in there to develop it. At least half of the features that are taken for granted now in MUSIC V were the result of my recommendations; it was a much more primitive thing when I got there. Then when I left Bell Labs I developed a system at Yale, and then I moved on to the Polytechnic Institute of Brooklyn and developed a system there. I was constantly dealing with that, and having to function as an engineer, spending more time at that, it always seemed to me, than actually composing. And that aspect of it got frustrating. It also meant that I had very little time to do anything else, any other kind of music. For example, I did some theater pieces and a few other things in the '60s, but not very much, so in a way, what was created there was a backlog of potential possible music in other media, which I just didn't have time to do before. And that backlog started me on a roll that went almost 15 years before I even went back and had the desire to work with the computer again.

Q: How important is the computer for you now in your composition?

TENNEY: It's very important. I've never actually counted this out, but I would say something like half of the pieces I've done since '84 involve the computer in one way or another.

Q: Could the time come where you might want to do another solo tape piece?

TENNEY: It certainly could. I recently had the occasion to work with another composer, Randall Smith, who freelances as a technician as well; he's got a great digital studio with Soundtools software. This was to prepare a tape that was not electronic music, but my experience of working with that software in putting this tape together was very impressive, so I can imagine that I might. It struck me that, with this kind of technology, it had finally become a truly plastic medium, the way Varèse envisioned it. And which it has not been; it's been this receding horizon for all these years. The interesting thing as far as I'm concerned is that it's digital technology that has been the breakthrough all along; that's what made it possible for me to really get to work in the medium in '61, and the potential now is just enormous.

Q: Can you describe the nature of your collaboration with George Brecht in creating the tape piece *Entrance/Exit Music?*

TENNEY: I got to know George through the Fluxus group — we were on concerts together, where he was doing his wonderful little minimalist pieces. In fact, he lived out in New Jersey near Bell Labs. He was a chemist professionally; he worked I think with DuPont. I got to know him in New York and we became pretty good friends. He was interested in the computer-music process as well, and he came up with that idea; he asked me, "Could you create a tape that begins with a sine wave and ends with white noise, and changes completely continuously?" And I said, "Well, let me try," and that was the basis of it. And then it was used frequently by Nam June Paik and Charlotte Moorman in their European tour; they used to open and close all their programs with it.

Q: The tape was really your first piece that was part of the Fluxus performances; after that came *"Chamber Music"* and your *Audience Pieces.* Was there an actual sense of joining a group or movement in your involvement with Fluxus?

TENNEY: Not really, no. In my sense of it, it was a bunch of individuals who liked each other and got along together and had ideas to collaborate in programs. The idea of its being a movement was pretty much in the minds of George Maciunas and Henry Flynt and a few people like that. Of course, now it's crystallizing into this historical object called Fluxus, right? That's taught me to suspect that most of the movements in history have been equally fluid and elusive and just accidental — or not entirely accidental, but nice confluences of different individuals. The notion of a movement is not the way I felt about it. These were just individuals; I was interested in their work, and there was mutual interest in the work, and we could do programs together.

Q: Your postal pieces of both the '60s and '70s show that you were involved in such a kind of composition because it was interesting to you, and not because it was contingent on any movement or circle of composers. Have you had the urge in recent years to knock off another quickie like those?

TENNEY: Well, in the last 15 years I have a few pieces where the score is so abbreviated — one or two pages, like *Saxony* and *Critical Band* — and these very compact scores are, in my mind, related to those postal pieces. And it's kind of a wonderful way of working, but I can't be limited to that. When I'm in the middle of the tedious working out of the other kind of piece, which takes untold hours of copying and this and that, I often say, "Oh boy, I wish I could go back — the next piece I'm going to do isn't going to be over one page!" But I can't plan that. These scores always are just what they seem to have to be, given the nature of the musical idea.

Q: There's a parallel in your work with the Fluxus performances and your involvement with the ensembles of Steve Reich and Philip Glass. There again, what the public is seeing as a defined movement involving contrary personalities was in reality a much more fluid and simple situation.

TENNEY: Absolutely. These were different, interesting, individual efforts. I first met Steve at a rehearsal for one of the New York Avant-Garde Festival concerts. He came in and somebody introduced us. (I forget who — maybe Terry Riley.) We talked a little bit and he played me a tape, and it was *Come Out*. And I said, "Wow, that's marvelous."

There are two ways these things get, as I said, crystallized into movements. One is the naming, which of course is essential — and most of the time the names are provided by critics, usually with negative intent. But frequently — and this seems to me a kind of European thing —there's also the idea of the polemic and initiating a new movement. That's a very European notion, I think. So somehow George Maciunas's European background strikes me as relevant: That was the way you did it. Whereas Americans are much more individualistic. Later on, if it's going to be useful to be attached to a movement, fine — I'm not going to go argue with anybody about it. But the reality is, it's a very fluid confluence of individuals. That's really how it can have been so lively and vital.

COMPOSITIONS

1952	*Interim* for piano	SP
1956-61	*Seeds I-VI* for flute, clarinet, bassoon, French horn, violin, and cello	SP
1958;71	*"Thirteen Ways Of Looking At A Blackbird"* (Wallace Stevens) for tenor, two flutes, violin, viola, and cello; revised for bass voice, oboe, alto flute, viola, cello, and contrabass	SP
1958;83	Sonata For Ten Wind Instruments	SP
1959	*Monody* for clarinet	SP
1961	*Collage #1 ("Blue Suede")* for tape	SP
1961	*Analog #1: Noise Study* for computer-generated tape	SP
1962	*Entrance/Exit Music* for computer-generated tape (in collaboration with George Brecht)	SP
1962	*Stochastic Studies* for computer-generated tape	SP
1963	*Stochastic (String) Quartet* for computer-generated tape or string quartet	SP
1963	*Dialogue* for computer-generated tape	SP
1963	*Phases* for computer-generated tape	SP
1963	*Ergodos I* for two computer-generated tapes to be played together or separately	SP
1964	*Music For Player Piano* for computer-generated piano roll	SP
1964	*Piano/Percussion Complement* for piano and percussion, with *Ergodos I* or *II*	SP
1964	*String Complement* for any number of bowed string instruments, with *Ergodos I* or *II*	SP
1964	*Choreogram* for any number of musicians with dancers	SP
1964	*Ergodos II* for computer-generated tape	SP
1964	*String, Woodwind, Brass, And Vocal Responses* with *Ergodos I* or *II*	SP
1964	*"Chamber Music"* for any number of instruments, players, objects, or events	FPM
1965	*Maximusic* (*Postal Piece #5*) for solo percussionist	SP
1966	*Collage #2 ("Viet Flakes")* for tape	SP
1967	*Fabric For Ché* for computer-generated tape	SP
1967	*Swell Piece #1* (*Postal Piece #6*) for any number of sustained-tone instruments	SP
1969	*For Ann (rising)* for tape	SP
1969	*Three Rags For Pianoforte: Raggedy Ann, Milk And Honey, Tangled Rag*	FPM
	Tangled Rag string-quintet arrangement (1974)	SP
	Milk And Honey arranged for mandolin(s), mandola(s), and mandocello(i) (1983, arranged by Larry Polansky)	SP
1970	*A Rose Is A Rose Is A Round* (*Postal Piece #2*) for voices	SP
1970-71	*Quiet Fan* for thirteen instruments or chamber orchestra	SP

1971	*Swell Pieces #2 & 3 (Postal Pieces #7a & 7b)*	SP
1971	*"Hey When I Sing These 4 Songs Hey Look What Happens"* for SATB	SP
1971	*Beast (Postal Piece #1)* for string bass	SP
1971	*(night) (Postal Piece #3)* "for percussion perhaps, or ..."	SP
1971	*Having Never Written A Note For Percussion (Postal Piece #10)* for solo percussionist	SP
1971	*Koan (Postal Piece #4)* for violin	SP
1971	*August Harp (Postal Piece #8)* for harp	SP
1971	*Cellogram (Postal Piece #9)* for cello	SP
1971	*For 12 Strings (rising)* for strings	SP
1972	*Clang* for orchestra	SP
1972	*Quintext I-V: Five Textures For String Quartet And Bass*	SP
1973	*In The Aeolian Mode* for prepared piano and variable ensemble	SP
1973	*Canon* for contrabass quartet	SP
1973	*Chorale* for viola and harp (or piano)	SP
1974	*Three Harmonic Studies* for orchestra	SP
1974	*Chorales For Orchestra*	SP
1974	*Three Pieces For Mechanical Drum*	FPM
1974;91	*Spectral CANON for CONLON Nancarrow* for harmonic player piano	SP
1974	*Orchestral Study: The "Creation Field"*	FPM
1974-75	*Three Pieces For Drum Quartet*	FPM
1975-76	*Harmonium #1* for variable ensemble	SP
1978-80	*Harmonium #3* for three harps	SP
1978	*Harmonium #4* for ten instruments and tape-delay system	SP
1978;84	*Saxony* for one or more saxophone players and tape-delay system; revised for brass quintet and tape-delay system; for string trio or string quartet and tape-delay system	SP
1978	*Harmonium #5* for string trio	SP
1979	*Three Indigenous Songs* for two piccolos, alto flute, bassoon or tuba, and two percussionists	SP
1980;83	*Chromatic Canon* for two pianos	SP
1981-84	*"Listen...!"* for three sopranos and piano	SP
1981	*Septet* for six electric guitars and bass	SP
1982	*Glissade* for viola, cello, contrabass, and tape-delay system	SP
1982-83	*Voice(s)* for variable instrumental ensemble, voice(s), and multiple tape-delay system	SP
1982	*Deus Ex Machina* for tam-tam player and tape-delay system	SP
1984	*Bridge* for two microtonal pianos, eight hands	SP
1984	*Koan* for string quartet	SP
1985	*Changes: 64 Studies For 6 Harps*	SP
1985	*"Water On The Mountain — Fire In Heaven"* for six electric guitars	SP
1986	*The Road To Ubud* for gamelan and prepared piano	FPM

1988	*Rune* for percussion ensemble	FPM
1988	*Critical Band* for variable ensemble and tape-delay system	FPM
1990	*Tableaux Vivants* for violin, clarinet/bass clarinet, bassoon, soprano saxophone/baritone saxophone, piano, and vibraphone	FPM
1991	*Three New Seeds* for clarinet/bass clarinet, trumpet, contrabass, piano, and two percussionists	FPM
1991	*Pika-Don* for percussion quartet and tape	FPM
1992	*Stream* for alto flute, English horn, clarinet, alto saxophone, trumpet, vibraphone, harp, and viola	FPM
1992	*Ain't I A Woman?* for two violins, two violas, three cellos, and celesta	FPM
1992	"Love Me Do" and "Do You Want To Know A Secret?" (Lennon/McCartney, arranged for piano by JT)	FPM

DISCOGRAPHY

1964
Analog #1: Noise Study
Decca 9103 lp

1969
Stochastic (String) Quartet
Decca 710180 lp

1984
Spectral CANON for CONLON Nancarrow
Cold Blue L10 lp

"Hey When I Sing These 4 Songs Hey Look What Happens"
Bennington 003 lp

Three Indigenous Songs (excerpt), *Phases, Quiet Fan, For Ann (rising), Spectral CANON for CONLON Nancarrow, Bridge* (excerpt), *Voice(s)*
Musicworks 27 cs

1985
Saxony
CRI 528 lp

1986
Collage #1 ("Blue Suede")
Musicworks 34 cs

Septet For Electric Guitars
Tellus 14 cs

1989
Harmonium #5
Artifact 002 cd, cs
EAR Magazine 1 cd (1990)

1990
Critical Band
Mode 22 cd

1991
For Ann (rising)
EAR Magazine 3 cd

Koan
What Next? 0005 cd, cs

1992
Collage #1 ("Blue Suede"), Analog #1: Noise Study, Dialogue, Phases, Music For Player Piano, Ergodos II, Fabric For Ché, For Ann (rising)
Artifact 1007 cd

"Love Me Do," "Do You Want To Know A Secret?"
Sony/EMI 8021 cd

1993
Chromatic Canon
CRI 637 cd

collaborations

with George Brecht:
Entrance/Exit Music (excerpt) Tellus 24 cs (1990)

BIBLIOGRAPHY

META∕HODOS: A Phenomenology Of 20th-Century Music And An Approach To The Study Of Form (1961) and *META Meta∕Hodos* (1975). Oakland, California: Frog Peak Music, 1988.

"On The Discriminability Of Differences In The Rise-Time Of A Tone." *Journal Of The Acoustical Society Of America*, 34 (1962).

"Sound And Cinema." Stan Brakhage, co-author. *Film Culture*, 29 (1963).

"Sound-Generation By Means Of A Digital Computer," *Journal Of Music Theory*, 7 (1963).

"The Physical Correlates Of Timbre," *Gravesaner Blatter*, 26 (1965).

"Edgard Varèse." *East Side Review* (January 1966); reprinted in *Soundings*, 2 (Spring 1974).

"Computer Study Of Violin Tones." Mathews, Miller, & Pierce, co-authors. *Journal Of The Acoustical Society Of America*, 38 (1966).

"An Experimental Investigation Of Timbre — The Violin." Report to the National Science Foundation (1966).

"Music And Computers," *McGraw-Hill Encyclopedia Of Science And Technology*. New York: McGraw-Hill, 1967.

"Computer Music Experiences, 1961-64," *Electronic Music Reports*, 1 (1969).

"Form." *Dictionary Of Contemporary Music*. Ed. John Vinton. New York: E.P. Dutton, 1971.

"Some Notes On The Music Of Charles Ives," *Soundings*, 2 (Spring 1974).

"The Chronological Development Of Carl Ruggles' Melodic Style." *Perspectives Of New Music*, 16 (Fall-Winter 1977).

"Conlon Nancarrow's Studies For Player Piano." *Conlon Nancarrow: Selected Studies For Player Piano*. Ed. Peter Garland. Berkeley, California: Soundings Press, 1977.

"Temporal Gestalt Perception In Music." Larry Polansky, co-author. *Journal Of Music Theory*, 24 (1980).

"Introduction." *Americas*. Peter Garland, author. Santa Fe: Soundings Press, 1982.

"John Cage And The Theory Of Harmony," *Soundings 13: The Music Of James Tenney*. Santa Fe: Soundings Press, 1984.

"Reflections After Bridge." Catalog for New Music America 1984.

"The Tuning Of Time." Casey Sokol, co-author. *Musicworks*, 29 (Fall 1985).

"About *Changes: 64 Studies For 6 Harps*." *Perspectives Of New Music*, 25 (1987).

A History of 'Consonance' And 'Dissonance.' New York: Excelsior Music Publishing, 1988.

"Crossings," *Musicworks*, 41 (Summer 1988).

"About Alvin Lucier," Catalog for Wesleyan University (November 1988).

photo: Gene Bagnato

"BLUE" GENE TYRANNY / Introduction

"BLUE" GENE TYRANNY was born Robert Sheff in San Antonio, Texas, on January 1, 1945. He studied piano with Meta Hertwig and Rodney Hoare, and harmony and orchestration with Otto Wick. By the time he started high school, Sheff was studying composition privately with Frank Hughes at Trinity University. He also met and became friends with an upper-classmate, composer Philip Krumm. Together, they gave a series of concerts at San Antonio's McNay Art Institute, performing (and in some instances, premiering) works by John Cage, Richard Maxfield, and Philip Corner, as well as their own music. In other concerts at the time, the teenage pianist was playing the musics of Bartók, Webern, Schoenberg, Satie, Ives, Alan Hovhaness, Christian Wolff, Yoko Ono, Dick Higgins, George Brecht, and La Monte Young.

At the urging of composer William Bergsma (who had heard him sight-read the accompaniment of a Richard Strauss horn concerto), Sheff interviewed at Juilliard in 1962, just after graduating high school. Although accepted by the school, he rejected Juilliard's conservative atmosphere and redundant curriculum, and decided instead to take a bus to Ann Arbor, Michigan. There Sheff rejoined Philip Krumm and became involved with the legendary ONCE Group, an association of performing composers which included Robert Ashley, Gordon Mumma, Donald Scavarda, George Cacioppo, and Roger Reynolds. Shortly before his eighteenth birthday, a piece of Sheff's was played at a ONCE Friends concert.

Prevented by residency restrictions from attending the University of Michigan, Sheff maintained his association with Ann Arbor's new-music scene while supporting himself as a statistician. He left Michigan in 1970, accepting Robert Ashley's invitation to teach at Mills College in Oakland, California. Besides giving classes on music history, theory, and recording-studio techniques, he was also a technician at the Mills Center for Contemporary Music. Around this time, partially in response to William Shockley's notorious theories of race and genetic inferiority, Sheff adopted the name "Blue" Gene Tyranny. Inaugurated while touring as pianist in Iggy Pop's band, that name would have claim to a considerable reputation by the early '80s, both for 25 years of composing electronic and instrumental works, and for collaborating on Robert Ashley's landmark series of video operas, *Perfect Lives (Private Parts)*. Tyranny's renown as an improvising pianist also took off then, with the release of his breakthrough performance of *The Intermediary* (1982). He has since performed concerts internationally, often combining his spontaneous pianism with interactive electronics, as documented in his collection *Free Delivery* (1990).

In 1983, Tyranny relocated to New York City, where he currently lives. He has continued his association with Ashley, participating in numerous premieres of his music, as well as performing as pianist for such composers as Laurie Anderson, Jon Gibson, Peter Gordon, and Ned Sublette. He has also created music for dances by Timothy Buckley, Rocky Bornstein, and Stefa Zawerucha; plays by Pat Oleszko and the Otrabanda Company; and videos by Kenn Beckman and John Sanborn. He has received two New York Dance and Performance Awards (Bessies) for his dance scores, and a New York Foundation for the Arts fellowship in Music Composition.

Providing so much music for so many different people and situations has sometimes obscured the range of Tyranny's own work. My book *Sonic Transports* (de Falco Books, 1990) attempted to correct that imbalance; readers are referred to its essays and interview for information regarding earlier pieces such as *Harvey Milk (Portrait)* (1978) and *The Intermediary*. For this volume of *Soundpieces*, I wanted to interview the composer about the status of two of his long-term projects. Speaking at my home in New York City on November 23, 1992, he described the 25-year history of his *Country Boy Country Dog* music, and outlined his work on *The Driver's Son (Insight)*, the first of a projected cycle of six audio storyboards for singers, instruments, and electronics.

"BLUE" GENE TYRANNY / Interview

Q: Could you describe your initial work on the *Country Boy Country Dog* music when you were in Michigan in the late '60s?

TYRANNY: I'd been recording natural sounds since I was a little kid in Texas. I had a wire recorder (World War Two technology!), and you'd edit by literally cutting and soldering the wire. Later in high school I earned enough money playing for voice lessons to get a tape recorder, and I did a lot of cut-up pieces with Phil Krumm when we started doing those concerts at the McNay Art Institute. I also just recorded all the time. I really liked it, but there weren't really any portable recorders then.

After I got to Ann Arbor from Texas in 1962, David Behrman said — I think it was 1966 — that he was editing the Odyssey series for Columbia Records and would I give him a piece? He didn't specify a tape or electronic piece, but I decided to do one with natural sound. I was very, very interested in the density of natural sounds. (There was this kind of synaesthesic thing with dimensional painting — I loved Rauschenberg's work from early on.) I thought that there was in the sound itself a music that was not generally regarded as music. It had none of the structural elements that we would call music, but nevertheless, it was sound and it was affective and caused emotions. People tend to just call them sound effects or environment effects for films or plays (of which I did several in Ann Arbor), or use the sound to represent some mythological scenario, as in many *musique concrète* pieces. At the time, like with all works that really mean anything, I was captivated and I didn't know why; it was doing something to me or I was entranced with it, and I didn't know why. This must be the same for everyone. You have experiences like this, and maybe much later on down the road, as they say, you figure out what you've been struggling to understand. So now, the way that I understand what was happening to me then, was that in daily life there was a certain spirituality; there was a real depth at the dynamic level — the movement and make-up of sounds, beyond images of behavior, beyond images of society, beyond language, beyond things you were supposed to think. There was this dynamic truth to the universe. There's a kind of an analog of it, which I recently read in a text on Mahayana Buddhism. The Mahayana idea is that nirvana is not separate from samsara, the world of phenomena; that nirvana is discoverable through it and is simultaneous with it. So it's not like having to wait to leave this veil of sorrows and go to heaven. This understanding seems to me to be fundamentally true; to my nature, that is a true thing. That idea may not appeal to another person, and that's fine.

So David asked me for the piece, and I recorded it for about half a year, all over Ann Arbor, with the idea of getting myself in places where I would normally listen, and in places where I would normally not be at all, at different times of day or at different distances. There was also the idea of different kinds of walks, random walks or very distinct geometries, which grew up with the idea of doing the piece. Since then, it's generated all the ingredients of a score that I've yet to formalize and put together on paper. I intend to do that by the time this record is finished.

Q: That score would be *How To Make Music From The Sounds Of Your Everyday Life*?

TYRANNY: That's what it was originally called. Now I'm having a problem just with the little words. (I wrote to Bob Ashley recently and I said, "I wish words were as easy for me as notes.") At one time, I wanted to call it *How To Make Music From The Sounds Of Your Daily Life*. What the title seems properly now to be, with the process and with the relationship of the person doing the piece to the sounds, is *How To Discover Music In The Sounds Of Your Daily Life*, rather than "make music," because we're always trying to make things and I don't mean that. What I mean is how to release music, how to discover aspects of it, how to discover the interrelationships of how the sound is working.

The initial tape piece was recorded and then organized into two channels that were each monophonic; two monophonic channels running at the same time. One channel is labeled "inside" and one channel is labeled "outside" by a voice at the beginning. This has to do with where they were recorded: a relatively inside space or a relatively outside space. It also can indicate something contextual or psychological, where one could say that this is an inside state or an outside state. I also wanted to deal with that idea: Toward the end the channels switch and then go back to their original positions. What I didn't have the equipment to do then was to cross-modulate the two channels — that came later because it required other electronics. But the initial tape piece, the *Country Boy Country Dog* piece, was just these two monophonic channels with a lot of editing. If I were to do it again, I would not edit because the editing gives it a little too much the aspect of collage and symbolism; I'd do it all in real time. So that was the piece I gave David.

Q: But it was never released on a Columbia Odyssey lp?

TYRANNY: It was never released. David released several pieces on the Odyssey label — a wonderful series that included Pauline Oliveros and Richard Maxfield. This was at the great outpour of new music in the latter half of the '60s, partly because the Beatles were interested in Stockhausen. People wanted to hear unusual things, so suddenly record companies of all sizes started putting out enormous amounts of new music. Columbia decided to experiment with their Odyssey label, but apparently David's producer thought the piece was not music, and he wouldn't let him put it out. Maybe it's just as well, because I've had the opportunity to work on other aspects of the piece and think about it over the years.

I realized that the sounds did not exist in exclusively separate inside and outside spaces. When you hear sound naturally, it's in a large field, and sounds are banging against each other and modulating each other and doing all sorts of things. So I wanted a way to amplify that relationship, and the only way to do it was to cross-modulate the channels. That possibility existed once the analog synthesizer came in. I learned the basic cross-modulation patch-up from Tom Zahuranec, a graduate student at the Mills College Center for Contemporary Music, who showed it to me on the Buchla synthesizer. The output of oscillator one goes to the program of oscillator two, and the output of oscillator two goes to the program of oscillator one. So you have an X, and that's the basic cross-modulation setup. That way you get very complex, almost unpredictable things, because you're setting up a field in which everything affects everything. That's starting to affect our intellectual life in the late part of this century, with chaos theory and fluidics — a lot of things where the activity of the whole field is being considered.

So I used that hook-up, but instead of applying it to oscillators, I used it for filters and for many kinds of different devices. A basic setup would be taking one of the channels of natural sound, putting it through a filter, and looking at just a very small bit of the frequencies — only a hundred cycles here, and then a hundred cycles here, and so on. So it was just a window, and there would or would not be activity there, according to whether there was any on the tape itself. Then that window would be translated into an envelope voltage and that would be the control and would drive a module of some sort. And I would do the same thing with the other device, and then set them up in that cross-modulation series. That enabled the process to do two things at once. One was to look at very fine aspects of the sound and derive melodic, harmonic, and rhythmic information.

Q: Information as electronic sound.

TYRANNY: As electronic sound, from the natural sounds. That was one step. The second step would be to see how the different electronic sounds, the "inside" and the "outside" channels, intermodulated each other in a large field. So I wound up with lots and lots of these analyses which I've called transforms — not because they transform from one state to another, but they were the intermediate state. (The idea of *The Intermediary* also works in here, as you can see.) All these transforms were done through the '70s — it required this new equipment and couldn't really have been done in the '60s. Some time in the future I'd like to design a portable, handheld device that would both create transforms in real time and also record them.

Most recently I've done several kinds of digital-sampling transforms — which also required new equipment. Tom Hamilton and I did this while working on the album. At this point now we're still working on it, but we've finished the natural-sound piece with several of the transforms — the original analog ones — plus a couple of these new digital transforms. And that would not have been possible except for the digital sampling available now and the very fine, step-by-step analysis. There are also several experiments that I want to try, such as matting and crossfading the entire retrograde of a transform precisely against the original forward motion, and producing phase phenomena; a shadow world at the exact point that "inside" crosses or meets "outside" (X marks the spot, so to speak); things that I have intuited about the sounds while working on them. "Intuit" doesn't refer to ESP; it's the sense that you don't find out things until you set the process in motion. Once activity starts, ideas then lead to other ideas, spontaneous things happen, etc. So things are hidden only in the sense that they're not activated to our minds, or in our minds, or in the world.

Q: The initial tape piece was called *Country Boy Country Dog?*

TYRANNY: Yes, but I didn't set out to do a particular contextual thing; I didn't set out to do a piece about country boys and country dogs. The piece is open contextually; the score is a procedural score — it just says that this is a relationship that you're working on with your daily existence, and it can have any content, whatever will be. It just happened that, in Ann Arbor, Michigan, in 1966, when I was in a rock band, people were saying jokes about "What a dog he is," jokes about boys and dogs, and there were the sounds of dogs and boys — and other rural sounds because Ann Arbor, although it's a college town, is surrounded by rural Michigan. That just happened to be what happened, and so I decided to call the piece something that described that temporary aggregation of sounds. But I didn't set out to do that particular subject.

Q: How does your 1981 score, *The CBCD Variations* for soloist and orchestra, fit into the series?

TYRANNY: By '79, I had many analyses or transforms or intermediaries, which were melodic or rhythmic and so on. Then Bob Hughes asked me to do a piece for the Arch Ensemble For Contemporary Music. At that particular time, I had been in the process of transferring into musical notation one of the rhythmic codes that had been derived. When you hear it, it's just this single note that goes bingbing-bing-bing-bingbing. It's very telegraphic. I was getting very interested in this idea of messages — I suppose codes too, but I was calling them messages — which eventually worked itself into *The Intermediary*. There was also melodic information and I thought about combining that with the rhythmic information — both of which were also used for a piece called *The Forecaster*. And then eventually combining harmonic and phase information.

Let me backtrack just a second. The basic working parameters for analyzing the sounds are aspects of the Doppler effect: amplitude, phase, frequency, and time. Those for me always describe very clearly the functions of synthesizer modules, and also of electronic music and music in general, even traditional music. So I described things in terms of those. This is a clear way for me to express to myself what's going on with the sound, its amplitude, phase, frequency, and time characteristics. If I was explaining it to other people, musicians, I would sometimes use those terms, but it's easier to refer to them as the traditional melody, harmony, rhythm, and so on — although those are more subjective terms.

So I was transcribing these transforms into musical notation to see how this same information could be expressed by acoustic instruments, before the commission came for the *Variations*. The melodies though were actually limited by the various tunings of the oscillators, and would slip and slide and so were difficult to notate simply. If I were to do it now, it would be easier because I could just feed it into a computer and get a notation read-out that would be very accurate. But at the time, I thought that it would just be too complicated for players. So I took the rhythmic information and set it up in bars of 5/4 — it seemed to graph out very nicely that way, and very accurately too, so that I could put on the tape, read the notation, and beat time along with it. (This procedure is different from the idea of music imitating natural sounds — you know, orchestral pieces that sound like birds, or *Pacific 231* which tries to sound like a train. Maybe it's the other side of that.)

What I did was essentially tune the orchestra to specific four-note modes: One was a "happy" mode and one was a "sad" mode. The happy mode was Eb-F-Bb-C, which is just open; it's sort of neutral. The so-called sad mode was G-Ab-C-D — the minor second gives this kind of interior, sighing quality to it. That partly came about because I was also teaching a jazz literature class at Mills, and I was very interested in Bessie Smith's remark that she sang only in these two modes, one of which was this happy mode and one of which was this sad mode. (These are not her modes that I used; they're different but they're also contrasting modes.) I was also very interested in the notion of mixed emotions within the same piece, that that was possible without them being contrasted. In a lot of Western music, you have a lot of happy stuff, then some sad slow stuff, and then some happy stuff. But in a lot of world music, especially Indian music, the mixture of the emotions is more subtle than that: They're not really contrasted, they're intermixed. And I happen to love Indian music. But I'm not an Orientalist in that I'm not trying to imitate Indian music. I think a music has to grow up in a certain place and culture and so on; I think it just belongs there. I think everybody should hear everything, but I think you should find your own music.

So the orchestra piece had as its working materials the modes which were then transcribed and rotated and modulated and stretched in certain ways as the piece progresses. This is a raga idea, that notes stretch or go back as the day changes, so you get different notes but they're not really different notes; they're just different tensions of the note, or different extensions in space, emotional and otherwise. A large structure was worked out for the orchestra, and then I thought, what is an orchestra? What is this ensemble of people? And so, from this large body of material that stretched over a certain number of measures — I knew that it would require this many measures, this large a time, just to express the materials — I also thought that I wanted to express a kind of a social/political notion of these people being together. So the material was grouped into three larger phases or movements to describe some possible interrelationships of these people. The first movement is the strictest — it's almost the most traditional — in that it's conducted and there are strict parts written, but gradually throughout it there are small sections in which notes are given with which people improvise in a kind of "chanting" style for a certain number of measures, while other people are playing the strict things. There's also a built-in short-term and long-term memory, in which a person plays a phrase of notes, then adds to that, but only after repeating something that was previously played in a more condensed, more neutralized or equalized form. It's this particular idea of memory in a controlled society, where memory is a flattening out of previous experience, of previous emotion, of previous images. And that happens within each part. The score is highly contrapuntal, but there's also this individual process going on with each line. In the first movement, the soloist is supplying notes and the orchestra echoes those notes. Then, within each part, as they echo the various notes, a person entering will summarize what has come before in another person's part, but summarize it in this very flattening-out context. It's like learning by imitation, but with surface values only; a reduced, neutralized version, sort of a bourgeois idea of mentality. In the second movement, this mechanistic activity is slowed down and at points stops, so there are just resonances, like meditations: Where are we at, what are we doing, what's going on? Here the orchestra is supplying notes and the soloist is echoing notes by a different process. The first movement is saying, in a sense, the society is more important than the individual; the second movement is saying the individual is more important than the society; in the third movement, everybody's the same — like Cage's idea of the ensemble of soloists. It's not written like John would have written it, of course, but it's very open, and at the end it has completely open phrases which people can handle any way they want.

Q: I understand that you include a performance of the *Variations* in this *Country Boy Country Dog* cd you're completing, but with some changes?

TYRANNY: It's only been reduced; it's still the piece. There were physical considerations — there weren't many strings in the ensemble, but the score as I learned later required a fuller body of strings. So I've duplicated some of that with a synthesizer. There were only one or two sections that I've left out. Some for reasons of proportion for the piece as a whole. In others I was trying for the image of a song — a large repeating loop — emerging from otherwise quasi-random activity, but I felt this image wasn't fully achieved.

Q: Around the same time as the *Variations*, you also created *The CBCD Concert*, in which you improvise at the piano to a tape of some of the transforms that you'd derived.

TYRANNY: Yes. They were combined in a structure on the tape where each of them was on for an equal amount of time, distributed in different ways in a matrix structure. But I'm still not satisfied with that piece. I just have to work on it — there were several problems, such as matching the micro-interval transforms with an instrument in standard tuning, namely the piano, and finding alternatives to that. Another problem was the characters of the transforms themselves — but I think there is a better timbre mix of some of the newest and oldest transforms now. Another thing I wanted to remove from the mix was the steady pulse — the illusion I was trying to create was that of an increasing pulse rate, where a change in the rate of a listener's scanning would make the exact same materials (upon which the scan was apparently imposed) seem to distort in some way: the classic foreground/background illusion that I had worked with in an early piece, *Silent Sound/Silent Talk/Silent Sculpture.* But in the first mix of the *Concert,* it began sounding to me only like an accompaniment figure. There's some other solution to be found, possibly in rhythmically gating the mix of the transforms, or modulating some other method of marking the passage of time.

Q: Will the *Concert* be part of the cd?

TYRANNY: No. The *Variations* will be on the cd, there'll be several of the transforms, the original tape piece, and the *Intro* which gives the basic tuning modes that I talked about before; that's a free canon in the traditional sense, and there'll be some piano playing with it.

Q: Your 1990 cd of piano performances, *Free Delivery,* has a performance of the *Intro* in which you play along with a tape of the modes. I was wondering if the *Country Boy Country Dog* cd would then appear without that section.

TYRANNY: There'll be an *Intro.* But the aesthetic for the cd is to go to the bare essentials. I like that very much, and it's sounding good. I think that, in the case of the *Intro,* we may just have a hint of a piano at the very beginning, and then never hear it again. I think we're probably just going to hear the six-part free canon. It's beautiful in itself, and I like it. Also it serves its function more clearly: It's a tuning, an introduction to the tuning of the orchestra piece. The pieces on the cd are arranged to describe the passage of a day, including dreams and daydreams "with and without images"; the *Variations* become a kind of evening concert where the musicians recall the events of the day under the starry sky of eternity.

Q: All but one of the tracks on *Free Delivery* are live performances. How interested are you now in performing concerts of solo-piano improvisations?

TYRANNY: My first inclination is to say it depends on the piece, but it always depends on the piece, so that's not much of an answer. I'm very interested in the idea of treating the keyboard as a calculation device, almost as if it were an abacus or a computer keyboard — *The Keyboard Calculation Etudes.*

I've stopped even thinking of the word improvisation — there's just music-making. I'm not being nitpicky about it. I think this weird situation has grown up in the last couple of hundred years or so, in which people make a big distinction between written music and so-called improvised music. I recently saw the movie *Tous Les Matins Du Monde,* about Marin Marais' music, and his teacher Sainte-Colombe who sat in a shed and improvised on the viola d'amore, and every once in a while wrote down a melody he liked. But when the notations were played, there was tremendous freedom: There was the whole practice of *notes inégales*, unequal notes, where even if the notes were written equally, they were played with tremendous rhythmic freedom, and then with so-called ornaments and embellishments — which are properly called inflections or gestures, because that's what's really going on; they pull the emotion, they don't merely ornament it. So when you ask about solo-piano improvisations, I would shy away from even using that word, and say instead solo-piano pieces, and of course they're going to be played with a lot of spontaneity. I don't mind if somebody says improvisations, but I don't in any sense distinguish them from the pieces that are written down. The writing down is just an intermediate act of notating simply to have something to refer to. But it's no different from a procedural score in which words notate things for you to do. In practice, in reality, there's no difference — at least for the music I make and for the way my friends make music. This doesn't mean that we don't play some very strict things sometimes. The line that I liked very much in *Tous Les Matins Du Monde* was Sainte-Colombe's remark to Marais when he first sat down and played: "Monsieur, you make music but you're not a musician." That means a lot to a musician, it really hits home. The guy's skilled in sound, he can read very well, he has all the technical abilities, he even pleases audiences, etc., but music isn't really in his soul, he doesn't give everything for it — it's an objectification of sound. It's not that the sound should express some static, internal, subjective state. For me, when you're making music, you are extremely sensitive to everything that's happening, and also to the linear flow of what's happened to that point, but not in a memory sense — or maybe in a very different sense of memory. In this case, the subjective is all the world, including you. The Upanishads say that the highest meditation, one of the greatest meditations, one of the most wonderful meditations, is when you consider everything as being subject; in a sense, apprehending the suchness of everything, including inanimate things — even a dried-up old stick that you come across in the woods can suddenly shock your soul. That's a completely different relationship to the world — not even a relationship, it's not even that abstract; just a way of going about acting and feeling, which we seem to miss in materialistic society.

That super-subjective state is really what happens when you're making the music. Any real musician will say that, when they're rehearsing, they always know they're not rehearsing to make it sound exactly like they're rehearsing. They're doing it only to work on the technical aspect of whatever has to happen. But they always know that when you get into that concert hall or wherever it is, when you start making the music, the music is something other than the notes; it's something other than the techniques; it's something other than any kind of images you have about the music.

Q: In the last few years, you've gotten a number of commissions for piano scores. How comfortable are you with writing music for other pianists?

TYRANNY: I know the people these pieces are written for, and I like their playing. They're all uniquely different pianists. Double Edge, the piano duo — and then individually Nurit Tilles and Edmund Neiman — are very different kinds of pianists. Lois Svard and Joe Kubera are also very different. I like things about each of their playing, which are not things that I would normally do.

Q: Does that enter into composing for them?

TYRANNY: In a sense, but in the most general way. Not like because they're good at playing scales, I then put a lot of scales in. No, it's not like that. In Lois's playing, I enjoy the lyricism of her tone and pacing, so I wrote the *Nocturne With And Without Memory* for her, which was about resonances and about making melodies vertical and various kinds of very odd things that start to happen.

What's happening now — if I can get just a little bit away from this, and then come back to it — is that I'm trying to figure out what my relationship to tonal music is and has been. That all fits in with the feeling that I always wanted to bring emotion and structure together in compositions. And they do come together in the dynamical properties of sound, and in many other ways. In emotional experiences — not just musical ones — it seems that there are truths hidden, not only ethical principles learned finally by the heart. Like when you get obsessed with something, for good or bad, there's something in it which you learn. Sometimes you just learn how not to get in those states; you see your mind at work and then eventually you just don't do that anymore. This is the peaceful experience of change, where you feel everything is devoid or empty of a specific self. You're always challenged to learn through life, you just are, whether you do or not.

And so tonal music, to me, has always seemed like modal psychology: within a tonal piece, there's a certain image, there's a certain emotion, there's a certain closedness to the experience. People talk about achieving closure, which is a yuppie psychological cliché that I think is kind of disgusting, to say the least. A cruel aspect of society is to turn people into characters and life into events in order to fit some program — to speak of people as economic units or misfits or too old to make the calculations, to speak of "closing" a relationship in order to "put it behind you," and to say, "If I ever get that way, I hope somebody will just shoot me." Closedness is interesting only in the intense dynamics of a relatively closed society, or a closed mental loop, which is a modal experience, and which means a certain emotion is being referred to. And aside from music, those experiences affect other parts of our lives, they're interrupted by other things — they're not closed. Otherwise, you don't learn, or truly feel. So it seems to me that tonal pieces are just like those things that seem relatively closed or relatively confined. But I wanted to find ways in which they would not be closed, where emotional things would extend into so-called intellectual things, into physical things — all the dynamical truths of the phenomenal world. And extend beyond ourselves too. Making the piece *No Job, No Warm, No Nothing* for Peter Gordon's concert

"Trust In Rock" was the first time that I very consciously tried to write a piece that was like a song, and then modulated it out of being a song: Aspects of it were taken, things were sampled literally, other kinds of musical processes that seemed somehow to fit with the song and which were part of the initial ingredient, but seem to extend that kind of relationship of the song to the world. The pieces I wrote for Lois, for Nurit, and for Double Edge all have this idea that there is a relatively defined emotional experience, the tonal piece, which is then extended into a dynamical world and we learn from that.

Q: We're invited to look beyond it, to go further rather than to stop.

TYRANNY: Absolutely. It doesn't stop. Actually, a piece of music never stops, if the truth be told. Even if there's a cadence, it doesn't stop. There's an old Chinese adage about music, where they say that the real music is after the musicians stop playing. And that's very true. What it's done to you is much more what music is about. I believe when we refer to transparency in music, we're referring to that experience. We value transparency not just because of Debussy's music or that wonderful recent performance of John Cage's *Atlas Eclipticalis*, but because that quality reflects the experience of feeling what the music has done to us after the sounds have stopped.

So to get back to writing the piano pieces. I don't want to write the music so that the other pianists sound like me. Of course my way of playing the piano, my choices, etc., will make them sound like me to a certain extent, but I'm much more interested in what they'll do with it, and also try to make it open-ended enough so that their choices of the moment come in too. *The Great Seal,* which I wrote for Double Edge, is much more like that. *The De-Certified Highway Of Dreams,* which I also wrote for them, is a summary of themes once composed for *The Driver's Son (Insight),* and contains no open sections, but is open to interpretation and original inflections.

Q: But other scores you've written have different performance freedoms or sections open for improvisation?

TYRANNY: Yes. The *Nocturne With And Without Memory* is notated in open notation, with no bar lines, so it's almost like mensural notation, in which things are relatively long or relatively short.

Q: Would you be interested in playing those scores yourself?

TYRANNY: Oh yeah. Well, I did with the *Nocturne* that I wrote for Lois: the *Five Takes* on it, which is on *Free Delivery.*

Q: That's not really the same thing, though, is it?

TYRANNY: It's not the same, no. It's just using the material from the first two pages. But I described to her how a lot of the runs, etc., even though they're notated equally in 32nd notes or whatever, should be just in the spirit of the moment — she can just stop on things and suspend time, and so on.

When I teach piano, I teach a kind of scanning method. You see a melody and it's all written out — say it's four measures long. Most of the students will play from the beginning of the melody, aiming to go toward the end of the melody, and that's its conclusion. What I do is point to some other place in that line and say, "This is what you're heading for now. Go toward this point, and then fall away from it." And suddenly it makes a whole different sense in the line; it's a breakthrough, and they start to realize that it's really them playing the music. And this works with almost any music: I taught a piano class at Bucknell University last year, and the kids would get up and play Mozart pieces, Bach, Alban Berg's Sonata. The first thing you'd have to teach them is how to relax, physically — that's always a big problem. And then to get them to be intellectually relaxed, to relax the brain muscle, so that they really get that idea that the music is not just the notation, and the notation is not even the expression of, say, Beethoven's initial desires — if we could even know such a thing, which I doubt.

Q: Beethoven might not even have known it.

TYRANNY: Now that's an intriguing idea. And things are supposed to change all the time anyway. Taking Beethoven as an example, we have all these letters saying, "Gee, the musicians now don't play the music any way near the way that we used to play it 20 years ago. They play it totally different." And here we are countries and almost two hundred years removed. I suppose it would be comparable to an acting class in which you read a famous speech by Shakespeare, with all sorts of different inflections, and with an unrevealed background emotion that drives the words dynamically, so that the actual meaning would be that background emotion, not the words that you hear. Of course, this doesn't mean that specific words or notes are in any way secondary. The whole process of sensory recognition, concept, and verbalization is necessary for what we call consciousness.

So back to the way I would play what I had written for Lois: I would just scan it in another way. And that may happen right at the moment of performance: I would suddenly feel that this chord or this moment or this point, this statement, somehow needed to be made or played at this time, even though I had rehearsed something totally different.

Q: You've been careful elsewhere to refer to *The Driver's Son* not as an opera but as an audio storyboard. Could you explain the difference between the two forms?

TYRANNY: An audio storyboard is like a procedural score, in that there are several possible realizations, one of which could be what we call an opera. But I could see *The Driver's Son* being a cd-rom maze or game; it certainly will be a recording; it could be a television piece — not a television piece of an opera, but a television piece; it could be a theater piece, in which case it would be more like an opera; it could be a novel; it could be a radio play. The material I'm working out is literally a storyboard, and it has to do with sound, ergo it's audio — that's pretty simple! Because it's a form which is a potentiality, I think it's more proper to call it an audio storyboard. Suppose I wrote it as an opera, and then someone wanted to make a film out of it, like they make *Carmen* into many different versions. Those versions really tend to be cartoons of the idea; they tend to be not what Bizet intended at all. I've nothing against writing an opera — or writing a piano piece — it's just that particular ideas like *The Driver's Son* and the other storyboards that would be associated with it, came to me in a form that did not say, "This is a stage work." I don't know what else to say about it. Whatever feeling and whatever process that made this piece emerge, this simply seems to be the proper way in which to express this idea.

Q: Do you see this piece as a special opportunity to write for voice?

TYRANNY: Yes. I haven't done many pieces which are based primarily on the voice, as, say, Bob Ashley's work is. I see the vocal information and the dynamic information, the instrumental and electronic information, as equal in this piece. Of course, our psychoacoustic mechanisms are all set up to receive the voice; its particular frequency range and inflections are associated with our primary existence and sense of meaning. When *The Driver's Son* is realized as a theater piece, I want the video-synthesizer information and the vocal information and the instrumental information to be equal.

Q: When you say "vocal information," do you mean the text, or are you talking about something more?

TYRANNY: I'm talking about the text and the singing and the electronic modulation that will happen to the voice. Those modulations will indicate very particular kinds of states. For example, the Narrator's voice is transformed by a kind of audio "morphing," a waveform interpolation, whenever he relates a story told in the second person.

Q: You've written that "the basic theme of *The Driver's Son* is the creation of the feeling of meaning through the visual sense." Is this idea treated just in the libretto, or is the feeling of meaning literally created in a visual way for the audience during the performance of the piece?

TYRANNY: The first at the moment; the second as a kind of a hope. I'm just starting to work on it, but the primary idea of the live video synthesis is almost like a paint-by-numbers set. There are all sorts of points of position information and momentum stuff which will appear on a screen for the video synthesis. Then that person will draw pictures and make meaning out of this neutral information, and that will be different in every performance, even though the dots are in the same place. Those dots will be like the notes for the musician: They will reflect the cyclic structure as well as the dynamic by-products of the vocal line — rhythms and melodies triggered by the vocal line. The audience should get the sensation either that something is being revealed (like an ancient message in a graphic code suddenly broadcast from the moon) or that the music is being made up at the moment. The piece I did for Nurit Tilles, *We All Watch The Sun And The Moon (For A Moment Of Insight)*, is based on a notion of combining physical and spiritual cycles of the sun and the moon with the growth proportions of a Saquaro cactus, to make a time schedule for gradually revealing a whole piece of music I previously composed. The piece is revealed very gradually by the interference of the cycles, which helped me pick out notes at certain points. But, to repeat, the sensation for the audience should be, depending on their particular psychology, either that something that's already been made up is being revealed, or that something is being made up at that moment. Or a mix of the two — the illusion of time from two directions simultaneously, like in *The Intermediary*. So it depends on whether the listeners are backward looking or future looking, I suppose. I call this compositional procedure "Sleeping Beauty In Camouflage," which is also the title of Act III, and is also a metaphor of the built-in dynamics of the mind, which reveal themselves in interaction with perceptions, the mind as a Sleeping Beauty in camouflage — in this case, not a catatonically passive heroine but one fully aware and waiting. Part of the psychology in *The Driver's Son* text is that things should be equally physically real and psychologically illusionary. If I can achieve it — that's part of the art, to do that. I'm interested in time. Music is fundamentally an art about the time sense, and I'm really trying to get at a way of expressing music through non-linear time. This compositional approach I think will create that — there's still the linearity of the performance, of course.

There are several new pieces for *The Driver's Son (Insight)*: music for Act II, called "The Happy Landing," the name of a roadside convenience store in the shape of a 1930s airmail carrier plane. This music is based on the image of large, out-of-control oscillations coming gradually back to rest, like an airplane (or maybe an intense emotional state) pulling out of a tailspin in an old war movie — leaping arpeggios statistically averaging out, a feel of Vedic chant combined with an imitation of an automated arpeggio setting on a synthesizer. Another structural element is "The XYZ Harmonic Paths" on the image of evolution as a spreading-out rather than as a hierarchical ordering (resonances from the big bang — another notion for a piano piece for Joe Kubera). And the other piece for *The Driver's Son (Insight)* is called "The Hitchhiker's Dream," based on a vertical reading of "The XYZ Harmonic Paths." In this sort of love song, gestures are sampled from the melody, which is made from high harmonics of the chords, and these samples are stacked up and modulated at different tempos all compressed into a small area, a sound somewhat like an earlier piece called *The Interior Distance* — matter perceived as being built up from flashes of energy in different intensities and tempos, from the molecular to grosser worlds. This mix is also notated as subdivisions in a single tempo, and the performers can pick which they want to read, although the results are not quite the same — in the first notation, the beat is externalized, and in the second, internalized. I'm also working on the form of the sixth and last audio storyboard in this series, which will be an interdimensional matrix — three-dimensional chess is an example — and will use simple transformational-lattice and rotation-fragmentation techniques from earlier pieces (the music for Phil Harmonic's *Stars Over San Francisco* and the music for "The Bar" in Bob Ashley's *Perfect Lives*, respectively).

Q: In reading the text for *The Driver's Son*, I was reminded of a wisecrack Thomas More makes in *A Man For All Seasons*. After explaining something, he adds, "I trust I make myself obscure." The libretto's flow of convoluted language and imagery really can't be picked apart as it goes by during a concert situation — I'm not even sure it can all be picked up in a single performance. Data accumulates which reinforces preceding information but which also tends to cancel it out because its own complexities have to be dealt with. Is that a fair description of what's happening, do you think, or am I misrepresenting the text?

TYRANNY: You're not misrepresenting it as it has been. I'm trying to make it simpler for the audience, and more graceful. But I do still want that sense of relationship to things that have come before, that there are these motifs, many of them (about 30 or 40 — I haven't counted), which must be referred to in each of the five acts of each of the audio storyboards, and expanded upon or added to, depending on the nature of the motif, from act to act. I do want there to be an experience of memory to the piece, a memory of comparison, a memory of addition, a memory of change. So there will be that density — like a landscape of potentially meaningful but well-defined images, including ideas as images. But I want the text to be much more graceful than it has been. I'm taking out a lot of the extraneous material and a lot of the syntactical material, and leaving the images, leaving more emotional connections than syntactical ones. There is not one single didactic message to "get," and the characters don't represent anything other than themselves. Instead, an environment, so to speak, is created in which the listener will experience the feeling of meaning being created through action described in visual terms, and related to the characters but without specific meaning being ascribed.

I wish the text was complete and I wish it was what I want it to be now so you could see it. But that'll give you some idea of what I'm working on. I agree with you, there is the immediacy of the new image of the moment, and a person would of course want to experience that. But I hope there would be enough space in which, just like in a good motion picture where something's going on, they could say, "Oh wait a minute, that refers to something that happened back then" — without the text becoming plot heavy. Plot is secondary in the piece. These motifs are very important, and depth of character is very important. The character of Tim, the biochemist and musician, and the character of John Prester, the auto mechanic and musician, come from very different backgrounds, different cultures even, but they are lovers and they've also been friends "for as long as they can remember" — or as long as they care to remember! In rewriting the script, I'm trying to make their feelings more overt. I didn't describe them as well as I had hoped, but I've thought a lot about them in the last two years, who they are.

After the *Harvey Milk (Portrait)* tape and *The White Night Riot*, I've hoped to create more pieces with gay characters, simply because we have to know more. I'm particularly interested in people like We-Wha, the Zuni berdache, where the role of the gay person — I even hesitate to use the word "role" — how their relationship with other people was very complex, was positive in many ways, was caring, and was very instructive. Because that's a kind of model for gay people, to think of their gayness as more than just a particular mode of sexual affection. (Which it is also, of course — there is a real physical and psychological connection of "id" and "libido," of the making of ideas and sex.) In many societies, gay people function as priests and intermediaries, or find themselves, in more banal situations, explaining husbands to wives and vice versa. We often find ourselves in those situations. I want to try to show examples of how gay people exist in the world, and what that feeling is. Harry Hay, one of the early founders of the gay movement, described gay consciousness as subject-to-subject consciousness. I think that's very true — at least in our behavior, which is not one set thing by any means. It's something that we kind of supply; it's saying, "I see you — you're more than an object, you're more than a situation, you're more than a victim of circumstance." That's the feeling and context I'm talking about — a more direct communication. Even if humans are set up, at least at the start, to see through a glass darkly, to know the world only as an imperfect reflection of their own desires, people — all people — still have the capacity to struggle out of that initial condition bit by bit, by everyday realizations, by social interactions and mutual aid, and in many other ways.

Q: What other pieces are you working on in this regard?

TYRANNY: I'm thinking of doing a song about Henry Cowell's imprisonment. I've always admired Cowell, as so many people have. He was the first person who was consciously avant-garde and talked about ultramodern music in the early part of the century. He very obviously did experimental music of many different kinds and at a very young age. He gave lectures and helped invent devices like the Rhythmicon. He wrote an incredible book, *New Musical Resources*, and helped set up the New Music press, etc., etc. The fact that such a compassionate and smart guy could be set up by some neighborhood hooligans who apparently accused him of having sex with an "underage" boy — I think he was 17, which wasn't that young! Then of course the conditions of it being in the 1930s, when homosexuality would hardly be mentioned. Plus Cowell's being, I guess, very private about that aspect of his feeling. He went to prison but while there he made the best of it. He created orchestras of the convicts; he corresponded with all the people that he had been working with; he was beloved by the people he encountered. He had so much internal strength and togetherness, even though this so-called "crime" was obviously something that he should have never been sent to prison for. He's certainly not the first well-known person who was assaulted for being gay. In this case, by a misuse of our legal system for that purpose; I regularly correspond with a prisoner who has had a similar experience. I would like to set that material about Cowell for many reasons.

Q: What text would you set for this piece?

TYRANNY: What I'm hoping for is to find much more personal writings of his. I would love to find something where he describes more of his feelings of the incident and how he was set up, and the fact of his different friends' reactions to it — certain well-known composers stopped talking to him after that point; other people did not abandon him at all. I guess what fascinates me is that he didn't treat himself as a victim of circumstance. But I would like to know if he ever wrote anything about the dynamics between him and the neighborhood kids who had set him up. This song would possibly be part of a cycle of three songs for Tom Buckner, about friendships under unusual circumstances, but I don't really know if this story is exactly part of that song series or not; it depends on what this relation was. I'm not quite sure what'll happen with the Cowell piece.

Q: Would the other songs in the series have gay themes too?

TYRANNY: No, not specifically. They are about friendships in unusual circumstances. The first song is *Somewhere In Arizona, 1970* which is about two guys who used to be very close friends but hadn't seen each other in 18 years. This is based on an actual hypnotic regression: One fellow showed the other what is apparently a secret base in Arizona, where several UFOs have been stored by the military. The song uses ten lines from the actual session conducted by Berthold Schwarz, and then I weave other descriptive material around it, without changing the facts. The music is built in arcs of increasing emotion, rhythm, and pitch sense — from open monologue, to chant, to full-blown song, and then the process re-starts; 12 mini-sections in all, grouped in four of these build-ups.

The other song is also about friendship, but will have very different content. It would be about Pope Sylvester II (whose earlier name was Gerbert d'Aurillac), who was what we would now call a natural scientist. He was before Giordano Bruno, at the turn of the first millennium, 1000 A.D. He emphasized scientific procedure in his writings, and may have invented a mechanical binary computer. But he also had a very strange, mythological history — not discouraged by the church — which described him as having studied magical arts as a youngster and having run away with the daughter of the magician that he studied with, and stealing a book of secrets. At night he slept suspended by ropes under bridges, so that he was neither on earth nor in heaven, and the stars could not see him so he could escape his fate. In the Campus Martius in Rome, there was a statue with a pointing hand marked with the words *Pecute hic,* "Strike here," which supposedly pointed to the hidden treasure of the Caesars. People would hit the hand and get no result. Gerbert finally figured out that the clue was where the shadow of the finger fell on certain bricks at noon. So late at night, he and his thieving chamberlain went back, dug up the bricks, and found a staircase that led to a room where a great banquet was set with gold implements. And the story goes on from there. I want to set this story, with some flashbacks to his having studied with the magician, and some reflections on his later-written, natural-science philosophy at the turn of the first millennium, his comments on the mass hysteria accompanying the imagined Second Coming at that time, the fear of the time. The early Christian texts tended to freely intermix eroticism, saintly writing, the occult, and materialism in the form of jewels and gold. All mixed together — you get a lot of this in Hildegard von Bingen's work, and apparently in the writings of this Pope too. But again, it's this friendship at a crisis moment which is the main theme.

Another piece I'm working on is called *Holding Hands (Broca's Area)*, which refers to hands being held in different positions. It's a formalization or amplification of an idea in *The Intermediary*, where I describe a lot of the music as prose music. Again, it grew from one of those impulses where you don't know at first exactly what you're thinking; it takes years to feel it out, to discover other things, to read what other people have written. Music is so beautiful that way. It's a research method which is not just objective; you can really bring all the information in. When I so-called improvise, I used to refer to that as prose music. Then, many years later, I read about Broca's Area in the brain, in which speech and hand movement are exclusively related; that's all the area deals with. There have been studies on the hand movements of infants, which show that in fact their hand movements are a form of language — which is something I've always felt. So a lot of this is starting to come together in this piece, which formally presents that idea but in an almost religious context, using formalized hand movements from the mudras from Indian Buddhism, from Javanese and Balinese dance, from ordinary gestures, from Tibetan Buddhist ritual readings, the way the mudras are used (and some are very hip — they snap their fingers and do things that look like what teenage kids in America do). There'll be one performer moving hands, and the other performer doing vocal gestures based on ideas about protolanguage, the mother language. The hand movements will be picked up electronically in a field by proximity detectors of various kinds, which will then trigger synthesizers and possibly other kinds of events, like light. Then that will be translated into realtime information, melodic and so on, for the singer.

Q: Would you want a dancer or a musician to do the hand movements?

TYRANNY: I was thinking of a musician — I think I'd do them. A dancer definitely could do them, but I don't want it to look like dance; I want it to look like a religious meditation of some kind. The piece should be very formal and almost meditative.

COMPOSITIONS

1958   *Music For Three Begins* for audiotapes and mixing engineer
1958   *How Things That Can't Exist May Exist* ongoing collection of
        theater/street events, including: *Do Not Do What You Are Doing
        At This Very Moment* (1958), *Penniless Australian Is Crated, Flies
        Home in 63 Hours* (1966), *Silent Sound/Silent Talk/Silent
        Sculpture* (1968), and *Random Arrest* (circuit design) (1973)
1960   *Ballad* for one to forty instruments/voices
1960   *The Interior Distance* procedural score; realization for orchestra, 1993
1962   *Meditation/The Reference Moves, The Form Remains* graph score,
        realization for chamber orchestra, 1963; for trio, 1991
1963   *Diotima* graph score, realization for flutes and audiotapes
1963   *Home Movie* animated score on film
1965   *Just Walk On In* theater piece, graph score
1966   *Closed Transmission* for IBM 7090 computer-generated sound
1967   *Country Boy Country Dog* for tape
1967   *How To Discover Music In The Sounds Of Your Daily Life*
        procedural score
1967   *The Bust* music for Megan Terry's play *Viet Rock*
1968   *Portraits* music for film by George Manupelli
1971-92 *The CBCD Transforms* electronic analyses
1972   Music for Phil Harmonic's *Stars Over San Francisco* procedural
        score (transformational lattice)
1972   *"How To Do It"* intentionally incomplete procedural score
1974   *Remembering* procedural score and realization for voice and
        electronics
1975   *My Song* episode in the video series *Klahoya* by Mary Ashley
1976   *A Letter From Home* procedural score; realization for voices and
        electronics, 1976; for trio — ascending series, 1991; for trio —
        descending series, 1993
1976   *No Job, No Warm, No Nothing* songs with modulation procedures
1976   *33 Yoyo Tricks* music for film by David White
1976-83 Harmonic/melodic material and piano improvisations for Robert
        Ashley's opera-for-TV *Perfect Lives*
1977   *Archaeoacoustics (Harmonic Fields of Unknown Peoples)* procedural
        score
1977   *PALS / Action At A Distance* procedural score
1977   *Taking Out The Garbage* videoscore
1978   *Harvey Milk (Portrait), Part I: The Action, Part II: The Feeling*
        for tape
1979   *The White Night Riot* for tape
1980   *The CBCD Concert* for soloist(s) and electronics

1981	*The CBCD Variations* for soloist and orchestra
1981	*The Intermediary* procedural score; realization for piano and computer with Joel Ryan, 1981
1983	*The Crack of Dawn* music for film by Philip Makanna
1984	*The CBCD Intro*
1986	*Proximology* music for dance by Timothy Buckley
1987	*Somewhere in Arizona, 1970* for voice and electronics
1987	*Extreme Visitations Just Before Sunset (Mobile)* for tape and piano
1987	*Brain Cafe* music for theater piece by the Otrabanda Company
1988	*Nocturne With And Without Memory* for piano
1988	*Labor of Love* music for dance by Rocky Bornstein
1988-89	*The Forecaster* for orchestra, decoding chorus, and time-transposing keyboardist
1990	*The Great Seal (Transmigration)* for piano duo
1990-93	*The Driver's Son (Insight)* audio storyboard
1991	*The De-Certified Highway Of Dreams* for piano duo
1992	*We All Watch The Sun And The Moon (For A Moment Of Insight)* for piano solo; orchestration for two string orchestras and piano solo
1992	*The Black Box* music for dance by Stefa Zawerucha
1993	*The Keyboard Calculation Etudes* for piano and other keyboards
1993	*Holding Hands (Broca's Area)* for voice and electronics

---

All compositions are in manuscript. Inquiries about scores should be sent to Performing Artservices, 260 West Broadway, New York, NY 10013.

DISCOGRAPHY

1978
Out Of The Blue
Lovely Music 1061 lp

1979
Just For The Record
Lovely Music 1062 lp
Performances of pieces by other composers: Robert Ashley's "Sonata," John Bischoff's "Rendezvous," Paul DeMarina's "Great Masters Of Melody," and Phil Harmonic's "Timing"

1980
Harvey Milk (Portrait)
Lovely Music 101-06 ep

1981
Real Life And The Movies, Vol. 1
Fun Music 21 cs

1982
The Intermediary
Lovely Music 1063 lp

The World's Greatest Piano Player
Antarctica 6201 lp

1984
Selected Pieces
Lantaren/Venster 8442 lp

1986
The More He Sings, The More He Cries, The Better He Feels ... Tango (excerpt)
Tellus 16 cs

Remembering
Mills College 001 lp

1990
Somewhere In Arizona 1970
Elektra/Nonesuch 79235-1 cs, -2 cd

Free Delivery
Lovely Music 1064 cd

1993
The De-Certified Highway Of Dreams
CRI 637 cd

Free Reading Of The Nocturne With And Without Memory (excerpt)
Nova Era 2002 cd

Country Boy Country Dog
Lovely Music 1065 cd

collaborations

with Robert Ashley:
Private Parts Lovely Music 1001 lp (1977); cd (1990)
Perfect Lives (Private Parts): The Bar Lovely Music 4904 lp (1980)

Music Word Fire And I Would Do It Again (Coo Coo) Lovely Music 4908 lp (1981)
Perfect Lives (Private Parts), complete TV opera in seven episodes, Lovely Music 4913-17 videocassette (1983); 4917.3 cd, 4913 & 4947 cs (1991)
Atalanta (Acts Of God) Lovely Music 3301-3 lp (1985)

guest artist

with Laurie Anderson:
Strange Angels Warner Brothers 25900-1 lp, -2 cd, -3 cs (1989)

with Robert Ashley:
Automatic Writing Lovely Music 1002 lp (1979)
Yellow Man With Heart With Wings Lovely Music 1003 cd (1990)
Odalisque Lovely Music 3021 cd (1991)

with David Behrman:
On The Other Ocean Lovely Music 1041 lp (1978)

with Jacques Bekaert:
Summer Music 1970 Lovely Music 1971 lp (1979)
Jacques Bekaert IGLOO 008 (Brussels) lp (1980)

with John Bischoff:
Silhouette Lovely Music 101-06 ep (1980)

with John Cage:
Cheap Imitation Cramps 6117 lp (1977)

with Jon Gibson:
Rainforest/Brazil (He Was Not Disappointed) Lovely Music 3021 cd (1991)

with Peter Gordon:
Star Jaws Lovely Music 1031 lp (1978)
Casino Italian Records From The World EX 8Y (45 rpm) (1982)
"Siberia" Antarctica 6201 lp (1982)
Innocent CBS 42098 lp (1986)
Brooklyn CBS 42379 lp (1988)
Leningrad Express Newtone 110 cd (1990)

with Phil Harmonic:
Phil Harmonic's Greatest Hits Lovely Music 101-06 ep (1980)

with Jill Kroesen:
Stop Vicious Cycles Lovely Music 1501 lp (1983)

with George Lewis:
Chicago Slow Dance Lovely Music 1101 lp (1981)

with Van Rozay:
From San Jose Golden Vanity 1 lp (1980)

with the St. Francis de Sales Cathedral Choir and Ensemble:
Those Who See Light Cathedral 1975 lp (1975)

with David Tudor:
Microphone Cramps 6116 lp (1975)

with Peter Van Riper:
Sound To Movement VRBLU 10012 lp (1979)

with David Van Tieghem:
Safety In Numbers Private Music 2015 lp, -4 cs (1987)

BIBLIOGRAPHY

"A History Of ONCE: Music At The Boundaries." Mark Slobin, co-author. *Lightworks*, 14/15 (Winter 1981/82).

"20th-Century Avant-Garde." *All Music Guide.* Eds. Michael Erlewine and Scott Bultman. San Francisco: Miller Freeman, 1992.

CHRISTIAN WOLFF

photo: Gene Bagnato

CHRISTIAN WOLFF / Introduction

CHRISTIAN WOLFF was born in Nice, France, on March 8, 1934. In 1941 he came with his family to America, settling in New York City. He received his B.A. and, in 1963, his Ph.D. in Comparative Literature from Harvard. He took piano lessons in his early years, and had a few weeks of formal composition studies with John Cage; otherwise, he is essentially self-taught as a composer, and has been writing music since 1949. By the early '50s, Wolff was actively associated with composers John Cage, Morton Feldman, and Earle Brown, and the pianist David Tudor. With them, he participated as both composer and performer in a series of landmark concerts of indeterminate music.

Wolff's music of the 1950s and '60s brought ideas of indeterminacy into a unique rhythmic area, through his composition of scores that require the musicians to cue each other for the entrances and durations of their parts (*Duo For Pianists II*, 1958; *For One, Two Or Three People*, 1964). He is also a pioneer in composing scores which are independent of instrumentation (*For Five Or Ten Players*, 1962; *Burdocks*, 1971); which are available to non-musicians as well as to professionals (*Play*, 1968); which offer systems for improvisation (*Edges*, 1968); and which are purely verbal instructions, with no musical notation whatsoever (*Prose Collection*, 1968-71).

In the late '60s, Wolff was active in the British new-music scene, becoming friends with Cornelius Cardew and the other composers in his circle, including John Tilbury and Christopher Hobbs. His music was played by the Scratch Orchestra, an experimental ensemble founded by Cardew in 1969. By the early '70s, stimulated in part by his discussions with Cardew and pianist/composer Frederic Rzewski, Wolff started composing music with overt political content designed to promote ideas of democratic socialism. *Accompaniments* (1972), written for Rzewski, initiated his commitment to these ideas. Political concerns have informed his music since then, both the pieces with text (*Changing The System*, 1973; *Songs*, 1973-75; *Wobbly Music*, 1976) and his solely instrumental scores (*Peace Marches 1, 2*, and *3*, 1984; *Black Song Organ Preludes*, 1987; *Mayday Materials*, 1989).

An active performer as both pianist and electric guitarist, Wolff has played with numerous new-music luminaries over the years. Along with the artists mentioned above, he has performed his own and other composers' music with Alvin Lucier, Jon Gibson, Michael Byron, Maryanne Amacher, Wendy Chambers, Garrett List, David Behrman, Gordon Mumma, Ned Sublette, Philip Corner, Annea Lockwood, Alvin Curran, Charlie Morrow, and Kurt Schwertsik, as well as with the groups AAM and Musica Elettronica Viva. Wolff has also written music for choreographer Merce Cunningham. In 1975, he won the Music Award from the National Institute/American Academy of Arts and Letters.

Wolff taught in the Classics Department at Harvard from 1962 to 1970. He has also taught music at Mills College and was composer-lecturer at the Internationale Ferienkurse fuer Neue Musik at Darmstadt in 1972 and 1974, and composer-in-residence at the DAAD in Berlin in 1974. Currently he teaches Classics, Comparative Literature, and Music at Dartmouth College.

Christian Wolff lives in Hanover, New Hampshire, but is a regular visitor to New York City. During one of his trips to Manhattan, I spoke with the composer at the home of one of his friends on March 24, 1991. In our discussion, I was particularly interested to learn more about his experiences as a teenage composer, as well as his ideas concerning the dynamics of writing music with the intention of communicating specific political ideas.

CHRISTIAN WOLFF / Interview

Q: Were you musically active as a child, or did that develop after you came to the States?

WOLFF: Well, I was a child when I came to the States; I was seven when I got here. And I started piano lessons at about 11, 12, something like that. We came in very reduced circumstances, so we had no piano with us in New York until I was about 14 or 15. I had to go out to other people's houses to play the piano.

There was music in the family. My father had musical connections and was a very good friend of Adolf Busch and Rudolph Serkin and the musicians around them. They both lived in New York at the time and my parents would take me along to all sorts of musicales and concerts, so I had a large, extensive exposure to classical music from a very early age. There were no long-playing recordings then, but there was radio: WNYC was already operating and doing a full day's worth of classical music, so you could hear a fair amount that way. Otherwise, you had to get your music by going to concerts, which I did a lot of as a kid.

I got interested in pianists when I was in school, and I would go to as many concerts as I could — I'd usually go at intermission, and would slip in for free! And I got to know the repertoire that way: Bach through Brahms, more or less.

Q: So you were particularly interested then in pianists and their technique?

WOLFF: Yeah, right. In fact, for a while I had this notion that I would like to become a pianist. But I just didn't have it, and that established itself fairly early on.

Q: When did you start getting interested in contemporary music?

WOLFF: We spent time with this Viennese family — they were psychoanalysts — who had a summer place in Vermont. They used to commute down to Tanglewood, which was fairly straightforward in those days. (This is long before they had composers there or anything like that.) But the Juilliard Quartet had just started to play Bartók quartets and the Viennese school, Schoenberg, Berg, and Webern. And we went to this concert because the people were Viennese; they didn't like the music, but they went because it was Viennese. So I heard this concert of Schoenberg, Berg, and Webern, and I was just absolutely taken with that; I really thought this was great, this was wonderful. Which was for me very surprising because I had been extremely conservative in my musical tastes — in fact, obnoxiously so: I would boo at new-music pieces in concerts! I was really dreadful!

But this stuff seemed to me to be something. And about the same time, it was clear that I wasn't going to become a professional performer, that I just didn't have the skills for performance. But listening to all that music, I wanted to do something. I didn't want to just take it in passively. So I started trying to compose, entirely on my own. Somebody had given me a basic theory book that was wonderful: It had almost all the information you really need. Using it at first — this is before hearing that new music — I tried to make Bach-like pieces (not very successfully). But then, when I heard this other music, I suddenly thought, yes, this is what I want to do; I want to do something that just doesn't sound like anything else. I didn't want to imitate just that music, but the whole idea of starting new, starting all over, that suddenly caught my fancy. So that's when I started.

Q: You would have been about 14, 15?

WOLFF: I was about 15, 16, somewhere in there, yeah.

Q: Did you start tracking down scores by Schoenberg or Webern to see how they had done what they had done?

WOLFF: You know, I don't think I did, curiously enough. I just listened to the music and then did my own, which had obvious echoes. The fact that they could do the kinds of things they were doing suggested to me that I could also write atonal music, use noises, do all these various things — unconventional things from a classical point of view. But no, I didn't do it very systematically then. The whole notion of analysis didn't come up until I met John Cage. He took me as a student and we had a very short session of teaching. Among the assignments I had was to analyze the first movement of the Webern Symphony, Opus 21. And you couldn't get these scores — you had to go to the library for them. But he had gone to the library and copied out the first movement himself and that's what we were using.

Q: Other than your piano lessons, those sessions with Cage were as close as you came to studying music with someone?

WOLFF: Essentially, yeah.

Q: Had there been a point when you'd wanted to find some other teacher?

WOLFF: It did occur to me. When I still thought I had possibilities as a performer, I'd considered going to a conservatory instead of college. But I was pretty much discouraged from doing that — rightly, in retrospect. In those days, there was just no music going on at the university which seemed to me interesting. I went to Harvard, where there was Walter Piston — who was a great guy, actually — and Randall Thompson. But musically, for my own feeling, it was a desert. So I thought, all right, I'll do something else. Also, the notion I'd gotten very early was that there was no way to make a living out of being a composer; that seemed to me to be totally out of the question. So I thought I'd better see about doing something else, and since I had a lot of literature in my background — my father was a publisher and so forth — that's what I did. I started out doing English, but then I thought, no, there's too many people doing that, and I drifted into of all things Classics as a way of making a living to support my composing habit.

I would have liked to study with someone who would have allowed me to do what I thought was the thing to do at the time, but I just didn't see that anywhere — apart from the luck of having run into Cage. The other composer at the time whom I knew — in fact he was a neighbor of ours, sort of a friend of the family — was Varèse. And I had thought of asking to study with him, but then the Cage thing came up instead, and that was that. And Cage was so encouraging — he didn't seem to think it was a problem. We worked formally for only about six or eight weeks, and the reason we stopped was because he finally said, "Well, the only point of studying music is to learn about discipline. You seem to be able to impose your own disciplines, so we don't need to go on with this stuff." And that was it.

In retrospect, there are times I think it might have been quite useful to have done it and to have certain kinds of facility in writing, which extended study obviously teaches. If you have to turn out counterpoint exercises for so many months of the year, you get kind of handy at doing that, and presumably that can transfer to your own work. But that I didn't have, and still don't — writing comes hard; it's just this really hard work.

Q: Did you find it was difficult to get a job teaching music at a university without your having studied formally?

WOLFF: No, actually. The one I got I got really by accident. I started out as a full-time Classicist, and I taught for eight years at Harvard. Then, when that job ended, I was looking around for another one. For various personal reasons I had this connection at Dartmouth, and I went up there to interview for a Classics job. While I was there, I met Jon Appleton, who knew of me as a composer by then, and he said, "If you're coming to Dartmouth, you really should be part of the Music Department too." And I said, "Well, that's fine if you can arrange it." We had an enlightened Dean who thought this was a great idea and was not in the least bit disturbed that I hadn't any official credentials. So that was very nice.

Q: Had you wanted to teach music at Harvard but been stonewalled by the administration?

WOLFF: No, no. I could have done a music thing and then taught music, which is what people do now. But I didn't want to do that. I like to teach a lot, actually. But I did not want to be teaching something that I was myself working in creatively — it was just too much of a distraction and would muddy the waters.

Another way of looking at teaching is that you become an established composer and therefore you teach yourself, so to speak. And I certainly had no notion of anything like that. Teaching people counterpoint and harmony, which I myself had no particular interest in or training in or skill at, seemed to me totally ridiculous. And as far as teaching composition, I still don't know how to do it. It's like teaching poetry. You can obviously teach certain tricks — you teach people how to prepare a score properly and check various technical things — and you kind of encourage them, but what else can you really do in this day and age? Since we have no fixed styles, no standards so to speak, I don't think it can be done.

Q: Has teaching Classics fed something into your work as a composer?

WOLFF: Not directly, no. I think the connection is that I'm interested in teaching, in pedagogy. As somebody once pointed out to me, a lot of my music has a pedagogical character to it. Which is not something I deliberately chose to do, but I think that is the case. If there is a connection, it's on that level.

Q: Your music was performed in the '50s when you were 17, 18 years old. Was there ever the reaction that you were too young to be a serious composer?

WOLFF: I don't think so. Within the circle in which I found myself, that was not a problem; with Cage, Feldman, Brown, David Tudor, and so forth, I just happened to be the youngest one. And I was the one who went off to college — I suddenly disappeared from the scene because I had to go to college! So that was a little odd. But Feldman was 26, 27, and the rest weren't that much older. Otherwise, the question of my being accepted or not accepted was not an issue, because what we were doing was off from everything else.

Q: If the musicians were hip enough to want to play it, they wouldn't be bothered by the fact that you were 18.

WOLFF: Exactly.

Q: Your compositional use of cueing the musicians strikes me as really unique in Western music. Before your work, it was largely a non-issue: A composer would orchestrate a piece, and have, say, the flute stop and the clarinet enter, but one player wouldn't have to listen to the other for a cue to start. In jazz or in so-called ethnic or folk music, this situation is more common, but not in concert music.

WOLFF: Well, it is there at a certain level, by implication. When a string quartet plays, obviously they have to listen to each other. But you're right, it was essentially written into the scores so that, theoretically, if you did exactly what was written into the score, that should take care of it.

Q: By reading the score and counting the beat, the players would know when to enter. But your use of cueing reminds me of Zeno's paradox of motion, where he continuously halves the length between any two points, demonstrating that an infinite amount of space resides within any distance. You've shown that there's a whole world of rhythm to explore in that space between when the flute stops and the clarinet starts.

WOLFF: Yes, and I was interested in that. I was interested in two things. One was indeterminacy and the other was this thing of being just slightly off a fixed point. The fixed point is abstract in any case, but in classical music the notion of fixed points is very important: bar lines and all of that stuff. What I got interested in was the idea of just being a little bit off of it. And you can do that. Cornelius Cardew has some scores with conventional notations, but the instructions are to play just off the beat. I've never heard those pieces and I don't know if it really works. It's hard to make people do that, because the other model is so deeply ingrained and difficult to resist. Grace notes come the closest; grace notes and fermatas, you might say, are the two models for the kind of rhythm I'm interested in. If you have a grace note and you remove the beat, which is one way of looking at it, or if you have only fermatas, that would be the situation in which I operate. I didn't think of it that way at the time, but in retrospect that would be one way to describe it.

Q: Had you been listening much to jazz?

WOLFF: When I was a kid in high school, I used to go listen to Dixieland a lot. Which is not the same thing: The beat there is very square, although the improvisatory feeling is certainly there. And I liked that music a lot. It was the first non-classical music that I got into. In the late '40s and early '50s, popular music for my feeling was nowhere, it was awful — unlike now when it's really interesting, or has possibilities and is diverse; that's really where things are happening. But jazz I found really moving.

Q: But it wasn't a question of hearing the jazz musicians and thinking of your performers cueing each other.

WOLFF: No, no. I just kind of stumbled on it. It took two steps. The first indeterminate pieces I did were not cued. They were in a sense conventionally scored, insofar as time spaces were determined. But they were very irregular. I did it with seconds, and so you might have a space of two seconds — OK, that's pretty clear. But you might have one of 7/8 of a second, or 5-1/16 seconds: really irregular ones. And they were only spaces, and you were to do things within those spaces. But you didn't have to describe the space; you didn't have to have something beginning at the start or stopping at the end. You had this space and somewhere inside of that you did something. This music was for two performers: Frederic Rzewski and myself. We didn't have time to write a fully notated piece, and so I just stumbled on this idea. And it worked and we really liked doing it. Each of us would prepare our parts, but then when we started playing together, because we had these variable spaces within which to work, you would respond, almost inevitably, instinctively. And then also consciously you'd be responding to the other player, and in a way other than normal ensemble playing because you'd hear something and you could either play immediately after it, try to play with it, or wait a little bit before you play. So there's a whole range of possibilities there, which form a kind of improvisatory situation. I think it must have been from that sort of accidental cueing that I got the notion of actually making it specific.

The next idea was again to have those fixed spaces but in units which could be of variable sequence: Essentially the score's on one page, and you can go from one point to any other. The model for that was that Stockhausen *Klavierstuck XI*. But that's a solo piece, and I always thought it was a little bit of a scam because what was supposed to determine the indeterminate sequence was your roving eye. Well.... The eye roves but you can also make it go, and the fact is you tend to shape it pretty much as you want to shape that piece. But if you have two people, and the response has to be something that you hear from the other person, which is unpredictable and over which you have no control, then you're really in a situation which is indeterminate. And that's how I got onto the cueing thing. You'd have these longer units that would be cued by a particular sound: "Play this section here after you have heard a loud, high sound." You can start somewhere where there's no cue, because you have to start, right? And you're in that, and then as you get to the end of that measured space, you have to start listening for cues, because you're meant to tack on the next section as closely as possible. You can't just sit around and wait, is the point; it's very tense!

So that's one kind of cueing, which is a sort of more generalized cueing. From there I moved — a fairly logical step — to note-by-note cueing, or events one note of which would become the cue for the other player. And then of course more than two players, which complicated the situation. The final step was to allow cueing which was in a way like the beginning: indeterminate insofar as, say, you sustain a sound and you cut off with the next sound you hear, but you don't know when it's going to come. That gets you into interesting situations, especially if you're a wind player! You may get cut off practically before you get to make your sound, or you may just sit on that sound. And occasionally you would get into dilemmas: Say it's a duet and each player is supposed to wait for a sound to cut off the sound that he or she is playing, but they're both playing! So you just sit forever on that! But I made rules to deal with that situation.

Q: Nevertheless, as you've pointed out elsewhere, mistakes can be part of the piece as well. Did that idea arise because you found that mistakes were inevitable in playing these works and couldn't be filtered out without changing the nature of the music itself?

WOLFF: I think it came from a number of things. One was the Cageian notion that music and sound, or music and noise, are not irreconcilable. When we were writing in those days, even in a fully notated piece, there was a lot of silence. And inevitably there'll be sounds and interruptions in those silences. The feeling was that those would in no way disturb the piece; on the contrary, they became part of the piece. So things which would be regarded as mistakes in a conventional context, became simply what happened and therefore became legitimate parts of what was going on.

The other phenomenon is that you play and you make a mistake, right? Well, you've made it! Unless you're recording and can take it out, you've made it. And therefore it authentically exists; it's there. The question then is one of attitude. Do you say, "Oh, this is a terrible performance because this mistake was made," or is the character of the music such that it can accommodate things that were not originally intended? And that was the view we took, that the mistake was like a noise, something that simply came from somewhere else but was part of the situation. And the music was such that it accommodated that. You can have a very tight, closed musical world where obviously mistakes will damage what's going on. But here, the music was not like that. Quite the contrary, it was meant to be comfortable in whatever environment you put it — which included that of making mistakes.

There's a familiar dilemma with all of that music: this feeling that performers somehow would get that they could do anything, basically. And then you would get terrible performances, traceable to a very simple cause which was that the performers were not doing what the instructions of the piece required. In spite of all the openness, each of these pieces had certain precise, minimal requirements. And they were designed — if they were any good — to function under those minimal conditions. And when something sounded funny, it was usually because somebody either misunderstood or deliberately ignored some condition of the piece.

Q: A lot of your scores are available to untrained performers as well as to professional musicians. Over the years, have you been better served by one kind of player over the other?

WOLFF: No, I don't think so. I like to operate on a number of fronts. I don't function very theoretically; I respond pragmatically to situations. And that notion of writing for non-musicians and/or amateurs originated when I was in England for a year and was asked to go around speaking about my music. In those years the places that were really interested were the art schools, so the audience was basically not musicians; I mean, most of those guys played guitars or something, but this was not a sophisticated musical audience. And I found that it was all very well to talk about music and play a little bit, play tapes or something, but I really got bored with doing that. These were basically creative, interesting people, and they would obviously learn a lot more and have a better time if they got to do some of the music. So I made music to accommodate that situation, and that's what got me started. And I liked the results a lot.

The next step was to work with students. When I started teaching music, I did a course that was essentially a workshop in experimental music. It allowed in anybody who seriously wanted to do something musical, whether or not they'd had previous training. To a certain extent that fits my own situation compositionally, in that I too am a complete amateur, am self-taught, and so I have a certain faith in that process. The other notion is that music is nice that way. Anybody can make music. Kids do it; children do all kinds of amazing things and somehow they lose that. There's this sort of mystique that's put around it. Now sure, there are very specialized kinds of music for which you have to go to conservatory for umpteen years and so forth. But we all have voices and can sing, we all can beat out a rhythm of some sort. So between the two of those, you've got quite a lot to work with. And after that you can make modest instruments and so on and so forth. And now, once you get into electronic resources, it's amazing what you can do with very little musical training. So that was also in the background, I think.

Q: In fact, you can usually expect a better performance from a non-professional who has a serious attitude toward the score, as opposed to musicians who have a vested interest in their training and techniques.

WOLFF: Exactly. Interest, devotion, willingness — that's the other nice thing about non-professionals: They don't have this vested interest. You give them a violin and they'll bow with the wood part or they'll pluck it on the wrong side of the bridge. They'll just try to get the sounds that they think they can get out of this object, instead of worrying about the regular ways they're supposed to do it.

Q: You've commented regarding *For One, Two Or Three People* that you wanted "to make a lively situation for the performers." Had the whole issue of performers become more important to you as a composer around that time?

WOLFF: Yeah, I was writing for performers and myself. The kind of music we were making clearly was not popular in any sense whatsoever. There wasn't much point in worrying about the whole question of the audience. Especially in the beginning, because even here in New York with sophisticated audiences, the concerts were invariably scandals of one kind or another. Most people hated them. Nowadays, it's really hard to think of John Cage being regarded as a total off-the-wall kook. He'd been around and he had friends and so forth, but most people just didn't know what to make of this stuff, or hated it. So the feeling at concerts was generally very mixed — at best. And then when I set out for the hinterlands of Harvard University...! Then I really thought, this is just crazy, and even had a slight chip on my shoulder about audiences. I just decided never mind, I'm just going to do what I want to do, and let the chips fall where they may and not think about audiences. And that left me with the performers, which seemed to me much more interesting and important. We've still got this historical division, but it seems to me that there should be a much closer connection between performing and composing. As it happens, I myself am not enough of a performer to realize that, and I miss it very much.

Q: Yet you've played all your life.

WOLFF: I have, and I like to play a lot — some of the amateur music is for me, so I can play too!

The other thing that seems essential to me in composing is that you do something that performers can get into; maybe they won't enjoy it initially, but that there's something in it for them and you just don't, as it were, use them. There's a lot of contemporary music of the '50s and '60s — and still, no doubt — where the performer is regarded as essentially some kind of reproducing machine for these elaborate scores. And that seemed to me really terrible; that sort of alienating of the performer seemed to me just about the worst thing you could do. That was another reason I thought directly of the performers and what they were doing.

Q: Regarding *For One, Two Or Three People*, you've said, the "music is drawn from the interaction of people playing it." Yet both recordings of the piece seem to deviate from that principle. The performance by David Tudor superimposes two tracks where he plays the keyboard and the interior of the organ. Had he recorded two perfectly good, solo versions of the score, or was each track made with an ear toward combining them into a two-person version?

WOLFF: I wasn't there when he made the recording, and I never talked to him about it, so I know just what's on the record sleeve. But from other things that I know about David — he knew the piece well and had played it with other people — my guess is that he did two solo versions with the image in mind of the other version. But not literally — I don't see how he could do it technically.

Q: He wouldn't have been listening to a playback of, say, his keyboard version while he was playing inside the organ.

WOLFF: I don't think so. I would be surprised if he did that. But that's a guess. I'll have to ask him — if he remembers.

Q: However he did it, he can't be surprised hearing what he'd already played.

WOLFF: Exactly. The one-person version of the score is a different piece, essentially. There are a few points in that piece, whether it's one, two or three people, where you have to coordinate with sounds not your own, sounds in the environment. That's the one sort of survivor.

The whole notion of cueing is obviously a dilemma when you're writing solo pieces. I addressed it once. I wrote a piano piece called *For Pianist*, in which I tried to work out situations that would produce cues that were not perfectly controllable by the player. What I did was set up situations in which the pianist was asked to do something which could not be totally predictable. For instance, "play as softly as possible": You either play not as softly as possible, you play as softly as possible, or you get no sound at all. Those are three possibilities, and depending on which one results, it cues a different line in the piece and takes you in a different direction. Or you'd make a very wide leap as fast as possible: You'd either hit the top note or miss it too high or miss it too low — three possibilities result. I generated a bunch of things like that.

One more thing about David Tudor's recording, which I think was his view and which I agree with, is that recording is simply a different medium from live performance, and you make the most of it. I think that's what probably was going on then.

Q: The other recording is by the Percussion Group-Cincinnati, and in their notes they remark that their realization is "relatively 'fixed' ... though no two performances by us are quite the same, they are now quite similar." Is this idea of creating a performing version of the score really in the spirit of the music?

WOLFF: Not entirely, no. But it's a beautiful performance, very dedicated. I think people use that material in a way that suits them. And that particular group used to work the way string quartets work, and rehearse every day. And it's hard to reconcile that with at least the initial idea of a piece like *For One, Two Or Three People.*

The other extreme with that piece, if you're working with people who are experienced with it, is essentially to do a reading. In that piece, the only thing you have to agree about is the distribution of the material on a given page: Player one will cover this amount of it; player two, that amount; player three, that amount. You can do that by mail, everybody then looks at their stuff and works on it, and you might do a run-through before a performance, or if you're feeling really good about it, just do it with no rehearsals. That's possible if the people doing it have done that before and are familiar with the cueing — you have to know what to do when there's no cue, or when you're not getting one if you're expecting one, and so forth. But once you've done that a few times, you can just go ahead and do it.

That's one end of the spectrum. The other end is to work on it over and over again, which as I say seems to be the ethos of this particular group, and come out with a version that you get to know and which you're comfortable with. And which will inevitably have little variations — that's partly inherent in the way you produce sounds with percussion, especially sustained sounds. That's the route that they took and I think that's fine if that's what they want to do. Especially if you're recording, because a lot of this music is not suitable for recording. Recordings are a documentation of a performance. Given the kind of uptightness people have about recording, where you're laying this stuff down forever, I can understand why one would like to work up a version that you feel is going to be OK and where you won't screw up.

Q: Are you also describing somewhat the recording of *Burdocks?*

WOLFF: Actually, that was looser — there I was working with people that I'd been working with for years. But even there, we did a lot of takes and edited them.

Q: That's not a single performance on the record?

WOLFF: No. I think we did five sections of it, and some of them I think we just did straight through, or shortened some. But it's not edited in the sense of taking out two seconds and putting in something else. We laid down a lot of material, and then made a selection to fill 20 minutes for one side of the record.

Q: If you as a composer go to all the trouble of removing your taste and memory from the music, and the performer comes along and puts his or her own taste and memory into the music, has the point of the score been lost?

WOLFF: No — it depends. *For One, Two Or Three People* is pretty abstract, so it's very difficult to put your tastes into it! It's true, you could do it on instruments the sounds of which don't really move me very much. Yet one of the most essential conditions of that piece is that you have to change the colors of the sounds all the time. So even if you're using sounds that I would really dislike, the fact is you have to do something with them. Invariably, you're required to do peculiar or unconventional things, and you're more worried about the task at hand than the actual sound in some aesthetic or emotional or symbolic sense. So the music will come out as I intended. Now there have been some performances that I preferred to others, obviously. Because sound is very important to me, the sonorities and noise they make. And yet hearing people perform tasks that are somewhat unusual in a musical situation is really what it's about, and that's going to happen if they perform the piece as it's supposed to be performed. So in that sense, the question of my taste or their taste doesn't come into it, really.

Q: Morton Feldman compared his graph scores to "a kind of roving camera that caught up very familiar images, like a historical mirror." By using traditional notation, he got the musicians to play what he wanted to hear, rather than what they'd remembered hearing elsewhere. Have you felt a similar limitation using graphic notation?

WOLFF: No, I haven't really. With the Feldman graph scores, what he left open were the pitches: He'd have high, middle, low, and that's it. It was open to a kind of dangerous extent, because once you leave pitch choices open, especially with certain continuities there, people can stick a tune in — nothing says they can't. The other issue, which is a deeper one, is the one of the performer's intent in playing the music. If they want to play the music and mess it up — you can do that to any piece of music: You can do that to Mozart. In Feldman's case, the notorious example was a piece for orchestra, where one section of the orchestra just decided to pick out the pitches of some tune. (I've forgotten what the tune was — "Yankee Doodle" or something.) Well, that takes a deliberate effort of sabotage. What we said at the time was that we assumed, as everybody has a fair right to assume, a measure of good will on the part of the performers, and that they will not deliberately set out to sabotage a piece. But on the other hand, I also thought quite clearly in terms of making a piece so to speak sabotage-proof. I would try to imagine the worst-case scenarios: Given these freedoms, what could somebody do from an aesthetic point of view totally different from mine? And I would try that. And if it still worked, then OK! Which isn't to say that, if somebody really wanted to, they couldn't circumvent it. But that's obviously not the point.

Q: So you haven't suffered much at the hands of performers.

WOLFF: I don't think so, no. The abuses have been mostly careless and sloppy performances — this thing we were talking about earlier, where people assume that, because certain freedoms exist, that others automatically exist, and therefore they simply don't pay attention to anything. The other thing that happens is that people assume they can put the pieces together very quickly, which is again a very dangerous assumption — especially with the cueing pieces, because that takes quite a while to get used to and is not at all easy. I've had some disastrous occasions where people thought they could basically read it onstage. I said earlier that some of us could do that — I've done it once with David Tudor and John Cage, for instance — but we knew exactly what was going on. But for people who've never tried that, it's hopeless. Things like that have happened, and they just couldn't do it.

In connection with Feldman and *Burdocks*: There are some areas in *Burdocks* which are very open, and there was a performance of *Burdocks* which Feldman attended — I wasn't there, as it happened. It was by that English group, the Scratch Orchestra, and somebody started to play a folk song. And Feldman I think even got up during the performance and said, "That's not Christian Wolff's music"! This was reported to me later, and I thought about it and discovered where that would have been possible. It wasn't recorded, so I haven't heard it and can't tell you, but I suspect that it's perfectly OK; especially given the nature of that particular group, that it would have been very beautiful. And *Burdocks* is in fact a much more varied piece than *One, Two Or Three*, which is very austere. *Burdocks* has a tune in it, which I wrote myself! So if somebody else wants to put a tune in it, that's not going to wreck the mold of the piece.

Q: I read that *Burdocks* was performed by some 40 musicians. Is that still the largest ensemble ever to play your music?

WOLFF: I think so. I have a couple of orchestra pieces that have been performed.

Q: Being played by a symphony orchestra is where you'd run into the biggest risk of sabotage.

WOLFF: Right. But those scores are actually conventionally notated. There's a piece called *Changing The System* which allows multiples of four, and I think has been done by as many as twelve multiples of four, which would be 48 people. It's all done with subgroups of quartets, and Bill Brooks once told me that he organized a performance in San Diego with — I don't know how many, but at least a dozen quartets. And I've been involved with performances of that piece by six or seven quartets. I like those performances a lot — they're really fun! I like two things, clarity and complexity, which are almost mutually exclusive. And those pieces address the possibility of having a lot of material going on. And yet I want it to be going on in such a way that you can still see through the piece, you can still hear what's going on.

Q: Did your *Electric Spring* scores come out of your playing the electric guitar, or did they lead you to take up that instrument?

WOLFF: I was surrounded by people like Gordon Mumma, David Behrman, and Alvin Lucier, all of whom were working with electricity in some form. And I thought, they're doing it and that's OK, so I don't have to worry about it; but on the other hand, I was obviously interested. And my modest way of trying to get connected was to go out and buy an electric guitar and play with it! Because I liked the sounds, and at that time I also was beginning to get interested in popular music. So it was for all those reasons, and that's how it happened that I made those pieces. In fact, I also needed a bass and so I built one: a kind of very crude electric bass from a board, which we used in the first performances of those pieces.

Q: I understand that Feldman wrote an electric guitar piece for you to play.

WOLFF: Yes, that's a very sad story — because it doesn't exist anymore. The trouble with guitars is that they get stolen, right? What happened was that I had this guitar and I wanted something that I could play on it. I thought it seemed like an instrument he might be interested in — you could play these very delicate, soft sounds, and I had a vibrato bar, so you could bend the pitches a little bit — and I said, "Morty, would you be interested?" And he said, "Well, bring it over, let's see." So I came over with my little amp and guitar, and I plugged the thing in and played a few things on it. And he said OK and sat down at the piano and played this chord. And he said, "Can you do that?" And by using both hands on the fingerboard and so forth, I could do it! So OK, good, and he wrote it down. Then he played another chord: "Can you do that?" And that one I couldn't do. All right, so he tried revoicing one of the pitches, and it was OK. And we spent about an hour, an hour and a half, and he made the piece right on the spot, and then gave me the manuscript. And that was it, that was the only copy. And I played it a few times. It was a very beautiful piece — it was Feldman and he writes beautiful pieces. And then I came down to New York on my way to somewhere else; I had driven down and had the guitar in the car with a couple of other instruments. I parked for ten minutes, just to drop in quickly on somebody, and came back and the car was cleaned out. The music I'd kept inside the guitar case — that was the safest place, I thought. And that was it. Feldman's lost guitar piece.

Q: Commentators have likened your scores of the '60s to games. Are you comfortable with that comparison? Do you see yourself as having constructed games for people to play?

WOLFF: No, I don't — it's music. Clearly that's a helpful analogy, because there are rules. I used to use it in trying to explain how the music worked: that you had certain fixed rules and that the game had a very distinctive character because of the restrictive moves and the results of those moves, but that each game would be different. And that's a useful way of describing the music. The whole notion that a piece of music is supposed to have a fixed identity and so forth, and what is that, baffles people; most professional musicians think of a piece as a piece, and to have a piece that changes character all the time is baffling. So that analogy helped. I can usually tell what piece it is. Not always — something like *One, Two Or Three* you can do it in so many different ways — but after a while, I sort of get the idea and figure out which piece it is. But obviously people who are not familiar with the music don't understand that and can't hear it. So the game analogy is helpful. But it's not really a game so much, in the way, say, John Zorn uses that idea. There are some connections, the cueing and so forth, but in his case, I think he really has a clear image of a board game or a video game or a sports event.

Q: Do you have any personal interest in sports or games?

WOLFF: Sports, yes. Growing up in New York, I saw a lot of baseball and played some basketball as a kid. I still follow those things and I like them, but they don't connect much to music.

One physical thing that does connect is dance. Merce Cunningham's dancing has had a tremendous effect on my music, I think. It's hard to describe specifically in detail, but just the way he structures the pieces, the combination of movements — it's the formal character of the dances, the combination of abstraction with very powerful evocative possibilities.

Q: You mentioned John Zorn before — he and Elliott Sharp and other free improvisers performed at a retrospective of your music in New York. That concert demonstrated just how congenial their music is to your own, and I wondered if you had been aware much of their work in the '70s and '80s?

WOLFF: I was aware but only at a distance. That's the problem with not living in the city and only coming down occasionally. I had missed most of that music — I just hadn't heard it. I'd heard about it; I mean, I'd read *The Village Voice* and stuff.

Q: Which would give only a distorted view of it anyway.

WOLFF: Well, very sketchy. I know enough to take that with a grain of salt. I also had a clear sense that, rather like much of the earlier music of the '60s, it doesn't record well, that the recording gives you a very different impression from a live performance. So I was hoping someday to catch up with it, and I was very pleased with that concert because it was my chance to catch up with the music of John Zorn and Elliott Sharp and so forth — as filtered through my work, but that's OK too.

Q: When did you first realize you could compose a score without regard to instrumentation?

WOLFF: I can't remember exactly which is the first piece that does that. A very early piece, even before I met Cage, I did for voice and percussion. The voice part was written on a single line, not on a stave and not pitched; only relative high and low was written. The percussion was basically just the rhythms; I think I may have specified the materials, but nothing beyond that. Now, percussion writing is almost always like that, unless you know the percussionist and his equipment. Otherwise, you're dealing in a variable situation where you have to go with what you're going to get. And the voice seems to me also like that, obviously, if you don't specify soprano, alto, whatever. And that's what I had in mind with this piece, that any voice could sing it, and therefore only relative pitches were fixed. That's a very early stage, but it seems to me both voice and percussion have that quality. Percussion is already an instrumentation, and yet the possibilities are very extensive. The same with the voice, even when it's pitched because there the individual character of the singer is so powerful; the person is the instrument, and each person is different, so each instrument is different.

Other than that one, I don't think I actually wrote such a piece until probably the early '60s. Partly it was a practical consideration: I might not have known in this particular case who would be available to play, or I would want to make something that could be used on other occasions when I didn't have a recorder, a bass trombone, and a clarinet. You know, you can write just so many of those pieces; they're once-off pieces and that's it. So the idea of making something useful and practical I think was probably as much behind that as anything else. Then of course once you get into it, you realize the very specific kinds of compositional and technical issues that arise, apart from just making it available to a lot of different players.

Q: Did you find that those pieces would be played more often because of that openness, or did they fall into pretty much the same patterns of performance as your other works?

WOLFF: *One, Two Or Three* has gotten a lot of mileage; *Edges* is another one. There I think it's also the fact that they can be done by different levels of performers, professional and non-professional. The other piece that I think has been played a lot is a piece called *Stones*. I had this little set of prose pieces, which was my first dealing with this whole non-professional-performer situation. And those have gotten a lot of play.

Q: Looking back 20 years later, does it still seem to you that there was break in your music from the so-called abstract pieces, *Burdocks* or *Lines*, to the so-called political pieces such as *Accompaniments*?

WOLFF: In some sense, sure. It certainly felt like a big break at the time. But it's like Cage's pre-chance music and post-chance music: Clearly there's a sharp break, and yet in certain ways you can see that they're all by Cage. The same thing I think applies to my work. And in fact, recently I've come back to using some of the techniques of the earlier period, but in contexts which are quite different. But at the time it felt like a big break, especially that piano piece *Accompaniments*. Mostly because, at the very simple level, there are so many notes in that piece; there are more notes in that piece, I sometimes feel, than there are in all the previous music I've written! Because most of my music is this very sparse, Webernesque kind of texture, and then suddenly there's this piece which has a thousand chords in the first five minutes!

Q: Nevertheless, every note in each chord doesn't have to be played.

WOLFF: Exactly, there are still a number of indeterminate features. And even the element of professional/non-professional is built into that piece, because obviously the pianist has to be good (it was written for Frederic Rzewski), but he has to use his voice — and very few pianists are accomplished singers, so they just have to do the best they can with the voice — and play percussion with their feet. Both elements are there, and the pianist is somehow forced to function also as a non-professional.

Q: Had you felt the need for a break from what you'd been doing up to then?

WOLFF: Yeah, I really felt I'd done everything I'd wanted to do with those techniques. I didn't want to be repeating them.

Q: That's what I wanted to know, if *Burdocks* and *Lines* seemed to you to have taken that music as far as you could.

WOLFF: Definitely, yeah. *Burdocks* is already a transitional piece; free as parts of it are, it has certain fixed forms. There's one part where the pitches are free, but clearly you have three-voice chorales! And I've done a lot of chorales since, in various forms in various pieces, but that was the first one. And then the tune with accompaniment; and then the possibility of looping things, diatonic patterns that can occur over and over again — there was nothing remotely like that in my earlier work; there aren't even opportunities for doing that in my earlier work. So to that extent, it was already moving into a different climate. But generally, it was a question of moving out of what I began to feel was a highly specialized area that I'd felt I'd done. The other thing, as you know, was that I got interested in politics, and that earlier music just seemed to have nothing to do with any political issue; it really seemed totally remote.

Q: The reason I spoke before about music being "so-called" abstract or political is because the misunderstandings seem to set in so quickly with those terms. I can't imagine a piece of music not being political — if it exists in the society, then it's political.

WOLFF: Absolutely. I'm in complete agreement with that. And the funny thing is that in the later '60s some people began writing about my earlier work, doing Marxist interpretations of it and finding that it was in fact very political; because of this interactive dimension, it was a mini-model of some kind of democratic/socialist thing. Which certainly wasn't in my head when I wrote it, but I was delighted — that was fine with me.

There's the politics of the existence of the piece (even its technical nature), all of which is very interesting. But then there's the other question — now we get back to the audience, which I sort of deliberately shut out for all those years. If there's some political content in the piece, then you have to think about who's it for, and under what circumstances is it going to be communicated. And then the musical part of that becomes more important. In those years, I began to spend time with real political people who had no musical interests at all. You go to a meeting or a demonstration or whatever, you're not going to play *For One, Two*

Or Three People! However politically correct you might by some fancy analysis regard that piece, it's just not going to wash. You're going to have to do a song, you're going to have to do a piano piece with a certain resonance.

So that's entered into my thinking too. But in a modified way. Obviously, I'm not a writer of popular songs — I just don't have it for that, I don't know how to do that. And the solution that, say, people like Rzewski and Cardew came up with at first, which was to write a kind of music very closely aligned to late-19th-century romantic music, on the notion that this is something that people could relate to easily, that never moved me too much either. So I was left in a kind of no-man's land.

Q: After Cardew became a political activist — about a year before you did, in 1971 — he was dismissive of his own and others' avant-garde compositions. Was he throwing the baby out with the bathwater, or were there inherent contradictions between political content and experimental music which he couldn't resolve — or which cannot be resolved?

WOLFF: It's so complicated...!

Q: There's also the tendency, when joining up with something new, to feel a need to recant one's earlier allegiances.

WOLFF: I agree with that. I didn't have that in me, but I think Cardew did. He was deeply involved with both Stockhausen and Cage, and he really felt that he had to kick those traces, and he did — quite explicitly with those famous broadcasts he wrote for the BBC: There was one essay about "Stockhausen Serves Imperialism," and there was one about Cage. And I think it was valuable to do that. It gave us all stuff to think about; very serious things to think about. We might or might not have agreed with either the tactics or the tone, but the fact is Cardew was a very intelligent and very serious person, so this was something you had to come to terms with. And I think it was good he did it. But I have a much more, I guess, accommodating nature! I didn't feel the need to do that. So I didn't.

Now, with the larger question you're asking, I usually fall back on the position of context. If you think about, say, the early years of the Russian Revolution, it was a time of tremendous flowering precisely in the experimental arts. Now, Lenin notoriously didn't know what to make of that stuff and was kind of embarrassed by it; he really liked 19th-century romantic music which he also realized was bourgeois music and not politically the right thing. So the problem exists in many forms, and that's one of them. In that case, you have a historical context where you have revolution in politics and you have revolution in the arts, and nothing could seem more reasonable and right and proper. Once the avant-garde evolves and becomes the preserve of rather specialized interests, is involved with heavy subsidy by AT&T and all these other things that we're very familiar with, then it becomes a less-obvious representation of politically interesting positions, and you have to rethink all of that.

I've been talking in large terms of historical context. More particularly, you would think about an audience situation. And there are all kinds of examples that come to mind. There was an organization in New York, I think in the early '70s, called the Musicians' Action Collective. They did something I thought was very interesting, although I never got to hear any of their concerts. It was a group of musicians who were politically interested, but they came from a whole range of backgrounds: There would be people who played in the Philharmonic, there would be avant-garde composers, there would be folk musicians, there would be jazz people — practically anything you could think of. And they decided, OK, we'll each do our thing, but we will do it in a context which makes some kind of political statement and is in aid of some particular cause. They set all these rules for themselves. And each concert was devoted to some issue: It might be the farm workers, it might be whatever. And they would try to get music that was somehow related to the issue, but not necessarily. And you'd have a program consisting of a Mozart woodwind quintet — the guys from the Philharmonic would do that; Rzewski might have some piece written for the occasion; Mike Glick or some political folk singer would also have something more or less related, and maybe a few other things as well; some jazz combo would play — jazz is, in some way, deeply political, and yet at the same time has never done much with the verbal aspects of the politics. So you'd have this whole range of stuff, and you'd have an audience which was really interesting: People would go either to hear their favorite group, and have no interest in the politics; or they'd go because the issue was important to them. You'd get this very variegated group, which was in some sense unified by the issues, and the people who, say, were really interested in the jazz group would also hear the Mozart. My view about that is that the Mozart would become a political piece in that context. That illustrates this whole issue of context as clearly as I can. And that's the way one has to deal with the whole question: Name the concert, name the occasion and who played.... And even the results. Again, Cardew was very good about this. He'd say, it's all very well to have good intentions, but if they don't work, you've missed it; you haven't got it. So he'd really monitor what was happening, which is good; I think it's a very sensible thing to do. It's hard to translate that back to the process of composing — I find it really impossible to compose and think, well, is this the right thing to do politically, write my E-flat or C-sharp? Notes are notes.

Q: Do you ever feel that you're being drawn into letting non-musical distinctions make musical decisions, or that you have to start thinking not as a composer while you're composing?

WOLFF: A composer's material can be very various. Some composers work from works of art; some work from texts, which are not necessarily set. But the answer is yes; that is to say, I use material which is not necessarily musical. But I don't think that's that odd.

Q: Have you suffered any adverse repercussions from writing music with an overtly political content? Have you been harassed by the government?

WOLFF: No, I don't think so. Not that I know of.

Q: Have you ever demanded the file on you from the FBI under the Freedom of Information Act?

WOLFF: No.

Q: I bet they've got one on you.

WOLFF: Maybe — I don't know. It would be nice if they did! Let's be realistic here: My work is not exactly widely known in the world, so I think that people out there feeling it as a great big threat seems somewhat unlikely. I've never had much luck in applying for grants and things, and there was a time when I possibly might have been a little bit too hardnosed in my grant application and rubbed some people the wrong way. I know that the feeling exists — mostly within our own musical world; it's not so much in the big world. The person I know best for this is Frederic Rzewski who's far more visible than I am, partly through his performing. I know he's had a lot of trouble, especially in this country, getting jobs and perhaps even gigs in some cases because of his politics. And that's not surprising. So it certainly happens. But I have not directly noticed it myself.

Q: Was there a loss of support among formerly friendly composers who'd felt you'd abandoned or betrayed them?

WOLFF: There was bafflement, certainly. Including my close friends, John Cage and Morton Feldman and so forth. I think mostly, though, they stood back and wanted to see what would happen next, so to speak. But there was a difficult time, and it was exacerbated by this moment when Cardew took his stand. He was a good friend of mine — I had friends on both sides of something of a divide, and it was very difficult because I stuck by Cardew and defended him. But that sort of worked itself out pretty quickly.

Q: When you composed *Accompaniments*, in which you set a text about revolutionary China, did you ever wonder what would have happened to a Chinese composer at that time had he or she written such a score?

WOLFF: I guess not specifically. Obviously, I was operating out of a very privileged and open situation. I was interested at the time that there was a lot of talk about music during the Cultural Revolution, with very interesting attacks on the classical composers. Beethoven and Schubert were specifically singled out as not to be used and were forbidden, which seemed to me really strange, but interesting as an idea.

I certainly had no notions that this music would ever be played in China, so to that extent I didn't engage with that idea. Now, the politics of *Accompaniments* has been totally discredited; to that extent, the piece is finished and I should withdraw it. The things that were actually going on in those years we're finally finding out about, and they were horrendous. I think there are certain principles I found in the text that I used, which I still believe in, so that part is OK; I will defend the piece to that extent. The interesting thing about political music is that its political character comes and goes. Operas that were initially extremely political, like *The Marriage Of Figaro* or any number of Verdi operas, now are just high-art entertainment. So things change, and that's interesting.

Accompaniments was a problematical piece, for all my good intentions, and it raised these issues for me very clearly. I would play it for people who were politically interested but not musically tuned in, and they wondered whether I wasn't making fun of the text by setting it that way. I mean, I thought I was making tremendous strides forward in my music, and to them it was just basically weird and therefore a kind of undermining of the text. It was very unsettling. And Cardew had the piece played. (He documented this in his book.) To be sure, he did a rather weird version: He set it to instruments so that the piece probably wasn't much like what I had in mind. But anyway he did it, and there were very mixed results connected with that, and he wrote a quite severe criticism of it as a result.

Q: Arguing that one factor against the piece was that it could be done in a way that could permit misinterpretation?

WOLFF: Yeah.

Q: Yet in the piece you went out of your way to let the text stand on its own.

WOLFF: Exactly — that is specifically required in the instructions, that you do that. In previous uses of texts, I might essentially have said, use this as sound material. But here I said, in spite of the repetitive patterns and loops, the general tenor of the text should emerge in the course of a performance. So performance is critical — not just with ordinary performance, but with political performance — and that's another issue. The quality of the performance and the dedication of the performer can make the world of difference. And again, that's the Mozart thing: If you play that Mozart badly in that political context, it will have a poor effect; if you play it exquisitely and if people see that there is a devotion there and a skill, they may be very moved by that, and feel that this has been done especially for them in some way. Rzewski has done concerts for labor-union organizations, and he'll play very demanding music, and they will be somewhat baffled by all this. And yet, at the same time, the fact that he's doing it, and the fact that he's doing it so well and so seriously, has an impact and makes an impression.

Initially I made the decision to associate a text with everything I was doing, and then eventually I slacked off from that. That was a rather crude decision, but I thought, all right, I'll do that and see what happens. And so you got *Accompaniments* and *Changing The System* and *Wobbly Music* — and that's almost it. I have a lot of problems working with texts — not problems, but I find it difficult. It's partly because I work with texts professionally, and so have a special feeling about them. The really best texts I think are best left as texts and not mucked up with music. So that's one problem, and the other is that I really like a text to be just right, and it's hard to find ones that work well.

But it's survived in the titles, you might say. I do use titles a lot now, which are evocative of either a song which is used though not actually sung inside a piece, or of somebody's name — I've got a whole series of name pieces: Those are more recent and are tributes to and evocations of people.

Q: Opera would seem to be ideal for communicating political content in a powerful way. Have you been attracted to that?

WOLFF: I think if the opportunity arose I would certainly take it. And I have in the back of my mind thought about what kinds of material to use. But it's the kind of thing that I wouldn't just jump into. It's like orchestra music, of which I have very little: There's just such an investment involved that to do it without some prospects of performance, let alone money.... Yet on the other hand I have a certain amount of faith. It's true that, at the moment, over the last years there's enough interest among performers in my works so that I'm always writing — usually for a commission or for somebody who has asked for a piece (and they may or may not have the money to pay for it). But occasionally I write pieces because I want to write them and don't worry about it. In fact, my first orchestra piece was like that: I finally thought, hey, here I am, 50 or whatever, and I've never written for orchestra, so let's try it. And I really had fun doing it. And I just set it aside, and three years later somebody called and said, "Christian, do you have an orchestra piece?" But that was a five-minute piece and the investment was modest — I didn't do the parts or anything until the time came.

But opera is in the back of my mind as a possibility. Again, the opera houses, you have to pay $60 or $70 to get in, so you're restricting your audiences; it's a rather specialized situation. But there are other situations: chamber operas, street operas, whatever.

Q: Your music has been criticized for not having swayed the bourgeoisie in any perceivable direction. Is that a fair criticism? Do you feel you've failed as a composer if you haven't swayed the bourgeoisie?

WOLFF: No, not really. And what does that mean, to sway them? This is so generalized and abstract a term.

I think everybody does what they can, right? I'm not President of the United States, I'm not even a big politico or a little politico. I'm just a composer working in very restricted circles. And I can do several things. If I felt I could do it, and felt strongly enough about something, then I should go out there and agitate or run for office or something like that. But the fact is, I'm a composer — among other things — and I don't think I have the skills and the gifts. My energies I think are best applied to what I can do. And then the political question becomes one of doing what I do with as much awareness of the possible political implications of it, and with every effort to make something of it politically — let's put it that way — in a general sense. And it has to more or less take place within the contexts in which I can operate. Which are partly academic, at school — I think I do more political work as a teacher of whatever it is I'm teaching. And it's not that I read sermons; you do it in very small and modest ways.

The same goes for the music. I do certain things that in some sense are crude — one way to try to convey something political is with a text. That's the guaranteed way, theoretically; actually, it's not at all guaranteed. I learned that too the hard way. But at least it's a start, because people will say, what do you mean? or what does this title mean? or where is that text from? You create an occasion in which political questions can be raised, or a little bit of modest education can take place. I wrote a piece called *Wobbly Music* and "Wobbly" refers to the Wobblies, a political movement at the turn of the century, of which many people — including myself, once — are quite unaware, and yet it's probably the largest-scale radical movement this country has ever experienced. And I thought it's time for people to be reminded of that, that we have in our history the possibility of doing that — and why it was destroyed and in what ways and what it accomplished before that and so forth. So to make a piece about the Wobblies becomes also — this is where the teaching comes in again — a kind of teaching exercise. Teaching is largely persuasion in uncoercive ways; in ways that open up people rather than shut them down.

Q: The idea of your having to sway the bourgeoisie seems to imply that if people don't storm out of your concert and burn down an Army recruiting station, then somehow you've failed.

WOLFF: Exactly. And I don't know of any political music that does that. Most political music, paradoxically enough, is for the converted; it's an instrument of cohesion for a group that already knows what it wants and what it's doing. There's hardly any that I know of which operates in this funny area that we've tried to get into, which is to raise people's awareness outside of the circle of those who basically agree with you.

COMPOSITIONS

1950	*Duo For Violins*	CFP
1951	*For Prepared Piano*	TP
1951	Trio for flute, trumpet, and cello	CFP
1951	*Nine* for flute, clarinet, horn, trumpet, trombone, celeste, piano, and two cellos	CFP
1952	*For Piano I*	CFP
1952	*For Magnetic Tape*	MS
1953	*For Piano II*	CFP

1954	Suite I for prepared piano	CFP
1957	*Duo For Pianists I*	CFP
1957	Sonata for three pianos	CFP
1958	*Duo For Pianists II*	CFP
1959	*For Pianist*	CFP
1959	*For Six Or Seven Players* (*Music For Merce Cunningham*) for trumpet, trombone, trumpet, trombone, piano, and double bass	CFP
1960	*Duet I* for piano four hands	CFP
1960	Suite II for horn and piano	CFP
1961	*Duet II* for horn and piano	CFP
1961	Trio II for piano four hands and percussion	CFP
1961	*Duo For Violinist And Pianist*	CFP
1961	*Summer* for string quartet	CFP
1962	*For Five Or Ten Players* for any instruments	CFP
1963	*In Between Pieces* for three players	CFP
1964	*For One, Two Or Three People* for any instruments	CFP
1964	Septet for seven players and conductor	CFP
1965	Quartet for four horns	CFP
1966	*Electric Spring 1* for horn, electric guitar, electric bass guitar, and double bass	CFP
1966-70	*Electric Spring 2* for alto recorder, tenor recorder, trombone, electric guitar, and electric bass guitar	CFP
1967	*Electric Spring 3* for violin, horn, electric guitar, and electric bass guitar	CFP
1968	*Pairs* for two, four, six, or eight players	CFP
1968	*Edges* for any number of players	CFP
1968	*Toss* for eight or more players	OUP
1968-71	*Prose Collection* for any number of players	FPM
	includes *Stones, Play, Song, For Jill, Sticks, Groundspace, Fits & Starts, You Blew It, Crazy Mad Love, Looking North, Double Song, Pit Music, X For Peace Marches* (1986)	
1969	*Tilbury 1* for keyboard(s), any number of players	CFP
1969	*Tilbury 2 & 3* for any instruments	CFP
1970	*Tilbury 4* for any instruments	CFP
1970	*Snowdrop* for harpsichord and/or other keyboard(s)	CFP
1970-71	*Burdocks* for one or more groups of five or more players	CFP
1972	*Lines* for string quartet or other string ensembles	CFP
1972	*Accompaniments* for piano (pianist also uses voice and percussion)	CFP
1972	*Variations (Extracts) On The Carmans Whistle Variations Of Byrd* for keyboard	CFP
1972-73	*Changing The System* for eight or more instruments (players also use voice and percussion)	CFP
1973-74	*Exercises 1-14* for three or more instruments	CFP

1973-75	*Songs* for solo or unison singing	CFP
	"Wake Up," "It Is Said," "After A Few Years," "Teacher,	
	Teacher," "Of All Things," "Freedom"	
1974-76	*String Quartet Exercises Out Of Songs*	CFP
1974-76	*Studies* for piano or other instrumentation	CFP
1975	*String Bass Exercise Out Of "Bandiera Rossa"*	CFP
1975	*Exercises 15-18* for any number of instruments including piano	
	and trombone solo	CFP
1975-76	*Wobbly Music* for mixed chorus, keyboard, guitar(s), and two or	
	more melody instruments	CFP
1976	*Bread And Roses* for violin	CFP
1976	*Bread And Roses* for piano	CFP
1977	*Dark As A Dungeon* for clarinet	CFP
1977	*Dark As A Dungeon* for trombone and double bass	CFP
1977	*The Death Of Mother Jones* for violin	CFP
1978	*Cello Song Variations (Hallelujah, I'm A Bum)* for cello	CFP
1978	*Braverman Music* for four or more instruments, or one or two	
	pianos	CFP
1979	*Hay Una Mujer Desaparecida (after Holly Near)* for piano	CFP
1979	*Stardust Pieces* for cello and piano	CFP
1979-80	Three Pieces for violin and viola	CFP
	Rock About, Instrumental, Starving To Death On A Government	
	Claim	
1980	*Exercises 19 & 20* ("Harmonic Tremors" and "Acres Of Claims")	
	for two pianos	CFP
1980-81	Preludes 1-11 for piano	CFP
1981	*Exercise 21* for piano four hands	CFP
1982	*Isn't This A Time* for any saxophone or other reed, solo or	
	multiple	CFP
1982	*Exercise 22* ("Bread And Roses, For John") for piano four hands	CFP
1982	*Exercise 23* ("Bread And Roses") for chamber orchestra	CFP
1983	*Exercise 24* ("J.C.'s Bread And Roses") for orchestra (orchestration	
	of *Exercise 22*)	CFP
1983	*Piano Song* ("I Am A Dangerous Woman") for piano	CFP
1983	*Eisler Ensemble Pieces 1 & 2* for clarinet/bass clarinet, violin,	
	cello, and piano	CFP
1983-84	*Peace March 1* ("Stop Using Uranium") for flute	CFP
1984	*Peace March 2* for flute, clarinet, cello, piano, and	
	percussion	CFP
1984	*Peace March 3* ("The Sun Is Burning") for flute, cello, and	
	percussion	CFP
1985	*"I Like To Think Of Harriet Tubman"* for woman's voice, treble,	
	alto, and low bass instruments (one of each)	CFP

1985	Piano Trio for violin, cello, and piano	CFP
1985	*Instrumental Exercises With Peace March 4* for two clarinets/bass clarinets, two keyboards/violin (1), percussion, cello/electric bass guitar	CFP
1985-86	*Bowery Preludes* for flute (also piccolo, alto flute), trombone, percussion, and piano	CFP
1986	*Exercise 25* ("Liyashiswa") for orchestra	CFP
1986-87	*Black Song Organ Preludes*	CFP
1986-87	*Long Peace March* for flute/piccolo, oboe, clarinet/bass clarinet, alto saxophone, horn, trombone, percussion, viola, cello, and double bass	CFP
1987	*For Morty* for glockenspiel, vibraphone, piano (two or three players; other instrumentation possible)	CFP
1988	*From Leaning Forward* for soprano, baritone, clarinet/bass clarinet, and cello	CFP
1988	*Digger Song* for violin, viola, cello, and percussion	CFP
1988	*Exercise 26* ("Snare Drum Peace March") for snare drum	CFP
1988	*Exercise 27* ("Snare Drum Peace March") for snare drum	CFP
1988-89	*Emma* for viola, cello, and piano	CFP
1989	*Mayday / Mayday Materials* for synclavier/synthesizer-generated tape	MS
1989	*Malvina* for solo koto (13 string)	CFP
1989-90	*Rosas* for piano and percussion	CFP
1990	*Eight Days A Week Variation* for piano	CFP
1990-91	*Rukus* for baritone/tenor saxophone, electric guitar, and double bass	CFP
1990-91	*For Si* for clarinet/bass clarinet, trumpet, two percussionists, piano, and double bass	CFP
1991	*Gib Den Hungrigen Dein Brot* for flute and piano	CFP
1991	*Look She Said* for double bass	CFP
1991	*Jasper* for violin and double bass	CFP
1991	*Ruth* for trombone and piano	CFP
1991	*Kegama* for clarinet/bass clarinet, percussion, piano, violin, and cello	CFP
1992	*Tuba Song* for Bb tuba (solo or duet)	CFP

DISCOGRAPHY

1962
Duo For Violinist And Pianist, Summer, Duet II
Time 58009
Mainstream 5015 lp

1967
For One, Two Or Three People
CBS Odyssey 32-16-0158 lp

1969
Summer
Wergo 60053 lp

1972
For Piano I, For Pianist, Burdocks
Wergo 60063 lp

Summer
Vox 5306 lp

1973
In Between Pieces, Electric Spring 2
EMI 1 C165-28954/7 lp

Edges
EMI 1 G065.02469 lp

1976
Lines, Accompaniments
CRI 357 lp

1981
For One, Two Or Three People
Opus One 80/81 lp

1982
Hay Una Mujer Desaparecida (after Holly Near)
Music From Dartmouth/Philo 200 lp

1990
Mayday Materials
Centaur CRC 2052 cd

1991
Eight Days A Week Variation
EMI 7345 cd

1992
For Prepared Piano, For One, Two Or Three People
Hat Hut 6101 cd

Malvina
Collecta 003 cd

BIBLIOGRAPHY

"Four Musicians At Work." *Trans-formations*, 1 (1952).

"Kontrollierte Bewegung." *Die Reihe*, 2 (1955); translated as "Movement," *Die Reihe*, 2 (English edition, 1958).

"New And Electronic Music." *Audience*, 5 (1958).

"Ueber Form." *Die Reihe*, 7 (1960); reprinted in *Kommentare Zur Neuen Musik*, Dumont, Cologne, 1963; translated in *Die Reihe*, 7 (English edition, 1965).

"Questions/Demande" (bilingual). *Collage* (Palermo), 3-4 (1964).

"Electricity And Music." *Collage*, 8 (1968).

"Elements Pour Completer Une Interview." *VH 101* (Paris), 4 (1970-71); reprinted in *Revue d'Esthetique* (Paris), 13-14-15 (1987-88); reprinted as "Elements To Make Up An Interview," *ex tempore*, 3 (1986).

"John Cage." *Dictionary Of Contemporary Music*. Ed. John Vinton. New York: E.P. Dutton, 1974.

"Statement" and "Burdocks" in *Merce Cunningham*. Ed. James Klosty. New York: E.P. Dutton, 1975.

"On Music With Political Texts." *Sonus*, 1 (1980); also in *Literatur Und Musik*. Ed. S. Scher. Berlin: Erich Schmidt Verlag, 1984; and in *Contiguous Lines: Issues And Ideas In The Music Of The '60s And '70s*. Ed. T. DeLio. Lanham, Maryland: University Press of America, 1985.

"Under The Influence." *Tri-Quarterly*, 54 (1982); reprinted in *A John Cage Reader*, Ed. J. Brent & P. Gena, New York: C.F. Peters, 1983.

"On *For One, Two Or Three People.*" *Percussive Notes*, 22 (1984).

"Open To Whom And To What?" *Interface* (Netherlands), 16 (1987).

"Robust Wie Naegel." *MusikTexte*, 11 (1987).

"On Dieter Schnebel's *Marsyas.*" *Schnebel 60.* Ed. W. Gruenzweig. Hofheim: Wolke Verlag, 1990.

"Floating Rhythm And Experimental Percussion." *Percussive Arts Society Proceedings*, 1 (1991).

LA MONTE YOUNG & MARIAN ZAZEELA

photo: Gene Bagnato

LA MONTE YOUNG / Introduction

LA MONTE YOUNG was born in Berne, Idaho, on October 14, 1935. He studied saxophone and clarinet with William Green at the Los Angeles Conservatory of Music from 1951 to '54, and composition privately with Leonard Stein from 1955 to '56. In 1958, he received his B.A. from UCLA, and went on to do graduate work at Berkeley, where he studied with Seymour Shifrin. He also attended Karlheinz Stockhausen's Advanced Composition Seminar at Darmstadt in 1959, and studied electronic music with Richard Maxfield at the New School for Social Research from 1960 to '61. Since 1970, he has been a disciple of master singer Pandit Pran Nath, studying North Indian classical vocal music.

By the late '50s, Young had left behind playing jazz as well as composing with serial techniques, and had begun writing provocative scores that employed long sustained tones, such as *for Brass* (1957) and *Trio for Strings* (1958). He also developed a series of compositions without traditional notation, which were primarily (and soon exclusively) verbal, including *Vision* (1959), *Poem for Chairs, Tables, Benches, etc.* (1960), *Compositions 1960*, and *Compositions 1961*. With these and related scores, Young became involved with Henry Flynt, Yoko Ono, and the group of Fluxus composers who were active at the time. The early '60s also saw the evolution of his playing on piano and sopranino saxophone into an original approach to the blues, related to his interest in staticism and drones. The result was a series of now-legendary (and still unavailable) recordings, in which Young played with Tony Conrad, Marian Zazeela, John Cale, and Angus MacLise.

These pieces provided the transition into the music for which Young is best known today: *The Four Dreams of China* (1962) for unspecified instruments; *The Tortoise, His Dreams and Journeys* (1964-present) for voices, various instruments, and sine waves, and what would become his magnum opus, *The Well-Tuned Piano* (1964-present). All these scores would involve improvisation techniques, complex tunings in just intonation, sustained tones, and lengthy time scales. Along with developing these works throughout the years, he would compose other pieces with similar concerns, most recently *The Lower Map of The Eleven's Division in The Romantic Symmetry (over a 60-Cycle Base) in Prime Time from 144 to 112 with 119* (1989-90) for unspecified instruments and sound environment and *Chronos Kristalla* (1990) for string quartet.

In 1962 Young initiated his Theater of Eternal Music for performances of *The Tortoise*. Its alumni over the years include Conrad, Cale, Terry Riley, Terry Jennings, David Rosenbloom, Jon Hassell, and Garrett List, as well as Marian Zazeela, who has participated as both musician and visual designer, creating unusual lighting and slide projections for the performances. They would eventually marry, and she would become indispensable to both the performance and the sound and light environments for Young's music. (She also became a disciple of Pandit Pran Nath along with Young, and like him has since taught and performed ragas.)

Young has received many awards over the years, including the Maharishi Award for the Development of Consciousness, the Nicola De Lorenzo Prize, and the Bank of America Achievement Award. He is the recipient of numerous grants from sources such as the Foundation for Contemporary Performance Arts, the Cassandra Foundation, the Lannan Foundation, the National Endowment for the Arts, and the Creative Artists Public Service Program. He has also received a Guggenheim Fellowship and a DAAD residency in Berlin.

La Monte Young and Marian Zazeela currently live in New York City, and I spoke with them in their home on June 10, 1990. Over the course of our conversation, I sought to learn more about Young's early development as a composer, his work with Pandit Pran Nath, and his experiences in composing and performing *The Well-Tuned Piano.*

LA MONTE YOUNG & MARIAN ZAZEELA / Interview

Q: I'd like to start with *The Lower Map of The Eleven's Division in The Romantic Symmetry (over a 60-Cycle Base) in Prime Time from 144 to 112 with 119*, which you premiered in New York earlier this year. Do you see this work, with its use of improvisation, sustained tones, and unique tunings, as a culmination of your efforts with those materials, or as one more step along the same road, an eternal road?

YOUNG: I think it's one more step on an eternal road. But each of these bigger pieces, such as *The Well-Tuned Piano* and *The Romantic Symmetries*, do tend to be culminations of earlier work. If I have an opportunity to continue with a particular composition, or subset of a bigger composition, it would tend to develop further. If I don't get a chance to work with it, it probably stays where I last worked with it.

I have ideas, for instance, about pieces that I've worked with before, which I haven't had a chance to realize, because I tend to realize in the course of rehearsing and performing. I really like to improvise, and I only like to write down broad, powerful, theoretical constructs. I find it very slow and time-consuming to write out through-composed works. I can do it, but I don't have very much inspiration to do it. I'm always afraid I'll get a commission and that I'll have to finish something in a hurry! Because the most important things I've done have developed over a long period of time. The works grow out of long series of rehearsals and performances. Whether it's a solo piece, as in *The Well-Tuned Piano*, or a piece such as *The Lower Map of The Eleven's Division*, with the Big Band of 23 or 24 people, it still tends to develop in rehearsal. The large constructs that I do compose in advance — in *The Well-Tuned Piano*, for instance — became more and more specific, more themes developed. Very specific chordal areas of course were there more or less from the beginning, but I composed new chordal areas as time went on. With the Big Band, it's more abstract, the themes are at a very early stage of development, and it's hard to say until I put it into the next series whether or not actual themes will develop. I consider the tuning for *The Lower Map of The Eleven's Division in The Romantic Symmetry (over a 60-Cycle Base) in Prime Time from 144 to 112 with 119* pretty finalized. But anything could happen. I try to work in a way in which I don't preconceive or determine what's going to come next. I try to really be open to the highest source of inspiration, so that information can just come flowing through me, and I try to be pure so that I can receive this information and allow it to become manifest. I've found that by that approach, I get the most remarkable gifts that I couldn't have preconceived. If you let your own mind get in the way too much, it can prevent some of these possibilities. Naturally, one has to use one's mind, one has to practice, one has to do all of the things that we do to develop our skills, our senses, our ability to exist on this planet and relate to other people. But when it comes to producing creative work, there's a point on top of all of these technical means, which has to let the technical means be ready and prepared, but not determining what the creative process and result will be. The creative result is something that I have found is most revelatory and inspirational and ultimately of greater value for all mankind, if the performer/composer can be totally open and pure, like the concept of the empty glass or the hollow bamboo tube, where you just have to be open and let the information flow. Then things come that are a result of the culmination of our imagination — which had to have the ability to understand what was coming through in order to let it happen — but they're really also beyond just pure imagination. They're an opening up to a higher level of information that can actually flow through you if you can prepare yourself for that flow.

Q: Is it more difficult to function as that kind of conduit in *The Lower Map of The Eleven's Division*, where the ensemble is much larger than any you'd worked with before?

YOUNG: Obviously, it's different. I won't say it's more difficult because these were hand-picked musicians; people who, in some cases, have worked closely with me for years, and in other cases, have worked closely with the people who worked closely with me. As a result, everybody in the group was like a disciple or a student or a colleague who had performed my music, or somebody who had performed or studied with one of them. It was almost like a large family.

Of course it's different, working with a group rather than working by yourself. When you're by yourself, you can be freer than you can be in any other way. But you can't sound like 23 musicians. Each situation has its rewards. In this case, I thought that the Big Band was just incredibly supportive and tuned in — they really learned how to support what I was tuned into, and they learned how to tune in themselves.

Something interesting that I learned from Pandit Pran Nath was what I refer to as a kind of organically evolving improvisation. It was not in my style of improvisation so much before I studied Indian classical music with him. I think it's of particular importance in the Kirana style of Indian classical music, and the way *alap* begins in North Indian raga. I think *alap* is one of the great contributions of Indian classical music; it's quite unique. When you consider our musical inheritance from throughout the world, *alap* is the only music I can think of that isn't tied in with rhythm. (There's chant, but even though it's not in meters, it tends to be rhythmic — you don't have these long, spacious situations that you have in *alap*.) I feel that this approach to meditation in sound, if you will, is really unique; I can think of nothing like it in world music anywhere, until we get way, way into the 19th and 20th centuries. There are things like the Schoenberg *Five Pieces For Orchestra*, the middle piece, "Summer Morning By A Lake — Colors," which has some really pretty static space in it. But the way *alap* evolves, you know, you begin on the tonic, on Sa, and the way Pandit Pran Nath does it, you more or less introduce one note at a time, whereas there can be an opening constellation and you develop outside of that opening constellation more or less one note at a time down the scale and then gradually up the scale, carefully introducing each note and then working with it. Each note determines how the next note will be and what the next rhythmic value will be. The kinds of improvisation that I had been doing, with my own group — for instance, on sopranino saxophone in the early '60s and in the early recordings of *The Well-Tuned Piano* from 1964 — were more like my "Cloud" sections of *The Well-Tuned Piano*, but without the lead-in to them: starting with a block of sound, already playing at breakneck speed. And you know I've always been very interested in the concept of stasis; the idea that music did not have to go somewhere and did not have to be developmental. I once played for Kyle Gann a recording by the Kronos Quartet of my *Five Small Pieces for String Quartet*, written in 1956, and he said something to the effect of how interesting it was that the pieces didn't have contrast to each other. And I said, "Contrast? Contrast is for people who can't write music!" So then he wrote that that would be the new motto of his column! But that's how I feel. Variety and contrast are like techniques you learn in the early stages.

Q: Implicit in those techniques is the idea that you have to hold the audience's attention, to divert them, which is not at all the point in your music.

YOUNG: That's right. The contrast I'm making here is that, whereas I'm extremely interested in stasis, what I really feel is happening in *alap* — particularly in the way Pandit Pran Nath does it — is something that is more developmental. It's static on the level that a raga uses only a certain set of tones. But the way each note is introduced, the way each rhythmic unit flows out of the last, is something that's more developmental. I think that it became yet another level of revelation to me to hear it happen the way Pandit Pran Nath does it. He does it in such a subtle, refined way that I began to realize that this approach could have extraordinary grace and beauty, and that it not only had a place, but in fact became the approach to improvisation which I used throughout most of the *Well-Tuned Piano* recording that I published on Gramavision. The "Clouds" are very static, but the Romantic approach to melody, the organic evolution of motif from previous motif, I think is in this more organically developmental approach to improvisation.

With the Big Band, I was teaching them something about that: how motifs would gradually get started. Maybe I would start it, or somebody would start it, and gradually it would be picked up and very subtly worked with, and gradually perhaps metamorphose into something else. They were incredible to perform with. I still have members of the Big Band coming back to me and saying, "Monday nights just aren't the same anymore!" I really want the the Big Band to go back into rehearsal — they would all like to rehearse. I simply have to find an engagement. You know, it was very, very costly — and I'm still paying for it — to present that series of concerts. Not only paying 23 musicians, and rehearsing, but publicity and promotion, recording it in 24-track, every rehearsal, in case we got something. I've made a policy, you know, that I record just about everything I do, because I feel that you never know when you're going to get the good one. Every rehearsal isn't the same. Half the rehearsals are just OK, they're just work sessions, working through something. Then suddenly everything clicks. And if you don't have the recorder running, you don't know when it's going to click. It's a costly approach to recording, but I find it produces the best results.

Q: It also makes the musicians feel that it's not just a rehearsal, but that they have to come up with the goods.

YOUNG: That's right. Also, it eventually helps them relax in a recording situation because they get so used to it — the thing is always running! After a while, it's no big deal: "We're going to record." "Oh, again?"

Q: In *The Lower Map of The Eleven's Division*, the musicians are isolating pitches on a spectrum from 112 to 127 — that range is the lower map.

YOUNG: Right. And as you know, several of those pitches are transposed down some octaves, so that the pitches are arranged over a range of around 3-1/2 octaves — maybe 4, because we have the lower bass in there.

Q: Can there be an "upper-map" version, using the pitches from 127 to 144?

YOUNG: Yeah, we could do only the upper map. Also, I'd like to do the whole *Romantic Symmetry* over a 60-cycle base. I think I would do that before I would do the upper map, because I'd like to keep the low notes in which I already have. I began to realize that I just didn't have enough players for high instruments to get into the upper notes. You know, we had 23 rehearsals for those concerts, and felt we were just beginning to know the notes we were working with! Everybody admitted it, it's the most difficult piece we had ever done. Hearing those pitch relationships was very demanding. Even with the sine waves going in the background. By the time you get all of those musicians going, the level is such that to pick your tones out of that, it's really something.

ZAZEELA: We also did some section rehearsals with smaller groups, just the voices, or voices with the horns, and you might say that was a little easier, it was a little more crystalline to hear where you were in relation to it, but it didn't have that big-group sound. I think the difficulty was to achieve a very good level of intonation and also have the range of sound which we were able to get with all the bass instruments.

Q: That demanded sticking to the lower range of pitches?

ZAZEELA: No, it didn't demand that, but that's how it actually worked out with the players.

YOUNG: To do the whole upper map, it would have been another eleven tones. Most of those notes require at least a violin; some of them require something even higher; very, very high notes.

Since I already had these musicians more or less developed, and had been working with some of them over the years, it seemed like that was the logical part to do.

ZAZEELA: When you work the way La Monte does, and you come up with a problem like that, you find a solution with what's available. Whereas another composer might say, "Oh well, forget this, I can't get all the pitches so I guess I won't do it."

YOUNG: I had no interest in working with musicians that I hadn't already developed a relationship with. It's no fun, it's not worth it.

ZAZEELA: There was a piece scheduled this fall with the Brooklyn Philharmonic. Now it's been postponed for a year, and La Monte's really quite leery about how it's going to work out. At least with the Brooklyn Philharmonic, he's hopeful that he can get them to hire a number of musicians he's already worked with, and bring them in. That's what they've agreed to do, but still....

YOUNG: The piece I've offered them is one of the *Orchestral Dreams*. I had proposed a version that would be for eight trumpets, eight French horns, eight trombones, and eight tubas — in hopes of using a large portion of my players. It's a piece that could be really strong, but it needs a lot of rehearsals, and it needs that understanding of my music which my players are developing. It remains to be seen how the performers of the Brooklyn Philharmonic will relate to it. I think they will relate well, because as brass players I think they will relate to my brass players; I think that the feeling will be transmitted. But I just mentioned 23 rehearsals with the Big Band —

ZAZEELA: — And he's probably going to get two with the Brooklyn Philharmonic.

YOUNG: Well, this is another reason why I'm always afraid I'll get a commission! I apply for these, and then I get them and I worry about how I'm going to turn it into what I really believe in, what I really want to do.

In large works such as *The Well-Tuned Piano*, I interweave themes and interrelated motivic material from different themes, over five or six hours, to create a tapestry that is loaded with interrelationships of remembrances and premonitions and profound musical structures which can't be achieved in the short length that you're required to write for an orchestra, with the limited amount of rehearsal time and the limited tunings and the limited ensemble. The ensembles I want to write for are ensembles of like timbres: eight tubas, eight trombones, eight French horns, and eight trumpets in Harmon mutes. I have no interest in writing for percussion and two clarinets and two flutes and three trumpets and two trombones and one tuba. It's totally disinteresting to me because I'm not writing that kind of hop-skip-and-jump music, where you've got the drums beating the beat and the bass is playing the bass line and the trumpet playing the melody and the flutes picking up the melody and then the whole string section singing with it. I'm writing music that is about very profound relationships in frequencies and in time and in listening, and I need to create large chords in like timbres and have sustained tones. One of the problems I immediately ran into with the Brooklyn ensemble was they said, "Oh, we have to bring in all these other players and then we've got our regular players just sitting there with nothing to do." I'm going to try it and see if I can get this one piece through and how it works and try some others. But it's a question of whether some of my music will ever get into the repertoire or not. I'm not sure that it should, but I'm trying to give it a chance. The reason that I'm not sure that it should is that I recognize how much better it is when it's performed in my own hands. I like the idea of having disciples that you turn the tradition over to, who then perform it and turn it on to the next generation. But that in itself implies a lot of responsibility. The disciples have to have the same commitment and clarity of concept which I have, and the ability to raise funds.

Once you start creating really imaginative work and then you try to take it on tour, you're just asking to compromise, you're just asking to fit it in to earn money. The most important consideration that I find in all of everything I do is to find the appropriate balance between creativity and earning income. It's possible to do things that are so creative that they're not even recognizable, let alone fundable. That's great, I'm all for it. But meanwhile, you create yourself out of existence because you can't bring in any money to do what you want to do. The other extreme is that you try to write just one hit after another, and everybody recognizes that it's a hit and you get your income — that has its problems too. The challenge is how to do extraordinarily creative work — I mean, so creative that it can't even be recognized — and still get funding for it. There's nothing substantial to be gained from compromising except income, and we have to consider that income is not substantial but it's necessary; it's a must, it's a given, you have to have income, somehow you have to get it to go on. But it's not one of the important things for creative artists, in terms of what the really important things are.

I've tried to offer the string-orchestra version of my *Trio for Strings* to orchestras. So far I haven't had much positive response, partly because I ask for a lot of rehearsal time and they just don't want to give it. And I know how hard it is for just a good string trio or a good string quartet to play my *Trio for Strings*, so I know it has to be much harder for an orchestra. Yet orchestras want to do it in one or two rehearsals. And when it comes to writing a piece in just intonation for orchestra.... That's why when I had that Brooklyn Philharmonic invitation, I immediately thought of this idea of an *Orchestral Dream* with brass, using a good portion of my brass players.

Q: Is the conventional concert-hall situation a compromise you accept with an eye towards the time when you won't have to make such compromises, or do you think it's useful to do it their way for the present?

YOUNG: It's a very good question, the perfect question. I guess the thought is, since I've never had anything orchestral played except by my own group, if a piece could be successful with an orchestra, it could perhaps get played in other orchestral situations and eventually be played properly. I'm supposedly going to get a whole half of a program, which would give me around an hour for my piece. For a regular orchestral concert, that's a pretty good length. It's definitely being done with the hope that it would break into some full-length La Monte Young concerts of orchestral dimension. It probably couldn't compete with the Big Band in terms of sincerity and commitment and everything, the final musical result. But since a number of the players will be from the Big Band, I have hopes that it can be really good. It's something I guess that I will try once and see how encouraging or discouraging it is. It could be that I'd be better off putting my own orchestra together. The trade-off is, if it's done with the Brooklyn Philharmonic, they have to pay for it! If I try to put my own orchestra together, I have to pay for it. Sure, if I put my orchestra together, it will be much better; there's no doubt about it. But they've got the audience, they've got some amount of funding. We have to consider it as a first try, to see if it can work. It's a test. I don't want to let it become a compromise.

ZAZEELA: The problem for people composing in just intonation is that the equal-tempered system is so entrenched; it's a very, very large establishment. And there's that huge body of literature which obviously is valuable and shouldn't be discarded.

YOUNG: No, the body of literature is very important. Money is always a factor. The person who has to raise the money or the person who is responsible for organizing it is always thinking, "how can I pay all these musicians," "how many rehearsals are we going to have," and "we have to hire such-and-such conductor." You put all these things together and he has a budget, and then somebody comes along and says, "Hey, I've got a piece in a brand-new tuning and I need twenty rehearsals or ten rehearsals or five rehearsals even," and he starts tearing his hair and saying, "Well, we can't do this; we've got to have things that we can do." It's quite a problem. I think it was in my nature from the beginning to change the system and not to fit in and agree and just do it because it was a possibility. As soon as I started, I was organizing events that needed at first a week of setup time on location. Well, that was unheard of in music, unless you were doing an opera or something. First it was a week, and then that became two weeks, then that became a month. Now, as soon as you talk to me, I say, "I need a month on location just to set up. And I need the space all to myself if you want *The Well-Tuned Piano* or the Big Band. And then I need at least another month to do the concerts." Concerts on this level — I can't play piano for five, six hours more than once a week, and I can't sing for three hours, hard, more than once a week, if I'm going to do it regularly. I can do it twice in three days, but then I have to rest after that. Because I do sing hard in these concerts.

Q: So then the impresario is in the position of having the hall tied up —

YOUNG: — for two or three months. If you want to do seven or eight concerts like I really want to do. We had done basically five concerts with the Big Band:

the press preview and four public concerts. And by the last concert, we were just really getting good, and the piece was taking off. I mean, it had taken off at every concert, but it was really taking off on a new level at the last concert, and that could have built and built and built. I was just craving four more concerts or eight more concerts. The Band needs a place where it can play every Monday night. My music needs a place where it can be heard, where it can go on and I don't have to keep setting it up and breaking it down. That really drives me crazy, it's an enormous expenditure of money and energy.

ZAZEELA: Even in that situation, there was the difficulty that the place had to be re-set up for the exhibition every week. All the microphones and auxiliary equipment for the Big Band had to be put up every week and taken down. And that was a big part of the expense.

YOUNG: But at least the environment didn't have to go up and down. That was what was to have been so incredible about the Harrison Street Dream House, and what was so incredible about it during the six years that it did exist. It was a place where we could get an installation up and leave it up and present a major series. At Harrison Street we had our own security. It was our own responsibility, so we didn't even take the microphones down between concerts; we left them up because our personnel was responsible. And practically nothing ever got stolen from Harrison Street. At the 22nd Street installation, the Dia security did a good job, but they didn't want to be responsible for the microphones. And it was a small-enough space that the stage setup kind of impinged on the environment during the week. So we chose to break it down for various reasons between each concert, and that was an expense. But at least we weren't taking down the whole sound and light environment, which was the basis for the concerts. Having a one-year installation there was very good from that point of view. There were restrictions about access to it, which made it harder for us to do things in it than when we had had the Harrison Steet Dream House, where we had 24-hour access to the space seven days a week, and we could really get work done. We couldn't work at the 22nd Street space at night; we couldn't go in on off-days, sometimes. They would let us in only when they had business hours, and some of those business hours conflicted with days when our sound and light environment was open. It wasn't as free and open as it could have been if it were our own space. We feel that the only answer for our music and light work to evolve and develop to the degree that our inspiration and imagination suggests is to have a long-term space. I might even say, permanent. But certainly some place where we can do installations that can be developed and finessed, rather than just taken down as soon as you've got it up; as soon as you've made a presentation to the public, you take it down for the next variety act that's going to come on.

Q: Which is simply not the sensibility behind your work.

YOUNG: That's right, I am really not interested in variety and contrast, as we pointed out. I'm interested in evolution and development and finesse and subtlety and levels of experience which have to grow out of a tradition that takes place in time. Some of the great, beautiful Romantic feelings have to do with the experience of time and remembrances of time and remembrances of things as they took place over time. And when you have an opportunity to deal with enormous complexes of time, you have an opportunity to present really profound relationships about time and space.

Q: With the exception of the *Five Small Pieces for String Quartet*, I've always heard your music performed in a special environment that employs Marian's lighting and sculpture. I think one of the implications of the Theater of Eternal Music was that the traditional concert-hall situation couldn't support the kind of feelings and experiences you were describing. Do you think you can somehow turn that around — or has it become more attractive to you now to try to function in that environment?

YOUNG: It's not attractive to me to function in the normal concert environment at all. I don't find anything intriguing or interesting about it. I'm going to try it with this commission to see if I can transform it.

We've done some very nice presentations of *The Second Dream of The High-Tension Line Stepdown Transformer*: at the 30-year retrospective, where it was an hour and 47 minutes; at St. Ann's Church, where it was the second part of the program — we thought that worked quite well; and once at Kennedy Center, where it was a full program, with four trumpets. And in each case Marian did lighting. I would say that's my most serious small-scale touring piece — in other words, when somebody asks me for something that's really me but that can be done easily. What I ask to do that is about two days on location before the concert; then they play it and we go.

ZAZEELA: And I try to do something with the existing theater lighting: Just set my colors or possibly set up the lights in such a way that I can cast the shadows of the performers on a backdrop. But not bring in mobiles or other sculptures. Just creating an atmosphere. At St. Ann's we just basically brought our colors into that space, kind of aimed them at the columns and let them fall. It made it sort of magical, I think.

YOUNG: *The Second Dream of The High-Tension Line Stepdown Transformer* I think is a really serious piece. It is one of *The Four Dreams of China*, which was my first piece in the style of the *Trio for Strings*, with long, sustained tones. This work was an algorithmic-based score, utilizing a set of instructions upon which the performers improvised. It's in fact *The Four Dreams of China* which was the inspiration for the idea of a Dream House. I believe that it was hand-in-glove that I composed *The Four Dreams of China* and then I had the idea that a piece could be forever, if you let the concept happen. That is, in this case I realized that since the piece had long tones and silences, that the beginning silence could be the beginning silence and the silence at the end could be the end until somebody else picked it up at that frequency again and began to play the piece again. Somehow, around that time, having that kind of thinking evolving, I got the idea that there should really be a space where a piece could get going and run continuously and not have these considerations of whether or not somebody picked it up again. An incredible piece could develop. Now that I've had the opportunity to do some long-term installations, I'm absolutely convinced that this is a direction that my music really must pursue. Finding the means to do it is the challenge: how to get the funding for a space that's big enough to do things on a substantial level and then keep the space running long term.

Q: The experience of your pieces in these sound and light environments differs from the experience of regular concert-hall music in the sense of intimacy and isolation offered to the listener. Unlike the traditional venues, there's never a feeling of being part of a crowd in hearing these works, regardless of how many other people are there; you're left alone with the music.

ZAZEELA: In our own environments, where we have control over the lighting and the design of the space and everything, I think that's a very realistic conclusion; it should be a feeling that you'd get. I think that the direction of my lighting and the sculptures is towards self-reflection and a meditative atmosphere. If you actually get involved in looking at the mobiles and the lights and the shadows and thinking about the whole transfer of images that you're seeing there, it forces you to be introspective and to reflect it back onto yourself.

The concert tradition, going to a concert and the stage is lit with generally white lighting and the audience area is darkened, is this predictable form. I think choosing some color and putting it into a space and letting lighting happen in one sense makes it more theatrical. But it does take it out of that expected realm. Just changing it in a major way like that I think could be a good thing.

YOUNG: I want to say something about how I became aware of the role of lighting in a concert situation. I did a performance of *Vision* at the University of California at Berkeley around late '59, early '60. The piece contains 11 sounds in a 13-minute time structure which can begin and end with a silence. In order to delineate when the piece began and ended, I decided to turn the lights out. The piece consists of very strange sounds. I had just returned from Darmstadt and was very inspired by having met David Tudor and heard him perform works inside of the piano. Also, I'd heard a recording of Cage's *Concert For Piano And Orchestra* and I had been reading a lot of Cage and thinking about Cage's ideas. In any case, *Vision* had very unusual sounds, and the instruments were located around the room, on the perimeters of the auditorium, in the balcony, and so forth. And the lights were turned out and there were some silences and then a strange sound would come. And the students literally went crazy: They just giggled and laughed and got all upset and didn't know how to relate to the piece at all. Then later, I wrote a piece in which you just announce that the piece will be a certain duration, that the lights will be out for that duration and then turned back on. I began to realize that, if the lights are out, something very special can happen because you get into that sense of being alone with yourself (which many people can't handle); and that most performers were in a very simplistic ego relationship to the audience — they needed immediate acclaim for their presence on stage. What it really was about was that — the music had almost become a vehicle for their going onstage in bright lights, getting acclaim, and having had acclaim, going off. As I became more and more aware of this performer-audience relationship and the composer-performer-audience relationship — the more I composed, the more I performed, the more I observed audiences — I realized that in order to get into really serious work, it was necessary to bypass that relationship, because that relationship was preventing anything serious from happening.

I met Marian in 1962 and the very first concerts we did together were at the 10-4 Gallery and they were in the afternoon. We didn't do anything visual with those: The sun was coming in and it was kind of nice. The first concert where we did sound and light together was at the Pocket Theater, and there we had one of Marian's light boxes with her mandala-like design suspended above the performers. And that really worked, that was really good. From then on, we just realized that by giving the people a visual focus that allowed the performers to exist without putting the performers up front, the music could really happen on a much higher level, and the people could get with the music better, because instead of their focusing on brightly lit performers, they were given visual information that was intuitively designed to relate to the music. In fact, Marian did most of the designs while listening to the music here at the studio.

ZAZEELA: All the old Dream Houses were presented with slide projections. That projection series was a very interesting and involved work.

YOUNG: The projection series was a major work. The only reason we stopped doing the projection series was because of the sound of the projectors. But it worked well with loud music, and with the Big Band, we considered bringing them back, because the Big Band is loud enough. But *The Well-Tuned Piano* was so soft and delicate that we couldn't do the projection series. The projection series can work if the projectors can be in a booth, but you don't always have that when you're on the road; you don't always have the right situation.

Q: I've heard about how loud *The Map of 49's Dream* was supposed to have been, and then I think, "Well, that was 1968, people were barely used to discos...." Was it really loud?

YOUNG: It was really loud. That's the one where Stockhausen had to stand outside, or something — it was too loud and he was worried about hurting his ears.

ZAZEELA: I don't know, though, compared to disco. But we don't really frequent discos.

YOUNG: Well, we were going to hear some rock bands then. We had heard the Who, we had heard Jimi Hendrix.

Q: Did those pieces answer the questions you had in your mind concerning loudness, or is it still an open book for you?

YOUNG: I think loud is still viable. Loud is of course not everything, but loud can create a world of feelings which can't be achieved in any other way. It's a trade-off, you know: You might damage some hearing, depending on a lot of circumstances. It's certainly very possible, and everybody I think wants to take that into consideration. But I felt that the experiences I had were so worthwhile that it was worth it. Also, in my case, we don't know if my hearing was ever really damaged by sound, because my hearing loss is theoretically an inherited loss: Three of my four grandparents had hearing problems; my mother is very hard of hearing and wears hearing aids in both ears; my father had to have an ear operation. It's possible some of my hearing loss could have been due to sound, but a lot of it is probably due to inheritance.

The experiences that I had with loud sounds were so incredible, that at this moment I wouldn't think of trading them in. Also, there's another approach: If you want something to last forever, you take it and you put it in a vacuum and you never go near it. So it's like, you have your hearing, and if you use it at all, it's going to work toward wearing it out. OK, somebody will step right up and say, "Yes, but if you use loud sounds, it's going to be much worse." And I have to say, well, maybe it will be. But it creates an incredible effect. Better to have heard it and lost than never to have heard it at all. I guess the balance between all things is what's very important. It seemed to me that it was necessary to go through very loud sound experiences to enjoy them and appreciate them, to have a more complete and full understanding of sound. OK, I'm lucky that there are enough hearing-aid devices around that I can still hear and get by — and there are some problems with my hearing that these devices can't solve. But I think it was important to experience sound fully. I think most musicians who have worked with loud sound would agree that you may lose something, and that something might be part of your hearing, but there's nothing like that experience, if it's the right sounds. You know, soft sounds are great too and a lot of kinds of sound can be great, but it was through loud sounds that lasted a long time that I developed that understanding of the concept of getting inside of a sound. It was a very physical thing to go, spiritually, inside of the sound. It's something like what Pandit Pran Nath has pointed out on perhaps a more refined level, because he speaks in terms of tuning. When the voice becomes perfectly in tune with the drone, with the tamboura, it's like leaving the body and meeting to God. To become so perfectly in tune, the sensation of being perfectly in tune is just phenomenal, especially if you're a singer, and the concentration is so great that you can't be thinking of your body, so therefore, in a sense, you have left your body. And I think that working with loud sounds is perhaps less refined than this approach to tuning which Pandit Pran Nath speaks of, but it's perhaps a more accessible way to get off into that world of the sound and to leave your body. And if the sounds are both loud and in tune, you've got more working for you!

A sound is a physical process and phenomenon, and if it's louder, you tend to become the sound. When we speak of a psychological state or mood that is created by a certain musical mode, we speak of a set of vibrational patterns which is set up inside of the nervous system, which becomes what we're concentrating on, and to the degree that we concentrate upon it, we become that. So if it's a louder sound, it's just a little easier to become that. But you know, everything in place and in context — you wouldn't want Pandit Pran Nath to be louder than he is, yet he uses amplification so he can be loud enough to reach the audience.

Q: You were talking earlier about the idea of organic improvisation coming out of your studies with Pandit Pran Nath. Are there other specific regards in which, as a composer, your studying with him has been beneficial?

YOUNG: Yes. I think that, over all, he heightened my awareness on all levels of music and imagination. It's very interesting the way he taught me. He only taught me Indian classical music and the spirituality of Indian classical music — never tried to teach me anything about my own work. But I absorbed his teachings, and his teachings raised the level of my musicianship and heightened my sensibility about what music could be. Also, one very important thing that I learned from him was how to live and train as a performer. It was something that I had really never received in my Western training; in my Western training, I would go and have a lesson and then go back home. But in this tradition of Indian classical music, if you're a disciple of the teacher, you actually spend as much time as possible with the teacher, which means actually live with the teacher and serve the teacher. So for the first, I don't know, 15 years that he was in the West, he spent 50 percent of his time right here in this loft. Not every lesson is a sit-down lesson where he says, "OK, now I'm going to teach you this." Ninety percent of the lessons are you just observing what's going on. In fact, Indian musicians take pride in the fact that their children learn to sing without lessons; that they just hear it around the house and start singing. That's considered the advanced way to learn: If you're fortunate and can spend time around the master, then you just begin to absorb the tradition.

Q: Discipleship is absorbing not just technique but an attitude.

YOUNG: An attitude and an entire way of life. And this is what he gave us, an entire way of life, which has been really quite phenomenal and extremely rewarding. Our lives have never been the same since. It's just incredible to watch him prepare for a concert series: the single-minded focus, the training. He won't speak on the day of a concert, won't talk to anybody — and gets quite annoyed if you try to talk to him! Even the day before, he starts to cut down on talking. There are other interesting things on a very high level: Before a concert, he won't let us practice the ragas he might sing, because he doesn't want his inspiration to be sidetracked or spoiled.

Q: What are your own ambitions as raga singers?

YOUNG: Oh, we definitely want to sing raga. One of the ways Terry Riley and I still perform together is in raga. We've done some private recitals together, and I think we have an interest in doing more-public concerts of ragas together. Our intention is to go more public with our raga singing.

Q: Is there any feeling that, simply because of ethnicity or cultural difference, you could never attain a certain level of mastery?

YOUNG: No. We don't have that feeling and Pandit Pran Nath doesn't have that feeling. It's a feeling that can be had, but we don't have it.

ZAZEELA: I think that East Indians would probably be doubtful that anyone outside of their own culture could really —

YOUNG: Not all Indians, no.

ZAZEELA: I think they would come with that bias.

YOUNG: They might come with that, but I think after they've heard it....

ZAZEELA: Yeah.

Q: That certainly isn't the way Pandit Pran Nath teaches it; that's not the attitudes he promotes.

YOUNG: He's very positive in his teachings. He's already told us to sing publicly. In fact, he was telling us to sing publicly back in the early '80s. We've just been very gradual about it, because since we already have careers as artists, we don't have a need to do it to get income or to get heard.

Q: In some ways, Western listeners might be more uptight that what they're hearing from an American raga singer is ersatz, whereas an Indian audience could be more appreciative of the singer's technique.

YOUNG: Well, we've been well appreciated when we sang private concerts in India; Indians liked us a lot.

ZAZEELA: They liked it, but I think they were also somewhat bemused.

Q: It can be off-putting when something of theirs comes back in this way.

ZAZEELA: I think so, yeah.

YOUNG: Sure.

Q: Especially if it's done really well!

YOUNG: Yeah, sure. There's always jealousy. For instance, there's a lot of jealousy in India over Pandit Pran Nath's spending so much time in America — his Indian disciples feel that they really have lost him. Among one or two of them, there was some jealousy that he was gone.

Q: Is there the idea that somebody is going to have to take his place when he stops teaching?

YOUNG: Yeah. Well, already we teach all of his East Coast students. He's had us teaching here since the '70s.

Q: When did you realize that you'd become not just students but disciples?

YOUNG: In our case, he didn't treat us like other students. He just gave us a few lessons and then he said he wouldn't teach us unless we became disciples. Because...

Q: He knew.

ZAZEELA: He knew, right.

YOUNG: And we didn't even know what it meant! We were asking his other students, "What is it?" One of his disciples, Shyam Bhatnagar — we had helped Shyam bring him over — was saying, "Well, he doesn't want to teach you unless you become a disciple." And we were saying, "What is it?" Because the concept isn't here in the West as much anymore; it's a lost concept. It was an Eastern thing.

ZAZEELA: He told us we'd have to start his school and everything, and we thought, he's out of his mind, you know? What is he talking about?

YOUNG: He was always very certain of what he was doing, and very sure, never doubtful. And he often said, "You can't be doubtful. You have to make up your mind about what you're doing and do it."

Q: What kind of reaction did you get from your peers and, more importantly, your teachers, when you wrote *for Guitar*, *Trio for Strings*, and *for Brass* back in the late '50s? And how did you feel about moving in that direction?

YOUNG: I personally felt very strongly that this was a direction I was supposed to move in. I felt very inspired when I wrote the *Trio for Strings* at UCLA. I guess I must have written it over the summer and finished it in September, just before I went up to Berkeley, and I finished numbering the bars in Berkeley. Even when I wrote the middle section of *for Brass*, which had long sustained tones, I felt this was very important. Dennis Johnson, who knew me at the time, and Terry Jennings — Terry Jennings I think liked it, and Dennis didn't like it at first, but then when Dennis heard the *Trio for Strings*, I guess he really liked that. Terry Riley liked the *Trio for Strings* when he heard it. Riley and I became very good friends, and enjoyed very much performing together: I would perform in his pieces and he would perform in mine. At that time, Terry was writing something like late Schoenberg, and I was talking to him about the latest developments in serial technique and also showing him my music. And I found him to be extremely talented and open and receptive.

I took the *Trio for Strings* to Berkeley and showed it to Seymour Shifrin, and he arranged for it to be played in a kind of musicale recital at his home, for his composition class. So first we heard it and then we did a lot of talking. He had asked what piece we wanted to analyze, and I had suggested that I wanted to analyze the Schoenberg Trio for strings, because I liked it. So I remember that night, drinking coffee at his house, having heard my *Trio for Strings* and then doing some work on the Schoenberg Trio for strings. Eventually, Shifrin and I talked about my *Trio for Strings*, and he told me that I couldn't write that way in his class or he wouldn't be able to give me a grade; that he felt I was writing like an 80-year-old man, and that I should be writing with youth and vigor, like a young man — music that had climaxes and line and direction. So I wrote *Study 1* for piano specifically to demonstrate to him that I could do that. It won the Nicola De Lorenzo composition prize at Berkeley, for which Shifrin was one of the people who sat on the panel.

Q: It's interesting that what Seymour Shifrin said he wanted to hear in your composition was already present in your piano and saxophone playing.

YOUNG: The jazz playing, yeah. But I had left jazz because I had felt that to play jazz — it's this old question that something has to be recognizably something for it to be considered something. I was moving in a direction of jazz that was much more rhythmically complex and harmonically complex and less obviously swinging, even though I was swinging. And I just decided, why did I have to be bothered with those constraints? At the same time I was playing jazz, I was writing *Five Small Pieces for String Quartet* and *for Brass* and *for Guitar* and *Trio for Strings*. I probably stopped playing jazz — seriously stopped — by around '58. I think I stopped around the time I left L.A. City College, which would place it around '56. The recordings I have of me playing jazz are from '55 and '56. Probably by '57 I was stopping. I remember I used to play at L.A. State College a little bit. (L.A. State was a transition between City and UCLA; in fact, I went back to L.A. City one semester.)

Q: I understand that Stockhausen used the *Trio for Strings* as part of a teaching exercise in Darmstadt.

YOUNG: No, that's not accurate. Maybe he later used it as a teaching exercise, I don't know. But I didn't show it to him until the last day I was at Darmstadt, because I'd had such bad luck with Shifrin — I showed Stockhausen *Study 1* for piano. But the day I was leaving, I showed him the *Trio for Strings*, and he said, "Oh, you should have showed me this sooner. This is extremely interesting." Stockhausen did devote a considerable amount of time, however, discussing my *Study 3* for piano, which I wrote in the class, during the seminar. Cornelius Cardew has written about that somewhat, that Stockhausen must have been impressed with my ability to organize abstractly. *Study 3* for piano was all based on the number 7, and it was based on this number in various abstract ways.

One of the most interesting things that happened about the class at Darmstadt was that there was a student recital at the end. David Tudor was supposed to play my *Study 3* for piano, and the day before the recital or the day of the recital he lost the piece, and found it the day afterward. And I was always very suspicious because it didn't seem like David Tudor to lose anything. But the piece did have some long silences in it. Anyway, there's been a lot of speculation about that.

Q: Did you have to go all the way to Darmstadt to first hear some of the Cage pieces you were describing earlier, such as the *Concert For Piano And Orchestra*? Had you much familiarity with Cage's work before then?

YOUNG: Well, Terry Jennings introduced me to the work of John Cage, I believe around the summer of 1957. He played for me the early Cage quartet, which I really like, and liked then very much, and the *Sonatas And Interludes* for prepared piano, which I didn't like as much then but liked later. But I never liked them as much as the String Quartet, which I think is really a very significant piece; in fact, I think it's Cage's best piece. It's a very imaginative piece and unusual.

Q: It's interesting how many of the Fluxus people came out of the course he taught at the New School in 1958. You, however, were on the West Coast at the time.

YOUNG: Yeah. I never took his course. In fact, I didn't ever formally study with John Cage, although I consider him a major influence on me, and a teacher, and one of the great musicians and musical thinkers of our time. I think there's no doubt but that his work made it possible for me to, for instance, compose my 1960 *Compositions*, which at that time were called word compositions and which I later called the Theater of the Singular Event, and which were I think the foundations for what Henry Flynt later created as concept art.

Q: I'm particularly interested in the transition from your notated scores of the late '50s to these '60s pieces, and the understanding that you could compose music by writing a verbal instruction for the performer.

YOUNG: *Vision* is mainly words, with some graphic notations to give the performers an idea of the sounds. *Poem for Chairs, Tables, Benches, etc.* is all words. *Vision* was composed in November '59, and *Poem for Chairs, Tables, Benches, etc.* in January 1960. All of those pieces happened after I heard Tudor at Darmstadt. I think I had read some of the Cage lectures before I went to Darmstadt. But I got copies of some of them in Darmstadt, or saw more things of Cage there than I had seen before.

When I came to New York in the fall of 1960, I had thought I would study with him and Richard Maxfield. But Cage was somewhere else, so I studied with Maxfield — and was very happy about that, because he really knew a lot about electronics and got me off to a really good start. Maxfield was a rare phenomenon, really good with electronics. After two semesters in Richard's class, I was no longer interested in studying in a formal way, until I met Pandit Pran Nath in 1970.

One thing that was really important about Maxfield is that he was probably the first American to compose with electronically generated sounds, as opposed to re-recorded *musique concrète*. He did some of that too, such as in *Cough Music* and *Steam* and *Radio Music*. But he did use electronically generated sounds, and his approach to composition with electronic sounds was quite imaginative at the time, and his pieces sound just as good today as they did then.

Q: But you didn't get into composing electronic music at that time; you were doing the instructional pieces.

YOUNG: Except that I did compose *2 Sounds* which is a tape piece consisting of friction sounds recorded by Terry Riley and me. In 1961 I did the 1961 *Compositions*, which were all "Draw a straight line and follow it." They were composed as a strong statement. It was a conceptual work in which I wanted to compose my entire 1961 output more or less in one stroke, and I did it by taking a composition I had already composed in 1960, and then counting the number of compositions I had composed in 1960 and then distributing that number of compositions throughout the year 1961, so that there was one composition about every 13 days. It was also of interest to me that I performed a number of the compositions before they were composed. I performed the entire series of 1961 compositions in two places, at Henry Flynt's concert of avant-garde music, which he presented at Harvard in March 1961, and then again at my series at Yoko Ono's loft in May 1961.

Q: You were also playing piano improvisations with Terry Jennings and Dennis Johnson around then.

YOUNG: That's correct. I was doing a lot of piano playing in the summer of 1961. Terry Jennings was improvising on alto saxophone, sounding just like Lee Konitz and doing it with complete freedom and ease and a real ability to hear the pitches. He could just hear anything: You could play some great big chord and he could run the notes up and down just as fast as you could play — he had an incredible ear. He had perfect pitch, of course, but it was more than that. He could identify anything you played, but what he played on top of it was so beautiful and soulful and Romantic. Terry was one of the few people that I used to like to play piano for; I would play piano for him so that he could play. We really enjoyed playing together. And he was the first person after me to write in the style of the *Trio for Strings*, to write pieces with long sustained tones, such as his String Quartet, which I published in *An Anthology*.

Around that time, I also played piano at the Village Vanguard or the Village Gate, on some kind of a peace benefit — does that sound likely? Was there any movement for peace in '61? And the audience really liked it. I played with Walter DeMaria on drums, and Simone Forti sang. I wonder if Terry was there.

Q: Was the piano playing closely related to what you'd be doing on sopranino saxophone in the next year or two?

YOUNG: It was that static, modal, drone-style of piano playing which I played behind Terry Jennings.

Q: And that was different from your jazz playing in the '50s?

YOUNG: It is different. What I was doing in jazz was jazz; I was playing in a style that was a combination of Lee Konitz and Charlie Parker. What I did on the sopranino saxophone is really totally La Monte Young.

Q: So the piano in a sense was a transition between your reed styles.

YOUNG: I guess you could say it was. I guess that's true.

Q: Will those recordings — "B-flat Dorian Blues" or "Early Tuesday Morning Blues" — ever be released?

YOUNG: I really want to release them; I'm very eager to release them. Right now, they're at a point where I have to work out a contract with the performers on the tapes, because they were recorded at a time when we never thought of having an agreement. Now I have to work that out and once that's worked out, we plan to release them. I think there's nothing like it, and I think it's very important to get it out. It's quite interesting that I stopped playing saxophone. It's interesting also to think of whether or not I had to stop. But at that time I felt I had to stop. I wanted to develop my voice, and I was interested in just intonation and felt that the saxophone had certain limitations, but with the voice I could sing anything I could hear.

Q: The genesis of *The Well-Tuned Piano* begins in 1964, and a lot of those sax techniques could have been fed directly into that style of piano playing.

YOUNG: Apparently they did, and the whole tuning of the piano grew out of how I played the saxophone. The opening chord of *The Well-Tuned Piano* is based on a chord that I was playing in "Early Tuesday Morning Blues," and I tuned the piano to E-flat. When I was playing "B-flat Dorian Blues," that's G on the E-flat sopranino saxophone, and that makes C as the IV chord. So the E-flat sopranino C seven chord is a concert E-flat seven chord, which is what I open *The Well-Tuned Piano* with, but it has no third, and that was a characteristic of my style, to have no third in it. There are no thirds in the *Trio for Strings* — in particular no major thirds.

I had developed a style of blues which I later called "Young's Blues," in which, if I was playing piano, I would stay on each chord for as long as I wanted, rather than for a certain number of beats or a certain number of measures. Basically, I like to play blues with a pattern of the I chord for 4 bars, and then the IV chord for 2 bars, then the I chord for 2 bars, then the V chord for 1 bar, the IV chord for 1 bar, and the I chord for 2 bars. So with that structure you really got the I chord for 8 bars.

But then I started taking that progression and staying on each chord as long as I wanted. And Terry Jennings would improvise over that. Later, when I started the Theater of Eternal Music with Tony Conrad and Marian and Billy Linich (later Billy Name) and John Cale, I taught them to sustain these chords in the background and occasionally to change them, and I would play sopranino saxophone over them. But in "Early Tuesday Morning Blues," I had reached the point where I was just sustaining the IV chord; the whole thing is over the IV chord. That's how *The Well-Tuned Piano* begins, on this IV chord. It has a ninth in it; it has an F in the E-flat chord, which is not in the chord I was sustaining by doing fast combination permutations on the sopranino saxophone.

Q: 1964 is the year in which both *The Well-Tuned Piano* and *The Tortoise, His Dreams and Journeys* begin, and the saxophone is set aside. Is it your recollection that something special happened for you in that year, or were you simply going on following what was interesting to you?

YOUNG: It was all tied in together, and I was following what was interesting to me.

ZAZEELA: La Monte was getting more interested in just intonation, and he started to tune the piano — we had a little spinet piano here that had been my piano when I was growing up, which my parents had given us. He had started tuning it into what was to become *The Well-Tuned Piano*, and at the same time he was getting increasingly frustrated with the saxophone. He bought some double reeds and considered trying to turn the saxophone into a shenai.

YOUNG: But I didn't find that to be working out too well.

ZAZEELA: Of course, double reed wasn't his reed. And he was thinking about trying to imagine what it would cost to have a special saxophone made that could play in just intonation. Somehow he just started to realize that his voice was right there.

YOUNG: It struck me that I could build one saxophone in one tuning, but then if I wanted to have another tuning, I'd have to have another one built. And I decided to make the leap and switch to voice. Which was quite a daring leap because I had played saxophone since I was seven years old, and I had all my technique, I had everything together on the saxophone. Although I had done a little singing — my father and my Aunt Norma started to teach me cowboy songs when I was 2, 3, 4, in that age, and to play the guitar — I hadn't really formally worked on my voice the way I had worked on saxophone.

I didn't know anything about classical music in junior high school; all I really knew was cowboy music. It wasn't until high school, when I became a music major at John Marshall, that you could say I had any kind of beginnings of studying classical music, outside of whatever had been in my lesson books as a saxophone student — and playing in orchestra and band, of course, in grade school and junior high. But my high-school harmony teacher, Clyde Sorenson, had studied with Schoenberg at UCLA, and I took five or six semesters of harmony in high school and really liked it; it was easy for me and I did well in it. He played, I believe, the Schoenberg *Six Small Piano Pieces* when I was a senior, and I remember finding those very interesting. The other thing that he did which I found very inspirational was he took us to hear the Bartók *Concerto For Orchestra* at the L.A. Philharmonic, some special afternoon rehearsal for high-school students, you know, and I really found that so inspirational. My main interest in high school was jazz — I was playing jazz and that was the main kind of music I was interested in — but I got to L.A. City College and studied with Leonard Stein, and he introduced me to contemporary music and I started to really like it. By the time Leonard had introduced me to Webern, and got me writing some things, and people started to think that I was a good composer, and one thing led to another and I got very interested in composition suddenly, I gradually stopped playing jazz, and decided that, as a format, jazz was not supportive of open-ended creativity. What was interesting about my playing sopranino saxophone was it was tying together my skills on saxophone and my knowledge of improvisation with my knowledge of composition. And then all of that just branched out more and more into many other things, and I did it with other instrumental forces.

But it was partly my interest in just intonation that led me to switch from saxophone to voice. Tony Conrad had been very interested in just intonation, and he had pointed out to me that, with the positive integers, you could have a way of labeling all of the O-tonalities, as Harry Partch refers to them. I hadn't realized that before, although obviously other theoreticians had known about it. Once I understood that — somehow I had missed it in my acoustics of music class at L.A. City College — I just took off into the harmonic series and into just intonation, and started thinking that way and composing that way. I had composed a scale and set of frequency relationships for a piece we later called *Prelude to The Tortoise*, then, slightly later, almost simultaneously, I composed the first tuning for *The Well-Tuned Piano*, and tuned it. By June '64, there's a recording of *The Well-Tuned Piano*.

Q: You were saying before that the style of playing for the "Cloud" sections dominated that earlier version of the piece.

YOUNG: Yeah, but there were some slow sections too, I have to admit. I should play the 1964 version of *The Well-Tuned Piano* for people again sometime.

Q: How long was that realization?

ZAZEELA: The one that we usually play is about 45 minutes.

YOUNG: All I remember is I played until the tape ran out.

Q: There have been longer performances of *The Well-Tuned Piano* than the one released by Gramavision; I understand it's gotten up to over six hours.

YOUNG: Yeah, six hours and 24 minutes is the longest performance I did, and that was at the last concert of *The Well-Tuned Piano*, which I performed in 1987, at my 30-year retrospective produced by the MELA Foundation.

Q: Did those realizations have sections which weren't in the Gramavision recording, or was it more a matter of spending more time with what was already there?

YOUNG: No, there were brand-new sections. Both approaches would have been possible. But I really surprised myself. Because when I got ready to do the 30-year retrospective, I said to several people, including Marian and Heiner Friedrich (who was helping us sponsor the series), "I don't want to play *The Well-Tuned Piano*, because it's recorded, it's done, it's out, I was really in great shape then" — I had just finished three series of *The Well-Tuned Piano* at the Harrison Street Dream House, and this recording was the last concert of the last of the three series. I said, "Number one, I will never be able to play it like that. Number two, since it's already recorded, I should be working on something else, I've got to get another recording out, which takes me forever!"

ZAZEELA: Also, that summer, as we were planning the 30-year retrospective, we were finishing up the preparations for the recording: doing the mastering of it, and the timings for that time-score in the program. To get that as accurate as it is, we went over it many, many, many times. We were listening to it all the time, for five hours at a clip. There it was, 1987, and the piece had been recorded in 1981, and we were pretty impressed! It was just so beautiful, it seemed like it was just a masterpiece. I think La Monte himself was just in awe of it, of what he had done, and thought "I can't measure up." Because in the meantime we had been booted out of Harrison Street and had to regroup, and had all these reversals and difficulties —

YOUNG: I was somewhat depressed anyway. But what I didn't realize was that, in listening to it all of those times through the mastering, I was really thinking about the piece. In any case, Heiner Friedrich insisted I play *The Well-Tuned Piano*; he really wanted to hear it.

ZAZEELA: And when he started, from the very first play-through rehearsal, he played longer than the five hours. Which was another thing too: Did he have the stamina anymore? Could he really play through the piece?

YOUNG: Then as I began to rehearse and perform the series, I started composing completely new sections at the piano, just like that. I guess there were seven concerts, and by the seventh concert, there were just all kinds of new sections. I really surprised myself. And I realized again how deeply in love I am with *The Well-Tuned Piano*; I am crazy about it. I really long for opportunities to play it, but I want to play it in the right way. I can't stand to just sit down at the piano and tinkle the keys. I have to be preparing for a serious presentation of the piece — it's too painful to get only a little bit involved with it. It's quite a commitment just to keep the piano all tuned up perfectly so that it's inspirational to play. My best performances come out of the best tunings, because the tunings actually inspire how I play. So I've taught my disciple of *The Well-Tuned Piano*, Michael Harrison, how to tune the piano. He now tunes it extremely well, so that I don't even have to hear the tuning once he tells me it's ready; I just walk onstage and play. Those chords that he's tuned the most perfectly are the ones that I linger on and do the most inspired, imaginative performances on.

If the piano is in that state of tuning and I have the time to really get into it — you know, when I'm just practicing the piano, I think nothing of sitting down and spending two or three hours in "The Pool." I remember once I was practicing in Rome and Fabio Sargentini said he just couldn't believe it: I had sat there and played for four and a half hours or something, just practicing. You have to have that kind of time to allot to it, and you have to have a reason to be able to allot that kind of time to it. Because I have a lot of other projects going on, and if nobody is going to pay me to do a performance of *The Well-Tuned Piano*, how can I do it?

ZAZEELA: One of the new sections is an "Hommage à Ravel" — it's gorgeous.

YOUNG: I think, for me, one of my favorite new sections is "Blues for Eurydice." There's also a new section called "Orpheus and Eurydice in The Elysian Fields." And there's another new section that might be called just "Blues in B-flat."

ZAZEELA: Another thing that somehow came in more strongly in that later series was a reinterpretation of the "Young's Blues," bringing in more of that rhythmic style that he had played in the early '60s, and doing what he called blues breaks.

YOUNG: I started introducing blues breaks. The other thing I did which was more along the other direction you mentioned, of spending more time with what was already there, was that I greatly expanded and Romanticized "The Fountain." It just became totally unbelievable — very beautiful. So I don't know when I'll ever get a chance to play it again. Nobody's knocking on the door.

Q: *The Well-Tuned Piano* has sections entitled "Hommage à Debussy." The Debussy connection in this music is clear, not just in the sensibility that results in references and titles such as "The Shimmering Pool" and "Sunlight Filtering through Leaves," but in attitudes about staticism, which Debussy worked with at the turn of the century. What I find hard to see is the Brahms connection, signalled by the "Homage to Brahms" sections. Is it a matter of a Brahmsian quality in those passages, or is there a larger link to Brahms which I'm missing?

YOUNG: I think it's only that I felt something about that theme really reminded me of Brahms. There isn't a larger link; I don't know Brahms that well. Of course, I consider Debussy a really profound and very creative figure. There's a quote of his, which I'm trying to find exactly written out, about composition, where he said "Listen to the words of no man. Listen only to the wind and the waves of the sea." I took that imagery very seriously. To some degree, in my music, the formal structure is inspired by how clouds move across the sky. I found that that really became a tremendously fertile source of inspiration for structural form. The wind, of course, was one of the first sounds I remember, and I've written about that. But I've never talked before of how it might have influenced my sense of form, because I've never thought about it before this instant, when I was thinking about the clouds. But it probably did. I just talked about how interesting it was and how it probably had something to do with the sustained tones, but it's usually not sustained at one pitch; the wind moves around and changes according to its speed.

Q: The time score included with the recording, which Marian mentioned before, reveals how busy the piece is internally: It's a 300-minute work with about 400 different sections. Yet the overall sound is calm and serene, even at its most dense or raucous.

YOUNG: That's why I think *The Well-Tuned Piano* is really my most evolved compositional achievement. I think that there, with some very specific and limited amount of thematic and motivic material, I've been able to create something that exists on so many levels that it goes perhaps beyond the level of most extraordinary composition. Because there's not a note wasted in the piece; it's all completely tied together, thematically and motivically, yet I'm able to do it in such a way that it all comes out sounding completely natural and spontaneous. Yet there are so many levels on which to enter the piece and experience the piece and dwell in the piece. And it shouldn't be me saying this about the piece, but I think I have to be responsible to myself and to the piece and say what I really think.

Q: Hasn't Michael Harrison performed *The Well-Tuned Piano*?

YOUNG: He's played it in recital in private concerts. I haven't let anybody take it into the world in a public concert, but he has played it for a group of invited friends, and he plays it very well.

Q: How important it is to you to have other people play the piece?

YOUNG: Well, after I die, I think it's important that it be carried on in that way — or after I can no longer perform it. But at the moment, I think my performances are the definitive performances. And the only thing that would come from letting other people play it is that they would go out and play it for one-tenth the price, and everybody would want to hire them instead of me and nobody would want to do the real thing — because people are very easily satisfied to get a name on their festival for less money. All that people want when they come to me to be on a festival is my name. They don't care about my music: If I say I want to do *The Well-Tuned Piano*, they say, "Oh, you've done that." And if I say, "But it has all of these new sections," they say, "Well, what have you got that's less expensive?" I'm thinking about the evolution of music and what music can be and what art can be and what it is that we're here for and how we can hear and what is the interrelationship of our existence to time and eternity and universal structure. And they're thinking of, "How can I get La Monte Young's name on a concert at a reasonable price?" Very few producers are thinking about what I'm thinking about. It's really a challenge because you can just knock yourself out and go running around and get your name all over the place. But in my case, I didn't take up music to earn money, because I would've taken up something else if my goals in life were really to earn money; you can earn more money with other things. I'm doing music because I feel I was created to do it and that I have a responsibility to do what I'm doing. And to structure the correspondence of ideas of this type with earning a living is very challenging.

COMPOSITIONS

1953	*Scherzo* in a minor for piano
1953	*Rondo* in d minor for piano
1953-55	*Annod* for dance band or jazz ensemble
1954	*Wind Quintet*
1955	*Variations* for string quartet
1955-59	*Young's Blues*
1956	*Fugue in d minor* for violin, viola, and cello
1956	*Op. 4* for brass and percussion
1956	*Five Small Pieces for String Quartet, On Remembering A Naiad* 1. *A Wisp,* 2. *A Gnarl,* 3. *A Leaf,* 4. *A Twig,* 5. *A Tooth*
1957	*Canon* for any two instruments
1957	*Fugue in a minor* for any four instruments
1957	*Fugue in c minor* for organ or harpsichord
1957	*Fugue in eb minor* for brass or other instruments
1957	*Fugue in f minor* for two pianos
1957	*Prelude in f minor* for piano
1957	*Variations for Alto Flute, Bassoon, Harp, and String Trio*
1957	*for Brass* for brass octet
1958	*for Guitar* for guitar
1958	*Trio For Strings* for violin, viola, and cello
1958-59	*Study* for violin and viola (unfinished)
1959	*Sarabande* for keyboard, brass octet, string quartet, orchestra, others
1959	*Study I* for piano
1959	*Study II* for piano
1959	*Study III* for piano
1959	*Vision* for piano, two brass, recorder, four bassoons, violin, viola, cello, and contrabass
1959-60	[Untitled] for live friction sounds
1959-62	[Untitled] jazz-drone improvisations

1960	*Poem for Chairs, Tables, Benches, etc.* for chairs, tables, benches, and unspecified sound sources
1960	*2 Sounds* for pre-recorded friction sounds
1960	*Compositions 1960 #s 2, 3, 4, 5, 6, 7, 9, 10, 13, 15* performance pieces
1960	*Piano Pieces for David Tudor #s 1, 2, 3* performance pieces
1960	*Invisible Poem Sent to Terry Jennings* performance piece
1960	*Piano Pieces for Terry Riley #s 1, 2* performance pieces
1960	*Target for Jasper Johns* for piano
1960	*Arabic Numeral (Any Integer) to H.F.* for piano(s) or gong(s) or ensembles of at least 45 instruments of the same timbre, or combinations of the above or orchestra
1961	*Compositions 1961 #s 1 - 29* performance pieces
1961	*Young's Dorian Blues in Bb*
1961	*Young's Aeolian Blues in Bb*
1961	*Death Chant* for male voices, carillon, or large bells
1962	*Response to Henry Flynt Work Such That No One Knows What's Going On*
1962-64	[Improvisations] for sopranino saxophone, vocal drones, and various instruments realizations include *Bb Dorian Blues, The Fifth/Fourth Piece, ABABA, EbDEAD, DEGAC, The Overday, Early Tuesday Morning Blues*, and *Sunday Morning Blues*
1962	*Poem on Dennis' Birthday* for unspecified instruments
1962	*The Four Dreams of China (The Harmonic Versions)* for tunable, sustaining instruments of like timbre, in multiples of four, including *The First Dream of China, The First Blossom of Spring, The First Dream of The High-Tension Line Stepdown Transformer, The Second Dream of The High-Tension Line Stepdown Transformer*
1963	*Studies in The Bowed Disc* for gong
1964	*Pre-Tortoise Dream Music* for sopranino saxophone, soprano saxophone, vocal drone, violin, viola, and sine waves
1964-present	*The Tortoise, His Dreams and Journeys* for voices, various instruments, and sine waves realizations include *Prelude to The Tortoise; The Tortoise Droning Selected Pitches from The Holy Numbers for The Two Black Tigers, The Green Tiger, and The Hermit; The Tortoise Recalling The Drone of The Holy Numbers as They Were Revealed in The Dreams of The Whirlwind and The Obsidian Gong and Illuminated by The Sawmill, The Green Sawtooth Ocelot, and The High-Tension Line Stepdown Transformer, The Obsidian Ocelot, The Sawmill, and The Blue Sawtooth High-Tension Line Stepdown Transformer Refracting The Legend of The Dream of The Tortoise Traversing The 189/98 Lost Ancestral Lake*

Region Illuminating Quotients from The Black Tiger Tapestries of The Drone of The Holy Numbers; The Ballad of The Tortoise or Pierced Earrings/Drone Ratios Transmitting The Manifestation of The Tortoise Center Drifting Obsidian Time Mists through The Synaptic Stepdown Barrier, 7; The Celebration of The Tortoise; Tortoise

1964- *The Well-Tuned Piano* for piano
present

1965 *Sunday Morning Dreams* for tunable sustaining instruments and/or sine waves

1965 *Composition 1965 $50* performance piece

1966- *Map of 49's Dream The Two Systems of Eleven Sets of Galactic*
present *Intervals Ornamental Lightyears Tracery* for voices, various instruments, and sine waves

1966 *Bowed Mortar Relays* for tape (realization of *Composition 1960 #9*), *Soundtracks for Andy Warhol Films* "Eat," "Sleep," "Kiss," "Haircut") for tape

1966- *The Two Systems Of Eleven Categories* theory work
present

1967- *Chords from The Tortoise, His Dreams and Journeys* for sine waves
present realizations include *Intervals and Triads from Map of 49's Dream The Two Systems of Eleven Sets of Galactic Intervals Ornamental Lightyears Tracery* sound environment

1967 *Robert C. Scull Commission* for sine waves

1967 *Claes And Patty Oldenburg Commission* for sine waves

1967 *Betty Freeman Commission* sound and light box & sound environment

1967- *Drift Studies* for sine waves
present

1978 *for Guitar (Just Intonation Version)* for guitar

1980 *for Guitar Prelude and Postlude* for one or more guitars

1980 *The Subsequent Dreams of China* for tunable, sustaining instruments of like timbre, in multiples of eight

1981 *The Gilbert B. Silverman Commission to Write, in Ten Words or Less, A Complete History of Fluxus Including Philosophy, Attitudes, Influences, Purposes*

1981- *Chords from The Well-Tuned Piano* sound environments
present includes *The Opening Chord* (1981), *The Magic Chord* (1984), *The Magic Opening Chord* (1984)

1983 *Trio for Strings* versions for string quartet; string orchestra; violin, viola, cello, and bass

1984 *Trio for Strings, trio basso version* for viola, cello, and bass

1984 *Trio for Strings Postlude from The Subsequent Dreams of China* for bowed strings

1984   *The Melodic Versions* of *The Four Dreams of China* (1962) for tunable, sustaining instruments of like timbre, in multiples of eight including *The First Dream of China, The First Blossom of Spring, The First Dream of The High-Tension Line Stepdown Transformer, The Second Dream of The High-Tension Line Stepdown Transformer*

1984   *The Melodic Versions* of *The Subsequent Dreams of China* (1980) for tunable, sustaining instruments of like timbre, in multiples of eight including *The High-Tension Line Stepdown Transformer's Second Dream of The First Blossom of Spring*

1984   *The Big Dream* sound environment

1985   *Orchestral Dreams* for orchestra

1988   *The Big Dream Symmetries #s 1-6* sound environments

1989   *The Symmetries in Prime Time from 144 to 112 with 119* sound environment including *The Close Position Symmetry, The Symmetry Modeled on BDS #1, The Symmetry Modeled on BDS #4, The Symmetry Modeled on BDS #7, The Romantic Symmetry, The Romantic Symmetry (over a 60-Cycle Base), The Great Romantic Symmetry*

1989-90   *The Lower Map of The Eleven's Division in The Romantic Symmetry (over a 60-Cycle Base) in Prime Time from 144 to 112 with 119* for tunable sustaining instruments in sections of like timbre, and sound environment

1989-90   *The Prime Time Twins* sound environments including *The Prime Time Twins in The Ranges 144 to 112; 72 to 56 and 38 to 28; Including The Special Primes 1 and 2* (1989); *The Prime Time Twins in The Ranges 576 to 448; 288 to 224; 144 to 112; 72 to 56; 36 to 28; With The Range Limits 576, 448, 288, 224, 144, 56, and 28* (1990)

1990   *Chronos Kristalla* for string quartet

1991   *The Young Prime Time Twins* sound environments including *The Young Prime Time Twins in The Ranges 2304 to 1792; 1152 to 896; 576 to 448; 288 to 224; 144 to 112; 72 to 56; 36 to 28; Including or Excluding The Range Limits 2304, 1792, 1152, 576, 448, 288, 224, 56, and 28 The Young Prime Time Twins in The Ranges 2304 to 1792; 1152 to 896; 576 to 448; 288 to 224; 144 to 112; 72 to 56; 36 to 28; 18 to 14; Including or Excluding The Range Limits 2304, 1792, 1152, 576, 448, 288, 224, 56, 28, and 18; and Including The Special Young Prime Twins Straddling The Range Limits 1152, 72, and 18 The Young Prime Time Twins in The Ranges 1152 to 896; 576 to 448; 288 to 224; 144 to 112; 72 to 56; 36 to 28; Including or Excluding The Range Limits 1152, 576, 448, 288, 224, 56, and 28; with One of The Inclusory Optional Bases: 7; 8; 14:8; 18:14:8; 18:16:14;*

18:16:14:8; 9:7:4; or The Empty Base

1991-   *The Symmetries in Prime Time from 228 to 224 with 279, 261,*
present   *and 2 X 119 with One of The Inclusory Optional Bases: 7; 8; 14:8;*
           18:14:8; 128:16:14; 18:16:14:8; 9:7:4; or The Empty Base sound
           environments
           including *The Symmetries in Prime Time When Centered above and*
           below The Lowest Term Primes in The Range 228 to 224 with The
           Addition of 279 and 261 in Which The Half of The Symmetric Division
           Mapped above and Including 288 Consists of The Powers of 2 Multiplied
           by The Primes within The Ranges of 144 to 128, 72 to 64, and 36 to 32
           Which Are Symmetrical to Those Primes in Lowest Terms in The Half of
           The Symmetric Division Mapped below and Including 224 within The
           Ranges 126 to 112, 63 to 56, and 31.5 to 28 with The Addition of 119
           and with One of The Inclusory Optional Bases: 7; 8; 14:8; 18:14:8;
           18:16:14; 18:16:14:8; 9:7:4; or The Empty Base

1992   *Annod* (1953-55) *92 X 19 Version for Zeitgeist* for alto saxophone,
           vibraphone, piano, bass, and drums
           including *92 XII 22 Two-Part Harmony, The 1992 XII Annod*
           Backup Riffs

All compositions published by Just Eternal Music, c/o P.O. Box 190, Canal
Street Station, New York, NY 10013.

DISCOGRAPHY

1968
5 VIII 68 12:17:33 - 12:49:58 PM, Drift Study (excerpt)
S.M.S. Issue No. 4 lp

1969
31 I 69 4:37:40 - 5:09:50 PM, Drift Study (excerpt)
Aspen Magazine Issue No. 8 lp

31 VII 69 10:26 PM from Map of 49's Dream The Two Systems of Eleven Sets of
Galactic Intervals Ornamental Lightyears Tracery / *23 VIII 64 2:50:43 - 3:11 AM*
the volga delta
Edition X lp

1974
13 I 73 5:35 - 6:14:03 PM NYC from Map of 49's Dream The Two Systems of
Eleven Sets of Galactic Intervals Ornamental Lightyears Tracery / *14 VII 73 9:27:27*
- 10:15:33 PM NYC, Drift Study
Shandar 83:510 lp

1987

81 X 25 6:17:50 - 11:18:59 PM NYC, The Well-Tuned Piano
Gramavision 18-8701-1 lp, -2 cd, -4 cs; 79452 cd (1992)
Just Intonation Network 002 cs (excerpt) (1992)

1990

89 VI 8 c. 1:45 - 1:52 AM Paris, Poem for Chairs, Tables, Benches, etc.
Tellus #24 cs

1991

*90 XII 9 c. 9:35 - 10:52 PM NYC, The Melodic Version of The Second Dream of The
High-Tension Line Stepdown Transformer from The Four Dreams of China*
Gramavision 79467 cd

guest artist

"Terry's G Dorian Blues" by Terry Jennings on *Jon Gibson: In Good Company*
Point Music 434873-2 cd (1992)

BIBLIOGRAPHY

"Lecture 1960" (excerpts). *Kulchur*, 10 (Summer 1963).

"Dream." *Dream Sheet*, Ed. Diane Wakowski. New York: Hardware Poets
Playhouse, 1965.

"Lecture 1960." *Tulane Drama Review*, 10 (Winter 1965).

"Two Propositions in Black." *S.M.S.* 1, New York: The Letter Edged In Black
Press, 1968.

Selected Writings. Munich: Friedrich, 1969.

"Untitled (Notes on Dream Music)," *Aspen*, 9 (1970).

"Singing of Pran Nath: The Sound Is God." *The Village Voice*, (April 30, 1970).

"Notes On The Continuous Periodic Composite Sound Waveform
Environment Realizations Of *Map of 49's Dream The Two Systems of Eleven Sets
of Galactic Intervals Ornamental Lightyears Tracery*," "Dream Music," "Le Chant
de Pran Nath: Le Son Est Dieu," *VH 101*, 4 (1970-71).

"Musique: Pandit Pran Nath et Le Style Kirana," *L'Autre-Monde*, 69 (1983).

"Der Eroffnungs-Akkord Aus *The Well-Tuned Piano*," Catalog for "Raum Zeit Stille," Kolnischer Kunstverein, 1983.

"Terry Jennings" (Peter Garland, co-author) and "Pandit Pran Nath." *The New Grove Dictionary Of American Music*. Eds. H. Wiley Hitchcock and Stanley Sadie. London: Macmillan, 1986.

The Well-Tuned Piano 81 X 25 Record Program Booklet, 1986.

"Notes on *The Well-Tuned Piano*," 1/1, 3 (1987).

Music and Light Box, Catalog for "Klangraume," Rheinisches Musikfest 1988.

"*The Romantic Symmetry (over a 60-Cycle Base) in Prime Time from 112 to 144 with 119*," 1/1, 5 (1989).

"Lecture 1960," excerpts from "Sound And Light Works" (Collected Notes Spring 1990), Catalog for 44th Venice Biennale exhibition, "Ubi Fluxus ibi motus 1990-1962," 1990.

photo: Gene Bagnato

JOHN ZORN / Introduction

JOHN ZORN was born in New York City on September 1, 1953. He attended Webster College in St. Louis, Missouri, where he studied composition with Kendall Stallings and researched material for a thesis about Carl Stalling, the composer of scores for the Warner Brothers cartoons. During this time, he also began playing the alto saxophone. Disappointed with his classes, Zorn left Webster and eventually returned to New York in 1975, where he became involved in the innovative theater of Richard Foreman, Stuart Sherman, and Jack Smith, and began giving his own series of theatical performances with the Theater of Musical Optics.

In the late '70s, he began composing game pieces for improvising musicians, such as *Lacrosse* (1977), *Fencing* (1978), and *Archery* (1979). His own playing was also transformed in this time, with Zorn splintering his instruments in the same fashion that he was dicing and splicing the musics of his fellow improvisers through the dynamics of his game scores. By the mid '80s he would be more well known for playing various game calls, water whistles, and sections of clarinet than for his chops on alto saxophone. But whether he was leading a group of improvisers or performing a solo, Zorn's interest always focused squarely on rapid and extreme juxtapositions of discreet, variegated, and usually very noisy sounds.

Between gathering players for his game pieces and seeking out musicians with whom he could improvise, Zorn became a central figure in the realm of free improvisation, networking with musicians at first throughout the East Village, and eventually throughout the world. He has worked with countless musicians, including Fred Frith, Elliott Sharp, Christian Marclay, Shelley Hirsch, Bill Frissell, Polly Bradfield, Eugene Chadbourne, Arto Lindsay, Zeena Parkins, Joey Baron, Guy Klucevsek, David Weinstein, Anthony Coleman, Jim Staley, Bob Ostertag, George Lewis, David Van Tieghem, Tim Berne, Sonny Sharrock, Charles K. Noyes, Butch Morris, Toots Thielmans, David Shea, Anton Fier, Jamaladeen Tacuma, Ned Rothenberg, Robert Quine, Wayne Horvitz, Diamanda Galas, Albert Collins, Ikue Mori, Ronald Shannon Jackson, John Patton, Derek Bailey, Bill Laswell, Peter Blegvad, Sato Michihiro, Ursula Oppens, Tom Cora, Nicolas Collins, Yamatsuka Eye, Mark Dresser, and David Moss.

Zorn has played in several bands over the years, including the Golden Palominos, Painkiller, Slan, News For Lulu, Locus Solus, and of course Naked City, for which he has composed some of his most memorable and extreme music: pieces ranging in length from eight seconds to thirty minutes, which cover the spectrum of sound from the wildest noise barrages to silky covers of John

Barry and Jerry Goldsmith. After the release of his album of arrangements of music by Ennio Morricone, *The Big Gundown* (1986), Zorn began to attract the attention of classically trained musicians, and has since received commissions for fully notated, non-improvisational scores from the Brooklyn Philharmonic, the Kronos Quartet, and the New York Philharmonic. His lifelong interest in cinema was also reciprocated at this time, with Zorn providing scores for such films as *She Must Be Seeing Things* (1986) and *The Golden Boat* (1990). He has also created studio compositions, such as *Spillane* (1987) and *Elegy* (1992), which explore his interest in atmosphere, allusion, and narrative.

John Zorn continues to perform internationally, dividing his time between New York and Japan. I spoke with the composer at his Manhattan home on September 1, 1991, and again on May 12, 1992. Once the site of the Theater of Musical Optics, the small apartment now seems to exist chiefly to house Zorn's thousands of lps, cds, and cassettes. Our conversations ranged from Zorn's involvement in New York's avant-garde theater to the business and politics of releasing recordings in America.

JOHN ZORN / Interview

Q: I read that you went to Webster College in St. Louis, but left after about a year and a half.

ZORN: Right.

Q: But it was while you were at college that you started playing the saxophone.

ZORN: That's right. I'd applied to a bunch of schools and I'd got rejected by a bunch of schools: Wesleyan, Bennington. All these hoity-toity schools rejected me outright. I didn't do good in high school and I was never good at tests. So I got accepted by Webster and Beloit and went to Webster. The composition teacher was really nice — Kendall Stallings. I'd sent him some scores and he said, "I'm favorably impressed, it'd be nice to work with you," blah blah blah. He seemed like a real open-minded guy and I went out there. The Black Arts Group was happening in St. Louis at the time — this is '72, '73. Oliver Lake was teaching at the school; Luther Thomas was a student there; Joe Bowie and Marty Ehrlich were actually in town at the time, but I never met them. It was a real hotbed for that AACM/Midwest/Black Arts Group from St. Louis. I remember an artist there named John McVicker who first turned me on to free jazz. He sat me down and played me *Free Jazz, Ascension*, the Jazz Composers Orchestra two-record box set with Pharoah Sanders and Cecil Taylor, and *Unit Structures*. And I said, "Yes, this is what I've been looking for — the energy and intensity is still there, but the structures are really interesting and complex."

I had studied all the Cage followers, Kagel, and Stockhausen, and a lot of what disappointed me about that music was there wasn't enough emotional chutzpah in there; they weren't kicking ass; it was all very intellectual and there wasn't enough heart in it. So I started to think of myself as a new Romantic. I wanted there to be more feeling in the music, more blood. I still wanted all those horrible noises, but I wanted an emotional basis for them, rather than just a stopwatch.

I went to some record store on Delmar and I was looking through some Coleman and Coltrane shit. The guy behind the counter said, "Hmm, well, you should check out these guys in Chicago, the AACM. They're doing some interesting stuff." So I went through the section and pulled out *For Alto* and *Baptism*. It blew my mind. On the inside of the record, Braxton named all the right names: There was one piece dedicated to Cage, one piece dedicated to Stockhausen, one piece dedicated to Cecil Taylor. And I said wow, this guy's got a great head, he's listening to all this different music. It all connected up.

Q: But you weren't playing sax then.

ZORN: Not at all. I had done the typical composer thing of learning a little of everything: I'd played flute; clarinet; bass in a surf band when I was thirteen; some guitar; tuba and trombone in a brass workshop in school. But I never really thought of myself as a performer until I heard *For Alto*. Up to that time, I was just one of these geeks who wrote scores and tried to convince musicians to play them. But I eventually realized that I never really developed a close-enough relationship with these people, because I wasn't a performer myself. There was something missing. I figured I had to be on the same level with them, so I picked up the sax and I stuck with it.

Q: Alto right off the bat?

ZORN: I started right off with alto, switched to soprano after a couple of years, and then went back to the alto. There was a few years where I just played soprano — I was really into Lacy — and then totally left it behind and picked up the alto.

Q: While you were at Webster, didn't you also write a thesis on Carl Stalling's music?

ZORN: I worked on research, but I never finished the thesis. It was supposed to be my four-year thesis, but I dropped out before then. The first thing I worked on was something that compared Webern with Machaut. I was really into early music at that time; I was really into compression, and Webern's miniatures. (I think that interest culminated in *Torture Garden*.) My long-term plan was to do something on Stalling; I was collating information.

Q: So you went to Webster already with that interest in Stalling and in composing with block structures?

ZORN: I would say block structures developed over the course of years, through the study of Ives, Xenakis, Stravinsky, film and cartoon soundtracks, and Stockhausen's "moment-form." My interest in quickly changing block structures, and in what I call cartoon trades — that was there when I was in college. Of course the seeds had been implanted years before. Cartoon music was something that we all listened to and that was in our subconscious. It came to the surface when I went to school at Webster — with a lot of other things.

Q: When did you first start hearing those scores as music and not just as part of the cartoons?

ZORN: I think I started taking it seriously when I was in college. I started collecting tapes around that time, clocked off the TV: waiting for Road Runner to come on and turning my cassette recorder on.

After I left St. Louis, I went to the West Coast and did solo concerts, working with whoever would work with me. I met Philip Johnston in San Francisco in '74 or '75, and we came back to New York and started working on music together — doing things that were related more to Foreman's theater and Stuart Sherman's performances: things that involved objects, and things that, for me, really started concentrating on the idea of the cartoon trade and the changing blocks. That was something I really felt was my personality, my style, something that was new in a sense, but ancient at the same time. Because it came from my interest in

Stravinsky and Ives, who always had worked that way. All composers use abrupt changes at times.

Eugene Chadbourne was really interested in that stuff as well, and he really brought a lot out. I wrote a whole piece called *The Book Of Heads* for him, which was just a series of short pieces that could be rearranged in any way. Several of those pieces were called "Cartoon Pieces." It just got more and more ingrained into my language.

My ideas were confirmed over the years, through working with Joel Forrester and Philip Johnston; with Stuart Sherman, who was a performance artist that came out of Richard Foreman's theater, where I used to hang out all the time. Not enough has been said about my connection to the performance scene here in New York. Foreman, Stuart Sherman, Ken Jacobs, Jack Smith — they were all seminal influences that really shaped the way I think, not only about music but about the world in general; my approach to everything that I do is shaped by these people's ideas and the worlds that they created.

Richard Foreman's work had very specific musical influences. His was the most visual portrayal of music I've ever seen. The way he worked in that space (on lower Broadway, at Broome Street), the way it was timed — it was really inspiring. His big dream was to write a musical melody, and what was so ironic was that, visually, he was doing it constantly with all of his theatrical machinations. Jack and Richard and Ken Jacobs really instilled in me the love for the underappreciated and the love for doing things under adverse conditions, on small budgets — how money can be like handcuffs rather than something that frees you up. These were really fundamental questions to a 22-year-old kid: What kind of art do I want to be making? What kind of questions do I want to be asking?

Jack was a symbol of purity, plain and simple. He never compromised in his life. It was not even in his vocabulary. He never even put himself into the situation where he could compromise — it was not even a question, it never even came up. He lived his life the way he wanted it to be. Being able to learn from the guy just from who he was — you'd just see him on the street and there it was, The Jack Smith Show, right there. His shows were who he was, but there wasn't a moment when he wasn't who he was. In a sense he was always playing a part, and in another sense he was the part. Whether he was onstage or in the street didn't matter; or in his apartment, drinking Turkish coffee and showing slides and burning incense and putting on records of Les Baxter. It was just really, really inspiring. It's something that's caused a lot of problems for me in a certain way, in that I have that love for living in this little apartment. I don't want to move into a bigger apartment even though I can afford to do so. I prefer to be here, down in the ghetto or whatever it is, in touch with that part of those people's work.

This is the kind of shit that was instilled in me at an early, formative age, hanging out in that world, that theater Richard had; Jack's world, his apartment or wherever he was doing one of his things — that became his space, his world; Ken Jacobs with his projections, the nervous system. Jack Smith was living a life, he had created a world. So had Richard, so had Ken, so had all these people at that time. They'd create a living world that other people could step into and become part of. You were yourself but at the same time, you weren't yourself. The same way that, when I go into the studio to record *Spillane* or the Genet piece, performers are who they are and they're not; they're kind of doing what I want but they're doing what they want. I really feel like I've created a small society: a way of working. People fit into it — they like it — they have time off and then they're called to perform and then they have a long time off and then they're called to perform. They're asked to do different things at different times. It's like Hakim Bey's concept of a TAZ, a Temporary Autonomous Zone: a moment separate from society, which creates its own rules. That's what Jack was like; wherever he went, he created a TAZ. That's what Richard's theater was like. That's what it was like when you were sitting watching Ken Jacobs do his film performances. These were TAZs, things where expectations are gone out the window. You're in a completely other world. Some people can enter it and some can't, but regardless of that, it has validity, it's organic, it's alive, it has life in it — you can see it and you can't deny it. That's what art is about. It raises questions in your mind about what the regular world is. What's going on in society? That's why I feel it's really important that artists stand outside of society.

Richard moved out of his lower-Manhattan theater in '77, something like that, and started doing things with Joseph Papp. At that time I went to a panel discussion he did. Philip Johnston and Louis Belegenis and I were sitting up in the gallery, and at some point Richard said, "My years of experimentation are over now. I don't have anything else to explore. I've defined a language now that I'm going to be dealing with, and I'm interested in how to take that language into the proscenium stage. I leave the discovery of the new to those guys up there in the gallery." That was really a crucial moment for me. Richard was supportive of what I was doing at a time when nobody gave a fuck. My first performances in New York were in his theater and in my own apartment. When he wasn't doing a play, when he was rehearsing for a new performance, he'd let Philip and me do a performance there in the evening, after rehearsals or what have you — in his space, his sacred space! I used to hang out there and answer the phone. He said, "If anyone asks, 'Tell me a little bit about the piece — what's it like?' say, 'It's not for you,' and then hang up"!

Q: You began giving performances of the Theater of Musical Optics in '75?

ZORN: Yeah, when I came back to New York. That was really a visual presentation of the cartoon idea — an ordering of events that are very different from one another — like the cartoon trades in *Cobra*. But what I would do is use little objects. I'd have a grid of 50 different objects — all very tiny, that I'd found in the street or in the garbage — which I would then recombine. I would take three of them and put them together and create a little sculpture; put it out for a couple of seconds, create another one, and then switch them. They were always being switched at different timings, and you'd just see one "sculpture" at a time. You'd also see the same objects appear again and again, recombining with other objects. It relates a lot to my ideas about form and structure, the idea of blocks, the idea of cartoons: Things that appear in succession, and are very different from one another, can spark thinking patterns. That's really where I cemented the idea of creating "nodes" that can be interpreted in a myriad of ways; each person creates their own narrative.

That comes through in an interesting way in *Cobra* because onstage it really becomes a psychodrama where everybody's personality comes out in very exaggerated ways. And in the audience, everyone's got their own take on what's going on. I accept and insist on that subjectiveness — I don't think there can be "objective" music. I think more of creating little prisms. When my single creative vision passes through it, it separates into all the possible colors of the spectrum. It's broken up into shards. There are many interpretations possible, and all of them are valid.

Q: It was in this apartment that the Theater of Musical Optics took place?

ZORN: In that room over there. It was painted black at the time. The very first place that the Theater of Musical Optics happened was across from the Public Theater in the Collonades Building, at the very top. The little black addition that was there was the first place I lived in New York — and it was $50 a month! It was beautiful, but when the rent went up to $75 I had to move here to Seventh Street because I couldn't afford it anymore. But I was there for about a year or so, and that's where the first performances happened. A lot of people came to see my stuff at that time: Jack Smith, Stuart Sherman, Stefan Brecht, Ken Jacobs, Richard Foreman. It was a really exciting time for me, because I was doing performances and I was doing music — I never stopped composing.

Q: In fact there isn't that sharp a break between your ideas of theater and music: "The Theater of Musical Optics." And one set of pieces was called *Experiments In Harmony and Polyphony*.

ZORN: That's right. I was going into outer space at that time, thinking that music was not about sound at all, but rather a certain way of dealing with a media; a certain way of dealing with time. Theater deals with time in a very different way. Music is very specific about it. The only theater I've seen that comes close to music in terms of the way it deals with time was Richard Foreman's. So I developed the idea of creating musical pieces that were completely visual and didn't use sound! I was trying to take everything to the furthest possible place I could. And that was about as far out as things have ever gotten for me.

Someone like Mauricio Kagel would understand what I'm talking about, and has made films with a musical sensibility. I think he comes from the same kind of place. He uses theater, he uses music, and the way he approaches either a visual or sonic element is the same; he has the same sensibility about it. What's interesting for me about performers like Christian Marclay or John Oswald is that they don't really have a very good sense of musical time. They are manipulating sounds, but their sensibilities come more from conceptual art. Their decision making is often quite curious. I love it.

Q: David Tudor's recording of Kagel's *Improvisation Ajoutée* is always mentioned as having put a fire under you as a kid.

ZORN: That's right, that's the one.

Q: But you also must have dug the old DG recording of Kagel's *Der Schall.*

ZORN: Of course — I just played that for a friend of mine the other day! Joey Baron was here and we were doing a listening session. I was playing him different stuff and he said, "Play me your favorite Kagel," and I put on *Der Schall.* That's still one of the seminal records, absolutely. It's an amazing achievement, and you know, what kills me is that it was written in 1968 or '69, and I heard it not much after that — I'm impressed with myself! I was right there listening to the shit, you know what I mean? Wow! You know the excitement of that? Like being there listening to Ayler. I never heard Ayler; I never heard Coltrane; I never heard Dolphy. But I heard Kagel when he was kicking out the jammies! And I was like 16! That's an exciting thing to be there when the shit's actually going down, and in a lot of ways, I think those kind of traumatic musical experiences are the ones that stick with you the longest, that may be at the very base of what you do — the deepest roots.

I like to say that I'm really rootless. I think that the music that my generation — Elliott Sharp and Wayne Horvitz and Fred Frith — is doing is really rootless in a lot of ways, because we listened to a lot of different kinds of music from an early age. And we were obsessive about it. We listened to soul music, we listened to surf music, we listened to classical music, we listened to the ethnic records we could get on the Explorer series, we listened to jazz, we listened to movie soundtracks. We listened to all different kinds of shit, and as a result we don't really have a single home.

Q: When you started playing here in New York, there weren't that many performers around who were on the same wavelength — there was you and Polly Bradfield and Eugene Chadbourne.

ZORN: That was it at the beginning. And then Tom Cora and then Toshinori Kondo and then Bob Ostertag and then Ned Rothenberg — bit by bit, people came together from all over the country and gravitated to New York.

Yeah, it was difficult at that time to find someone who listened to all the different shit that we listened to. We could find someone who was into Ayler, but never heard of Cage or didn't care about that shit. Or we could find someone who was into Cage, but didn't give a fuck about music from Oaxaca.

This is where the Reich/Glass/Terry Riley/La Monte Young minimalist period becomes important for me, because they began to break with a lot of the traditions of closed-mindedness. There had been people like Hovhaness, who was into ethnic music, and Partch — there are always people that stand out. Lou Harrison was a great composer and a fine ethnomusicologist. But the thing that connected with me as a movement in general was the minimalists, because they talked openly about ethnic music: They talked about the influence of Indian, African, Balinese, Japanese music on what they were doing. And they created bands and worked with the same musicians over and over. Admittedly, the music was completely different from what I was trying to do, but it hit me really hard when I first heard Glass, when I first heard Reich. And I started doing very derivative pieces — I've got some tapes you wouldn't believe! Stuff from 1974 with wine glasses and vibraphones, repetitive patterns that were improvised but go on for an hour and half. That was an interesting period.

And Cage, of course, I mean, I love Cage's music, and he's an important influence for me. A lot of what I do comes directly from threads left hanging in the '60s by people like Earle Brown, Wolff, Cardew, MEV, and of course Cage himself. When I criticize Cage, what I'm really doing is criticizing the people who have put him into the position of some kind of God or guru. That's bullshit. I like to be someone that pops people's balloons. That's why I'm really blunt about Cage, and that's why I'm blunt about certain people that have somehow ended up in these positions of worship. It really pisses me off. You talk to the minimalists, and they're always so damned reverential to Cage — they're all ready to give him a blow job. There's something so sterile, so precious about it all. I like some of his pieces, I don't like other ones. I don't appreciate his chance approach — that's the antithesis of what I'm trying to do. I'm interested in decision making; he's interested in giving the decision making up to chance, and I think that's a cop-out. He can put out reams and reams of music, hours and hours of tapes, and he doesn't have to do a goddam thing but throw a coin. That's bullshit. The music that I'm most consistently drawn to is music that through the years has been produced through blood and sweat, whether it's Van Gogh or Joyce, Beethoven or Brian Wilson — people that really had to fucking sweat over each decision and say, "Am I crazy doing this? Does this make sense? This doesn't make any sense. I can't do this. But I have to do it." But don't mistake my irreverence for disrespect or lack of humility! I love Cage. He's one of the great American mavericks, and he still has the ability to piss people off, but let's pop the goddam balloon. He's no holy man.

Q: We live in a time when the music press encourages either that kind of adulation or else a total denial of a composer. The scene is constantly being reduced to a few heroes and heavies, who's in and who's out, in order to sell newspapers and magazines — that is, if anyone gets written about at all.

ZORN: Yes. It's a shame when they pick out one or two people from a whole generation of musicians to turn into gods. It happened with Reich and Glass; it happened with Cage. God forbid it should happen to me, but of all those musicians — Elliott and Wayne, Anthony Coleman or Chadbourne — I'm the one that keeps getting the play, and it's not fair. I come from a pool of musicians that collaborated, that shared ideas. I learned a lot from the years that I spent with Chadbourne. And from Fred Frith. And from Bill Frisell. I worked with Chadbourne from '76 on; with Fred, from '78 or '79 on; with Frisell, from '82 or so on. It was a real melting pot of people who felt the same way but created completely different music. I know Glass and Reich feel the same way, that they get all the attention and a lot of good people have been swept under the rug. It isn't fair, and it's largely a matter of the press — they love doing that, and it's a drag. I think it's important for people who find themselves in the public eye to try to diffuse some of that attention to other places, and give support back into the community that nurtured them in the first place. It's a responsibility I became very aware of years ago when the press started jumping on me in the mid 1980s.

The big turnaround was that Morricone record. That was the mistake of my life! I never should have made that record.

Q: You'd resisted doing it for a long time, hadn't you?

ZORN: And then I broke down because it was a chance to go back into the 24-track studio. That was the only reason I did it — purely selfish reasons. Sure, I wanted to pay tribute to Morricone, but that can be done by lip service in interviews. I wanted to bring a whole new generation of musicians together and give them a chance to play with each other, but they were only making $50 apiece per session — I couldn't afford to give anybody more than that. And I was using people like Robert Quine, Diamanda Galas, Toots Thielmans, John Patton — everyone got the same money. That was good, but it was also a rip-off in a lot of ways. To tell the truth, I never made one cent from that record!

It also more or less permanently affected the way people think of what I do — because now many people see me more as an arranger rather than a composer. They listen to originals from Naked City, and they say, "Oh, nice arrangement of the *Batman* song of Neal Hefti" — as if it has anything to do with that! Nobody thinks of the music on *Torture Garden* as being composed, they take it for granted as if it came down here from outer space. It's actually a series of compositional etudes — almost every fucking note is written down!

Q: Was there the idea that *The Big Gundown* was worth the effort because you'd be able to include an original, "Tre Nel 5000," along with your covers of Morricone's music?

ZORN: No, not at all — that was an afterthought. Originally I had planned to do an arrangement of "Tre Nel 3000," which is one of the most eclectic scores he ever did. So I created this grid and said, "Out of 30 events, 10 will be arrangements of moments from the score, and the others will be my crazy stuff." We'd do a little bit of it at the end of every session: I'd get some of the musicians together and say, "You play in this section like this, you play in that section." And at the end I said, "This doesn't sound anything like an arrangement of Morricone. This is mine, let's just call it mine and that's the end of it!"

Q: You said this record brought you back into the 24-track studio — the previous time having been the recording of "Shuffle Boil"?

ZORN: I guess the previous time was "Shuffle Boil." The recordings I had done with Whiz Kid for *Locus Solus* were my very first 24-track experiences. Then Hal Willner paid the bill for "Shuffle Boil," and I said, "I've got to work in this medium again — there's a lot of possibilities here in the studio." Yale Evelev was willing to foot the bill, so I went for it, and made *The Big Gundown*. In the middle of that I did the Kurt Weill arrangement; the Morricone took a year and a half to record, and the Weill was done somewhere in that time. I'm really happy with that piece. When Yale heard it, he said, "I've got to have a piece like this on the record. We've got to do a piece this complicated. This is what it's all about." I said, "Great. Give me $10,000 for one five-minute piece of music, and I'll give you a piece like that." He just didn't understand the time involved.

Q: You've spoken about the qualities of Monk — the humor, the dissonance, the sense of timing — which you were focusing on in "Shuffle Boil." Which qualities in Weill's music were you trying to bring out with "Kleine Leutnant"?

ZORN: The decadence of Germany in the '20s; the rise of Naziism; German Romanticism; the Broadway influence; his use of folk instruments and folk musics; cabaret theatre; his work with Brecht and the idea of confronting the audience and making things very real. The instrumentation meant using the snare drum a lot; the use of the trombone; banjo and accordion — folk instruments; the harp representing his classical connection; sprechstimme (another thing that was going on in Germany around the time he was working). The reason I used Japanese — why the hell did I use Japanese? Was he multilingual? That could have been it. I don't know. I cut the score up to change the structure a bit, but the piece's integrity remained intact.

This was also the first time I used my punch-in method — I basically developed it for this piece. It's the same way that I recorded *Spillane* and the Godard piece. I give the musicians the music for the section that we'll be working on, for example, the first section of the piece — in *Spillane* it was a scream; in the Weill, I think it was snare drum followed by four trombones. We'd rehearse it, get it perfect, and then record it onto tape. Then I'd give them the music for the second section of the piece. Bit by bit we'd build it up. An additive process, with the musicians concentrating on the details of one section at a time, but relatively blind, as far as where the piece is going. Like a director in film, only I would have the overall perspective. We'd roll the tape back, listen to the previous section recorded, and then just where they're supposed to come in, I'd cue them and they'd begin performing. It's like a series of short live performances put directly onto tape. No tape splices, no splices ever. Everything just put right into place on tape using A-B sets of tracks so that you never actually cut into the previous performance. Sections literally overlapped, with the reverb of the previous section dying behind the beginning of the following one.

Q: What was it about recording with Whiz Kid and M.E. Miller for *Locus Solus* that got you into overdubbing?

ZORN: It was just by accident. We went out to Long Island to pick up Whiz Kid the day of the recording session, and he bailed on me; he wanted me to use his protegé "Cheese Whiz" instead. Fuck that! We rescheduled the date and spent that day in the studio recording the drums alone, and a week later added my sax and Whiz Kid. So it was really a matter of logistics. That was the first time I was in a 24-track studio, using the 24 tracks for what they could do. Before that, I was one of those Derek Bailey/Evan Parker purists: "Live to two-track — I don't want anything to get in the way of the music," you know? "No reverb, completely dry"! I was a real fucked-up asshole!

Q: That's how you recorded the first *Classic Guide To Strategy*?

ZORN: That's right — I can't wait to re-master that record, and add some EQ, compression, and reverb. The second volume was done a couple of years later, in a completely different way: It used my A-B tracking so I could get faster changes: ten seconds, then five seconds, then 15 seconds. I built the pieces a bit at a time. I'd let it go for a minute or so, and then stop and put in a little one- or two-second blast, and then go on. I couldn't change from the alto to the duck calls fast enough, so I used double-tracking techniques on the second record.

Q: With your lps of long single pieces such as *Archery* or *Pool*, is there kind of a reverse-Stalling effect for you, in the sense that with Stalling, you appreciate what kind of a composer he is when there's no visuals and all you have is the music; whereas when we don't see your players making decisions and trading cues, a certain homogeneity creeps into the piece?

ZORN: Perhaps. Not too much, I hope. I never thought of that before, but it makes a certain degree of sense. I've always said in the past that I wanted to do game pieces behind a screen because the interactions distracted you from hearing the music — it becomes a spectacle. But that's what it is! It is a spectacle! And now I get into the theater quality of it; that's part of its essence. An important part. In training the musicians to do the piece, I try to encourage the players to think of the overall musical shape — to step outside and look at the big picture. I want their decisions to be musically motivated. But once we start, who knows what's going to happen or where it's going to go. That's where the spectacle comes in. What happens to people when they are given power has been well documented historically. The volatile nature of game pieces like *Cobra* creates a situation where often people find it hard to control themselves. It becomes psychodrama.

Q: The original score of *Track & Field* called for the role of prompter to go to different players over the course of the piece, but in some of its later performances, there'd be a full-time prompter. With *Cobra* that job is always done by one specific person. Had you found in playing these works that it was better to have one person stick to being the prompter?

ZORN: I think it's best that way. Ultimately, I'm the best prompter there can be, because then I can be a complete fascist! Only someone who really knows the rules can be a good prompter; someone who is extremely hyper, omniattentive, and can make split-second decisions when three people are raising their hands and each one wants something different. A lot of times, people make calls that I know are going to end up in a train wreck, and I have to know when to say no. It's like a coach.

Someone who does it again and again and again will get better at it, but some people are naturally born to it and some people are not. Jim Staley would be a horrible prompter. Can you imagine Bill Frisell being a prompter? It's just impossible! The prompter's role requires a specific kind of talent. It's the same way that I choose the musicians in the band: You want to pick someone not just because they can play well, but because they have a good sense of humor, or they get along with the guy across the room; because they believe in democracy, or because they don't believe in it; because they want to subvert the shit or because they want to just sit back and do what they're told; because they have a lot of compositional ideas (and maybe play awful) but they're going to make good calls. There's a lot of reasons to call someone into the band in a game piece. And for the prompter, it's the same thing: You've got to pick the right person for the job. It's crucial. The prompter can make or break a performance, no matter how inspired the band is. The prompter is a direct source of energy and inspiration for the entire group.

Q: In the cd of the studio version of *Cobra*, you included pre-recording chatter and even a flubbed take.

ZORN: I like that shit. It's very personal. It's like bringing the audience inside — letting them in on it all.

Q: It makes the studio version seem more "live" than the live version, which has nothing extraneous or imperfect in its various sections.

ZORN: It's true. That's right. It adds life. But that was totally subconscious.

Q: Did the studio version use the punch-in techniques?

ZORN: No, not at all. It was just live to two-track.

Q: And the separate sections on each of the two cds?

ZORN: Those are separate pieces. "Versions," if you will. *Cobra* is something that can end at any time. What we did was we'd talk in the studio and say, "Let's do various lengths of pieces: some one minute, some six minutes." So if we did a lot of five-minute pieces, I'd say, "Let's do something much shorter"; if we did a lot of

short ones, I'd say, "Let's try for a long one this time." Everything on the *Cobra* cd
are complete pieces that I ordered after the fact.

Q: *Spy Vs. Spy* was recorded in two days, which is mind-boggling in light of the
speed and precision of the playing. How much rehearsal time had been put in
prior to those sessions?

ZORN: We had gone on tour for about three weeks in Europe. And Tim Berne
and I had been playing that music for four or five years before that.

Q: I had read that you and Berne were playing Ornette Coleman's music back in
'84. How close was that playing to what's on *Spy Vs. Spy?*

ZORN: My relationship to Ornette's music is an interesting one. Again, *Free Jazz*
is one of the first records that turned me on to that music. I started listening to it
when I was in college in '72. When I picked up the saxophone, I practiced to
Ornette all the time — and I practiced to Eric Dolphy and Jackie McLean. That's
why I play so sharp; I'm so fucking sharp on the horn because I practiced eight to
ten hours a day to people who played incredibly sharp! That's what sounds right.
When I play in tune, it sounds flat to me! It sounds boring, dull, it doesn't sound
like a saxophone — it's so sick!

Anyway, I started doing concerts of Ornette's music because you could play
the head and then just blow and not worry about what to do on top of the chord
changes. And you didn't have any neurotic bebopper from the old days saying,
"You're not cuttin' it man, run the changes!" So we'd just play — rhythm section
and two horns, kind of like the way he did it — for years, from when I picked up
the horn in '73 or '74, till '80, '81, '82. And then with Berne in '83, '84, '85.
The first few concerts I did with him were just side of beef, side of beef, side of
beef, side of beef, you know? Blowing, and we'd each take solos.

Then I stopped practicing the horn completely, around '82 or '83. But up to
that time I had practiced eight hours a day, literally. I was so neurotic, I'd bring
my horn into the bathroom while I was pissing and keep playing! I finally got sick
of it. I woke up one morning and I said, "I'm not going to practice again, ever. It's
over. I'm going to start going to movies, learning about life, go out there and
shop," blah blah blah. That was the best thing I ever did, I don't regret it at all.
But it made me insecure about my playing, and when I started doing the gigs with
Berne, I became very unsatisfied with the way I was playing Ornette's music. And
I remember saying to him, "Why don't we solo together, both at the same time?"
Kind of in the tradition of *Free Jazz,* a Dixieland kind of thing, instead of play the
head, then you solo, then I solo, then we play the head. I felt Berne was blowing
me off the planet on the solos. My solos were boring, I hated them, and this was a
way of getting around that. We started doing that and it felt great, it got the energy up. I also started getting more into thrash music around '85 or so, and the idea
of doing Ornette in a thrash style started to germinate in my mind and I began
pushing it — especially when I realized we were going to make a record. If I'm

going to do a recording of Ornette's music, I want it to be the way I did the Morricone. I've got to bring something new to it, I've got to bring it up to date; but it's got to come from the *inside* — not a totally alien agenda imposed on it from the outside. So I made a list of everything that Ornette's music was to me, which included that intense energy and that real bluesiness it had. But when it first hit the scene, it was a shock. People didn't even think it was jazz: Someone once described Ornette's music as "one long squeak." What are they thinking about? It's melody from beginning to end. So I said, "If I'm going to do a record of Ornette, it's got to be a punch right in the face, it's got to shock people" — the way his music did in the early '60s, because that was an important part of what that experience was, it was so different. So I said, "It's got to go all the way. Let's bring the energy up more, the thrash." And that's how it happened. There's still a lot of blues in that record, if you listen to the second side. Most people don't even get to the second side. Halfway through the first, they go, "Fuck this! It's bullshit!" The second side is a lot of blues and a lot of melody. I'm really happy with *Spy Vs. Spy*. I think it's the best tribute that I could have done to someone who was absolutely one of my biggest heroes. And whether he likes it or not, I don't care. I really feel I did his music justice.

Q: I understand you've heard that he didn't think the music was done live.

ZORN: That's right. Bob Hurwitz told me this. He went into Hurwitz's office at Nonesuch, and Hurwitz said, "What did you think of the *Spy Vs. Spy* record?" And he reportedly said, "Well, they could never have done that live." But we'd done it live, over and over, and we still do it live. That certainly created a big controversy, and it was the beginning of the end of my getting respect in the jazz world. I went into the Church of Ornette Coleman and laid a fart! Sacrilegious! Recently, the Sonny Clark group with Wayne was meant to get a gig at the Vanguard. Max Gordon's widow, Lorraine, is running the place now. Wayne called her up and said, "So, is it going to happen? We'd like to do a week. Did you hear the record?" And she said, "Well, you know, I listened to the record and it's great. Wayne, I really want you to play at the Vanguard. But I feel that Max is looking down at me and he's saying, 'What are you doing to my place? How can you have these people in my place?' John Zorn, I respect what he does — but not at the Vanguard. I can't bring myself to have him at the Vanguard. Max would never forgive me."

Q: Do you practice now on saxophone?

ZORN: No.

Q: Rehearsing to get up to speed for projects like *Spy Vs. Spy* or *News For Lulu* is one thing; just practicing your instrument is something else.

ZORN: Those bands rehearsed on the bandstand — on tour in Europe. That's not the same as practicing at home, and I don't think I'm ever going to do that again. I really don't see myself as an instrumentalist. In a lot of ways, a lot of my problems have been because I play the saxophone and because people see that as a jazz instrument. I mean, how can something like *Torture Garden* go into the "Jazz" section? It's unbelievable, but there it is! I play the saxophone. What the hell do you want from me?

Q: How much of your music would you call jazz?

ZORN: Jazz was a music that I listened to and loved and paid tribute to and learned from. It's one of several musics that I learned from. I learned from Cage and his followers. I learned from the European Kagel/Stockhausen school. I learned a lot from Japanese music. I learned a lot from rock — I've listened to it since I was a kid.

Q: You also must have learned a lot from listening to animal sounds.

ZORN: Animal sounds, absolutely. And sound-effects records.

I play a lot of different things. And I pay tribute to a lot of things that I really respect. I'm inherently rootless. I don't fit into the jazz tradition. I don't fit into the rock tradition. *Torture Garden* does not fit into the rock tradition. It's got thrash elements in it and there are a lot of hardcore kids who get off on it. But is it hardcore? No. There's a certain set of rules which you have to obey. And with most scenes, the most important rules are the least important to me: attitude; stance; posture; the clothes you wear; where you play. All the trappings of the music. I'm not a skinhead with tattoos on my arm, who goes and slamdances at CB's. I'm interested in the music those people are making. The same thing with the jazz scene: Their trappings are not my trappings. The classical scene too: I don't obey those rules. I'm interested in music, and not the bullshit trappings that surround so many of the scenes, and which people are convinced are the tradition of the scene. So when I play a jazz phrase in the middle of an improvisation with Derek Bailey, am I playing jazz? Am I playing jazz phrases? Am I imitating jazz? What am I doing?

Q: These aren't questions you're asking yourself.

ZORN: No. But obviously critics are asking themselves, and a lot of them are coming up with very rude answers that oftentimes say more about the writer than what they're supposed to be writing about.

The ultimate answer is, you can't put what I'm doing or what Elliott does or what any of these guys do into any kind of a box like that. Inherently it's music that resists categorization because of all the influences we've had. And we've been listening to these musics for years and years and years. We were brought up on it. This is the first generation of composers that was brought up on a range of music as wide as this — available to us because of the recording boom. There's the rub: What is it? I don't know. Is it jazz? No. Is it classical music? No. Is it hardcore? No. It's none of them. But it draws on what we've learned and it's sifted through our own aesthetic. We're not really "the downtown improvisers"; we're not really "the New York noise musicians." We're not really any of that. We didn't fall into any fashionable trend. As a result, we have longevity. But also as a result we have complete incomprehension. We've mystified everybody. They still don't know because they can't grab it. And ultimately, I think that's to our benefit. Because we're all so different.

Q: Isn't the incomprehension more a critical and press problem than an audience problem? If the audience likes it, then they've understood it.

ZORN: For me, if they've heard it, they've understood it. They don't even have to like it. I like to think that my works are open to many interpretations, and more often than not, those varied interpretations speak more about the interpreter than about the work being perceived! There is a crucial difference between "perception" and "understanding," and of course I don't expect people to understand what I've put into a work on the first listening. But I think what I put into a work and what the work becomes are really on different levels. I mean, do you really have to know all the details of Alban Berg's love life to understand what's going on in the *Lyric Suite*? Great works can be understood on many levels, and with the greatest works, those levels reveal themselves and are discovered through deeper investigations and through time. Stravinsky said that music is unable to express anything at all — it simply exists. All it has to do is reach open ears, through the recording medium or in a concert or even in a record store, being played in the background. There it is. That's it. That's all there is to it. Unfortunately, most critics have padlocks on their ears in the form of prejudices, preconceptions, and the like. Often, even the best music isn't meant to function as a skeleton key — and these padlocks remain in place forever.

Q: Has it been hard to get the Kronos Quartet to improvise?

ZORN: They don't improvise. On *Forbidden Fruit*, for example, or on moments of *Cat O' Nine Tails*, they're given a certain amount of freedom within a certain context or framework. They're told, "between this written piece and that written piece, you have six seconds to fool around with col legno." How much is that improvisation and how much is that composition? It gives a certain freedom and it gives a certain feeling to that moment, which it wouldn't have if I had notated all the col legnos. But a lot of times what I find classical musicians doing — it's second nature to them — is they'll try something once and then stick with it. They see that a version works and they just keep doing it. No matter how much you say to them, "No, I want you to try something different," that's not their nature. I think that's why a lot of Cage's music fails in that world for me. To give unsympathetic musicians something they don't want to do creates a kind of tension — which maybe Cage is interested in, similar to Anthony Coleman who's very interested in that kind of tension, that kind of drama, that theater. But I'm not. I work with musicans and I try to get the best out of them. And when I write music in the classical mold, I play the game according to their rules: I write every note down and minimize choices. What I want to do is to gas them. I want to get the best performance I can out of any musician I work with, whether they're improvisers or whether they're classical musicians. And for the classical musicians, you have to write in a certain way, so that it's "comfortable" on the instrument they play; it's got to be challenging, but it has to pay rewards in some way. A lot of music doesn't pay any rewards — it's boring, dull music. It's not fun for them to play and it's not that interesting to listen to — Wuorinen is a good example of that. When they talk about that "Serious Fun" shit, I think that they've got it completely ass-backwards: They're talking about the musicians up there being serious, and the audience having fun. Forget it. I think the musicians should be having fun, and the audience should be taking it seriously. That's really what my music is about in a lot of ways.

For classical musicians, what I like to do is integrate quotations of literature they might or might not know within the lines that I'm writing. So that a violinist over the course of say, eight bars, will play a couple of bars of mine, then there'll be a bar of Mozart and they'll say, "That sounds familiar"; or there'll be a bar of Messiaen, and they'll go, "I've heard that somewhere before." And then it's back to my stuff. So it's like a little game in a sense. A lot of the ways I deal with classical music is in terms of theater, or of thinking of it like a family — sets of relationships. It's a cultural approach, instead of manipulating pitches in some kind of mathematical system — which has been the tradition for years and years and years, and still continues with some composers today (although for me it pretty much died out with Elliott Carter). I don't think that's going to be a prime mover in classical music anymore. We're basically hearing from intuitive musicians who write what they hear or who use many systems at the same time. What I try to do is, instead of dealing with pitches, I deal with phrases, shapes, genres, quotations, gestures — a lot of the way Ligeti dealt with gestures, or Xenakis with cloud sounds, or Penderecki (who is not a great composer, but who also dealt with gesture). There are many ways to unify a compositional structure — I like using dramatic subjects. Music is not just notes on the page, it's not just pitches in the air. It's got to have some kind of cultural resonance to it, it's got to tell a story in some way. Every piece on *Torture Garden*, for example, has some kind of subtext to it; a story that's being told. In *Spillane* it's more obvious, but even with something like *Torture Garden*, there's a story there. The titles help with that too, they give the pieces a cultural resonance, something that can get thinking patterns going, which someone can identify with or not identify with or get pissed about. My record covers are involved in this too. You try to create a package that really tells a story and says something within a larger context than just the abstract world of sound or pitches.

With the classical pieces, I draw upon what I consider to be the great composers; I use Berg, Schoenberg, Webern; I use some Stockhausen, Boulez; Stravinsky's used quite a bit; Bartók, Varèse, Ives, Carter, Messiaen. These are the people that I listened to when I was a kid. It always comes back to that period in the late '60s where I was really solidifying — all my germ ideas were coming together. I've returned to the same scores I bought when I was 16, 17 years old and extracted information. Sometimes in my string quartets I'll have one of my own lines in the first violin part; the second violin, I'll say, "improvise using glissandos"; the viola part will be from Boulez, *Le Marteau*; and the cello part will be a retrograde inversion of Stravinsky from some orchestra piece. All stacked in one bar. And then the next bar goes on to something else.

That's one technique I like to use. Another one is the use of genres: tango, blues, jazz, country. Also tributes to famous composers — in other words, writing in the style of the great masters. Or taking all the pitches from one bar of *L'Histoire Du Soldat* and putting them in a different rhythmic matrix. I enjoy codes and games like that. It gives a piece a strange kind of resonance — a relation to the past. I try to write music that's challenging to play but within the realm of possibilities. Someone who works with, say, synthesizers and sequencers and computers can lose touch with that and give people things that are technically impossible — and a lot of times, not worth the effort. Really, my concern in the classical world is that I gas the performers, it's fun for them to play, and challenging to listen to.

Q: How interested are you in introducing yourself into the world of orchestral and chamber commissions?

ZORN: It's definitely the next step for me. I've got the foot in the door: the Brooklyn Phil, the Kronos. I did a second piece for Kronos and I'm working on a third one. I've just finished a piano piece for a Boston pianist named Steve Drury, called *Carny*, which is a pretty crazy piece. New York Phil has commissioned me for a five-minute fanfare piece. It's a long time ago I got the letter — I've got to start working on it!

Q: *For Your Eyes Only*, your Brooklyn Philharmonic piece, was performed at the '90 New Music America, but there were no notes for it in the program, and your NMA bio included a big slap at the festival and the Brooklyn Academy of Music. The impression created was of someone who wanted to come into that scene but wanted to remain outside at the same time.

ZORN: I can tell you exactly what happened — it's never been made clear. The press went out of their way to make it look like I was some kind of hypocrite who had taken the money and ran. The reality of that situation was, I've been boycotting New Music America since I first performed in it at Hartford in '84, because I thought that whole situation was bogus: It was like a convention. But the Kronos commissioned me to write a piece. They pay me from money that they get from a lot of different sources, and then they have the exclusive rights to play that piece for two years. They decide that they're going to do the piece at the New Music America in Florida. I say, "I don't want you to." They say, "You can't tell us what to play or not play." They play it. The Brooklyn Phil calls me, commissions a piece. I write the piece. Then they say, "We're going to do it at New Music America." I say, "No, you can't," and they say, "You can't tell us where to perform this piece or where not to perform it." That concert was going to happen at BAM, and I had an absolute aversion to BAM since our Morricone thing: They'd treated us like shit — it was like they were afraid something would get stolen because these "downtown sleazeballs" were in their place. So I said to Yale Evelev who was involved in the thing, "No, I don't want it at BAM," and he said, "Well, we have to do this concert. They do it at the Majestic anyway, it won't be at BAM." I couldn't tell them where or where not to do the piece. I wasn't paid by New Music America and was not involved — in fact, I was in Japan at the time. The press had a field day making me look like a hypocrite. But it wasn't my place to defend myself. Fuck them. If they want to think that, fine.

Yuji Takahashi recently conducted the piece in Japan and now the Kronos is going to do it on the West Coast, so I'm getting more performances. When I write a classical piece, I want there to be a lot of performances. If you do some big thing with a lot of extra performers, which has improvisation or anything like that in it, it's only going to get one performance and then it's going to be shelved. That's not what that world is about, there's no point in that. If you're going to do something like that, you should start a new orchestra. Which is something I was thinking of doing: People who can improvise and read classical music, people like Jim Staley and George Lewis in the trombone section; Steve Bernstein on trumpet. You could get a really great group together. I'd like to do that — get good composers, commission them, and then really have a mix of wild noise improvisation with exactly notated, written music played by people who were into doing it. That's the only way to get that thing happening.

Q: In the early '80s, you were fond of quoting yourself from the score of *Hockey*: "My concern is not so much how things SOUND, as with how things WORK." Has that emphasis changed for you over the years?

ZORN: No, it's the same, absolutely the same.

Q: Is it true for Naked City as well?

ZORN: I think what I was talking about in that quote was more about the game structures. And in that sense, it's less true of the classical pieces or the Naked City pieces than it is of *Cobra* or *Archery*. If I have to be completely truthful, Naked City is about performing things that I hear — it is about sound. It's about composition. Naked City is like a little machine. It's a picture of my brain. With the *Spillane*-type pieces, there's a sense of collaboration involved in the studio. I'll say, "Go in and do a car crash," and the musicians are actually coming up with sounds that I take as a point of departure and try to refine. But we're talking about an incredible exactness and precision in manipulating the kinds of noises and sounds that are inherently unnotatable from the start. I mean, this music has progressed far beyond the capabilities of our language to describe or notate it. I think there's an important difference between asking a musician to simply "improvise" and trying to communicate in a coherent way to another musician a complex, unnotatable sound that you've got in your head. Sometimes the best way to coax such sounds from an "improvising" instrumentalist is to say, "Go in and do a car crash," and take it from there. Sometimes you need to be more technical. It depends on the player — you've got to know what is going to excite and inspire them. With Naked City, the ratio of actual written pitches is much, much higher. Each piece is presented on one sheet of paper. These are my contributions to the world of song "charts" and "Fake Books."

I never thought of myself as someone who hears music in their head and then it translates it to musicians who play it and then someone experiences it. But I am one of those people too. I think that part of the musician's role is to hear sound and work with it. You improvise with people and you hear what they do and you like it and then you have it frozen in your mind and you want to bring it out of them again — or out of someone else, and it gets translated again, like a game of Telephone. But it's true — there are too many sounds logged in my head! And sometimes it's a real pain in the ass to have to write it down. Skritch Skritch Skritch.

For my Genet piece, I hooked together the classical stuff with my file-card compositions. And it was so successful in the studio, it blew my mind — and I was working with musicians I'd never, ever worked with before (except for David Shea). I think it's the best thing I've ever done.

Q: What was the origin of that piece?

ZORN: It came out of my rereading Genet. I'd read *The Thief's Journal* when I was 18 but I didn't know what the fuck was going on. I took a look at again more recently, and it connected, really, really intensely. Originally the piece was called *Elegy.* Enough of this *Spillane* shit, you know what I mean? I'm just going to do an abstract piece called *Elegy.* I know that it's about Genet, but I'll tell nobody else. Then it came out that it was about Genet, and everyone was talking about it. But I don't even think I'm going to put Genet's name on the outside; I'll just put *Elegy* and maybe a picture of him on the inside or a quote from the book.

I found really great ways to structure compositions in the past year. *Elegy* is based a lot on *Marteau Sans Maître* by Boulez, which is one of my favorite pieces of all time. I updated the instrumentation: Instead of alto flute I used bass flute; instead of acoustic guitar, I used electric guitar; the three percussionists I made a turntable player, a sampler player, and a classical percussionist playing mallets and noise percussion. There's a violist and a vocalist who does occasional screams and vocal sounds. So the first connection is using that kind of instrumentation, but the resultant sound, forget it — it's completely different. I used some of the record of *Marteau* in sampling, little bits here and there, but it's hard to tell. There's a lot of written material in the Genet piece, exactly written for the classical players, and a lot of that was generated from pitches in the score of *Marteau.* Not in the sense that I would actually take phrases out, lift them, and have them like quotes. I used the score the way Schoenberg would use a 12-tone row or a serial box. I used it as a point of departure. Sometimes I would reverse pitch sequences; sometimes I would use every other pitch from the viola part and give it to the flute; sometimes I would take rhythm from one instrument and pitches from another and put them together. All different kinds of things that worked with my ear; all done intuitively, using my ear for what I wanted to hear. But intellectually using another person's composition, another person's pitch-set world, the sound of that particular pitch organization, as the elements for the piece I'm working on. It helps give a piece unity. *Spillane* has a unity in the sense that each element deals with some aspect of Mickey Spillane's world. But in terms of sound and pitches, what's going on there? I use maybe six recurrent themes that come back and forth in different ways, and one set of chords which is reused again and again and again. You try to give a composition a coherent sound, the way Varèse used three pitches for *Octandre*, or the way Carter uses intervals. Now I'm working on a piece for Kronos and all the material is derived from the *Lyric Suite*. I'll circle certain areas that I like and reuse this material in a myriad of ways. It's never a case where I'll just take a whole bar; it's more like, this is just raw material that I'm using — this scale, this set, this multiphonic, etc., etc. It's incredibly organic; it makes so much sense, it blows my mind. And it's very natural to me because it's something that I did when I was first writing music, when I was 14, 15 years old. I would use other people's things and copy them out, putting different things together from different compositions, because I'd like this bar, I'd like that chord — same fucking thing, only now to another level. It also creates a real interesting game of analysis for musicologists in the future, a new kind of analysis. I'm using a lot of the techniques I used from studying Schoenberg, Webern, Berg, and how they manipulated 12 tones, but I'm using those in a completely different way.

It's an exciting time for me right now. A lot of times you're really not able to step back and analyze what you're doing, being so inside it — and that's an important part in what I do: I really try to just follow my instincts, whether it pisses off people who are trying to be politically correct, or who are concerned with a certain musical tradition. That cannot concern me; I can't think about trying to censor my work. I've got to follow through wherever my crazy mind takes me. Artists stand on the outside of society. I think that's an important point: I see the artist as someone who stands on the outside; they create their own rules in a lot of ways and shouldn't try to be socially responsible; being irresponsible is the very point of their existence. That's what makes that person able to comment on what's going on around them, because they aren't restricted by the censors or the powers that be — or in the case of what's happening in the arena today, the Big Brother that used to be watching in the '60s is now your next-door neighbor. Now what you've got is the mind-set of censorship appearing as political correctness. I have colleagues and friends coming to me, and they're not just saying, "Hey, I don't like this work, it doesn't engage me," or "Oh boy, here John goes again with that crazy stuff." They're saying, "This is wrong. This is not progressive. This is Neanderthal. This happened years ago and you should know better than this. You shouldn't be doing this. This shouldn't be out there." Things are getting confused. It's a scary time. Nevertheless, I feel right now is a real strong time for me. I'm figuring a lot of shit out, drawing my moral line, and saying, "Fuck you. I don't need this. I've got to follow my artistic vision, whether you think that it's repulsive or anti-women or anti-Asian or whatever. I have to follow it through."

Q: Has your music been the problem for Nonesuch, or have all the difficulties been about packaging?

ZORN: It's packaging, completely. But with me, the packaging is essential — that is my artwork, making records, and I want to give people as many clues as I can. I don't want to mystify everybody; I'm not into making some kind of cult. I'm trying to be as clear as I can, and when I put the pictures on the covers that I do, it's really to tune you in to what's going on, rather than to turn you off, and that's what business people can't understand. They're only interested in how it will sell. So my attitude toward Nonesuch was, "If you don't understand what's happening with the covers, then you don't understand what's happening with the music, because they're both coming from the same place. We don't really have a relationship here — what are we, just sucking each other off? I'm getting publicity, and you're getting some kind of perks for having a weirdo on your label?" It didn't work.

In terms of artistic creativity, they want their hands on something; if it's not in the studio, making a suggestion or something, then it's on the cover. The bottom line is always the cover, and it's always been too important for me to give up. I was spoiled from the beginning, with *School* and *Pool* and *Archery*, doing it all myself. I was rubbing them the wrong way by insisting on the imagery being the way it was, and by just out-and-out saying, "Look, who do you think you are? You're not an artist, you're a businessman. I make the records, you sell them — let's leave it that way."

Naked City was what they were putting most of their eggs into. They were really excited, they really felt they could sell the record.

Q: Did they? Were they behind it to your satisfaction?

ZORN: I don't care whether they get behind it or not. I'd rather that it was in the stores, but I'm not like a lot of musicians who get pissed: "Oh, they're not pushing it, they're not selling it the way it should be sold." I just want to document the shit, and then where it goes, I really couldn't care, to tell you the truth. So I was perfectly happy with what they had done with all of my records. They'd been doing a lot of publicity with the Naked City album, and sold 60,000 of the goddam things. I'm not going to knock that — of course, I haven't seen a cent in royalties or mechanicals!

The question was more of a moral issue for me. I put out *Locus Solus* on a small Japanese label in December, and already I'm seeing royalties. Can you believe that? It's amazing. They are so honest. I've known the guys for years, and I feel really comfortable supporting them because they take the money and put it back into the business. They don't go and buy an expensive apartment or some Robert Motherwell painting that they're going to stick in a vault. They're really involved in circulating and keeping it going. The first thing the people at DIW said to me was, "Of course, we want you to take care of all the covers; you're in total control of the covers." Not only that, they gave me a whole label, Avant, and carte blanche to produce anyone I want. You can't ask for more than that. I find that working in Japan suits me really well. I like the people and I trust them. They're not all that way; I'm sure there are a lot of crooks in Japan working in record companies. But the three companies I've found are exceptional people: incredibly honest; trust you completely with the music, they're not going to give you any second-guessing, you're in charge; and they're honored to have your music on their label. It's a great situation. The only thing I regret is that my music won't be available here for quite a while. Unless a licensing deal can be worked out — I'm not sure. Nonesuch is obviously interested in it, but who knows what's going to happen in the future.

Q: Had there been trouble with the other covers? Mark Beyer's art for *Spy Vs. Spy*?

ZORN: There were troubles, sure. If we'd done the original *Spy Vs. Spy* cover that I wanted, it would have been a little more controversial and had a little more impact. It was a black figure and a white figure, drawn by Mark, who were embracing and about to stab each other in the back at the same time. That was really what *Spy Vs. Spy* was about, the friction: me doing Ornette's music, the whole black/white jazz thing. That was something I was addressing in that music which didn't become clear because the cover didn't spell it out. They did not want any kind of politicized cover. I went for something else, and there are some good elements in it. But I don't feel I compromised. They feel that they were had; they also feel that they were taken advantage of on the Naked City cover. I think they're still really upset about the drawings. I told them that I would not put out a Naked City record without Maruo Suehiro's participation; that he was integral to the package of Naked City the way that Yamatsuka Eye is integral to the band — I'm not going to put out a Naked City record without Yamatsuka Eye on it. He is a member of the band, as far as I'm concerned. And they just couldn't handle that at all.

Q: Is the termination of Naked City an outgrowth of these difficulties?

ZORN: No, it's a musical thing. That band was meant as a compositional workshop, but I'm just not hearing the band anymore; I stopped hearing new compositions for them. And I didn't want to travel around and regurgitate the same pieces over and over; I didn't want to become a repertoire band, presenting a music. If I was no longer getting something out of it, in the sense that I was hearing new music and new ideas being played right there, then I just don't see any reason for it to be around. That was the major reason why I decided to hang it up.

The other side of it was that I was really beginning to lose touch with who I was, as a musician, as a composer. The band was being seen as a "band," and compared to other "college rock" bands like Sonic Youth or the Lounge Lizards or Nirvana or Hüsker Dü or what have you. I was never that kind of musician. It was something that I dabbled in; ultimately, I look at Naked City as my pop-band experiment which worked for four years and then I went on to something else. It was really confusing for me to see *Torture Garden* on the college CMJ report — what the fuck is that supposed to mean? Who am I? What kind of musician am I? Am I now stuck doing this kind of thing? What are we doing when we're onstage? We're alienating the hardcore people with the jazz shit; we're alienating the jazz people with the hardcore shit; and then there's the movie soundtrack stuff that nobody likes. We also were doing game pieces on this last tour: We did *Lacrosse*, my first game piece, and it was great, man! But the audience didn't know what the hell to do.

The point of that band was not to confuse people or to create a satire of 20th-century culture — although a lot of people think it was. Nobody really understood what that band was about. For me, it was about writing; it was about having a machine that could play back anything that I came up with. And that was exciting, to know that I could write a piece in the morning, bring it into the studio, and record it that day with a band that understands just what I'm talking about. It was about trying to get precision instead of my slapdash, one-rehearsal hit situations; it was about doing the same pieces over and over and over and seeing how that worked, how musicians could deal with it. And it was astonishing to see Joey, Bill, Wayne, and Fred come up with something different, every night; every fucking night something different happened on the same tunes that we did 20, 30, 50 times. Amazing!

Musically, Naked City was like the compilation tapes I make from different tracks on the cds I buy. That's what that band was about: This is what I like to listen to at home. It was also something I'd never done before, compositionally, in those 3-minute song-form ideas. I mean, if you sit back and listen to that shit, it's pretty twisted! What has it got to do with jazz or hardcore? It's got nothing to do with any of that. It's the weirdest kind of mutant. We've got six more records: *Heretic*, which is an all-improv record; the *Leng-Tch'e* record, which is the 35-minute hardcore piece, as an ep (we might include a live version of it as well); an ambient record called *Absinthe*; a record of covers; a record of my 3-minute originals, called *Radio*; and *Grand Guignol*.

Q: None of which will be on Nonesuch.

ZORN: No. *Bar Bands* is my last official Nonesuch record. That's already been years in the making and there's nothing I can do about it. But that record does not need anything that's going to upset them. Again, the music determines what the covers will be. For me, that's really what it's about. That music needs something that's softer, so I'm sure they'll agree with what the cover will be. That's in the works now; they've seen the elements of the package and have agreed to it, and that'll be out in September.

Bar Bands is perfect for Nonesuch because of the ethnic connection. It's a series of game pieces, but they're given a strong theatrical context that harks back to my connections with the New York performance scene, with Ken Jacobs and Richard Foreman and Jack Smith. There's a theatrical element in the way it's set up, and in the dynamic between the woman narrator and the two male performers. I'm really happy with those pieces, and those are pieces that I think have been the most difficult for people to understand. Nobody knows what's going on there. I think people are totally baffled by those pieces. I don't know why those in particular. They're not like game pieces, because they don't have that wild, crazy, theatrical thing; they're not like my *Spillane* pieces; they're not like Naked City pieces. They're not like anything I've ever done, and some of them are really like almost fucking New Age: The third movement of the *Bar Bands*, called "Qûê Trán," is a Vietnamese narration with two keyboard players. It's long and slow, very hypnotic. It relates more to La Monte Young or Terry Riley than to anything else. Those three pieces have yet to be really dealt with. They've been slagged for years, since I started doing them in '84. This suite has taken me six years to put together. For me it's really a major opus.

Q: A few years ago, you said, "I'm at the point now where maybe I can make somebody cry with music. That's been a dream all my life. It's almost possible now." Have you gotten closer to it?

ZORN: The end of *Spillane*. Every time I hear that, I get choked up. Every time I hear it: The big buildup, and then the thunder, the drone, and then Bill's guitar on top with the rain coming in. It really sets a mood, it sets the whole thing up. And every time I hear it, I just go, "Man, this is it. This is the shit. I finally did it." Like the fourth movement of Ives' Fourth Symphony: something that's got this mood, this expansiveness to it. It almost sums up a whole history of a certain kind of music, in a sense. That does it. I did an arrangement of Debussy's piano piece "Engulfed Cathedral" for Naked City, which I think also reaches that. That's an arrangement I'm quite proud of.

COMPOSITIONS

1976-78 *The Book Of Heads* for guitar solo
1977   *Lacrosse* for between four and seven players
1978   *Fencing* for three of the same instrument
1979   *Hockey* for three players
1979   *Pool* for four players
1979   *Archery* for twelve players
1979   *Tennis* for two keyboard players or two percussionists
1980   *Jai-alai* opera
1981   *Croquet* for sixteen players
1981   *Go!* a play of roles
1982   *Track & Field* for any number of dancers, performance artists, and musicians
1982   *Locus Solus* tactics for rock trio
1983   *Rugby* for five players
1983   *Impressions Of Africa* for soloist and two drummers
1983   *Darts* for five dancers and five musicians
1983-84 *Sebastopol* for three trios (rock, classical, and improvising)
1984   *Cobra* for ten or more players
1985   *Xu Feng* for six players
1986   *Road Runner* for solo accordion
1986   *Spillane*
1987   *Forbidden Fruit* for string quartet, turntables, and voice
1987   *Ruan Lingyu* for three narrators and eight musicians
1987-89 *New Traditions In East Asian Bar Bands*
         "Hu Die" (1987) for two guitars and Chinese narration
         "Jang Mi Hee" (1988) for two drummers and Korean narration
         "Qúê Trán" (1989) for two keyboards and Vietnamese narration
1988   *Cat O' Nine Tails* for string quartet
1988-91 *Torture Garden*
1989   *Bezique* for nine or more players
1989   *For Your Eyes Only* for chamber orchestra
1990   *The Castle / The Trial* for two keyboards and turntables
1990   *The Dead Man* for string quartet
1991   *Grand Guignol*
1991   *Carny* for solo piano
1991   *Elegy*
1992   *Leng-Tch'e*
1992   *Memento Mori* for string quartet

soundtracks

1986	*White And Lazy*
1986	*She Must Be Seeing Things*
1987	*The Bribe* (radio play)
1988-89	*Cynical Hysterie Hour*
1990	*The Golden Boat*

All compositions published by Theater of Musical Optics, 61 East 8th Street, #126, New York, NY 10003.

DISCOGRAPHY

compositions

1978
Lacrosse
Parachute 4 & 6 lp

1980
Pool, Hockey
Parachute 11/12 lp

1981
Archery
Parachute 17/18 lp

1983
The Classic Guide To Strategy, Volume One
Lumina 004 lp

Locus Solus
Rift 007 lp
Eva 2035 cd (1992)

1985
Cobra
Bad Alchemy No. 3 cs

Godard
Nato 634 lp; 53004-2 cd (1992)

1986
The Classic Guide To Strategy, Volume Two
Lumina 010 lp

Rugby
No Man's Land 8538 lp

1987
Spillane
Elektra/Nonesuch 79172-1 lp, -2 cd, -4 cs

"Blues Noel"
Nato 1382 lp

1989
Cynical Hysterie Hour
CBS/Sony 24DH 5291 cd

"Purged Specimen"
Eva 2010 cd

"Nuit Blanche Pour Les Gorilles," "Spirou Et Fantasio A New York"
Nato 1715/1774 cd

Sawtooth
Enemy 12001

1990
Film Works, 1986-1990
Wave EVA 2024 cd
Elektra/Nonesuch 79270-2 cd, -4 cs

1991
Cobra
Hat Hut 60401/2 cd

1992
Road Runner
CRI 626 cd

Sebastopol
Einstein 001 cd

For Your Eyes Only
Fontec 3151 cd

Elegy
Eva 2040 cd

arrangements

1984
"Shuffle Boil"
A&M 6600 lp

1985
"Der Kleine Leutnant Des Lieben Gottes"
A&M 5104 lp

1986
The Big Gundown
Nonesuch/Icon 79139 lp, -2 cd, -4 cs

1989
Spy Vs. Spy
Elektra/Musician 60844-1 lp, -2 cd, -4 cs

"Hard Plains Drifter"
Elektra/Nonesuch 60843-2 cd

1992
"Akunin Shigan"
Toshiba 6496 cd

Naked City

1990
Naked City
Elektra/Nonesuch 79238-1 lp, -2 cd, -4 cs

Torture Garden
Shimmy Disc 039 lp
Toy's Factory 88557 cd
Earache MOSH28 lp, cs

1992
Heretic (Jeux Des Dames Cruelles)
Avant 001 cd

Grand Guignol
Avant 002 cd

Radio, Vol. 1
Avant 003 cd

Leng-Tch'e
Toy's Factory 88604 cd

1993
Absinthe
Avant 004 cd

bands

with Deadly Weapons:
Deadly Weapons Nato 930 lp (1987)

with Golden Palominos:
Golden Palominos Celluloid 5002 lp (1982); cd (1991)

with Locus Solus:
Island Of Sanity No Man's Land 8707 lp (1987); cd (1991)

with News For Lulu:
Kimus #1 Hat Hut 6000 cd (1988)
News For Lulu Hat Hut 6005 cd (1988)
More News For Lulu Hat Hut 6055 cd (1992)

with Pain Killer:
Guts Of A Virgin Toy's Factory 88561 cd (1991)
Earache MOSH45 lp, cs, cd (1991)
Buried Secrets Toy's Factory 88569 cd (1992)
Earache MOSH62 lp, cs, cd (1992)
"Marianne" on *Koroshi No Blues* Toshiba 6496 cd (1992)

with Slan:
Live At The Knitting Factory, Vol. 3 A&M 75021-5299-2 cd (1990)

with Sonny Clark Memorial Quartet:
Voodoo Black Saint 0109 lp (1987)

improvisations

with Derek Bailey, Fred Frith, Bill Laswell, Charles K. Noyes, & Sonny Sharrock:
Improvised Music New York 1981 MU Works 1007 cd (1992)

with Derek Bailey & George Lewis:
Yankees Celluloid 5006 lp (1983)

with Yamatsuka Eye:
"Cowlick Pussyman" Arrest 003 cd (1992)

with Fred Frith:
"Houston Street" ESD 80462 cd (1990)

with Ikue Mori, Lindsay Cooper, & Fred Frith:
[untitled] Tellus 15 cs (1986)

with David Moss:
"Hand Tech," "Husk When Time" Moers 2010 lp (1984)

with Charles K. Noyes:
"Augury" Zoar 12 lp (1982)

with Valentina Ponomareva:
"Koseinenkin Hall II" Leo 175 cd (1991)

with Ned Rothenberg:
Trespass Lumina 011 lp (1985)

with Sato Michihiro:
Ganryu Island Yukon 2101 lp (1985)

with Jim Staley:
OTB Lumina 008 lp (1985)

with Tenko:
"Improvisation" *Bad Alchemy No. 3* cs (1985)

guest artist

with Andrea Centazzo:
First Environment For Sextet Ictus 0017 lp (1979); New Tone 6707 cd (1992)
(excerpt)
USA Concerts Ictus 0018 lp (1979)

with Eugene Chadbourne:
The English Channel Parachute 7 lp (1979)

with Nicolas Collins:
100 Of The World's Most Beautiful Melodies Trace Elements 1018 cd (1989)

with Jad Fair and Kramer:
Roll Out The Barrel Shimmy Disc 84912 cd (1989)

with Fred Frith:
The Technology Of Tears SST 172 lp; Rec Rec 20 cd (1988)

with David Garland:
Control Songs Review 95 lp (1946)

with God:
Possession Virgin 910 cd (1992)

with Half-Japanese:
"Should I Tell Her?" Shimmy Disc 001 lp (1987)
The Band That Would Be King 50 Skidillion WATTS Half 8-1 lp (1989)

with Wayne Horvitz:
Simple Facts Theater For Your Mother 004 lp (1980)

with Frank Lowe:
Lowe And Behold Musicworks 3002 lp (1978)

with Mr. Bungle:
Mr. Bungle Warner Brothers 26640-1 lp, -2 cd, -4 cs (1991)

with Butch Morris:
Current Trends In Racism In Modern America Sound Aspects 4010 lp (1986)

with David Moss:
Dense Band Moers 02040 lp (1985)

with Bob Ostertag:
Attention Span Rift 33 cd (1991)

with Sato Michihiro:
Rodan Hat Art 6015 cd (1989)

with Sovetskoe Foto:
The Art Of Beautiful Butling 1st 084-93232 cd (1992)

Japanese recordings

with Friction:
Replicant Walk Wax 32WXD-110 cd (1988)

with Hikashu:
Live Puzzlin' 001 cd (1989)

with Jagatara:
Sore Kara RCA R32H-1076 cd (1989)

with Fusanosuke Kondou:
Heart Of Stone BMG B29D-14102 cd (1990)

with Koichi Makigami:
Koroshi No Blues Toshiba 6496 cd (1992)

with Seigen Ono:
Comme Des Garcons, Vol. 1 Tokuma 407 cd (1989)
Comme Des Garcons, Vol. 2 Tokuma 408 cd (1989)

Nekonotopia Nekonomania Crammed Disques 30057 cd (1991)

with Ruins:
Early Works Bloody Butterfly 004 cd (1992)

with Jojo Takayanagi:
Experimental Performance Mobyus 005 lp (1986)

APPENDIX: KEY TO PUBLISHERS' ABBREVIATIONS

AMP
Associated Music Publishers, Inc.
see GS

B&H
Boosey & Hawkes, Inc.
24 East 21st Street, New York, NY 10010
(212) 228-3300

BB
Broude Brothers Ltd.
141 White Oaks Road, Williamstown,
MA 01267
(413) 458-8131

BCP
Bowdoin College Press
Bowdoin College, Brunswick, ME 04011
(207) 725-3747

BMI
BMI Educational Journal Canavanguard,
1971

BMP
Belwin-Mills Publishing Corp.
see TP

CFP
C.F. Peters Corp.
373 Park Avenue South, New York, NY
10016   (212) 686-4147

DLP
Deep Listening Publications
156 Hunter Street, Kingston, NY 12401
(914) 338-5984

EAM
European American Music Corporation
P.O. Box 850, Valley Forge, PA 19482
(215) 648-0506

EBM
E.B. Marks Music Corp.
see TP

ECS
E.C. Schirmer
138 Ipswich Street, Boston, MA 02215
(617) 236-1935

ET
Edition Tonos
c/o Seesaw Music Corp.
2067 Broadway, New York, NY 10023
(212) 874-1200

FLP
Fallen Leaf Press
P.O. Box 10034, Berkeley, CA 94709

FMC
Fujihara Music Co., Inc.
18206 51st Avenue South, Seattle, WA
98188   (206) 246-9880

FPM
Frog Peak Music
Box A36, Hanover, NH 03755
(603) 448-8837

GB
Gerard Billadout Editions
see TP

GCM
Golden Croak Music
3338 17th Street, NW, Washington, DC
20010   (202) 462-4580

GS
G. Schirmer, Inc.
225 Park Avenue South, New York, NY
10003   (212) 254-2100

HBP
Hermes Beard Press
see FPM

JP
Jenson Publications, Inc.
c/o Hal Leonard Publishing Corp.
P.O. Box 13819, 7777 West Bluemound
Road, Milwaukee, WI 53213
(414) 774-3630

LCK
Lim Chong Keat
see FMC

LG
Lawson-Gould, Inc.
c/o G. Schirmer, Inc.
225 Park Avenue South, New York, NY
10003   (212) 254-2100

M
Mills
see TP

MCA
MCA Music
see TP

MFP
Music For Percussion
c/o Plymouth Music Co.
170 NE 33rd Street
Fort Lauderdale, FL 33334
(305) 563-1844

ML
Mills College Library
Oakland, CA 94613

MM
Marymount College Library
Palos Verdes, CA 90274

MP
Media Press
Box 250
Elwyn, PA 19063

MS
manuscript

NM
Norruth Music
available from MMB Music
10370 Page Industrial Boulevard
St. Louis, MO 63132   (314) 427-5660

OUP
Oxford University Press
200 Madison Avenue
New York, NY 10016   (212) 679-7300

PA
Pavilion: Experiments In Art & Technology
B. Kluver, J. Marin, & B. Rose, eds.
New York: Dutton, 1972

PSO
Peer-Southern Organization
810 Seventh Avenue
New York, NY 10019   (212) 265-3910

RK
Robert King
7 Canton Street
North Easton, MA 02356

ROP
Paul's Blues. New York: Red Ozier Press,
1984

SN
Soundings (January 1972)

SP
Smith Publications
2617 Gwynndale Avenue
Baltimore, MD 21207   (410) 298-6509

SR
Source, 4 (January/July 1970)

TP
Theodore Presser Co.
Presser Place
Bryn Mawr, PA 19010   (215) 525-3636

Z
Zeitschrift (Spring 1979)

INDEX

ABOUT THE AUTHOR

COLE GAGNE (B.A., Fordham University) is a writer, musician and video artist living in New York City. He is the co-author (with Tracy Caras) of *Soundpieces: Interviews With American Composers* (Scarecrow, 1982) and the author of *Sonic Transports: New Frontiers In Our Music* (de Falco Books/Samuel French Trade, 1990). His writings about music have also appeared in *Option, BMI Magazine, Brutarian, Ear, Op,* and *Keyboard Classics.* He is librettist and co-composer of Plastic Music's opera *Agamemnon* (1992), in which he also performs as singer and instrumentalist. Currently he is completing a critical study of the films of John Huston, and collaborating with "Blue" Gene Tyranny on a book about the legendary 19th-century American composer Anthony Philip Heinrich.

1